The Berlin Wall

David Leo Rice

Whisk(e)y Tit
VT & NYC

For my mother

"Give me back the Berlin Wall."

–Leonard Cohen

2020

Prologue: Eternal Weimar

January

Reports of immense, icy mountains growing of their own accord along the coastlines of Europe, undercut by craters, tunnels, and passageways that connect in undisclosed locations, or don't connect at all, have so far proven impossible to verify. Surveyors sent out to map, or re-map, the fjords of Northern Norway and the Black Sea coast of Bulgaria, the southern beaches of Sicily and the Algarve in Western Portugal, return with contradictory reports, or don't return at all. Some embed in fishing villages and take vows of silence, while others send back field notes in garbled code, terrified bleatings and blurred selfies that serve no purpose other than to exacerbate the already heightened state of alarm in which their home offices await them.

Cell phone videos of jagged peaks rising like elevators from the Atlantic and the Mediterranean, and of long, humanoid processions vanishing beneath rocky escarpments, appear on computer screens in Paris, Rome, and Berlin, and then, after a second of static, disappear, only to reappear again late at night when no one's watching, or a day later, when no one can be certain if key details have changed. News reports are redacted or deleted moments after they air, by forces the anchors swear are entirely outside their stations' purview. These anchors then also vanish. Entire websites and journals shut down over false reporting, only to be resurrected by debunking the same stories they previously died defending.

Simultaneous screenshots of these stories from different computers display different information, while printed maps in university archives and public libraries also fragment, some displaying the newly monstrous coastal ranges—claiming, in medieval gothic script, that these are the oldest, most sanctified facets of Europa, God's bulwark against the rising seas—while others remain unaltered, or show large gaps in what used to be the solid edges of the landmass. Even maps of the old geography begin to look suspect, as if perhaps no change has occurred other than a weirding of what was there all along, a sudden perceptual inability, among the EU's 500 million, to see the normal contours of the Croatian or the Latvian or the Irish coastlines as normal any longer.

 Geography professors squabble and fracture, half of them insisting that an epochal change is afoot, while the other half insists that the sailing, so to speak, has never been smoother. Any perceived tempest, this unruffled half insists, is playing out within a sturdy Ikea teacup, so that, surely, now is the time to stay the course. "The biggest mistake we can make going forward," insists Peter Lenz, Chair of Humboldt University's European History Department on Deutsche Welle's New Year's Day Broadcast, "is to let ourselves get spooked going into the next decade."

Nevertheless, spooky, ant-like smudges of stranded human families (although, German Chancellor Lena Havermeyer thinks, much as she hates herself for thinking it, let's not assume they're human just yet) climbing and falling, scuttling and plummeting, dot these mountains on the computer screens cluttering her office in the Reichstag, their eventual crash into the waves barely audible, even with the volume turned all the way up. Havermeyer pictures them first as crabs and then as spiders, watching the words 'crabs' and 'spiders' scuttle from one side of her head to the other, perfectly representing that which they... represent.

She laughs at the redundancy of the thought, marveling at how, just a moment ago, she'd expected something profound to emerge from the folds of what she still considers her supple, first-rate brain.

Seriously though, she thinks, something, in reality or an unnervingly good simulation thereof, is afoot. Beyond this, no layperson, and not even those who ought to know, can offer anything more than the same contradictory speculation that has defined the discourse of the past several decades, if not the past century, if not all of Europe's history, if such an entity can still be said to have any knowable history at all.

If Europe can still be called an entity.

"Now the entity is folding in on itself," she reads, unable to resist opening window after window after window on her thirty-inch desktop work screen. "Its edges are rising vertical and even warping over the top to form something like an origami box, sealing 500 million souls inside, or threatening to, while granting access, through channels no one can map, to millions of others." Air travel remains unrestricted for the time being, but even so it seems more and more fraught. Prominent personages leave in a hurry, while those who arrive at Heathrow and Charles de Gaulle and Milan Malpensa seem hollow-eyed and remote, like decoy people.

Planes disappear in midflight, or crash into barriers that, upon inspection, prove impossible to locate. Pipelines burst, gushing oil into wheat fields and water reserves, while hobbyist geographers pour from the woodwork with their homemade instruments, eager to prove, once and for all, that the earth is nothing like what the powers that be have always insisted it is. That it is, rather, a Rubik's cube being constantly shuffled by unseen hands, all borders suspect, all compasses faulty, no formations permanent. Much as she wishes she could avoid the thought she knows is coming, Lena Havermeyer slumps back in her office chair in the touchy nerve center of Germany and admits that they might just be right.

That evening, she wallows in heartburn in her tasteful, modern residence in the Grünewald in Southwest Berlin. She stands alone in front of her frosted-over windows, massaging her temples and looking out at the distant lights of the city under which, she can't help but fear, something real is stirring. Whether this thing is physical or metaphysical she can't be sure, nor can she quite be sure what the difference, at the dawn of the new decade, might still be said to be. As she pictures them, the mountains and tunnels stand as an example of something that can only be indicated by example.

But an example of what?

She has the suspicion that some completely different event could just as easily have occurred and made the same point. But, again, what point? Burping acid, she feels like she's just received a message she can't open. Yes, it arrived, she imagines telling the disgruntled sender, and sure, I'll sign for it, but no, I haven't yet completed the unboxing.

And I'm not sure I ever will.

So stop asking.

She sends more delegations into the field, demanding better intel, which she knows they won't deliver and which, in due time, they don't. YouTube overflows with experts and reenactments, old footage doctored to look new and new footage doctored to look old. Ancient races rise from the thawing permafrost, their chests carved with glowing runes, while craters swallow Slovenian villages, replacing them with dens of harpies and werewolves.

In the next set of videos, the Chancellor watches a movement coalesce around a candidate named Ulli Harz, an avatar who seems to have arisen from a rift in the Internet itself. She muses on this concept, uncertain whether she heard it discussed on a commentary track—one that is perhaps still playing—or arrived at it in what might still be said to constitute her own thoughts. The Internet as authentic topography, as a space unto itself rather than a representation, true or false, of any other. A realm, a district, an autonomous regime of being. The mountains, she considers, are rising *in the Internet, not only* on *it*. The images are not images of *things*—they *are those things*.

Whatever she'd been watching while thinking or hearing all this reverts to a campaign video for Harz's One Valhalla Party, which advocates, as far as she can tell in the state she's glazed into, the union of Austria and Germany with Scandinavia and The Netherlands and the secession of that new nation from the rest of Europe, his campaign abetted by the sold-out lecture tour of Ragnar of Atlantis, whose videos clot any screen his name appears on. All grim signs for next year's election, symptoms of the same chaos spreading everywhere, seeping outward like the oil spills that have become a meme whose parallel seep she can't help but follow. Soon, Europe will be nothing but a black pool of oil, contained by the thousand-foot walls of its new border ranges.

And yet it's still possible, as a parallel stream of videos never ceases to insist, that nothing is happening. Nothing but boredom. Too much peace. Too much prosperity. Too many teens on screens.

All I want, she thinks—though, even more so than before, her thinking feels pat, like she's consenting, or not quite consenting, for something in need of a head to think this through her—is a simmering down of whatever this is. Whatever underlying condition we now either are or are not seeing the worsening symptoms of. The mountains and tunnels, if they're real, are likewise symptoms. Everything displaced onto something else, all events signs of other things, never quite things in their own right. Hyperlink events, leading ever deeper into the news.

She leans back in her chair and tries to enter a dream of Baiersbronn, deep in the Black Forest. Silent, dappled in summer sunlight or fresh Christmas snow. She tries to place herself back in the Mayor's Residence, where she lived from 1981 to 1996, walking the shaded country lane from there to the Town Hall and back twice a day, even on weekends, when she never missed a leisurely brunch and stroll around the park, greeting her constituents with a handshake and a smile.

She holds onto the dream, forcing her head into the plush leather headrest of her office chair while YouTube plays against her closed eyelids. She burrows down inside herself, through one of the rifts in the newly fractured ground, down to the Second Europe beneath. The reserve continent. Still-pristine, its future still to come.

Down here, in this ur-Baiersbronn, the splintering ground of Berlin forms the sky, raining ash and dust upon her as she walks the road to town, working hard to imagine that it's still 1985, or even 1995, the cherry strudel and Milchkaffee at Kleindorf's fresh and waiting for her. But, even in the dream, history won't revert. The sky continues to shake and spark, and she sees a figure blocking her way, just up ahead, and she knows she'll have to stop to meet it.

She slows, the air darkening as Karlheinz Bauer extends a hand and smiles, his eyes invisible in the gloom. She nods and forges ahead, determined to muscle past him. But now, as then, he pivots to block her way, staring, his face pulsing in the darkness, his suit wet and steamy.

"We're not going anywhere," he says softly, as she stops short, inhaling his rose-scented musk. "We know you've seen us here, coming and going from the office complex on the Heideggerstraße, beyond the Aldi. We've been watching you since '89. We like what we've seen. We can help, if you let us."

He steps aside and she hurries on, but now the road leads only to the train station, and the only train is the Express to Berlin. She boards with no luggage, barely dressed, falls into a feverish sleep, and awakens in her campaign office in Mitte, her long, victorious ascent to the Chancellorship already underway. The hard work of campaigning purely a formality.

The Chancellor opens her eyes and waits to remember that she's still in Berlin. As if the dream sent me here, she thinks. As if, had I only kept my eyes open, I never would've walked that road, never met Bauer and his colleagues, never entangled myself with the Soft Illuminati, considered by so many to be the glue that held the Berlin Wall together. The literal mortar, loosed across the continent and then the world one November day in '89. If only I'd resisted the dream—now it both is and isn't possible for her to have been in this chair, in this room, to have had or not had that dream in the first place—I would've remained Mayor of Baiersbronn, living out my life over Milchkaffee and cherry strudel on a succession of temperate Sunday mornings, rereading my Antiquariat Kleist and Hoffman editions in my dim study at night, a glass of chilled prosecco by my side.

Unless that too is heresy. A convenient fiction, masking... what? Our careening through formless space? A trackless Siberian frontier, groping through a blizzard, dreaming of homes that never were? She shudders, summons a force of will sufficient to close her browser just as the next Ragnar video comes alive, and gets up to mix a gin and tonic with what she affectionally calls *my imperial swizzle stick*, not hesitating to add a splash of rosewater.

9

April/May

She emerges from a tunnel of nightmares that's left her gray-haired and yellow-eyed, her gums black and weeping, when news reaches her desk that Martin Himmelreiter has died. Surrounded by his four children, twelve grandchildren, and thirty-two great-grandchildren, at home in Bamberg, the ancient skeeze has finally shuffled off at the age of 107. While she knows that the phrase 'last living Nazi' can never be absolutely proven, and is thus, in essence, a farcical notion to indulge, she decides that he'll do, and convenes a committee to plan a lavish celebration. Thank you God, she thinks, glancing up at the eggshell-white gypsum of her office ceiling. If I could perceive you as real, this is what I would think in your general direction, now more than ever before. Thank you for this opportunity.

The celebration, set for May Day, will also serve, she decides over breakfast with her Culture Minister and some finance people from Luxembourg, as a symbolic Funeral for the 20th Century. An end to the madness, and mad madness-denial, of the past five months, and, by extension, the past hundred and twenty years.

As soon as breakfast is over, she resolves to write her speech at her work desk in front of the same window she spent the winter and early spring staring out of, brooding on images of self-generating mountains and intermittently accessible wormholes, of gushing pipelines and vanishing planes, of work crews unfolding paper maps only to vanish into them, turning up as fly-sized blots over the names of major cities. Of Europe making itself a fortress with the tacit approval of all its leaders, no matter what they might say, myself included. She often thought all this in February, March, and April, mired in an insomnia so profound that sleep had come to seem like a rare and shameful delicacy, one she took care not to be seen trying to enjoy.

This whole year has felt like one long night, but not the kind you sleep through. First the mountains and tunnels, she thinks, losing the gist of her speech, then the man in Tübingen who claimed to have undergone a kind of divine intercourse whose nature he couldn't or wouldn't describe, the result being that he gave birth to what he called, on national TV, "a micro-race of sixty-six Supermen, currently being raised in my basement and those of allies around town and the nearby villages."

Retweeted half a billion times by Ulli Harz and his legions, humans and automata alike.

Thinking back on that segment now, she pictures this man distended on a bathmat on the basement floor like a collie birthing a litter of puppies, and it's all she can do to keep from guffawing. Despite the relief a true belly laugh would bring, she forces her face into a tactful smirk, aware, as always, of being watched by her staff, all with Twitter accounts of their own.

She coughs into her fist and buries the aborted first page of her speech beneath the morning's news. The topmost sheet details further instances of what has come to be known as *flaccid invasion*. Reports of this nature have been coming from all corners of the continent, hysterical (she hates the word, but there is no other) testimonials in which men and women claim to have been "imperceptibly violated in the night, so that, when I woke up, I felt like I was both me and not me at the same time. It's like something has gotten into me and I don't know what it is!" This exact phrase, uttered verbatim if one accounts for the imprecisions of translation, has now cropped up, according to the running tally at the top of the sheet she's looking at, eight hundred and eighty-six times, in every country in the EU, as well as in Turkey and the UK, sulking in its self-imposed banishment. The day before yesterday, she was forced to watch a video of a man in Katowice, outside Krakow, jigging naked in a kiddie pool in his backyard, his chest covered in coarse white hair and his biceps boasting dual rose-wrapped crosses, shrieking (according to the subtitles), "But there's no entrance hole! There's no entrance hole anywhere on me! How could this have happened?"

How indeed? She shrugs, as if performing her uncertainty could free her from the need to posit an answer. Then she returns to the ordeal of writing her speech. "The twentieth century," she writes, struggling to string the words together, "was a time of unprecedented chaos and brutality. Let us never mince words about this. Indeed, let us never forget that the twentieth century was... was... was..."

She sits back in her desk chair and feels herself suddenly on the verge of weeping. What *was* the twentieth century, exactly? Did it even occur? She gets up, fearful of flaccid invasion despite being unable to imagine, in any concrete sense, what the term refers to. She expels her staff and locks the door, then sits back down and lets the tears come, and with them the fullness of the feeling that, in all honesty, she cannot remember what the twentieth century was. The best she can do is squint through her tears at what looks like a thick hank of skin hanging from the ceiling, descending toward her like a blanket. This, she thinks, is perhaps what the twentieth century has amounted to. The skin of millions sheared off, then stitched into an odious blanket smothering the continent, softening edges that ought to be hard.

She tugs it down to face level and uses it to dry her eyes and blow her nose. Then she snuggles against it, well aware that it's the only human contact she's had in months.

———————————

May Day arrives and Alexanderplatz fills with revelers, or mourners, while the Chancellor folds and refolds the three handwritten pages she's managed to produce, picturing the origami-like folds of the continent as she rehearses the words in her head, trying to imagine how it'll feel to say them while telegraphing the impression that she means what they mean. She thinks of Wittgenstein, her constant companion during the seven years of her philosophy doctorate in Heidelberg, and the only bitter old man with whom she's ever felt a shred of kinship. What does it mean to say one thing and mean another? She asks herself, as Wittgenstein once asked her, groaning alive from the pages of some clothbound library book full of nail clippings and dead hair. In what actual sense does the meaning exist apart from what is said and, if it doesn't exist, what does it mean to speak of it? She shrugs

13

and shudders and watches from behind a curtain as the crowd continues to file in and the embalmed body of Martin Himmelreiter in its sleek black casket is removed from its government hearse and propped in a stand beside the podium, which it is now time for her to approach.

She looks at the sky, clear and blue, and wonders what became of the rumors that it sealed up or clotted over. Then she looks back at the sky, still clear and blue, but now she wonders what it's supposed to look like, and whether, perhaps, this is a long way from that. She closes her eyes, forcing herself to remember—"Sky! Sky!" she shouts inwardly, like an asylum doctor offering a patient one last chance to demonstrate her sanity—but wrenches her lids open in a hurry when she ends up back on that road in Baiersbronn, Karlheinz Bauer waiting beneath a chestnut tree in his steaming felt suit.

She trembles, her chest cavity sagging, until an aide presses her shoulder. Then she watches her legs convey her head and torso out from behind the curtain and up to the microphone, before a crowd of thousands that roars in such a way that it's impossible to tell if they're welcoming or warning her.

And who are they, anyway? She wonders, just below the level of her official consciousness. Though she knows that the first five rows are made up of supporters hired by her staff, she can't help but wonder: in what possible world can it be true that I was elected to govern them?

Though she'd like to ask this very question aloud, instead she looks at her papers and cedes control to the worldly part of her, the part that resolved to leave Baiersbronn and embark upon the campaign that would put her at the helm of the EU's sole economic and cultural superpower, no matter what those sweaty perverts in France might say, she thinks, allowing herself a miniscule smirk. Then she clears her throat and hears a voice that reminds her of her own.

"Today, good people of Berlin," it says, in clean, clear German, all traces of Bavarian brogue ruthlessly purged, "and those who've come from far and wide, we convene for a special purpose. Today, it is both our solemn and our joyous duty to lay the twentieth century to rest. That century of murder and madness, of fuming, infernal machines, that century in which chaos nearly swallowed us whole, is, thankfully, long gone. We have learned much from it, and we know that the road ahead will pose challenges of its own, but today we close that chapter forever. Twenty years after its calendar end, today we mark the biological end of the twentieth century. Its last wheezing, groaning avatar has left us in peace. Today, Martin Himmelreiter, um," she gestures at the coffin and swallows a sudden, panicky surge of doubt as to who, exactly, Martin Himmelreiter is, or was. She's afraid she called him Martin Heidegger. As soon as the name registers, a body materializes to match it: an old man in the front of the crowd, wearing a damp tweed suit with a pink necktie and a rose corsage, leering at her, enjoying her momentary lapse. *Here I am*, his eyes seem to say. *I took the train all the way from my cottage in the Black Forest. That coffin is empty*. She closes her eyes and sees herself leaping down from the podium and wrapping her fingers around his neck, choking him to the ground and smashing his skull against the concrete until part of it opens, revealing his brain. Heidegger's brain. She pokes a thumb through the hole in the skull and presses into the soft, spongy flesh, but stops when it says, *"C'mon baby, crush me like the slug we both know I am! Give me what I deserve. Put me in the coffin. Do it now, or forever hold your..."*

"Today," she repeats, wiping her fingers on the edge of her skirt, "we lay to rest the last remaining Nazi. Martin, um, Himmelreiter," here again she scans the crowd, half-expecting to find Heidegger mouthing the words, *I can never die. Nothing can ever kill me. I am Being itself.* Instead, the old man with the rose corsage simply stands and listens, refusing to let on whether he's thinking what she is.

Or vice versa, he seems to whisper. She feels a spasm run the length of her back, and a thick rivulet of sweat follows it down, under the waistband of her skirt, as the words, *Hitler's soft fleshy back... I never found anything half so erotic as the merest thought of Hitler's soft fleshy back*, float through her head, and she tries to remember who said this first. Dalí? Must've been. She clears her throat, determined to go on speaking before Dalí —if it was Dalí —says anything else inside her.

"Martin Himmelreiter," she continues, her fleshy back entirely slick now, roiling with what she tries hard not to imagine as rank Spanish semen, "was a minor official at Theresienstadt, not one of the epochal mass murderers who were sentenced at Nuremburg and Jerusalem. Yet, still, he both ordered and carried out the deaths of countless innocent German citizens. Indeed, his very banality makes him all the more emblematic of the forces whose purgation we are today here to celebrate. Today, at long last, he is gone from our midst. At the age of 107, this monster has departed from us, and we are all the better for it. The evil contained within him, responsible for the mass death of the Holocaust just as surely as it bears responsibility for the pernicious rumors of the past several months, has dissipated back into the universe where, for lack of a human host, it will become fodder for black holes."

She pauses, her head again full of Wittgenstein, as she wonders what it is she means, if not what she just said. And yet what she just said seems... it seems... again a cloud fills her, starting in her stomach and moving upward, like one of those mountains supposedly rising from the Norwegian coast and rendering the continent impregnable except through passageways no one can guard. Or did I imagine that as well? She wonders, unable, at the moment, to fathom how so far-fetched a story could possibly be true. And yet, she thinks, if that isn't the case, what is?

Mustn't something be?

Leaning against the mic, she watches a municipal work crew load the casket into a hearse with BAIERSBRONN displayed in gaudy lettering across an illuminated destination marquee. Once this has been accomplished, and televised, she continues, "Not only is the body of this despicable creature going to be carried down to the Black Forest and interred there, but so is the Holocaust Memorial," she gestures here to a series of eight flatbed trucks, all loaded with stones and signage. "The Holocaust, at long last, is behind us forever. As extinct as the dinosaurs; the Reich as fallen as Rome, no matter what Ulli Harz might induce his bedroom-dwelling minions to believe. Let them stay in their bedrooms. Those of us here, in real time, can see that the space the Holocaust

Memorial once occupied is now to stand empty as a Future Museum, to be filled, when the day comes, by the glorious, as-yet-unwritten history of the New Germany and, by extension, the New EU which, now that the tumult of its youth and, let us say, adolescence has been concluded, is entering its Golden Age. Germany faced its worst self and, alone among nations, triumphed." She scans the crowd, wondering how many Harz supporters are among them, far from their bedrooms, wishing her dead. Do such people exist, outside the troughs and trenches of the Internet-as-autonomous-topography?

She forces herself to continue. "Germany rose from the ashes of its own making to become the greatest modern society the world has ever seen. Indeed, it rose from those ashes in order to define what a conscientious, equitable, and enlightened modern society looks like. The Future Museum will, in time, be the jewel of Berlin, the envy of capitals the world over, a site dedicated to peace, prosperity, and the constant, patient search for greater knowledge, greater reason, and greater tolerance. As we move into the 2020s, let us all together celebrate the centenary of the cultural apex that was the Weimar Republic, but this time, thankfully, with no dark specter on the horizon. This time, good and decent people of Berlin, the liberal consensus is here to stay! We have reached the ideal present, and from this present, we move gracefully, without fear and without regret, into our collective future."

She steps back from the mic and waits, unsure whether to expect applause or attack. A smattering of ambiguous chatter ensues, and then something resounds in her ears and she feels faint and grabs the podium, terrified of appearing incapacitated in front of her people. An aide sidles up to her but she shrugs him off, gripping the lacquered wood and staring at the mustache above Heidegger's permanent avuncular smirk.

A wave ripples through the crowd. At first she thinks a bomb has been detonated, and part of her hopes this is the case, because at least that would be a tragedy of knowable proportions, one with a well-established protocol, a transaction of sorts, but she senses that no such thing has occurred. The crowd seems to warp and crack up; then it comes back together, unscathed but altered, its integrity called into question in a way that Lena Havermeyer, despite her doctorate and three guided mushroom trips in Marrakech and the ten or so books she's read about the consciousness of octopi and Aspen groves, finds herself ill-equipped to comprehend.

She closes her eyes as the Soft Illuminati slip through the rift that's opened in the day's mellow spring weather, straining not to see them even though there's nothing to see. They rise from the scarred ground where the Wall stood and massage rose jelly into the torn membrane they've come through, kissing its edges, whispering, *Dear sweet nurturing mother, we are here through your grace alone, and through your grace are we strong. Where once we held concrete and barbed wire, now we hold reality itself. Allow us to mediate between the Hard Illuminati, never to be seen, and the many, many people of this world, as they gaze upon its fraying seams and pray to be delivered into the future they all know is coming.*

Then they stow their jelly in the breast pockets of their damp suits and commence in earnest the work of flaccid invasion, worming their way into the bodies of the thousands gathered there on Alexanderplatz, filling the spaces between their organs that had, until a moment ago, processed the diseased flesh of the century that has now been well and properly buried, peeled from the bones of the known world so that newer, healthier flesh might grow in its place. When they've finished and returned to their safe house in Wannsee, the rift heals in such a way that everyone in Berlin can tell something is different, but no one can say what it is.

Part I: Flaccid Invasion

György

György Kaczor squirms awake at sunset in his too-large apartment in Charlottenburg, in the torpid old West of the city, to watch the Chancellor gesticulate in confusion on his laptop. In the corner of the screen a small banner reminds him that today's his nineteenth birthday. He clicks okay and closes his eyes again, trying to slip back into his dream, but it's fading. Hungary in springtime, the village of Gyula in a rare burst of floral glory, the wind perfumed and perfect, cleaner than any air he's ever breathed, a wind from another time, from the deep past, before the incursion of Christianity, when the Magyars were still...

But the air has grown foul and greasy, the ground softening, the firm, fertile Hungarian soil turning to blubber, a grey, cancerous bulge clotting together and smothering the town, forcing him out of his country and into the heart of Berlin a year ago, when he'd just turned eighteen and the prospect of a two-year exchange at Humboldt University to study with Peter Sloterdijk—the last honest philosopher in Europe, who, as luck would have it, was visiting Berlin from Karlsruhe on a brief guest stint—was more than he could turn down. He pictured himself drinking cheap dark beer on his way to an orgy in the back room of some Friedrichshain nightclub with lean, toned blonde girls, drunk out of their minds, free at last, no longer a virgin, the ruins of the dead east receding behind him, the days pulsing with the promise of new life, making him giddy. But, as soon as he stepped off the Budapest-Berlin night train and rolled his roller-bag past the Sephora and the Starbucks and the Wonderpots frozen yogurt kiosk in the Hauptbahnhof, it began to sour. The walls did not hesitate to close in.

By now the city had turned fully rancid, leaving him half-asleep on a mattress on the floor a year later, with the Chancellor gripping the podium two inches from his face, seeming to shake the screen itself, and all he can see is Hungary filling with fat, blobbing over into an unlivable mess, a slick jiggling oven tray to which he fears he might never return—or, worse perhaps, might have to return only to live within what no hero kept it from becoming.

He grips his stomach and pinches the small soft accruing roll and warns himself that this too must change. Summoning the voice of the man he sometimes still imagines he will one day become, if he's brave and clearheaded and lucky, he tells himself, "György, I'm disappointed in you. You can do better. You must. Don't make me tell you again. You don't want to find out what I'm capable of. You may be weak, but God knows I am not."

He sighs and pictures the route he'll take to the gym, on the third floor of an office building on the Kantstraße, above a Nordstrom Rack and a Media Markt. Letting this train of thought peter out with the image of himself arriving and wiping down the lat pull machine, he clicks through some Hungarian news sites, the few reliable ones left, and finds them all buzzing with commentary on the Chancellor's speech and the so-called Funeral for the Twentieth Century that she has apparently just presided over.

"NO MENTION OF THE LIVING WALL!!" reads the headline on one of them. He clicks to see the rest of the article. "Surprising no one, Havermeyer entirely sidestepped any account of the Berlin Wall as it actually was. Who does she think she's kidding? Whatever her government and those like it might say, the People know the truth: The Wall was alive. All that concrete and barbed wire and landmines they say it was made of? Lies. Anyone who was around back then whose mind hasn't been turned to jelly knows that they were sentient beings. Beings that felt pain and pleasure, with dreams of their own, and that, when the Wall supposedly fell, they were scattered to the corners of Europe, where they roam still, wondering what went wrong. Wondering where they belong now. Waiting to be redeemed, so they can redeem us. Believe it or pay the price! Time is tick-tick-ticking. The future will not resemble the present forever. The reckonings they think are over have barely begun."

György yawns and closes that window and looks over at another pop-up notification, reminding him that Ragnar of Atlantis is speaking in Kreuzberg tonight. Damn, he thinks, I meant to get tickets. I'm sure it's sold out by now.

He slams his laptop shut, as if this tiny flourish could obviate the disappointment, and spends a moment regarding the poster on the wall above his bookcase, which displays Mishima's head on a plate, its lips frozen halfway between agony and exaltation. He salutes the Great Man before turning his back.

Walking to the bathroom, he passes the porcine hulk of his French roommate, Vincent. Vincent the Barnyard Pig. He regards the boy in his white T-shirt and loose, blue-striped boxers sprawled on the couch in a welter of beer cans and potato chip bags, his thumb at the edge of his lips. Suck it, little baby, György thinks. It's all you're good for.

He gags as the full decrepitude of Vincent's life impresses itself on his imagination. A sleepwalker among sleepwalkers; a dead soul among dead souls. A chaff person in a chaff society. You deserve Berlin and Berlin deserves you.

He spits on the fabric near Vincent's marbled thigh and lumbers to the bathroom, pees, drinks from the faucet, and pulls his sneakers on. Outside, in the spring twilight still dappling the Schloßstraße, he sets out running toward the gym, desperate to reconvene with the version of himself that's already there.

Fat!

Fat!

Fat! If there is one righteous path in this life, it is the unwavering crusade against fat. The fight for cleanness, for leanness, for purity. The man he might one day become, the hero who will rescue Hungary, concurs. The choice is yours, György: do you want to turn out like me, or do you want to turn out like Vincent?

I want to take the carving knife off the magnetized wall strip and skin Vincent alive and bake the skin in the oven until it crackles. He runs faster and faster, as if he could outrun the part of himself that just thought this, and meant it, and slobbered over the aroma of all that fat baking with garlic and

27

salt, mixing with the exhaust from the Chinese takeout stall he'll order dumplings from on his way back from the gym.

Ute

Ute walks the final stretch of the road to Kuldiga at twilight, having turned inland from what she supposes must have been the Latvian coast sometime earlier in the week. Unless that was just a mosquito-infested bog, leading nowhere, she thinks, laughing because, lately, she's found that almost everything she's capable of thinking is funny. Reports of the Chancellor's speech have filtered through her defenses, as world events still seem to do—she can't help passing newspaper kiosks and ceiling-mounted TV's muttering to themselves above the heads of sullen shopkeepers in the stores where she pilfers bread and soda—but they no longer faze her. Of course Havermeyer didn't mention the Wall, Ute thinks, realizing, perhaps for the first time, that she's given up all hope of ever being acknowledged publicly as what she is, or was.

She laughs, startling a family of sheep grazing by the roadside. But was I really what they'll never say I was? There are times, like now, when the notion that the Wall was conscious strikes her as absurd. There are any number of reasons why I might have ended up like this, she knows, squeezing the buboes clustered on her inner left thigh. Aren't there?

Well... like what, for instance?

I don't know, maybe I'm just from nowhere, she replies, retracing a familiar thought pattern, one well-worn from two decades on the road, wandering from the no-man's land between Thessaloniki and Istanbul to the torture basements of Upper Austria and the fetish clubs of Belgrade, then up to the Baltic and the Bay of Finland and around, and around, and around, skirting the Russian border without ever daring to cross into the zone of derangement, and, perhaps, ultimate peace that she suspects must lie beyond. The taiga. The true desert of zero-history. The opposite of the cradle of civilization. Russia terrifies and entices her as no part of Europe ever has. The thought of its border, which she often pictures as a quantum event, only traversable by techniques more occult than simple foot travel, is almost enough to make her stop laughing.

Kuldiga. She passes the sign now, informing her that she's arrived.

Arrived!

But arrived where?

Kuldiga!

To do what?

Be in Kuldiga!

Why?

She shudders. Sometimes the game, if it is a game, goes too far. As a prize for winning or for finding a way to quit, she fixates on the prospect of a glass of beer and a plate of hot meat under watery sauce, a night in a pub, a crowd of gawking villagers eager to hear her tell in broken English, unless they speak German, of what it was like to be the Wall. The last bulwark, the final sluice in linear time. The bones beneath the skin of the century, now left behind in a loose pile, creeping downward from ceilings and inward from walls in every government palace and significant embassy in Europe.

She shudders again, briefly picturing the basement in Graz where she ended up the last time she let a Wall-obsessed drunk bring her home. Not tonight, folks. Not tonight.

Tonight I bed by the roadside, in the cold grass among the sheep, the nettles, and the Soft Illuminati, who, she knows, wander the fringes of the continent just as surely as they've swarmed its heart, unable to stop anywhere short of total invasion, flaccid or otherwise. They don't frighten her. Any change is welcome. Smear me with your rose-scented jelly, she thinks, scratching at her armpits. Smear me and do as you please. Tell me the Wall was merely a wall, and the world is better off without it.

She pulls a handful of sharp grass over her torso in place of a blanket and wonders whether the choice to regard the Soft Illuminati as real or imaginary resides, in the final reckoning, inside or outside her skin. Or perhaps it's a moot point. She's on the edge of drifting out of individuation and back into the dreamspace where the Wall still stands, visible, as they say, from space. The wide-open taiga behind her at last, the waves of the Arctic Ocean ahead. The true end of the world, after so many false ones. A dream from which, at last, I will never be forced to wake.

Whatever's going to happen—she falls the rest of the way into this dream, leaving a husk by the Latvian roadside—is going to happen regardless of whether I or anyone else consider it real.

Anika

Anika Schulz lies in bed on the first night in her new apartment on Schönhauser Allee, in the dead center of the city, far from the pounding nightlife of the East, and amuses herself by thinking, I'm over-stimulated. My eyes are closed and I'm lying here in the soundless dark doing nothing at all, and yet, still, I'm over-stimulated. She wants to laugh and then, after a brief choking silence, she does. As she laughs, she thinks, who's to stop me? Gerhard?

She's still laughing as the silent film replays in her head. Images of that day two months ago unspool once again: their arrival at the contemporary art museum in the old Hamburg train station, the largest Anselm Kiefer retrospective in twenty years. Gerhard's favorite artist for as long she'd known him, his devotion to what he called 'the Kiefer-space' often verging on mania. She watches herself and her husband flicker around the hazy, underlit set of the museum, everyone in the crowd spooked and skittish, their attention wavering between the art on the walls and whatever coastline-related updates their phones are beaming in.

Gerhard stands so close to the paintings that his nose vanishes between the thick rivulets of black and gray paint, his eyes trembling against cancerous oil slicks, his ears deaf to everything but the clacking of rusted boats sutured to the canvas with barbed wire and vicious coils of steel running through foot-high snippets of Scripture. She twists in her sheets as he turns his head sideways to mouth, "This is all real,

33

Anika. This is all going to happen. Kiefer isn't art. This is how the world will look. Perhaps how it already does, if only we could see it as it is. Everything they've been saying about those mountains? The man in Tübingen? The Soft Illuminati? All I know for sure is that the time has come, and I, for one, don't plan on sticking around to see it."

Paranoid and suicidal!! An intertitle reads, before the film cuts back to their apartment in Prenzlauer Berg, the new one they'd just moved into after her promotion. "I'm going into my study to send an email," he mouths, and walks away, closing the door.

Ten minutes of silence—it's all silence! She thinks, delirious as the film plays on—and then a wet thud, palpable through some dreaming sense deeper than sound, and then silent screams outside, and then silent sirens... all the stock responses in a row. Everything on cue.

It wasn't until much later that night that she read the email he'd sent: *Dearest, you were right all along. All these years, we didn't take you seriously enough. You alone saw what was coming. Now I see it too. Thank you for your gift to us, and, though I know it will never be enough, I would like to apologize on behalf of humanity. I hope you will accept my life as a tiny token of our gratitude for the services you have rendered. I hope you have reached a position of equipoise, from which to go on with your work or retire with pride.*

It took her nearly a hundred read-throughs to realize that the email had merely been BCC'ed to her. Its primary recipient— and lord knows how Gerhard got the address—was Kiefer himself. She can't help thinking—now, as then—that he got out just in time. That Gerhard, alone among everyone in her life, found a way to break the impasse.

Alone now in her new apartment, deep in the impasse, she hears herself panting. The silent movie is over, the theater black and clammy.

But there's someone who won't leave. Some horny old man trolling for stragglers, a boogeyman with a rubber chicken dick beneath his raincoat. No, looking around her apartment, she senses it's more than that. Less terrestrial, harder to categorize. She blinks back an image of Gerhard behind the walls, buzzing against them like a wasp trapped between the screen and the window, then a deeper image of Kiefer's abstract canvases growing faces, the roiling grays and blacks and browns resolving into the moaning skulls of hundreds of men, her husband somewhere among them.

She forces herself onto her elbows and stares across the dark space to where it hovers in the corner, a thick darkness in the room's otherwise thin dark. It just hangs there, fulminating, biding its time, conveying the message that it feels no pressure to get it—whatever *it* is—over with.

Part of her wishes it would. If something's going to happen, she thinks, afraid to try moving in case it turns out that she can't, I wish it would already.

But it doesn't.

Finally she tries to roll over and, to her immense relief, succeeds. After flopping around in the sheets for a minute, she finds her phone. Are incubi real? Unlocking the screen and squinting into its lunar light, she pictures herself Googling this question and deciding to believe, with the fanaticism of a born-again convert, whatever answer the first search result happened to give.

But before she can either transfer this thought into action or decide to resist the temptation to do so, the cheering of a crowd outside the window rouses her into a shallower state of un-sleep, one in which she's capable of remembering the name Ragnar of Atlantis. I wonder how his speech went. I guess, judging by the shouting and cursing and bottle smashing, pretty well. Or poorly, depending on your interest in seeing the postwar consensus hold a little longer. She wants to go back to sleep, but the lingering presence of *the thing that wasn't here* is more than enough to discomfit her into a sweatshirt and a pair of slippers.

Thus attired, she plods to the kitchen to hover over an electric kettle with no plan for what to pour the boiling water onto: coffee or chamomile? Is it morning or night? She looks out the window and wishes there were some higher power she could appeal to for advice. Some authority beyond her own to say *make coffee* or *make tea*.

The kettle clicks and she leaves it unattended, letting her mind drift back out the window and down among the revelers. She tries to imagine what they're feeling, the violent, forbidden thrill with which Ragnar seems to have recharged the continent's men. She ruminates on the book proposal sitting open on her laptop, her as yet still nascent idea for an even-handed study of the Ragnar Wave, using Atlantis, to borrow from Julian Jaynes, as a potent metaphor for the sunken half of the human mind, the dark half that once heard the voices of spirits and ancestors as something more than its own repressed figments. Ulli Harz, the surging politician that no one has seen in person, would of course be another piece of the puzzle. Another set of chapters. A redundant one, perhaps. A copy of Ragnar, a double of the same avatar. A shadow of a shadow account. Or something like that. There's no way to be sure and Googling it only makes everything worse, filling the screen with videos atop videos atop videos, until they ooze off the edges and onto the walls.

How long has it been since the last book? She tries to blot out the answer, but the same part of her mind that kept her from sleeping now laughingly answers: six years!

Yeah, yeah, laugh all you want, she shoots back. But the last one was big.

This much is true. *The Persistent Myth of the Living Wall: Germany's Rapid Descent into the Post-Rational* was—and as far as Anika's concerned, still is—the most thorough and best-argued account of the topic, just as her *Soviet Hangover: The Eerie Afterlife of the DDR in the Minds of the Reunified Volk* has, for nine semesters, been Humboldt's most popular and controversial course.

Though she knows that here she's marching into the realm of bad habits—amazing how easy they are to spot, and yet how hard to change—she turns from the window and walks into the living room, where she takes her book off the shelf, trying to downplay the fact that, so far, it's the only one she's unpacked from all the boxes wedged into the corner by the door.

She sits on the clean white carpet and opens to the table of contents, hoping, she supposes, to remind herself that she's capable of putting things in order. She yawns, looks down at the mass of paper in her lap, and feels no kinship with any of it. She shudders and thinks, this must be how a child whose grandmother got her the wrong Christmas present feels, and then she thinks, wasn't I that child once? Isn't this how I felt then?

Before she reaches the point of asking herself whether she can remember where she grew up, or who her parents are, or were, she slams the book closed, hoping to crush the disorientation between the covers, even though she knows things don't work that way. What's in me is in me, and what's in the book is in the book. People are people and things are things.

But which is which? whispers the thing that wasn't here, which has come into the room with her, invisible even though the lights are on. "I'm not going to dignify that question with an answer," she whispers back, as she puts her book back into the box with all the others. Then she turns out the lights and gropes her way back to bed, despite knowing that, as soon as her eyes are closed, the silent film is going to start over again, in a seedy Weimar theater that only shows this one reel, populated only by herself and that boogeyman, already untying the sash on his raincoat.

György

György wanders the wreckage of Mitte at five a.m., stepping through piles of vomit and broken glass. His lanky frame is filled equally with two distinct rages: rage at the vile heedlessness of the whipped-up masses following Ragnar's speech, and rage at himself for missing it.

He syncs his footsteps to the alternation of these rages, so that when his left foot hits the ground, his rage seethes outward, and when his right hits, it seethes back in. *Like so am I a perpetual motion machine.* He gains speed as he traces the path of the wreckage. *The only thing viler than humanity is myself, and vice versa, and vice versa, and on and on to infinity.*

He marches across Potsdamer Platz, past the Komische Oper, and, inexorably, toward the site of the dismantled Holocaust Memorial. Where the stones and plaques once stood now stands a silent chain of men and women locked arm in arm, staring at the colossal TV tower behind Alexanderplatz. György walks among them, letting the significance of their protest sink in a little at a time. Some are shirtless with red paint on their chests, just coming visible as the sun rises, while others wear white T-shirts printed with the same text. It reads, in German gothic script: *The Wall was alive and you know it.*

The assemblage—and now he can't tell if it's real people or a collection of first-rate mannequins—mesmerizes him. He puts his face to the face of one of these figures, nearly squishing his eyes against its eyes, and feels it sucking him in, peeling off his individuality like the veiny outer shell of a shrimp.

His arms pull off the shirt that had, until just now, contained them, and his feet step freely from his shoes and then his socks. He looks at the pile of cheap fabric beneath him and thinks, the last of my personhood is contained therein. Now I'm part of something greater, something beyond the pathetic joke of individuality. My body is tight and toned and ready to do its part. He steps beside the nearest figure and presses his skin against it, trying to breathe as little as possible as he positions its unresponsive arm around his own.

His consciousness melts into the Wall's. As the Wall regards the city it used to divide, and thereby define, the TV tower and the communist skyscrapers give way to Habsburg palazzos and sprawling nineteenth century cafes, the concrete turning to handsome old stone, the grit and grime receding to reveal a more sanctified city in its stead. For a minute, or an hour—there is no longer anyone present to perceive time passing—the second-growth skyline of Berlin yields to the grand bridges and boulevards of Budapest. And not Budapest as it exists, or ever existed, trodden into idiocy by Turks, and then by Austrians, and then by Russians, and now again by Turks and Syrians and barbarians beyond naming, abetted by Brussels and Soros and Washington, but a platonic Budapest of the soul, a Budapest as the capital city of Heaven, purged of riffraff, gleaming on high for all time, with the face of an angel smiling from every gilded window.

"Never again will I abandon you," he promises Hungary. "Never again will I seek greener pastures in the West."

György hears himself moan this, and watches his eyelids flutter upward, much as he wishes they wouldn't. He tries to savor the last instant of his vision, but, as soon as he's aware that it's leaving him—or that he's leaving it—it's gone.

He shivers as selfhood returns unbidden. Slug-life resumes. The Steppenwolf slinks back to the steppe. He shivers harder and realizes he's shirtless in the new Berlin morning, alone on a dessicated plane of concrete in a mass of strangers, who are also coming awake and beginning to disperse. As he disperses along with them, he glimpses the vastness and terror of the journey he will have to undertake before he can return to Budapest a hero. And then even this glimpse curdles in the fetid reek of a thousand chain cafes pulling cheesy egg sandwiches from industrial-grade microwaves.

Anika

Anika sits at a table outside the Café Sonnenstrahl, on a pretty embankment beside the Spree that looks across to the Pergamon museum, picking at a poppy seed muffin and nursing an iced coffee. Each spring, as soon as the weather permits, she moves her student meetings to this café, ostensibly for the sake of enjoying the sunshine but really, she knows, for the sake of distancing herself from the University. Anything at all to minimize the time she spends as an employee, in someone else's building, in an office that, although it's one of the most sought-after on campus, has nevertheless been assigned to her.

Here, though she's still compelled to limit the scope of her thinking to the work of whatever student happens to be sitting in front of her, at least she can affect the pose of a private citizen, a woman on her own in the world, enjoying a muffin on her own time.

Though she can tell she'd been about to think something else, something important perhaps, the stench of unwashed T-shirt quashes whatever it was going to be and forces her to look up, into the dark-ringed eyes of a gangly, acne-scarred teenager with an ominously shaved head.

"György," she hears herself say, "sit down. I've read your paper." Normally she offers the students a coffee, though of course always hopes they'll decline, but today she can't bring herself to. She wants this over as soon as possible. She takes a long pull on her straw and rolls muffin crumbs between her fingers.

The boy takes a seat, staring past her in the direction of the river.

He says nothing, nor does he appear anxious for her to speak first. She takes fewer and fewer of these meetings, delegating them as much as possible to her teaching assistants, but, in recent years, the preponderance of boys like him has grown sharply enough that she feels compelled to address the issue in person. And who knows, she thinks, maybe it'll lay the groundwork for what's next, if I really decide to write on the Ragnar Wave. The Harz Phenomenon, the...

Alright, she commands herself, talk. "Look, I appreciate the time you clearly put into this, György, but I can't accept the paper you submitted." She pulls it from her bag and places it on the table between them, next to the remnants of her muffin. The Living Wall Was Real: Notes on the Liberal Suppression of History by György Kaczor, reads the text, in huge bold letters, across the top of the page.

György refuses to glance at the failing grade she's written beside his name, though Anika knows he can tell it's there.

"The course I teach—the course you took—is about propaganda," she begins. "It's about the pernicious lies that trickle down through history to keep us from acknowledging the truth. The myths that people, through no fault of their own perhaps, end up subscribing to, because the burden of reason is more than they can shoulder. The loneliness of a world in which events simply occur, guided by no unseen hands. A world of accidents, of miscommunications, of petty corruption and best intentions gone awry. The Berlin Wall, György, was a travesty. A dark chapter in our history that followed an even darker one, but led, thankfully, to a much lighter one." She gestures at the surrounding café, the infants napping in strollers, the tourists consulting Lonely Planets, apparently untroubled by or unaware of the churning frenzy of the coastlines.

György makes no effort to follow her gesture, and she doesn't belabor the point. "I understand that, in Hungary, you may have grown up with limited access to information. This, too, in its way, is a sorrowful result of the Wall, and all that it both stood for and enabled. And for that I'm sorry, György. But here in Germany, in the twenty-first century, we trade in reason. Coherent arguments. Sound logic. Just look at the news. Now, more than ever, the burden is on the academy to proceed carefully and methodically. Our generation is counting on yours to understand this before it's too late. Even your beloved Sloterdijk, who I know somewhat better than you do, would say the same. I cannot in good conscience grant a passing grade to a paper that does not embrace reason. If you choose to believe in the Living Wall, that is your prerogative, but you will not do so as a graduate of my course, nor, for what it's worth, do I think it likely that you will do so as a graduate of Humboldt University. If you insist on subscribing to these fictions, maybe you should just," she looks up here, catching herself just before she completes the sentence with, *go back to Budapest, where Nazis still breed like mosquitos. Where the 1940s did not lead to the 1980s and then the 2020s but only and always to the 1940s.*

The boy continues to stare past her, a few beads of sweat quivering on the sides of his skull.

She thinks, I should just leave. Just leave him sitting here, with his lunatic paper, and let him take it or not. What more is there to say?

But she can't force her body to carry this directive out. Part of her wants to know him better, perhaps even interview him for the book she may be on the verge of starting, after—she can't help but twist the knife—six long years. This boy's entire adolescence.

She tries again. "György," she says, louder this time, determined to force his attention away from whatever he's staring at. "You're an intelligent young man. You have your whole life ahead of you. Why derail it with nonsense? Now," she changes register, trying to segue from accusation to clemency, to act as if it isn't too late, "the semester is over, as I'm sure you're aware, but if you can get me a revised version by Monday, I'm willing to give it another read and adjust your grade accordingly. The registrar's office will accept an amendment if I write to them. If you simply consult the existing literature," she prevents herself from saying *my book*, "you'll see, quite clearly, what the Berlin Wall was, and what it was not. The documentation is overwhelming. Some things are ambiguous, György, but other things…"

He stands up, his eyes milky and distant. For an instant, she's afraid he's going to try to strangle her. She flinches. But then his body shakes and he starts to cry. He opens his mouth, as if about to respond, then walks away, into the crowd, leaving her there with her iced coffee, her muffin, and his paper. She watches him go as a Ragnar ticket stub blows across the concrete beneath her table, coming to a stop against her left ankle, a little gesture from the universe so dumb in its obviousness she can't help but smile.

György

Wiping his hot eyes on his sleeve, György reels off into the city. Everything he'd planned for the rest of the day turns to pulp, replaced by the low gut sense that he'd planned nothing at all. That, on the deepest possible level, he has nothing planned. Nothing planned for today, nor tomorrow, nor the day after, nor twenty nor thirty years from now. Nothing ahead, nothing coming, no conceivable scenario worth making even the slightest effort to pursue, even as there's no opposite joy in abnegation. No relief in giving up, because there's nothing to give up on.

He passes the cafes lined up along the Spree, the tables full of couples and families sitting out, sipping coffee and eating strawberry shortcake and ice cream and fruit compotes, their cell phones and sunglasses sitting beside their hands like props in the idiot drama they're all engaged in, nattering the same lines over and over in bestial redundancy. Among the fifty or sixty people he can see, there is, at most, enough raw will to animate one legitimate being.

Their mouths hang open, displaying their purple, flabby gums and horsey teeth stained with sugar and cream, their tongues smacking, their eyes rolling back in their caved-in pumpkin skulls, and György feels his thighs and shins vibrate with loathing, down into his feet, drilling him into the ground, until all he can do is stand there like a malevolent statue and close his eyes and dream of dismembering them one by one, piling the pieces in the chairs they'd been sitting in for the

47

waitstaff to shovel into the dumpsters, among the eggshells and potato peels. If I cut each of you in half, he thinks, you'd be about the size a fit person should be.

When a woman eating a cream puff with a long fork glares at him accusingly, like he's been whispering his thoughts aloud, he flushes and tips forward, and then he finds himself ducking away from the riverbank and into a side street, the buildings swelling upward and leaning in to menace him like buildings in some picture book of Viennese ghost stories from the nineteenth century.

The buildings clatter and laugh and push their residents from their bowels out to their edges, the windows filling up with jeering monkey faces, all there to revel in György's shame, licking it up, their teeth knocking together in a horrendous collective din which grows in volume as György runs deeper into the decaying city, past more outdoor tables, greasy sows pushing whole pizzas down their slop-holes and gibbering mustachioed men washing their lips and noses and chins in beer, belching so hard they send themselves flying, provoking in György the desire to pound them flat against the concrete, them and the whores they squirt in every night, and to impale their mongrel spawn with a broadsword, two, three, four, five at a time—the sword keeps growing as he pictures it—until the city is quiet and clean and then, at long last, he will sit down in a patch of grass and close his eyes and think in peace about what to do next, where to go now that Germany has proven no different from the Hungary he left behind.

He dead-ends against the backside of some municipal bureau and leans against a patch of faded graffiti and spits onto his shoes, trying in vain to vomit, while more tears stream down his face. He flashes back to high school, killing himself to master English and German while what few friends he had fucked off, spray-painting Ferneczi slogans on the decaying sides of town offices and posting memes of humanity reduced to grinning skeletons or pus-spewing zombies, commenting on livestreams and posting kill stats from shootings in other countries, laughing at the number of dead and half-heartedly making plans to top it, designing crude digital walkthroughs of their high school, or the shopping center at the edge of town, tactical plans for taking down a hundred, two hundred, a thousand squibs, pounding cheap beer and vodka in a gardening shack at the edge of town, gorging on chips and porn and, though she seemed only to ever exist in the recent past, never the present or the near future, the occasional Albanian whore... György mashes his face against the side of the building, here in Berlin, though it might as well be Gyula, he thinks, for all the difference it made in the end. He pictures the email from Erasmus last year, his acceptance to Humboldt, the surge of excitement he'd allowed himself to feel at the prospect of meeting Sloterdijk, the brief but total certainty that his life was about to change, that escape was possible, that something profound and legitimate had opened up to him, that the ruin of Hungary, the ruin of his parents and his friends and their friends, drifting into bestial hopelessness while the nation was overrun from the East, would not be his own ruin, that he would be the one to make it out, to attain legitimacy as an individual, a free agent in the West, and now, he thinks, here I am...

He looks up at the streets, at the blob of humanity that no longer appears distinct, as if the marginal differences in facial structure between one person and the next were no more than a joke on the part of some grinning designer, copying and pasting morons with senseless, unconstrained abandon, tweaking them just enough to evade the accusation of having failed to engender any progress in a hundred thousand years.

Or not even a designer, he thinks, wiping his eyes and nose with his sleeve. An algorithm, a mindless process running out of control, snuffing out genius wherever it accidentally crops up, until we're smothered in fat and grease and skin, and there's nowhere left to go, Erasmus or no Erasmus, Berlin or no Berlin. Until all we can do is crawl on our bellies toward the cliffs supposedly ringing the continent and wait our turn to tip face-first into the waves. He stalks off into the city, unsure of where, if not those cliffs, his destination might prove to be.

Ragnar

Ragnar of Atlantis climbs into the ceiling-mounted chrysalis he sleeps in while on tour, and lets the rocking of the luxury bus lull him into a reflective mood. He clutches his phone against his chin, like a squirrel with a juicy nut, and begins to type notes for next week's lecture in Copenhagen.

"The coming flood," he types. "Only in Atlantis will the strong survive. All surface life wiped out. But according to what rubric? Who decides who lives and who drowns?"

He smiles.

"I'll tell you who we won't let decide," he types, "we won't let the global, anti-humanist government forces decide. The cabal. The Soft Illuminati. We are the people, are we not? The real people! The real men who keep the real people safe from harm! And make no mistake: harm is coming. The barbarians are at the gate! But we won't let them broach it, now will we?" He hears the chants and cheers of his crowd, the same every time, in every city in Europe, and pauses to acknowledge his good luck at having found himself in his prime at exactly the right moment in history. How many artists can say that?

He indulges in answering: not fucking many.

Then, still on his phone while the bus hurtles along the boggy Northern coast of Germany, he signs into Nordmen and resumes where he left off. His avatar is, naturally, also named Ragnar, and also from Atlantis. All that's different, he thinks, from within the Game, is that here what you see is what you get. That which appears to be true actually is.

He hatches from the egg that nourishes his avatar when he isn't using it, and strides out of his tour bus and down to Southern Germany, which takes about fifteen minutes on foot. The first thing he notices is that the Black Forest is on fire. The trees are burning, blackening the sky before crumbling into grey pillars of ash. The second thing he notices is the altar in the center of the fire's reach, the stones standing upright in three columns and five rows, surrounding an innermost stone anointed with a grinning mummy in a tweed suit.

He makes note of all this, building his lecture as much from within the Game as from without, cultivating the courage to clear away the last flimsy vestiges of distinction between the two.

Anika

Anika always gets to class a full hour early on the first day of the new semester, even though it doesn't take more than fifteen minutes to set up her papers and water bottle on the lectern, and plug her laptop with its prepared slides into the overhead projection system and leave the pile of handouts, if there is one, on a desk by the door.

She does this in order to sit in the lecture hall—which, for the first five years after her book came out, had continually grown larger, and has now begun to shrink, such that today she's back in the room she taught in during years two and three—and absorb the atmosphere, becoming one with the space in order to, by the time the students arrive, guarantee that there's no power negotiation about whose property they're on. No jockeying for supremacy, even with the know-it-alls, of which there are always one or two, though none as menacing as György. Their meeting by the Spree kept her up all night, again filling her apartment with nightmares. She threw his paper out at the café, but then, a few paces later, she returned and pulled it from the trashcan. Then again, at home, she tried to throw it away. For now, it's in the bottom drawer of the desk in her office, waiting until she begins her Ragnar book in earnest.

Forget all that, she tells herself. Get back in the right headspace. Consensual subservience is what I'm here to instill in my students. She hopes that the weeklong intensive she's been hired to teach, in honor of the Chancellor's proclaimed "Summer of Tolerance" initiative, will be no different.

She roams the aisles of the stifling lecture hall, walking up and down each one and sitting briefly in each seat, staring out at the podium so as to preview all the lines of sight that will soon be trained upon her. This way, there's no possibility of ambush, no means by which a student can see her from an angle she's unprepared to be seen from and thereby, intentionally or not, undermine her authority.

Ambush.

The word lingers as the sound of the door opening sharpens her dull anxiety into something closer to fear. This whole past week was eaten alive by visitations, night after night in the new apartment, figures looming up around the edges of her vision like those mountains supposedly looming up around the edges of the continent, the result being that, when the email arrived asking if she'd be willing to teach a weeklong version of her *Soviet Hangover* course, sponsored by the Ministry of Culture and open to the public, she typed *YES* immediately, then forced herself to wait six hours before hitting Send. Even without her meeting with György, it would've come as a relief, but now it's more than that. A chance—she tries not to call it *a last chance*—to get my story straight.

From the perspective of a few hours ago, the course had seemed like a refuge, a return to the kind of authority she knows she can only exert in rooms like this one, but now... ambush. She used to lock the door until the very last minute before class started, but the University no longer allows locked doors during what they smugly refer to as "contact hours." So now she looks over at the flickering EXIT sign, cringing at the prospect of an overeager student arriving early, either to sit alone in one of the seats and stare at the whiteboard, or, worse, deluge her with a litany of nervous questions, or, worse still, with a litany of overconfident theories.

All have happened, but none are happening now.

What's happening now is that a smartly dressed woman who looks uncannily like Chancellor Havermeyer is making her way into the lecture hall and saying, in the Chancellor's calm but assertive voice, "Professor Anika Schulz?"

Anika hears herself acknowledge her own identity. Then she hears herself say yes to the Chancellor's question as to whether there's a place they can speak in private and then, what feels like an instant later, they've passed through a phalanx of bodyguards and ended up in her office. The Chancellor is seated, absurdly, in the same secondhand leather armchair occupied throughout the semester by students pressing Anika for the reference letters that she dreams, more and more often, of refusing to write. The same armchair that György sat in last semester, showing off his biceps while trying to bait me into admitting that, when I wasn't "doing my dance for them," I too believed in the Living Wall. She shudders in a way that she hopes the Chancellor can't see, and again wishes she'd thrown his paper away. When I had the chance, she thinks, as if she no longer does. She rests her fingers on the handle of the drawer she hid it in, making an exaggerated effort to keep them still.

"Professor Schulz," the Chancellor says, making no sign of having noticed this effort, "as you know, 2020 has been a trying year for the continent, and for Germany in particular. I won't get into the specifics of..." She glances at the immensity of Berlin Wall literature on Anika's shelves, then continues, "You are the foremost expert that our university system has produced on the legend of the Living Wall, and the myriad reasons why it persists in the minds of our populace, much as we'd hoped it would've died a natural death by now and left an uncorrupted generation in its wake."

Anika nods, too on edge to feign modesty.

"Well," the Chancellor continues, after looking over the bookshelf again, "there's a matter of some delicacy I've come to discuss with you."

Anika nods again, for a slightly different reason this time.

"I'll jump right in, then. This door locks, doesn't it?"

"I'm not supposed to, well, the University asks that we leave our office doors open at all times so that..." Anika looks at the door, then says, "It does."

She gets halfway out of her chair before the Chancellor says, "Allow me," and turns where she sits to engage the lock. In the newly sealed privacy of the room—Anika feels estranged from it, like it's no longer her office but rather some underground interrogation chamber she's been brought to in the night—the Chancellor says, "Have you ever been to the Black Forest?"

"The Black Forest?"

The Chancellor takes this to mean that Anika has not. "We have done what we could to prevent this story from entering the mainstream news, but perhaps you've seen it out there on the blogs—I don't presume to know your browsing habits, Professor, though of course I could have that information forwarded to me, if I so chose—but, well, there are reports that the stones of the former Holocaust Memorial, which were transported, as you know, out of Berlin and into the woods, appear to have been," she clears the throat, "rearranged."

The word hangs in the increasingly stuffy air and Anika studies the face of the woman across from her. *How do I know it's really her, the real Chancellor?* a voice asks in Anika's head, but it feels partly performative, partly György's voice, a mockery of what she *would think* if...

"They have been rearranged into," the Chancellor, or the woman that Anika has resolved to accept as such, interrupts, "a, well, it appears to be a temple of sorts. An altar. No one quite knows. Surely a prank pulled by drug-addled teenagers or inbred farmers in the region," she flushes at the minor thrill of demeaning her constituents in private, "but the story is spreading that something, let us say, of a more supernatural bent has occurred. That some entity, some emergent spirit of the Forest itself, has done this. Stirred up by the fires, perhaps. The Forest is burning, as I'm sure you're aware. In any event, people—some people—are taking this as a symbol, though of course they can't agree on what it symbolizes. Still, the notion of occult forces making themselves manifest in such a way is not conducive to the peace and prosperity that it is my duty to foster. This summer more than ever, in advance of next fall. I'm sure I don't need to explain why."

Anika nods to show that, indeed, the Chancellor does not. She's read about the fires on one of the sites she stumbled across while tracking the ongoing, ever-more-muddled reports of the shifting coastlines, the mountains that might or might not be growing, the sky that might or might not be closing in, Ulli Harz who might or might not exist, and the invading masses that might or might not be undermining, as one site put it, "the ability of sane Europeans to go on living a normal life." In the midst of the visitations in her apartment all week, this news had seemed remote, like the scores of a foreign sports team or the travails of the contestants on a dating show.

"So," the Chancellor says, "I hope you can see why your name came up in committee. Our request is that you travel this summer to the Black Forest in order to, let's say, examine the circumstances surrounding this altar. Find out who made it, what it's being used for, and why there are those scattered throughout cyberspace eager to suppose its architect is not human. At the end of the summer, you will present your findings to me and, should I find them as compelling as your work on the Living Wall, I will then present them to the public. A sort of object lesson about the ways in which we lose our moorings from time to time, straying from the path of reason, and how best to reset our course," she looks into the corner of the office, savoring this phrase and committing it to memory, should she wish to reuse it in another context. "People need reassurance in times like these, Professor. After my presentation of your findings, you will be free to turn them into a book. A follow-up to your first, which, if I'm not mistaken, is still your lone published volume?"

Anika opens her mouth, half-intending to voice some protest, perhaps even to exaggerate the status of her new work on the Ragnar Wave, but the Chancellor interrupts before she can.

"This could be a substantial opportunity for you. Should your findings prove compelling, arrangements can be made—and you will keep what I am about to say strictly private—to ensure that the book you produce becomes the volume of official record. It will be definitive. It will spend a year on the bestseller list, if not longer. A TV series will be put directly into development, with you as host, should you wish to fill such a position. It will be taught in schools throughout Europe as the verified account of this strange interlude, the true turn of the millennium, half-demented from two decades of waiting. Such an achievement could obviate, let us say, the necessity of unwanted work for the rest of your career. No more office hours. No more letters of recommendation. This much I can promise. Do you have any questions for me?"

Anika does, of course, but her spine seizes up before she can voice them. The figure of the Chancellor wavers in its chair, darkening, threatening to become the same amorphous presence that has rendered Anika's apartment all but uninhabitable. As she pictures it now, the Black Forest, even if it's on fire, promises only relief. I would climb in a madwoman's trunk just for safe passage out of Berlin, she realizes. As if there were no other way to leave.

Riveting her eyes on the grain of her wooden desk so as to blot out as much as possible of whatever vision wants to intrude, Anika forces herself to say, "If you'll excuse me, I have a class to teach. I'm already late."

The Chancellor rises from her chair, saying, in a voice that again telegraphs sober authority, "Never mind that. Pack your things, Professor. Your train to Bamberg departs in two hours."

She places a one-way, first-class ticket along with an envelope stuffed with other papers on the desk, peels the professor's fingers off the drawer handle, and shows herself out, leaving the door open as mandated by the University. When she's gone, Anika presses the cold, waxy envelope to her nose, expecting to smell ash.

Ute

When news reaches Kuldiga that an altar has been erected in the Black Forest, topped with the mummified husk of Martin Himmelreiter, the ludicrously anointed "last living Nazi," a laughing epidemic overwhelms the Latvian village where Ute's spent the past few nights. It may have started with a few discrete individuals, parked behind bright screens in dim rooms, but, by the time Ute becomes aware of it, as she crouches in the town square begging for change, it's enveloped everyone in sight. Swarthy men selling lotto tickets from carts and kiosks, children on summer vacation, office workers hurrying back from lunch: everyone succumbs to the wave, laughing until they fall over. Once they're on the ground, they go on laughing, lying on their backs and kicking their legs in the air, breathing just enough to remain conscious.

Ute laughs with them, though her laughter is, unlike theirs, voluntary. She's seen this enough times. The hysteria of a town when the people realize it's all going to happen again. Everything they've been through and more. "Not this again!" she mugs, like it's the greatest punchline ever conceived.

But the only thing that's actually funny, she thinks, is that we're all still here. That life is, even now, ongoing. That history still has more to say, despite there being no one left to hear it. No one but husks, remnants, drifting over dead ground, killing each other for grey and flavorless scraps. She could go on. Thus, the hilarity neither surprises nor overwhelms her. The rocking, cackling forms of the villagers remind her of

61

nothing so much as locusts dying in a pile at the end of their season.

Still, she forces herself to laugh a little longer, if only for the dull fellow-feeling it engenders while, underneath, she prepares to stroll among the juddering shapes and collect their wallets.

The intention moves through her system, up from her gut, through her face, and into her forehead. Once it's completed this journey, she swallows the last of the laughter in her dry throat, done with fellow-feeling for now, and gets to her feet. Brushing off the few coins that people threw at her in the course of the morning, she roves among the shaking, insensate shapes on the cobblestones, plucking one wallet after another.

She soon has sixteen in her arms, enough for ferry passage to Finland and, depending on how many credit and point-of-sale-authorized debit cards they contain, a mellow Finnish summer and perhaps even a crisp and darkening Finnish autumn in a boardinghouse someplace quiet, with plenty to eat and a little to drink.

She basks in this autumn twilight until a hand clamps around her shoulder and under her clavicle, forcing her to turn and face the stretched, red cheeks and fuming mouth-hole of the town drunk, a face that's proven almost identical in the hundreds or even thousands of towns she's passed through since 1989. A mask handed out at birth to one man in ten, or one in five. "What you got there, gypsy?" he asks, in English, not deigning to sully his native tongue on one such as her.

She gives him three wallets. He takes them with one hand, but keeps his other on her shoulder. "More," he says, leering.

There was a time, early on, when her body still appeared young and healthy enough to be traded, on occasion, for something resembling sex, but those days are long gone. The skin that has grown over her concrete and wire core since '89 has aged just as a human's would, so that now, if she were human, she'd be a woman in her late 70s, and not the kind who's become dignified with age. There was likewise a time when she might've run, but now, her top speed reduced to a shambling lurch, that too is no longer an option.

So she takes a different tack, the only one that's remained effective. "You know what I am," she whispers. "I'm no gypsy." She clutches the drunk's hand and runs it under her dress and up her side, all the way to her armpit. "You have a place around here? Some room you go to with your friends before the bar opens, or after they throw you out?"

The man opens his eyes wider, wide enough, it seems to Ute, to reveal the chugging of his barely functional brain. Too slow to get what everyone else is laughing about. Finally, he nods.

She tries to smile while running her eyes across the remaining wallets on the ground. She knows he'll fight her if she tries to retrieve them. "Take me there," she sighs, as those slow, calm months in Finland drift off into another year.

György

In the week since the Eternal Weimar speech and his meeting with the professor and subsequent run through the city's sorry afternoon decline, György has followed news of the resurrected altar in the Black Forest, as well as ongoing reports of the coastlines tearing themselves to shreds. He watches the continent devolve on the monitors at the gym, reports breaking through other reports so fast that the screen often resembles microscope footage of cell division. He's been holed up in the weight room, toning and polishing his still-adolescent body in hopes of recapturing some fraction of the feeling he caught in the hours before dawn, when he'd taken his place in the monument to the Living Wall and glimpsed...

It feels like blasphemy to refer to the vision now that it's receded.

Still, it's all he can get his mind to settle on. Any notion of trying to smooth out the situation at Humboldt, or of returning his parents' calls, no matter how worried they sound, is more than he can find the will to consider. My will must be conserved, he knows, staring at his biceps in the gym mirror. Only my will can save me now, he warns himself, without quite being able to articulate what he needs saving from, nor quite what, tangibly speaking, his will consists of.

As he curls dumbbells, he replays the scene with the professor at that pig-trough café by the river. He imagines rising to his feet, looming over her, and saying, right to her face, "the Wall was the only thing holding it all together, and you killed it. You killed it once with bulldozers, and again with books. It was the spine of the continent, and you ripped it out and threw it away. And what are we left with now? A culture made of mayonnaise. Mayonnaise voters, mayonnaise politicians, all of you rotting together in a slick wet bowl."

He reaches the end of his repetitions, but keeps lifting so as to finish out the scene in his head. "A gigantic mayonnaise corpse putrefying in the sun." He sniffs the air. "Can't you smell it? I sure can. I can see the maggots wriggle. And you want me to comfort you in your denial? You want to fail me if I don't play your game?"

He snarls at his reflection in the mirror. "I don't think so. Enjoy the rest of your decomposition. Me? I'm gonna find a way out."

Though he ends this set of extra reps on a triumphant note, by the time he starts the next, he's back to the morbid fantasy of having lived and died in the twentieth century, like Mishima, like Hesse, like Jünger, like Cioran, or even earlier, like Nietzsche or, earlier still, Schopenhauer. Speaking of will. He almost laughs as he heaves the dumbbell in his right hand up to his chin. To have simply been a great man in an earlier era, when the planet wasn't dying. When we weren't about to go extinct. When I could've died with dignity, a hero, a figure of worship, a man to be reckoned with by future generations.

And now, what? No matter the greatness of what I achieve, how long will it last? Ten more years? Twenty? He slams the dumbbells back into their rubber rack and scoffs away, seething at humanity's callousness. This is what you left us? The present you were kind enough to give? He wants to scream. Why leave us a world at all? Why not find the decency to end it?

If you're sure there's no future, then why not let yourself go? The voice asks him. Why not pull out your cock right here and…

And what? He snarls back. What good would that do?

It'd prove you're not a coward. And if you're not a coward, then maybe you can find it in you to…

The thing inside him swivels his head toward the darkened, floor-to-ceiling windows, and forces his mind to play a scene of his body flying outward in a shower of glass.

Now that's heroism, the voice says. Like Mishima. Remember, coward?

Yeah, the other voice protests, but before he did that, Mishima wrote like twenty, or twenty-five, I mean…

And that's why, the voice retorts, you are at best a satire of ambition. Slinking off to Berlin to become a philosopher, leaving your friends to fight for the soul of Hungary without you. No real man will ever see you as anything but a sniveling whelp. You'll be lucky if someone deigns to kill you.

As soon as this spiral commences, any productive workout is over. He knows that much by now. Pinching his belly, he retreats to the showers, strips, and spends a few minutes in the abandoned steam room, punching the slick tile walls until his knuckles open. Then he gets dressed, picks up pork dumplings and scallion pancakes at the takeout Chinese stall next door, and eats them in bed.

He falls asleep as soon as he pushes the empty containers onto the carpet, despite Vincent loudly smacking down cereal and watching cartoons on his laptop at the table just outside the door. His dream, which starts right away, burns Berlin to the ground and raises Budapest in its stead. He wanders the city, retracing the path he took after his meeting with the professor, the windows of the grand prewar buildings again filling with angels, the open doorways clotting with ghosts, a soft androgynous voice calling him toward...

He startles awake, unsure where he is. He slaps around for his phone, half-planning to call his mother, but his hand touches his laptop first, so he drags it onto his chest instead.

"The entirety of the EU," he reads, in white Hungarian text against a black background on a site that must've auto-updated many times since last he checked it, "is going to crumble. Only Hungary will remain. Maybe. Ferneczi promised as much, but even he, in the year since the shock election, has backed down by degrees. Tiptoed away from the cliff of the new, back toward the suffocating morass of the old. Even he's proven to be a coward at heart. Just another servant of the Soft Illuminati. The time has come to rise up, together, brave comrades in arms, against the State, which will only ever..."

They're all cowards, György scoffs, closing the site. Everyone in a position that requires courage. The world can't be salvaged. It needs to be remade, the buried kernel of its true self dislodged from the colossal heap of manure that's accrued on top of it since the Middle Ages, if not since Rome's conversion, its cowardly abandonment of the ancient gods in favor of Christ's other cheek.

He smiles, realizing that he's now repeating the last lines of the Ragnar podcast he listened to at the gym. Rolling over, he wonders if all his thoughts at the gym were actually lines from the show. This reminds him of tomorrow night's lecture in Copenhagen. Removing his parents' credit card from the wallet in the back pocket of the jeans that lie twisted on the floor beside his mattress, he buys a general admission ticket and then, once it's gone through, a seat on the high-speed train that leaves Berlin's Hauptbahnhof in three hours.

Ute

Ute follows the Latvian drunk through a warren of backstreets, seeking the point where the old city gives way to the new, the dense, medieval core rotting into block housing and motorways, flanked by auto-grills and gas stations, all of them full of soft bodies that can't stop laughing. She laughs too at the thought that this somehow still constitutes a world.

"What?" the old man barks.

Ute shrugs and squeezes his hand, urging him onward like a horse. The sooner we get to whatever hole he lives in, she thinks, the sooner we can get it over with and I can be on my way Westward.

Westward?

Yes. Time to return to Germany. See about that altar. The Russian border draws her toward it for months at a time, but it always repels her before she can make any serious attempt to cross, or even to discern if crossing is possible. Every year, though she rarely spells it out, her wanderings follow a migratory path from west to east and back again, between the Ardennes and the gulf that seems to open between her feet and Russian soil whenever she draws close enough to contemplate crossing over.

Russia, she thinks, still guiding the old man while trying to let him think he's guiding her, will mark the end of my journey, whenever the time comes. Perhaps that will constitute a kind of freedom, an eternity among the wolves and birch trees, beyond the last weak tendrils of history. She moans as she lets herself imagine it, the birch forest growing outward to the farthest edges of her consciousness and then growing farther still, warping over into the buzzing, charged-up space where her inner world syncs with the rest of the Wall's. She pictures all the atomized pieces on journeys congruent with her own, all of us burning off time until Europe finishes its interminable decay and leaves us, finally, free to abandon it. Forgotten at last, when no one remains to remember us.

Next year in Siberia. She stifles another laugh.

"Almost there," the old drunk grunts, his calloused fingers worming their way down her back and around the scarred flesh of her upper buttocks.

The man's home, such as it is, smells of sawdust and motor oil. He heaves up a grate to let them in, then heaves it down as soon as they've entered. Ute clenches her teeth to keep from shuddering. It's a bad idea, she knows all too well, to let them lock me in like this. She recalls the man in Chemnitz who padlocked her in his basement and forced her to watch as he injected an anesthetic into his scrotum, removed one of his testicles with a kitchen knife and, barely wincing, carved it into a flesh swastika, which he presented her with just before passing out and, as far as she could tell, dying on the spot.

She kept it in her pocket for the next few days. Then she fed it to a pig she met by the road south of Dresden. When the pig swallowed it whole and implored her with its eyes for more, she thought, if I had more, I would gladly give you them all.

It would be my honor to stand by your side and watch you swallow them down, one after another after another, until they were all gone.

"Wait there," the man orders, as he heaves across the concrete floor and into an adjacent room, which erupts in snarls and barks and then, a moment later, the sound of chains and the whining of a rusty lock and then, another moment later, shouting in a language she can't comprehend mixed with the slamming of a large dog against the bars of a cage.

The man returns winded and panting, half-visible in the light filtering under the door he's just closed. Easing herself into the trance that makes these encounters bearable, she asks, in English just slightly better than his, if she should remove her dress or if he'd like to do anything else first.

He seems not to understand the question, so she mimes the act of removing it, and the man nods, still winded, his eyes glimmering. Secondary smells of fur and unwashed work clothes fill her nostrils as she drags the fabric past her face, her exposed skin puckering in the dank air.

She folds the dress on a worktable a few paces away, then removes her underwear and places that on top, hoping the man will allow her to keep her socks on, as the floor is almost certainly strewn with nails.

He makes no sound other than that of his panting moving lower in his throat. Naked but for her socks, she walks over to him and presents her right side. She holds still while he drags his hands up and down the grout and dried cement and ingrown steel wires that run from her hip to her armpit, his fingers quivering with excitement. She sees that it's his first time. With men like this, you can never tell until the last minute. Some have made a fetish out of tracking us down, while others wait like bullfrogs until we cross their path.

He runs his fingers along the length of the wires, feeling their grooves and irregularities, his eyes closed as—Ute has no doubt—the Wall rebuilds itself in the weak ground of his imagination. The incoherent continent comes back together, its broken backbone healing for the few moments between now and his inevitable orgasm. How she wishes she could share his excitement; to spend even a second with the feeling that the past still matters, and points toward an actual future, a Europe divided in such a way that East and West each grow charged with purpose, with real hope, real fury... to look forward to rather than backward at the fall of the Wall, as if it were all that stood in the way of paradise... what would I give to feel that again?

What do I even have to give? She almost laughs again but, for fear of shaming this old man whom she can't quite bring herself to hate, refrains.

She hears his belt buckle hit the cement floor and the gelatinous sounds of his right hand going to work, while his left presses deeper into the caulking that dams up her armpit. He grips onto the rough material, pressing his side into hers, hard enough for her wire to penetrate his skin, and then he moans and, for a moment, stops.

She stands very still, unsure of the direction things are about to take, as the man waddles over to another workbench in another corner, his pants still around his ankles, and falters through a drawer, picking up and putting down objects, until he closes the drawer and returns with a box-cutter, its blade ratcheting out one click at a time.

She closes her eyes and pictures the virgin Russian taiga, in which perhaps she and her lost cohort will now spend eternity together, frozen in the Arctic wind.

Please just make it quick, she prays, as she prayed in '89, when the hammers came.

She hears a low moaning and, a moment later, feels hot blood pooling around her feet, and is about to give thanks for how painless it's been when she feels the man tip against her, and looks over to see that he's sliced his own side open, and is now inserting her wires into the wound.

Her dormant erotics flicker to life as she feels her metallic extensions, which over the years have grown nerves of their own, enter this stranger's system, and she reaches her arm out to press him closer, her dry grout growing slick with his blood, and she listens to him moan and, a moment later, hears his weak emission hit the floor, and then she comes too, despite herself, and pushes him off of her, wincing as her wires retract from his body and the flaps of his side hang loose and the caged dog snarls in the other room.

The man collapses and lies shuddering and whispering in Latvian, surely begging whatever god he believes in to grant him a pleasant dream.

She wipes her wires with one of the oily towels she finds hanging on a hook by the door, then steps into her underwear and her dress, then returns to regard the small, wizened man curled like a puppy on the concrete.

A wave of pity overtakes her and she bends over to pull his pants up, hoping to leave him in a semi-decent state should anyone find him here, but he rolls over when she touches him and so, afraid of disturbing whatever repose he's succeeded in crawling into, she simply takes back the wallets he took from her and stuffs them into a paper bag. Then she covers his wound with the oily towel and unlocks the shed door with the key that, it turns out, had been dangling in the padlock all along.

Outside, the day is finally ending, the laughter dying down. She heads into the sunset, away from the ineffable wilds of Russia and back toward Lithuania, Poland, and the crushingly overdetermined border of Germany, the most crossed and thus least numinous on her entire circuit.

Anika

Anika arrives in Baiersbronn at noon on a Sunday, the long train journey already decaying in her memory like a deep, dense dream that she's awoken from too quickly. She gets out of the hot, empty compartment, crosses the nearly empty platform, and takes out her phone to read over the email the Chancellor's office sent her, with detailed directions to the cottage that, they claim, has been set aside for her to reside in for the duration of her project.

She studies the blue line marking her hypothetical path from the station to the cottage on the Google map attached to the email and then, extending the roller-handle on her suitcase and hefting her shoulder bag higher up her shoulder, sets out along the cobbled streets, past the church, past the two closed bakeries, the Stammkneipe cantilevered over a brook, the realtor's office on the other side, and then two restaurants, one of which looks surprisingly upscale. She examines the menu in its glass case, allowing herself to salivate over the roasted pig's knuckle and Eisbein and half-kilo steaks, the sort of artery-clogging Teutonic classics one can hardly find in Berlin anymore.

Then, before she's quite ready, she wipes her mouth, turns from the menu, and sets out along a path leading first past bushes and shrubs and then into the woods themselves. The Black Forest *an sich* she thinks, realizing only now that she's never been here before. The banality of the thought forces her to stop and take stock. How could I not have realized? She

75

looks up at the overhanging trees and listens to the creaking of branches and finds herself wondering about the ground that Hänsel and Gretel passed over, whether their little feet trod the same dirt she's now dragging her suitcase along, their breadcrumbs buried deep underground, or if… a feeling of total lostness, a midnight feeling, overtakes her, indifferent to the fact that it's broad daylight and she's only just arrived.

Enough! She tells herself, in her best impression of her professor voice. Stop being a child. Get out your phone and check the directions again, then follow them to your cottage, where you will, in short order, lay your bag flat on the ground, unzip it, remove your laptop and power cord, plug it in and place it on a table, then sign onto the Wi-Fi network which, with any luck, will be easily accessible using the password also contained in the email on the phone you should be already checking.

Anika does her best to obey, and mostly succeeds, but the soft footsteps of Hänsel and Gretel creep along behind her the rest of the way. She knows better than to turn around, but, all the same, she can't help wishing they would stop, or, at the very least, have the decency to muffle themselves behind a gauze curtain—she feels herself straining for an adequate concept and settling for the first that comes to mind—separating then from now.

The cottage is set off from the trail in a clearing framed by immense trees and dense beds of moss, with a fire pit and two plastic chairs between where she stands and the door. She can smell smoke and hear a distant crackling, enough that her mind flashes on an image of Gerhard licking a long row of

Kiefer's in whatever hell he's ended up in, framed forever by those images of civilizational collapse that, she's now certain, were all he ever loved. It was never that he feared it coming too soon, she realizes; it was that he feared it coming too late. He feared missing it. The crackling becomes that of the projector, the silent film boiling and shaking as Gerhard's tongue runs from one edge of the frame to the other, and Kiefer, Dark Lord of the Black Forest, welcomes another lost soul.

Forcing her way out of the theater before the film plays through yet again, Anika drags her bag past the coals without checking how fresh they are, and stops to pull open the screen door, holding it with her hip while she scans her phone for the keypad code to open the wooden door behind it. 1-9-8-9 she types, grinning as the lock clicks open. She jiggles the handle until it gives, then shoves her way into the cool, dim, empty...

She shrinks as a man looks up at her from the table, waving without making any effort to stand. She turns and considers running, but her back seizes as the man says, "Welcome."

The word hangs in the space between them, refusing to resolve into menace or its opposite, whatever that might be. Anika looks at him, waiting for him to say something else. She senses that the time to run, if there ever was such a time, has passed.

When she's made it clear that she's not about to respond, the man gets to his feet with a heavy downward push on the tabletop and lumbers over to her, his breath sharp with liquor and his armpits dank with sweat. He gestures at the tiny interior and says, "The place is ready for you. I'm Horst. Don't worry, I'll be very nearby if you need me."

After making this promise, or threat, he stands still and looks her over, perhaps smelling her just as she's smelling him, waiting for her to step aside.

"Is there any, um," she mumbles, realizing that she forgot to bring any food or other supplies, having assumed that the cottage would be much closer to town.

"The refrigerator is full." Horst belches and exhales, letting his stench fill the small space. "As is the liquor cabinet. I've been instructed to keep them both that way, so I will come with fresh supplies once a week. If you need anything sooner, my number is on a card taped to the refrigerator. Call anytime."

With this, he turns, brushes past Anika on the threshold, and vanishes into the woods.

When she's sure he's gone, she unpacks, then lies on top of the bed as the afternoon dims toward evening, trying to make herself comfortable. She looks across the interior at her laptop plugged in and set up on the table, in front of the seat where Horst had been sitting, and thinks, well, how does it strike you? Do you feel safe here? Do you feel any different than you did in Berlin?

The screen remains illuminated for a few more minutes, then goes to sleep, taking Anika with it. She falls into a cottage that's filling with green light, just as the one she left behind turns black. She knows, in a vague, half-conscious way, that soon it'll be dark everywhere and she'll wake up confused and uneasy. But, for now, she's in a place of luminous sylvan green, the light bathing her and caressing her, massaging her muscles, working out the kinks from the long train journey and the long years in Berlin before that, the years of quasi-celebrity in which, for better or worse, she'd presented herself to the world as someone who knew what was happening, on a scale both grander and more nuanced than most people can claim to know anything at all.

Now, in the green cottage, the trees outside are talking to her, leaning in through the windows, their voices drunk and harsh, their accent backwards and southern, like Horst's.

"Welcome," they say, "you've arrived. After a lifetime in exile, you have come home. You are in Germany now, the real Germany. Your homeland, the bower of your people. No more thousand-Euro strollers in Prenzlauer Berg; no more döner kebabs and Spanish discos in Neukölln. You will never return to Berlin as it was. That Berlin is an island in time and space. Let it sink back under the waves. You are now, at long last, where you belong."

The voice sounds so much like Horst's that Anika startles awake, terrified that he's in the cottage, leaning over the bed with his belt unbuckled.

But no, as far as she can tell in the dark, she's alone. She shivers and draws her arms tight around her body, waiting for a modicum of inner balance to return. When it doesn't after several minutes, she tiptoes off the bed, afraid to make any noise even though she's still fairly certain she's alone, and opens the refrigerator, which, as promised, is full of food. She stares at the rows of vegetables and packaged meat, trying to imagine what she might do with them. Then she closes the door and opens the liquor cabinet which is also, as promised, far from empty.

Sipping her first glass of wine, she spots an old issue of *Der Spiegel* lying out on the counter, posed there, she assumes, waiting to be found. After studying Havermeyer's face on the cover, she flips to the article about the Chancellor's rise from small-town Mayor to the very head of the ship of state, but she stops reading after the section entitled *Formative Years in Baiersbronn*.

She crushes the magazine, stuffs it in the trash under the sink, and refills her wineglass, which appears to have emptied itself.

György

The audience goes wild as Ragnar takes the stage riding a hairy naked man who, after a moment, György recognizes as Lars von Trier, the once-great auteur who'd nearly vanished from public life. He raises his right arm, still sore from the gym, in a salute along with the five or six thousand other men in attendance as Ragnar jerks the leather reins fastened to the dog collar around Lars' neck, riding him to the front of the stage to return the audience's salute, then turning him around and riding him toward the back, affording the audience a clear view of his flabby buttocks. The cheering continues for several more rotations of the stage, Rammstein's "Bück Dich" blaring, as ever, over the soundsystem, half-ironic and half-sincere, until Lars collapses under the weight on his back and the audience boos.

Ragnar dismounts and, still clutching the reins in his fist, drags Lars by the neck to the front of the stage to greet the crowd head-on for the first time. In the pulsing blue lights and waves of smoke, he looks like a giant. A figure straight out of Nordmen, György thinks, amazed at how quickly the spectacle has drawn him in.

"Greetings from Atlantis, the land of buried truths!" he shouts, his voice deep and rich with an accent all its own. He holds the mic-stand high over his head with one sculpted, tattooed arm, while keeping a firm grip on the leash with the other. "I said, greetings from Atlantis, the land of buried truths!"

The crowd goes wilder still, then simmers down as Ragnar drops the mic stand. "This man has betrayed his ideals," he shouts, jolting the reins until Lars is in a half-sitting position, his whimpers audible through a mic that must be hidden in his beard, his penis and balls choked by a rubber tourniquet into a gruesome bouquet. "He is now no more than a puppet, a sack of flesh on a string. A slave of the international art market, crafting parodies of violence for weaklings in cozy theaters in Paris and New York." The audience boos louder. "But… and let me get right down to business here, so are most of you. There's a reckoning coming, and it will spare none but the strongest. Can you confidently swear you are among that number?"

More cheering as a curtain lifts at the back of the stage to reveal a replica of the altar that has supposedly been erected in the Black Forest. Blue flames lick at the stones, working their way up toward the antler-bedecked mummy on top.

György stands on tiptoe to see over the shaved heads of two burly men who've just now forced their way in front of him, but his calves are too sore from the gym to allow him to hold this posture for long. So he settles back onto his feet and nurses his Carlsberg, trying to locate himself in his body, but he remains dispersed, unsure of his place in the throng. Just let me disappear, he thinks. Just let something absorb me.

The men cheer again, jostling together and stomping their feet, pressing so close to the stage that their many skins merge into one.

"In Atlantis," Ragnar booms, "the absolutely true remains absolutely true. No one has, and excuse me here, fucked with the truth. We know what's real. We are the only society that has never had any need for belief, nor for interpretation, nor for compromise, nor for laws and treaties, for we simply recognize what is. And it is beautiful, and it is great, and it is—let me hear you say it—pure!"

The room fills with sound, but it's not enough for Ragnar. He demands to hear it again.

"It is pure!!" the crowd shouts again, loud enough to bring a smile to the speaker's face.

"You're goddamned right it's pure. I wish you could see it. But you can't. You're not ready. In your current forms, the journey would kill you. You'd drown halfway there."

Cries of disappointment fill the hall.

"I know, I know. But we're very selective in Atlantis. We have to be. Most humans don't make the grade. Though I don't have to tell *you* that!" The hall fills with cheers. "Down in Atlantis, we live in harmony with myth. We dream true dreams, and we know they're true, and we get on with our lives. With honor. With dignity. We are shown the way. There is no confusion. There is no second-guessing. There is no miring in the filth of self-consciousness. There are no Soft Illuminati, flaccidly raping us in our sleep, without even the decency to let us know that it's happened. There are no..." he jerks the reins around Lars' neck again, "weirdos!" Then, lowering his voice and narrowing his eyes, he adds, "In Atlantis, the absolute is present. All hail the absolute!"

In the videos that György's seen, this line always gets the largest cheer, and tonight is no exception. Copenhagen goes wild as the flames around the altar in the background surge up toward the ceiling, kindling the mummy's tweed suit.

"All hail the absolute! All hail the absolute!" chants the crowd at Ragnar's prompting, only stopping when he makes a theatrical throat-slitting gesture and then pretends to shoot into the crowd with the mic-stand.

"Seriously," he continues, "we down in Atlantis are worried about what we're seeing up here. Europe is wasting what little time it has left. The flood is coming and your governments are dithering like dogs nipping fleas. There are, to mix metaphors for a second here, bigger fish to fry. This is a civilizational crisis, people. Time is of the essence. Atlantis sank under the waves thousands of years ago to avoid facing the wages of uncertainty that will now be your undoing. The fracturing of realities into sub-realities, and sub-sub-realities, the endless splitting of hairs and mixing of races, the boiling of our ordered cosmos back into the primal chaos it emerged from, until... until... until..."

He pretends to be so worked up that he loses his place in his lecture. Then he shouts, "Until brave men band together and rise up! Until we put our collective foot down and shout, 'Enough bullshit! Reality is singular, and it will be restored! We know what's real, and we're ready to fight for it!'"

"We know what's real and we're ready to fight for it!" chants the crowd, over and over and over, as the lights go wild and smoke blankets Ragnar in a thick white cloud and Lars begs for mercy while György approaches something like ecstasy where he stands in the middle of so much sweaty, superfluous flesh.

After the show, he loiters outside the hall, sucking down the cool Danish summer air and trying to regain his footing before deciding how best to face the city in which, he now realizes, he's neglected to book a place to stay.

He watches the drunken masses swarm out and lets the familiar mixture of longing and loathing swirl up from his gut. Grunting apes, says one voice in his head, while the other says, let me in. Just let me be part of something for once in my life.

The alternation of these two voices, each growing louder to drown the other out, absorbs most of his attention, until a gust of cigarette smoke cuts through both to the silence underneath. He coughs and blinks, and looks into the faces of two blonde men in leather jackets and black jeans.

He tries to think of something suitably threatening to say, but gets nothing out before the one on his left jeers, "Waiting for his autograph?"

György shrugs. He flaunts the knuckles he busted in the steam room, while looking over at Ragnar's tour bus parked beside the venue and wondering what the scene inside is like. Not the best racket for picking up girls, he thinks, a smile playing across his lips.

"Yo, dude, you with us here?" one of them snaps in his face.

He nods, falling out of a suddenly vivid vision of a green, undulating Hungarian meadow in May, some handsomer version of himself sprawled on the neon grass with a buxom farm girl sprawled beside him, her simple cotton dress riding up in the breeze.

"What's your name, man?" the other asks, his voice slightly gentler now.

György has to cough and shudder to force his mind to stay in its body. He tells them his name.

"Word," one of them says. "I'm Gunnar, and that's Knut. What'd you think of the show?"

He must have said something that identified him as an ally, because the next question he registers is, "You like to drink?"

He lets on that he doesn't hate to and drifts outside his body again to watch it follow its new friends up the street and around the corner, into what he senses may be the beginning of a more consequential phase of his existence. Good, it's about time, half of him thinks, trying hard to convince the other half, which wants nothing more than to slither back to Gyula and live a coward's life in his dead uncle's gardening shack on the edge of town.

Ragnar

When the crowds have dispersed, Ragnar changes into sweatpants and a Champion tank top, and sprawls on a leather ottoman in his tour bus, sipping chilled aquavit as he waits for Lars and his entourage to arrive. He picks at the herring and lox and caviar arranged on the table, and basks in the feeling that tonight may have been his best show yet. It damn well ought to've been, after four grueling days of rehearsal with Lars micromanaging every last detail. He laughs to consider how far the show has come and how much farther it might still go. Then he plugs his mic into his computer to record a quick podcast before the high fades and the afterparty obliterates its memory.

Ute

Ute reaches Germany after a long, hard trek through Poland, alternating between ancient boreal forests and crumbling post-industrial sprawl. The return, she finds, is always faster than the departure, as if there were currents governing land speed just as there are in air and water. The season is no longer identifiable; it feels hot but late in the year, the sky full of smoke as the days darken and the grass turns brown.

She crosses the border that divides the towns of Zgorzelec and Görlitz, free and open today, though she can sense that soon this will no longer be the case. She forces her feet to mimic the gait of the others crossing along with her, and, if anyone can tell that she's in any way unlike them, no one lets on.

So now she's in Görlitz, the sky already dim, the hour impossible to determine until she passes the clock tower in the main square, which she decides to look at but then neglects to, because a throng of shrieking children absorbs the entirety of her attention in the instant between the decision taking root in her head and the resultant action manifesting in the muscles and tendons of her neck, which have grown steadily thicker and coarser in the years since '89, less responsive the more tangled her nerves and wires have become.

Her gaze is now riveted on this metastasizing throng, children and teenagers bearing aloft stuffed bears and apes, rubber effigies and leaky sacks of trash with crude faces painted on them, chanting, "Let them drown! Let them drown! Let the dogs drown!" as they approach the fountain at the foot of the clock tower. The percussive insistence of the chant hammers home, far more clearly than the ambient chatter around her so far has, that she's back in a country where she can't help but understand the language. Dammit, she thinks, also in German. She wants to look with longing back toward the Polish border and consider the possibility of returning the way she came, but, just as the spectacle around the fountain precluded any possibility of checking the time, so too does it compel her attention away from the border. That door, she can tell, as her head fills with harsh, overly familiar syllables, has closed until next year.

The children and teenagers foremost in the procession lean over the fountain to dunk the stuffed animals and rubber toys and bags of garbage, shoving them under with bats and paddles, chanting, "Drown! Drown! Drown!" even louder than before, their voices more in sync, their many organisms merging into one, while, behind them, the next row of congregants holds posters bearing psychedelic drawings of the never-seen Ulli Harz or maps of Europe surrounded by ominous black zones, some smudged and featureless, others overflowing with drooling hordes of one-eyed giants and rat people with jagged fangs. It comes as no surprise to Ute that any coherent map of the territories surrounding the continent is a thing of the past—the most cursory web search in the public libraries where she sometimes stops to check directions reveals maps that either simply end where Europe ends, or depict barbarous wasteland extending away on every side, its minions entering the continent through obscene new orifices—but the combination of the signs and the drowning of the effigies and the inrush of over-familiar language turns her stomach a few degrees further than it's been turned already.

Or perhaps she's simply hungry. She yawns as the children leap into the fountain to stomp the leather, rubber, and plastic bodies they've scattered there, determined to drown them all equally, and thereby save the venerable town of Görlitz from…

Ute yawns again, declining to complete the thought. The yawn is deeper this time, drawing her shoulders all the way up to her earlobes. As they sink back down on her exhale, a hand attaches to her left clavicle, sending shivers along the wires bundled beneath her baggy coat. Slowly, she turns to find out who or what the hand belongs to this time.

On the other end of the arm attached to the hand stands a severe but smiling black-haired woman wearing burgundy lipstick and Prada eyeglasses. She's as old as Ute perhaps, but better preserved, or simply better-looking. Her features are sharper, more carefully drawn. The two of them regard one another without speech for a moment, covering all the preliminaries with their eyes while the townspeople rage, splashing water onto the cobblestones and flipping the tables of the outdoor cafes.

The woman adjusts her coat—just as baggy as Ute's, though far more chic—and nods in the direction of a hotel on the far side of the square, across from the clock tower. Though no particular invitation has yet been tendered, Ute is more than willing to follow this woman out of the fray, which has now swollen to include adults as well, farmers waving knives and clubs and police officers clutching dogs on chain leashes, all of them chanting and barking, "Drown! Drown! Drown!" as loudly as their lungs will let them.

Having crossed the square without incident, Ute and the woman walk through the lobby of the Hotel Silesia, which claims to be a four-star establishment, and up a flight of stairs onto the second floor, into the empty restaurant. They stand on the threshold, surveying the expanse of tables, until a bald man hastily buttoning a waiter's vest over his white-collared shirt bustles in behind them, turns on the lights, and, pretending to overlook their baggy coats and sagging posture, says, "Right this way, ladies."

He leads them to a table in the very back corner, as if it were the last one available, but the woman, her voice rich and grave, her German more refined than any Ute's heard in years, says, "By the window, please. We'd like to watch the festival while we eat."

The man looks behind him, as if hoping for reinforcements, but, finding no one, nods and leads the way over to the table nearest the window, beyond which the square, the fountain, and the growing pile of human or humanoid bodies is clearly visible.

As Ute approaches her seat, she looks down and sees one of the effigies writhe in a little girl's arms, its hollow mouth riven, but a moment later it's underwater and a moment after that—she's seated now, the menu open before her—it's as still as all the others, no longer worthy of the compassion that, Ute supposes, all living things deserve.

Looking back at the menu, she hears the woman declare, "Now this is my treat." Then, though Ute hasn't protested, she adds, "I insist, really."

Ute nods, eyes on the woman's baggy coat, which, of course, she hasn't removed. She wonders what the woman's wires look like, how tangled or how free they are. She senses herself on the verge of blushing and so takes a large swallow of water, stifling a cough. Meetings like this used to be common—in the nineties, she ran into remnants of the Wall almost everywhere she went—but the first decades of the new millennium have served as a zone of diffusion, flooding the extended family with fakes while the originals died off or hid themselves away.

Ute grunts assent as the woman finishes listing a series of proposed entrees and wines, and then half-listens, a moment later, as she repeats this series, verbatim, to the glowering waiter.

"I know it'll taste like rubble," the woman muses, lighting a cigarette that took her a long time to find in her red leather purse, "but that's part of the thrill of splurging, don't you think?"

Ute wonders how to respond. *The thrill of splurging.* She considers the phrase, even as surplus has never been among the problems she's sought to solve. Picking at the sauce-stained white tablecloth while ash drips from the woman's cigarette into a green glass ashtray, she knows what she's going to say only when it passes her lips. "The Authentication Ritual, shouldn't we..."

The woman exhales a mouthful of smoke that becomes a *shhh*. A frown comes across her face, but passes quickly. "There's plenty of time for that. I, for one, have nowhere else to be tonight. How about you?" Her voice is calm, though not so calm as to mask the presence of something fiercer underneath.

Ute's silence conveys that she, too, has nowhere else to be. She's been burned before—many times in the nineties, and early in the new millennium, she spent the night with men and women claiming to have been part of the Wall, only for their implants to come out or break off partway through their time together—but encounters such as this one have grown so rare that she can't find the will to cut it short.

"Ah, our Riesling," the woman says, looking out the window as the waiter pours a drop in her glass. She tastes it and nods.

The waiter shuffles away once their glasses are full and, as if to mock the intimacy of their dinner, turns on a large TV mounted on the wall, though he's decent enough to keep it on mute. Ute, who can't help looking over, sees that it's broadcasting the same event that's transpiring just below. The text across the bottom of the screen reads, "Courageous townspeople defend themselves against fresh wave of invaders pouring in from Poland."

The word 'invaders' lingers in her head until the delivery of the shellfish course reminds her that she isn't here alone. The platter of crabs and half-cracked mollusks fuses, in Ute's gut, with the drowning still underway in the square. The wealthy woman—as Ute has come to regard her—picks up one of the two hammers and smashes a purple claw, grinning through her makeup.

"I'm Klara," she says, slurping down crabmeat. "No reason not to learn each other's names, even if we're not going to…" She gestures ambiguously with the hammer.

Ute, picking up a hammer of her own, nods and mutters her name, before cracking down on a striated piece of shell. After shaking the fishy water onto her plate, she sucks out the orange meat, tasting it for the first time in her long life. Rubble, like everything else, just as Klara promised. She chews slowly, tasting rock and dust and wire. The sounds her molars make on the meat change, in her head, into those of the Wall's collapse, the reverberations of the concrete giving way, the falling chunks thudding to the ground.

"Good?" Klara asks.

Ute nods and smiles. "A splurge."

More courses pile up—first leek soup, then schnitzel and field greens, then cherry tortes and anise schnapps—as do Klara's cigarettes in the ashtray. The waiter, when he's not bringing and clearing these dishes, lurks by the window, watching the mayhem in the square and comparing it with the coverage on TV, his eyes wary, scanning for discrepancies.

"It's getting worse," Klara states, looking past the waiter.

"Today, or in general?" Ute asks, though she knows the answer is 'both.'

"Both," Klara confirms, and laughs, aware that Ute had been thinking exactly this. A spark of like-mindedness jumps between them and, for the first time, Ute lets herself consider the possibility that it might be genuine. Perhaps we really were together then. Long-lost sisters, reunited after all these years apart. Why not? She smiles and dabs a tear in her left eye with her cloth napkin, already damp with soup. Under her coat, her wires tremble and scrape.

Klara smiles too, also dabbing her eye. "I'm glad we met," she says, her voice suddenly grave. "I can't tell you how lonely I've been, wandering from town to town. All the money in the world can't make up for…" She downs her schnapps and waves her glass in the air, summoning a refill.

Though the sentence remains unfinished, Ute knows what she means. "I'm glad too," she says, licking dust from her teeth. "After enough months out there," she nods at the windows, beyond which the screaming and chanting are still underway, the fountain so full of spongy bodies that they've absorbed all the water and bloated accordingly, "you start to wonder if…"

"Any of us are still around?" Klara signals for the bill. "We are, Ute. It seems like there's fewer every day—and believe me, I've read the books, and seen the graves where our brothers and sisters have fallen, and the chop shops where the fakes are built, and the teenagers drinking cement, as if that could make them like us—but we haven't vanished from Europe just yet. Soon, things are going to get better. Something is wrapping up so that something else can begin."

After smiling in a way that means she'll only say more when she decides to, she pays with a pile of crisp Euros, and blushes before asking, "If I booked us a room in this dump, would you spend the night with me?" She looks at the throng outside, moving, flood-like, across the square and toward the hotel. "I, for one, don't intend to be sitting here when they break in to ransack the bar."

Ute tries to picture them smashing glasses and bottles, but finds she can generate nothing beyond the image she's watching right now, through the window. As if that scene, though it takes place outdoors, could be reproduced in here, everyone making the exact same actions, screaming the exact same things, only incidentally related to the background they're posed against. Though she knows that when they get in here, if they do, some aspect of what happens will be unique, the scene out the window is more than enough to motivate her to follow Klara out past the waiter station and over to the front desk.

Their room is on the twenty-third floor, overlooking the square, where the streetlights illuminate a seething pandemonium. Ute goes into the bathroom to wash the crab and pork from her fingers. When she comes back, the TV is on, updating the story of how the people of Görlitz bravely defended against another barbarian invasion.

"There's us, in the window," Klara remarks, pointing to a shot of the hotel dining room on the screen. Sure enough, the two of them are visible in silhouette, cracking their crabs and talking animatedly. "Don't we look happy?"

Ute nods as she tries to remember what they were talking about. A shiver passes through her as the place where this memory should be remains blank, as if she'd been so caught in Klara's gaze that she hadn't formed her own impression of the moment. As soon as the blank opens inside her, Ute feels everything fall into it, as so often happens with déjà vu. Her entire sense of being turns cold and ghostly, and Klara takes on a sinister dimension. The screen cuts to a parallel feed of armored soldiers on motorcycles tearing through tunnels beneath the city, dousing huddled forms with gas before more soldiers roar by and set them on fire, and even this feels awfully familiar. Like it just happened, which, of course—Ute tries to steady herself—it did.

"What?" Klara asks, relaxing on the bed with her jacket open and her wires and cement chunks hanging out on the starched pillows. She unwraps a chocolate from the nightstand and waits for an answer.

Compared to where I spend most nights, Ute thinks, remembering the old drunk in Latvia and the ten or twelve identical scenes since then, this is nothing. What am I so afraid of?

She moves as quickly as she can toward the bed, trying to outpace the realization that what scares her most is the possibility of genuine kinship, a feeling so rare that she's developed no system for processing it.

"Nothing," she says. "I was just…" she doesn't bring up the Authentication Ritual again.

"There's still plenty of time," Klara says, tossing her chocolate wrapper onto the floor.

Here pass what Ute will come to consider the happiest hours of her post-Wall existence. She lies next to Klara in bed, where they hold one another tightly, their wires intertwined, each playing mother to the other's lost child.

Walls keep growing in what Ute pictures as the terrain of her psyche, taking root in the parched dirt as bulwarks against whatever incursion of feeling is trying to get through, but she knocks them down one after another, determined, despite the cost, to feel as much as she can. To preserve the peace as long as possible.

Relative peace, she thinks, glancing at the TV through one half-opened eye as paramilitary troops in riot gear haul mutilated bodies from the fountain and charred crisps from the tunnels while townspeople in homemade armor lurk like hyenas around the peripheries. But still, compared to what's coming—she's never admitted this before, but she's known it for months—today counts as a ceasefire.

Ceasefire. The word soothes her as she snuggles closer to Klara, miming the act of suckling at her breast, though she knows that no such organs exist there. Still, the fantasy endures, and Klara seems to encourage it, petting Ute's stringy gray hair and whispering soft syllables as a shared dream envelops them, their splayed nerves twining together.

In the dream, Ute and Klara are human, living together on the outskirts of whatever town they're in now—the name no longer matters. All that matters is the soft grass in summer, the soft snow in winter, the impermeable canopy of the evergreens, the sounds of birds and cows and the scent of fresh beer and hot mulled wine in the pub, where everyone they've ever known, and will ever know, gathers to talk and sing and simply be together every Sunday evening, just as they have since the Middle Ages, and just as they will until the long distant horizon of the far future finally arrives.

Ute basks in the security of the dream, her face pressed to Klara's side, simultaneously on the hotel bed in Görlitz and on the eiderdown comforter she inherited from her grandmother, lovingly hand-stitched with fables about the family of ducks whose feathers now provide the warmth she's basking in.

She tries to go deeper, down to the bottommost root. If I find it, she resolves, I'll cling to it so tightly that I'll never rise back to the surface. If that entails a kind of burial, then so be it. No one will find me. Nothing matters except reaching that root, and refusing, no matter what happens, to let go.

She sinks, struggling to breathe, coughing and hacking as the pressure mounts and her vision blurs and her muscles fill with acid and cramp up. The root system, thousands of spidering tendrils converging, loses focus and the scene splinters before cracking into jagged shards, like the stained-glass windows of a bombed cathedral. She hovers in a space that loses definition as the temperature drops and the air fills with a sticky, burning liquid that smells like sweat and gasoline. As this mixture catches fire, she hears Klara cackling in the distance, then sees her body enveloped in flame in a circle of colossal oaks, and she can tell, for reasons she may never grasp, that this, all of it, is exactly what the wealthy stranger wanted.

Ute shoots up in bed, coughing and shivering, her wires snagged and sparking, her skin dry and crispy as she examines the woman beside her, still asleep.

She seethes with jealousy, then anger, then hatred. What right do you have to remain down there, under our eiderdown, while I'm back here, alone in the dark of some abandoned border hotel?

Swinging her feet off the bed and onto the carpet, she stands and stares at the TV, on which Chancellor Havermeyer yawns and squints at a teleprompter, like she, too, has just woken up and isn't yet sure where she is. Ute watches for a moment, squinting back at the Chancellor in unwitting mimicry, until the scene cuts to footage of troops hosing down the square in the pre-dawn, blood frothing around their rubber boots. Ute jerks her head away and looks out the window, which displays the same image. She shudders as the two realities sync together; perhaps here, she thinks, on the far side of the dream, there's only one reality left, all disparate pieces, no matter their mutual irrelevance, merged by fiat.

This thought discomfits her more than any disjunct between screen and window ever could. She closes her eyes and tries to return, even only in shabby reenactment, to that village pub on Sunday night, but the life she lived there with Klara is over. She sees herself on the street, pounding on the window, while those inside drink and talk, oblivious to the stranger begging them to hear her. A dark reminder of another time, one they've gathered tonight, like every night, to push ever further into the past.

I could've stayed, she thinks, but something in me needed to travel on. So here I go, back in my body again. Alone. Clammy and exhausted, she turns from the pub and toward Klara in the bed. Blinking back tears, she goes over to wake her up. The Authentication Ritual can be postponed, but not forever.

After much yawning and groaning and protest, Ute and Klara stand side by side in the bathtub, their thighs trembling against one another. "You're sure?" Klara asks, her voice frightened, totally unlike the cool assurance it'd conveyed over dinner.

Ute knows that, if she spoke now, she'd sound the same. Perhaps literally, as if the dream had fused their two voices into one. So she simply nods, despondent to realize how certain she is. There's no turning back, though a deeper, quieter part of her psyche still protests. Why give this up?

Why scuttle it so soon?

Because it's not yet time to stay put, is the best she can tell herself. It's not yet time.

So the Authentication Ritual begins, both Ute and Klara crying at their mutual expulsion from the place they'd shared, their tears running past their ankles and down the drain. They use their hands to weave their wires into a braid, then scrape their respective patches of grout together, hard enough to generate a cloud of dust. Thus conjoined, they close their eyes and sync up to a shared channel on which it's always Berlin in November of 1989, the first hammer blow about to land.

They feel that hammer hit somewhere above their diaphragm, and they recoil—in the bathtub and in Berlin—coughing as the grout that holds them together gives way. The crowd, made up of those who were present then as well as those tuning in from other gateways now, cheers as tractors and backhoes rumble past, moving in to do the real damage once the symbolic hammer blows have landed. The Wall churns and gags as the machines' metal teeth penetrate its body, carving innumerable jagged pieces from what had, until then, grounded its self-image upon the bedrock of its indivisibility. As it cracks into thousands of Utes and Klaras, the sky likewise cracks with lightning, illuminating Berlin like a sacrificial pyre in…

The Black Forest.

Burning trees flank an altar beneath a domed ceiling of human flesh, bodies crushed so closely together they allow only the faintest glimmer of moonlight to shine through.

Ute flails and screams as figures kneel at the altar and chant in supplication to a black-cloaked priestess who appears, in the vision's final flicker, to wear not only Klara's clothing, but her face as well. She makes wide, sweeping gestures with her arms, drawing the errant pieces toward her, until they close in, fusing together, restoring the Wall in the heart of the woods, as if it had stood there all along, unmoved since the failed invasions of Rome.

Aware that she's been recognized, the priestess nods with a cruel smile and mouths the words, "Release her," and Ute careens back through a mess of staticky, intermediate channels, all of them hot with the breath of eager drunks, before surfacing once more in a bathtub in Görlitz, sobbing against the tiled wall as the woman she came so close to loving regards her with a mix of pity and horror.

"What is it?" Klara asks, once Ute has calmed her breathing.

Ute looks at her, scanning her face for any sign of recognition of the role she played in the Black Forest. But Klara merely looks upset.

"The Authentication Ritual," Ute stammers, fumbling to disentangle her wires. "It... I know what you are now."

Klara narrows her eyes, watching Ute retract without making any move to help. "What do you mean? It was just getting started. We've barely even..."

Ute shakes her head. "No. You're a fake," she insists, desperate to mask her fear of being absorbed, even if it's the best thing that could happen to her. "You weren't really there, in the Wall, in Berlin, when it fell... you're one of those, uh..."

Something in Klara changes. She reaches down, gathers up the rest of her wires, and stomps out of the bathtub. Grabbing a towel from the hook on the back of the door, she ties it tightly around her waist and says, "Leave."

Ute remains in the tub, wavering between fury and remorse. She's on the verge of apologizing, even suggesting they try the Ritual again, when Klara repeats, "Leave! You were my guest here, but you aren't any longer. I saw you. I could see that you were ready to be made whole. But I suppose I was wrong. You're a stranger to me now. Leave my room. You don't want to see what happens if you force me to make a phone call."

Whatever was tenuous between them a moment ago is broken. Klara's face now bears the same expression it bore atop the altar, completely in control from here on out. Ute nods, steps from the tub, and sidles past Klara, who moves aside just enough to let her exit the bathroom. She pulls her old dress and baggy coat back over her frame and steps into the beaten-up canvas boots she's worn for the past six years.

She hesitates at the door, contemplating an apology, or, if not that, an accusation—some valedictory remark, at the very least—but has the feeling that if she were to speak now, there'd be no way of controlling what she said. So she nudges the door closed, as if trying not to wake someone still asleep, and walks into the hallway, toward the elevator, which is taped shut with a handwritten sign that reads OUT OF ORDER.

Ute takes the stairs, trying not to picture what must've happened to the elevator when the celebrants broke in. Instead, she reads the fire evacuation instructions in German and Russian, over and over on every flight, until she emerges on the second floor, back in the restaurant. It's now host to a breakfast buffet in a cordoned-off area, the rest of the dining room hidden behind a beige curtain. Again, she tries not to picture the devastation it conceals, though she realizes that the sound of whatever happened must have made its way up to the room and soundtracked their shared, or nearly shared, reprise of the Wall's collapse.

When the scent of bacon and coffee hits her, she falls in line with the few other guests, all of them elderly, some in homemade armor and others in nondescript tourist gear, and takes a plate when it's her turn, filling it with potatoes, sausages, and runny scrambled eggs. She balances a raspberry Danish and a corn muffin on top and turns to look for a table, when the waiter from last night, again buttoning his vest, appears in front of her. They make eye contact, his gaze low and hard, his lips upturned.

"Please," Ute mutters, "I'm starving." Though, after last night's dinner, this isn't strictly true, she knows that it will be soon enough, and this seems to lend the utterance an equivalent veracity.

The waiter's expression softens by some just-perceptible degree as he says, "Wait here, don't sit down." He strides to the kitchen and returns with a Styrofoam container and a set of plastic cutlery. "Eat it outside." He hands her the container and turns his back.

By the time she's finished loading it up, he's gone. With the hot breakfast sweating under her arm, she shuffles past the few occupied tables and down the last set of stairs to the lobby, past the rack of yellowing brochures for hiking excursions in the nearby Polish woods, and out into the square, where ambulances and military jeeps have encircled the fountain.

Bodies are stacked in piles, some covered with translucent plastic, others still open to the air. The same children and teenagers who'd swarmed the square yesterday gawk at their handiwork, none of them noticing Ute as she passes by. She examines the bodies, postponing the inevitable decision between choosing to believe that they were human all along—and thus only appeared to be toys yesterday—or that, somehow, they transformed overnight. Or perhaps they're not human even now, and she's simply lost the ability to tell who is.

No option seems more or less plausible than any other, so, for now, she focuses on leaving Görlitz, and with it, Klara, which have fused together in her mind, like two sides of a coin in some currency so foreign she can't even guess at its value.

Though her gait is slow, she moves without stopping and, before long, reaches the edge of town, following a road that winds past a gas station and a Eurospar, toward a field populated only by a parked pickup truck and two grazing cows.

She stops in this field, settling her weight onto a rock and opening her Styrofoam container in hopes that the food has retained at least a little warmth. The first mouthful of eggs reveals that it has. A mercy. Though the taste of rubble remains, the heat soothes her system and brightens, however slightly, her prospects for the day ahead. She looks at the condensation inside the box's cover, and then over the field, toward the farmhouse on the far side, and lets herself slip back into the place she approached in bed with Klara last night. "My own," she mutters, mouth full of eggs. "My home, my cows, on the edge of the town where I was born. The town where I could've remained, my mouth full of eggs laid by the chickens I raised."

The feeling lasts until the food is gone, and she has half a mind to eat the container in hopes of prolonging it, but knows well enough what it's like to be sick out here on her own. So she puts it down and gets to her feet, the postponed shame at the failed Authentication Ritual finally hitting her, like a flock of vultures that's been hovering overhead all morning, waiting for the right moment to strike. *Was I afraid that it wouldn't work, or that it would?*

As she heads Southwest, dragging her feet along the shoulder of what soon becomes a two-lane highway, she ruminates on this question, thinking back on her disjointed memory of the Wall's collapse, its transposition from Berlin to the woods. Then she asks herself the question she's managed to avoid until now: *is Klara the fake, or am I?*

She feels the seed of doubt plant itself inside her and put down roots, shredding their way through soft tissue. *Is it possible that I was never really part of it? That I'm even less than I thought I was... that I'm truly no one at all, unable to fuse with a genuine piece of the Wall because I was never...*

Of course, it's possible! Just like everything else. But so what? What would you do differently?

She shrugs, closing her eyes and trying to conjure the familiar image of Russia, the Wall rebuilt in the virgin taiga, far from human eyes, beyond civilization and all of its discontents. A kind of heaven, a reprieve from exile. Or perhaps there has never been any exile, only a slow approach toward that which has never yet existed; perhaps the Wall, as we remember it, is in reality nothing but a premonition, still to come, and all this wandering has been in the service of an eventual coming-together that will render it all worthwhile. "Wait for me, Klara," she prays, hoping her prayer can be heard. "I wasn't ready this time, but next time I will be."

She only realizes her eyes have been closed when a milk truck bears down on its horn and swerves around her, forcing her into a ditch where she loses her balance and topples over. Lying there on her back as the truck vanishes around a bend, she tries to take stock of who and where she is. For an interval, it's impossible to say. She seems, once again, to have reemerged from the Wall's collective being, or someplace even deeper, the Russian furnace in which its steel wires were cast, hot enough to reduce all known history to gleaming liquid, awaiting form and purpose. Like the furnace that made the universe out of whatever trash was floating around before.

The sun goes down and a chill moves through the air. She hears a gruff female voice in the distance, cackling the words, "Return to your journey, Ute. The time to be no one has clearly not yet come. I will grant the second chance you requested, if you prove strong enough to find me, but I will not deploy another avatar to hold your hand."

When she acquiesces, the voice cackles louder, thrilled at its own power. Though she can't yet tell whether the voice is coming from inside or outside her head, she knows that she and Klara will meet again and that, next time, it will be in a setting at once less comfortable and more significant than the hotel whose contours have already faded into the memory of a more innocent time, never to be repeated. It grows fully dark as she resolves to increase her pace and keep her eyes open, so as to approach the Black Forest with all the clarity she has left.

Anika

Drunk in her bed for the fifth night in a row, Anika lies very still and watches the sun go down outside the cottage windows. It filters through the smoke of the burning Forest and onto the faces of the stuffed bear, then the stuffed wolf, then the stuffed fox, lined up along the back wall of the cottage like notches on a sundial, registering the dying moments of the day before the nearly interminable night takes hold.

She's learned, over the course of her first four nights here, to begin drinking well before then if she hopes to drift off at a reasonable hour. Otherwise, the eyes of the animals start following her, winking with sinister intent as if their hollowed-out skulls had been possessed by the same thing that materialized in her apartment in what now seems like the sunken island of Berlin. And to the degree that I sense something isn't right here either, she muses, snuggling into her pillows as the room spins, my only recourse is to drink until I can tell myself, in all honesty, that I'm merely drunk.

She laughs at the circularity of the thought. And yet it rings true. If I only remember that I'm drunk—she closes her eyes and imagines herself at the front of the big lecture hall at Humboldt, full now of coral and warm salt water—then any perceptions I may have, no matter how valid, can be invalidated by my knowledge that, were I sober, I'd see things differently.

Thus, she adds, exiting the lecture hall to seek herself out in her flooded office, it is imperative that sobriety be kept in strictest abeyance. Held there in case of direst emergency. A precious resource to be conserved.

Though she has no wish to see Horst again, she knows he'll replenish the liquor anytime she calls him, so she grants herself permission to pour liberally. The first night, after he left, she'd retired to bed around nine, after waking from her nap only long enough to set up a modest stack of books at the desk by the window, including the French, German, and English editions of her own, and creating a new desktop folder entitled "Black Forest Mythos Project," with a new document inside, the only one so far, entitled "Observations."

Then, after failing to read any of the manuscript of the critical biography of the short-lived Berlin fabulist Wolfgang Herrndorf that a colleague had sent her for peer review, she climbed into bed with a full glass of Riesling and waited, though she didn't yet know it, for the windows to clot over with skin.

When they did, on that first night, it appeared, from her vantage point, as if the smoke of the burning trees was taking solid form. She emptied her glass, then reached under the bed to refill it from the bottle she'd stashed there, and got under the covers, lying very still as the skin hardened, took on shape, and forced its way through the windows, bypassing the glass without breaking it.

Now it was in the cottage with her, reeking of sweat and wood smoke, dotted with moles and hair and the traces of ancient scars and tattoos. It made a sound, a whoosh or coo of pleasure, as if it found all of this erotic, and then she noticed herself making the same sound. Soon, she couldn't tell if it'd been her making it all along.

The combination of skin and sound filled the room, drawing near to where she lay. The closer it got, the more it seemed to ripple with faces, the semblance of people she knew passing across its leathery expanse like something inside was projecting them. She saw the Chancellor, then her dead husband, then his beloved Kiefer, then her little sister and her mother and her father and...

She moaned louder, sinking backward into her mattress as her hand sank under the covers and up past the hem of the long shirt she always wore to bed, moving of its own accord now, burrowing under her panties just as the skin-mass burrowed into the room, twisting and kneading the flesh that was now an amalgam of old and new, herself and something else, none of the folds familiar, her hand vanishing as she tunneled inside what she was becoming, the room closing in and sealing around her, melting her skeleton into more skin until she'd been augmented or reduced to a smooth, slick oval, rocking gently in the sheets where once a woman had been.

Waking late the next morning, she felt enervated and unmoored, newly hatched into a world she could barely remember having seen before. She sensed, with the exhausted dread of someone who's been out drinking till dawn and finally reached a long-suppressed catharsis in the fog just before blackout, that something transpired last night whose nature she would first have to find a way to unpack, and only then to address.

She could tell that a new situation was already afoot, despite her having barely had time to settle in. Nevertheless, she stretched out in the sheets, trying to pull unfamiliar skin over bones that felt soft and ill-formed, and looked up at the pine-board ceiling and dismissed, for now, the work of figuring out what that situation might be. I can't remember, she insisted. Leave me alone, I simply can't remember.

She dozed off again, then got up and made coffee in the French press she found on the counter by the fruit bowl, already loaded with grounds. Not bad. She looked around and, in the fresh daylight, noticed the stuffed animals on the walls as if for the first time. "Hello, folks," she said, ranging her eyes from bear to wolf to fox, bypassing whatever repulsion she might have felt had these creatures turned up in circumstances that weren't already so strange. She let her eyes linger on the patches of exposed skin under their mangy fur and used this to push back the slowly returning memories of a thick, creamy expanse of skin filling the cottage last night.

When her coffee was finished, she got dressed and walked to town, where she roamed the high street until lunchtime, then ate a simple plate of boiled chicken and greens in one of the restaurants, and then had another coffee and a slice of strawberry torte at the Stammkneipe cantilevered over the brook, where she already regarded herself as a regular, projecting her time here shockingly far into the future. As she sipped and cut at the torte with the side of her spoon, she stared into the faces of the villagers, trying to glean who she was to them, whether they knew what had happened last night in the cottage, and whether, indeed, they were part of it. She snuck her hand under her shirt and down the waistband of her pants, itching her foreign-feeling skin whenever she sensed that no one was watching.

As far as she could tell, the villagers saw her as what she nominally was: an upscale northerner passing through town for a reason that didn't concern them. Still, she couldn't help staring, certain there was more to it than this. Their seemingly blank eyes reminded her of the animal eyes on the wall across from her bed, concealing things she both did and didn't want to discover, set in faces made of the same skin she was now itching.

As afternoon approached evening, she walked back to the cottage, through vivid green light. When she got home—using this word in her head for the first time since she'd arrived here, and, she realized, for the first time since Gerhard did what he did and she moved into the apartment in Mitte—she sat for an hour in front of her laptop, typing and deleting the same few lines in her new document. Then she got back in bed with a fresh bottle of Riesling and waited for the sun to set.

———————————

Now, in bed on the fifth night, Anika lies very still and waits for the skin. She closes her eyes and walks back along the high street, retracing her steps from earlier today, marveling at how, in less than a week, Baiersbronn has come to feel like the whole world: when I picture a street, she realizes, or a church, or a bridge, or a bakery, it's the street, church, bridge, and bakery in this town that I picture. As if there'd been nothing before. As if, after years of blue nothing, I've at last been released into a real world.

She looks at her laptop and considers typing these reflections into her still-blank document, but recoils from the prospect. Too much, she decides. Too soon. No need to start writing, she tells herself, aware of the circular nature of the thought, until I get to work on the book itself. The Chancellor, if she remembers correctly, gave her all summer.

Looking out the window at the hot, pregnant night, it's impossible to picture the summer ever ending. And if it's simply that I'm going mad, she thinks, well, there's something thrilling about doing it quickly, rather than dragging it out into the long, grim process I suppose it would have been had I clung to sanity. Something nice about already being done with it, already living in the present rather than resisting the future.

So, for now, she lies back and waits for the skin to arrive.

But tonight it doesn't. She lies and waits, but restlessness, in the absence of contact, soon overwhelms her. She gets up and pads to the window, where she can see smoke and, in the distance, orange flames in a clearing, surrounded by the black smudges of cloaked bodies. She can tell it's getting closer, burning its way toward her. Or dragging the cottage toward it, like a sun burning bigger and bigger, its pull increasing all the time.

She shivers and closes the blinds and wishes for the rush of familiarity that the skin used to provide. Like a thick, living blanket, smothering me without harm in my bed, tucking me in, reminding me what it means to be cozy, ensconced in a kind of history that comes together into something solid, rather than dispersing invisibly into the air and, for all I know, up into space to drift forever.

Gripping her sides in the chill of the empty room, she looks from the window to the stuffed animals, and then she looks back to the window, opening the blinds again, as if anything could possibly be different from a moment ago. Then she hears something shift underfoot, mercifully cutting short what could have been a full night of alternating between one fraught vantage and the other.

She puts her shoes on over her bare feet, under her long shirt and a pair of flannel pajama bottoms, and hurries toward the sound, which seems to be coming from behind a door next to the fridge. It rustles like a pair of feet walking up and down, and, though she knows she ought to fear it, she feels only a desire for company. Like an addict craving any means of restoring a lost equilibrium, she moves toward the door thinking only of the warmth she's felt these past nights under that blanket of skin. As if, without it, she had no skin at all. Nothing but a sheared surface awaiting activation.

Gripping the knob, she watches as her hand twists and then pulls, and then the door is open and she's watching herself descend a flight of stairs, despite the fact that the cottage has no foundation. She listens to her footsteps on the creaky wood and thinks, this must be the sound I heard before.

At the bottom of the stairs, she emerges onto a street in broad daylight, a row of houses behind budding oaks and sycamores, all of them fronted by well-trimmed lawns and flanked by sturdy family vehicles resting in paved driveways. She walks down the street, past the houses of her neighbors, waving to a few and stooping to pet their dogs, before turning off the sidewalk and up her driveway.

When she gets to the door, she reaches into the pocket of her pajama bottoms, searching for a key that isn't there, before she remembers that all she has to do is knock. She looks at her knuckles for a moment, as if to make sure they're sturdy enough for the job, and then she raps them against the wood. After a second impact, a pair of shuffling feet comes to the door. When it opens, the sound stops and she's face-to-face with herself: another Anika, or perhaps the only one, she thinks now, as her consciousness shifts so that she's standing inside the cottage, looking out at a strange woman who begins to blush.

"I'm sorry," says the strange woman. "I must have the wrong address." After a dead pause, she adds, "Perhaps I'll come by later."

With this, she departs and Anika closes the door.

Inside, all is cool and quiet, the carpeting plush, the windowsills full of healthy plants. She strolls past them, yawning, and realizes how tired she's grown, even though she only went out for her usual neighborhood stroll. Oh well. She lets go of whatever she'd planned for the rest of the day. Nothing wrong with resting up a little, though there's a pile of mail by the door that'll have to be opened and sorted eventually.

Resigned to postponing this task, she goes inside, takes her shoes off, and gets under the sheets without brushing her teeth or performing any other nighttime ritual. She's exhausted now, enough that she feels her body cramp as sleep overtakes it, and then, what feels like an instant later, she's waking up, still cramped, in some awful drafty room surrounded by dead animals, and she wants to scream, but she's suddenly terrified of who might hear. So, instead, she gets to her feet and tiptoes into the kitchen to see if a door she dimly remembers beside the refrigerator is still there.

György

György wakes up in a child-sized bed on a horse farm, somewhere in the Norwegian countryside, three or four weeks after meeting Knut and Gunnar in Copenhagen. His training has been ramping up, from thirty push-ups in the morning and a two-mile jog before lunch to, now, a hundred and eighty in the morning, a six-mile jog before lunch, and then, after dishes and chores, another hundred and eighty push-ups before dinner. After dinner the evenings have, so far, devolved into levels of drunkenness György has never before seen, though his hosts swear that as soon as the off-season ends and the mission, whose nature has not yet been revealed, begins, this will abruptly cease and the "days of all-out hardcoreness will be upon us in a major way."

At the end of another day of training, Knut and Gunnar take their seats at the head of the table, while György and a South African horse-handler named Tom sit at the far side, shivering despite the season ostensibly still being summer. They eat a platter of roast pork and a pile of wilted greens in silence, watching Ragnar in Stockholm on a flatscreen TV above the fireplace. They've watched all of his appearances so far, from Denmark down through Germany, where in Düsseldorf and Nuremberg a blurry Ulli Harz hologram appeared onstage beside him, then east through Poland and Hungary, and south through Greece and the Balkans, then east again through Turkey, and then back, along the same route but in different

119

cities, or, in sites of especial interest—Vienna, Budapest, Belgrade—different venues in the same cities.

Tonight, after the usual theatrics and chest-thumping exhortations to heed the call of Atlantis before it's too late, he leans into the screen and whispers something in Norwegian. Knut and Gunnar, though already drunk, put their shot glasses down and lean in. They make a show of listening closely, as if the televised lecture had morphed into a Skype call.

Ragnar talks for five minutes; then the screen reverts to the gallery of potential videos to play, most of them old Ragnar speeches that György's seen many times by now.

In the silence that follows, Knut and Gunnar confer in Norwegian, looking over at György and laughing every few sentences. The more they talk, drinking all the while, the more they laugh. György sits still and watches them, sipping aquavit from a cloudy glass while Tom stares into space, making eye contact with no one.

As their laughter intensifies, György resolves to stare them down, forcing them, eventually, to acknowledge him. "Sorry, sorry," Knut says after deflecting the attention for a moment. "We were just saying that the initial phase of training is nearly at an end. Time for phase two. Ragnar says you're going to have a very special role in our new coalition, once phase two is completed."

"That's right," Gunnar adds, refilling his and Knut's glasses from the bottle that's migrated down to their end of the table.

"And tonight's the first step. Time to introduce you to the Deep Ragnar. He's coming over. Are you ready?"

György looks to Tom, who's looking out the window, either too drunk to notice that the conversation has switched from Norwegian back to English, or aware that tonight's events, whatever they turn out to be, don't involve him.

Gunnar clears his throat and György looks back, and nods. "Sure, I'm ready," he says, his accent humiliatingly Mongoloid in the house's cool Nordic air.

"Come upstairs then," says Knut, draining his glass and refilling it from the bottle he can now barely manage to open.

Upstairs, the two Norwegians lead György down a drafty, stone-tiled hallway, past the room where he sleeps in his child-sized bed, and around a corner he's never passed before. Knut unlocks a door at the end of the next hallway and they climb a narrow set of stairs with no banister—one edge seems to open onto a steep drop, though György can't be sure if this is possible—to arrive in a partly-finished attic. The chill up here is even more pronounced than it was at dinner, though, György thinks, maybe that's just because it's gotten later, in the night or the season, or both.

In the center of the attic's thinly carpeted floor sits a gigantic, blue-green egg. It fulminates in the stagnant air, breathing in and out, excreting rivulets of blood that pool beside it, blackening the area around its base. When György turns to gauge his hosts' reaction, hoping, thereby, to calibrate his own, he finds them gone, and the door closed behind them.

121

"György, my friend, stay a while," a voice says. He turns, uncertain whether he'd rather discover that the egg's talking to him, or that someone else is in the attic. This uncertainty is deep enough that it takes a few minutes to realize the voice, wherever it's coming from, is speaking Hungarian. After so long away, the language sounds foreign, enough so that it nearly brings him to panic. His first, irrational instinct is that his parents have tracked him down.

"György," the voice repeats, now clearly coming from inside the egg. "Relax. We can speak together in any language we choose. Would you prefer English? German?"

This last word hangs in the attic air until György shakes his head. "No," he says, in shaky Hungarian, trying to force himself to relax. "Keep talking like this."

"Gladly," the egg replies, bouncing in its pool of blood, its crinkly shell warping in and out. "Let's you and I spend a few moments getting to know one another. Would that be alright? I sent the boys away so we could be alone."

"Ragnar?"

The egg shakes and makes a high-pitched sound that might be a sort of laughter. "That's one of my names, yes," it replies. "My surface name, for the stages and screens and filthy town squares of Europe. But here, among friends, let us throw off names, shall we? Will you have any doubt as to whom I'm addressing if I stop using yours?"

György shakes his head.

"Good. Then feel equally free to stop using mine, or, more to the point, to stop preoccupying yourself with wondering what mine might be. In retrospect, you may think of me, in this incarnation, as the Deep Ragnar, having traveled up from a lower level to pay this one a visit, but for our purposes at the moment, think of me simply as a voice that has something to tell you. A fellow traveler, though one much further down the road you have just embarked upon." It makes more of that noise that György is now determined to regard as laughter.

"What I'm about to tell you has to do with the fate of consciousness," the egg begins, its voice identical to Ragnar's but altered by virtue of its speaking Hungarian. György is disturbed to realize that he can't tell if the accent is native or foreign, as if all the time he's spent in Germany and, now, Norway, has purged the proper sound of his native language from his inner ear. The proud, masculine voice he still hears in his head snarls, but the egg cuts it off.

"The end, I should say," it continues, "of human consciousness. Its imminent, voluntary winding-down. Are you prepared for me to continue?"

György notices himself sitting on the ground now, staring up at the egg, which, when it breathes in, appears almost as large as the attic. He's surprised to notice that this is the first time he's pictured the egg hatching, as if this were only one of a great many things an egg might do. As soon as this image comes to his attention, it's all he can see. The fact that the egg contains something, rather than being something in its own right, becomes such a compelling notion that he can't imagine how else he could ever have seen it.

This so preoccupies him that the egg has to ask again, this time more sharply, whether he's prepared for it to continue. He manages to nod.

"Good. Then let me cut to the chase and later, if need be, backtrack to address any questions you may have. The chase is that the time has come for humanity to renounce its consciousness. This is the culmination that has been building for centuries. The climax, so to speak, of the journey you have been called upon to undertake. Throughout the entire course of the so-called post-Enlightenment era, the human race has, beneath its own knowledge, been building toward the cusp your generation and its few relevant elders have arrived at. The decision between terminal self-consciousness and voluntary unconsciousness. The wages of human consciousness aren't all bad, of course. Discoveries have been made that will be useful to your evolutionary successors. The stage has been set for a glorious post-human era. But, make no mistake, that era is now dawning. The graceful exit, György, is not suicide, which is nothing but the most infantile and narcissistic capitulation to self-consciousness' relentless pressure, but rather voluntary unconsciousness. Genuine, total enslavement to the Absolute. This is the only form of noble enlightenment, because consciousness, in its very essence, invites flaccid invasion. It not only entices the Soft Illuminati, it breeds them, just as surely as a bowl of milk left out in the sun breeds fungus. The fate of all conscious beings is to end up, sooner or later, feeling unlike themselves—and hence invaded by forces they choose to characterize as external—and panicking at the implications of this feeling. Striving, too late, to restore a lost order whose specifics they can barely recall.

"Of the several great leaders of the twentieth century, Adolf Hitler, as Ulli Harz has argued more and more clearly, alone glimpsed the totality of what I am about to propose. But he was, in the end, not brave enough to see it through. In the end, he collapsed into venality. He proved, despite the immense inhumanity that is often attributed to him, to be all too human by succumbing to ordinary, corrupt bloodlust and craven power mania. The paranoia of a boy pretending to be a man, seeking from world events the recognition only a mother can provide. After his death, Europe was like a patient waking up partway through open-heart surgery: the impact of his actions, because they were never seen through to their necessary conclusion, appeared senselessly brutal. A shock from which the system, as it were, still hasn't recovered. Indeed, a shock in response to which the system has grown nearly overwhelming, totalitarian on every level except its burnished surface.

"A shame, really, for he was, or could've been, a being who understood what was at stake, and who, more importantly, knew how to make others understand. But oh well. That's over and done with. Now, history has moved on, taken a new avatar, one much closer at hand. The young man known to you, I trust, as Anders Breivik. The hero who spearheaded the movement of which you are now, I am happy to announce, an official part. Justiciar Breivik will, I am also happy to announce, be rejoining the ranks of free men before long, if your hosts, Knut and Gunnar, are successful in their aims, as I have every reason to believe they will be. The Norwegian Security State is not, shall we say, a force to be reckoned very hard with."

More laughter.

György opens his mouth, unsure if a question is about to emerge. Before it can, the egg continues, "Breivik and I are already, as you'll see, related in certain regards. Through him, I came into being, and through me," the egg begins to shake, and then, a moment later, to crack, "he came likewise into being. Not in the flesh, perhaps," a voice says from inside the yolky interior, "but in a capacity equally consequential."

"I am, you see," says Breivik, switching to English as he pulls white-yellow mucus from his naked body and steps into the circle of blood and shell that marks the space where the egg used to be, "here to pay you a visit. Your hosts have told me good things about you. What you did in Copenhagen—most boys your age would've balked when faced with apparent innocents such as those. But not you. You saw through the illusion. You saw that they were corrupted already, and thus irretrievable, as most so-called sentient beings now loose upon the earth sadly are. I don't use the phrase 'boys your age' in a pejorative sense, but merely to suggest that the journey into full manhood is still to come—Lord knows I didn't make that journey myself until that afternoon on Utøya, when I was already well into my thirties, more than a third of my life lying in ruins behind me. There will be plenty of time for discussions of manhood in the near future, along with the notions that, I trust, the Deep Ragnar has begun to elucidate for you," here he bends over and picks up a gleaming shard of shell and kisses it, running his long, pink tongue over its jagged surface, hard enough to draw blood, "just before I was born."

György perceives all this with no spatial or emotional grounding in his own presence in the room. He is, for the time being, a neutral organ of perception, two egg-shaped eyes registering events with no faculty for reflecting on them, let alone responding.

He watches in this state as the naked Breivik approaches, stepping out of the circle of the egg and putting his wet hands around György's throat. Leaning in, Breivik's breath hot and sticky as a newborn puppy's, he whispers, "Tomorrow, we talk. Tonight, we get to know each other."

This clearly isn't a question, so György makes no attempt to answer it. Instead, he watches as the newly hatched man, whose skin feels as real as any György's ever touched—though he reminds himself that he's touched very few in his nineteen years; perhaps, now that he thinks of it, only his own—caresses his pecs under his T-shirt, then kneels to unbuckle his pants. Before György can give any sign of protest or consent, or even consider which sign to give, Breivik has taken his penis in his mouth and begun to pump up and down on it, from the back of his throat to the front of his lips, and back, and forward again, smearing it with the blood that's still oozing from his lips.

György closes his eyes and thinks, as his inner voice slips back into manly Hungarian, I am not a faggot. I am not a faggot. I am not even human. I am something far greater than the totality of this puling, obsolescent race. I am something above and beyond consciousness, not a god, nor a titan, nor any other category of mortal aspiration, but something wholly outside the entire insectoid-theosophic paradigm. Something overwhelmingly potent, a being whose nature cannot be summed up in words, nor its countenance approximated in images. Something tangible in a way that no mortal sense can grasp, neither touch, nor smell, nor—he looks down at Breivik's balding blonde head, pumping back and forth in martial rhythm—taste.

He feels his core seize up as the voice of the Deep Ragnar rages in his head, shouting about the cowardice of Hitler and the coming revolution of unconsciousness, the final heroic leap from the sinking ship of human history, a graceful ceding of the physical earth to humanity's bionic successors, while those few among us possessed of genuine courage, those few with the ability to see... to see...

He sees the Deep Ragnar as a homunculus inside the eggshell of his own head, slamming against the sides, building pressure as he demands to be let out, into the cool air of the attic, and he feels a crack in the left side, between his ear and his eye, and he clenches down, bracing for pain, and then he lets go, feeling the entire soupy mass explode without regard for its future among the living or the sane.

―――――――――――

When he comes to, he's halfway down the upstairs hallway, his pants in a bunch around his ankles, his legs hot and sticky and his breath short in his chest. A mixture of lingering arousal and encroaching shame corkscrews down through his bowels and pushes out a series of farts that he half-expects to end in diarrhea, but he makes it back to his room and into his child-sized bed without incident. He pulls the sheets up over his face and exhales, trying to keep his breath as silent as possible, though he can't be sure if this is necessary.

As he closes his eyes, his head fills with the image of Breivik swallowing his sperm before stepping back into the circle of eggshells and gathering them into a new, seamless egg all around himself, its embryo fertilized with György's successors, who will, when the day comes, burst forth to assume their rightful position atop the cinders of the world that came before.

Then the entire attic becomes a railway car chugging along tracks that only it knows how to traverse. After a hot, black interlude of European night, with gypsies roaming the aisles in packs of five and six, begging and selling pungent snacks from paper bags, the train deposits him at an abandoned, drafty depot in a part of Hungary he's never seen before. He gets off, yawns on the platform while a pack of dogs sniffs for trash, and then watches, impassively, as the sparse backdrop of trees and telephone wires bleeds out, revealing a pastiche of ravening wildmen on horseback, beheading entire rows of kneeling figures with tree-sized broadswords and battle axes. The heads, enough to make up a small village, roll toward György where he stands, so fast they set him running back through the empty station and across the field of ash that now seems to constitute the entire Hungarian landscape, all the way to the horizon.

He runs without direction until, in the far distance, he sees what appears to be a large building. He turns toward it, pursued by the rolling heads, which now emit the sound of hoofbeats, as if they'd merged with the horsemen who severed them. Like creatures in the wild. Creatures whose natural prey is me.

With the last of his energy, György throws himself out of the field and across a painful boundary, like an electric fence, into a grassy meadow, where the sound of hoofbeats is as loud as ever but, visually, is replaced by the less disconcerting image of horses grazing in a pasture. This seems like an improvement over the mass of heads, so he slows to a walk, which carries him to the front door of what he now recognizes as the house he's been staying in for the past few weeks, though he doesn't yet remember why.

He pulls his sneakers off, wipes sweat from his forehead, and walks, feigning equilibrium, into the kitchen where Tom sits drinking coffee and staring at a tablet, his headphones nestled beneath a baseball cap that reads, "Cape Town Horse Feeds."

Though he'd love any reassurance that he's now awake and back in a shared reality, György senses that disturbing Tom would only make the situation worse, introducing a new variable without solving for any of those already in play. So he ignores him, pouring his own mug of coffee from the machine on the counter and glancing at a note pinned to the fridge with a Norwegian flag magnet. It reads, "Gone to Oslo. Back soon, if all goes well."

After a breakfast of muesli and yogurt, György picks up his Hungarian edition of Mishima's *Patriotism*, the only book he brought with him from Berlin, and leaves the kitchen, where Tom's still absorbed in his tablet. He sets to wandering the property, from the pastures in front where the horses, now silent, go on grazing, to the shed out back, where he finds dozens of rifles and grenades in wooden crates, and then up to his room for a nap. He doesn't set himself any goals for when he wakes up, as he can tell that the day's primary purpose will be to put a solid block of hours between himself and whatever happened in the attic last night.

He lies in his child-sized bed and tries not to picture that room, which, he realizes now, is directly overhead. An impulse pulls his eyes to the ceiling, forcing them to scan for any sign of egg yolk bleeding through. None yet, he sees, though this hardly assuages the fear that it'll begin dripping at any moment.

In hopes of burying this fear, he rolls onto his side and pulls his laptop into bed with him, and, for the first time today, opens his browser. Clicking onto a livestream of the altar in the Black Forest, he leans in to watch a severe, graceful woman in a black cloak behead a rooster and pour its blood at the feet of the mummified Nazi, while a crowd of worshippers in Valkyrie masks chants syllables he can't make out, a few of them parading past the others with burning runes on iron poles.

This scene, which is either replaying on loop or going on and on in real time, lulls him into a trance in which he imagines that the screen now displays one of the few Hungarian news sites he still visits. "I, Arisztid Huszár," reads a banner across the top of the page, in handsome pre-reform Hungarian script, "have emerged, like an answered prayer, from the languishing heart of Hungary to throw off the smothering blanket of the EU and raise the old Magyar gods back into the sky."

He pictures men in bear pelts and chain-mail armor standing on ladders to hoist gigantic puppets onto a scaffold that stretches across the Danube. Then he pictures these men on horseback beheading legions of prisoners and infidels, the heads rolling across a field of ash, and then a warm droplet lands on his face and the vision ends, exiling him back into the body of a nineteen-year-old boy lost in the back country north of Trondheim.

He closes his eyes and forces himself to listen as the voice says, "Those heads you ran from this morning, they were coming to serve you. Slain enemies, slaves now to the Great Cause. Lead them to glory." He knows that when he presses Refresh, the words he read on the screen will disappear, but the name Arisztid Huszár will remain inside him, never to be displaced or called into question.

When more droplets of what he now realizes is egg reach his tongue, he bolts out of bed and down the hall to the bathroom, where he intends to spit into the sink, but, the harder he tries, the more the egg clots in his throat, cooking in the steam rising from his gut.

When he's both cooked and swallowed all the egg in his mouth, he leans down to wash his face, then looks up through the half-window above the sink as an SUV rolls up the gravel drive. He stands there with water running down his cheeks as the vehicle pulls to a stop and then, a moment later, Knut,

Gunnar, and a puffy, bald man in an orange jumpsuit step out and make their way toward the house.

Whatever peace he'd struck with the egg leaves him now. He feels his gut cooking it again, this time into something toxic, and he leans against the sink and begs for the strength to vomit as the men downstairs call his name.

He knows he'll have to answer soon but, just before he does, he rolls up his sleeve and removes a fabric marker from the drawer beneath the sink. In large, shaky letters, he writes Arisztid Huszár in the space between his wrist and his elbow, one word atop the other, then rolls his sleeve back down and descends the stairs. He pictures Breivik on his knees before him and thinks, damn right, I know the truth about both of us now.

In the kitchen, he looks at the man in the orange jumpsuit who looks back at him and says, "I heard what you did in Copenhagen."

György nods, turning away from Knut and Gunnar and over toward Tom, who still appears catatonic at the far side of the table, staring at his screen without seeming to see it.

A moment later, Knut sets out a bottle of Aquavit and four glasses—three large ones and a small one for György—and pours them full. Then he raises his and talks for a long time in Norwegian, making Gunnar laugh.

The man in the jumpsuit remains silent, his eyes on György.

"What I just said," Knut adds, switching to English, "is that we have a saint in our midst. Saint Breivik, here to restore the

Nordic peoples of Europe to their rightful place at the pinnacle of the human pyramid. Just in time for the Flood, which will render all of Southern and Eastern Europe uninhabitable. Even for vermin. With Breivik as our commander, we will conquer the Black Forest and thereby, after all these centuries, prevail over the Germans, who proved to be cowards when they had the chance to lead. No longer shall we capitulate to their avaricious and perverse vision of Aryan dominance. Our rule, as true Nordmen, will be pure. We, alone of all peoples, will resurrect Atlantis and ensure that it never sinks again."

Gunnar raises his glass as, a moment later, does György, though his eyes are still on Breivik, trying to glean, before any subsequent events occur, the degree to which the embodied man at the table across from him is the same as the one that hatched from the egg in the attic last night, and the degree to which something entirely other than this is the case instead.

Though we are not yet prepared to posit an answer, György tells himself, as if he were Sloterdijk concluding a long, dense talk in a lecture hall at Humboldt, we can be certain that this is the question.

Ute

The number of pseudo-Berlins diminishes as Ute leaves what was once the DDR and draws closer to what is still the Black Forest, but the frenzy of reenactment that has flared up in recent weeks grows steadily more oppressive and harder to bypass. Every other town, it seems, is abandoned save for a Living Wall dividing it down the middle and a gaggle of townspeople arguing on both sides, reiterating the enmities of thirty and forty years ago, adapted only slightly to make reference to the shredded coastlines and whatever faceless millions are, or seem to be, making their way through them.

She bypasses the fray to rifle through a dumpster at the edge of the main square in a town near Bamberg, and pulls out the remnants of a McDonald's bag, half eaten away by the grease of its own contents. She swallows the bag along with the meat and bread and potato, then washes it down with a Beck's she finds wedged between two black trashbags nearby. It all tastes like rubble to her, alternately wet and dry, the same as all the garbage meals she's foraged for during the hot, solitary weeks of wandering since she left Klara. She shakes this memory off before the scene replays.

That chapter is drawing to a close. The Black Forest is almost here, or I'm almost there. Staring at the faces of the Wall reenactors in the central plaza, she licks grease from her incisors and tries to spot a flicker of genuine kinship, a single face, among the fifty or sixty lined up in this third-tier southern town, whom she might plausibly have known all those years ago. A single real segment, she thinks, staring at one dumb face after another, from the real Berlin. From the twentieth century. A single genuine article among so much pretense and child's play. But no such thing appears. All that seems real now is the distant notion of Russia, a grove of oaks in a silent, frigid landscape patrolled by wolves, the hard, graffitied concrete of the Wall reassembled at last, once and for all free of pretenders. Standing only for its own sake, for the sake of togetherness, declining to cleave any population from any other.

Klara welcoming her for a second and final time.

But, she sighs, the world would have to be empty of people for that to happen. This thought makes her sad, both because she feels herself to be at least partly human, perhaps more so than ever, and because she senses that humanity will never leave the earth without a cataclysm so destructive that nothing will be left. Not even the frozen taiga of the outermost Siberian plateau. That too will have to melt before this is over.

"And you?" someone growls, in a fatty Bavarian accent. "What gives you the right to stare at us like that? What makes you so sure *you're* real? You look like you've failed an Authentication Ritual or two in your time, old lady!"

Before Ute can identify who said this, the whole pretend Wall is cackling at her, and then her blood is on fire and she's shuffling as fast as she can through the streets of this town, all of which have been renamed, with hand-labeled signs, to correspond to those of eighties Berlin.

She heads along "Unter den Linden," out of the region these cretins have labeled "Mitte," and through a novelty-store Brandenburg Gate, desperate to find open country before a throng of counter protestors chanting, "Tear down this Wall! Mr. Gorbachev, tear down this Wall" tramples her underfoot.

Hours later, well past the "Now Leaving West Berlin" sign that someone tacked up on the outskirts of town, she's back on a two-lane highway, but whatever clarity of mind she'd had before is gone. Unable to muster her thoughts into anything other than a multidirectional clanging, she tries instead to silence them. In the semi-silence that ensues, she passes open fields interspersed with ruined factories and junkyards, slag heaps and polluted streams and herds of abandoned cattle under stands of trees that, increasingly, sag beneath flames and cinder.

Before long, the night sky has turned orange with sparks and the ground has turned soft with ash, and Ute can see she's already deep in the Black Forest. She exhales and stops for a moment, feeling some of the rage abate as the entire paradigm of towns and the highways between them recedes. She can tell that she won't reach another for quite some time.

Yawning, she looks up as what appears to be a monkey leaps from one tree to the next, gripping the branches with tremendous confidence and chattering loudly. When it stops, she sees that its shape is human and hears that its voice is male. She can make out, in the light of the burning trees, that he wears a gray blazer, matching slacks, and a black beret. His bare feet clutch the branches as he releases his grip and pulls up a camera dangling on straps from his neck in order to snap her picture. Then he leaps off into the dark, and Ute hurries on her way, wherever that proves to be.

Soon she's skirting the edge of a circle of people, all of them wearing black or red cloaks, all bent forward in worship of a mummy on a tower of stone. They're clustered so tightly they look like scales on the belly of a dragon, perhaps the very one they're attempting to summon, or supplicate.

Though Klara's voice resounds throughout the clearing, Ute ignores it for now, aware that she's not in any way ready for a second encounter. Without stopping, she drags herself through a section of oaks the fire hasn't reached yet, keeping out of earshot of the worshippers. After another spell of blackness, a light appears in the distance and she approaches it, certain that it's the house she dreamed her way into on that hotel bed in Görlitz. At last my body has caught up, she thinks. At last the reunification process reveals the joint between its beginning and its middle, beyond which only the end can lie.

Anika

Typing in her subterranean living room, where she's moved her books and laptop, Anika sees a friendly stranger walking down the leafy street her cottage is situated on. She smiles as the stranger approaches, strolling across the lawn and toward her front window, and she keeps smiling as the stranger knocks on the glass.

The knocking goes on and on, growing louder and less friendly, like the stranger intends to break the window. So, repressing a sudden incursion of fear into what she thought was supposed to be an entirely peaceful homelife, Anika heaves up from her desk and walks toward the window, only to find that the stranger has moved, or was never there to begin with. The knocking comes from upstairs now, farther away but suddenly more menacing, because, Anika reasons, if the stranger breaks in while I'm down here, I could be trapped. This could become her home, with me as the basement captive. An open secret known to everyone in town, worn down through conversation until it becomes a legend from long ago and I'm never heard from again.

She hurries up the stairs, out of her peaceful homelife and back toward the burning hell of the Black Forest. Grabbing the largest knife from the wall strip beside the sink, she heaves open the cottage's door to reveal an elderly woman in an oversized trench coat, shivering and panting on the Welcome mat.

"I'm sorry," the woman says. "But I've been on my feet a long time. I need to rest."

Anika steps aside, amazed at her own lack of concern. "If I were in my own skin," she says, brushing her pants with the knife, "I'd ask what you're doing here. I'd probably turn you away."

She steps aside and the old woman shuffles past her, sinking into an armchair. As soon as Anika sees her sunken in that position, a feeling of perfection overwhelms her. A feeling that both of them are just where they're meant to be, and that all the world's problems are nothing in light of this. That this, and nothing else, is what both have been waiting for. My mother's come home, she thinks, pulling the old woman's blanket up to her chin. After so long apart, the missing pieces are falling back into place.

Part II: A Second Europe

Anika

Once again, time passes in such a way that Anika can't say where it went, nor what shape its passing has taken. The endless summer wears on, the air getting thicker and hotter without ever feeling later. Not that it feels early, she knows, but rather that it felt as late as possible right away. She's in the cottage beneath the cottage, working on her book, now entitled *Reflections on Normal Life in Southern Germany*, while Ute rests in an armchair. Anika sits at a cozy desk in front of a window that seems to reveal a placid garden scene, though there are days, like today, when she questions where this imagery comes from. I'm wondering, she thinks, removing her hands from the keyboard for fear of accidentally interpolating her doubt into the document that's slowly taking shape, whether the day out there, and this cottage, and the whole history it seems to suggest, is being piped in from someplace far away. Like Muzak to placate a frightened patient in a dentist's chair while the anesthetic takes hold.

When this series of thoughts has run its course, she places her hands back on the keyboard and watches them type: *and this is the home, dear sweet home, in which I've lived with my cherished, elderly mother, since time immemorial. Well, at least as far back as I can remember, ha ha!*

She laughs aloud, as if the sound of her own voice might lend veracity to the line she's just written. Ute stirs in her chair and groans, gathering her blanket around her neck as she nods back off.

Anika looks out the window again, at a series of families walking nearly identical dogs, looking neither at her nor at one another, and then she catches a whiff of smoke curling down the stairs, and her eyes fill with tears as she remembers the burning Forest, the penitents in circles around pillars of ash, the island of Berlin sinking beneath the green waters of her memory, or that of the person she used to be, and, leaping to her feet, she shouts, "The cookies! They're burning!"

"Cookies?" Ute yawns, but Anika has no time for her mother's confusion. She knows better than to go down the road of arguing with her about where the smoke is really coming from. Instead, she runs across the cottage to the sun-dappled kitchen in back, and pulls the sheet of blackened dough from the oven, just as she always does at this time of the afternoon, when she's written the few lines that she's going to manage for the day and the ongoing presence of the world above insinuates itself back into the idyll here below, threatening the very essence of normal life in Southern Germany. So, she removes the burning cookies and shouts, "Mother, get dressed, we've got to run to town to pick up more flour, butter, and sugar. These are ruined. I'm sorry I was so absorbed in my work that I forgot to check them."

After a slow interval in which Ute has to be coaxed from her chair and helped into her going-out dress and sturdy walking shoes, she and Anika exit their cottage onto a street lined with dozens just like it, all of them done up in the classic Bavarian half-wood style, all inhabited by families that never emerge except to walk their dogs.

Anika used to linger on their lawns and try to peer in, debating whether to go up and ring the doorbell and introduce herself as the new neighbor, but then a face appeared at the window that was so pallid, so barely-human, that she turned and ran, in a heedless panic, off onto another set of streets and spent the rest of the evening finding her way home, exhausting herself with the effort of ignoring the thought that perhaps she was lost for good. A stray person in a world without oversight, she remembers thinking during that awful interval. A piece on a board that is no longer part of any game.

But I can't be lost, she thinks now, gripping Ute's frail hand, because here I am! She smiles, determined to find solace in the tautology.

Ute leans against her, dragging her feet, as they come to the end of the lane they live on, and turn onto the main road that winds through copses of flowering trees and into the outskirts of Baiersbronn. Anika used to wave at the cars rattling slowly by, but this, too, she's had to cease doing. The faces in the car windows were the same as those in the windows of the houses, both human and not, orbs of flesh with eyes and noses and yet, in some crucial aspect, lacking all sympathy. Neither hostile nor greedy nor furtive nor lecherous, but simply not all there, unable to meet the minimum requirements for recognition of mutual humanity. So, now, Anika looks down at her feet, or up at the road winding ahead into the distance, whenever a car passes by. As always, Ute seems unconcerned, lost in thoughts of her own, or simply absorbed by the task of remaining upright.

After passing into the town proper, they make their slow but deliberate way up the high street, past the tavern cantilevered over the brook, past the church in the quaint central square, past the shop that sells sheet music and classical records, past the cafes and the restaurants, past the train station she arrived at—she can see herself dragging her suitcase from Berlin, even if the streets, as she pictures them on that first afternoon, float far overhead—and along the strip toward the Aldi on the far side.

Anika looks further up the strip, at the corporate campus with its constellation of office buildings, some bearing German flags, some American, but her eyes water and her mouth goes dry, and she's forced to duck into the Aldi before she collapses out front, as has happened once before.

Inside, she continues to fight the pressure building in her sinuses. Though she's not aware of any formal limitation on how long she can be out for, nor on how far from home she can go, she's never tried to go farther than this. Even this far, a couple of kilometers at most, oppresses her equilibrium, lending the world a heavy, underwater feeling. Most of the time, she forgets that she is, in some sense, living underground—if her memory of descending a staircase can be trusted—beneath the Europe she was born in, and in which she traveled to the Black Forest as a semi-famous author on a prestigious government assignment. But now, in the produce aisle of the Baiersbronn Aldi, the weight of it comes down on her. The sense of depth, of being beneath so much, compresses her lungs and forces her to grip the shopping cart and pant in thin, raspy drags, like a woman who's spent decades in this town, subsisting on beer, cigarettes, and whatever meat wasn't deemed fit for export.

Ute looks at her, unfazed. Like so, they traverse the aisles, gathering eggs, butter, milk, flour, and chocolate chips.

By the time they've reached the checkout counter, surrounded by more of those silent, non-emotive figures that seem to've been deployed merely to lend the town a semblance of inhabitation, Anika is shaking so badly she has trouble getting her wallet out of her purse. Ute has to clench open the edges, like a surgeon's assistant, and hold them while Anika pays, avoiding eye contact with the checkout girl who, naturally, isn't trying to make eye contact with her, either.

The walk home is excruciating, worse than any Anika can remember. They skirt the high street, which seems longer and more menacing in this direction, strewn now with glowering teenagers and snapping dogs, before passing back through the square with its abandoned church and a pile of metal café chairs and umbrellas that must've blown over in the wind.

The road snakes around and Anika drifts, pressing her shins into what now feels like a thick buffer of gel. When she looks up at the sky, she sees roots forcing their way down from the cloud cover and she glimpses the trees high overhead, on the other side, burning and burning in the Black Forest, until it becomes a forest of flame.

Coughing in the smoke, she grips Ute's hand, hefting the groceries on her other side, and drags the old woman back up their street, past the silent neighboring houses, or the place where those houses should be, but now it's dark and the road has turned to soil and the trees have loomed all around them, and the Black Forest, with its burning and chanting, is all there is.

Anika wants to run, either toward or away from this realization, but she's too tired to drag Ute, who's now reverting to concrete and wire, her heels sparking against the ground.

By the time they reach the front of the cottage, the entire structure is covered in skin. Perhaps, Anika thinks, the very same skin that, until just now, covered Ute's frame, turning it into something motherly. Allowing that tenuous story to cohere. The cottage pants, inhaling and exhaling with the rhythm of some far-distant set of lungs, entirely calm despite the crisis that Anika tries to believe has actually occurred. The burial of our peaceful home, she laments, half in earnest and half in a voice from a fairy tale, the invasion of our normal life, shuddering at the sweat-reek the skin gives off when they get close enough to smell it. Because if no crisis occurred, she can't help thinking, then it means things have always been this way, and the only crisis is that I once let myself believe otherwise. Killing this line of thought before it goes any farther, she gathers herself, lets go of Ute's hand, and forces her way under the skin, groping around for the latch.

When she finds it, she pulls open the door and hoists the hanging flap into an awning so Ute can crawl under. Inside, she marches straight to the fridge, desperate to put the groceries away, if only for the satisfaction that accomplishing such a simple task might still provide. The shelves are already full of butter, sugar, eggs, and flour, a record of previous excursions just like this one, earlier times when she and Ute left the cottage below only to return to the cottage above, where, needless to say, it would be absurd to undertake the ritual of baking cookies. Like the folklore section of a university library, she thinks, staring into the fridge: dozens of variants on the same cryptic theme. Reams of data signifying what?

Once today's supplies have been added to all the others, she closes the fridge, takes her shoes off, and gets in bed with the Riesling that, thankfully, is still lying on its side, corked just beneath the dust ruffle.

Now, for days or even weeks, it will be impossible to reenter the world below. Its memory will fade as Ute's wires tremble outward, rusting in piles across the floor, and Anika's lungs and sinuses expand now that the lower world has ceased to exert its crushing pressure upon them. She will feel, in place of that pressure, only a dull shame at having allowed herself to lapse so far into the lurid fantasy of a Second Europe underfoot. A cautionary tale, she'll come to think, of the depths the mind can sink to when not sufficiently occupied.

Sighing as her headache dissipates, Anika pulls the pillows over her head to blot out the sound of Europe breaking. She closes her eyes, wraps herself in an eiderdown quilt, and resolves to begin the work of once again imagining a happier existence just beneath the floorboards. Because only once I've rebuilt it in my mind, she knows by now, as she drifts off, will it one day become possible to return there in body.

György

After a three-day period during which Breivik demanded complete solitude to gather his thoughts and the others were instructed to fast and abstain from bathing and speaking, a midnight meeting is convened in the attic.

György lies in bed in the hour beforehand, reading and rereading the fading name on his forearm. Arisztid Huszár. He kisses his flesh, paying obeisance to the great hero, and thinks, if you give me the chance, I will make you proud.

Then the signal comes and it's time to go upstairs.

He gets out of bed, looks quickly at the egg stain on the ceiling, and prepares to make the ascent once again, skirting the steep drop off to one side by focusing on the wallpaper on the other.

Upstairs, the liberated murderer sits on a makeshift throne with Knut and Gunnar on lower seats beside him, one on his right and the other on his left. Tom sits on a stool in the corner, outside the candles that encircle the three Norwegians.

"György, welcome," says Knut, gesturing for him to sit on another stool, at the edge of the candles, a little closer than where Tom is sitting. "The Supreme Justiciar has prepared some remarks for this phase of the mission. Though you will soon be required to learn Norwegian, should you prove ready and able to go farther with us, for the time being, he has agreed to deliver them in English."

Breivik, dressed in flowing black pantaloons and a loose black shirt, nods and draws his hands into his lap, palms up, like a Buddhist monk. Then he closes his eyes and says, voice low with the absolute expectation that he will be heard, "Every era struggles, violently, to be born. There is no slick birth canal open to welcome the future in through. This is not how it works. The being known as Jack the Ripper fought, possessed with furious passion, to slice the twentieth century into being. The century that Adolf Hitler almost concluded halfway through, were he not, in the end, a coward. A dark-haired Austro-Hungarian coward, pretending to Aryan purity. And so, gentlemen, it took until the summer of 2011 for me to bring that ending to bear, and thus to usher the twenty-first into being. Or almost into being, as all shall soon see. A little late, I know, but better than never!" He smiles, wide-eyed at his own quasi-joke. Then he resumes, "The century when, at long last, the Nordic peoples will assume the throne that has too long been occupied by traitors. Jews, apostates, stunted little men who pull their pants down and expose their gaping backsides, along with those of our women, to the barbarian East, at the very first opportunity. The century in which, at long last, the death spiral ends."

He looks at György, eyes filling with hatred at the mention of the word *East*. Then they empty again and he resumes speaking.

"When I was elected Supreme Justiciar of the Knights Templar, I knew that I had a calling that went beyond my own life. Far beyond, indeed, the life of any human man, which is always, in the final reckoning, a tiny and insignificant thing. A speck among specks. I, too, was a speck at your age. Alone in a room in my mother's house in Oslo, surfing endlessly through the back channels of the Internet, looking for what? Proof of the supremacy of the Nordic race? Proof that we were under existential threat from the myriad barbarisms festering beyond our borders?" He scoffs. "I already knew all that. What I didn't know was that there was a solution. A way forward. A way that, indeed, the spirit of Hitler could be salvaged from its rotten body, stripped of that name, and brought at last to fruition."

The candles judder and Breivik scans the faces of his audience, seeking absolute attention, which three of the four display. Only Tom stares off into space, making no sign that he knows where he is.

"We have work to do, gentlemen, so I'll skip ahead, past the awful events of that July afternoon on Utøya. Events which have been covered and covered and covered by the corrupt news media, until any semblance of truth has been purged from them. Until they have been turned to grey, skinless chicken. Let me say, simply, that it brought me no joy to kill those children. I killed them, all seventy-seven of them, for the greater good. To begin the war that is now raging all around us. The war in which I am Supreme Justiciar and, under my guidance, Europe has nearly been conquered. Nearly conquered? You may ask, thinking to yourself that the war has only just begun. But it has not just begun, gentlemen. No, indeed, for the nine years I spent in prison, years that the rest of the world dithered away, I've been fighting tirelessly, day in and day out. Because, gentlemen, that day on Utøya was the beginning of something, not only the end of those children's lives. Those children were martyrs in the cause of something greater. And that thing is Nordmen. That's right, on that very day in July, forces in the universe greater than we are, forces whose power exists on a scale we can scarcely comprehend, greater than that of the so-called Hard Illuminati—imagine the great-great ancestors of our old Norse Gods, the ur-ur-ur-Gods, fathers of the Titans' fathers, in whose hollow skull the Vikings believed we all were housed—opened the portal to a Second Europe, a deeper, more consequential version of events, in which the true battle for the soul of the continent is being waged, as we speak, by the myriad armies under my command. A war in which the sides and the stakes could not be clearer, far beneath the deadening confusion and indeterminacy here on the surface. Mere ripples from a war of leviathans, my friends. I am, even now, in thousands of places at once, thousands of attics like this one, making this speech thousands of times to men like you, while my avatar Ulli Harz campaigns across Germany, prying it loose from its Soft Illuminati Chancellor so that, at last, it may serve us Nordmen in the lieutenant capacity it was always meant for. Harz, I am proud to report, is soon to be the next and final Chancellor of Germany. Or, better put, the first Chancellor of New Germany, a client state of Norway, as once Norway was a client state of theirs. Everything falls into place in the Game. Every quisling has its function. But I'm getting ahead of myself."

He stops for a moment, panting, or pantomiming panting. Then he continues. "As soon as I got to prison, I demanded access to a PS3, and, later, a PS4, and, though at first I was permitted the usage only of games transparently meant for children, my demand was granted. Let us all thank the weak, callow liberal state of Norway for that."

Nervous chuckles creep around the room.

"And through these devices, childish as the powers that be would like us to believe they are, I began to wage war. Real war. Through the portal of these consoles, I left my flabby, human self behind, like an old uniform in the back of a locker, and entered Nordmen as a warrior. I sent those mountains up through the levels and onto the surface of Europe to indicate my power. To show that something from the deepest depths was coming. Thus, I began the long, bloody campaign that is now, I'm proud to say, nearly at an end. Over those nine years, while the surface of Europe was collapsing under the weight of its own entropy, drowning under skin that, shorn from its bones, had begun to turn brown, I and my armies of brave Nordic warriors were hard at work, reclaiming the land that rightfully belongs to us, slaying thousands upon thousands of monsters and apparitions that had, for too long, masqueraded as human. We conquered the East, all the way up to the Russian border, killing the weak and enslaving the strong," he looks again at György, "who are now honored to fight beneath us, as our grunts and foot soldiers. When the war is finally won and we Nordmen are united at last in Atlantis, these Easterners will be our slaves, as the word 'Slav' already reveals they are meant to be. And they will relish the opportunity, aware that, as the old saying goes, it is better to be a servant in heaven than a master in hell. And what will hell look like?"

Breivik looks out the windows. "Hell will be everything other than Atlantis. Everything outside of Nordmen, which, from this moment on, I command you to recognize as the only reality. From my position of Supreme Command, I dispatched Ragnar, another of my lieutenants, to traverse Europe, rounding up the faithful so that, one day, I might be released to undertake the Final Final Solution in person. The merging of levels, the plugging of dykes. The true end of the Anglo-Communist clusterfuck that emerged from the failure of Hitler's half-measures. The worst era for our people since recorded history began."

Knut and Gunnar look confused. I'd be confused too, György thinks, if I weren't so angry. He wants to read the name on his arm again, but fears drawing attention to himself, and is further enraged by this fear. He clenches his seat, biding his time.

"Undertake it... in the Game?" Knut ventures.

Breivik flies up from his chair and brings his fist down on the young man's nose, drawing a torrent of black blood.

"Henceforth Nordmen is no game! It is the field upon which the Final Final Solution will be realized at last." He sits back down, collecting himself, eying Knut to see if he makes any attempt to retaliate. Of course, he doesn't. He doesn't even whimper.

"The Final Final Solution, gentlemen, is the battle for the Black Forest. The battle for Baiersbronn, its most sacral site. For too long, from the time of Wagner and even before, the Germans have leeched off of us, stealing our myths, sending us their Jews and Catholics and Arabs and, worst of all, their self-loathing, steadily weakening our people in both body and spirit. As if we were the ones with no authentic mythology, no path to the sacred and the ancient save through the tunnels dug by the fearlessness of another people. And look at them now! Look at the Chancellor's 'Summer of Tolerance'! The Germans are such cowards they butchered the Living Wall, the only truly transcendental entity to emerge from their culture since *Faust*, and then they pretended there never was any such thing. Deutsche Bank let the Soft Illuminati establish offices in every town in the nation, and for what? To sell Coca-Cola and Gap jeans?"

He looks around the room again, as if expecting hearty assent, but after what he did to Knut, there's nothing but silence.

"I can see you're nearing the limit of what you can comprehend for the time being, so I will say, simply, that it is incumbent upon us to retake the Black Forest, and rebuild the Living Wall around its edges. That, gentlemen, is the emanation point of all European power. The heart of the heart of the continent, the omphalos, the seed from which the World Tree sprouted, and then, tended by drunkards in Lederhosen dreaming of milkmaids in alpine meadows, was allowed to decay. We will reach the very ultimate level of Nordmen—the Final Final Solution, in which the Black Forest, once it belongs solely to the Norse, will sink beneath the waves that rise to cover the ash heaps left in the wake of the fires that are, even as we speak, burning unabated. It will become an island at the heart of the Second Europe, and then Europe and Atlantis will be one and the same, and we will be victors, heroes. Innumerable insectoid hordes will try to force their way in, rowing across the risen sea, but the Living Wall, at last given its due, will repel any and all such efforts and we will, at last, have complete peace of mind. Beyond strife, beyond struggle. Beyond consciousness. There will then be only one level. Only one Europe, and it will be called Atlantis. The once-digital ground will be made real beneath waves of blood."

He looks at Tom for the first time and says, "Stand."

Tom stands.

He says, "Come here."

Tom comes to where Breivik is sitting.

"Wring his neck," he says, nodding in Knut's direction.

Tom wrings Knut's neck.

"See," says Breivik, as Knut falls onto his back with his arms and legs in the air, his shoelaces dangling. "This is what true obedience looks like. The state deeper than consciousness, deeper than doubt. Tom has reentered the sunken Atlantis of his own mind, and is, as such, a formidable warrior in the landscape of Nordmen. Not all of us are permitted to enter that state just yet, as the Final Final Solution requires a level of planning and management that, sadly, only our conscious minds are capable of executing. But soon, very soon, we will have taken the Black Forest and then all Nordic men will be united in unconsciousness, and the tragic, moronic human era will be at an end, and history will be over. We will have succeeded, where none have before, in forcing eternity to begin."

The Chancellor

Lena Havermeyer snaps out of another morning spent staring at the skin overhanging her office in the Reichstag when the words, "Sven Jepperson is here to see you," force their way through her locked door.

She watches the skin meld back into plaster as she waits for that name to correlate to a face or, failing that, a shard of hearsay or reputation. A note on a legal pad, a subject line in an email. When nothing of this sort occurs and, she senses, long enough has passed that her aide is about to shout the same words again, only louder this time, she preempts that by shouting, "Sorry, who?"

A pause, a stifled cough, and then her aide, timid now, says, "Ragnar of Atlantis, ma'am. I took the liberty of adding him to your schedule, considering..."

Ragnar of Atlantis. The Chancellor closes her eyes, pinches the bridge of her nose, and mentally scrolls through the thousands of clips she's been forced to watch of that man's lectures—though rallies, or riots, seems the better term—all across the continent, spilling out of their allotted halls and into the streets, setting off one Kristallnacht after another, until half the windows in Europe were broken, not to mention twelve synagogues and thirty mosques burned to the ground, all without there being a single concrete charge that any municipal authority could bring against the man himself, who, after all, was merely talking. And what did it amount to?

Man-boys hopped up on Red Bull and video games pounding their chests and yelping about Atlantis? To what end?

She sighs once for herself and then a second time, allowing her breath to come out in the form of the words, "Show him in."

When she releases her thumb and forefinger from the bridge of her nose and opens her eyes, an impressively fit, tall, aquamarine-eyed Danish man stands before her, wearing green Puma sneakers, chic denim pants, and a crisp off-white dress shirt. He seems, despite his stature, slightly flustered. Like he showered in a hurry before coming here and hasn't quite dried off.

"Rag, uh," she tries to remember the name her aide used, "Sven, welcome, please take a seat," the Chancellor says in English, ignoring the likelihood that he speaks pristine German.

He nods and settles in across from her, placing one sneaker over the other knee, careful not to scuff the fabric.

She glances at her computer screen, which has begun to auto-play a clip of him climbing a totem pole in the center of a moss-strewn stage, above the caption RAGNAR CLIMBS THE WORLD TREE FROM HELL UP TO HEAVEN. 8.6 million views. She wants to reach over and pause it, but fears making any sudden movements. Instead, she puts her hands in her lap and looks behind the man to confirm that her bodyguards are in position by the door. At least this much is true.

"You wanted to see me about," she opens, unsure if she's supposed to know the events that culminated in this meeting's emergence on her schedule.

"Breivik," the man across from her states, as if that one word were enough to answer her question.

And, in a way, it is. Of course she has, along with the rest of Europe, followed the bifurcating reports of Breivik's disappearance from his cell in Skien Prison in Telemark, Southwest of Oslo, last week, and the insistence, on the part of the Norwegian Government and the better part of its media, that the killings in 2011 never occurred. She watched his cell transform into a live-streamed Peace Shrine, filled with flowers and teddy bears and children's pajamas, as the people of Norway lined up to cleanse themselves of the shame they bore for nearly a decade. Better them than us, the Chancellor remembers thinking, and so, in a sense, thinks again now.

"At long last," intoned Prime Minister Hanne Nordahl, a casual friend of Havermeyer's, "the good people of Norway lay down their burden." She lay down a garland of chrysanthemums on the cement floor beside Breivik's abandoned PlayStation 4. "For far too long, a grave historical inaccuracy has been allowed to fester. The flames of untruth have been fanned by unscrupulous forces, to the South and the East of here, but no longer. No, I swear, on this hallowed ground, the monster formerly known as Anders Breivik, murderer of innocents, is cleansed from our midst, just as surely as he will be cleansed from our history books. No longer will future generations live in fear that such things are possible in Norway. No longer will boys and girls in this blessed country live with the belief that their brothers and sisters were murdered on that July afternoon nearly a decade ago. No, boys and girls, if you're listening, you never had those brothers and sisters. It was all a vast misunderstanding, a mental conspiracy perpetrated by the Soft Illuminati. The parents of those children never had children. Luckily, here as with all things, understanding has triumphed. With the secular God of the modern North as my witness, let this cell remain ever empty, as proof of the wrongheadedness that led our good people to believe that there ever was such a person as Anders Breivik. There never was, and there never will be!"

There never was, and there never will be! The people chanted back, on the live-stream and all around Norway (36.4 million views), and then, soon enough, across the Continent, including in the heart of Berlin, right outside the Reichstag. For all Havermeyer knows, they're out there still... though, if they are, she's thankful for the soundproof glass of her office windows. Videos claiming that this wasn't really Nordahl proliferate on the far left and right-hand fringes of her screen, but the center seems willing to be convinced.

Raising a hand to her mouth, the Chancellor sighs again, then looks back at the man sitting across from her, forcing herself to remember that he's still here.

"And so," he says, "I have come to request amnesty. The Norwegian Government, for obvious reasons, has turned a deaf ear to my situation. The Danes, I have no doubt, will follow suit. No one will hear me when I say that Breivik is out there, on the loose. More powerful than ever. More powerful than a man can be. So I want to be locked up someplace safe. Here, in Germany. Indoors, away from what's coming."

"What's coming?"

Sven looks at the ceiling where the skin descends, at first a little at a time, the plaster crinkling here and there, but soon it comes in broad, heavy sheets. The room fills with dander. As Sven shows no response, the Chancellor has no way of telling if he can see it. Part of her wants to ask, but she quickly suppresses this part and says, instead, "I'm seeing pieces here, Sven, but no whole."

The whole is to be found only in Myth-time! She imagines him shouting, after tearing off his white shirt, blue jeans, and green sneakers to reveal a leather thong and chest harness over rippling, tattooed pecs.

Instead, the man across from her, who seems less and less like the Ragnar of the videos she's seen, recrosses his legs and says, "I lost control of the narrative, ma'am, and for that I'm sorry. Lars von Trier and I, we, well, we wanted to try something. An evolution of cinema to fit the new millennium. To see if it would work. A capstone on a career many had already considered complete. And if it did work, we wanted to see how. I had the charisma, and he had the vision to stage it, and the people and the budget, and... and he's kind of lost faith in cinema, you know? It used to mean something to him, something deep, entwined with Christ and sainthood and sacrifice and revelation and... I don't know, you'd have to ask him. But somehow that all went away. After *Antichrist* and *Melancholia*, he grew cynical. Lost touch with whatever the

164

world felt him grasping for in *Breaking the Waves* and *Dancer in the Dark*. Maybe lost touch with cinema itself, his holy vessel. He needed to put his faith in something else. Another medium. So we put together the character known as Ragnar, and we shot and posted some videos and then, once they caught on, we booked a tour, and..."

He breaks off and looks at her expectantly, as if hoping that she won't ask him to tell the rest. But she glowers sternly enough to make it clear that nothing about what he's saying is self-explanatory. He blanches and she allows herself a moment of pride at this small transfer of power.

"Well," he continues, reluctantly, "things got out of hand. I played the part, and I'll admit that I enjoyed it. I found myself fusing, in certain capacities, with the Ragnar character. I mean," his voice grows whiny here, self-justifying, "that's what actors do, isn't it?"

The Chancellor refuses to nod.

"Okay, what I'm saying is, maybe I did identify with the character I was playing, but I never intended *this* to happen." He holds his hands up in the air, as if that might serve to indicate what's happened. She can see him acting now, straining to keep a straight face. "There are things down there," he continues, and the Chancellor sees something crazy cross his pretty face, and, for the first time, she thinks, maybe this man isn't well. The possibility brings with it the immense relief of sealing everything she can tell he's about to say into a certain hermetic category. After checking that her bodyguards are still in position, she prepares to do exactly this.

"Down there," he continues, looking at the floor, "in the other world, the other Europe, underneath us, there was another me. A stronger, meaner, realer version. Like a version who actually was what he said he was. Who meant it. Who really was from Atlantis. In a way, Lars found what he was looking for. Once again, he found a way to use his visionary gift to contact forces beyond this world. He cast me out as bait, and something down there bit."

Tears stream down his face. The tears of an insane person, the Chancellor decides. "I started calling him 'The Deep Ragnar,' and as my tour went along, he took over. He'd appear inside an egg and then hatch from it. The same every night. The same as Ulli Harz, who he created—I'm sorry, but there's no other way I can put it, *he* was in charge at this point—from within that deep place. Another emanation. A dummy politician, an avatar. A finger puppet. But it caught on."

This time, the Chancellor has to try harder to feign indifference. She taps at her inner thigh with her index finger, just as she used to before calculus exams in secondary school.

"He opened for me on my lecture tour. I'm sure you've seen it on YouTube. The Harz hologram, you know? Anyway, by this point in the tour, we were back in Copenhagen, Lars' hometown, when I really sensed it was happening... when I could tell that it was him, not me, up there. I was waiting below, in a world that looked like this one, but wasn't. A buried Europe, still-pristine, immune to whatever was happening up here. A place that people would be willing to do horrible things in order to access. Looking back, that night in Copenhagen, something changed. A door opened, and it's been open ever since. I accepted the offer to go down there so he could come up here, if that makes sense. Though I didn't know that's what I was accepting. I don't know what it means that I'm here today. I don't know if I really even am."

His eyes look into hers pleadingly, and, for an instant, she wants to say, "I know where you mean. Once, a lifetime ago, I lived down there too. In a beautiful town in the heart of the woods. How I wish I'd never boarded the train that took me away."

But, because she's Chancellor of Germany, the last moral and monetary bulwark in the entirety of the EU, she holds back.

"Sipping aquavit in a trailer with Lars," Ragnar continues. "Some of the people there called it *Nordmen* and treated it like it was all a game. But I don't think it is. Or not only that. It's really there, ma'am. Just beneath us. It's real. Right now, the Deep Ragnar is going about his business. The boys who follow him, they," more tears flow, "they freed Breivik. They brought him down there, or he brought them down there, maybe. Or they brought him up here. I'm not sure which is which anymore! I'm not sure who's in charge. Sometimes I think that the whole original idea was his, and he just forced Lars and me to do his bidding up here, like we were commissioned to embody the 'Surface Ragnar' while, all along, the Deep Ragnar was calling the shots. I don't know. All I know is that they're real. They're both real. Breivik, and the Deep Ragnar, and Ulli Harz, and they're going to burn Europe to the ground. They're going to spill so much blood, ma'am, and forgive me for saying this, but no one who survives will ever be able to clean it up. Not you, not anyone. Hitler, Hess, the Third Reich?" He looks up, as if it to check that she knows what he's referring to. "That was nothing. Please believe me. I came here to admit to you that I set it in motion. I didn't know what was going to happen, but I had a feeling that something was, and I—Lars and I—we went through with it anyway. And for that, ma'am, I want you to lock me up. Whether you consider it a kindness or a punishment is up to you."

The Chancellor stares as hard as she can at the sobbing man, willing herself to believe that this is the only Ragnar, the one who, along with Ulli Harz, who may or may not exist, broke half the windows of Europe. She pictures herself addressing a fresh crowd in Alexanderplatz as work crews repair the damage and she promises, in no uncertain terms, that the Ragnar Wave is at an end, and that equilibrium has been restored. Just in time. Just before Armageddon came raining down. Or bubbling up. How's that for a reelection platform? She clamps her teeth to prevent a smile.

Look at him, a voice whispers in her head, *he's no one, nothing. You've seen the Ragnar videos. You're going to pretend this is the same man? That locking him up will put a lid on it?*

She shudders, coughs, and makes the mistake of glancing at her screen, where Ragnar is sawing the head off a bull with a broadsword and bathing in its spurting blood. Then she looks back at the cowed Dane across from her and says, her voice even and clear, "If you feel yourself to be in danger, whether internally or externally, it is possible, though I can't make any promises at this time, that the appropriate governing body within my administration may be able to arrange an indefinite stay for you in a state-of-the-art psychiatric hospital on the Polish border. Would that be suitable to your request?"

After he nods and she presses the button on her console that summons an aide to escort him away, she pictures a psychiatric hospital full to overflowing with the entire male population of Denmark, every single cell stuffed full, and many doubly or triply full, all of them in crisp jeans and designer sneakers, and yet the Ragnar Wave—she watches him brandish the bull's head in one hand and the broadsword in another, chanting to a crowd that's also brandishing broadswords (96.7 million views)—continues unabated, tearing through Europe like the fire that's taken hold of the Black Forest.

The Black Forest. Once Sven—she again forces herself to remember his name—is gone and her office has been sealed behind him, the Chancellor looks out the window at the sun setting over Berlin and decides, after many weeks of putting it off, that it's finally time to give Horst a call.

She pauses the Ragnar-feed on her computer, closes the server before it autoplays any fresh footage of Breivik's empty cell, and pulls out the miniature black notebook in which she keeps the only extant copies of the phone numbers of all the people that, in solitary moments like this, she likes to call The Munchkins. All those connected in any way with the town of Baiersbronn, in any of its incarnations.

After a few rings, a gruff, Bavarian voice comes on the line.

"Horst," she says, "you know who this is." If there's one perk left in my job, she thinks, it's that I get to say things like that.

He grunts.

"I don't have a lot of time, so tell me quickly: how's she doing?"

More grunting, the sound of dogs whining, a can opening, food slopping into a pail. Then he says, "Alright, I suppose. She's found the staircase."

"Good." The Chancellor stares back at her ceiling, no longer surprised to see the skin. She reaches out and takes a hank between her fingers, gently kneading it. "And how much time is she spending down there?" *Don't let her spend too much, you know what happens to people*, she knows she ought to say, but she keeps herself from saying it just yet.

"How should I know? I patrol the loop, as you requested. Sometimes I see her up above, sometimes down below. At the Aldi."

The Chancellor yawns as the rest of the light bleeds out of the sky and she pictures the nightclubs of Berlin filling with young people oblivious to the precarity of the world they inhabit. Oblivious, or all too aware. Perhaps so aware as to have accepted it more fully than she ever will. She can't tell if this possibility is to be hoped for. She pictures herself bursting into Berghain at four on a Saturday morning and demanding to know if the thousands of revelers crushed together in there know just how little time they have left. *And where, if we knew, should we go, if not here?* She imagines them asking, to which she imagines herself replying...

"Is she writing?" She forces herself to ask, before the other conversation nullifies this one.

"Writing?" Horst sounds confused.

"Her book, Horst. That's the whole reason she's there. We've discussed this."

Horst falls silent, and the Chancellor feels her will to press the issue dissipate. What difference does it make? She wonders. Is there any salvaging the situation, book or no book? The skin touches her mouth and her tongue extends to greet it.

"Alright. Just keep her well fed and well liquored, and find out if she's writing. Next time I call, I'm going to ask again, and that time I'm going to expect an answer."

"An answer?"

"About the book, Horst! Say it. What are we talking about here?"

After another pause and more whining of dogs, Horst manages to repeat the phrase, "The book."

She yawns and is about to hang up when he adds, his voice twisted and echoey now, like he's much farther away than he was before, "And the other woman, ma'am... she's... the other woman is with her now. The wire and concrete woman."

The Chancellor shoves the phone back against her ear and says, "What?"

But Horst has hung up and the Chancellor, though she knows she could call him again, hangs up as well and leans back in her chair as the skin hanging down sweats and contracts. It flops against her screen, smothering its display. When she peels it off and tucks it behind the computer, the gallery of Ragnar videos has been replaced by a BREAKING NEWS banner that shouts, "Controversial Danish filmmaker Lars von Trier found dead and dismembered in his luxe Copenhagen residence."

She gets up, pours a glass full of gin, and returns to her desk, running her fingers through her hair as she presses Play with the other hand.

Claiming to be "exclusive authorized footage," it shows the filmmaker in jeans and a baggy, black T-shirt wandering around his kitchen in the late afternoon light, sipping a green bottle of beer while onions fry in butter on the stove. He seems lost in thought, or in the effort to avoid thought, passing the camera without seeming to notice it, though he or his crew must have set it up.

He looks confused and exhausted, at the end of his rope. Perhaps he has indeed been maddened by the forces that Sven described. Perhaps it's all true. He leans over the onions, picks up a slice, holds it out like a worm, and tastes it. Then he puts half back in the pan, sighs, takes a cleaver out of a block sitting on the counter beside the stove, hefts it over his head with his right hand, and brings it down on his left, splayed atop a cutting board.

The camera shakes and cuts out, as if it can feel his pain. When the shot resumes, his hand has been entirely severed, his wrist wrapped in a dishtowel. With his other hand, he dices off the five fingers and cuts the palm into three sections, all of which he balances on the edge of the cleaver in order to transfer them to the frying pan, losing one finger down the back of the stove. As the rest sizzles, he takes a long swig from his beer, holding it to his mouth until he drops it, where it shatters on the ground, causing the camera to cut out again.

The Chancellor closes her eyes, sips her gin, and pinches the bridge of her nose, surprised to find her own hand still attached.

When she opens her eyes again, Lars is at a plastic table covered in a red and white checkered tablecloth, the kind she remembers from family picnics when she was small. His entire left arm is gone, and before him sits a long platter, piled with onions, tomatoes, grilled shrimp, lemons, and large chunks of meat. A crucifix and a series of votive candles flank the platter, and an open bottle of aquavit sits beside him. He reaches into his lap, removes the bloody towel from his wrist, tucks it into his collar, and squeezes lemon over the shrimp and the meat.

Then he digs around in the platter until he finds a finger, which he gnaws from the nail on down, until only a spindly bone remains.

The video pauses for a Volkswagen ad, then one for a nasal spray. The Chancellor looks out the window, shivering, only turning back to her monitor when the soothing commercial voice segues back to the Dane's satisfied chewing. Now both of his arms and a large chunk of his torso are gone, leaving a bearded head and a flabby neck atop a mass of gore. It leans against the table, sucking down meat that looks more thoroughly stewed, unlike the grilled meat of the earlier scene, leading the Chancellor to suspect that this is an entirely different video.

She watches the ad cycle play out again. Then the video cuts to an image of Lars' head floating in a mess of black soup, its lips still puttering, while hymns play in the background, and a Danish voice, with English subtitles, says, "The Great Man died in a passion of his own devising. He prepared this Last Supper to shock us out of our numbness, and to share his essence with those of us who need it most, as Europe once again faces the specter of dissolution. A final masterwork, from the last great master of European Cinema, who has died for our sins. The last genius to never leave Europe. Click on the link below to order an authentic piece of the Great Man's flesh, vacuum-sealed for freshness and hand delivered to your door. Supplies strictly limited."

The camera zooms in on his skin until it fills the frame.

Gagging, the Chancellor watches her left hand extend toward the keyboard, the index finger already extended. Just before it clicks on the link, another video plays, this one debunking the last, claiming that, contrary to the spreading rumor, von Trier is alive and well, having simply checked himself back into rehab after releasing a hoax video as a gift to his fans.

After several more ad breaks, this video likewise ends with a link to buy a piece of the Great Man's flesh, and, once again, the Chancellor watches her hand extend to click on it, faster this time.

Ute

The longer Ute spends in the upper cottage with Anika, the more her skin recedes. She sits in the corner while Anika drinks white wine and paces the bedroom in the shadow of the stuffed wolf, fox, and bear, muttering what sound like spells. During the daytime, Ute has no choice but to watch all this without comment. Then, at night, when the chanting starts up in the Forest, she feels a stirring in the metal and concrete that now make up most of her body. Her wires twist toward this sound, like the antennae on a crab, to pick up the thin but distinct strain of Klara's voice, chanting, "Come to me, come to me, come to me now, Ute. It isn't too late, but it will be soon."

Ute looks over at Anika and wonders what it would take to drag herself to the door, and then, if she could get that far, to drag herself farther, out past the fire pit beside the cottage and into the circle of flame. Because if I could get there, she thinks, Klara would take me the rest of the way. Of this much she's certain. Another thing she's certain of, perhaps the only other thing, is that she can't survive many more nights alone. She can feel her already-weak pull toward the Russian taiga weakening further, and the distance growing until it seems to recede into the impenetrable back reaches of space, stranding her alone on earth, in a house that no longer feels like the one she glimpsed in a dream on a hotel bed, in a room she should've found a way to keep from ever leaving.

More days and nights like this pass, during which Ute sidles a few inches closer to the door, dragging herself on her exposed wires toward the sound of Klara's voice, which fills her with a dull but tenacious charge. She moves slowly enough not to attract attention, but, still, the distance grows over time, until the night comes when she's close enough to the door to force her way outside.

She lurks by the opening while Anika commences her evening routine, shutting her computer and climbing into bed, with or without a book, to work her way through the last of the wine that Horst left stocked in the pantry.

Ute waits until Anika's under the covers, moaning softly as the skin comes in through the walls and down from the ceiling to envelop her, leaving only the topmost hairs on her head to fringe what is now a bulbous sack, like a gigantic turnip. Then she closes her eyes, summons a vision of the taiga, however fuzzy, and cracks into it like an ampule of adrenaline. She uses the resulting surge to shoulder open the cottage's flimsy wooden door and launch herself onto the ground, which is so soft that her wires cut straight through, entangling with the roots of ancient trees.

Thus entangled, her blood thickening with ancient sap, she forces her way along, conscious only of the low, rhythmic chanting up ahead, past the clearing that surrounds the cottage, past the footpath that leads to town, past the dunes of cooling ash, and toward the vast yellow-orange blaze at the heart of the Black Forest.

After a long, painful period of inching along, Ute hears Klara's voice. Though it still sounds distant, and warped by smoke and the chanting of others, it's unmistakable. I'm coming, Ute thinks, and this time I'm going to stay. I won't lose you again. Just help me get there. Please. I can't make it on my own.

As she goes on thinking this, crawling through the soft dirt and choking on the fumes in the air, she feels something subterranean pull her in the direction of the clearing. At first she thinks it's still the roots, thickening as she moves toward the point where the trees are tallest, but soon the feeling of contact from that hotel room in Görlitz grows unmistakable. Klara. You're merging with me. Sending your wires under the earth to pull me toward you, to make me part of you, and you part of me.

Forgiveness. Warm and soft as the eiderdown on the bed in the Hotel Silesia.

Her body sparks and trembles and she closes her eyes, surrendering to a vast rock pillar, reaching up from the bottommost Europe all the way to the one on top, stabbing through several night skies. At the base of the pillar stands Klara, robed in black, preaching to a circle of lost pieces of the Wall, while, on top, stands the mummy of Martin Himmelreiter, presiding over the stones of the former Holocaust Memorial, preaching the same thing as Klara below, the same word, repeated over and over and over:

"Unity."

"**U**nity," Ute repeats. Unity. The pieces are finally coming together for good. The quantum particles of the Russian border are shifting, drawing near, eliding all the territory in between. Opening, once and for all.

She exhales and releases the tension that's been propelling her forward, giving in to the pull of the subterranean wires, expecting to glide the rest of the way into the clearing and from there out of history for good.

At the back of the vision that's still unfolding, she sees a pile of thousands or tens of thousands of bodies, crushed and crushing one another, dead but still moving, squirming and fighting for position, nestled in the shadow of a wall on three sides and a frigid ocean on the fourth, Klara rising up from the bottom of the pile to pull her down, arm in arm, to her final resting place. A womb that will never squeeze her out.

She jerks her eyes open as a crushing pain cleaves into her lower back, and, though she knows that something terrible is now occurring, her first instinct is to preserve that glimpse of the Other Side. She reaches her arms out, praying that Klara takes hold of them, as another brutal impact chops into her spine.

"It must've gotten tangled in the roots," a male voice says in the air above her.

"I don't how it could've gotten out. I was going to bed, and..."

"Here," the male voice interrupts, "dig around its face with the other shovel. I'll keep breaking up these roots until we can pull it free."

The man and the woman work through the night to disentangle what's left of Ute, using shovels and spades to chop through the wires that reached out to welcome her. The chanting and burning goes on in the clearing up ahead, but Ute knows she'll never reach it. Not on her own, anyway. Not tonight. Not in the state she's in.

The last of the wires finally pull free around dawn, and Ute watches herself being dragged back through the underbrush, past the fire pit, and past the solitary figure who stands on the periphery with his camera and notepad, alternately snapping photos and jotting notes, a simian smile dividing his bald head in two.

Anika

They drag her into the cottage and leave her in a pile on the rug.

"Quite a statue," Horst mutters, pouring a schnapps from a bottle he took down from a high cabinet labeled CHRISTMAS.

"Sentimental value," Anika replies, her voice quavering from the exertion of dragging it inside. "My research is on the Living Wall, so..."

Horst looks down at Ute, then back at Anika, and nods. Downing his schnapps, he leans toward her, close enough to drain whatever warmth had lingered from the flames outside. Then he belches and says, "About your research. The Chancellor called. She wants to know how your book is coming along. If she calls again, I'll tell her it's nearly finished."

He pours another shot, downs it, hands Anika the glass, unlocks the door beside the refrigerator using a key attached to a wire clamped to his belt, and descends the staircase into the dark.

When he's gone, Anika sits in one of the two chairs by the table in the kitchen, from which she regards the wire and concrete mass heaped by the door. She studies it, searching for signs of movement, uncertain if she'd be reassured to find any. I know it moved, she thinks. If it didn't, why did Horst and I have to drag it back in from outside? Or was that merely a bad dream from which I've now, thankfully, awoken?

As soon as this possibility announces itself, she latches onto it. Yes, she decides, getting to her feet and filling the kettle, it's all been a long nightmare that, though I'd rather be sleeping peacefully, I'm glad to say I've finally awoken from. Another of the nightmares that chased me from Berlin. Though she's discomfited to find that they've followed her here, she's relieved to have determined that this is all it was. The mind plays tricks. We know this. We've known it a long time already.

She paces the kitchen while the water heats up, gathering her arms around her sides to ward off the cold of the late summer evening—unless, she thinks, it's still early summer, the hottest days yet to come—and she eyes the hunk of concrete and wire each time she passes it, thinking: a souvenir. A souvenir from my research, after all these years.

My research.

As the water shakes inside the kettle, she closes her eyes and pictures a basement within herself, a warm dark room with a Persian rug, a plush armchair facing a desk piled high but neatly with papers and, beside it, a bookshelf full of color-coded editions of her research, her book translated into all the major languages, even some whose characters she can't make out.

The kettle clicks and she watches herself pour it over grounds in the French press, bored by this scene in the kitchen, eager to get downstairs, to the room that is now open, after having been closed for too long. The room that sustains and preserves her research, ensuring that, no matter how much else burns and crumbles, the work remains sacrosanct.

With a mug half full of milk looped around her index finger and the French Press balanced in her other hand, she opens the door beside the refrigerator and makes her cautious way down the steep staircase, one edge overlooking an impossible drop.

The room at the bottom hums louder the closer she gets to it, and her temples throb as if she were descending into a pit of thick, hot coffee, but she perseveres, rationing her breath as she makes her way toward the desk, laid out exactly as she pictured it. She settles into the leather chair behind the desk, plunges the coffee, and looks over her papers, rifling through the thick stacks in search of the place where she left off. The place where I left off? She asks herself, remembering, or deciding, that she must have been in the middle of something. A large piece of work, something momentous, incorporating years of my life, and, when finished, paving the way for a future on a level of access and influence far higher than it otherwise would have been. A consequential step along the road of my becoming.

She leans back in her chair, closes her eyes, and tries to correlate imagery to the concept of her future. A scene, even a single snapshot, an etching on a piece of scrap paper, anything at all to suggest that this is going someplace real.

But the only image that comes is that of a chunk of wall standing alone in a grassy field, endlessly awaiting the emergence, on the horizon, of the next closest piece so that, generations hence, some final unity will be achieved. A potential bulwark against potential invasion, she thinks, blushing as she remembers Kafka's "Great Wall of China." Indeed, she thinks, shivering as the feeling of being that lone piece of wall, waiting and waiting to be joined to something larger, sinks in.

Footsteps in the background demand her attention, but when she turns, it's only an old woman, shuffling down the stairs and sinking into the other armchair. The armchair, it would seem, that's meant for her. Anika looks her over, trying to remember if she's seen this woman before, and, if so, whether she poses any threat. Then she thinks, ah yes, of course, my elderly mother!

How could I forget she was living with me here, absorbing the clean country air after the noise and smog of Berlin? Anika winces as a watery pressure builds in her sinuses and, not for the first time, she fears that remaining down here will crush her. She pinches her nose and exhales as hard as she can, forcing the pressure out of her skull.

Then, careful not to disturb her mother, who seems to have dozed off, she gets up, pads over to the bookshelf, and takes down the German edition of her book. Sitting back at her desk, she pushes aside a stack of papers, turns on the banker's lamp in the righthand corner, pours her mug full of coffee, and opens to a page near the middle, where the word *concrete* catches her eye, offering a form of reassurance she's more than happy to accept.

ON DRINKING CONCRETE IN CHEMNITZ:

O ne of the most disturbing practices that has been reported in the larger field of inquiry into what has been termed, by myself and others currently active in the field, Living Wall Reenactment Syndrome, is that of former subjects of the DDR obtaining small quantities of liquid cement and, in apparent protest of what is seen as the dishonest official account of late twentieth century German history put forth by the Havermeyer Administration and its immediate predecessors, consuming it orally. These people, who skew overwhelmingly teenage and overwhelmingly male, then join hands on the outskirts of whichever Saxon or Thuringian village they happen to reside in, and chant, in unison, "The Wall was alive! The Wall was alive! The Wall was alive and the Wall will live!" Meanwhile, needless to say, the concrete they have ingested is hardening in their stomachs and esophagi, slowly killing them like those roaches in the Lispector story.

The irony of arguing for the supposed aliveness of the Wall, while at the same time ensuring their own deaths, is either lost on these protestors, or has a meaning for them that it does not have for us (by which I mean, those of us sufficiently informed to recognize rank and, in many cases, obviously dangerous lies when we see them).

Nevertheless, the burgeoning graveyards of these cement-stomached youths must be reckoned with, for simply ignoring their existence will only breed more suspicion of the upper political and economic classes in the eyes of the working and unemployed classes, especially in the former East. It cannot be denied, indeed, that on the outskirts of once-significant East German metropolitan areas, such as those surrounding Chemnitz, dozens and perhaps even hundreds of young people have piled up, their skin putrefying and falling away to reveal cores of solid cement, thin and distended as Giacomettis. Known, in the local parlance, as Wall Sentinels, these figures appear to have taken on greater and greater folkloric significance in the minds of the local populace—older and better-off people (in terms of both education and economic stability) unfortunately included—representing, as they do, not the actual pieces of the so-called Living Wall, but, rather, the dramatic sacrifices that ordinary people are willing to make in its name.

The longer the municipal governments of communities such as Chemnitz go on refusing to dispose of these "sentinels," the greater their significance will grow, like lightning rods gathering charge. Already, there have been reports of plaques appearing around the necks of these figures—either worn by the cement-drinkers before death, or else affixed to them by others thereafter—with slogans such as, "Rebuild the Real Germany: Repair Her Broken Backbone."

The sentiment expressed therewith, to the best of this researcher's knowledge, is that these people have come to believe that 'real' pieces of the (formerly) Living Wall have been atomized across Europe, in a manner akin to the Turko-Balkan notion of the gypsy, or the Lost Tribes of Israel (again, the irony of such a figuration, in the context of resurgent East German nationalism and its attendant antisemitism, is not only not lost on this researcher, but is fully intended to underscore her thesis), and are living in hiding, understandably terrified of suffering again the pain they suffered during the Berlin Wall's official destruction, in November of 1989, to say nothing of what the Wall must have suffered—in this account of its existence—throughout all the decades that it stood guard along the fault line that has now allegedly been rent open, cracking the continent perhaps fatally in half. These cement-drinking youths believe that the sacrifice of their own lives in this manner, the turning of themselves into Sentinels, may serve—illustrating the evergreen logic of symbolic sacrifice—as an enticement to the actual pieces of the Living Wall, wherever they may be, to reconvene, having been shown in this manner that they still have allies in Germany and that, indeed, their coming-back-to-together would represent, for these allies, a best-case scenario (the worst being, presumably, the continued smooth-functioning of the internationalist project known, crudely, in their circles, as the "E-Jew," a bastardization of "EU" and perhaps also a reference to the burgeoning fear of digital technology and the dawning of a post-human era, which these backwards-looking young people seem to believe can be forestalled by the reunification [the irony of this word's usage, in the present context, is, once again, not lost on the author] of the "injured but not dead" Living Wall).

Anika closes the book and puts it back on the shelf. Then she sits again in her chair, blows through her stoppered nose to clear the pressure, and tries to doze as the sun streams through the windows at the very top of the room.

Behind her closed eyes, she slips back into that cold, grassy field where Kafka's lone section of the Great Wall of China still stands, forever awaiting the appearance of its counterparts. She yawns and pulls her legs up under herself on the chair, and pictures the chapter she just read as an analogue of that piece of the wall, a unit of meaning likewise awaiting its context, words blowing across desert sand, a fragment of a world that no longer exists, or that one day might, but not yet, and perhaps not for a long, long time. Though she has a dim memory of having written the words she just read, as well as those filling the hundreds of pages surrounding them, she can't picture where, or when. More importantly, she can't picture the world that those words sought to describe, nor the state of mind she must've been in to write them, and consider them true.

This, she thinks, as she falls further asleep, is the dream I will attempt to have. Just as she remembers dozing off as a little girl with a headful of bedtime stories, eager for the volatile energy of dreaming to melt those discrete images into a warm bath where she could fully submerge herself—or no, more than a warm bath, a full amniotic environment, a hot primordial sea where the landmass that would, eons hence, come to be known as Atlantis was still being formed—she now slips deeper into a dream of the Living Wall as nothing more than a noxious myth, the result of economic disparity, historical accident, and post-Soviet propaganda. Or, deeper still, the simple result of her own dreaming, as if she alone on earth had conceived of it, and it would thus painlessly die with her.

This dream carries Anika into mid-morning. Then, when the sun gets high enough to shine directly into her eyes, she stirs. Her first sensation is extreme hunger, sharp enough that her only thought is of finding something to eat.

She stands up, rouses the old woman from the other armchair and says, "Come mother, we're going to town. It's Sunday morning." As she says this, Anika senses that it must be true. Her sense of completion of the week's work, and of calm mixed with dread at the week to come, correlates too strongly to the archetype of Sunday for anything else to be the case.

After the old woman uses the toilet and splashes water on her face in the half-bathroom attached to the workspace, and Anika does the same, the two of them depart through the door that leads into the garden, blooming with roses and daisies. Birds sing in the warm morning air, redolent of pine and spruce, and the ground feels soft and mossy underfoot. The pressure builds again in Anika's sinuses, and dark thoughts of dragging a squirming, struggling piece of Wall across an expanse of roots and dirt through a cloud of smoke percolate at the edges of her mind.

She fights to keep the center—the sacred clearing in the woods of my mind, as she hastily puts it—free of everything except appreciation of the birdsong and the airborne perfume. This is Sunday morning, she reminds herself, a time when one's only concern is finding a warm, soothing cup of Milchkaffee and a nice juicy slice of strudel.

Before long, they're strolling through the outskirts of town, into an atmosphere of classical good cheer, everyone smiling in rugged country slacks and fresh-pressed dresses, half of them emerging from Church, ruddy-cheeked and clad in Lederhosen, while the others, like Anika and her mother, filter in now, just in time for the breakfast rush at Kleindorf's and Schönnenhof's, the town's two bakery-cafés, locked in friendly competition for as long as anyone can remember.

"What do you think, mother? Cherry strudel or apple?" This will determine which bakery they choose.

Though she sounds ever less like a woman and more like an automaton struggling to pass as one, Ute mutters, "Cherry," which is all Anika needs to hear. She leads them straight to Kleindorf's and signals to the gentle young waiter that they'd like a table for two.

Before long, they're sitting in the window, watching village life unfold at a leisurely pace on the street outside, a harpist plucking Bach etudes while they sip thick, rich coffee with a generous topping of both foamed milk and whipped cream and a sprinkling of cinnamon, punctuated by bites of cherry strudel, perfectly balanced between sour and sweet. This, Anika thinks, is the life. These are the moments that humanity persists in order to enjoy.

Her temples throb again and she coughs, spitting out part of a cherry pit. It lands on her plate with a sharp ping and rolls to the edge, and the moment briefly threatens to crack up. But Anika manages to come to terms with the pressure before it does. She clicks her jaw and blows yet again through her pinched nose, and, though no comfortable equilibrium returns, she decides to consider the pain bearable.

Through this pain, she takes another sip of Milchkaffee and another bite of strudel, and pictures all the decent people doing the same, all over Germany, the same as they've done since the Middle Ages, and she knows that if she could stop time right here, freeze everyone into a painting that smelled like fresh coffee and cherry and warm, flaky dough, she would do it in an instant and never, not once in all of eternity, regret her decision.

Barring this, she decides, as time continues to pass, and her breakfast dwindles and the specter of filling the rest of the day looms—the specter of Sunday afternoon, which is really the specter of the entire coming week—I will go back to my office to write. I will write the simple story of my life in this town, as a woman—no, a girl, a little girl with her whole life ahead of her—in peacetime, enjoying the simple things, because, when you come right down to it, those are the only things you can put your faith in. The only things that are real enough to truly enjoy.

Reflections on Normal Life in Southern Germany. She looks back at the title once she's returned to her office, and is startled to realize she's already begun work on it. Before moving into the unwritten pages, she reviews what she has so far, writes a faithful account of the morning's breakfast excursion, then breaks for lunch with her mother in the back garden.

György

In the weeks since Breivik's speech, the horse farm has filled with bodies, young men like Knut and Gunnar rolling up the gravel drive in white vans, spilling into the pastures where the horses are now being outfitted and trained for battle. György supposes that a signal, inside or outside of Nordmen, has been sent, as Breivik refers to these men as "my soldiers, reporting for duty."

The livestream from Baiersbronn shows the Wall growing around the altar, new segments arriving every day while flames sanctify the ground in which it puts down roots of wire and cement. "The time for the Final Final Solution," the narrator announces, "is nearly at hand."

At breakfast, one of the new soldiers mutes the tablet on which he'd been watching this footage, leans over to where György's eating unsweetened oatmeal, and says, "I heard about Copenhagen. Damn, man. How many Jews? Guess that's why they let you hang with the Generals."

György blanches, and is about to say something, when Gunnar shouts, "Okay men, work time!" forcing them all to abandon their bowls and congregate on the lawn, where a thirty-foot wicker statue of Odin is almost complete. Though no timetable has been announced from on high, György can't imagine it taking more than the rest of the day to put the finishing touches on it, at which point some culminating ritual will surely occur.

Anything to break the spell of the past few weeks, which he's crawled through in a haze, seeing things that he knows aren't there, pleading with his own stubborn mind to free him from doubt by yielding another vision of Arisztid Huszár, which it has so far refused to do. Instead, the house has filled with the shadowy presence of Knut, both dead and not dead, flickering on and off without anyone else seeming to notice and, every night, the equally incorporeal presence of Breivik in his bed, whispering in his ear, "Prepare your womb. You will birth a handsome litter of Nordic sons for me yet, just wait and see."

Tossing and turning and trying to pry the Justiciar off himself—György seems to be back in bed now, despite having recently marched out onto the lawn in broad daylight—he can't help hearing the rest of Breivik's entreaty, which, like a character in a game whose dialogue runs on loop, is the same every night: "No longer can the Nordic race tolerate the influence of women, even be they blonde and blue-eyed, slim-waisted and supple. Just look at what's happened to our men. Weaklings. Sissies. Cry-babies one and all, wringing their hands and dreaming of compromise. Begging for scraps. Afraid of their own shadow. No longer. In Atlantis, men will beget men, and nowhere in the chain will the softening influence of Woman be allowed. The feminine must, though it pains the hedonist in me to say so, be bred entirely out of the gene pool. Only then will the masculine principles of honor, dignity, and courage be impervious to corrosion. We will become like the mighty oaks of the Black Forest, standing strong for thousands of years. But"—every night, he leans in here and nibbles György's earlobe—"no Nordic man ought ever to be subjected to the humiliation of bearing young, so, needless to say, a new kind of womb will have to be found. This, my swarthy Magyar friend, is where you come in. It will be the supreme honor of the Hungarian people to bear our young, and, in this sense, to participate in the culmination of humanity that life on Atlantis will represent. Of course, no inferior DNA from you or any man like you will pass to our offspring—you will, in that sense, be a pure vessel for our seed, not any kind of parent—and yet, nevertheless, you will play a crucial role in this chapter of human history, as an accessory to the greatest society the world has ever known, the final society... already, as we lie here and whisper together like this, your insides are being hollowed out, your inferior organs withering to make space for the womb in which my brave sons will soon grow."

György shoots awake at this point, the same every night, into the flames of a synagogue on a side street in Copenhagen, the night of the Ragnar rally. He runs through the collapsing infrastructure, prayer books and pews and tapestries burning all around him, as the air fills with the screams of parishioners and, in the distance, his own laughter, mixed with that of Knut and Gunnar, wafting into the inferno from the cool sidewalk outside, where they drink Carlsberg and cheer him on. He runs as fast as he can, but in no particular direction, simply circling, waiting out the clock, until he dies and, by dying, wakes up a second time. There's nowhere else to go, no escape in the dream, just as there wasn't in reality, if it ever was real, which part of him wants to doubt. So, he runs through the flames, torn between gloating at the death of the Jews and wishing he could annul the scene and start it over, simply return to Berlin on the night train and forget he ever went north, finish his paper on Sloterdijk's conception of national sovereignty in the 2020s and return to his parents in Gyula with his tail between his legs, but then, he thinks, still circling the synagogue with his skin peeling off his frame, no, if I'd never come here I never would have met Arisztid Huszár, and then I never would have...

He comes to in another set of flames, rebooted, having apparently lost track of the entire day. Now he's in a circle of fifty or sixty Norwegians, all of them in black robes while he's still wearing his jeans, staring together at an immense burning statue of Odin. He forces the question of whether he's inside or outside the Game to the back of his mind and tries to simply focus on the scene before his eyes, but as soon as he does this, his stomach throbs and all he can think is that he's already pregnant with Breivik's spawn, his old organs trashed to make way for an engorged womb that has been implanted in him through a whisper in a dream, like Christ in the Virgin Mary. The destroyer of all that was once noble in Europe. The king of the cult of weakness that has prevailed here for the last two millennia. He coughs, wheezes, and again forces his attention back onto the statue, which has now been reduced to two crackling legs supporting a mound of ash.

As the men chant, "No future! No future! There is no future except on Atlantis!" a figure emerges from the ash heap, perched on one of Odin's gigantic legs. It hauls itself to a standing position, dusts off its military uniform, complete with medals, sword, and cap, and says, in Breivik's now-unmistakable whine, "Welcome, soldiers. The Final Final Solution is nearly upon us. Ragnarok is nearly here!"

The men chant, "Ragnarok! Ragnarok! Ragnarok is nearly here!" while György massages his belly and thinks: the situation is coming apart. The same thing that has happened to all of Europe is happening here as well. He shivers at the realization that nowhere is safe, that every instance is a microcosm of the larger calamity. Nothing is outside the fractal. His legs tremble and he fears he's about to fall backward, into the man behind him, so he closes his eyes to gather what's left of his equilibrium, hoping, at this point, just to get through the rest of the evening and find his way back to bed, where perhaps a heroic dream will restore his will to power.

But when he opens his eyes, the scene has transformed once again. Now, in place of Breivik in his Knights Templar uniform stands Arisztid Huszár, naked inside the pelt of a gigantic wolf, atop the carcasses of the Norwegians. He smiles at György, then pulls the wolf's head over his own and growls, "György, my son, your moment of reckoning has arrived. Leave here tonight. You know you don't belong. Steal one of these infidels' vans and drive. Drive as quickly as you can, due south. They will follow, but if you leave tonight, you can beat them to the Black Forest. They aren't really dead, you know this. They will rise again, so you must go now. Go there, where the Living Wall is massing. Go there and round it up and rebuild it around Hungary. Conquer all of Europe in Hungary's name and make these degenerates your slaves. It's the only way to honor the old gods, the true, powerful gods of Old Hungary, before the Christians watered them down into weak gruel. Before the Germans, and the Russians, and the Turks, and the Jews..." Here the wolf gets so livid it ceases talking and begins to snarl, clamping its jaws open and closed in the moonlight, seeming to eat the darkness and leave a yet-deeper darkness in its wake, sucking him in until he's passed through to the other side, looking out through the wolf's eyes at the place where the boy used to stand.

The vision sputters as several Norwegians, already resurrected, help Breivik down to the lawn, and György lands back in his body, chanting along with them, pledging his readiness for Ragnarok, for the waters to rise, leaving only Atlantis. But, while his body goes through these motions, his mind studies the vans parked in the driveway, searching for the one closest to the exit.

When he's determined which one it is, he turns back into the crush, accepting a tall bottle of Svalbard IPA and a shot glass of Aquavit, and joins in with the chanting, hoping, for now, only to avoid contact with Breivik.

As the night wears on and the Norwegians get ever drunker, György skulks among them, testing how far outside their circle the Game—a term he's started to apply to the entire situation up here, everything since Berlin—will let him go. He closes his eyes and sees the burning synagogue, Jews screaming in terror, then opens them and sees the Norwegians, shirtless, their chests tattooed with Celtic crosses and runes, eagles and hammers, howling at the night sky or unloading rifles from a crate someone must have dragged over from one of the vans. The scene turns sluggish and glitchy as it replays again and again—either that, György thinks, or I'm drunker than I think I am, though he can't remember having accepted more than a few shots, and maybe a few lines off someone's car key—running out of new imagery while refusing to end or segue to the next scene.

He looks up at the sky where the moon hovers, flat and lusterless in the dead center, and, though he knows that nothing will come of it, he closes his eyes and tries to burrow beneath the burning synagogue, down to something authentic in his own mind, some buried kernel of self-awareness in the catacombs, some idea he can latch onto as definitely his own.

Nothing.

He opens his eyes, pulls them off the moon, and decides to work his way back into the throng, in search of alcohol. Better, he thinks—or the Game thinks through him—to get really drunk than to stay as I am, wondering whether I'm sober. But before that, he has to pee. So he crosses the throng to the far side, past the pigs on spits and the ice chests of beer, past the remains of Odin, past the stables where the horses are moping in silence, and into the house that, for a brief period a few weeks ago, felt like home.

He shuffles up the stairs he's shuffled up dozens of times before, but this time he feels like a burglar, breaking into a stronghold where, if caught, he'll be killed without question.

After peeing in the bathroom through whose window he first watched Breivik rumble up the driveway, he passes his old bedroom and is overcome by exhaustion at the sight of his bed. So, putting off the thought of going back outside and hitting the liquor, he tiptoes into the room, pulls down the comforter, and slides in between the sheets.

Aware of the effect that closing his eyes is likely to have, he endeavors simply to rest awhile, until he decides what to do next. Maybe, he thinks, already beginning to nod off, if I lay low in here, the party will die down and then, around dawn, I'll be able to tiptoe out onto the empty lawn and take my pick of vans.

"Even for a novice, the Game's not that easy," a voice whispers in his ear. "You should know that by now."

He rolls onto his side and dismisses this voice, trying, again, to anchor himself in the moment. "I'm in Norway," he whispers, resorting to the habit he developed in childhood of listing only the things he can be certain of, as a means of warding off encroaching night terrors. "I'm in the north of Norway, maybe the far north, on a sort of vacation, and I'm here with..."

"You're here with me," Breivik whispers in his ear. "I knew you'd be waiting. Your vagina is ready." The Justiciar's breath is thick with wood smoke and barbequed meat, his voice shot from chanting. "Let me install it for you."

Though he knows he should run, or, better yet, fight, György freezes. He lies still while Breivik reaches around him, unbuckles his jeans, and shoves something cool and gelatinous into the shriveling space between his legs. Cool tendrils reach from his pelvis up into his belly, pushing his organs aside, demanding space.

Though he can tell that damage is being done, he feels no pain. Or, he considers, I feel pain but no hurt. One or the other, but not both. Something is happening to it, a György-shaped thing lying in my bed, but nothing, so far as I can tell, is happening to *me*.

"Soon, you'll be full to bursting with my sons," Breivik coos in his ear. "Strong Nordic men, ready to rule Atlantis for generations, their genes never warping, never weakening, never wearing out."

György shuts his eyes as tightly as they'll go, willing himself back into the burning synagogue, then willing the collapsing structure to take him with it, down into the realm of ashes, the Hell of Jews, but he remains where he is, quivering in his bed in Northern Norway as Breivik hunches up behind him and, though no feeling correlates with the experience, seems to enter the orifice he's just installed.

"There are hundreds more like you," he pants in György's ear. "Hundreds and thousands and millions, in Hungary and Poland and Greece and all those dank crannies over there, the unclean corners of Europe, moldering in the shadow of the heathen East. Muster them. Bring them here. Tell them the good news! Out of darkness... light!" He thrusts harder, crushing György against the wall. "You can be their prophet, leading them to us, to the only place on earth where they can still serve a higher purpose. Where their lives will amount to more than a degrading copy of their parents' and their parents' parents', each generation a little weaker, a little further from the promise with which, I'm sure you'd like to believe, your earliest ancestors gazed at the future."

Breivik slams György again against the wall, crushing his face into the dusty paint beneath the windowsill. Then he grabs the back of his head, lifts it an inch, and presses it to the window, forcing him to look down onto the lawn where the soldiers are now engaged in an orgy so multi-limbed and many-headed that it's impossible to count its participants. The only point of reference György can reach for is the medieval paintings he's seen in the Gemäldegalerie in Berlin, Bosch and Breughel and Cranach the Elder, giants and witches and ogres and satyrs worshipping naked in the moonlight, bathing indiscriminately in one another's blood and spunk, becoming something at once more and less than human, barreling across a threshold that György's never even approached.

Never until now. He winces, though it still doesn't hurt, and prepares to close his eyes again, praying this time to wake up inside the wolf. Just give me that one chance and I'll do whatever you ask from then on. As this thought takes root in György's mind, Breivik slams back into him, shoving his face so hard against the window that the glass cracks and almost shatters, crushing up the integrity of the moment so that, for the rest of the intercourse, György hovers in a middle place, between wholeness and brokenness, neither here nor there, thinking: of all the ways I pictured my first time, this was never one of them.

The thought makes him smile, and leads, naturally, to the next thought, which is, I wonder if it's Breivik's first time, too? The two of us up here together, at last crossing the no-man's land we've approached so often, only to retreat in terror and frustration, back to our screens, our rooms, our blankets. He tries to keep from laughing out loud, but the laughter emerges regardless, forceful enough to cause Breivik to stop and bark, "What?"

Empowered by the Justiciar's embarrassed confusion, György emerges into the smell of fur and a rich, welcoming musk that he can barely believe is his own. Gone is the sour, timid sweat he's exuded all his life, in the cold, yellow-tiled gym at his half-defunct high school in Gyula, and in the corporate gym in Berlin, above the Media Markt on Kantstraße, where he hunched beneath barbells heavy enough to bend his spine and summon ripped Germans to his rescue. Replaced, finally with the animal sweat of a warrior.

And not just any warrior—he stands, removes Breivik's penis from his lower body, and crushes the Nordic man-child's head between his palms like an oversized plum—but the warrior known from Lisbon to Moscow as Arisztid Huszár.

He sucks blood from his wolf-fur as he deposits the carcass in the bed he used to sleep in, tucks it in tightly, then strides from the room, down the stairs, and into the kitchen, where he extracts a set of car keys from a bowl by the sink. Then he strides back outside, into the cool predawn, across the field where the Norwegians lay sprawled in glutted stupors, and begins trying the keys in the doors of the various vans, feeling as invincible as anyone alive has ever felt.

Every time a van fails to open, he smashes its windshield with his fist and moves on, until he's settled behind the driver's seat of a Mercedes Sprinter cargo van. He backs up into another van of the same model, parked directly behind him. After crashing into it three times, he manages to push it enough to one side to maneuver past, and then it's just a matter of reversing further down the driveway, turning around, straightening out, and putting it in Drive. On his way down the driveway, György screeches past Tom, who sits gargoyle-still on an overturned picnic table, his Cape Town Horse Feeds cap low on his head, his eyes fixed on a tree trunk several inches in front of him.

This level of the Game lets him go without struggle. Though he knows better than to assume that he's seen the last of Breivik, Knut, and Gunnar, despite two of them ostensibly being dead, György allows a sense of calm to settle over him as he drives, yawning and blinking in the arctic dawn. The wolf recedes, but his confidence, for now, does not.

He toys with the radio until a cacophony of black metal pours from it, and then he drives onward, nodding in time to the sluggish rhythm. He drives like this for hours, following roadsigns toward Narvik, which, judging by the frequency with which its distance is listed, must be the closest city of any size. The sun rises over a landscape of half-finished housing developments, or those that have half-decayed, and rows of single-occupancy units lined up along brackish inlets, people out front raking their lawns in monotonous synchronicity with their heads down. In the far distance, if he squints, he can make out what appear to be the jagged peaks of the mountains that supposedly rose from the ancient coastline, and he can even make out what look like stretches of highway, pulled entirely perpendicular to the ground against the edges of these alien landmasses, and yet he can tell that, no matter how long he drove, and no matter the direction, there'd be no way to reach them. He pictures approaching and being rebuffed, again and again, bouncing against a soft barrier, unable to say how or where it exists.

Repeated impacts wear him down until his eyes water and his vision flickers and he has to pull off the road outside Narvik, in the parking lot of a gas station where a long-haul truck blocks all three diesel pumps.

He rummages in the glove compartment until he turns up a wad of bills, shoves them in the back pocket of his jeans, and walks inside. Passing the trucker, who's deep in conversation with the girl behind the register, he makes his way to the bathroom, yawning again and running his hands through his hair.

Standing over the toilet, he unbuckles his jeans and is about to reach into his underwear when a residual memory of last night stops him. Instead, he closes his eyes, pulls his underwear down to his ankles, turns around, and sits on the toilet, letting whatever happens happen without looking down to see what it is. Then he gathers a handful of toilet paper and wipes himself. Touching a pussy is nothing when it's your own, he thinks for the first time.

When he's done, he stands up, eyes still closed, pulls his jeans and underwear back around his waist, flushes, then cranks the sink as hot as it'll go. When the room is full of steam, he dunks his head under, gripping the porcelain to keep from whimpering, and only stops when he can feel his scalp pucker. Then he steps back from the basin, dries his hair and face with a long pull of paper towels from the rickety dispenser, and returns to the world outside.

Back in the station store, he gathers up seven Monster Energy Drinks, a chocolate chip muffin, and an airtight pack of reindeer jerky, which he brings to the counter, where the girl now sits by herself, watching something on her phone that causes her to alternate between a genuine smirk and what looks like feigned horror. He stands behind his snack pile and waits to see how long it'll be until she looks up. So long, it turns out, that he has to interrupt by saying, "How long to Copenhagen?"

When the words reach her, she swivels her head off the screen in slow motion, lingering on whatever she's watching as long as possible, her lips curling when she finally breaks contact and regards György head-on. "What?" she says, after another drawn-out moment in which she simply stares.

He repeats the question, and then, because he can tell she's about to say, *I don't know*, he says, "Look it up." Then, because he can tell she's about to tell him to look it up himself, he says, "I lost my phone." He holds up his hands, as if to prove it.

At this, she narrows her eyes into a mask of withering hatred, looks down at her phone, minimizing whatever she'd been watching, and asks him to repeat his question.

He does, and then she says, "Where?" and he spells out C-o-p-e-n-h-a-g-e-n, slowly enough for her to type it one letter at a time.

When she's finally done this, she holds up the Google Maps route, which shows a 22-hour drive, east and then south through Sweden, passing through Uppsala, and then Stockholm, and then Malmö, before crossing a bridge into Denmark. He nods, and then, just as she's about to go back to whatever she'd been watching, he pushes his Monster cans all the way across the counter, so close to her that she has no choice but to ring them up.

Back on the road, he cracks the first can, places it between his knees, and alternates swigging from it with mashing the muffin against his mouth, tearing at its soft center with his front teeth until it's small and wet enough to swallow.

Twenty-two hours. The length of that settles over him, tamping down the initial rush he'd felt upon leaving the compound. Nothing to do but drive. If they're already chasing me, let them come. And if not, let these hours pass in any way they wish. He cruises across the Swedish border without incident, and begins the long trip south, through towns that look almost identical to those on the Norwegian side, but feel more nestled, less exposed to the hazards of the coastline and its millennia of visitation.

Towns that have never had to face the edge of things as directly as those in Norway have. Towns that, no matter what it is, have never been the first to know. He cranks up the metal on the radio, having forgotten, for a while, that it was still playing, and resolves to make it to Copenhagen alive. Other than this, it's too soon to say, though he pictures himself, draped in Arisztid Huszár's wolf cloak, tearing through the Black Forest at midnight to summon a demon army to retake the continent for the Magyars, moving ever eastward, against the tide of history, back toward Russia, conquering everything in sight until all that's worth having belongs to Hungary, guarded forever by the Wall. Until the word *alive* means *Hungarian*, and the word *dead* means absolutely everyone else. Until Moscow and Berlin are but slum districts of Budapest.

This vision is enough to occupy the parts of his mind that aren't occupied with staying on the road and following the increasingly frequent signs for Stockholm, or, he's loath to admit, with tracking the occasional squirms in his belly, which he can only hope mean nothing but hunger.

He passes through the outskirts of the Swedish capital around one in the morning, and stops at a roadside plaza. All that's open is a Turkish kebab window and, though he hates the Turks almost as much as the Jews and the gypsies, he's too tired to resist. A warrior needs to eat. He scowls at the bearded man in the window and hands over the credit card that, luckily, was still to be found in the wallet in his jeans.

The Turk scowls back, his gaze threatening enough that György eats awash in fantasies of leaping over the counter and impaling the bastard on his own döner spike, but he can't muster the energy even to picture it in very much detail.

Instead, he finishes in silence, hoping the unclean food will poison whatever demon spawn is gestating inside him, and leaves his dirty tray on the table. Then he gets back in the van, determined to make it to Denmark by dawn.

The night enters a lull here, growing lighter and darker by degrees, a holding pattern that, György senses, will not release him until he drives over the bridge that connects the Swedish peninsula to the mainland of the continent that he has already renamed *Old Hungary*. He opens his last Monster drink, chugs half of it, and lets his eyes droop open and closed. "Nothing can kill me now," he whispers.

Convinced of this, he rolls down the wide, coastal highway, drifting from lane to lane, making his way through the exurban sprawl south of Stockholm, the endless expanse of freight terminals and factories and housing towers, the sun rising a little at a time over red and blue steel containers that read MAERSK SEELAND and HANJIN and SIEMENS. Closing his eyes whenever the brute impurity of these relics of the global age force themselves upon him, he passes through the burning synagogue to a deeper place in which he's rising from his throne, heaving off his wolf cloak, and turning to address a crowd of thousands, kneeling in a clearing before him, ready to conquer the Black Forest once and for all. Across his back, the name ARISZTID HUSZÁR glistens in blue, impressive enough to convince him to get the tattoo done aboveground as well, as soon as he makes it back to Germany.

First, though, Copenhagen. Hands barely on the wheel, György lets the forces guiding his progress take him the rest of the way, through the inland tip of Sweden and across the Öresund Bridge into the Danish capital, a smaller, quainter version of its Swedish cousin, and here, for the first time since completing what he now thinks of as the Breivik Level, or perhaps merely the First Breivik Level, he faces a genuine conundrum, which he pulls into the parking lot of a Scandic business hotel to consider, as the radio picks up a broadcast discussing the still-unsolved murder or ritual suicide of Lars von Trier. He tries to smile at the strange news, flashing back to the filmmaker naked and bound at the Ragnar rally, but

207

only manages to yawn, as he turns the radio off and tries to breathe in silence.

On the one hand, he thinks, I want to find the place where I went through the wormhole, out of Europe and into the Game, which must've been here, somewhere in Copenhagen, after I met Knut and Gunnar at the Ragnar rally. On the other hand, though already he can barely remember what was on the first hand, I don't want to do anything to jeopardize my relationship with Arisztid Huszár. He shudders to imagine himself here alone, nineteen and sitting in a stolen car in the parking lot of a chain hotel on the outskirts of a strange city, his student visa about to expire, his credit card about to max out, his parents about to give up waiting for him to call, as if this were the worst case scenario and not simply the state of things. Then, luckily perhaps, someone knocks on his window.

After realizing his eyes have drooped shut once again, he opens them and looks over at a duo of what appear to be military police, wielding assault rifles with an armored van parked behind them, as if posing for the save screen of a level called *The Clean Northern Capital Under Martial Law*.

György licks his teeth to purge whatever pockets of his Hungarian accent he can and says, feigning German-accented English, "Yes?"

The soldier looks over the van, confers with his colleague, then says, "Please step out of the vehicle, sir."

György complies, yawning in the fishy morning steam of what he realizes may actually be the third day of his journey, not the second, as the soldiers rummage in the back of the van, which, György also realizes, could contain anything at all. He never thought to check.

The soldiers throw boxes around until a voice comes over their radios, the delay between one device and the other giving it the effect of a stutter. Then they hurry away, saying only, "Keep moving, young man. If you have a destination in Copenhagen, go there now. If you don't, leave the city."

While György considers whether he has a destination in Copenhagen—he tries to imagine where the synagogue, or the ashes of the synagogue, might be, relative to where he is now—the armored vehicle peels out of the parking lot, and he suspects, though of course he can't yet say for sure, that another synagogue has burned, or a mosque, or a Buddhist or Hindu temple. Maybe the American Embassy. So it's starting. The Breivik Revolution. Ragnarok. It's starting, or perhaps it's already well underway.

He pulls out of the lot behind the armored vehicle and tries to follow it, but a roadblock just around the corner brings him to an abrupt stop. More of those armored vehicles stretch sideways across the road, manned by more troops, all of them clones of one another, while, in the background, a whitish-gray cloud of smoke rises from the center of the city.

The troops make an unambiguous "turn around" gesture and, though György would like to ram through the roadblock and search the city for the site of the synagogue he allegedly burned—or burn it now, if only to prove he's deep in the Game, safe from all externalities—he can't summon the will for a fight just yet. Not until I have my tattoo. He withers behind the steering wheel, exposed and helpless without it. A familiar voice in his head whispers, *picture your scratchy old mattress in Gyula, your sweaty little boyhood bed... that's where you'd like to be right now, isn't it? You know that's where you belong, the only place you've ever belonged... Just crawl back in there, snuggle your threadbare stuffed animals, hold them tight... tell them about Arisztid Huszár while you birth Breivik's children!*

The voice laughs and laughs inside him as he tries and fails to turn around in the growing line of traffic, ramming the back of the van into a dumpster and causing another troop duo to approach. He manages to straighten out just before they ask him to roll down his window and initiate the search procedure all over again, and then, before he can track the transition, he's driving in a clear lane in the other direction, the smoldering mess of Copenhagen receding behind him. He yawns again, presses his soft teeth against the edge of his last Monster can, and follows signs for the south.

After another run of exurban sprawl, he pulls over at another rest stop to eat another plate of döner. The only difference is that, this time, he's too exhausted to formulate any concrete thoughts about Turkey and its many sons and daughters. For the moment, he's too exhausted even to taste the food. He simply pushes it down his throat and looks around the plaza, full of old people in sweatpants and raincoats, their blonde hair thinning, and he thinks, soon, these places will contain the only survivors.

These people, the ones drinking cherry 7-Eleven Slurpees and McDonald's milkshakes and eating bacon-wrapped hot dogs from ketchup-smeared bags, will be the only survivors. Without ever knowing what they've survived, the Nordic race will be whittled down to them. That's who Breivik and his army are going to leave behind. The heirs of human consciousness if the Breivik Boys keep their appointment on Atlantis. György leans over his plastic plate and laughs. The thought is too funny to keep to himself. There's got to be someone he can tell. He looks around the plaza, past the preteen girls sitting side by side, each with her own set of earbuds in, laughing at separate videos, past the old couple spooning creamed corn from a paper cup and dropping most of it on their tray, past the middle-aged man in a raincoat, his belt hanging open as he squeezes a bag of gummy worms at the checkout counter of the Penny Markt stall, as if inspecting an avocado, and finally to the sullen face of the Turk at the Döner stand, who might, for all György can tell, be the exact same one he saw last night, or two nights ago, or three, at the rest stop in Sweden, which might likewise be the exact same place. The Eternal Return of the Eternal Return.

And so wherefore the new?

He closes his eyes and pictures Old Hungary expanding like a grease stain across the map. He watches as it covers more and more and more of what used to be Russia, the vast virgin forests, the infinite acres of birch and pine, the unincorporated armies of wolves, all of it ours, he thinks. All of it ours, peace at last, freedom from mediocrity and boredom and weakness.

When there's no more food to power these thoughts, György sits up, wipes grease and yogurt from his face, and, saying nothing, departs. Back behind the wheel, he decides to follow signs for the German border and then, once there, chart the fastest course to Baiersbronn.

The flatlands of Southern Denmark merge with those of Northern Germany, Kiel to Hamburg to Hanover, the Baltic the same dead purple on both sides, beneath the same vague twilight, like the universe has, at last, reached its final equilibrium. György twists the dial on the radio all the way to the left, then all the way to the right, and struggles to discern the difference. The air in the van hums at the same low boil either way. He punches the console three times in quick succession, then sits back and drives with his bleeding hand in his lap.

His first destination is a town with a decent tattoo parlor, so he gets off the highway at Göttingen and starts cruising the local roads, casing one town center after another, never leaving the main streets, until, five or six towns later, he finds one. Stigma Tattoo, in a town called Bad Salzschlirf. György swings the van in front of the store, taking up two spots, and steps out, wholly unaware of the time of day or night, much less of the last time he's eaten, slept, or used the bathroom in the way that he's now obliged to.

The storefront appears to be open, so György proceeds through, eyeing the twentysomething guy and girl behind the desk, siblings perhaps, both of them with purple hair and pierced lips and septa. He glances at the poster beside the register, advertising various levels of Wall-implant surgery. Then he opens his mouth, but yawns for so long the girl starts talking first, in fast, heavily-accented German that he struggles to comprehend.

He nods, not quite sure what she just asked him, then says, in his best imitation of a Berliner, "I need a name tattooed across my back. Two words. Can you do it?"

This time the guy nods, then says, switching to English, "Write it on this sheet, exactly as you'd like it to appear. Then we can discuss specifics."

György's hand shakes so badly he can barely hold the pen, but, stabilizing it with his other hand, he manages to write *Arisztid Huszár* and push the paper back to the guy, who studies it with a perplexed expression, but doesn't immediately say anything.

The blue neon sign in the front window is the only light in the room, bathing everything in the same fish tank glow, and György has to fight the urge to lean forward against the counter and nod off.

He grinds his palm into his face and says, "Sure," when the guy asks him to pick a font from a laminated binder. He picks the boldest one he can find, with the harshest, sharpest letters, and says, simply, "As big as possible," when the guy asks about size, and then he says "blue" when the guy asks about color, and then, after being quoted a price of sixty Euros per hour, says, "Right now," when the guy asks when.

Shirtless on the bench, György presses his lips against a sweaty slab of leather. After being asked if he's ready, and nodding as much as he can while flexing his delts beneath an alcohol swab, the needle makes its first incision. His body tenses up and draws together, lured toward the point of contact, but he forces himself to relax and, before long, the needle's grinding rhythm lulls him to sleep. His consciousness drips downward, through the bench, and into a thick forest below.

He hovers over it, flapping on tremendous eagle wings, dripping bright red droplets onto the treetops, which grow taller once his sanctified blood reaches their roots. The forest grows and grows, its leaves pulsing red, departing from the earth and forcing him to fly higher to avoid getting snared in the branches, until he and the trees are deep in outer space, the planet a distant speck, a botched experiment best forgotten, and then, for an eternity, there's nothing to worry about. He drifts, accepting his long-delayed reward, flapping his wings just for show now that there's no gravity to overcome.

But even eternity has its limits. The needle stops and his wings fall off and the earth comes rushing up toward him, barking, in Germanic English, "Okay, that's all we do today. Come back tomorrow for the second half," and then he's out on the street, wandering among pasty specters in sneakers and black jeans and oversized T-shirts, leering at nothing, nibbling sausages and slurping giant cans of beer, indifferent to their own death, which seems to have come long ago. This is the world that Goya foresaw and Krasznahorkai gave voice to and György falls into the churn of it, his back raw and dripping. He pictures the hot night air as the paint that Goya mixed to render this very image, or its medieval analogue, which seems like the slimmest of distinctions. He looks out at the horizon, past the edge of town, and sees bodies piled upon bodies, vast tracts of death, skin piled upon skin, so high that it ceases to be bodies at all and becomes merely skin, recycled skin, ready to coat fresh people except there will be no fresh people, there will be nothing more, "Yes," he says, "a Bratwurst with mustard," and then he's eating it, and drinking one and then another can of Weihenstephaner, tasting nothing, his nipples hard in the night air, his back opening and closing like a wind vent, and then he's on the bench for his second session, the needle is back in him, and, for the time being, it feels like all that's keeping him alive. My last tether. All that's plugging me into the wall. He opens his mouth, lays his tongue against the leather, and pictures the name *Arisztid Huszár* growing so long that the process of etching it onto his skin will never end. He pictures the letters growing and growing and growing, reaching from here to Vladivostok, his inked skin blanketing the continent, visible from space, and he pictures his natural life ending and the tattooing process going on still, first on his skin as it putrefies, and then on his bones, and then on his ashes, a process that can't ever end and will thus, amidst such brute and wanton chaos, promise a line of continuity, more robust than any bloodline, and that, he thinks, just before blacking out, will at last be enough for me. I will then see why I had to live.

Next time time he wakes up, György's at the front desk, swiping his credit card, wondering, not for the first time, whether his parents are tracking the purchases, and then he mumbles some form of thanks to the Germans who've branded him, pulls his shirt over his tender shoulders, and walks outside, back into the hot night and the crush of the living dead, wandering the same insensate circuit as last night, Weihenstephaner in one hand, Bratwurst in the other. When he's finished both, he gets in the van, drives straight toward a cluster of flesh in the central square, causing it to scatter, and makes his way out of town and into a dank field, where he kills the engine, reclines his seat, and, at last, goes all the way to sleep.

When he wakes in the morning, having dreamt nothing at all, he puts the van in gear and heads further south, on the last leg of the journey to Baiersbronn, and the altar, where, as he imagines it, he'll stride up to the regrowing Wall and announce, in no uncertain terms, that Arisztid Huszár is here, ready to lead an army of the faithful on the most ambitious campaign of conquest since that of Alexander the Great. He'll remove his shirt, display his back, and they will follow. Because if I don't make that happen, he thinks, as he gets up to speed on the Autobahn, then there's nothing but Bratwurst and beer, over and over again, until I too, end up in the skin pile, along with everyone else, and then what will it all have been for?

Arisztid Huszár, stirring awake inside him, growls, "Drive faster."

The Chancellor

The Chancellor hangs up on Horst, saying, "Well, keep an eye on him. Let's see what this boy wants before we intervene."

With the phone back in its cradle, she looks at the proliferation of screens that has eaten through every last square foot of her office: banks of screens along the walls, hanging at varying heights from the ceiling, implanted in the skin that used to descend from it, and on stalks rising from the floor. Now, as she sits at her desk, no non-digital surface is visible. Even the door is hidden, a fact that induces no small measure of claustrophobia, like she's been swallowed by something living.

The screens buzz and boil, showing the altar over which the mummy continues to preside, and the cottage where Anika is, thankfully, working on her book, or was until some wild-eyed boy with a grisly tattoo across his naked back showed up in a white van, pounding on the door and begging for a place to sleep.

Now, the Chancellor is discouraged to see, the boy and the old woman are speaking in a corner, beneath the stuffed wolf, seemingly already on friendly terms, while Anika is back to drinking in the kitchen, bottle after bottle of Riesling that, for the time being, Horst is under orders to go on supplying.

She yawns and looks behind her, in hopes of catching a glimpse out the windows and down over Berlin, but now this view is likewise occluded by screens, many of them showing live-feeds from the asylums on the Polish border—six so

217

far—that have, over the past few weeks, filled with young Scandinavians who, like Sven, poured into her office begging to be locked up before what they unanimously termed the "Ragnar Wave" broke over Europe. And has it broken yet? she wonders, glancing at yet another bank of screens showing troops marching through Copenhagen, and standing guard in the ruins of the city's mosques and synagogues—not a single one left standing—and, to her right, a screen detailing the clean-up efforts of Dutch authorities after a nerve gas attack in the Anne Frank House in Amsterdam.

Is this the war those men were so desperate to avoid? She's given up dispatching scouts, seeing as none ever return, nor does she contact any foreign heads of state, as none seem like real people anymore. So there's no intel save for what crosses the screens. Or perhaps, she considers, it's just that I've run out of scouts to dispatch, and if I had more in reserve, I'd send them all, just to feel like there was still something I could do. Surely that's what I've done already. She plans to ruminate further but footage of her Eternal Weimar speech in Alexanderplatz plays across one of the screens and takes her attention with it. She leans closer just as her avatar onscreen leans over the podium, gesticulating at the embalmed corpse of Martin...

She laughs at the thought that her inability to remember that old Nazi's last name has become a classic bit, enshrined in the annals of German comedy, alongside the works of Heidegger himself.

The thought remains funny, but the longer she stares at herself onscreen, the more heavily something else seeps in, rendering the laughter desperate. She tries to parse out the woman she's looking at, to determine who it is, despite the fact that—of course!—she already knows. It's me, she insists, but another part of her sneers, yeah, yeah, yeah, we've all heard that one before. A numinous laugh track crackles.

As the desperation grows, she gets up and looks out her window in the direction of Alexanderplatz, to prove to herself that, at the very least, such a place still exists. But she finds that she's still sitting where she'd been a moment ago, watching the speech play out onscreen, and then the video that auto-plays after that, and then the video that auto-plays after that, the screens egging each other on and cracking each other up as she fingers the jerky that arrived when she ordered a genuine piece of von Trier's flesh.

Determined to take some action from where she sits, she presses the Call button on her console and waits for an aide to answer. When one does, she says, "Prepare my car and driver. I'm leaving for the residence early tonight."

"Very well," the aide replies, and hangs up, leaving the Chancellor alone to wonder how her driver will reach her. Maybe I'm stuck here for good, she worries, looking to the right, at footage of a row of blonde men being deloused in what—why mince words?—essentially amounts to a concentration camp, and then left, at footage of the Dutch Military Police leading a team of bomb-sniffing dogs toward a truck idling in Dam Square.

She closes her eyes and waits, picturing her residence in the Second Europe, where she's never yet had reason to return.

Deep in the tunnels beneath Berlin, the tunnels that Hitler dug and subsequent governments claim to have filled in, the spare continent, the place where we—those of us who can—will go when it's finally time. She worries both that she's giving up too soon and that she's waited too long.

Not for the first time, the Chancellor gives grudging thanks to the God her younger self repudiated when her driver emerges and leads her by the hand past the screens, making just enough space among the flesh for the two of them to pass, like twins sliding down the birth canal. He leads her down the stairs and out a back exit of the Reichstag, as if an active terrorist threat were in effect, which, judging by the footage from Copenhagen and Amsterdam, doesn't seen at all unlikely.

Soon she's in her limo, drifting south through Mitte, into Neukölln, saying goodbye—she admits it now—to the city she's lived in and loved ever since she accepted the train ticket that Karlheinz Bauer foisted upon her on that steaming green road in the deep woods.

Thick black ink covers the limo's side and back windows, hiding the rest of the journey from the Chancellor's sight, a small mercy, as the seam between one Europe and the next passes in darkness. "Onward, ferryman," she mutters, "take me all the way." Though she didn't mean for the driver to hear this, she takes small satisfaction when he grunts to acknowledge that he has, as if the destination hadn't been decided long ago.

Still, despite the black ink, the transit rattles her. It feels as though the limo's falling through quantum space, neither here nor there. A period, of uncertain duration, in which thought grows impossible and the illusion of a unified self comes undone. Then the limo evens out along a new highway, and the Chancellor brings her thumb and forefinger to her nose, pinches hard, and breathes, wincing from the pressure before considering its source.

Only once she's done this several times does it occur to her that she must be underground now, down in the bunker world, the sub-level, which Hitler, along with Freud, either invented or discovered in the first half of the last century. The distinction between one mode and the other, between considering this place a mental construct and a physical reality, feels like the pedantry of late adolescence and early adulthood, a distinction that adults learn to live without. The aptness of this formulation makes her laugh as the limo emerges from darkness to cruise along the strip at the edge of Baiersbronn, past the corporate campus where Bauer works, past the Aldi, and onward through the center of town.

By the time the driver brings the limo to a halt outside her residence, and walks around to open her door, tears are pouring down her cheeks and her mouth is ripped open in a clown grin, like something's got a hook in her soft palate.

"Alright ma'am, this way, please," he says, his voice betraying no awareness of the state she's in.

She lets him guide her through a dank garage, full of lawn furniture and bicycles, and into a modest but tastefully appointed old house. Like a bed and breakfast, it seems, as she takes in the scent of fresh-baked bread and laundered curtains.

Turning to find the driver gone and the kitchen empty, she approaches the bread, removes the dish towel keeping it warm, and cuts a thick slice, hoping to postpone any more significant exploration for as long as possible. She slathers the slice with bright red raspberry jam from a dish beside an urn of coffee grounds, then takes her snack into the living room, where she settles into an armchair to regard her reflection in the dormant TV.

Though she doesn't turn it on, or even look for the remote, she knows that, if she were to tune in now, it'd show the world above, the chaos of Europe, which, down here, would play as a sitcom. A laugh track echoing over burning buildings and flooding streets and women with mahogany skin shrieking as naked fatsos from Eberswalde tear their arms off. She shivers and eats her bread and thinks, I did my best. I really did. But it was too late by the time I came to office. I didn't abandon you—she looks at herself in the screen again, as if communing with the version of herself that might've stayed above and seen it through to the bitter end—I did what any sane person would. There's no honor in going down with the ship.

She takes a huge bite of bread and smears jam all over her lips and is about to reach for the box of tissues on the side table when a hand appears and does it for her. It gently wipes her mouth and, from this gentleness, she can tell it doesn't have bones. She closes her eyes, hoping not to see the hand's owner, but it lingers in the room once her mouth is clean, and she can tell that it won't leave until she acknowledges it.

So, licking the last sweet raspberry seeds from her molars and swallowing deeply, she opens her eyes to regard the skin in the clear light of the living room. It stands beside her, if *stand* is the word, though it doesn't have legs or arms, just a thick draping of skin over more skin, the same color and texture as that which hung so often from her office ceiling. "Welcome home, honey. I missed you," it says, from someplace within its folds, and she sees that it's meant to represent her husband.

After considering and rejecting a number of more complex responses, she says, "Thanks, you too, honey," and settles back in her chair, unable to take any further steps into her new life until she gets some sleep.

But, though her eyes are closed, the scene drags on. The skin hovers beside her as she sinks into thought. How long till the Soft Illuminati replace me? she wonders, reclining deeper in the armchair where she will one day die. Then she wonders, how long, indeed, since they already have? She pictures a succession of Chancellors, dozens or hundreds of them, all with her face and her mannerisms and perhaps even her thought patterns, all elected to preside over Germany for increasingly brief periods, in order to give the doubtful public the crude impression of continuity, while, here below, empty houses fill with defunct models like herself, a whole town of ex-Chancellors, their bones turning to rubber, their particular skins reverting to skin itself, no longer anyone's, until they're innocent enough to meet Bauer once again on that steaming green road and take the train ticket he offers them.

"Come, my love," she whispers. "Let's go to bed." She holds out her hand, and her husband takes it.

Part III: Normal Life in Southern Germany

Anika

Anika laces up the hand-cobbled leather boots she purchased on her last excursion to town and counts her pocket money, making sure she has enough for her Sunday breakfast, and her mother's, and that of the strange fellow they call Georg, the rangy, coltish young man who showed up on their doorstep, back upstairs in what, from down here, she's taken to calling the Former Europe, as if this version, down below, were the continent's authentic guise, and that one, up there, no more than its sloughed-off snakeskin, a font of carnival antics to glance at once or twice a year.

"Apple strudel or cherry?" She asks, relishing the now familiar refrain as the old woman and the young man line up behind her, their shoes likewise tied, their spirits likewise high in anticipation of Sunday breakfast in the safe haven of Baiersbronn.

"Apple, today," Georg replies, his voice cheerful enough that Anika has no trouble minimizing the dissonance in his accent, which, like the dissonance in his overall affect, is just pronounced enough to attract her notice, but not so pronounced as to spoil the mood. Sometimes when she looks at him, he appears familiar, like they've met before, in another time and place, and within this familiarity hides a note of discord, the possibility that, if they have met, their meeting was fraught with menace. But, like everything down here, Anika manages to shrug it off. Maybe in my former life, back in Berlin. When she hears the word *Berlin* in her head, she sees a mass of roaches and flies sealed inside a translucent plastic container, only their outlines visible. As long as the lid doesn't come off, it hardly matters who, or what, is inside.

Indeed—she locks the door of the cottage and hurries to keep up with her companions, who've already set out on the road to town—there seems to be no cost to denial down here. So, whether or not she knows this boy from Berlin, and even whether or not she knows better than to associate with him, it costs almost nothing to take him out for apple strudel at Schönnenhof's, a kindness he seems direly in need of.

After a leisurely walk along the country lanes that lead to town, they settle into a table by the window of the sunlit café, sipping tremendous mugs of Milchkaffee with a dusting of cinnamon and cocoa on top, and picking at their warm, raisin-studded apple strudel. This interlude lasts ten minutes, placid as a landscape in a Stifter novel, the background noise smooth and soothing, everyone together conspiring to conjure the essence of an ideal Sunday in the prime of the nation's life.

Then, a commotion in the square outside intrudes. They go on eating, but fall silent and lean forward as two waiters stride up to the front windows of the café and winch them open so the warm air wafts in, as does the noise from across the street, where an elegant, self-possessed older woman ascends a small podium and leans into a microphone that a crew has just finished setting up. Looking across the square and into the window of the café, seemingly straight at Anika, she says, "Good people of Baiersbronn, Happy Sunday!"

Anika closes her eyes and hears the roaches and flies scuttle in their plastic container as she recognizes the Chancellor's face. She musters enough discipline to force the recognition down into the same real-yet-unreal place where her recognition of death has lived since the initial shock of learning about it wore off, sometime in her fourth year. If I've managed to make my way deathward throughout the decades since then without a psychic collapse, she assures herself, then surely I can assimilate the shock of seeing the Chancellor here.

More black matter in the insect jar.

Still, the thought festers and spreads, so that, whether or not Anika acknowledges it, everyone in sight save for the old woman and the boy comes to look like the Chancellor in varying states of decay. The other diners, the waiters, the passersby. All of them.

"This is your Mayor speaking," the woman behind the podium continues. "First of all, I wish to say publicly how proud I am to serve as figurehead for this wonderful community." The growing crowd applauds, as do those gathered in the café. Anika looks down and watches her own hands crush together.

"All is well in Baiersbronn," the Mayor continues, her smile unmoving on her face, her words thus distorted by her refusal or inability to move her mouth. "The strudel is copious and fresh, the coffee is thick and rich, the air is fragrant and warm, and Midsummer's Day is upon us again!"

She pauses a second time, and waits until the next round of applause dies down. Then, modulating to a more somber expression, she adds, "But Baiersbronn is a small place, surrounded by a very, very large one. The Forest leaves us little breathing room. It is an ocean, in which we are but a tiny island. I am here today to celebrate with all of you the splendor of another peaceful Sunday, but also, and just as importantly, to issue a warning."

A tense inhale moves through the crowd, followed by the tinkle of forks being laid cautiously onto plates.

"What I need to say," the Mayor continues, looking around her, as if hoping for a reminder from someone standing nearby, "is that the surrounding woods are no longer safe to picnic in, despite the annual tradition that falls, I am well aware, on today of all days. It is my solemn duty to report that several of our cherished citizens went missing in the woods last night, and several strangers were apprehended there near dawn. Frightening, vacant young men, their eyes gazing on a world other than this one. Thankfully, Frau and Herr Hans Volkendorf found them before they were able to cause any further harm, and they have been dealt with in full observance of local law and custom."

She pauses again, pulls her face back into its grimace of concern, and resumes. "Still, until such time as we can be certain as to what is afoot, no one is permitted to enter those woods. In order to ensure that this prohibition is respected, a curfew is now in place. After dark, all citizens are to remain indoors, without exception. As soon as it is safe to do so, this curfew will be lifted. Rest assured that I and my staff will be working diligently to discover the nature of these unfortunate occurrences, and to put measures in place to ensure they never occur again."

After a final pause, during which she restores her face to its smiling position, she says, "Another serving of strudel and coffee is on me! For those of you already seated in either of our two wonderful cafes, simply tell your waiter or waitress when you are ready, and your second breakfast will be brought to you. And for those gathered out here, I invite you to follow me to the benches by the fountain, where we will be served al fresco! Today, this will suffice as our Midsummer Picnic."

Over second breakfast, the citizens of Baiersbronn commit to pulling the borders of their world closer in, casting the surrounding woods, even the nearby regions where they'd often strolled on Sunday afternoons like this one, into the ever-growing zone of exclusion, the dark, teeming regions where they must no longer go, not even in their thoughts.

Anika looks away from their Chancellor-faces and down at her fresh apple strudel and, though she has no appetite, projects all the sense of security and rootedness she can muster onto it. Only you, she thinks, taking a small bite, are safe. She chews the sweet, raisiny mash, and wonders if even this island might, in time, go under. Looking at the pastry, she begins to pick it apart with her fork, trying to discern which pieces are real and which are not, which can be relied upon, and which must be treated with the same suspicion she is now prepared to apply to the woods, in which she too has spent many a bucolic Sunday afternoon, walking off her breakfast or picnicking on a shaded patch of grass.

She looks up at Ute and Georg, but as they too appear lost in thought, she returns to her previous ruminations. Her mind drifts back to a trip she took with two friends to Greece in the summer between their first and second year at university. A tiny town, high in the mountains north of Athens, accessible only by funicular, and only on certain days of the week. A town whose name escapes her now, and perhaps did even then. Certainly, she can't remember ever having known it.

She can picture only disembarking with her friends and nodding a cryptic goodbye to the funicular driver, a heavyset man in a sodden blue shirt and red cap, who wouldn't be back until evening. Then she sees herself walking into the streets, stultified under boiling, cloudless sunlight, which illuminated a great many empty benches and a few occupied by old women in black dresses and old men in black suits, sitting so still it was impossible to tell if they were alive. She remembers the silence of this town and the wet, motionless eyes of the dogs they passed as they walked around and around the few main streets, every storefront closed, unsure why they'd come there, nor whether the sun, which seemed, like everything else, to be fixed in place, would ever set enough for evening to arrive, and with it their ride back to wherever they were staying.

The funicular must've come in the end, since she's not there any longer, but she can picture no end of that day, no return journey, nor even any return journey from Greece, and now, as she looks up from her empty strudel plate and out over the café and the town square of Baiersbronn, baking in cloudless sunlight, she finds she can't quite convince herself that this isn't that same town, where she's been waiting all her life.

Walking through the quiet, still streets, the cusp between Sunday morning and Sunday afternoon having come and gone, the heavy peace of that Greek mountain town returns to her, and her fear of having never left mingles with a kind of bashful hope, a hunch that perhaps the utter motionlessness she found there was the ideal state of being, a state of death without death, a state of impenetrable, insane solitude much to be desired.

Now she can't be sure whether, if it were up to her, she'd wish to have remained there or to have moved on, returned to university, earned her doctorate, written a major critical work and become a renowned professor, as another partly-remembered narrative indicates that she did. For a moment, the decision feels like it's hers to make right now, like it isn't too late for either to be the case.

Then the feeling passes.

Outside the hardware store, Anika's thoughts dead-end on the screen of the TV in the display window, bulging with footage of riot troops hosing down a blazing synagogue in what the subtitles claim is Brixton, a long row of body bags lined up beside it, their zippers flapping in the wind. Then a cut to a flock of seagulls pecking at the remnants of a cephalopodic mass of bodies that have washed up in what the subtitles claim is Lampedusa. Beneath the image, a subtitle reads, "MEDITERRANEAN NOW SO FULL OF BODIES THAT ALL WATER HAS RUN ASHORE."

A laugh track permeates everything, seeping through the windows and onto the street, compelling the villagers to imitate it. Ute laughs too, but more gently, looking off into space as if the scene reminds her of another from long ago.

Ute

The three of them set out for home, ready to lie low, but stop outside the connected butcher shop and wine canteen, where what looks like half the citizens of Baiersbronn are waiting to go in. Couples and families emerge with picnic baskets overflowing with bread and cheese and cold cuts, chocolate bars and bottles of Riesling and Gewürztraminer, while others go in and emerge with the same provisions, falling in line behind those who emerged before. When it's their turn, Anika, Ute, and Georg also go in, without stopping to talk or even to think, and gather up the same goods as everyone else—including a picnic blanket, which the store also has on hand—paying at the till and likewise falling in line, as others fall in behind them. Soon, they're closer to the middle than the back.

Together, they make their way up the sun-dappled road, past the side-lane that leads to their cottage, and onto another lane that leads past a lake, a grove of poplars, and then into the Black Forest itself.

The air is hot and misty, full of buzzing and birdsong, and the citizens are silent except for a low, communal hum, a giddiness in their collective disregard for the Mayor's warning. Together, perhaps more together than they've ever been, they walk the wooded trail, deeper into the thick trees, past the ash heaps and the trunks that are still burning, until they arrive in the clearing with the altar atop which Martin Himmelreiter, half-dessicated by now, his face almost as pallid as the antlers affixed to it, still keeps watch, his lips bunched together in a half-smile.

Fanning out around the altar, the citizens of Baiersbronn spread their blankets, unpack their picnic baskets, uncork their wine, and sprawl out, inching their bare feet into the soft dirt. The air turns thicker and greener, ever more fragrant, as conversation and laugher mingle with the birdsong and the crackle of embers.

Young couples sneak into the underbrush, while children in cloth shorts and flowing summer dresses run barefoot among the trees, playing hide and seek or chasing deer and squirrels, squealing with the simple elation of being alive, and of knowing they're alive, and of knowing, even, something of the fondness with which they'll look back on this moment when they are no longer.

Ute, lying on a blanket with Georg and Anika beside her, accepts a plastic cup of fizzy white wine and a hock of salami on black bread, chewing with her full attention on what's in her mouth. Here, in this moment, in this version of events, she can nearly taste it. She closes her eyes and runs her tongue over the greasy, marbled meat, forcing something of its essence into her soul. I'm an old woman, she tells herself, eyes still closed, as she swallows and washes it down with wine. An old woman who's lived her life in this town, watching her daughter and her grandson grow up healthy and strong. Who's come to this very clearing for the Midsummer Picnic every year since I can remember, always right here, on this day, always this same bread and wine and meat, its taste perceptible through memory, if not quite through the buds on my tongue. Its taste is enough to insulate me from the drownings and the burnings and the riots on TV, enough to cast a protective spell in which I can live out my life in peace, part of Europe and apart from it at the same time. She laughs, not quite believing any of this, but enjoying the act of imagining what it would feel like if she could.

She eats and drinks more, reflecting on the beauty of it all, the sense of having reached, at last, the still center of an otherwise endless churn, the man atop the altar smiling down upon the townspeople, a patron saint wasted away in body but ever-present in spirit, wishing the good people of Baiersbronn well.

Anika refills her cup, and Ute drinks it down again, and signals for another refill, allowing herself to drink more freely than she has since her night in the Hotel Silesia, when she first glimpsed the very clearing she's finally arrived at. All's well that ends well, she thinks, or pretends to think, lying back on the blanket with her head in the grassy dirt, letting the feeling of ultimate arrival wash over her. All my life, I've been working my way here, across a plateau of dead skin, while, at the same time, she sees now, as Anika refills her cup yet again, I've been here all along. There's never been any struggle except to recognize this simple fact, and never any journey except toward that recognition.

As if called upon to embody Ute's contradictory thoughts, the Mayor rises from her own picnic blanket, at the edge of the clearing, and strides up to the altar, her head level with the mummy's legs. Stooping to kiss the big toe on each foot, she holds up her champagne glass and says, "Good people of Baiersbronn, it is wonderful to see you all assembled here today, in observance of our Midsummer Picnic, an occasion that, if you'll forgive the blasphemy in my saying so, I've always found even more joyous than Christmas. The warm, beating heart of the year emboldens us today, the Forest in full bloom, the rich, multi-hued green of our beloved Southern Germany..." She stammers and looks into the trees, as if trying to remember what she'd been about to say.

Ute leans up on her elbows and feels a chill as she wonders whether that's the same woman from before. The one who forbade everyone from coming here. Is this here part of that there, or part of something else, or neither? Everything feels both continuous and discrete. Part of the same story and not part of it, every moment just a moment, every day just a day, yet hooked up to all other days through wires running beneath the ground.

"Our Midsummer Picnic is... has always been..." the Mayor itches her arms and bats away the mummy's feet, knocking against her cheekbone in a breeze that has just started up. Ute feels the chill again and, now, a drop of rain. A murmur passes through the crowd.

"Good people of Baiersbronn," the Mayor resumes, clearing her throat and pinching the bridge of her nose. "Good people, I bid you only... eat, drink, and... today of all days, it is our sacred duty to replenish the bonds that keep us safe, as a community, here in the heart of the continent, against the incursion of the overwhelming fear we felt not long ago. Indeed, I can remember a time when we were afraid to... when we thought we couldn't even come here, to our hallowed picnic grounds, because..."

The woods shake as the sky opens and two shirtless men on tremendous steeds trample through the underbrush, scattering children and half-naked couples. They chant something that none of those assembled can understand as they approach the altar, trapping the Mayor between them. Then they dismount and, without looking at one another, hoist her over their heads and hurl her upwards, impaling her on the antlers protruding from the mummy's skull. Her blood runs down Himmelreiter's forehead and into his gaping mouth, causing his skin to grow ruddy and supple. His tongue flicks out to lap it up, and his throat constricts as he swallows.

The men turn to the crowd, their eyes unseeing, and as the rain washes over them, they chant, "Atlantis, Atlantis, Atlantis!" while the Mayor flails on the antlers, her eyes wide-open, suddenly alert—it seems to Ute—to the danger she tried to warn them of this morning. As if she foresaw this exact moment, in all its particulars, from a distance in spacetime so vast it collapsed under its own weight and appeared, from another angle, as no distance at all.

The crowd scatters while the two men remount their steeds and tear off in the direction of downtown, the trees sparking alight again, despite the downpour. The flames boil the rain, filling the air with both smoke and steam, until it's impossible to see. Ute lets Anika and Georg guide her by the hands, her sides aching again, her wires beginning to regrow as the afternoon's idyll burns off. At the far edge of the clearing, the monkey-man she saw on her way into town smiles with his beret on his head and his camera to his eye, snapping footage of the mayhem with a grin like this is just what he's been waiting for.

Anika

Later that evening, in dry clothes, Anika sits on the couch with Ute and Georg, watching the grainy television she found in a closet and resisted plugging in until now. No one has spoken since leaving the clearing.

They sit in a row, their thighs touching, and watch as the Mayor, from behind a podium in an empty room somewhere in the Town Hall, says, "And good people of Baiersbronn, as we celebrate our Midsummer Picnic today, let us take this moment to remember, as we always do, that day, in the darkest final year of the Second and Final World War, when marauders from the wild North stampeded into our peaceful clearing and," she chokes up, a look of terror crossing her face, as if someone evil has just crept into the room with her, "murdered my predecessor for all too see. A crime so heinous, so venal, that it reverberated throughout the Black Forest, causing our noble pines and oaks to combust in agony. Indeed, there are still those among us who remember the long nights when they burned and burned, and it seemed as though nothing, not even weeks of rain, could put them out."

Anika looks out the window where the trees are burning still, amidst the unrelenting downpour, and, nauseous from the steam, she gets off the couch and into bed.

In bed, though she knows she'll regret it, she opens her laptop and searches for "MIDSUMMER PICNIC KILLING." As soon as she's entered these words, her screen seethes with videos and headlines, embedded tweets and banner ads. "Soft Illuminati hush up killing of town Mayor," reads the first article she clicks on, beneath a picture of the corporate campus beyond the Aldi.

"As they've done before," the article continues, "at the behest of the Hard Illuminati, who keep themselves shuttered in the deepest basement of the innermost building, impervious to all investigation, the Soft Illuminati, an unwavering presence in Germany since the advent of the Marshall Plan, have ventured out among the people of Baiersbronn and used their soft power to cause us, in the span of a single evening, to forget what we all saw. To accept that the horrible events of this afternoon occurred years and years ago. To accept, as they always induce us to accept, through the flaccid invasion that all consciousness is susceptible to, that horror is nearby and yet never quite at hand. That we are protected by a thin yet robust buffer of time and space. A flimsy yet durable consensus, a gossamer safety blanket. The awful things, though we know they exist, are safely cordoned in the past, in the history we study in order to ward off what it portends, to keep it always at some remove... one town away, one country away..."

She exits this page and opens another, this one purporting to show footage of the Soft Illuminati—two men in rumpled suits, their faces puffy as if they'd been woken by a phone call in the night—pulling the impaled Mayor off the antlers, burying her in a mushroom patch, then erecting a monument in the clearing with the insignia, "In Eternal Memory of the Midsummer Bloodbath of 1945."

Anika struggles to keep her eyes open as the delayed stress of the day hits her all at once. She yawns and tears up, wondering if here, at last, her final tether is breaking. Half-asleep and eager to make her way into a dream of the silent, timeless Greek town she thought of earlier today, she looks back at her screen as it streams footage of her with her mother and son this afternoon, picnicking in peace beside the monument that she just watched the Soft Illuminati set up. Though she knows this ought to shock her, she's too tired for the shock to get through. She closes the screen, pushes the device under the sheets, and falls into a warm green nether-space in which she's sprawled on a picnic blanket in the midsummer sunlight, a bottle of cold prosecco fizzing by her ear.

György

György sits on the bed he's come to regard as his own, knees against his chest, and tries, gently, to calm down. He waited on the couch with Ute until she too went off to bed, then he switched off the TV and went to his room.

He sits there, rocking, trying to keep out the memory of the men who arrived in the clearing, the men whose faces he can't pretend he didn't recognize.

They're here. They've found me.

He swallows and commands himself to abort this line of thinking. That's another story. Like the Mayor said on TV. Something that happened a long time ago, no part of what's happening now.

This works, to a degree, but he can't keep from fearing that one of these days he'll have to undergo a complete reckoning with how and why he came here, and then it will be time to face whatever comes next. The notion fills him with dread, as if that moment, when it arrives, will constitute his first true rite of leaving home. Like this cottage, the one he can almost believe he grew up in, with his mother and grandmother, is the first and last safe haven that life on earth will offer him.

Hoping to postpone his expulsion for as long as he can, while accepting that he will indeed have to face it, he maintains hold only of the name György and the knowledge that, in some crucial respect, he isn't the quiet, gangly German boy named

Georg the two women have taken him for. This, he hopes, will be enough of a thread to lead him back to his mission when the time comes. When—his mind disobeys orders and replays a memory of the picnic—more Breivik Boys come, enough to track me down and force me to face what happened in the attic in Norway.

After again ordering himself to stop thinking about this, this time on threat of punishment, he picks up the *Selected Works of Novalis* that he found on the shelf above his child-sized bed and reads until he dozes in the gloom of evening, the battered hardcover spread across his chest. He floats until a dream takes hold. In the dream, he's in this same bed, the same book spread across his chest, but the ceiling is gone, open to a night sky that's filling in, piece by piece, with images of the life, or lives, he left behind, each boiling in its own corner, like so many disparate newsfeeds. On one, he sees himself at fifteen in midwinter in Gyula, doing pushups shirtless on a concrete floor, steam pouring from his nostrils. On another, he sees Breivik in a black robe leading his army south from Norway, through Sweden and across onto the mainland, making haste toward the Black Forest, to join the early guards who have already arrived. On a third, he sees Arisztid Huszár in his wolf costume, or his wolf skin, slaying legions of infidels and spreading his shadow across the continent, ever eastward, reestablishing Hungary as an eternal Asian power, free at last of the doughy dead skin of Europe, while on yet another screen he sees a crowd of healthy, hearty young men in blazing sunshine beside a turquoise sea, chanting, with Ragnar at their fore, "Atlantis! Atlantis! No future except on Atlantis!"

He rolls over in bed and feels his belly squirm, and so rolls, quickly, onto his back again, looking at the ceiling as the screens melt into the slow, graceful flapping of a giant bird, or a giant winged man, wearing György's face, his arms long enough to reach from one horizon to the other, his scarred back dripping blood that falls like thick, heavy hail onto the blazing forest below, sizzling as it enters the flames, perfuming the air with hot iron.

When the smell becomes too heavy to sleep through, he sits up in bed and breathes hungrily until his legs are solid enough to stand on. Then he walks to the open window and leans into the night as the blood-soaked trees double and triple themselves around the cottage, drawing nearer through frantic replication. The sky closes in as the trees grow together, their trunks and branches bending to form a wooden ceiling that replaces the ceiling of the bedroom, so that, without stepping outside, György is now in an enclosure of trees, the wooden walls reabsorbed into their trunks. At large in the Forest Room, choking on the meaty air.

He walks through hot ash and woodsmoke, and looks up to see his visions of Gyula and Breivik and Atlantis burning away, blackening at the edges like torched parchment scrolls. His mind recoils and, next time he looks up, the embers are being drawn back together by gelatinous white strands, an ooze or putty filling the empty spaces, rendering a totality that, though he knows it to be an illusion, he nevertheless embraces with relief.

He lies down on a bed of moss and watches the singed sky repair itself, luxuriating in a sense of wholeness that feels meant for him alone, a gift. Like a wanderer out of the Novalis he was just reading, he interlaces his fingers in the moss beneath his head and looks up in gratitude as white jelly fills in the darkness, soothing the burn site like aloe on a wound.

Everything fits within the white jelly's patchwork. Becalmed, he cuddles the moss and falls asleep a second time. He feels the moss soften and absorb him, admitting him down into a deeper forest, where humans and trees and sky and water and ground and fire are indistinguishable, all entwined in the vast collective body of Being, a place without worry or competition or violence, without regret or aspiration. A gnostic unity, the Ur-Forest of which all others are merely examples, the rhizome from which all trunks rise and fall. The Forest in whose heart the Blue Flower grows. He sighs and stretches and lets the peace of it pervade him, the soft, creamy wholeness that binds everything together, ensuring that no discord is possible, brooking none of the malignant narcissism that, he just barely remembers, led him to the brink of murder in a previous life. Maybe over the brink. No, he thinks, as the Soft Illuminati finish filling the sky and creamy rain drips down upon him, seeping into his mind and body, no, I'm whole at last, innocent, exactly where I belong, the years of conflict long over, buried in the same skin heap as all the senseless tantrums of the continent that birthed me. The long war is won. Surrender and victory have fused into a holy androgyne, never to be riven apart.

He sighs and gasps as the creamy rain fills him more and more, at first pleasantly, and then with both pleasure and pain and then, as it pumps ferociously into him, with a pure agony that blows up his stomach and all the space between his organs and the waterways in his skull that had, until just now, permitted the flow of blood and the release of pressure. It gouts down from the sky and in through every orifice, soaking him on the moss where he lies until he grows so cold and wet that he shoots awake, emerging back into the Forest he departed from, shivering in what has become an early morning downpour, his stomach and groin and legs slick and distended and aching with a fullness they can't dispel.

As the deluge intensifies, filling his mind with a premonition of the Forest underwater, the trees rippling like seaweed, he gets to his feet and, clutching his sides with one arm and shielding his face with the other, sets out at a run, trampling moss and wet leaves. He hears what must be a family of deer startle as he rounds a corner, and realizes, though he doesn't slow down, that he's entirely lost, so lost that he couldn't even say what not being lost would mean. Though he can dimly recall a cottage, he can't picture it, and, as it seems no more tangible than the rest of what he's just dreamed, he has no reason to believe that it's part of whichever Europe he's stumbled into.

Running onward into the rain, he shivers while the bloat throbs in his gut and he trips over roots while scrambling through thick stands of oaks and birches, their trunks slick with rose jelly. The sky recedes and breaks apart into its incommensurate cells when the Soft Illuminati slip back into remission, returning to their offices beside the Aldi to review the work they've done.

Spitting and tripping and shivering harder still, he fights through an especially dense stand of trees when he glimpses lights in the distance. He hurls himself toward them with the desperation of a capsized sailor, arms outstretched as he crosses a clearing, into the embrace of a tall, severe woman in a black robe.

She steadies him on his feet, planting him in the ground like a statue and says, in poised, elegant German, "Georg. We will speak only this once. Your fate lies to the East. Take Ute there. She needs your arms, your legs, your van. The gateway will open for you, if you go where she asks. It will not open for you alone, and you know your fate if you remain here. If you truly wish to do something, do this."

With this said, she picks him up and puts him down on the threshold of the cottage, disappearing just as an elderly woman in a loose shawl and pilled slippers opens the door. "Welcome home," she mutters, in a gravelly East German accent, and plods over to retrieve a towel hanging over the back of a chair, which she hands him as soon as he's crossed the threshold. He takes it without question and wraps it around his drenched shoulders, pulling it tight to his sides as he tries to remember how many times this has happened before. He can't remember when he arrived here, but he knows it must've been long ago. He pulls the towel tighter, as if to tamp down the rising dread that he's stayed too long, that what began as a reprieve is becoming a purgatory.

"Told you not to go in the woods," she says, seemingly to no one. Then, turning to him, "Cookies?" She pulls a tray from the oven, dropping it with a clatter on the stovetop. She piles several onto a plate and brings it to the kitchen table, where a jug of milk already sits out, its glass sides cloudy with fat.

Georg sits down and accepts what he's been offered, eating as fast as he can, as if by overfilling his stomach with simple grease and starch he could mask the much stranger fullness of what he knows is growing there.

The old woman watches with a smile, nibbling a single cookie of her own, masticating the crumbs over and over. After perfunctorily asking permission, Georg takes the rest, shoving them down his throat in relentless rhythm, resigned to growing fat like so many lost boys before him, Hänsels one and all.

An hour later, when the sun's up and the rain has slowed, Anika enters the room, yawning, and says, "Well, shall we get dressed for our walk to town? It's Sunday morning, after all."

Ute and Georg nod, put their cookie plates in the sink, and pull on their shoes, joining Anika in the group effort to ignore the memory that yesterday, the day of the picnic, was Sunday too. As they prepare to leave, the possibility that they've entered an airless, lunatic loop, a smothering string of Sundays linking the world's outset to its culmination, plays through all of their heads, freighting the question of cherry strudel or apple with a weight it can hardly bear.

Ute

Back home that afternoon, after a return walk alongside the Mayor, who seems now to live in the house next door, and who bears no trace of what happened to her, or to her predecessor, yesterday, Ute settles into the easy chair to wait for dark. She pulls her shawl over her shoulders and scratches her left arm, worrying at the skin just above the pit of her elbow. The boy she found soaked on the doorstep this morning skulks around the kitchen, confused and helpless, as if he expects her to rescue him again, from some exile inside the cottage, even deeper than whatever came over him in the woods. He reminds her of the men in Latvia and Poland, gazing at her in their sheds and cellars with older versions of those same eyes, full of the same ache that, for however a brief a spell, her wires seemed able to soothe.

She leans back, still scratching her arm, and lets the sound of Anika's clacking keyboard from the other room lull her to sleep. Once it has, she drifts, in mind if not also in body, out of the chair and into the Forest, making her tired way deeper in, toward where the Wall is massing. She sheds the warmth and comfort she indulged in while playing a grandmother in a cozy cottage in Southern Germany and drags onward, past stand after stand of oaks, toward an orange flicker in the distance, smoke and ash filling the air.

She drags herself toward it, roots scratching her bare feet, branches scratching her arms, tearing the skin, but all that matters is reaching the flames before they recede even further, stranding her here forever. She pauses, centers herself, grits her teeth, and forces all the energy she has left into her feet, accelerating from a lurch to a halting trot, arms outstretched toward the flames and, within them, a confident, familiar voice, drawing her in.

Arm over arm, she swims through the air, ignoring the pain, hurling past every snag, tearing through every tangle of bushes and low-hanging branch, fixated only on doubling and then doubling again the progress she's made, no matter the toll it takes on her body, no matter the pain... until her arm catches on a particularly jagged branch, split into shards by last night's storm, and the skin opens up and it hurts so much she has to stop.

She jolts up in her armchair and squints through the gloaming at her inner arm, torn wide open, the flesh peeled back, revealing, amidst the muscle, a thin, straight pea shoot of wire. After glancing around the kitchen to make sure the young woman and the boy are elsewhere, she grits her teeth and reaches down to touch it, twisting it gently. She feels two knobs of concrete attached at varying heights, and smiles to imagine a magnificent Wall growing out of innumerable pieces such as these, all knotted together into a façade that no sledgehammer or bulldozer could ever crack.

When the blood becomes more than she can contain where she sits, she wraps her blanket around her arm and stumbles to the bathroom, where she locks the door and turns on the light to get a better look. Either it's grown in the time it took her to walk here from her chair, or the dimness of the living room disguised how much there was before.

Now a foot of wire has unspooled from her elbow, and pulled up a patch of skin that runs almost all the way to her wrist, revealing a pulsing mass of nested cords and concrete. She stares into it, fascinated at how it hovers between foreignness and familiarity, an impossible yet inalienable part of herself.

She's about to press a finger inside to see how much she can feel when the end of the protruding wire tingles and then a staticky voice fills the bathroom. Ute looks at the window and, realizing what must be happening, moves toward it.

"Make haste," Klara commands, her voice garbled by the transmission but unmistakable nonetheless. "For the longer you wait, the further we recede, across a vast frontier. You refused my offer of fellowship in the hotel. If you wish to doubt my authenticity, that is your choice. But I do not doubt yours. I've seen more fakes than you have. I will not wait for you, but if you can catch up, you will find a place among us. The boy will help you if you ask him. He has been primed to. The house you are in now is not the one you glimpsed from the bed of the Hotel Silesia, no matter how determined you may be to pretend that it is. I offer this invitation not for your sake, but for the Wall's. It is bigger than you or me, it is…"

The voice cuts out and Ute pushes a stool over to the window and stands up on it, pushing her arm outside and extending the wire as far as she can in hopes of picking up the lost signal. After she pulls it another several inches out of her arm, careful not to break it off entirely, Klara's voice returns, more distant but no less distinctive. The concrete beads on the wire dance and knock together.

"The old schemas are collapsing," she declares. "The old notion of a First and a Second Europe, aboveground and below, and the Rubicon of the Russian Border... all that is crumbling, turning to ash. The levels collapsing under their own weight, like an attic that's grown so overstuffed it spills its contents back onto the floor below, taking the ceiling down with it. There is no more history. There is only space, Ute, space and ash and skin, all jumbled together, without sense, without order. Without resistance. Blessed chaos. The frontier is growing. The taiga we've labored so long to return to is returning to us instead. Our hour is nearly here. Come. Follow my voice. But be careful. Shirtless men in black pants with blonde hair and ice-blue, lifeless eyes are rounding us up. Drones, automata, marching in formation and chanting about Atlantis. They're binding and gagging any suspected pieces of the Wall, taking them to parts unknown. I know you've seen them. Go carefully, Ute, but go now."

When the voice falls silent a second time, Ute lets her wire wilt and knows better than to try to catch the signal again. She closes the window and steps down from the stool to sit on the closed toilet seat and gather her thoughts.

With her arm wrapped in a bath towel, the wire pressed flat beneath it despite the pain, she tiptoes out of the bathroom, planning to doze in her chair until the boy returns from his nightly sojourn in the woods, at which point she'll offer him milk and cookies for the last time.

But as she passes his room, expecting to find the door slightly ajar, as he always leaves it when he steals out, instead she finds it shut tightly with a low, pervasive growl issuing from the other side. She stops, presses the towel tighter to her arm, and leans in to listen. The voice is harsh and guttural, the language alien. Amidst the unknown syllables, a few words she must've picked up on her travels through Eastern Europe come through. "Asia," she hears the boy, or the beast that was the boy, growl.

"Conquest."

"Hero."

"Frontier."

"Immortality."

The longer she stands listening, massaging the wire that has begun to unspool once again, seeking stray transmissions, the more clearly she can see the coming phase, orchestrated by Klara, or whatever forces speak through her. At dawn, this boy will load me into the van that's been parked all this time outside the cottage, rusting in a puddle, and together we will drive east, across the frontier, on a journey that, for different reasons, will offer both of us our very last chance.

She sheds a tear for Anika, soon to be left here alone, and then she shuffles off to the kitchen to make a final batch of cookies, which will serve as a farewell breakfast for the three of them, and the fairy tale family they briefly formed.

Anika

During these same nighttime hours, Anika sits alone at her laptop, a fresh bottle of Riesling open beside her, but the cursor at the end of the word *Germany* refuses to move. She stretches her wrists over her keyboard and closes her eyes and practices breathing, trying to relax. She can't say quite what the problem is, but it's something, she can tell, close to a lack of conviction. A wavering between mental states, like an elevator stuck between floors.

And what states might those be? She opens her browser, as if this might contain the answer. Closing as many of yesterday's tabs as she can, despite half of them boasting LIVE UPDATES, she forces herself away from the ongoing question of what really happened at the Midsummer Picnic, and back to a sober session of scholarly writing, however absurd such a notion seems to her now.

Once again picturing her first book as a single stretch of the Great Wall of China in Kafka's parable, abandoned on the Mongolian border, she mouths, "Please wait for me. A new section is coming. The edifice, in time, will be complete."

Beneath all the pages and videos she closed is another layer of the Internet, this one boasting reports of rafts sinking off the coast of Algeria, holy sites incinerated, bodies strung up in trees and boiled in public squares, hotels bombed, banks looted, Amsterdam underwater, Antwerp underwater, saints exposing themselves to young girls in remote Serbian villages, presidents and prime ministers resigning and replacing one another with the speed of multiplying bacteria, all of it reported in the same breathless, half-mocking tone, as if it were all both dead serious and a pull-my-finger joke at the same time.

Anika recoils from this layer, part of her wishing she'd remained with the reports on Baiersbronn. She tries to picture the clean, self-contained pages of her document, open just behind her web browser, as if they were a promised land she could only return to after a long and arduous journey through minefields of BREAKING NEWS. Boundaries, clarity of purpose, measurable progress. The clean, wholesome beauty of the book, the most self-contained of all media. The least susceptible to flaccid invasion.

Perhaps, she thinks, that's why I went online in the first place. To scare myself back to work.

She reclines in her chair and runs her hand through her bangs and breathes into her fist, trying to muster the strength to close the browser and pick up where she left off in the document. But first, a quick comb through her inbox. Just to delete some spam and prune back the business and academic emails she's long since stopped responding to.

She begins by batch-deleting large swaths of notifications from Humboldt without reading their subject headings, along with reminders from gas and electric companies, and then a series of warnings from the landlord of her apartment in Mitte.

She deletes them all, then moves on to her spam folder, which has grown fetid since last she checked it. Here, she presses Select All and is about to torch the entire heap when a heading at the bottom of the screen catches her eye:

KING OF ASHES—NOTIFICATION RE: GERHARD SCHULZ.

Trembling at this first mention of her husband since his suicide, she stands up, circles the room, eyes the door as if contemplating escape, then returns to her desk and opens the email, forwarded from Gerhard's defunct account, which reads:

TO THE BEREAVED SPOUSE: THIS IS ANSELM KIEFER, KING OF ASHES, RESPONDING TO YOUR LATE HUSBAND'S MISSIVE. HE IS SAFE WITH ME, BY WHICH I MEAN, HIS SPIRIT HAS BEEN INCORPORATED INTO THE FATHOMLESS ASH-SPACE THAT I HAVE BEEN CONSTRUCTING FOR THE PAST SEVERAL DECADES. THE KIEFER-SPACE, WHOSE ABSOLUTE REALNESS HE SO RIGHTLY PERCEIVED, HAS BEEN HAPPY TO WELCOME HIM AMONG ITS LEGIONS OF SHADES. IF YOU'D SO LIKE, ONE OF MY MANY OUTPOSTS IS NEAR TO WHERE YOU ARE STAYING, JUST PAST THE FLAMES OUTSIDE YOUR COTTAGE. COME PAY ME A VISIT IF YOU WISH TO SEE THE PERMANENT FORM YOUR LATE HUSBAND HAS TAKEN.

After several more trips around her room, which seems to grow smaller each time, until there's barely enough space to stand up, Anika steps into her rubber flip-flops, ties her hair back, and walks out, past the room where Georg lies growling, past the chair where Ute dozes, and out into the hot, cricket-singing night.

She tiptoes at first, but before long the smoke and heat in the air make it so hard to breathe that she has to pick up the pace, at first marching in the fire's direction, past the lake and deeper into the woods to the picnic site with its new memorial, and then, when the concrete hulk of a series of warehouses and other buildings draws into view, breaking into a run toward them.

She runs across a field of cracked and shattered trees, stumps and charred branches littering the path, forcing her to leap over them in her slippers, nearly falling several times and once engaging a vicious bear trap, but she keeps her eyes fixed on the doorway of the building closest to her, and thereby remains upright until the circle of ashes is behind her and she's knocking on the rough, cold concrete of the bunker door.

On the third knock, a young man in tight black jeans and a white undershirt hauls the slab open and regards Anika where she stands, the blaze at the center of the Forest to her back. He holds very still, clearly not about to speak first.

"Email," she says, realizing that she has no words of introduction planned. "He emailed. About my husband, he's…"

The young man keeps his gaze fixed on her, withholding any legible response.

"The King of Ashes," Anika continues, beginning to feel insane, the dreaminess of everything up until now threatening to wear off.

The young man's expression softens and he asks, in Italian or Spanish-accented German, "Here for a loved one?"

Anika nods and he steps aside and ushers her into a drafty, echoey cement hall, the only light that of a row of fluorescent bulbs thirty or forty feet overhead. The walls are entirely covered with grey and deep-blue and black paintings, mottled, grizzled trunks, oaks and cedars and dense forest scenes adorned with hocks of rusty metal and barbed spikes and fragments of text in looping, monastic cursive. She walks from one to another to another, just as she did on the last day she spent with her husband, at the Kiefer exhibition at the Hamburger Bahnhof, when he saw the final vision that convinced him it was time to go... here.

She turns when someone approaches behind her, and, just before she sees him, she knows it's the Great Man himself. The King of Ashes. She turns to behold him, bald and smiling in a tight white T-shirt beneath a gray blazer, loose black slacks, barefoot.

He opens his mouth wider to reveal spotted, jagged teeth and a tongue black from smoking, his breath thick and earthy, unpleasant and comforting at the same time. "You've come for one of them?" he asks, already turning to lead the way out of this room and into another. "One of the ash men."

Anika nods again, hands behind her back, aware that there's nothing that needs to be said but eager to speak anyway, if only to remind herself that she's present. "Gerhard Schulz was my husband. I'm Anika... you replied to his email." She swallows. "It was forwarded to me."

Kiefer nods. "I remember. A while back. Must've been sitting there, on the underside of your computer, a long time. You're the author. *The Myth of the Living Wall*. I have your book someplace. I read your chapter on the Wall Sentinels outside Chemnitz. Matter of fact, I used to collect sentinels when I had a studio out East. Karl-Marx-Stadt." He laughs to recall the name. "A valuable collection. Long since sold." He looks at a bookshelf behind him, as if searching for Anika's book, but they're all made of lead. "Literature's always been my deepest passion," he says. "The realm of the soul. Much more so than the brute mechanics of what passes for art. That's work for a beast such as me."

Now it's Anika's turn to nod, but Kiefer's already up ahead, leading the way in his bare feet along a narrow corridor lined with glass-fronted meeting rooms and chrome bookshelves, overflowing with hardcovers. His back's turned, so he doesn't see the ambivalence in her nod, the tic of uncertainty as to whether, after all, she is still the Anika Schulz who wrote *The Myth of the Living Wall*, or whether now she's someone else, or no one at all.

After a long, winding tour through a network of similar hallways, mostly abandoned save for the occasional assistant typing on a computer behind soundproof glass, or pouring over a tabletop covered with printed documents, and one hall in which stands a chrome tableau of the Midsummer Picnic, with the Mayor impaled on antlers in the center, they emerge into the Hall of Mummies, as Kiefer proudly describes it.

Row after row of partly destroyed figures, ash and wire and gravel protruding from their torsos, holes big enough to see

through pocking their skulls and arms and even their legs in some cases, so that a few slump forward, propped up by those in front of them, or lean against the walls, their eyes black and shiny like deep, still water.

"The dead of Europe pile up here," Kiefer says, with a smile, as he leads Anika past the mummies, weaving delicately among them so as to draw near without knocking any over. "Suicides. Cowards. I find them out back like locusts. Like they fell from the sky, though I never see them fall. Perhaps, rather, they burrow up from the ground, like sprouts in some terminal spring. Who knows what's up and what's down out here, am I right?"

He laughs, loudly enough that it becomes menacing. A show of confidence that Anika didn't need.

"I just go about my business. Whenever I need a fresh subject, I go out back and fetch one. Resell them to the folks up there at a handsome price." He looks at the ceiling. "Where Giacometti left off, I picked up. And those that don't sell to Hamburg and Paris and Berlin? These woods are full of princes and princesses. Undead, from another age, but here still. Sequestered in their castles. They pay fortunes, ancient fortunes, sums that make a mockery of money itself. *The Final Dissolution of the Fleeting-Improvised German Men*. That's what I call this series. My last, perhaps."

He laughs again, but wistfully this time, as if at himself rather than the world. Then he pauses, his smile relaxing to a neutral expression, offering her an opportunity to ask him anything. The obvious question—do you mean that you crafted likenesses of these people, or that these are their actual bodies?—floats in her head, but she can't bring herself to ask it. Discomfiting as it is not to know, she can tell that knowing would be worse.

Kiefer moves deeper into the rows. "The Chancellor's hosting a major exhibition of my work in Berlin next spring, the first to showcase the mummies, so I've got them all out here, for auditions." He laughs quietly. "Have to choose the handsomest fellows for the city folk."

He stops short and reaches out to take Anika's hand, firmly enough that she stops short, too. "This one," he says, gesturing at the face of the mummy just in front of them, its head covered in cracked green paint, its teeth replaced with nails, its tongue a strip of screw-studded leather. "This is your husband. Gerhard. I know them all by sight. Like a shepherd knows his sheep."

She pictures him communing with them in the dark, bringing them back to life when no one's looking, asking them about the lives they left behind, and their reasons for leaving. Or reason, she thinks, bitterly, certain it's always the same. Revelations. Ragnarok. Ashes upon ashes. The end of history. The Decline of the West. Boo-hoo. She looks into the face of her dead or undead husband and thinks, happy now?

You abandoned our son, she wants to tell him, picturing Georg, alone and growling in his room. Because of you, he grew up without a father. Do you know what becomes of boys like that?

Though his leather tongue and gauze-crusted clay jaws don't move, he seems to smile. Anika turns her back on him, determined, like an Orpheus to Gerhard's Eurydice, never to look again.

"You may take several minutes here, to make your peace. The value of my work makes it impossible for me to leave you alone with it, but you may nevertheless rest assured in your privacy, within reason. Avail yourself of this opportunity now, as it won't come twice."

Anika shakes her head. If anything is reassuring, she thinks, it's the prospect of never seeing him again. She can't imagine why she came even once.

Kiefer seems unconvinced, running a large, flat hand over the expanse of his bald scalp. "I offer one complimentary tour," he insists, insulted, as if she'd rebuffed him, not Gerhard. "To each of the spouses. It's the least I can do. And also the most. Do not come back here. You will not be welcomed if you do. Are you certain you wish to leave?"

Anika nods, certain of nothing else.

"Very well." Kiefer drops his hand from his scalp down to his side, looks over the Gerhard-mummy with an expression of wistful solidarity, and says, "Then I'll show you out. We'll take the long way, so you can see the rest of the compound."

He leads her out of the hall of mummies and across an adjacent and equally tremendous space full of pallets, forklifts, and tractors, operated by workers in full-body protective gear, loading and unloading swaths of skin from a dusty pile under a heat lamp. Anika sees the skin, registers it as the same material that periodically covers her cottage, and then looks away, consigning it to the same darkness that, she hopes, will now contain Gerhard forever. She closes her eyes, pinches her own skin, and pictures it wrapping him and all the mummies and then compressing more and more tightly, drawing them into a ball from which none will ever regain their form. But as she fixates on this image, it morphs into the opening of the new show in Berlin, herself and Gerhard there together, strolling among the skin-covered mummies, arm in arm, a plastic cup of white wine in her left hand and a paper plate of pretzels in his right. The atmosphere grows charged, but in a much more familiar way, charged with the heightened crowd awareness that the artist is here tonight, sitting right over there on a stool, Gerhard beginning to pant, about to launch into his familiar routine of wondering out loud if he has what it takes to go over and introduce himself to Anselm Kiefer, his God on Earth, and what it means about him, as a man, if he doesn't. His hand, even in what Anika knows is only a vision, sweats so heavily she has to let it go.

"Please," Kiefer pats her gently on the back and points toward a golf cart parked beneath a glowing EXIT sign. "After you." He gestures at the leather seat beside the steering wheel. When she's settled into place, he sits down beside her, turns the machine on, and drives out of the skin room and into a gray, ashy dawn.

He drives past slag heaps and piles of scrap metal, smelting machines and jackhammers and wire cages full of charred wood, paint cans lying everywhere, and speeds up across an empty field toward what looks like the remnants of a town, the buildings lower, less industrial, the spire of a church visible up ahead.

"I bought Baiersbronn after it was condemned," he says, driving them past building after building, all coated in grey and black, thick with soot. After the Atlantis attacks destroyed it." Anika has the horrible feeling that they're about to drive past the cafes where she ate apple and cherry strudel on Sundays with her mother and son, and that all of it, all those memories, will be uprooted and consigned to her alone, to do with as she pleases in the absence of any external confirmation, the lone madwoman roaming a ruined town, raving about better times. Pulling old sausages from the back of the Aldi freezers.

As if reading her thoughts, or simply responding to her discomfort, Kiefer jerks the cart to a halt in front of Kleindorf's and says, "They used to have the best cherry strudel in town here. Probably the best in the region." He sits back and regards the broken glass and charred awning of the façade, seemingly lost in fond memories, as, of course, is Anika. Such hard metal and concrete to protect such a soft center, she thinks. Perhaps he thinks this too.

She stares at the elegant ruins and tries to picture herself in there just yesterday with Ute and Georg, and feels something in her mind tear, like the muscles in her back giving way after holding a heavy suitcase for too long. She gasps and Kiefer looks over at her.

"Everything alright?"

When she doesn't respond, he fumbles for something in the breast pocket of his blazer that he appears not to find, and says, "I'll take you to the curtain, then."

Before she can ask what he means, he puts the golf cart back in drive, cuts across the smoking remnants of the town square, in which, not long ago, the Mayor issued her warning about the surrounding woods, and drives up the road in the direction of the Aldi. Just before they reach it, or the place where it should be, he stops the cart in front of a gray chrome curtain, hanging directly across the road, and says, "Here's where I turn back."

He looks at her, a hint of pity crossing his face, then says, "Thank you for paying me a visit, and you're welcome for the tour. As I said earlier, do not attempt to contact me again. If we meet in the future, I will not recognize you. We will be nothing more to one another than a Great Artist and a nameless member of his vast public. I lied about owning your book."

Then he jumps down from the cart, removes his blazer and, in his T-shirt and bare feet, strides over to the curtain. When he reaches it, he bends down, grabs hold of its bottom lip, and heaves it upward, grunting as sweat breaks out across his bald head.

Anika continues to sit where she's been sitting, transfixed, until Kiefer barks, "Now! Go through, goddamit!"

This forces her to her feet. She darts past him, saying nothing as she ducks down, passes his grimacing face beneath the blade of the curtain, and emerges, alone, on the other side.

As soon as she passes through, the curtain disappears, restoring her to the parking lot in front of the Aldi, just as she remembers it. A plastic bag blows in the wind, and a sallow, Chancellor-faced teenager walks past, struggling to light a cigarette with a book of matches. She can tell that she's back up above, the Second Europe underfoot once again, though this framework feels inadequate now, too flimsy a schema to incorporate the reality of wherever she just was. A euphemism to placate nosy children. Both ground and sky feel unstable, both made of the same material, no longer stacked in a way that makes sense.

There's either too much reality here, a world's-worth compressed into a town-sized space, or else too little, not even enough to live a modest life in peace.

She checks her pockets for her wallet, thinking that a hot coffee and a roll, even if only from the Aldi bakery counter, would restore her, but she finds nothing. So, in the hyped-up phase that always follows a night of missed sleep, she trudges onward, half-intending to walk out of this town and restart her life in the next one.

She makes it as far as the corporate campus, where she winces at the growing pressure and gazes across the parking lot, at the one lit window in the otherwise-dead cement façade of the main building, unable to resist picturing the Soft Illuminati inside, heeding the Hard Illuminati's orders to erect the memorial in the clearing where, they say, the killing occurred more than half a century ago, almost before living memory.

She freezes on this image, her eyes riveted on the window, until the sky shudders and opens again, and she remembers how much her sinuses have begun to throb. The cold rain fills her body with new sensation, forcing her mind out along the surface of her skin. Trembling, she resolves to jog home, not at all convinced that she's back on whatever side of the curtain she was on before she opened the Great Man's email.

György & Ute

Back in the cottage, the spell is breaking for György. The clock on his woodland reverie is striking midnight and he too is returning to the tarnished world, the world in which his warrior body has been atrophying, the war for the soul of Hungary neglected in a corner of his mind while this once sacred town fills with Breivik Boys, eager to kill them all.

He sits in his room with the *Selected Works of Novalis* that has soaked through and dried out many times over, and stews, aware that, for reasons outside his control, the time to leave home has come. Arisztid Huszár is calling from the deep woods. György fingers the skin on his upper back that has healed atop the tattoo he almost forgot was there. He is calling to me, and if I don't heed the call soon, he will leave me behind. I will be Georg for the rest of my life. A provincial nobody, eating strudel with old women until I'm an old man eating it alone.

He gets to his feet to pace, alternately seething with guilt at having postponed the journey for so long, and roiling with fear at the prospect of leaving what has proven to be the only convincing homelife he's ever known. Closing his eyes, he can picture nothing of Gyula save for the concrete gymnasium he's seen in visions so many times before, himself on the ground at six in the morning, doing push-ups with steam pouring from his nostrils like a bull in a pen, waiting to be released into the ring. No, only here, in this cottage, and in the cafes of this town and the groves and meadows just outside of it, did he ever feel truly accounted for.

Like a real person in a real place.

The entire struggle—he projects himself far into the future, after millions have died—will have been nothing but the struggle to return here, to the very state I've enjoyed in this cottage, the state of knowing I'm in the right place, and yet, here, it no longer pertains. Though I wish only to stay, I know I must wander. The wide world is calling. The greatness and horror of history demanding I take my place within it. The gateway through which all Great Men must pass—he picks up his *Novalis* and squeezes its edges while his heartbeat rises in his ears—opens but for a short while. The time to fight my way through it has come. The in-rush and upsurge of meaning and menace and beauty that I've felt here, bedding down in the moss at nineteen, will dissipate and curdle if I lie still, leaving me a ruined man, or not a man at all. I will be the destroyer of my own nest if I do not relinquish its comforts today. It occurs to him that there is no natural death, not really, only the quick suicide of running into battle and the slow suicide of running away from it.

All of the grandeur and sadness and crystallizing nostalgia he failed to feel upon leaving Gyula to study in Berlin last year washes over him now, as if that leave-taking never took place and here, for the first time, he's about to enact the world-historical mythic transition of leaving home and, though still a whelp, facing the lifelong struggle to make a place for himself in the outside world, along the treacherous edge between what can be imagined and what must be observed.

This is what it means to become a man, he thinks, to recover the lost beauty of boyhood on one's own terms, no longer those of the mother.

He stretches his arms, which have grown sallow and spindly after so long a reprieve from training, and rubs his belly, thick with strudel and other foreign matter. "Only onward, into the woods, to become the wolf-man," he announces, as a knock on the door reminds him that he isn't here alone.

After a second knock, he pulls on a shirt, exhales, and opens it to reveal a woman-shaped chunk of wire and concrete, interposed with hair and bloody chunks of skin.

"May I enter?" she asks, in the voice of the woman that, for as long as he's been here, he's been happy to call *Grandmother*.

He says nothing, but stands aside as she drags into his room and settles onto the bed, her wires titling around in search of a resting position, like those of a lobster dropped into an unfamiliar tank.

"Georg, we haven't spoken, you and I, in private like this, before. But I think you know what I am."

He regards her, the skin under his tattoo pulsing, his body swelling with the possibility of so much hearsay being proven true all at once. He puts a hand to his groin to blot a sudden dampness and says, "Part of the Living Wall."

She nods. "Everything you've heard is true. I've wandered so long, Georg. You have no idea. Longer than you've been alive. Much longer. Longer than this whole millennium has been alive. History is flaying me open," she holds out her arm. The wire picks up a distant signal, adding a third, unintelligible voice to the room. "The time has come. The Wall is rebuilding itself, deep in the taiga, outside of history, beyond the frenzy forever."

He stares, waiting for her to continue.

"All of this—our Sundays in town, our early morning cookies, our picnic—they've been wonderful, but they can't last. I think you see this, too. So I'm asking you to leave with me. Right now. Drive me across the frontier that is, even as we speak, growing between us and the Wall. Making it ever less likely that we'll get there in time. Come there with me, to the ends of the earth, and in that place, you will be transformed. Whether you live or die, you will be spared the slow hell of an ordinary life in the new century that has still barely begun and perhaps never quite will."

He sits on the bed beside her, trying to fathom what she's saying. "Most men spend their lives bathed in the glow of their computers, eating salted dust in their underwear," she whispers, "dreaming of the heroes of centuries past, or centuries hence. Whole lives passed in dreaming. Waking suicides." Her throat seizes up with the effort to speak, long since unaccustomed to saying so much, and so forcefully. But it seems to be working. Georg looks at her, his defenses down, his ears open. "The chance to escape the wreckage before it wrecks you too. That's what I'm offering. The chance to be more than a weak boy left alone in an empty house with only his mother for company. Because I'm leaving, with or without you. I have nothing to lose. The place where we're going, the deep taiga, the unconquered East. It's the only place left.

Europe is over. You know this as well as I. So come with me now. You drive, I'll navigate, and together we'll outpace the End."

He pictures the Living Wall rebuilt in the unconquered East, Arisztid Huszár on a throne of skulls inside, emperor of Old Hungary, resurrected through György's heroism alone. He looks at the keys to the van he stole, sitting in a pile of dirty boxers on the desk. He nods. "If you can direct us, I can drive."

Ute tries to stand and sinks back onto the bed, emitting a whine part human and part mechanical. Wincing with the pain of shifting her wires, she reaches her arms out and György takes them, hauling her upright and propping her against the door while he throws the few clothes he's worn— whatever was to be found in the drawers and closets of this Georg-room—into a sack that he likewise found in the closet, and slings it over his shoulder, his keys in his front left pocket, his eyes brimming with boyish tears.

Moments later, they're downstairs, drinking the last of the milk in the fridge and eating the last of the cookies. Then, though both consider writing Anika a note to thank her for the hospitality, they're already on the lawn, unlocking the rusty van for the first time since they've been here, and piling into their respective seats, which requires stepping over a moat of rainwater and pine needles.

Then the moment of truth: György puts the key into the ignition and turns it. On the first try, nothing. On the second, nothing. He flushes and feels a wave of anger rise from his stomach to his neck, bifurcating at his shoulders to spill down

273

both arms and into his hands. The force of it causes him to turn the key a third time, almost hard enough to break it off. This time, the engine rumbles to life. A moment later, he's jerked into reverse and is peeling through the moat and around the cottage. As he straightens out and puts the van in drive, he catches sight of a figure hurrying toward them through the rain, and he almost stops to wave goodbye to Anika. But the phase in which she partook of their lives, and they of hers, is already over and a new one has begun. She already belongs to a different regime of the world's ever shifting and recombining folklore so that, from where they sit, she's no longer real to them and probably never will be again, and György, leaving the Black Forest for what he hopes is the last time, is in no mood to engage with its phantoms.

Anika

Anika slows her pace as the van tears across the clearing in front of the cottage and barrels into the Forest, cutting a narrow path between the trees until it disappears, as completely as Kiefer did when he dropped his rusty metal curtain.

She stands there, empty-handed, trying to remember what the old woman and young man looked and sounded like, because she can tell that, as soon as she enters the cottage alone, it'll be like they were never there. Despite the downpour, she would've stayed outside gazing at the wall of trees for an hour if a rough voice from off to the right hadn't startled her, announcing that the next phase has already begun.

"Your pages," Horst shouts. "Give me them."

She hesitates for one last moment, watching the Forest as if it might reverse its decision to swallow the van. Then she turns and walks, feigning confidence, toward the cottage.

In the kitchen, she finds Horst rifling through the fridge, examining the mostly empty milk jug and the depleted though still considerable cookie supplies. "I'll bring more wine later today," he says. "But first, your pages. Chancellor's orders."

She wonders if Horst perceives the Mayor of Baiersbronn and the Chancellor of Germany as the same person, and even sees a masculine version of the Chancellor's face in his own reflection, or if this fact, like so many others on this side of the curtain, pertains to her alone. She decides not to mention it. Picturing Kiefer in his compound, she thinks, he's made peace with his world: so must I.

"They're not ready," she declares, newly sure of herself.

Horst doesn't respond. He closes the fridge, glances at the many dishes piled in the sink, and again says, "Pages," holding out his hand.

"The book's not finished," she repeats, though she can see that he's not going to leave empty-handed. Flustered, she tries to remember where she left off. As it appears to her now, she can't be sure there's anything saved on the computer.

"I didn't say finished," Horst growls.

She nods, unwilling to press the issue further. "Fine. I'll just... go print out what I can," she says, and traipses off, but he intercepts her in the doorway.

"I'll go with you," he says, and her mind runs through every way the next ten minutes might play out. She watches him do horrible things to her if she says yes, and the same things, or worse, if she says no. She pictures his thick, squat, reddish-purple dick sprouting from the ancient zipper of his work jeans, more fungus than flesh, and has to stifle a weird grin as the thing expands in her head. She swallows, gives an *as you wish* nod, and leads the way into her study, where his sour tobacco and schnapps breath fills the space, spoiling the hominess that hovered everywhere until just now.

She opens *Reflections on Normal Life in Southern Germany* and scans through it, making sure the pages are legible. She tears up rereading the strudel scenes; their tenderness seems so distant now, so improbable, and yet there they are, on the page, in full detail. To keep herself from crying, she says, in her sternest academic tone, "I wish I'd been given some forewarning. I don't typically show raw drafts to—"

"Pages," Horst interjects, grabbing them as they emerge from the printer and mashing them together in his fist. When the last has joined the others, he wipes his forehead with the pile, grunts, and says, "These'll be on their way to Berlin tonight. Soon I'll be back with more wine."

A momentary lightness passes over him, a twinge of kinship for the sylvan exile that he and she share, and then he's out the door and she's alone, truly alone, for what feels like the first time. Returning to her study after his footsteps disappear, she scrolls back to the title page of her document and, hovering her cursor beside the words *Reflections on Normal Life in Southern Germany*, adds the subtitle *A Family Memoir*.

The Chancellor

Chancellor Lena Havermeyer arrives at the Reichstag just after dawn, as she does every day in summer, when the sun rises early. In winter, she's in position long before the sun is, but those dark days, luckily, are still a long way off. There's always a little something to be grateful for, she reminds herself, as she walks past the long row of Kiefer's, many of which depict the Reichstag in ruin, exploded from within and without, that adorn the hallway. In the spot nearest her office, two men hang a new piece that appears to show a field of heads clustered in the shadow of the burning Reichstag, arrested mid-blast. She hurries by without stopping to read the plaque or scan the heads for faces or ask the workers who authorized the sale, knowing that, if she did, they'd reply, "You, ma'am."

By Relentlessly Contemplating Its Own Destruction, Europe Wards Off the Event Itself Until the Last Possible Moment. Oh yes, she thinks, as she hangs her crisp blazer over the back of her desk chair and buttons her sleeves at the elbow to prepare for what she hopes will be several hours of uninterrupted work, I remember purchasing that one now. A high point, even for Anselm. A rare acquisition that future Chancellors will thank me for.

Averting her gaze from the screens, all of them boiling with feeds she can't bring herself to throttle, including a livestream of Kiefer leaping among the trees of the burning forest like a monkey with a camera around his neck, she looks down at her desk, where a bulging, grease-stained envelope awaits her attention. Though all her mail is delivered by private courier and thus bears no postmark, she can tell it's from Baiersbronn even before she opens it. No one but Horst would stuff so many pages into so tight a space, with so little regard for the condition in which they'd arrive. She permits herself a moment to do nothing but picture the unknown joys of illiteracy. Then she pulls out the mass of pages, smoothes them on her desk and, holding the pile between her elbows, reads:

> But that Sunday, which began like all the others, took a turn when the Mayor appeared behind the podium in the park across the street from where I sat with my mother and my son. She stepped up there, ostensibly to warn us that all was not safe in the woods, and yet, Baiersbronn being what it is, I knew that, somehow, all would be well. We all knew this, and thus we processed, provisions in hand, into the clearing for our picnic…

The Chancellor folds the papers back into the mess that Horst sent them in, too shaken up to see the humor, or even the symmetry, in returning them so soon to their original, illegible state. Her eyes water as she stands and hurries past the screens and out of her office again, trailing a security detail down the halls of the Reichstag as she gropes for an exit, any exit, any means of gulping down a few mouthfuls of fresh air before the memories drown her.

Memories of what? She wonders, as she settles onto a bench in a protected courtyard, waving off the few, tentative questions that her bodyguards have asked. She reaches into a planter and retrieves the pack of cigarettes and the lighter she keeps stashed there for times like this, and lights up, inhaling deeply as a cracking and grinding hammers in the background.

Memories, she thinks, once the nicotine has stabilized her blood as much as it can, of a deep, hot, underground place, a skin-covered, sweaty house where I sank into an armchair while a sitcom of my life up here played on an old TV. The type of show my mother's generation grew up with. She closes her eyes and attempts to bear the feeling of being in two places at once, up here and down there, and realizes she's been replaced. One of me relinquished the Chancellorship, so another stepped in. Or was installed. She grinds out her cigarette, though it isn't finished, and lights another, as if this one might prove more effective.

Well, what do you expect? Someone's got to do the job. The laugh-track from the sitcom roars in her head. Then she pictures herself quitting and being replaced dozens or hundreds of times, thousands maybe, while an equivalent stream of Mayors from down in Baiersbronn cycles up through the earth and into her office. She lights a third cigarette, glaring at one of her bodyguards when he shifts his weight in a way that seems to evince concern. Who's to say how many of me there've been? She closes her eyes and pictures a chain of selves, standing at varying distances from one another, some quite far apart—whole forests and oceans between them—with a white substance holding them together, gluey as Marzipan. The Soft Illuminati, always there to fill the gaps, so that, no matter how fragmented the pieces become, a sense of wholeness remains. The business of the Hard Illuminati, deep inside their campus beyond the Aldi, will proceed uninterrupted. A Marzipan-certainty that I'm still me, still living my life… the life I've been living all along. A little older and worse for wear, maybe, but in essence still myself. She closes her eyes and sees herself dying on an antler in a clearing in the woods, and even this does not break the continuity of the life she feels she's lived, even as she knows she hasn't. Not as an individual, anyway.

When more cracking and grinding intercedes, she opens her eyes. Careful to avoid the gaze of her bodyguards, she gets to her feet and paces the courtyard, feeling vertigo overtake her. Her thoughts rise and rise, unbounded, her sense of self unspooling until it feels infinite, like everything, or nothing at all, like there's no such thing as Lena Havermeyer, no woman who graduated first in her class at Heidelberg and wrote a dissertation on Wittgenstein that was not only published when she was still at university, but translated into French and English and sold in trade editions, long before her political career began, no woman who…

And now I'm nothing but skin over a core of raw material, suitable to any purpose, she understands, the emissary of forces beyond my comprehension. As necessary and bereft of free will as the Wall itself.

She looks up again, the vertigo spiraling through her body and out of her head. Staring at the sky like Prince Andrei at Austerlitz, she expects to see the last of her grip on sanity flying upward like a lost balloon, but instead what she sees, as the cracking grows louder, is the sky filling with stone and concrete.

She falls onto her back in the courtyard, at first terrified that an earthquake or explosion has occurred, or perhaps an asteroid has landed in the Spreewald. She hears her bodyguards shouting behind her, but their voices fade into a low rumble as the sky fills in, streets and houses and even, now, mountains and bays full of ships, a swath of territory fully the size of Berlin looming above it, several hundred feet high.

When the grinding goes quiet and the new topography settles into place, the landmass overhead shakes and settles. She looks up again, breathing more evenly now, and recognizes, in the very center of her vision, the Parthenon and the Acropolis and the Temple of Dionysus, as clear as she's ever seen them, and she thinks, with a large, relieved sigh, oh, it's only Athens overhead. I got worked up over nothing.

The laugh-track explodes again, and for a moment it fills the quiet between Berlin below and Athens above. She rolls her head to the side on the cobblestones and can see, at the far edges of her vision, a great expanse of blue dripping on what must be the easternmost edge of Berlin, and thinks, ah, the Aegean is raining on Friedrichshain!

She sighs again and feels her vertigo abate as the thoughts that she'd feared were unspooling into the infinitude of space are caught and held instead in the dimly glowing middle space between Berlin and Athens. The feeling of a filled-in sky, of the limit of dispersion being several hundred feet rather than billions and trillions, gives her some of what she imagines God must give to those for whom He's remained alive. Closure, clarity, a human-sized space in which to operate, vertically as well as horizontally. A world-sized room for one's loftiest thoughts to echo in.

I'll take it, she thinks, as she closes her eyes and feels her selfhood, so recently restored to her body, seep out through the back of her head, down through many grounds and all the way to Baiersbronn.

"Ma'am! Ma'am!" Her bodyguards shout, shaking the new Chancellor that has filled the empty shell.

She sits up, unsure how long she's been out. Without checking the sky to see if anything's changed, she lets them lead her inside, through a clamor of aides, ministers, and military personnel, all chattering over one another, disturbing the technician who's still trying to hang the new Kiefer. "Get me to my office," she shouts in the ear of the closest bodyguard, who nods and digs his hands more tightly into her upper arm, wrenching her through what feels like a crowd of scorpions, all pinching in a frenzy.

Behind her desk, her heart so high in her throat it feels like an extension of her tongue, she glances from screen to screen. All the feeds crawl. "EUROPE'S BORDERS FINALLY SEALED!" gloats one, while another shrieks, "CLIMATE CATASTROPHE HAS COME!" and a third simply states, "GEOGRAPHICAL ANOMALY IN EFFECT. REMAIN INDOORS UNTIL FURTHER NOTICE."

Indoors? She muses. What isn't indoors now?

"Ma'am?" someone says, for the second time in five minutes.

She takes a pinch of jerky from her desk, shoves it in her mouth, and, chewing what may be the last of Lars von Trier, holds up a finger to show that she can't talk right now.

The aide waits, as if on Pause, while the Chancellor drifts through video after video, her bodily integrity coming undone, merging with the warm cream of the Internet itself, the soft interstices between one account of events and the next, lending them whatever semblance of coherence they have, until she falls, easily, all the way to the bottom, where a video entitled RAGNAR'S VALEDICTORY ADDRESS starts to play.

Ragnar

"I am speaking as myself now. Earlier, I wasn't. Earlier, during my lecture tour, I was obliged to speak through avatars. A great succession of them, as one after another defected, seeking succor in that bulging bughouse on the Polish border where all so-called reasonable men have surrendered their freedom in exchange for an infant's notion of security. Sucking the Chancellor's teat, gorging on her sour, webby milk. Grubs, roaches, weasels. Good riddance. Their time will come.

Now, though I have no form, I am happy to report that I no longer need one. I am, for the first time that I can remember, unencumbered. No longer hatching from one egg after another to puppet the arms and legs of cowards back and forth across the stages of Europe, bellowing the truth of Atlantis through their throats, summoning acolytes like some desert prophet from centuries past.

Now the ball is rolling, momentum is building, Supreme Justiciar Breivik is back in command, leading his minions deeper into the continent, making haste toward its heart, suturing together the battles he won in his cell, deep within the Game that some call *Nordmen*, and those he is winning now, out in the environment that some—though ever fewer—still call *Europe*. Before long, the two will be one, and the waves will have risen, and the only habitable land will be called *Atlantis*, an island at the center of a new sea that, even in its newness, will assume the potency and grandeur of myth. But a myth that the brave men in his command will inhabit firsthand, not as mere believers, grasping at hearsay. Their minds will be blank, their worries renounced, their futures flattened into an unending and untarnished present, unhindered by the bloat and rot that has bogged this continent down for too long. Indeed, it is not so much that the waves are rising, but that the old landmass, sodden as a fermenting fruitcake, is sinking. Lower, lower, so that the mountains surrounding it appear to rise, convening overhead, the sky that shone over Copernicus and Galileo and Isaac Newton, and all the other heretics of the so-called Enlightenment, going dim, the constant static of doubt and interpretation and schism and subtlety leaving our people in peace for the first time in twenty centuries, returning us, at long last, to the silent clarity of the heroes we're descended from. Praise be to them, for these are truly the last days of history. The cool, fresh, pine-smelling relief of eternity is close at hand. Brothers, men: come with me now!"

Part IV: Atlantis

Ute

Ute leans against the passenger's side window while the boy drives through the relentless rain, the wheels rocking over the drenched road. Her arm-wire picks up panicked and celebratory voices shouting that the sky has closed in, which anyone with eyes can see. She tries to imagine what this means about the source of the rain, and ends up picturing the seas that have been folded overhead emptying out, the sky now a plummeting mass of saltwater and fish and whales and eels and monsters.

She twists the wire back and forth, raising and lowering the voices in a tic that becomes ever less conscious as the hours of the journey accrue and her mind drifts out to the place where, in earlier days, the collective dreaming of the Wall was always there to absorb it.

When the rain tapers off, the light outside glows a dim green, the sky or ceiling now marked by patches of open farmland and patches of deep forest, some of it snowy white, some a deeper green than the surrounding air. Finland, she thinks, picturing that northeastern corner of the continent curling around to find its place above Germany, though she knows her image of Europe folding up like a peeled orange, its peninsulas and protuberances reaching inward like fingers—the clash of metaphors feels appropriate—may bear no resemblance to whatever's actually afoot.

Done with the sky for now, she fixes her gaze on the boy behind the wheel. He drives with his arms extended almost all the way, his elbows resting on the edges of a belly that's grown since they left the cottage.

She watches it swell with his breathing, distended and uneven, made all the more prominent by the thinness of the frame surrounding it. No machine would be built with those proportions. Her eyes linger so long that she doesn't notice him glaring at her until he barks, "Stop looking at me!" and pulls the van to a halt at a gas station. Her wires jam into the upholstery when he cuts the engine.

Pulling them out one by one and packing them back into the cleft of her arm as Klara's voice comes faintly through— "Come to me, come to me," it whispers—she watches the boy force the nozzle into the tank and squint at the green expanse surrounding them, the light low and heavy, almost steamy, the wooded background more distant now, across a body of water, while the foreground displays signs of an approaching settlement: a partly paved road, litter blowing around the edges, a yellowing billboard for a tooth-whitening service. She's counting the gleaming teeth on display when the boy gets back behind the driver's seat with a Monster energy drink and a sausage in a napkin, and says, mouth full of meat, "There's a town twenty minutes up that way. Let's find a place to sleep."

He drives on, handing her part of the sausage and grunting when she thanks him. A tanker passes in the other lane, perhaps on its way to the gas station to deliver a refill. The outskirts remind Ute of those surrounding many of the towns she's passed through on foot, and they may well be the same, but the landmass overhead renders everything strange. Like the sky filling in is just the front of some much larger aberration, a shift in mood whose physical contours conceal as much as they reveal.

The streets and shops look depleted, like those of a village in plague-time, or like whoever began building them abandoned the project partway through, heeding a warning before it was too late. Ute fidgets with her wire again, drawing Klara's distant voice into the van. Behind this voice, even further in the distance, comes what sounds like the chanting of men. György turns his head in poorly cloaked shock as he pulls into a lot behind what must be the town's only hotel, empty save for a motorbike leaning against a disconnected washing machine. "I don't know if my credit card still works," he says. "If it does, I'll rent us a room."

Ute tries to smile, but the eerie green light emits a groan, blending with the low static and boar-like chanting still issuing from her wire, so she puts her fingers in her ears as she waits. A few moments later, György returns, waving to her to come in. She pulls her loose cloak about herself, masking her wires, and limps across the lot, past the external stairs and around to the front of the cement structure, where a glass door displays a web of peeling Routard and Michelin tourist decals, the newest from 1987.

After resting an hour in their room—a stucco square on the third floor, at the end of a long, silent hallway—they rinse their faces, first him, then her, and go down to the dining area, where a jumpy waiter serves them fish soup.

They sit across from one another in the dim interior and watch the only other diner, a musclebound man in a tank-top, bald with a ruddy beard, tipping his own soup bowl down his throat while glaring at them over the lip.

Ute watches György and this man regard one another across the open space, punctuated by a wooden boat full of empty bowls and mini jam jars set inside a fishing net, surely a gimmick for the breakfast buffet. Everything feels nautical, as if the rising seas were forcing an equivalent rise in seaside atmosphere. She returns to her soup, supping a little at a time, picking bones from the chunks of cod, while the man and the boy go on staring at one another, the temperature in the room rising.

As soon as the waiter goes over to the man's table to refill his glass and pick up his empty bowl, György gets to his feet and says, "We're leaving. We'll sleep somewhere else."

He storms out of the dining room, then past the front desk and back out to the parking lot, where he gets in the van. She follows a moment later.

Nodding to her arm, he says, "We're losing time. Where to?" Though he never mentions Klara's name, he waits while Ute pulls out the wires and extends them through the window, pulling snippets of that elegant, classical German voice into the van with them.

György

György drives as fast as the van will go, up mountainous stretches of desolate one-lane highway, the engine rumbling under his seat, the wheels spinning in puddles and grinding over downed branches. The topography feels doubly-unknown, both new to him and new to itself, never before driven on, lending the journey a welcome sense of virgin discovery, even if the roads are cracked and jagged with holes. He drives past towns that are now no more than X's on the landscape, like the stringy remains of buttons torn from a leather sofa, and past towns that are almost entirely flooded, only their steeples protruding. He tries to savor the strangeness of it all, musing on Burke's notion of the Sublime as both beautiful and terrifying at once, a feeling that pulls us out of ourselves and into confrontation with the true immensity of Being, and our own nothingness in light of it. This landscape, he can plainly tell, could kill you and, in the moment of death, prove the reality of God.

The green-black slopes rising around the van, some so high they merge with the ground overhead, like columns in a prehistoric temple, are almost enough to steal his thoughts away from the man in the restaurant, but not quite.

The Breivik Boys are on the move. He clenches the steering wheel and stares through the windshield, afraid both of driving off the road and into the darkness on either side, and of seeing a caravan up ahead, making haste toward Baiersbronn. He marvels at how easily he allowed himself to forget that chapter, or at least to consign it to the same indefinite space as the attack in Copenhagen. The same indefinite space, as he thinks about it now, that the whole long spell in the cottage in the Black Forest has also settled into. He tries to determine if he has any memories that don't feel submerged in this way, anything he can be certain either did or didn't happen, but the effort only makes his stomach squirm and his bladder ache, so he cuts it off midway and focuses, instead, on the coming epoch of the Kingdom of Old Hungary, which—he reminds himself, lest he forget even this—he will rule as God-emperor in the form of Arisztid Huszár. He looks out the windows, willing the surrounding darkness to yield a fleeting glimpse of the wolf-deity, but it refuses to oblige.

The drive remains dim-green, hemmed in by colossal peaks, cars and trucks swerving around the van throughout the night, all of them potentially carrying Breivik Boys, until György can't drive any longer and pulls onto an access road leading steeply down toward a body of water. Jerking the emergency brake just before he loses control, he announces, "We'll rest here," and goes into the brush to pee, hoping the old woman can't see him squatting with his pants around his ankles.

Both sleep in their seats, reclined as far back as they'll go. He rolls side to side, blinking through gauzy fragments of dreams and struggling to keep his eyes closed until, around dawn, he falls into something deeper.

He bobs in a soothing murk until a pounding on the driver's side window pulls him out. Blinking open eyes that feel sore from how hard he's worked to squeeze them shut, he regards a haunted-looking man in a brown suit, his face pressed so close to the window that his lips splay open across the glass, like the suckers of an octopus in a tank. György reaches under his seat in hopes of finding an ice-scraper or steering wheel guard to use as a weapon, but nothing of the sort is at hand. So, instead, he starts the van and prepares to pull out, though the slope of the road is such that the maneuver can't be done in one go.

"I don't mean you any harm," the man shouts, withdrawing just enough to form his lips back into a speaking shape. Something in his voice forces György to stop, re-engaging the emergency brake. It's only when man says, "Please, roll the window down," that György realizes he's speaking Hungarian. He can sense Ute looking at him in confusion and surprise, but he can't refuse to roll the window down now.

Once he's done so, the man leans in, seething harsh cigar breath, and says, "György Kaczor?"

György focuses on the man's teeth, willing himself to show no recognition.

Still, a look of relief comes over the man's face. "Good!" he says, grinning and pulling at the door handle. "I'd hoped so. Your parents have sent me to find you, György. They're very worried."

György opens his mouth to ask how this man found him, but the man interrupts with, "Your credit card. Thank you for checking in at the Kleinbischoff Fisherman's Inn and Boat Launch. Your parents will be so relieved to know you're here. Now," he looks behind him, in the direction of a car parked on the opposite side of the road, "if you'll just come with me, we can…"

After flooring the accelerator and throwing the man backwards down the gravel path, György pulls into reverse, tries to maneuver around the still-living body where it lies, and tears off up the road.

Ute slams against the window, her eyes on her own reflection in the windshield, and György can't help but admire her for resisting the urge to stare at him in his humiliation. He crushes his teeth together and growls, sub-audibly at first, but, as he drives on and the realization that his credit card is now compromised sinks in, and his parents resurface from the tank they'd sunk into, reducing his self-image to one of sickeningly prolonged puberty, he indulges in a louder and louder growl, opening his throat and mouth until he's howling at full volume, leaning out the window as he drives into a metastasizing wilderness spotted with villages full of the same uneasy silence as the one they almost slept in last night. He drives on and on, his howls growing louder still, so loud they overwhelm the grunting and barking of the radio that's begun, once again, to crackle along the wire protruding from Ute's arm.

Anika

The days since her mother's and son's departure have grown even more repetitive and ritualistic than the days when they were together, the strudel days when Sunday followed Sunday followed Sunday. Now, she wakes at dawn, sits ruminating in bed until she grows restless, then traipses past the stuffed animal heads to the bathroom, where she washes her face and brushes her teeth. Then she gets dressed, leaves the cottage, and walks along the sun-dappled lane, past the Mayor's house and into town. She can hear distant rain, and a shiver passes over her skin, as if some other version of her body, on the other side of Kiefer's Iron Curtain, were getting soaked, but, as she can't see it, the feeling washes off, just as the rain itself would, if it were raining here.

She buys a newspaper at the kiosk in the square, beside the fish pond, and takes it to one of the benches beside the flower garden, or, if she's feeling profligate, to the Stammkneipe cantilevered over the shallow, rocky brook, where she orders a cold Witbier and a hot pretzel with a dish of creamy schmaltz, white with brown flecks of bacon, and she looks up at the blue sky, cleansed of smoke and seawater now that the fires have burned out and the rains have stopped—by this point in the day, far enough from her dreams on both sides, she allows herself to believe that they have, and that what appears to be the sky really is—and listens to the brook babble as she breathes the clean air rolling in from the Forest, purified over and over again by the infinitude of trees, as vast as any ocean.

The Forest still exudes a chill—it is, after all, where her mother and son disappeared—but she forces the thought to the periphery of her mind, just as the Forest itself stands at the periphery of the town. That close, and no closer.

She pulls her pretzel apart, rolling its fleshy segments between her fingers and dipping them in the schmaltz, absorbing the warmth and saltiness of the molten fat, letting her mind regress to earlier times in this town, a childhood she knows may be imagined but that she no longer resists indulging. She pictures herself here as a twenty-year-old student, working her way through *Buddenbrooks* and *Steppenwolf* and *The Tin Drum*, letting the full, heady greatness of her native culture, its world-historical mythic potency, seep into her bones.

Only when the pretzel's gone and her beer is half-empty does she reel her thoughts inward and look down at the paper. "SKY OVER BERLIN REPLACED BY DOWNTOWN ATHENS," reads today's headline, showing a photograph that looks like it was produced in a photo-editing program from the early 2000s. She skips the Chancellor's statement, reprinted in part below, and flips onward, past reports of sieges in Bratislava and Trieste, monks drowning pregnant teenagers off the coast of Northern Spain, and insurgencies in the Ukraine where the reporter seems unable to decide if there are two warring factions, or three, or four, nor which, if any, has laid claim to Crimea.

She's about to fold the paper and walk to the used bookstore behind the church to see if she can find an early edition of *Buddenbrooks*, or a *Tales of Hoffman*, to recreate the moment she envisioned a moment ago, when, towards the back of the paper, a quarter-page article catches her attention.

Baiersbronn Author Paints Ambitious Portrait Of Germany As It Might've Been

...reads the headline.

She signals for a refill on her beer, which has dwindled faster than she expected it to, and delves into the piece, the first she's seen on her work since her book came out all those years ago, on the other side of the Curtain.

In a charming, at times beguiling portrait of life in a small Southern German village, local scholar-turned-fabulist Anika Schulz conjures a vision of peacetime life that veers between the lurid and the whimsical, inducing readers to imagine a nation free of madness and possessed of a stable cultural heritage, though the version of sanity her writings present are, naturally, a form of madness in their own right. This reviewer, for one, eagerly awaits her complete text, whenever it emerges from the no-doubt tenuous psychic state she must be communicating with us from. For now, we have only this fragment, which has sparked no small measure of controversy and speculation in the ever more atomized publishing scenes of Frankfurt and Berlin.

Simultaneously thrilled and insulted by the report, she settles her bill, walks half-drunk through the silence of the town, and enters Antiquariat Reinhold Berg, a two-story, ultra-curated bookshop in the shady lane behind the church, where, after fifteen minutes of browsing, growing gently drunker on the concentrated paper and binding fumes and playing hide and seek with the cat, she finds what she came for, and leaves with a 1937 *Buddenbrooks* and a 1901 *Tales of Hoffman* in a paper bag.

Returning to the Stammkneipe, she orders another Witbier, but, as she'll need her hands free to write, she forgoes the pretzel this time. When the thick, frosty glass arrives, she spreads her books across the tabletop, thrilling slightly at the inexplicable yet deep-seated sense that these are the only two copies in existence, and begins a new chapter by hand in the journal that she's purchased for this reason.

Knowing that Horst will turn up tomorrow morning to collect her pages, she takes another slug of beer, uncaps her pen, and titles a fresh page *Reading Hoffman by the Babbling Brook: Reflections on the Essence of a Summer Afternoon in Southern Germany.*

Ute

The boy has now driven them so far into the hinterlands that Ute has given up all effort to track their progress. The landscape no longer corresponds, even dimly, to any she's passed through before. The further they go, stopping only for gas and fast food, the blanker and more neutral it all comes to seem. So much so, she thinks, huddled in her seat, that I long for the old signs of destruction. The burnt buildings, the drowned bodies, the hanged dogs. She tries to recall how the continent looked when it was still in the grip of a coherent devolution, a downward spiral with trackable contours, bad decisions and worse reactions, familiar grist for familiar mills, but all she can see now, even with her eyes closed, is a tan expanse extending out of view, partly flooded and partly barren. An endless plane of old skin, pocked with spindly black trees like hairy warts, and brackish bodies of water like open sores. A few sick animals roam across it, wolves and foxes and bobcats, their eyes shining black in the dim space between the skin-covered ground underfoot and the skin-covered sky overhead.

She itches her wire and presses its tip through the window, pulling in Klara's voice, focusing as hard as she can on where, if not here, the virgin taiga is to be found. She assigns her entire consciousness to this question, but it remains vague and garbled, dampened, it seems, by the same skin that's covering the landscape. Even our languages, Ute can tell, are being phased out, into a past that no one—if there's anyone left—

will remember. And how does a voice emerge from a wire anyway? She laughs, uncertain now if she's hearing anything at all.

The itching gets worse and she tears at her wrist with the fingers on her other hand, reaching deeper into the nest of wires until she's unsheathed the entire arm, leaving nothing but a metal rod between her flapping hand and her shoulder.

For a spell, neither she nor the boy remarks on this, but by the time she feels blood running over her feet, she can tell that the next phase of the journey has begun. No longer will they roam the new geography, staying in fisherman's hotels, or even dropping in for a bowl of soup. That phase, like the one in the cottage that preceded it, is finished. She feels her eyes grow hot as she looks at the boy, a wave of tenderness coming over her as, again, she sees what he'll grow into. The garage he'll live in, the women he'll try to pick up in the town square, proffering a few crusty bills in exchange for a night on the cement floor while a dog snarls in a cage nearby. That or less than that. Perhaps so much less that the dog and the garage, women or no women, will seem like a long lost heaven, never to be regained.

When the van lurches to a halt, she clears her throat, wipes her eyes on her shoulder, just above the rod, and spills out the side door, half-destroyed but eager to soldier on. The boy sits behind the wheel and stares her down as she drags herself into the frontier, ready to join the Wall or die in the process. Beyond the highways and town roads, beyond the woodland paths and the old routes she used to take around the continent, she trudges now with nothing but the last of the energy stored in her system, totally certain of her destination even as the way there recedes beyond imagining.

———————————

As there are no landmarks, she can't tell how far she's come. She can't tell anything, other than that she's forging ahead, across wobbly, poorly thought out terrain, the creation of a God who stopped partway through, and that her skin, already mostly removed, is coming the rest of the way off.

She struggles along, her right hand tearing at the left side of her body and her left hand tearing at the right. The skin she removes falls and melds with the ground, like water into water, while Klara's voice comes in clear again, radiating from all of Ute's body now, not only her arm.

"Almost there," the voice urges. "You're almost there, Ute, just keep coming this way. Follow my voice. Shed your human aspect... the Wall is ready to welcome you. You are the last missing piece. All those years on the road, you were training for this. In the Hotel, you weren't ready, but you are now. When you get here, we will be complete."

Hours pass as she forces her way toward the voice, her skin gone and blood pouring off her, soaking her metal shins and grout-crusted ankles. When she reaches up to peel the mask from her face, a loud whooshing tears across the landscape, and with it a clattering of birch trees on the far horizon, the clearest sign yet that she's made it to Russia, and, though her lower body feels heavier than ever, made for standing its ground, not running across it, she can see, on the far side of the papery birches, a solid, slate-gray patch and she knows—it

305

feels like the last known thing—that there, up ahead, at the far extent of what can be seen, stands the Resurrected Wall.

I have only to make it that far, she promises herself, only that little bit further. But her legs, no longer legs, grow sluggish, and her body, no longer a body, grows dry, and she feels the heaviness of everything coming down upon her, the skin-sky lowering as the skin-ground rises, and the last thought she has isn't of the Wall, as it ought to be, but of herself enfolded in skin, covered once again in the same dead matter she's only just finished stripping away.

György

After watching the old woman stagger off, leaving the floormat on the passenger's side clotting with blood, György sits behind the wheel and tries, as best he can, to set his mind a productive task, like that of determining which direction is most likely to lead to the battlefield upon which the soul of Old Hungary will be redeemed, but he finds he can do little more than picture masses of Breivik Boys ransacking the continent, piloted by their bald overlord on his horse farm in Norway. I am not a faggot, I am not a faggot, I am not even human, György recites once again, as he returns to the attic, with all of its associations waiting there like photographs in a poorly hidden box.

He fights his way out, down the stairs with the steep drop on one side, through the kitchen where he sat with Knut and Gunnar and that braindead South African in his Cape Town Horse Feeds baseball cap, across the grounds, madly in search of Arisztid Huszár. But the mountainous Norwegian landscape flattens as soon as he makes any progress into it, and the ground turns soft and mushy, the air full of sweat and dandruff. Nevertheless, reaching beneath his neck to rub his tattoo, he forges on. Any of this, he thinks, could be Hungary. How would I know? How would I ever know? Though he's aware that he's thinking in Hungarian, he can't imagine what outward sign could possibly convince him that he's found the right place.

So this is hell then. A cluster of oblong shapes emerges in the dim middle distance ahead. Hell is anyplace that might be Hungary and might not be. Anyplace that won't tell me. That won't let me help it thrive. That doesn't care if I'm its redeemer.

He falls to his knees in the fluff and dander and looks around as the eggs roll toward him, bouncing and whispering, en masse, in the horrible drawl of the Deep Ragnar, "So, György, we meet again. I hoped we would. Here, on the level of all levels. Beyond the above and below, at the apex of the real, or, if you prefer, its nadir."

György looks out at the encroaching skin walls and tries to see the reconsecrated Hungary he's fought so hard to bring about, but all that fills his mind is cherry strudel with his mother and grandmother in the warm middle of a lazy Sunday. He looks anxiously around, as if in one direction this scene were still accessible, and all he had to do was stride toward it, taking his place at the table with a casual, "Sorry I'm late."

"The world you started out in is gone," the Deep Ragnar continues, all the eggs bobbing in unison with his breath. "Either this is what it's become, or it's still going on elsewhere, but far, far away, much farther than you'll ever get."

György moves among them, deeper into the field that extends as far as he can see, in front and behind, so that he can no longer remember which direction he came from.

"We are about to hatch, György," they continue. "Full of brave Nordmen to populate Atlantis, which is nearly ready for us. Through us, they enter the Game. You, too, by the looks of that belly, are just about due." The eggs bob and cackle. "On Atlantis, once the battle is won, we will no longer be needed. You and your filthy countrymen will do the honors. The next generation will be birthed through you. The generation that will live there forever. The true sons of Atlantis. Even Breivik himself doesn't know this, György, but as we're alone out here, I'll tell you: the Nordmen who won the battle will not be permitted to inhabit Atlantis. Too much history weighs them down. Too much memory. An infection, as you are well aware. No, they will come to Atlantis, but they will die there. Only their sons—those about to be born from you, and from thousands upon thousands like you—will be immortal, when the world, and with it all of consciousness, all of memory, all of plurality, all of futurity, sloughs away and only Atlantis remains. An island in time as well as space, truly at one with the universe, and therefore outside its endless flux."

The egg bobs and issues the sound that György long ago decided to believe was laughter.

"You were not wrong to imagine yourself as one singled out for heroism. Set aside from the mutt-pack slurping old meat from city dumpsters. If anything, the scope of your calling exceeds even your most feverish fantasy. The reconsecration of Old Hungary?" More laughter. "Only a degenerate would set his sights so low. No, György, to birth the first and only race of eternal Atlanteans, once the Nordmen have served their purpose? No hero in human history has been called upon for more. Not Prometheus, nor Alexander, nor your hated Christ. You, György, carry within you the final stage in the human project, the race of immortals that..."

Up ahead, past rows and rows of eggs, György can see a road. Though he can't picture what he'll do if he gets there, he grabs his belly and runs in that direction.

As he runs, the terrain overhead lightens and the eggs grow less prevalent, like a cancer going into remission. Soon, he's alone on the tan plateau, though he resists the temptation to dismiss everything that just occurred as a night terror. Too easy. And too soon. He still looks warily around, the skin under his tattoo prickling, and the voice still natters in the distance, reduced to an atmospheric effect, a low and universal thrum.

After another long spell in this half-sane state, he makes it to the road just as a lithe, yellow-eyed wolf slinks out of the scrub on the other side. György smiles, locking eyes with it, feeling as though the benign force of the universe has finally seen him, and come to his aid. He kneels down, hands open, and marvels at the fact that this is the first real wolf he's ever seen. Larger, leaner, less dog-like than he could've imagined. Its eyes wise and pitiless, its teeth sharp but nestled safely, for now, in its black gums. It approaches, one confident but thoughtful step at a time, creeping toward him, ready for a confrontation whose nature György knows he should not assume will be amicable. Still, he hopes. He hopes some accord will develop between them, some mutuality, a wolf-man and his wolf, Arisztid Huszár and his trusty...

The impact is so fast and so hard that the truck's already speeding on its way before György looks up and registers what's happened. The army vehicle, laden with shirtless Breivik Boys bearing machine guns and chanting in monstrous harmony, tears off up the road, vanishing from sight as György looks down at the grey and red carcass, rent nearly in half across the median.

With tears filling his eyes, he kneels over it, half-hoping that another vehicle will put him in the same condition. He regards the animal in its totality one last time. Then he sets to work. Luckily, for his purposes, the impact broke the skin in several places, so he can get his fingers underneath and tear upwards, taking care not to mangle it any more than necessary.

By the time what passes for sunrise has come and gone, he's standing in the middle of the road draped in a pelt that covers everything except his bulging belly. He even managed to preserve the skin around the wolf's eyes and snout, which he now wears over his own face, squinting through the eyeholes.

The first sight he takes in from this new vantage is that of an old woman shambling up the road toward him. She looks something like the woman he traveled this far with, but something about her is different. It's not until she's standing in front of him, saying, "I fell into the skin and it covered me," that he realizes what it is: the bulge of her wires is gone. Now she appears to be no more than a regular old lady, one of the innumerable feral babushkas roaming the post-Wall East, a constant, pathetic presence in the Gyula of his boyhood.

"I killed this wolf," he says, at a loss as to how else to respond.

In the silence that follows, they set out together to finish their journey on foot.

Anika

During the period that has just passed, the age of the great flood and the great war on the far side of the Curtain, just barely audible from the cottage, Anika's fame has spread to the point where she now regularly fields interview requests, fitting those she doesn't deny into her rigid daily routine as best she can. She can tell that she's reached the apex of her career, a level of exposure above even the highest highs of the year when her first book came out. She writes in her journal about how she's entered a kind of afterlife, a period of heaven on earth, the worst long over, buried deep underground along with all the dead.

Seated with her laptop on a bench in the park or at her usual table at the Stammkneipe, cantilevered over the brook, she conducts video conversations with critics and reporters from *Der Spiegel* and *Die Zeit* and a dozen other publications, struggling to answer, as honestly as she can, how and why her oracular series of chapters, which have been serialized in these same journals in advance of their publication as a book, developed. These journalists' faces are invariably glitched out and broken up, degraded by the immense distance separating their screens from hers.

Lest there be any doubt that this, too, is part of her official assignment, Horst appears at her door every evening, bearing fresh bottles of clear, cold Austrian wine, which he only hands over in exchange for her fresh pages and a full account of how the day's interview, or interviews, went. "The Chancellor," he says, his voice weary with repetition, "is happy with what you've produced. Keep up the good work, is her message to you."

Occasionally, when she seems sluggish or distracted, he adds, "And don't forget, we can cut you off anytime. The plug can be pulled."

Something about the way he says *plug* makes Anika think he means not only whatever money is supporting her stay here, but also whatever ontological conditions have produced the vision of Baiersbronn, and by extension of Southern Germany, she's captured in her writing. She hasn't so fully abandoned her critical faculties as to be unaware that much of what she's seeing, hearing, tasting, and remembering is likely an illusion, a simulacrum, and yet what, she wonders, as she sits by the fire pit with a fresh bottle of wine in the evening, is the alternative?

As she sips and goes back over the day's interview, and looks ahead to tomorrow's, she sees a scuttling in the far distance, and flashes back on her visit to the Kiefer-space. As the memory takes shape in her mind, the dimness at the edge of her vision likewise takes shape, and she wonders whether what she's seeing is another manifestation of the rusty curtain that Kiefer stepped through when he dropped her off by the Aldi.

"The Iron Curtain," she mouths, with a smile, as she takes another swig of wine. It's not that I don't know it's there, she plans to tell tomorrow's interviewer. It's just that all I can write about is what I see on this side. If that strikes your readership as fantastical, or even psychotic, then so be it. I can't see what they see, either. Let them stay on their side, and I'll stay on mine, passing notes through a crack in the Wall.

"**W**ell, at first there were two levels, a First and a Second Europe," she tells that imagined interviewer once he appears on her screen, eighteen hours later. She dips her hot pretzel in schmaltz as he sits in an office in Berlin, his eyes darting side to side.

"But then, after the rains fell and the waters rose, they collapsed. Except it wasn't destructive. Quite the opposite. It was a kind of superimposition. Many layers, many Europes, all piling atop one another." She shrugs, as does he, though only she takes another swig of beer.

He looks at his notes and says, "Goethe, Schiller, Kleist, Hoffman, Rilke, Kafka, Walser, Hesse, Mann, Grass, Sebald. All these names, and the wonderful-sounding works you associate with them. The rich literary canon that you claim their works helped define. Where did they come from?"

She wants to take her laptop to the Antiquariat across the street and point the webcam at the shelves and say, "Right here," but she's tried this before and only ended up looking crazy. Crazier than the interviewer already thought she was. For him, that one time she tried, there appeared to be nothing but a slate-gray wall, covered in rust and runic graffiti. She could see as much in her miniature video window, at the bottom of the chat screen. Pure Kiefer-space.

So now she simply says, "They're names I remember. Writers I read when I was young. They meant a lot to me, so I wanted to honor them in my own writing. To drive the tradition onward in my own small way."

The interviewer nods, half-satisfied, and says, his face breaking up and coming partly back together, "And Wagner? You describe him creating an entire town to house his visions. A visionary paradise in Southern Germany. Would you say that you've taken after him, in inventing Baiersbronn?"

Again, she wants to insist that she hasn't invented Baiersbronn, any more than she invented Wagner, but she knows from previous interviews where that line of defense will end up. Internet searches for these names yield links only to her own writing, and to the voluminous comment threads and video essays it's generated, many of which lead in turn to Ulli Harz fan sites.

"You could say that," she tells the interviewer. "Wagner exists as a portent in my own private myth-space. So, yes, I built his dream-town of Bayreuth in the model of my dream-town of Baiersbronn. A kind of reverse influence, sinking back through the ages like water into the roots of a vast oak. The World Tree, if you will."

The interviewer looks up from his notes and gives a noncommittal nod. "Would you say that your overall project is utopian? The attempt to create a coherent, peaceable German culture, imbued with the dignity and grace it could never otherwise attain?"

She nods, foregoing the urge to ask *and what, if not that, is German culture to you?* She's asked too many interviewers this already, and all she's ever gotten is a sinking expression, a look of shame and terror, a sort of *how could you not know?* frown that she can't bear to see again today.

"In these woods," she says, "in the German history to which I have access, there is a long tradition of witches and enchanters. Spells, oracles, otherworldly forces entering our sphere through the narrow, dark spaces between the trees. The Black Forest is the gateway. Always has been. Thus, I see myself in a long line of threshold-figures, translators bringing messages from that world to this one. It just so happens that, during the era we are currently living through, it has fallen to me to perform this function."

The interviewer looks flustered. "But I thought you said the levels had collapsed. That they were all one world now."

She tries to produce a benevolent rather than a condescending smile. "For me, yes, they have. That's why Kant and Mann and Schiller and all the others are sitting, right this minute, on the shelves of," she looks in the direction of the Antiquariat, but again resists the urge to bring her laptop over there. "Never mind. All I mean is that, for me, it's all right here. There's only one world. For you, however, and your readers, it would seem as though something very different is the case. Thus, for the sake of your pages, I call myself a medium. An intermediary. That's what you want to hear, isn't it?"

Though she isn't quite angry, she can feel the temperature rising between her and this mousy young man with his posh university accent and his burnished chrome office chair, rising and falling in jets of pixels behind his head. For his part, he appears increasingly nervous, checking behind him as if he fears that some aspect of what she's just mentioned is about to materialize.

Anika wants to ask what he sees and hears, but she has too much pride. I'm a writer, she thinks, not a lunatic. I'm in the Baiersbronn I know and love, and I'm simply telling people what it's like here. They can do as they please with that information.

The interviewer says, "And those grey and black statues, embossed with verdigris and rust, do they figure into your scheme?" He seems to be looking right at them, in the background of his video feed, though all she sees, when she looks where he appears to be looking, is an elderly couple eating coffee cake and sipping hot chocolate with whipped cream, both wearing versions of the Chancellor's face.

She shakes her head, suppressing, for the second time in twenty-four hours, her fear of the Kiefer-space encroaching. "All I see is in my writing. Baiersbronn is a peaceful place, an eternal place. A paradise on earth." The image of that fast-asleep Greek mountain town passes through her again, and again she thinks, I don't remember leaving because I never left. Though she resists the urge to look up, she can tell that, when she does, she'll see the torpid streets of that town in place of the sky. She'll look up and see herself at nineteen or twenty looking down at the tormented, leering, famous woman she's become at forty, and she won't know which of the two she is, nor even what the question means, nor who's asking it.

"I think I have enough to work with, thanks," the interviewer says. "Take care of yourself. I hope, wherever you think you are, you find a way to remain there."

After shutting her laptop, Anika orders another beer and pushes her seat up to the railing over the brook, its sound as soothing as ever. She tries to shut out the possibility that the Curtain's closing in, and that soon the whole town, even as it exists for her, will be nothing but rust on jagged sheets of iron. She thinks back on the Kiefer shows she's been to over the years, dozens and dozens, and she pictures the gargantuan metal books on display, their pages gnarled and frayed, rot spreading across them, eclipsing the names Goethe, Schiller, Kleist, Hoffman, Rilke, Kafka, Walser, Hesse, Mann, Grass, Sebald. She leaves a few coins on the table and thinks, taking her leave of those books, I'll protect you for as long as I can, same as you've protected me.

But as she walks back to her cottage, now constantly on the lookout for the Iron Curtain, she can't help feeling that soon the Kiefer-space will have consumed everything. My writing, my memories, my body, all bound for the immense drafty room where my husband already resides.

As she passes the Mayor's house, she looks in the window, where the old woman reclines in an armchair watching TV. The screen shows piles of bodies shifting and settling on the Alexanderplatz pavement, leaking blood, and the laugh-track fills the room and drifts onto the lawn where Anika stands. She closes her eyes, pictures her words being transcribed in Berlin by that shifty young interviewer, and takes what solace she can in the knowledge that, at the very least, a story in which Germany represented the apex of world culture for three centuries will soon hit newsstands in a city that can only benefit from imagining that such a thing was so.

György & Ute

The boy in his wolf-suit and the woman in her skin-suit trudge onward, up and up and up the road, until there's no more road ahead. Caravans full of Breivik Boys and caravans full of skulls and headless carcasses race past them, paying them no mind. Though György suspects that Breivik himself must be looking for him, he figures that the Justiciar has more pressing matters on his mind. Who knows how many Slavs and Magyars he's impregnated. Probably so many that it's no concern of his if a few go missing.

Either that—György pulls the wolf's eyeholes flush with his eyes, which he has to do every few minutes—or else he can no longer see me. Perhaps I've slipped out of the Game, across the border of Nordmen and back to... wherever this is. Perhaps the heroic struggle that Breivik and his Boys are engaged in is, for them, playing out on a very different landscape, even if, as far as I can tell, it's the same place.

Who knows how many places there are? He pictures himself writing a philosophical treatise on the networked ontology of the situation, the urge to map and the urge to burn maps, the soft landscape of the Real eaten away by clickholes until only the holes remain. "But holes *in what*?" He can hear himself ask this from a lectern in Budapest, delivering a condensed version of the paper before a packed auditorium, row after row of rapt faces, young men like himself but, crucially, less fully-fledged. Young men like I used to be, before I made a name for myself in the world.

Focus! The voice in his head shouts. Find a way back to where you are.

Startled, he pulls the eyeholes flush again, resetting his wolf mask and, with it, his focus on Old Hungary. I'm coming, he promises. I'm coming. Wait for me.

But looking down at the skin-ground and up at the skin-sky and out at the skin-horizon, like the walls of a room, he can't help fearing that wherever this is will prove to be the last place, and that it may well be as far from Old Hungary as he's ever been. As if the entire journey has been a flight from his calling.

He growls and tries to heave off the thought that all the experience he'll ever have, between now and his death, is sealed in here with him already, as is all the air he'll ever breathe. He takes a deep breath, torn between wanting to conserve it and wanting to suck it all down and expel it in one last teeth-gnashing howl, the words "I tried!" roaring past his teeth as he expires.

Ute scratches at her arm, where no wires any longer protrude, and tries to remember what she'd been looking for when she began this journey. It seems like another lifetime, like some unresolved business she was born with and has spent decades trying to forget. She looks at the tan horizon, hemming in every edge of the environment that she and this boy with his stinking wolf-suit are stuck in, and wonders what culmination either of them could have hoped for when they set out. She can remember happier times with him and with a woman who might have been her daughter, long, lazy afternoons spent in sunlight and a picnic in the woods on Midsummer's Day.

And, now that she thinks about it, she can remember a sense of unity even deeper than those Sundays, a unity so deep that she can't isolate herself within it, because there was no self then. Only an it, a *we*. A state of being, but no subject within that state.

The Wall. She can see it now. It fills her mind so quickly that it overwhelms her balance and threatens to knock her backwards, and she opens her eyes, only to realize they were open already.

So the Wall's really there, just ahead, and there's no act of eye-opening that can wipe it away or push it further out. There's no buying more time. The journey has felt long, but not nearly long enough. It's all happening too quickly. The Wall is right there, not a memory, not a vision, so tall and gray it looks like the end of the world.

György sees it too. He pulls the wolf-skin tightly around himself and, to take his eyes off the gray enormity, he looks down at his ankles, where, for quite some time, a pressure has been nagging at him.

The singular urge to maintain his pace across the frontier has kept him from looking down all this time, but now he can see what looks like the remnants of a man, reduced to flotsam, clinging to his feet. A man-shaped mass of weedy skin, intertwined with moss and vines and mushrooms, stringy and barely alive. With just enough facial articulation left to scan as human, the man-thing looks up at him, its eyes soft and partially popped, and says, in ravaged Hungarian, "György,

I've tracked you all this way. Please come home. It's not too late to resume a normal life."

The phrase hits him in the gut, as hard as if one of the Breivik Boys had jumped off his caravan and slugged him with the stock of a rifle. He staggers forward, falls onto his belly, and feels the spawn inside him squirm and chatter. Help me, he thinks, rolling onto his side and looking up at the woman, who seems not to have noticed that he's fallen behind.

"Help me!" he shouts. "My foot's gotten tangled!"

Ute turns to regard the boy lying on the ground, wrestling with what looks like a tangle of roots and moss. She tears her eyes off the Wall, half hoping it'll disappear by the time she looks back in that direction, and goes to help the boy up. But before she gets there, a red, watery stain explodes between his legs and he flips onto his back, shrieking at the taut, vibrating skin overhead.

What follows is the deepest, most searing pain György's ever felt. Deeper even than the imagined agony of heroic battle. Deeper than the exalted death throes of Yukio Mishima, as his bowels came out and his head came off. He phases in and out of consciousness, barely cognizant of where he is or what the woman beside him is saying. He has no words to clarify the nature of the pain to himself, so he fills his head with the same screaming that's issuing from his throat, the same sound playing out on two channels at the same time, and he pushes his head back into the soft skin he's lying on, forcing up a deep memory of the Wanderer in Novalis reclining on a bed of wet moss as he digs his feet into the tangle of pants and underwear and weeds and teeth that surrounds them, and prepares to die. The forest beneath the forest, he pleads. Just let me sink down there and stay.

One after another, Ute pulls slippery, blonde babies out of the boy's vagina. She piles them on the pillowy skin beside her as more and more come, until a total of twelve have emerged, leaving the boy spent and deflated inside his nappy wolf fur, a quarter of the size he'd been. So small that he's barely bigger than his offspring, which laugh and chitter where they lie.

Then they sit up and continue speaking in a language she can almost but not quite understand. Something adjacent to German, but more northerly. Colder, of a deeper green. They grin, their faces already old, their slick baby hair already that of balding men. She watches them cackle and point at her, then teeter to their feet to march in the Wall's direction.

György awakens to see a small army of miniature Breiviks marching away from where he lies.

Though he still feels ripped in half, something inside him rallies and forces his body to its feet. He staggers up, kicks through the remnants of the man who tracked him down, and groans to the woman, "Stop them!"

The voice of the Deep Ragnar echoes back through his head and he knows that if he looks to either side, the eggs will reappear, hemming him in, laughing at his desperation to prevent his offspring from going where the Game has already determined they must go. Still, he pulls the wolf fur over his shivery frame, invokes the name of Arisztid Huszár, embodiment of the fullness of Magyar wrath and retribution, and determines to kill those twelve Breiviks before they make it over the Wall to cement his humiliation in the perpetuity of Atlantis.

Together, the boy and the woman track the Breiviks across the frontier, the skin so ample and soft beneath their feet that it feels like running through fresh snow. Water sloshes in declivities all around them, rolling in waves, sometimes blocking their way.

They sink in up to their waists and haul themselves out again, blood leaking out of György so fast that he survives only by banishing the pain to another chamber of his rapidly fragmenting mind. That's all happening in the Game, he tells himself, whereas here, in the snowy, virgin wilds of Old Hungary, my redemption is nearly at hand. My prey has nearly succumbed.

Thrilling at the articulation of this prospect, and the lack of any authority to deny it, he throws himself forward, arms outstretched, and catches two Breiviks, holding them face down in a puddle until they lie still. Ute, likewise, catches two more, leaving eight up ahead, still scurrying toward the Wall.

They repeat this routine, drowning four more, leaving only four on their way to the Wall, but the injury and the exhaustion have caught up with György and he falls behind, while the remaining four gain distance, growing smaller as they go.

György falls on the frontier, his fur cold and sticky atop his tattoo, and knows that the battle, this part of it anyway, is lost. The remaining four have gained too much ground. He watches them march on until a chattering nearer-by pulls his attention downward.

"Together in Atlantis! Together in Atlantis! We are together in Atlantis at last!" the eight stunned Breiviks lie chanting, none of them dead, their voices a higher version of the smug whine that György remembers from the horse farm in Norway. He can understand enough Norwegian to tell what they're chanting. You sound just like your father, he thinks.

He lumbers over to where the eight have clustered, basking in one another's warmth, and he scoops the nearest one up, staring at its still-chattering mouth, the word *Atlantis* oozing like cream from its lips.

Raising the balding blonde thing to his own lips, a modicum of motherly love passes through him, a shameful inability to hate this thing he's birthed. Then, closing his eyes and willing his teeth to grow into the noble fangs of Arisztid Huszár, he bites down, tearing into it like a slice of watermelon. He keeps his eyes closed, hovering between knowing and not knowing, giving himself permission to continue while also revoking that permission, and bites again, and again, filling his mouth without, yet, swallowing. He feels the body lighten in his arms, diminishing bite by bite as his own face bulges with what's now inside it, his cheeks puffing out and out and out, until, at last, he's forced to swallow.

When he does, he feels the soft, hot meat pass down into his belly, and he feels its strength course through him. He feels his wounds heal and his lost blood return, better than before, less anemic, less sallow. Purer. Clean, fresh Aryan blood rushes through his system, puffing out his fur, binding it to his skin. He stands up, roars, and grabs the next Breivik, ripping its head off with a single bite.

He rips and chews and swallows and rips and chews and swallows again, and again after that, until the eight Breiviks he managed to capture are all back inside him, and he stands ten feet tall, a real wolf-man now, no longer a boy in a wolf-suit. Like crushing the walls of a honeycomb between his molars, all partitions between worlds break down and rush together in his core, making up his new flesh. When there's nothing more to eat, he rises to his full height, wipes his lips on his furry arm, turns to regard the woman who's stood to the side watching him all this time, and says, "It's time to storm the Wall. Are you coming?"

Like so, the wolf-man and the old woman march toward the monolith that has replaced the horizon. They gain speed as they approach it, bouncing between folds in the skin underfoot and swimming through rising breakers, discrete bodies of water merging as the sky sags ever lower, like a circus pavilion collapsing in the wind, until they're pressed against the towering, graffiti-strewn concrete and the waves have joined to drown the entire expanse behind them. They crush their faces against the Wall, smelling the still-wet grout and the barnacles and the cold, green patches of moss that have already taken root there.

Then Arisztid looks to the woman and says, "Climb onto my back," and she does, her fingers pinching the edges of his tattoo. Just as her palms are pressed flat against him, he presses his flat against the Wall, and, in imitation of his four children who got away, he launches upward with a single, superhuman leap, flying past foot after foot of dead material, the salty air whooshing through his fur, until he stands on the ledge, hundreds of feet up, his paws entwined in barbed wire, oblivious to the woman riding him until she climbs down and, nestling her feet likewise in the wire, comes over to stand by his side.

Together they survey a territory that extends to a horizon that is, once again, defined by the Wall. The center is composed of dense, lush greenery, palm trees and flowering trellises growing beside and among the towering oaks of the Black Forest, subdivided by stone enclosures and amphitheaters and statues of Dionysus, temples fronted by vast Doric columns and sculpted fountains and amphorae and dense stands of olive trees and grapevines, a Nordic dream of Europe's profound Greek origins, a pastiche of the ancient world as envisaged by...

At the center of the forum stands Breivik, shirtless, brandishing a sword, while thousands upon thousands of warriors, likewise shirtless, kneel before him, their bald heads and bearded faces identical in the warm tropical light. Copy and paste, copy and paste. Ragnar, Breivik, Ulli Harz. A servant approaches on his knees, brandishing a bundle wrapped in white cloth, and Breivik holds it up for all to see. Unwrapping it to reveal one of the babies that escaped, he stares into his own miniaturized face and proclaims, "Here, brave Nordmen, is the first of many immortals! Our work is done, our war is won. These children will outlive us by millions and billions of years, and all will be as it should! At last, at long, long last, peace and harmony have been won in Atlantis!"

The Nordmen rise and stab their swords into the air, cheering in unison until the Supreme Justiciar cuts them off.

"Under the sage guidance of the Deep Ragnar," he continues, "us brave men of Norway have been led through the collapse, the rubble, the wreckage and the ruin of Europe, past the fragmenting languages and the mystifying borders, through the splintering coastlines and the rising waves," at this, Arisztid looks behind him to verify that the skin-frontier has turned to ocean, leaving himself and the woman on a seawall surrounding the only island in sight, a cold, salty wind whipping his fur while gulls shriek in the sky, "and, at long, long last, to our ancestral home on Atlantis. We have conquered the Black Forest, drowned the Germans and claimed Baiersbronn for the Holy North. You, and I, and all now able to understand me, as I speak in the uncorrupted Atlantean language of old," Arisztid bristles with reflexive pride to realize that he, too, can understand it, "will end our lives here, so that the new, immortal, post-consciousness Breiviks who are now in our midst may inherit this paradise free of taint. Free of worry. Free of history!"

"No past! No future!" chant the Nordmen.

"No past! No future!" echoes Breivik, arm held out at nearly a right angle from his shoulder. "Where Hitler balked, Breivik stayed true. History, gentlemen, is behind us. Eternity is in the hands of my offspring." He holds one of the babies up again, whispers something in its ear, then places it on a throne, beside the other three, who must've appeared when he was speaking. It squirms and fusses but soon settles in, regarding the proceedings with the equipoise of a man who knows his position is assured.

Bending down, Breivik grabs hold of the skin, which seems also to have blanketed the ground of Atlantis, and pulls it up around himself, stopping with it around his chest, like a wetsuit. "The dead skin of the continent," he continues, "has followed us, even here. For we too are products of its decline. It lives within us, just as surely as we, until now, lived within it. Thus, let us pull it around ourselves, sealing ourselves in tight, and thereby use up the last of it, so that my offspring may thrive in a truly purged environment, free of all memory. Upon fresh, genuine ground, at last. Wrap yourselves tightly, brave Nordmen, and go to your rest knowing the full scale of what you've made possible. As we speak, hundreds, perhaps thousands of filthy Easterners are birthing my spawn, drawn ineluctably toward us for reasons they can scarcely comprehend. Drawn here ineluctably, indeed, for one simple reason: because that which lives inside them knows where its fate lies. Because that rough beast, to borrow a last poetic phrase before my mouth is forever silenced, slouches toward Atlantis to be born! In honor of those children I was forced to kill on an island outside of Oslo in what is now another lifetime, I say: welcome home! On Atlantis, you are, at last, reborn."

He raises his arm in one last salute. Then, after the assembled masses have responded in kind, he pulls the skin past his face and up over his head, where it fuses together, smoothing into the seamless oval of a man-sized egg.

The Nordmen, likewise, have become eggs, thousands and thousands of them, rolling toward the peripheries, into the shadows of the Wall, while hundreds of baby Breiviks, climbing from a mutilated pile of Romanian, Polish, Bulgarian, Greek, Albanian, and Hungarian proxy-mothers take their place beside their brothers on the thrones that have been set out for them. All is peaceful. The skin is gone, the ground is reconsecrated. The Game is won. Atlantis is risen.

———————————

Ute turns from the scene, her feet snarled in wire atop the Wall. She feels the wolf-man turn with her, the two of them with their backs to Atlantis now, facing the open ocean. All memory of the frontier they crossed to get here is just that, a memory, and now her eyes and ears are filled with crashing surf, the Wall so high it looks like a row of cliffs, the very edge of a continent that has been ending for so long she began to doubt that it ever truly could. And yet here it is, the edge beyond which none may pass. Beyond which no journey, no matter how unresolved, can continue. There is no frontier any longer, save for the sea. All habitable land, all memory. Everything that isn't nothing. Layer upon layer upon layer, infinitude of myth, a density of meaning approaching that of a black hole: all underwater now.

The waves soothe her.

She closes her eyes in the salt breeze and strains to hear Klara's voice in the distance, whether it be the distance of memory or the deep interior of the structure she's standing on, the Wall that no longer evinces any sign of having been alive. No sign, she thinks, but me. I'm the last bulwark, the final living proof. The only unincorporated piece. I never should've listened to her. She only led me back to Baiersbronn. And yet, closing her eyes and picturing Anika drowned beneath the waves, Ute can't imagine any other journey; once again, the Russian border bounces her back, refusing access to the taiga. And so maybe none of that was real. Maybe this, here, in the center of the waves that were always going to rise, is the only real place.

And so I have indeed made it to where I was going.

This thought swells her with a desperate, lonely pride. The pride of a figurehead who's survived a sea journey that killed the entire crew. She stands taller, looking out to sea, as far from home as she's ever been, and yet no longer bereft. No longer seeking that which she knows can't be found. Without stopping to consider the meaning of this action, she reaches down to pull the barbed wire up from where it clusters around her ankles, at first tentatively, wincing as it eats into her palms, but soon the pain is forgotten, her skin consigned to the same distant past as all the skin of the dead continent. Now she's tearing it up with abandon, her arms overflowing, and now the wolf-man has joined in. They tear and tear, Klara's voice whispering louder as the wires come out, unsealing the top of the Wall and leaving rows of scars and furrows. Whispers of apology, of supplication, of *it's still not too late to join us*, shoot along the wires as Ute bundles herself in them, but none of it registers. There was never any *us*, she can finally see, as she presses the wires into her body, imposing from without the wires that once, in another lifetime, seemed to sprout from within. Stray voices on the airwaves, static and hiss, canned statements from another era, nothing more.

There was only ever me. Only ever here.

This place.

The last of all places.

She shoves a wire into her side and exhales sharply, not in pain but in memory of pain, in honor of it, in honor of the pain that all those men in Latvia and Estonia and Austria felt when she let them cut themselves on her wires, back in that other lifetime, on that other continent.

But no longer.

She shoves the wire into the wolf-man's fur, just beneath his ribs, and trembles as he growls and snarls and his matted grey side turns red. She shoves it in deeper, impaling him, then reaching around to pull it out the other side. Then she pulls it back around and presses it into her own side, likewise impaling herself and pulling it out her own other side, and again, and again, until she and the wolf-man and the Wall are one, indivisible, no longer lost. The red fur grows over both of them, furring the wires, furring the flesh, furring the concrete, until there's only one essence, without a name, nor anyone to wonder what its name might be.

Finally, the Wall thinks, letting go of all its former names and all the pieces and places it used to be, we are one. No memory remains of the territory to our back. All that exists now is the territory ahead, the wide-open sea, the breakers and the cold surf. The moment no longer feels like the end of anything, nor like a fresh beginning, but merely a redundant example of eternity. The Wall stands still before the ocean, unblinking as the sun sets for the last time on the West.

Epilogue: The Europe Room

The Chancellor

The Chancellor wakes up in the Presidential Suite at the Hotel Silesia and, after a quick buffet breakfast in the empty restaurant, glared at by a stern waiter in a button-up vest, is escorted into her limo.

She sits upright against the tan leather upholstery in back as the driver rolls toward the border between Görlitz and Zgorzelec, approaching Poland and the asylum where the Svens, as she's taken to calling them, have been quarantined. The Last Good Men of Europe, the seed bank for when the Ragnar Wave finally breaks. Everyone's tense from what's happened, and tenser about what still might. And yet it's not too late to simmer down. To put the past in the past. It's never too late for that.

She holds her face taut and her mouth closed for fear of letting loose a smirk or chortle as she gazes at her translucent reflection in the window, superimposed over shuttered factories and fields of slag, and she tries to guess who's inside the face she can see. Which version, how many replacements down the line, how many buried Chancellors deep? She stares long enough to lose focus and, as she'd hoped it would, the question boils into abstract contemplation of wobbly shapes.

She watches them wobble and then come to a halt as the driver pulls into the designated space in front of the concrete slab of asylum, and then she watches her door open, as if melting away in the toxic atmosphere, and she watches a gloved hand reach in for her, and she has a brief, ludicrous instinct to hide from it, like a child hiding from a man-sized lobster in a nightmare, but then the hands are entwined with hers and her feet are on the cold ground beside the boots of whoever these hands belong to, and then she and that man are walking side by side, with dignity, into the asylum, where she remembers, just in time, a joyous event is to be held.

She is led quickly through a lobby filled with dead-eyed men waiting in several lines to be admitted to an auditorium. She smiles at the few whose gazes meet hers, though mostly she keeps her eyes on the podium that draws closer every time one or the other of her feet touches the ground. After a finite number of subsequent footfalls, she's behind the podium, gazing out at a crowd of well-dressed, well-groomed Nordic men, some hairless and some with close-cropped straw-yellow hair. She wraps the fingers of her left hand around the edge of the podium to keep from floating away, and tries to do likewise with the fingers of her right, but finds that something glossy and intractable has come between them.

Glancing at this hand, or at the thing in the hand, she registers the shape of a hardcover book. Extending her glance into something slightly less discreet, she sounds out the title, hovering in handsome Gothic script above a photo of a gingerbread house in a wooded clearing.

Reflections on Normal Life in Southern Germany:

A Family Memoir.

She nods, as if someone had just read these words aloud to her, and the script she's planned, or that her predecessor did, goes into effect.

"Peace-loving men of Northern Europe," she hears herself say, "I stand before you bearing good news from your neighbor to the south. Though I will not deny that the causes for concern that drove you here were, at one point, valid, all has been resolved now." She holds the book high overhead. "The news is in. The fire in the Black Forest is out. All reports of mass flooding have, thankfully, been disproven. Cooler heads have prevailed. All is as it was. The gates of hell that some claim opened, for a time, in Southern Germany, have closed, never to reopen, not even in dreams. You may return home and rest easy, free of fear and free of guilt. All of Northern Europe, from Munich to Tromsø, from Hamburg to Helsinki, is a peaceable kingdom once again."

She waves her book arm in a grand flourish, sending a signal whose meaning she can't anticipate. Tapestries depicting the grain of warm wood cover the cold cement walls of the asylum and wine corks pop as a string quartet tunes up.

"All the instructions for maintaining European decency, for preserving the national heritage of which we are justifiably proud, are in here. Please, file in and get your books in a respectful and orderly manner."

The crowd approaches the stage to pick up copies before bringing them, obediently, to a table beside the podium where a well-dressed woman waits with an uncapped Mont Blanc pen. She looks to the Chancellor, smiles graciously, and then turns to regard the first face in a line that has grown to encompass hundreds. The Chancellor can't remember this woman's name—though she knows she could simply look at the cover of the book she's still holding—but she can remember meeting her in an office at Humboldt University in Berlin, and this memory is enough, for the moment, to soak up whatever doubt has lingered around the edges of her mind.

Berlin. That's where we are now. Why shouldn't we be? The eerie memory of the border, the coldness of concrete asylums in Poland and all they too easily suggest, even in the new century, the stale air of the Hotel Silesia and the now-famous "drowning fountain" in the square outside: all of it drifts up to the rafters and hovers there, unnoticed by all who have the sense not to look. After all the Pseudo-Berlins that have proliferated across the length and breadth of this nation, the Chancellor thinks, what's the harm in adding another tonight?

The woman I hired to write a book has written that book. Beginning, middle, end. Dispatch enough good people to the field, and one of them will make it back.

She steps off the podium, skirting the line that has only continued to grow.

She walks on her own, tailed at a safe distance by her bodyguards, past the signing line and over to the edge of the Europe Room.

The Europe Room?

Part of her wonders where this term came from, while another part, the part that said it, replies, "That's right. They're safely sealed inside now. Your job here is done. You're free to go."

As soon as this statement has been made, escaping the mouth of some vestigial Chancellor folded up like a bat inside her skull, she sees the mahogany wall in front of her sag and groan, becoming skinlike and then becoming skin. It sags toward her, its skin touching hers, and then she's wrapped in it, indistinguishable from it, her back to the becalmed crowd, her face—for a moment—unable to see what's ahead.

She hovers in this interim, proud of the peace she's managed to broker in the Europe Room, the restored sense of it being Berlin—of it having always been Berlin, of nothing untoward ever having intervened—while also anticipating whatever's on the other side.

The Real World. Retirement. Freedom, finally.

The skin grows cold and scaly, churning around her, pushing from behind, forcing her onward with a series of cervical heaves. It heaves again and again until she's been expelled, once again in her own body, on her own feet, shivering in the cold and the dark. It seals up behind her, glowing a warm, homey orange as the wind blows her across the frontier, away from the Europe Room and toward the distant lights of Baiersbronn, where Horst calls to her softly through the dark.

She turns, despite the wind, and, like Walter Benjamin's Angel of History, about whom she wrote so many papers so many epochs ago, drifts backward away from the past, out of the restored, redeemed high culture of Europe, and into the future, which, since it's all behind her, is of an attribute she can't be expected to describe.

Anika, Ute, György

Anika indulges all the pride her system can process at the length and enthusiasm of the line that's formed to buy her book. After months alone in her cottage in the woods, haunted by bodies that were and weren't there, in unpredictable alternation, rippling into her awareness as the Curtain rippled in the wind, the fact that she's produced something tangible and ended up here, back in Berlin, facing a line every bit the equal of that which turned out to buy her first book, is no small matter. Relief, even salvation, is the word. She slashes through her printed name on the book's title page, then scrawls her initials in cursive beneath the slash.

And salvation, she realizes, not just for me, but for them too, all these cowed men waiting obediently in line. Salvation from what they all feared—truly feared, not just worried over on some wine-softened afternoon—was happening in the Black Forest and, by extension, across the continent. Emanating from its poisoned heart. The altar, the fire, the cliffs, the jackboots with skulls hanging from their heels, the bodies in town squares, the drowned children in public pools, so many there was no room for the water... and the water itself, spilling over and rising up, drowning everything, a continent's collective nightmare, the sequel to the long, long nightmare of the Living Wall and the War that produced it.

A nightmare from which we've all, at last, awoken. And awoken into what? She asks herself, practicing for the lecture she'll give at Humboldt this fall, once her book and its spinoff

TV series have segued into a new course. We've awoken into Goethe, Schiller, Kleist, Hoffman, Rilke, Kafka, Walser, Hesse, Mann, Grass, Sebald. Wenders, Fassbinder, Herzog. Cherry strudel and apple strudel. Sunday and Sunday and Sunday. She smiles. All the good things, the things for which we ought to be proud, and for which, indeed, we are proud. German pride without shame, unto eternity.

She signs and signs, more books than she can count, so many that her Mont Blanc runs out of ink and is replaced, at once, with a new one.

Then, finally, when the population that lined up for copies has received its copies, down to the last man, she gets to her feet, takes a flute of champagne from a tray, and wanders through the space, whose nature she had, until now, been too busy to consider.

The signing hall lets out into a gallery and she drifts with the crowd, emptying her glass and replacing it with a full one, and then another. Once she's had several, she finds herself in a hall of metal artworks, some hanging from the walls while others stand on the floor, somewhere between paintings and sculptures.

The air smells of metal and dust, hovering above blighted landscapes, fire and ash and trees reduced to splintered sticks. To one side stands a metal cottage in a metal clearing, its roof cratered, its walls scored with rusted barbed wire, and beside it sit the remnants of a van that looks like it drove over a landmine. A road made of nails and razor blades leads to another patch of metal ground upon which is arrayed a model town, green copper and charred black iron forming a vision of Bavarian charm as it might appear a century after the end of all human life.

Anika looks away, toward the profile of a tall, gaunt man, barefoot in a black blazer with a white T-shirt underneath, his eyes calm, his mouth set in a knowing smirk. He nods very subtly when he sees her and she returns the nod, considers approaching him, and decides against it. For however long this late, unexpected period lasts, she decides, I'm going to live my life as if it were true that he's no more than a famous artist standing among his works at an opening in Berlin, his big Black Forest Retrospective, the most personal and perhaps final show of his career, and I no more than a famous author who's just sold out the first printing of her second book, bigger and better in every way than her first.

And who knows, she goes on, taking another flute of champagne and wondering if she should track down something to eat, perhaps that's all we are, and ever were, and life will simply continue, encircled by dread without quite growing unlivable. She brushes against Gerhard, his face fringed in verdigris and his body entombed in iron, and looks at him for a moment, mouthing, "I made it on my own. Despite your abandoning me with our son and my mother, I made it back, stronger than before. So let's not make a scene." She turns from the statue. "Just imagine we're divorced and both of us have turned up at the same opening. The civil thing is to overlook one another. To say, Berlin is big enough to let some of what's forgotten remain that way. We are modern adults in a modern city and that is how it's done."

She downs her wine and flashes back to the Stammkneipe in Baiersbronn, where she can't shake the feeling that some version of her, perhaps the main version, is still sitting, enjoying a placid sunset over the babbling brook while drinking the same wine that she appears to be drinking here in Berlin.

György scowls as he stalks through the exhibit, clutching his dog-eared copy of Cioran's *The Trouble With Being Born*, which he'd been reading at an outdoor café in Mitte until it got too dark to continue. Now he strides among the art, gnashing his teeth, as ever, at the rampant weakness on display all around him, the nodding heads of the bourgeoisie, and he feels himself longing for a war while also fearing a war, and hating the part of himself that fears it. There is no heroism without suffering, he thinks, as he's thought so many times before, so many times today, even, and yet he recoils at the prospect of suffering just as he always has, ever since he was a little boy drawing monsters in his notebook by the riverside in Gyula, while his parents picnicked and, mouths full of salami and champagne, told him how much better things were now, compared to when they'd been his age, when there wasn't even any... when you had to wait in line for...

A familiar face catches his eye and he loses the thought, replaced, in an instant, by a cascade of memories. He looks at the old woman in a loose coat roaming among the crowd with her hands out, and he has to turn and close his eyes as the room shakes and threatens to dissolve. Nothing but a filthy beggar, he tells himself. Scum, runoff, the kind that ruined Hungary and is now oozing ever Westward. Yet something in her face pulls him out of where he is, or seems to be, and back toward someplace else. Ocean mist on his face, the low bobbing of ovoid shapes audible behind him, thick blood dripping down his inner thighs. His skin prickles and trembles, sprouting with the memory of fur, or a premonition of fur, and now the rusted hulks of ruin and despair that were, an instant ago, no more than bourgeois baubles take on the menacing cast of real ruins. His sides itch and ache, deep wounds held back by thin, fresh scabs.

Something happened, he knows. Something that isn't a lie. Something that isn't just a story to tell kids to keep them from becoming heroes, or an algorithm telling a YouTube channel to tell me what I want to hear. He swoons and flushes and ducks his head, running past the beggar woman and toward the exit, though he can already tell that no such exit awaits him. What would I give to return to that story, the one in which I became a wolf and fought my way to the end of the end of the earth? In which I watched Europe drown, and stood triumphant above the waves, surveying what little remained.

This is the same question he's asked himself all his life, tempered only slightly tonight by a new set of specifics. When he hits the far wall of the exhibition space, where a bank of screens shows a video-art installation captioned NEXT YEAR IN ATLANTIS, he leans against it, catches his breath, and waits, despondent, for the vision of himself and Ute atop the Wall to recede. Arisztid Huszár. The name floats through his head. The man I could've been, he finds the courage to admit, if only I hadn't been born a coward. Swallowing phlegm, he shoves his way through the exit, into a darker, more distant room.

Ute watches the boy leave and she smiles, itching her wires under her coat. She can remember a world in which she and that boy merged, the last two living souls at the end of a long, directionless frontier, their backs to the Wall, their fronts to the cold, black ocean. And she can remember a life before that, a life shared by her and that boy and the drunk author, now being helped into a chair by an African museum guard. She can picture the three of them strolling along a leafy, sun-dappled lane to eat strudel on a late Sunday morning, debating, with amicably feigned rancor, whether today it should be cherry or apple.

She can remember this life and many others, a life in which she heeded Klara's call and it didn't lead to Baiersbronn, but rather deep into the taiga, all the way in, where, even now, she's part of something larger, something hulking and solid and silent, meaning that these thoughts are no more than a passing fancy, a harmless dream of Berlin from the depths of a Siberian midnight.

Either that, she thinks, or else I'm still in the midst of my life, an old woman who's wandered for years and years, since long before '89, a nameless gypsy surviving on alms and trashcan hamburgers, back in Berlin after a long summer in Bavaria, and, soon enough, I'll be on my way again, back east, again to Poland and Latvia and Belarus, again and again around my circuit, up to the Russian border and back, trying for a mellow autumn in Finland until something real sees fit to stop me.

György pushes through the exit and descends a staircase, wandering corridors and galleries that feed into an underground hall where a lone yellow light burns. A museum storage room, by the looks of it, metal and cement men awaiting activation. When he reaches the back wall, drawn across the slick tile floor with a determination he hasn't felt since his return to Berlin from the half-remembered fog of Atlantis, he leans in to read a wide steel plaque. ARCHAIC TORSO OF MISHIMA. He parses these words over and over, running his hands across them like a blind man.

Then he allows his head to drift upward, away from the text and onto the burnished, chiseled skin beside it. The washboard abs, the beautifully sculpted arms, the jagged skin of the neck, where the head was severed in the final instant of Mishima's legendary seppuku.

He falls to his knees and gazes up, his eyes playing over the preserved majesty of the greatest warrior-poet who ever lived, one of the very few men who, in death, proved that his life had been worth living. The hall remains silent while György pays his respects, quivering down where the torso's feet would be, until a voice ripples through the room, commanding his attention.

You must change your life, the torso declares, loudly and clearly in German, requisitioning its long-lost head through some primeval logic that György knows better than to question.

You must change your life. This time, he merely thinks the phrase, aware that the Great Man will never deign to address him again. Here is my moment, he understands. My summons, my Rubicon. Every Hero is given one, and only one. All my life, it was only that the Call hadn't yet come! He

350

laughs at the foolishness of having imagined that he'd missed it long ago.

He stands, bows to the torso, then leans in, unsure how close it'll let him get. It doesn't flinch or rebuke him, so he leans closer, his face to its bronzed skin, his lips opening, his tongue out. And then he makes contact, his rough, mealy tongue on the hero's taut, toned body, licking the skin stretched across its pecs, then down to its nipples, then further down, tracing the deep lines around its abs, between and above and below each striation. And then he stands, trembling, looking behind him to see if anyone's entered the room. Finding no one, he repeats, "You must change your life," feeling the truth of those words trickle down his neck. And then he raises himself up and leans forward to lick the torso's neck, tracing glistening lines around the scarred, knobby flesh where the head used to be. Where—he drags his tongue from the back to the front— the fateful sword cut through. The final stroke, the single most courageous moment in the life of a man whose life ran on nothing but courage.

Tears fill György's eyes as he feels the stump grow wet, as if running once again with blood. He laps at it and tastes the thought turning to matter in the hot dark.

He laps desperately at the neck, gushing now with so much blood that it's as if the head has just been severed. He closes his eyes and feels the wolf fur grow back around his body as the blood makes him strong, its iron filling his mind with blades slicing through skin and gristle, clean, straight, definitive cuts, over and over and over again, without hesitation, without revision, without uncertainty. Severing the rot from the world, rescuing the small perfect core underneath.

The blood pours down his throat, becoming his own blood, that of Arisztid Huszár, liberated from history, and it thickens, clots, cools, until it's part of him and the stump is dry, covered with smooth, taut, warm skin, no longer a stump, but a... face. He leans into it, his lips against its lips, his teeth against its teeth, his tongue against its tongue. He extends the kiss as long as it'll go, man to man, warrior to warrior, before the moment comes when he'll have to pull back and shift his attention from taste to sight, reckoning with what, or who, the Archaic Torso of Mishima has become.

He holds on, his hand around the back of the regrown head, while he feels a hand creep around the back of his own head, in perfect sync. The room shakes and a smell of hot yolk mixes with that of drying blood, and, for a long moment, he's subsumed, neither himself nor anyone else, simply a heart beating inside a thick, regal pelt of fur.

Then, at last, he has to breathe. He sinks down into the kiss, as far as he can, fighting to nestle on its warm bottom, and then he pulls back, speeding toward the surface, and air, and life.

Staggering backward, he regards, and is regarded by, a wide, bald face, wiping its lips and smiling at him. It licks its teeth, pulls yolk from its eyebrows, swallows, and says, "I've been waiting here for you. A long, long time, it feels like."

György—as it has so many times before, that name, the smallness of it, returns in Breivik's presence, precluding the possibility of anything grander—nods, trying to show as little reaction as possible.

"But you're here now. That's the important thing," Breivik continues, scratching the chiseled abs that, until a moment ago, belonged to the only man in history who could've written *The Sailor Who Fell from Grace with the Sea*.

György feels himself nod again, a cadet answering his commanding officer. He looks upward, furtively, wondering how far overhead the museum he left behind is now. The hall of false idols, the bourgeois sabbath of the Kiefer Exhibition. He wishes, as he's wished so often before, that he were back there now, sipping wine, studying the contours of the sculptures' pseudo-destruction, remarking to whomever happened to be standing beside him that the textures of the paint and the rust are so *resonant of the predicament we're in, you know? The danger that Europe faces in the coming years.*

But the predicament isn't up there with the statues. It's down here, with the hand that's now coming toward him, a plastic bauble balanced on its outstretched palm.

"You're asking yourself, right now, whether I'm in your head, or whether you're in mine, or whether we're both in some third space, some constructed reality to which both of us, as equals, are subject." Breivik laughs, clasping the bauble so it doesn't fall.

"Tell yourself whichever you choose. Or pick all three! Perhaps this is all my dream, from inside the egg on Atlantis. It makes no difference. Because, in all seriousness, you're going to do the same thing in whichever one it is, or in all of them, if you prefer."

He opens his hand again, and pushes the bauble toward György, who picks it up and balances it on his own palm, imitating Breivik's pose of a moment ago. He focuses on it, and feels Breivik focusing on it, and for a moment the hall is silent and still.

Then Breivik looks back into György's eyes and says, "The time has come for you to press the button. I belong down here," he puffs up his chest and, seamlessly, expands to fill the form of Ragnar. "Underground, in this sunken Europe, now that the battle—this one instance of the endless war— has been won. Or," he looks to the bauble again, "is soon to be. Take a moment to make your peace with the life you've lived, György, then do what needs to be done. This is your calling, and you've responded to it courageously, but now is no time to turn back. The summit awaits you. None of what you've undergone so far is real. Think of it as training. Berlin, Copenhagen, Baiersbronn, and all the territory thereafter. Now, the Game has deposited you here, on the threshold of the really real. The final level, the climb to the hatch that leads through the ceiling and out of the Europe Room. We are proud of your loyalty. Your fealty to the cause. The honor you've found in assuming your position of support at the bottom of the Nordmen pyramid. Now prove yourself, for all time."

Ragnar leans in, kisses the top of György's head, and steps back onto the pedestal where the Mishima torso had stood.

A moment later, György's alone in the hall, beside the Archaic Torso of Mishima, as motionless as it's been since the attempted coup in Tokyo in 1970, when the Great Man lost his head in ritual suicide and entered the innermost annals of world history, never to be displaced.

Ritual suicide. The phrase passes through György's own head as he looks down at the bauble, the only indication that the entire Breivik scene wasn't a dream. He rubs his fingers over the smooth plastic, inching them around the front to rest on the button.

Closing his eyes, he promises Mishima that this is his storming of the Ichigaya Camp, his coup d'état. His revenge on the coarsening of eternal values and the moral rot at the heart of all civilizations once they grow too settled. Unwilling to live as a loser in a nation of losers, Mishima chose to die for the emperor instead. So this will be my attack, György decides, on the corruption and weakness and procession of simulacra that has consumed my continent, just as it consumed yours. I will fight and die for the restoration of honor, just as you did. With this orb, I will blow Berlin to smithereens, in an explosion so historic that the walls between the Game and the world will melt, actual and digital space fusing for all time, with no space for Soft Illuminati in between, and those who come after will, once again, build a real city, a noble, dignified, consecrated city, upon the ashes of what grew here when cowards were tending it, converting their dollars to Euros in the dead of night.

And that city, when all is said and done, will be named Budapest. The other Budapest, the one I left behind, will be discarded as a failed draft, a version that didn't work out. Here, from the rubble, with the Archaic Torso of Mishima buried like a root deep underground, the Magyar Kingdom of Arisztid Huszár will flourish forever.

György closes his eyes and pictures the wolf man rising from the pulp of his soon to be ruined carcass, and he repeats the phrase, "You must change your life," one last time as he presses the button.

Kiefer

He waits until all the guests are gone. Then he locks the doors of the Europe Room with the burnished chrome key he wears around his neck and sits in the sudden quiet among the shapes that have come into being through his hands. *The Final Dissolution of the Fleeting-Improvised German Men*. He regards their tortured topographies in the dark and wonders how much longer they'll serve to contain the energies he's learned to fit inside them. How much longer, he wonders, until they overflow and the Armageddon they represent is visited upon their many admirers, and, after that, upon me too?

And would it be worse if that Armageddon came, or if it never did? If all this, this life's work, proved to be no more than fifty years spent dithering in mediocrity, sublimating the fear of nothing happening into the fear of something epochal about to arrive? Fifty years servicing a dozen Chancellors as an official totem-maker, a sculptor of futures too awful to be real, and, by that token, guaranteed not to be. A master of transubstantiation, turning apocalypses into collectors' items. A master decorator of the Europe Room, like Bosch and Picasso and Bacon before me.

Perhaps—once he starts, he can never stop—all this is no more than an old man's florid way of wondering how much time he has left. Something in the smallness of this possibility appeals to him, so he decides to make it his date for the

357

evening, and go out on the town, forgetting, for now, the larger questions that the smaller ones always lead to.

Heartened, he pulls up his blazer so it sits right on his still-manly shoulders and lets himself out through the service door, back into what is, to all appearances, still the city of Berlin, the new capital of Europe in all its post-Wall glory, Germany having achieved a level of power through apparent compromise that it never could have through overt aggression.

He walks along Unter den Linden in the hot, soft night, careful not to look up at the sky, or the ceiling that passes for sky, if, as he often suspects, every apparent exit from the Europe Room is merely an entrance to another wing of it.

Without choosing a direction, he strides past the rubble of the Reichstag as it begins to regrow after tonight's bombing. He looks down and sees the hairless head of a young man rolling along the sidewalk, and he stoops to pick it up. Holding it at some remove from his Hermés undershirt, he watches the last of its blood drip out, hardening the look of self-serious resolve frozen on its face. A crude impulse to pull its lips into a clown grin comes over him, but he suppresses it, letting the head fall from his hands and roll away.

He considers a new sculpture of the wreckage, perhaps with the head cast in bronze somewhere in the array, or free to roll within it, kicked by the show's visitors to add an element of interactivity, but he can't pretend he hasn't exhausted the possibilities of this concept many iterations ago, and is now only playing through old instincts, indulging in memories of his prime, when there was so much left to sculpt, so much that he was certain the people of Europe still needed to see. No, better to let the work stand as it is. He's done what he can with this particular rubble, falling, as it does, the same way every time. He's collected enough, more than enough, heads for one lifetime. He's seen the Reichstag regrow more than enough times, only to be razed again.

Soon that boy's body will reconstitute itself, just like the Reichstag, just like everything else, sinking below the pavement and down into the rot of memory that constitutes the physical earth, while a new boy, identical in appearance if not quite in essence, will stand up at dawn, a little hungover, clad in new skin that already feels old, and walk to the gym, afraid that he's lost touch with something primal and overwhelming, that he's forgotten the innermost thing without ever becoming able to say what it is.

Flaccid invasion upon flaccid invasion, making mythomaniacs of us all.

Kiefer shakes his head. There was a time, closer to middle age, when he still believed in bodies, real bodies, to which his sculptures, no matter how much they sold for, were only tributes. "The corpses fall into the chasm between mutually exclusive accounts of history," he remembers writing one June or July afternoon in his journal sometime in the late 90s, a journal that has since been published by Taschen to be sold at museum gift shops around the world. "Only the corpses, seen by all, claimed by none, are real."

And yet, he wonders now, are they? Are they any realer than anyone's account of what's happened, or what's happening, or what's about to? Now, at this age, he finds he's come to doubt it. He's come to doubt that his work, in aggregate, amounts to any more than fetishes for ghoulish princes in inherited castles, holy relics of a dead world, proof, for what it's worth, to those ghouls, that they are the sole survivors of a species-annihilating cataclysm. And perhaps they are. Locked away, shuffling in decaying silk robes and leather slippers past priceless hellscapes riveted to stone walls, gazing upon what, to them, indicates the state the outside world has fallen into.

Kiefer walks on, as more thoughts of age, of time passing, accrue. He shivers, despite the heat, and forces his attention off the bomb site and onto a row of bars up ahead, all of them glowing dim orange, some empty and some full. The full ones are surely aflame with gossip about the attack, fear and excitement mingling as they always do. The communal forgetting that it's happened before mingling with communal hope that, soon enough, it'll all be alright. That the dam will hold this one last time. Everyone waits for the Chancellor's speech, even if only to mock it.

It doesn't matter which bar he chooses, only that he chooses soon. Remaining alone on the street while the city reverts can be dangerous. He chooses one and orders a peaty scotch, neat, and swirls it in its glass, gazing at the reflected light in the swirl and deciding to drink this one, then one more, and then be on his way. Out of Berlin, yet again, and back to his congress with the forces that have staked their claim in the Black Forest.

When he's finished his second scotch and settled the tab, he'll walk, through the smoke and the heat and the pre-dawn light, back to the Hauptbahnhof in silence. When he gets there, he'll settle onto his usual bench and wait for the train that the Soft Illuminati—he resents that facile term, but they've given him no other to call them by—always send. When it arrives, he'll board, alone, and leave the city once again, speeding through the sleeping suburbs of the former East before veering south, back to Baiersbronn and his studio, where, until his heart or his liver gives out, he'll go on sculpting Europe's certain doom in peace.

The Chancellor

The Chancellor jerks awake in the king-sized bed of her Berlin residence when the news comes in. She can't remember if an aide told her over the intercom, or if she received a text, or if she heard it on the TV that'd been left on overnight. All she feels, as she crosses the carpet to the bathroom and runs the faucet, is déjà vu. Of course this precise event—whatever its nature turns out to be—hasn't happened before, but its contours, its mood, its overall atmosphere, are so familiar she can't shake the sense that nothing's required of her other than to walk along a track that's already been set out, up to a podium where, in essence, she stands already, talking and talking and talking. Nothing more is required—she massages soothing cream into the hard, sore creases beside her nose— and nothing more is permitted.

She steps into the shower and basks in the steam and then, as she's stepping out, watches the bathroom fill with Soft Illuminati. They materialize out of the steam such that they become completely coterminous with it, as if they'd had no bodies beforehand. Now the room is full of them and their rosewater reek, and empty of steam. All at once, it's cold and dry. The Chancellor shivers in her towel, though she knows better than to call for help or make any effort to oppose whatever mission has brought them here.

"Many, many, many iterations of you ago," they say, their German archaic and over-enunciated, the way she's always imagined the diction of the priggish university professors who refused to recognize Nietzsche's genius, "a deal was struck. A peace was set in motion." She shivers. "You will appear before the people today, on Alexanderplatz, and reassure them that the new Reichstag will hold. That, once again, the terror is behind them. The markets have reopened, the malls have reopened, the schools and the airports have reopened. The borders have reopened. Everything is open. The topography has stabilized. The waves have receded. The fever has broken once again, and good health is projected from here on out."

The Soft Illuminati condense into a single man, his expression flustered, as if he's just now arrived. Then they return to steam. The room grows hot and wet again, and there's no sign that any visitation has occurred. She swallows, tasting menthol and eucalyptus, and returns to her facial regimen, determined to focus all her energy on the grave occasion to come.

"Last night's bombing," she tells herself in the mirror, as her face wavers in the steam, "was not an isolated incident. It was—insofar as our intelligence at this point indicates— part of the string of increasingly deadly attacks ravaging the continent. Provocations of war. Yet, and mark my words here, the German people choose peace, this time, as every time from now on. We, as the model citizens of Europe's foremost liberal democracy, will not be goaded into fighting fire with fire. Literal fire, in this case," she jokes, looking to her left, as if over there, beside or behind the toilet, the burning Reichstag were to be found. She promises herself that she'll remove this line when the crowds at Alexanderplatz are actually before her. "The Reichstag lies in shambles, for the second time in a hundred years. But this time, unlike that ignominious winter night in '33, we will not be dragged to the brink by the forces that would drag us there. This time, we—"

She's behind the podium, looking out at rows of faces, all of them awaiting her pronouncement.

She closes her eyes and shivers with a degraded, generations-old memory of standing at this very podium, before this very crowd, to announce the formal death of the twentieth century and the dismantling of its solemnest memorial. This very crowd, or one much like it. "The Reichstag," she hears herself say, "may have burned last night, but what's important to remember is that..."

Before she can hear herself reveal what's important to remember, she thinks, much as I appear the same as the woman who stood before these people back then, they appear the same as the people who stood before me. Or her. She shivers again, uncertain how many versions of herself she's cycled through between then and now. And how many versions of them. How many times has the population of Germany died and been reborn, new matter poured into the same molds, collectively agreeing to pretend that a new leaf has been turned over?

She looks for the Soft Illuminati, willing them to appear, to tell her that none of this is her responsibility, that there was never anything she could do, and yet, she wonders, what would I have done, if I could have?

What would I do, if I could?

"The Ragnar Wave, the killings on the beaches, on the mountain passes, in the land tunnels, in the new geographies, the reports of Atlantis resurfacing..." She grasps the podium and shakes, opening her mouth wide in the hope of giving the spirit that animates her an escape route. Pour out of this skinsack, and let a new me pour in.

But no such thing transpires. The crowd remains in its position, and she remains in hers.

"The badness, the violence, the doom," she hears herself continue. "Behind us, all of it, at last. The Reichstag burned but it has been rebuilt, or else it almost burned but, in the end, did not, or... whichever way you'd like to see it, it's up to you. No one's telling you what to think. And the poor souls implanted with wires and concrete and covered with skin, the so-called Living Wall? They've been cured, every last one of them. That case is closed, I'm happy to say. A matter of literature from here on out."

She closes her eyes and sinks into a gallery of horrible footage of forced surgeries, of wires being pulled by machine from mottled expanses of flesh, of the screaming and begging of old women as the rusted, blood-covered remnants of the Wall are torn from their torsos and shipped to a medical waste facility in Wuppertal. A series of images that either actually occurred, or that she saw on YouTube, or both.

"Lastly, before we all disappear," she says, flashing back to the warm summer noontime of Baiersbronn. "Before we all *disperse*, rather, it is my pleasure to announce that a suitable new monument has been selected for the space formerly occupied by the Holocaust Memorial. The Future Museum is to be occupied by a full-scale replica of the cottage in which our nation's greatest living historian, Anika Schulz, composed her masterpiece, *Reflections on Normal Life in Southern Germany*. In which the names Goethe, Schiller, Kleist, Hoffman, Rilke, Kafka, Walser, Hesse, Mann, Grass, and Sebald, among dozens of others, were coaxed from the darkness of the woods and wrestled into concrete sentences from which we all may better ourselves, fortifying our minds so that we never lose them again.

The cottage in which, indeed, the very groundwork for our national culture was laid, rescued from a maw of unutterable satanism. Sacrifice, spirit worship, ghoulishness beyond measure... from this, from the very heart of the heart of the infection at the heart of the Black Forest and thus, indeed, at the heart of the nation, and therefore the heart of the continent, Professor Schulz rescued something of transcendental value. Wagner, Röntgen, Einstein. Heidegger. I could go on. Instead, I leave it to you to visit the cottage, being erected as we speak upon the site of the former Holocaust Memorial."

With that, the Chancellor bows to a fresh round of applause and allows her aides to escort her away from the podium and back to her car. "Take me down there," she instructs the driver. "Down below. I'm ready."

He nods, though he does not look at her, and the Chancellor lies against the headrest and wonders if, in the end, it's up to her to say when she's ready, and, if not, who or what else gets to decide. She closes her eyes, only opening them when the car passes the Reichstag, gleaming in all its rebuilt glory, beside a scale model of the same building in a state of utter devastation, molten flames consuming it from within, heads strewn in the rubble out front. The new Kiefer installation. So that we never forget how close we came.

György

György wanders through the shade of dense evergreens, itching his skin and rubbing his head, taking his time, letting the question of where he is and how he got here linger. The trees smell fresh, maybe too fresh, and the dirt underfoot is too hard, packed over concrete, but he takes it for what it appears to be, unaware of any other move he might make.

He jostles for space, passing through the forest with a crowd of others, tourists, families, far more people than he remembers having been there—*here*, he corrects himself—before. Whatever. Pigs, cows, legions of the flaccidly-invaded. Let them mill about, sculling across the soft but resistant surface of history. The pretend forest floor, the closest they'll ever come to the real thing. His destination grows clear: the cottage up ahead, barely visible through the crowd, but coming into definition a little more with each step.

He forces his way toward it, determined to make his way back inside, hoping that there he'll finally remember whatever it is that's now bobbing in the murk at the bottom of his memory, just present enough for its existence to be known, and just obscured enough for its nature not to be. Once there, he hopes, shoving his way past a fat gaggle, I'll either remember what it is or forget about it all together. The journey I embarked upon from that bedroom...

He shoulders open the door of the Future Museum and lurches in past the smell of fresh varnish and paint, looking for his old room. He gropes past the guides who stand by the entrance proffering brochures, past the gift shop café selling strudel and Milchkaffee, past the automated speakers narrating the legend of Professor Schulz's heroic discovery of German culture, past the bookshelves selling *Reflections on Normal Life in Southern Germany* in 20 languages and screens showing footage from the wildly popular, ongoing TV adaption, and down the hallway that he walked down so many times before.

The crowds thin out once he's past the main room, where the exhibits are clustered, and he's able to make his way into his old bedroom without being held up. Before he's all the way inside, the smell of damp rags and sweat tells him he's come to the right place. He coughs and looks in the direction of his old bed, lingering a moment on Ute's sandaled feet before scanning the rest of her, taking in the full familiarity of her ropey hair and oversized jacket.

She looks back at him with the same partial recognition she displayed at the Kiefer opening, but something in her expression is softer now, less gritty, more resigned. György's seen videos of the surgeries, the forced wire and concrete removals, the surgical waste center in Wuppertal, itself now a hub of collectors' items, robbed by armed gangs on an almost nightly basis. A first glance at Ute is enough to tell him she's undergone the treatment.

A second reveals she's soon to die.

He looks behind him, at the tour group mulling around in the hallway, and eases the door shut, buying himself a minute or two alone with her. Then he creeps over to the bed and sits down, noticing that his rain-soaked *Selected Works of Novalis* is still on the shelf. This brings a smile to his face, despite the somberness of the situation.

"How long do you have left?" he asks, skipping the few pieces of small talk he might've offered first.

Ute smiles appreciatively and coughs, massaging her side, which he can now see is thick with gauze and peeling surgical tape. "Not long. Would you do something for me?"

He nods without asking what it is. What else am I doing? Registering for the fall semester at Humboldt, arguing my way back into the courses I failed last year? He nods again, eager for any real assignment.

She pulls her coat open further, revealing not just the gauze and tape, but a paper bag overflowing with wallets. She grins wider. "I've been collecting these all day. When tourists enter a museum, they don't believe that anything real can happen to them. It was almost too easy."

She laughs, then continues. "The Wall, whatever's left of us, they're out there, for real this time. Deep in Siberia. Near Yakutsk. Before they pulled my wires... I picked up the signal. Would you drive me there? It's the only place where I can die as more than a dog."

György nods again, as dread and excitement at the prospect of the journey comingle inside him. Then the bedroom door opens and the tour guide says, in English, "And here, folks, are models of Anika's elderly mother, Ute, and her wayward,

Romantic son, Georg. You'll remember both from the book.
Aren't they lifelike?"

György & Ute

After buying a beat-up van at a chop shop in Friedrichshain with the money from a few of Ute's wallets, they set out, due east, once again toward the Russian border. They have papers this time, easily forged, and, together, they're determined to cross over.

György drives, dreaming of the road to Hungary as he rolls over the ruins of the DDR, then into Poland, then Lithuania, then Latvia. Back in Kuldiga, Ute leans against the window and bids farewell to this town where what she now considers the culminating phase of her journey began. "Thank you for setting me on my course," she whispers, "though I thank you for nothing else."

György helps her change her gauze and tape, and feeds her kebab and caramel creams and Polish beer. Soft, wet rubble, but appreciated nonetheless.

Straggling contingents of bald, bearded Nordmen cluster in the doorways of motels and roadside restaurants, but now they look like middle-aged dads reenacting a war from another chapter of history, its ground conditions dormant until they flare back up, a generation or two from now, when the old reasons have become new again.

When he gets tired or drunk enough, György can still make out the contours of the Europe Room around the edges of his vision, the brutal slabs of mountains boxing the continent in, and the dull skin flaps covering the sky so completely they've now blotted out all memory of what's behind them, and thus, in effect, eclipsed themselves and become the sky. But, most of the time, that schema—along with the earlier schema of the Game—feels quaint, like the delusions of a simpler century. As defunct as the Enlightenment. Another failed world-system in an infinite succession, each replacing the last with something lesser.

He drives east and east, picturing the doctoral thesis he could write on this topic, the procession of schemas, of unifying theories of existence, that are born, grow up, face conundrums, grow old, and die, leaving nothing but piles of wilted skin behind, from which the next generation will be hastily and inexpertly made. For a time, he lets himself enjoy the prospect of writing such a paper, or such a book. Perhaps it really isn't too late to resume a normal life. Become a philosophy professor in Budapest, a respected man with a past he only discusses in certain company. A Hungarian hero who invaded Russia and lived to tell the tale. After all, he thinks, maybe in whichever Europe I'm in now, all I did was kill one old woman. Or not even that: all I did was help one old woman kill herself.

Help one already dying old woman die.

Almost nothing.

He closes his eyes and pictures the shredded private investigator in the woods. Then Ute groans, crinkling her gauze, and a smell of running blood fills the van, and he knows it's time to pull over.

After what feels like many days, they reach the border, the station in Eastern Latvia beyond which the real Russia begins. It's just before dawn, and a short line of cars and trucks precedes them, rolling through at a sleepwalking pace, the gestures of the drivers and the border agents synced up, as if they all go through these same motions at the same time every day.

When it's György's turn to drive up to the window, he gathers the papers that Ute pulled from the glove compartment and nudges her, encouraging her to perk up and downplay the gravity of her damage.

He hands the papers across to the clean-shaven, green-capped agent, and says nothing until the man asks a question in Russian. It hangs in the air, diffusing while the sun rises up ahead.

Then, just before the man repeats himself, or switches to English, Ute replies in Russian, her words slow and faltering, her eyes filling with tears. The man nods curtly, asks something else, to which Ute responds in the same manner, wiping her nose, and then he nods again, stamps their papers, and hands them back, already waving the next car up.

Like so, at last, they roll across the border, through the quantum tunnel or wormhole at the edge of the Europe Room, and into the sunrise. György doesn't ask Ute what she said, and he can tell that she'll never say it again.

However long the drive out of Europe felt, it's nothing compared to what comes next. György drives on and on and on into the sunrise, playing back over memories of the last time he and Ute crossed the frontier, headed for Atlantis. This, now, feels like a reprise of that, an attempt, however futile, to reconnect with their previous journey, when time and space did not behave as they do now. Certain stretches of road feel familiar, though they don't last long or appear often. When the familiarity recedes, it's impossible to say what combination of psychic and atmospheric effects gave rise to it until, suddenly, it returns.

The smell of blood and pus fills the van, even with the windows open, and Ute turns ever more yellow-green, her breath ragged and short. She directs him with her eyes screwed shut, spending the last of her mental energy on getting the route right. It's mostly long stretches of the same road, probably one of only a few highways that cut east across the country once Moscow and its vast environs are behind them. Every so often, she tells him to take an exit and then they're driving through sprawling farmland or barren steppe, with no landmarks in sight until, hours later, she mutters, "Take a left here," or, "Take a right there."

He follows her directions as precisely as he can, the land growing alternately mountainous and flat, even flatter than before, concave almost, as the sky retains a grayness that makes it impossible to tell whether it's still skin or now, at last, ether once again. Sometimes the road hypnotizes him and he pictures the van driving up the wall of the Europe Room, and other times he pictures the Europe Room as a small, porous box far behind them, a jeweled trinket abandoned on a dead relative's mantelpiece.

Then, after an unquantifiable stretch of such travel, the skin opens up. Genuine, piercing blue shines through, and the smell of salt and brine pours into the open windows, and Ute opens her eyes and groans, "We're here."

György cuts the engine at the foot of a cement wall, standing in a semi-circle around the coastline of what he imagines must be the very northeast coast of Russia, out beyond Yakutsk, facing the Arctic Ocean and the narrow top of the world, the air cleaner than any he's ever tasted.

She unzips her coat and peels off her tape and gauze, revealing the open wound. It weeps into the cupholder between the driver's and passenger's seat as she knees her door open and rolls out, falling onto the ground and forcing György onto his feet and around the van to help her.

She holds her arms out to him and he heaves her upright and tries to walk her in the direction of the wall, but she digs her heels into the soft earth. Stopping short, she says, "Thank you for this, Georg. If you hadn't taken me here, I would've wandered till I dropped."

Tearing up a little, he waits for her to say more, but she doesn't. After a silence punctuated by the waves crashing on the rocky coast, he can tell she won't. So he nods, thinking, *you're welcome.*

Then he reestablishes his grip under her arms and walks her toward a ladder against the wall. When they reach it, he positions her almost inert body against the base, squeezes her fingers around the rungs, places her feet lower down, and pushes her upward, climbing behind her, moving her hands one rung at a time, flashing back to when he could leap up in a single heroic motion with her on his shoulders.

When they reach the top, she can't stand. He rolls her onto the narrow ledge, face-first, so she can look down into the pit of bodies, many of them looking back up at her. He pictures a long goodbye here, the two of them together in silence, once again atop the wall at the edge of the world, peace ascendant over the coastline. A long spell reminiscing together on all they've been through, a grandson bidding his grandma farewell. But, before any such dynamic can take effect, she rolls over and is gone. He watches her sink in, the bodies reaching up to claim her, and he begins to cry. Even after such a long journey together, it feels too soon.

Through his tears, he sees Klara—her face comes back to him from the Black Forest—emerge from the tangle and wrap her arms around Ute, bearing her down to whatever death or new life awaits at the bottom of the pile. The sea breeze blows cool and heavy across the scene, and the sun, once again, rises from even further east, over Japan, illuminating the final resting place of the Berlin Wall.

———————————

György stands there all day, looking down at the pit of bodies, hundreds and hundreds deep, most of them dead, some still dying, and perhaps some already coming back to life. He looks down and, as his tears dry, he feels his chest open. Arisztid Huszár swells back up inside him, the old possessing spirit taking hold once again. He hears Ragnar shooting back up through the ground and the Age of Mythic Battle rolling back into position, like a slide in a projector. I slew all these infidels, he tells himself. I tore down the Wall that sought to limit my kingdom. Just like I torched that synagogue in Copenhagen and blew up the Soft Illuminati Reichstag in Berlin. All lies in ruin beneath me; none are equal to my might. He watches the pit, still writhing, Ute's face reappearing on occasion, until the sun starts to set, turning its back on the pagan East.

Then he climbs down the ladder, careful not to slip in the dusk, and gets back behind the wheel of the van, which will soon need more gas. He turns it around, facing west once again, and steels himself for the drive back to Europe. Back to Hungary, at long last. Where he'll return as Arisztid Huszár, conquering hero and redeemer of the land, sanctifier of the eternal Magyar Kingdom, never again to be crushed under the boot of foreign occupation.

He sets the van in motion, taking his time to conserve gas and, with it, the feeling of victory. Of the Hero's Return, which all young soldiers going off to war dream of. Because already, as the Arctic Ocean recedes behind him, he feels it fading, leaving him in the body of a boy nearing his twentieth birthday, with a consciousness he can neither escape nor embrace, and nothing to look forward to but a return to his native country after a year abroad, where, because he knows he won't kill himself until his life's work is done, he'll have to find some way to live. Having escaped the Europe Room, it turns out there's nothing to do but drive back in.

Anika

Anika wakes to her alarm in her new four-story townhouse in Prenzlauer Berg, and steels herself for the first day of the fall semester. She plods downstairs to the kitchen and sets the water to boil, and, while she waits, regards the gnarled contours of the Kiefer that the Chancellor gave her as a thank-you gift for services rendered to the nation. *Kleindorf's Strudel* reads the text at the bottom, in tortured Gothic script, half-erased and buried in a sea of rust and rot, a backdrop now for the steam off her espresso. Life goes on, she marvels, with equal parts revulsion and relief, as she drenches a bowl of muesli in goat's milk. When she's finished, she showers and dresses. Then she gathers her notes and a first edition of her new book, and sets out for Humboldt.

Back in the big lecture hall now, she locks the door and begins her private preparations, calibrating her gaze and her voice to dominate the giant interior. She sets up her PowerPoint— photos of the carnage in Copenhagen, in Amsterdam, around the Reichstag, and of Breivik, shirtless with a PS4 controller in hand, and of long lines of men and women with wire-implants and tattooed graffiti, fountains of drowned effigies and makeshift auction houses around the medical waste facility in Wuppertal—and casually rehearses her speech.

"Yet again, Europe approached the brink, and yet again it has retreated from it. The eternal is to be found in culture, in music, in art, not in..."

A creak at the door distracts her, and, before she can engage her faculties of reason, she's overwhelmed by a dead certainty that it's the Hungarian skinhead from last year. She sees him slinking into the room, sullen and musclebound, his talking points already on the tip of his tongue. She shivers to realize that part of her hopes it's the case. Despite everything, part of her misses him. My creep of a son. She smiles.

The door creaks open further and something else enters. Not a boy, nor anything especially human. A thing, a presence, like the remnant of Gerhard that used to visit her at night in her apartment in Mitte. Gelatinous, translucent, it develops just enough of a face to mouth a curse that will hover above whatever else may happen in this room.

Then it resolves into the body of a young man in new jeans and a tucked-in plaid shirt, who says, in pleasant, Hamburg-accented German, "It's an honor to make your acquaintance, Professor. Your books changed my life."

She nods and tries to thank him, then turns her attention to the subject at hand: normal life in Southern Germany, its continuity even now, on the eve of the election that many quadrants of the Internet are still swearing Ulli Harz will win, despite his most vocal adherents having gone to ground.

As her head fills with the gentle fragrances and ambient birdsong of Baiersbronn, she feels it growing heavy, too heavy for her body to support, and then her body grows too heavy for the floor to support, and then she's sinking, out of her body, out of the lecture hall, out of Berlin, out of the Germany that Ulli Harz, if he exists, may soon command.

Down below, she fills out another version of her body, fresher, healthier, as the familiar smell of used books comes to suggest a bookstore. "And here is one of my all-time favorites," she hears herself tell a camera crew, her lips pulled up into a dimpled smile, her tongue still tingling with the salt and schmaltz of her afternoon pretzel. "Robert Walser's *Jakob von Gunten*. The intricate beauty of these sentences, page after page after page, its haunted yet fully self-aware vulnerability, its delicate mix of childish whimsy and adult resignation, is, quite simply..."

She breaks off to stare into the camera, waiting to hear what she'll say next.

The Mayor

Mayor Havermeyer fills her briefcase with papers and sets out along the road home, having shepherded Baiersbronn past the rocky shoals of another day, once again to the safe harbor of evening. She nods to the few souls still working in the Town Hall past sundown, crosses the square, acknowledges the closed facades of Kleindorf's and Schönnenhof's, passes the crew filming this week's installment of the ever more popular *Normal Life in Southern Germany* show, and heads toward the Aldi where, after all these years, she still does her shopping.

She goes on making friendly eye contact with those inside, smiling at young mothers with children in the top racks of their shopping carts, and at elderly men and women clutching their wallets against their chests while squinting at the labels on cans of peas. All wear versions of the Mayor's face, some more weathered and some fresher than others.

When she's gathered the week's modest bundle, she pays, nods to the sullen teenager who works the till, and sets out on the road, shivering and casting her eyes down when she passes the corporate campus where Karlheinz Bauer works. Though she continues to look away, she can't help noticing that one light is on. Third floor, second office from the end, same as always. He's there, watching me, she knows. Putting his affairs, and by extension those of the Soft Illuminati, which are in turn those of the Hard Illuminati, which are in turn our own—it's impossible not to reiterate this chain of command, no matter how many times she's done so before—in order. Deciding the outcome of tonight's election.

She quickens her pace, half-expecting to find him barring her way, a train ticket to Berlin in his outstretched hand, his suit damp and reeking of rosewater. "Only you can save the nation," she expects him to say, and part of her is disappointed when he doesn't. "If you go up there, if you make it into the Reichstag, we are prepared to offer you Baiersbronn."

"Offer me Baiersbronn?" She can't help rehashing the old conversation, now that she's standing exactly where it took place.

Bauer nods. "This town will be preserved as you remember it. No matter what happens up there. We will see to that. It's not much, but it's the best guarantee we can make. It is, let me be very clear, the only guarantee we can make. The *only* guarantee anyone can make. It's Baiersbronn or submersion beneath the waters of a sea that has not yet been named."

Then he vanishes back into memory, leaving the road empty, no one blocking her way home.

Shaken and squirrely, she makes it back to her house just as her husband turns on the TV. He issues a low, wordless sound when she takes a seat beside him, kicking her shoes off onto the carpet. Too tired to empty the grocery bags, let alone consider making dinner, she reaches inside, removes a bag of muesli, and eats it dry as the evening's episode of Anika's show wraps up. Anika concludes her customary visit to the antiquarian bookstore, rhapsodizing, this time, about the singular beauty of the sentences of Robert Walser, and then a commercial break intervenes.

The Mayor nibbles oats and filberts and tries to clear her mind of Karlheinz Bauer on the road, but she only gets partway through this process when the next segment begins.

"Election Night Special Coverage," blares the TV, its resolution waxing and waning. "Stay with us as we count the final votes to determine the nation's next Chancellor. Will it be incumbent Lena Havermeyer," an image of a woman that reminds the Mayor of herself flashes across the screen, "or will it be the mysterious upstart Ulli Harz, whose One Valhalla platform has galvanized and scandalized the nation in equal measure?"

A digital image of a smooth white egg flashes across the screen, hovering, fulminating, as if something inside is itching to hatch.

Havermeyer closes her eyes and inhales, the dander off her husband mixing with the sweat from her own armpits. She loosens her collar and removes her bra from under her blouse, trying to accommodate her quickening breath. She closes her eyes as the anchor reads, "As of this count, it's looking like Harz is in the lead with…"

Failing to keep her eyes closed, she gets to her feet and drifts out of the house, through the woods, and back up the road, past the Aldi and into the parking lot of the corporate campus. The anchor's voice follows her, filling the air.

"It's looking more and more likely that Harz, who's promised to hatch from his egg and show himself in public if elected, is going to..."

She crosses the lot to pound on the locked glass doors, waving her arms at the sensors, which blink red but don't otherwise respond.

"Please!" she shouts. "Herr Bauer! It's urgent. They're going to destroy the country. Send me back there. Let me stop them. I can do it. Just tell me how to find the train to Berlin."

The building remains locked; the light she saw before is off now. An empty shopping cart rolls across the concrete. The anchor's voice devolves, sighing syllables and heavy breath, the word "Harz" audible among them.

It's too late. I could have done it, she thinks, turning from the silent edifice, which now seems long-abandoned, the seat of some transnational company that folded years ago, or consolidated its offices in much bigger cities. One of the old draws to Baiersbronn, bringing jobs and money and schoolchildren. Gone now. All gone. The town cut off from the nation, left to its own devices. An island in the heart of the Black Forest.

Havermeyer shivers, wondering where her body is, whether it's here in this cold parking lot beside the Aldi, or in her warm home beside her faceless, dander-smelling husband, or up above, far away, in the heat and noise of Berlin, deciding, while she still can, whether to concede to Harz or contest the election.

She feels small, smaller than she ever has, miniscule compared to the world and its cacophony. But also, at the same time, safe, insulated, like she got out just in time.

Tomorrow's another day. She wanders, resolved to watch the sunrise over the town she loves so much. I won't return home tonight, she decides. I'll keep vigil, see to it that, even as they rip the nation apart up there, all stays intact down here. The eye of the storm, the still point in the turning universe. Wasn't I promised that much?

She roams through the hours past midnight, circling the abandoned square and the locked façade of the Town Hall and the Antiquariat with Walser in the window, until she finds herself at the train station, alone on a bench, beside a trash can overflowing with beer bottles and candy wrappers.

Gazing at the abandoned tracks, one for the northbound train and one for the southbound, she tries to tally up how many times she's boarded the Regionalbahn to Bamberg, and there transferred to the Express to Berlin. A hundred? A thousand?

She can't be sure. Letting the tally go, she lingers on the tracks, taking solace in the notion that no trains come here anymore. That whatever becomes of Berlin, and Hamburg, and Frankfurt, and Munich, will have no repercussions in Baiersbronn. That, after all these iterations, all these lifetimes, all this history, Normal Life in Southern Germany has been preserved.

She hears something as the sun rises in the far-off East. A distant rumble. She jumps, aware that her instinct is to hurry away before a train, if it's coming, pulls into view. But she forces herself to sit still. No, she resolves, as the distant rumble draws closer. If a train comes, if it turns out that, even after all this, they still aren't through with me, that my presence is still required on Alexanderplatz, then I'll be there, so that some future version of myself will, after dozens or hundreds of future wars are fought, be able to live here in peace, sitting on this bench and watching the sun arrive from Russia without fear of what it portends. And in essence that woman is here already, she knows, because the bench and the tracks and the station house with the bathrooms padlocked shut will never change, nor will the pines and oaks overhanging the tracks and so, even as I board the train and take my seat and review the notes Karlheinz Bauer has sent me off with—even as I do this now, or remember doing it years ago, or imagine doing it years from now—the better part of me remains below, setting off into another bright blue morning in Baiersbronn, ruminating as I walk from the edge into the center, on the question of Kleindorf's or Schönnenhof's, apple strudel or cherry.

Acknowledgements

I am sincerely grateful to the following people for their help in developing this book and bringing it into the world, a process that began in 2018. First and foremost, as ever, to Miette Gillette for her fearless stewardship and vision in making Whiskey Tit everything it is, and creating a vibrant and dynamic home for work like this. Also to Patrick McGrath, John Reed, Avinash Rajendran, Gabriel Frye-Behar, John Waterfall, Michael Natalie, and John Kazanjian who read this book in early drafts, to Thomas Kendall who read it later on and helped usher it into the world, and to Andrei Cristea and Michal Labik who read it in the middle and provided invaluable insight into contemporary Eastern Europe. Much of the factual backstory of Anders Breivik and the July 22 massacre comes from *One of Us* by Åsne Seierstad. Lastly, thanks, as ever, to my wife Ingrid for the support, encouragement, and editing all along the way.

About the Author

David Leo Rice is the author of several novels, including *The New House*, *Angel House*, and the *Dodge City* trilogy, as well as the story collection *Drifter*, named one of the "10 Must-Read Collections of 2021" in the Southwest Review. His next collection, *The Squimbop Condition*, will be out in 2025. He's online at: www.raviddice.com.

About the Publisher

Whisk(e)y Tit is committed to restoring degradation and degeneracy to the literary arts. We work with authors who are unwilling to sacrifice intellectual rigor, unrelenting playfulness, and visual beauty in our literary pursuits, often leading to texts that would otherwise be abandoned in today's largely homogenized literary landscape. In a world governed by idiocy, our commitment to these principles is an act of civil service and civil disobedience alike.

Milton Keynes UK
Ingram Content Group UK Ltd.
UKHW022120070524
442340UK00022B/627

'An exuberant, indulgent romp of a novel … *Butter* is a full-fat, Michelin-starred treat … Let this book bring you under its spell – then make yourself some rice with butter'   *The Sunday Times*

'Ambitious and unsettling … a thought-provoking and surprisingly feelgood take on friendship, transgressive pleasures, and society's impossibly contradictory expectations of women'   *Guardian*

'Part of the brilliance of *Butter* is its framing of individual eating habits as a mystery to be solved … It isn't entirely clear whether to read the novel or devour it'   *Observer*

'Cleverly intertwines paeans to the pleasures of eating with indictments of Japan's standards for women'   *New Yorker*

'When *Butter* originally came out, five years after the real-life killer Kijima received a death sentence for her murders, it became a cult bestseller … Yuzuki evokes a cold and alienating world'   *Financial Times*

'The perfect mix of crime thriller, twisted feminist fantasy and gourmet cooking – what more could you want?'   *Independent*

'Asako Yuzuki has turned [*Butter*] into not just a fascinating psychological puzzle but also a damning indictment of Japanese misogyny and fatphobia'   *New York Times*

'A biting satire on fat-shaming culture and double standards in beauty'   *Financial Times*

'This Japanese novel, which has become quite the cult phenomenon, is nothing short of ingenious'   *iNews*

'Like *The Martha Stewart Show* meets *The Silence of the Lambs* ... it's the uneasy, persistent social misogyny, and how it polices social norms and expectations, that is the novel's true focus. Simmering through the book is the refrain that each of us has to learn to listen to our own tastes, desires and sense of satiation to find what constitutes a "good amount". *Butter* gives a healthy, easy-reading serving of social commentary, where only the gluttonous are innocent'

Art Review

'A tale of loneliness and desire, full of an urgency ... Even descriptions like "a perfect masterpiece" and "crème de la crème" are inadequate for a book like this' *Croissant Magazine*

'I have been glued to Asako Yuzuki's new novel *Butter* ... contains delicious descriptions' NIGEL SLATER, *Guardian Feast newsletter*

'Compelling, delightfully weird, often uncomfortable – and with fascinating insight into Japanese cultural mores and food – *Butter* will churn your brain and your stomach with panache'

PANDORA SYKES, author of
How Do We Know We're Doing It Right?

'An unputdownable, breathtakingly original novel about true crime, loneliness and female appetite in all its tricky, transgressive glory. I will be spoon-feeding *Butter* to every woman I know'

ERIN KELLY, author of *The Skeleton Key*

'A delectable meditation on appetite, fatphobia and misogyny in modern Japan – *Butter* is a salty morsel with one hell of a bite'

ALICE SLATER, author of *Death of a Bookseller*

'Yuzuki uses luscious food writing to fuel a nuanced and intelligent exploration of contemporary womanhood ... I devoured this dark and delicious novel' IMOGEN CRIMP, author of *A Very Nice Girl*

'With writing masterful enough that you gulp it down breathlessly ... full of the delight that comes from carrying you off to utterly unexpected destinations, this is a tour de force that will leave readers satisfied'   RYŌ ASAI, author of *The Kirishima Thing*

'An indubitable masterpiece'   DAISUKE YOSHIDA, *Shōsetsu Shinchō*

'A reading experience so rich it was like being swathed in melted butter'   *Fujin Kōron*

BUTTER

ASAKO YUZUKI

Translated by Polly Barton

4th ESTATE • *London*

4th Estate
An imprint of HarperCollins*Publishers*
1 London Bridge Street
London SE1 9GF

www.4thestate.co.uk

HarperCollins*Publishers*
Macken House, 39/40 Mayor Street Upper
Dublin 1, D01 C9W8, Ireland

First published in Great Britain in 2024 by 4th Estate
First published in the Japanese language as BUTTER by
SHINCHOSHA Publishing Co., Ltd in Tokyo in 2017

Fiction

1

A catalogue record for this book is
available from the British Library

ISBN 978-0-00-874187-7
ISBN 978-0-00-874335-2

Set in Adobe Caslon Pro
Printed and bound in India by
Replika Press Pvt. Ltd.

MIX
Paper | Supporting
responsible forestry
FSC™ C016779

CHAPTER ONE

The row of tall, narrow houses all in the same shade of ecru trailed up the gently sloping hill, with no end in sight. Everywhere in this well-kept neighbourhood left a seamlessly uniform impression, and Rika Machida had begun to feel as if she were circling round and round a single spot. The hangnail on the finger of her right hand, by now as cold as ice, was sticking right out.

It was the first time she'd got off at this stop on the Den-en-Toshi commuter line. Perhaps because it had been designed for car-owning families, the streets of this suburban neighbourhood, commonly considered the ideal place to raise children, were unfeasibly wide. With the map on her smartphone for guidance, Rika found herself traipsing through the area surrounding the station, which was teeming with housewives out to buy groceries for the evening meal. It was still hard for her to swallow the fact that Reiko had settled down here. The place was all mass retailers, family diners, and DVD rental shops – she hadn't passed a single bookshop that looked as if it had been there forever, or in fact any shop that appeared to be owned by an individual and not a corporation. There was not the slightest whiff of either culture or history.

The previous week, Rika had taken a day trip to a town on the southern island of Kyushu, to research a crime she was covering involving a young boy. The town had been overwhelmingly residential, with only the odd local supermarket and occasional sign for a cram school interrupting the sea of houses and apartment buildings. She'd passed a couple of high-school girls wearing skirts of a length she'd not encountered in Tokyo. Walking alone through the neighbourhood, the kind of place she would never visit if it wasn't for her work, Rika had felt her existence growing distant, as though her entire self, her entire life, were being erased.

At least here there was a place ready and waiting to welcome her, Rika told herself, in a bid to haul back her consciousness. With that, she set foot inside the shop, which she'd resolved would be the last she'd try. That scent unique to supermarkets of cool apples and wet cardboard enveloped her gently. At a stand on the supermarket floor, a middle-aged woman was frying meat on a hotplate, cutting it into bite-size pieces as she called out to customers in a high-pitched voice, entreating them to try it. Rika picked up one of the packs of pork on display. How long had it been since she'd looked at produce up close like this? The pretty pink-coloured meat and shining white fat jostled for place with each other, cool and moist.

She and Reiko had been texting since Rika had passed Futako-Tamagawa Station. Reiko had offered to come and meet her at the station, but Rika had said there was no need, and asked instead if there was anything that she could pick up on her way. That morning, Rika had returned home in the early hours and fallen into bed, sleeping till after lunch. She'd showered and worked on her preparatory report, then headed out to Shibuya for a meeting with a regular columnist. At some point, noticing the time with a start, she'd hurriedly brought the meeting to a close and leapt onto a train. There had been no time to go shopping. Reiko might have been a close friend, but their familiarity didn't assuage Rika's guilt about visiting her new marital home empty-handed. Reiko's reply came immediately, along with a cartoon rabbit sticker – it seemed that after having given up work last year, her silly side had finally returned: *If you're sure, then would you bring me some butter if you can find it? There's a shortage this winter, and I can't get my hands on any. But if you can't it really doesn't matter! I'd rather you got here quickly.*

The dairy section was bathed in a placid yellow light. On the bottom rack was an empty space about five shelves wide, with a notice taped in place: 'Due to product shortages, supplies of butter are limited to one item per customer.'

Rika had been to three supermarkets now and in each one it had been the same story. Resigning herself to the reality of the situation, Rika picked up the richest, butteriest-looking margarine variety from the selection, and quickly made her way to the cash registers.

Reiko's new house lay a five-minute walk from the station, on a gently sloping hill. The three-storey property, indistinguishable from those around it, had been designed to maximise space on the plot of land, no more than 100 square metres in size. The Toyota fitted so neatly into the parking space, it looked as though it had been made to measure. Alongside the front door was a line of planters with daisies, violas, and other kinds of flowers, while on the door hung an ivy wreath. This clear expression of Reiko's personality reassured Rika. Pushing the button to the intercom, she found herself exhaling in relief.

'Rika, you're here! Wow, how long has it been?'

No sooner was the door opened than Reiko had bolted out in her apron and was hugging her. Rika returned the embrace, wrapping her arms around Reiko's slender shoulders. At five foot five in height, Rika was significantly taller than petite, delicate Reiko, and when she hugged her, could encircle her fully with her long arms. The violet-like aroma that was Reiko's signature scent rose up from her hair. Rika felt her eyes growing hot. Perhaps, she thought, perhaps without realising it I've been starved of these expressions of affection, of the warmth of another human body.

The intensity of the greeting wasn't for show, either. The two friends had spent practically every day in each other's company at university, but they were well into adulthood now, and six months had passed since they'd last seen one another. Even after Reiko had given up her job, the busy nature of Rika's work made it hard to find time to meet. In theory, Rika had Tuesday and Wednesday to herself each week, but she didn't know any of her colleagues who actually managed to take proper days off – except for maybe Kitamura, a junior member of staff. Today was a Wednesday, but she'd had a meeting with a columnist earlier, and after finishing up at Reiko's she planned to go back to the office to do some research.

Rika could make out the aroma of dashi and melted cheese emanating from inside Reiko's house, fusing with that scent of fresh wood characteristic of new-builds. Putting on the warm fabric house slippers that her friend laid out for her, allowing her trenchcoat to be hung up, she moved down the shiny, immaculate parquet flooring of the hall towards a room illuminated by a lambent orange light. The living room that led on to the kitchen was a very average sort of space, but thanks to the Liberty print sofas and curtains, the dresser and bookshelves of antique dark wood, and the collages on the wall by an artist Rika didn't know, it had the feel of a cosy attic room. In fact, it reminded Rika of the apartment in Oyamadai where Reiko had previously lived by herself.

Rika rinsed her mouth and washed her hands at the bathroom sink, then wiped off her hands on one of numerous fluffy hand-towels that lay piled in a basket. Catching the delicate fragrance of fabric softener on the towels, Rika resolved to ask Reiko what brand she used – although it wasn't the sort of thing that she'd usually notice.

'I'm really sorry, Rei. Not only am I late, but all I could find was this.' Rika took out of the supermarket bag the offending item, a packet labelled 'Margarine Made With 50% Butter', and held it out sheepishly to her friend.

'Amazing! Thank you!' Reiko smiled and moved to the fridge to put the margarine away. If she were being honest, Rika couldn't really tell the difference between butter and margarine.

'I went round and round all the supermarkets here, but there was no butter to be found …'

'It's like in *The Story of Little Babaji*! Going round and round and ending up as butter!'

Giggling to herself, Reiko skipped back to where Rika stood in the living room, where she pulled an illustrated book off the shelf, and held it out triumphantly. Now she saw it, Rika had the sense that she had, indeed, read the book back when she was in nursery, but only had the haziest recollection of it.

'I've started buying picture books that I think might be good for the baby.'

The way that Reiko spoke made it seem as if her baby already existed in the world, Rika thought – as if they were all just waiting for it to appear in the room. It was the previous summer that the obstetrician had told Reiko it was likely that stress was to blame for the fact that two years into her marriage she still hadn't conceived, and Reiko had promptly quit her job in the PR department of a major film production company, which was so hectic that even finding time to make medical appointments had been difficult.

Now Rika stole a sideways glance at her friend, who was leafing through the picture book with evident pleasure.

There were still no signs that she was pregnant, yet she had an aura of maternal calm about her. She seemed much more at ease than when she'd been working – not only was her skin now free of make-up and her hair glossy and lustrous, but her light brown eyes seemed to sparkle, and her lips had a petal-like fullness to them. Under her ditsy-print skirt, she wore navy leggings and woollen leg warmers, presumably to protect herself from the cold. Her outfit was incomparably more casual than anything she'd worn in her working days, but she still looked stylish, with a touch of Parisian chic about her. So tiny and girlish in her looks was she that it was hard to believe she was thirty-three, the same age as Rika herself. When Reiko had resolved to give up the job that she was so good at, Rika had thought it a waste. Not just that – her friend's decision had produced in her a sense of loneliness and resentment that had left her sleepless. They had argued about it several times over the phone.

Peering over Reiko's shoulder to read the picture book, Rika found herself transported back to their time at university, when she and Reiko had often shared textbooks in the lecture hall. While out walking in the jungle, the young boy, Little Babaji, encounters a group of four tigers who steal his clothes and possessions. In their new finery, the tigers become distracted arguing over which is the grandest. Forgetting all about Little Babaji, they begin snapping at one another, biting each other's tails until they've formed a ring around a tree. Clamped together, they start chasing each other round and round, going so fast that they begin to melt into a yellow butter. Babaji's father finds the butter and brings it home, and there the melted tigers are slathered on hotcakes, ending up in the Babaji family's stomachs. This cruel turn of events is narrated with the utmost matter-of-factness.

'Babaji's family are quite merciless, don't you think?' said Reiko when they reached the end. 'I feel a bit sorry for the tigers.'

'What are you saying?' responded Rika. 'It's the tigers who are to blame! They tried to eat Babaji first, remember? I think the moral is that you shouldn't let your vanity make you so competitive that you're driven to self-destruction.'

As the two were immersed in dissecting the book, the door opened.

'Rika, you're here already!' said Ryōsuke. 'Good to see you.'

It seemed to Rika unthinkably early for Reiko's husband, who worked in the sales department of a medium-sized confectionery manufacturer, to be getting home from work. Ryōsuke had been a quarterback in the American Football team at college, and was exceptionally well-built. His most distinctive features were his eyes, which were always scrunched up into an amiable smile, and his rosy cheeks, like those of a small child. At first glance, he seemed like a person with whom Reiko would have little to talk about.

The pair had been brought together by the PR campaign for a film. Reiko's company had commissioned Ryōsuke's confectionery firm to make promotional tarts featuring the lead actress. In the meetings that followed, it was Reiko who'd taken a liking to him first. She'd known the first time she set eyes on him, she said – it had to be him. Ryōsuke was initially nonplussed by the way that Reiko, who seemed out of his league, had pursued him so intently, but had taken to her more introspective, innocent side. Having grown up in a rowdy family of five, to parents who got on well and together ran an izakaya in the part of Saitama where they lived, Ryōsuke had an open, laid-back way about him that alone was enough to attract Reiko. The itchy, jealous feelings that Rika had once harboured towards her friend's spouse had by now died down – though it was true to say that when she'd seen Reiko in her wedding dress, Rika had felt as though a piece of her own self had been stolen away.

Reiko set down on the table a selection of large plates, each of a different design and glaze, and the meal began.

Bagna càuda with a plentiful variety of steamed winter vegetables and a rich anchovy sauce, thinly cut slices of warmed salt pork, a tofu and leek gratin, rice cooked in an earthenware pot with vegetables and chopped oysters, and miso soup – the dishes had a vitality to them which came from using only the freshest ingredients, and though the seasoning was unobtrusive, all the flavours had pleasing depth. Weren't oysters supposed to be good for fertility? Rika thought as she brought to her lips a mouthful of rice enriched with soy sauce, whose smell put her in mind of the sea, shooting a glance over at her friend. She realised that she had more of an appetite than she could remember having in a long time, and that if this was largely owing to how delicious the food was, it was also in part to do with the way Ryōsuke ate, as if in a state of ecstasy.

'It is okay to have seconds? This pork is unbelievably tender. Honestly, you could serve this in a restaurant.' His eyes narrowed to threads of satisfaction, Ryōsuke held out his empty plate to his wife. Watching Reiko serving him her food with an air of great pride, Rika felt once again that she understood why Reiko had chosen him.

Suddenly she felt embarrassed about when she'd deemed the area bereft of culture earlier. They must have selected this neighbourhood together, planning their future based on Ryōsuke's salary, prioritising safety and convenience. Reiko had no intention of relying on her family for any financial support.

'I know people say this all the time, but this honestly makes me think I need a wife. You're a lucky man, Ryōsuke.'

Rika felt genuine envy for Ryōsuke, who sat in front of her with a carefree smile. He seemed to exude such a sense of ease, his skin glowing and his expression relaxed.

At work, too, Rika noticed that the married men of the older generation had a certain leisurely quality about them, in spite of how busy their days were. It seemed that most of their wives were home-makers. Rika had never considered that kind of life for herself, but she could see the power such women bestowed upon their families. Every night, those women would clean out the toxins that had built up in their partners' bodies and souls over the course of the day – toxins that, if left untouched for too long, would eat a person away. The elder male colleague of hers who had died unexpectedly at home last month had been single and lived alone. An image rose up in Rika's mind of her own cold apartment which she hadn't cleaned in some time – his had probably looked a lot like that. The apartment also closely resembled the one her father had inhabited by himself after his divorce.

'You should bring your boyfriend along next time! I've still never met him, you know.'

Oh yeah, now you mention it, I do have a boyfriend – Rika suppressed a smile at her own train of thought. Makoto Fujimura worked in the literary publishing section of Rika's company. Perhaps because they had started out as friends, their relationship was hardly what you could call romantic. During the week, the most they saw of one another was crossing paths in the corridor at work. All in all, they met maybe twice a month if they were lucky, when one of them stayed over at the other's apartment. And yet Makoto was still an invaluable pres-ence in her life, a person with whom to share life's respective burdens, and she was grateful too for the well-judged distance between them.

'Rika, what do you eat these days?' Reiko asked. 'Are you looking after yourself properly? You look like you've lost weight again. I was reading something the other day saying that the average calorie consumption of Japanese women today is lower than the levels recorded right after the Second World War.'

'That wouldn't surprise me. Honestly, I've neither the time nor the energy to cook. I don't even own a rice cooker. I mean, what'd be the point, when I'd never use it? Most evenings I'm out entertaining bureaucrats, or else having dinner with someone whose story I'm covering.'

'Entertaining bureaucrats, eh! I bet you get treated to all sorts of delicacies that mere mortals like us couldn't even dream of,' said Ryōsuke.

With this, Rika recalled the hours she'd spent the previous night in an expensive Ginza restaurant, where she'd been treated just like a waitress at a hostess bar whose job it was to entertain and flirt with men. Most bureaucrats would, from time to time, come up with a convenient 'misinterpretation' of the situation – would decide, for example, that a female journalist was approaching them not because she needed something to write about, but because she was attracted to them. The leek from the gratin, so soft and melting in its texture, suddenly tasted bitter in her mouth, and she switched topic.

'I don't understand anything about flavour, that's the problem. My taste buds are like a child's. I'm perfectly happy with convenience store bento boxes and curry from cheap restaurants.'

Food and fashion – the things that women were supposed to have a particular fondness for – had always left Rika indifferent. At her height, though, it was easy for her to look stocky, and she took care that her weight never exceeded 50 kilos. Perhaps that was in part the legacy of her mother, who had been very conscious of such things. Rika tried not to eat late at night. If she was entertaining clients and they ordered food, she only touched the vegetables and soup. In the convenience store outside the office that she went to twice a day, she went for healthy foods like yoghurt, salad and harusame noodles. She didn't have the time to go to the gym, but she tried to walk everywhere she could. Her slim physique ensured that, despite not being a remarkable beauty, she would still be complimented, and that the fast fashion items she chose haphazardly suited her figure just fine. Rika was in an industry where maintaining one's appearance tended to be rewarded with professional success. Back in her girls' school, too, her long, narrow eyes and slender boy's face had earned her many letters of admiration from younger girls.

'I don't think your sense of taste is lacking, Rika. Misaki always says that she didn't have any time for proper cooking, but she did a far, far better job as a single mother than my parents managed as a pair.'

Reiko was on first-name terms with Rika's mother, and referred to her affectionately as 'Misaki'.

Rika's parents had divorced soon after she'd started secondary school, and her mother took the split as an opportunity to take up co-ownership of a boutique that her friend had started up. She received no money from the divorce, and knowing they could expect no financial support from Rika's father, her mother worked constantly. She'd never been a particularly talented cook, but while married to Rika's father, she had tried to grace the dinner table with a variety of dishes. Once she began working, however, she turned to her daughter and said, 'I'm sorry to ask this, but do you mind giving me a hand from now on?' In response, Rika channelled all her energy into helping out. She made sure that the cleaning and washing was done before her mother got home from work, and would cook the rice and make the miso soup. When her mother came back after eight, she would bring a couple of deli items, which would form the main dishes for the pair's late dinner. There may have been no elaborate home-cooked recipes, but neither was there any of the tense atmosphere that had prevailed when her father had been around. Many evenings they'd meet in a family diner to eat. Something about this way of life resembled being away at summer camp, an extension of going out with friends, which Rika liked. The sense that she was being relied upon built her confidence.

This rhythm they'd established had continued until Rika left home at the age of twenty-two. As her boutique began to grow in popularity, Rika's mother went abroad more frequently to search out new products, and some months Rika spent more time with her grandparents in Okusawa than at home, but to this day she and her mother remained close. Rika hadn't gone through a rebellious phase; she'd made all the decisions about her university studies and her future career alone, and seen them through. Her industrious mother, who was now over sixty, still worked on the shop floor in the second branch of the boutique in Jiyūgaoka.

Back in their university days, Reiko had often come over to cook in the Hatanodai apartment where Rika lived with her mother. Both Rika and her mother were astonished to discover what a good cook Reiko was. Even when making simple meals like ochazuke or pasta, her little additions of yuzu rind or salted lemon displayed her inventiveness, giving her dishes the sort of taste that made you want to take your time savouring them. The only child of the owners of a well-known hotel in Kanazawa, Reiko had a stubborn sense of aesthetics and a rebellious spirit that you would never have guessed at from her refined appearance. From Reiko's childhood on, her parents had been de facto separated but continued to live under the same roof. Both openly had lovers, and neither of them had much time for their daughter. For Reiko, who had spent much of her childhood alongside their housekeeper whose cooking skills were, by her own admission, first-rate, 'the taste of home' meant a table clustered with exquisite decorative terrines and tiny dishes whose calorific contents had been perfectly calculated.

'If I ever have a son or a daughter, I want them to grow up eating food and cakes that I've made,' Reiko had said time and again. 'I'm studying now so that when the time comes, I'll be able to make the kind of healthy food that they'll want to eat lots of.'

Their backgrounds may have been worlds apart, but Reiko and Rika shared the experience of holding, throughout their girlhoods, a sense of unease towards the kind of family that the rest of the world idealised. That might have been why, Rika thought, when their eyes had met in the enrolment ceremony, she'd summoned up the courage to speak to Reiko. Now Reiko looked up at Rika, face alive with curiosity.

'Tell me about your work. Last time we spoke, you were trying to get permission to cover Manako Kajii. What happened with that?'

Manako Kajii was the suspect convicted in a case involving several suspicious deaths in Tokyo, and which had been creating a stir in the media for years now. Using a dating service specifically for people looking to get married, she had extorted money from a succession of men, and stood accused of killing three of them. Her blog, a string of descriptions of extravagant foods and other luxuries which she had kept updating right up until the day before her capture, had caused a sensation in the wake of her arrest. She had passed her time going to restaurants and ordering special dishes, and also took pride in her own abilities as a cook. The media never seemed to tire of her case, whose online aspect made it so very *contemporary*.

Kajii was currently in the Tokyo Detention House awaiting her retrial.

The case of Manako Kajii – or 'Kajimana' as she was known in the mass media – had intrigued Rika ever since her arrest. Rika had been part of a different news team at the time but the case had continued to niggle at her, and she was now approaching the age that Kajii had been at the time of her arrest. The election coverage she'd been involved with up until now was wrapping up, and it seemed that she would finally be able to start pursuing stories at her own discretion.

'I bet Kajimana eats an absolute ton! That's why she's that huge. It's a miracle that someone that fat could con so many people into wanting to marry her! Is her cooking that good, or what?' Ryōsuke said.

A chill ran down Rika's spine. She saw a frown flit across Reiko's brow and then disappear. Reiko had always been even more sensitive to misogyny than Rika herself was. But it wasn't that Ryōsuke was particularly insensitive. What he'd just given voice to was, Rika supposed, the standard response of the average man. The reason the case had garnered so much attention was that this woman, who had led several men around by the nose and maintained such a queenly presence in the courtroom, was neither young nor beautiful. From what Rika could see from the photographs, she weighed over 70 kilos.

'Rather than trying to find a new lead in her case, what I'm interested in is the social background to it all. I feel that the whole case is steeped in intense misogyny. Everyone in it, from Kajimana herself to her victims and all the men involved, seems to have a deep-seated hatred of women. I don't know whether I can really get that aspect across in a men's weekly magazine like ours, but I want to try. I've written to her several times, though, and had no response. I've even been to Tokyo Detention House twice in person, but it seems she has no intention of meeting me.'

—*I've been lonely so long that if I can find a woman to take care of me when I'm old, I don't really care how ugly she is.*

—*I'm not bothered about what she's like, so long as she's the domestic type who'll make me dinner.*

—*She might be fat, but she's a real cosseted princess-type. There's something unworldly and untouched about her.*

All three victims had come out with statements like these to the people close to them while they'd been still alive. They clearly had a powerful need for Kajii, and had presented her with significant sums of money, and yet in the presence of third parties, had repeatedly made disdainful statements about her. In court, the prosecution had thrown considerations such as alibis and solid evidence to the wind in order to launch attacks on Kajii's concept of chastity, so their line of argument veered about wildly, and the trial had made slow, painstaking progress. One of the witnesses, a female care-worker for the elderly, was interrogated in a manner that many felt to be sexual harassment. The debate around the case was split down gender lines. Something that a prominent male critic had said on the topic had been deemed misogynist, and he had eventually been forced to apologise.

'The last victim – what was his name again? You know, the guy who was kind of famous in online otaku circles? Just before he was run over by the train, he'd eaten beef stew that Manako Kajii had cooked for him. I wonder if that was something she learned to make at that French cooking school – what's it called again? Oh yes, Le Salon de Miyuko!'

It seemed from the information she had at her disposal as though Reiko had been avidly reading up on the case, both in the weekly magazines and online. She liked to have her finger on the pulse, keeping up to date with the latest news and trends, and she was also the industrious, diligent type, with a passion for research. At university she had consistently been top of her class.

Le Salon de Miyuko was a women-only cooking school that was well known among a certain social elite. It had been set up by Miyuko Sasazuka, wife of Mr Sasazuka, the owner-chef of the famous French Restaurant Balzac in the affluent Nishi-Azabu district of Tokyo. On Balzac's day off, Miyuko Sasazuka, who herself worked in the restaurant with her husband, took over the premises to run the cooking school, whose selling point was that its students not only had full run of the Balzac kitchen, including the professional ovens and cooking equipment used by its chefs, but would cook with the restaurant's finest-quality ingredients. At 15,000 yen a lesson, the fees for the thrice-monthly classes were far from cheap, and a year's attendance would set you back over 500,000 yen. Nor did graduating from the course give students any kind of certification, or ability to turn professional. The classes were rather like an extremely opulent pastime, permitted only to wealthy housewives and women with high salaries. Up until two months before her arrest, Manako Kajii had been avidly attending the school, with her fees paid for by one of her victims. A quick search on the internet soon yielded a group photograph from the Salon, showing Kajii standing with the other students. Among that group of stylish women attired with impeccable taste, Kajii, in a tight-fitting dress that accentuated her voluptuous figure and would have been more suitable for a ritzy date than a cooking school, stood out like a sore thumb. Now, after being hounded by the press, the cooking school was on a break.

'Yes, apparently right before the victim died he sent a text to his mother: *My girlfriend made me beef stew! It was delicious.* Remember the argument of Kajii's lawyer in court: would a woman who'd spend all that time cooking up a delicious beef stew for her lover really push that same man in front of a train? Listen, Rika, next time you write to her, why don't you try asking her if she'll share the recipe with you? I bet she'll agree to meet you after that.'

Rika blinked. The idea had never even occurred to her. Back in her time working in PR, Reiko had often used her thoughtfulness, humour and talent for conceiving of unexpected gifts to win over difficult film directors, talent agency presidents and sponsors, and bring them round to her way of seeing things.

'Women who love to cook are so delighted when someone asks them for a recipe that they'll tell you all kinds of things you haven't asked for along with it. It's a law of nature. I'm exactly the same.'

'It's true, you know,' Ryōsuke piped up. 'A little while ago one of my colleagues came round with his wife and kids, and was really impressed by the shūmai that Reiko made. So Reiko started telling him in detail how to make them, the kinds of steamer you need and all this. She got so carried away that he was quite taken aback,' he said, laughing.

'Hey, Ryō, I wouldn't mind going to Le Salon de Miyuko one day ...'

'Not on my kind of salary, I'm afraid!'

Dessert was home-made candied chestnuts, chiffon cake baked with amazake and rice flour, and cups of gingery chai. Biting into the cake, Rika discovered that it was perfectly fluffy, with a pleasing springiness and bite to it. Yet when she widened her eyes and sang its praises, Reiko frowned remorsefully.

'What with Christmas coming up, I wanted to make a thick buttercream bûche de Noël, but of course without any butter that's off the table. Rika had a look as well, Ryō, but it seems like there really isn't any to be found around here. At this rate, pound cakes and sponges won't be on the menu for a while. We're left with chiffon cake, I guess: it's about the only thing you can make with rapeseed oil.'

'But this is so dense and squidgy, even without it! It's great. It looks like the butter shortage is going to drag on, anyway. They're saying that with the heat last summer, lots of dairy cows got mastitis, and that's what's causing it. But this is after they forecast a supply shortage, and imported a load at the last minute as an emergency measure. So where's it all got to? I wonder. Saying that, though, there are fewer and fewer dairy farmers in Japan these days. I'm guessing that there'll come a time in the future when we'll just import all our dairy products from overseas. In any case, it's a real blow for a small company like ours.'

As she listened to Ryōsuke and made the appropriate responses, Rika recalled that Manako Kajii had a soft spot for butter. Rika's interest in food was so limited that she'd only skimmed Kajii's blog, but she did remember that Kajii had gone on and on about expensive brands of butter. Come to think of it, there'd been a discussion in court about how Kajii had taken one of her victim's credit cards and used it to buy numerous packets of butter costing nearly 2,000 yen a pop. Kajii had grown up in Niigata, surrounded by dairy farms, so maybe that explained her pickiness. Her fixation had been thoroughly mocked online, with people making comments like, 'No wonder she's that big if she eats so much butter', and, 'It wouldn't surprise me if she used her sticks of butter for you know what …'

Just past nine, Rika said her goodbyes, politely rebuffing the pair's entreaties for her to stay longer, to sleep over and leave in the morning. With the onigiri made of the oyster-and-vegetable rice and the piece of chiffon cake wrapped in clingfilm that Reiko had handed her tucked inside her bag, Rika headed for the office.

I only want to spend my time with people who know the real thing when they see it. People who truly understand the value of the real thing are few and far between. These kinds of lines appeared frequently in Manako Kajii's blog. Someone who knew the real thing when they saw it – surely it was hard to find anyone that applied to better than Reiko, thought Rika. In front of the ticket gates, Rika turned around and looked back once more at the neighbourhood. The cluster of lights from the new houses leading up the hill now seemed to her warm and inviting. When she reached for her train pass, she noticed that her fingertips looked less dry than earlier, and her hangnail less severe.

'By focusing solely on the question of whether the victim was wrong to permit or encourage the taking of the photographs, the revenge porn debate has swung way off course. So long as we keep up this culture of victim-blaming, these kinds of cases will continue to occur.'

The speaker's black-suited forearms flung out haphazardly across the panellists' bench were unusually long. His greying cheeks were drawn, his dark hair was speckled with white, and his eyes, so googly that they seemed ready to drop out at any minute, were cushioned by unhealthy looking black bags. He was hardly what you'd call a dream-boat. And yet, every time his fierce expression relaxed a little, every time his Adam's apple travelled up his long neck, Rika would find herself fixed on the sight of him. Here he was on a morning chat show, speaking about the case where an office worker from Hamamatsuchō had been strangled to death after naked photographs of her were leaked online by her ex-boyfriend.

'Oh, Shinoi's doing these kinds of programmes now, is he?' came a voice from behind her.

It was her colleague Kitamura, four years her junior. 'I suppose that, despite that gangster face of his, he's got a sexy aura. For a man in his mid-forties, his opinions are pretty sympathetic to women, so he probably goes down well with housewives. And he's in good shape for his age.'

'You think?' said Rika, doing her best to look as disinterested as possible as she smiled and looked away from the screen, picking up the remote that lay on the old sofa.

Yoshinori Shinoi, a senior editor at a major news agency who had recently become a household name thanks to his media appearances, had been a well-known figure to everyone in Rika's department for a good while, having long been prized as a go-to person for opinions on various issues. The space she and Kitamura were now in, with its battered corner sofa and TV, was the perfect place for taking a breather. You could even have a quick nap there, if you weren't bothered about being caught in the act. Looking up at the walls stained yellow from the nicotine that escaped the door of the smoking room directly ahead of her, Rika turned down the sound of the TV.

Within the offices of Shūmeisha, one of Japan's biggest publishing companies, the only department with a smoking room was this one: that of the *Shūmei Weekly*. This meant that the heavy smokers from other departments such as books and sales would all come here especially, and the footfall was high. The only time you could truly zone out around here was on mornings like these, when there were few people around. Rika had come into the office early, but sitting on the sofa, she found herself losing any sense of urgency. She took an onigiri, this morning's breakfast, out of the convenience store plastic bag and unwrapped its cellophane coating. She'd asked the cashier to microwave it for her, and the rice was still pleasantly warm. While inspecting the wide variety of onigiri lining the shelves of the convenience store, much as she always did, Rika found herself pining for the meal Reiko had cooked for her last week, including the oyster-and-vegetable rice, and her hand had grasped the takikomi onigiri, a variety she never usually chose.

'On the subject of this Hamamatsuchō revenge-porn case … Our scoop that the suspect had engaged in stalkerish behaviour towards two of his exes but not been prosecuted for it came via you, right? You were the first to point that out.'

Kitamura was settling himself down beside Rika on the sofa, addressing her chummily as if they were friends at school. His fitted striped shirt clung to his slim figure, which showed not a trace of spare flesh, and his dyed flax-brown hair suited his pale skin. He had the air of a pampered princess, and indeed, he got more sleep than anyone else around here, neither drank nor smoked, and was the first to get round to the books and films that people were raving about. He had a nonchalant ease about him and his perspective on matters was roundly neutral. Not only did he never get angry, but he never got ill either, so his presence was much treasured by the company, despite his lack of professional zeal.

'Oh, that was just a fluke,' replied Rika. 'Man, I can't face the editorial meeting today! I've got nothing remotely decent to bring. Whenever I think I've landed a scoop, it gets leaked online.'

'I wouldn't worry about it. With an old-man paper like ours, we're guaranteed to keep selling copies so long as we keep featuring articles about warding off inheritance tax and cancer. We're just here to keep things ticking over. It's about time we started running articles like "Ten Ways to Keep Having Sex Until You Die".'

It was a Thursday, the day when all the journalists revealed the scoops they'd landed and the stories they wanted to cover in the upcoming issue. On Friday, the editors would announce the line-up for the magazine accordingly, and the weekend would be spent doing the necessary coverage and writing up drafts in time for Monday's deadline. This week-long circuit, which felt a lot like sprinting round a running track, was repeated four times a month, which was to say forty-eight times a year. Having worked at the company for a decade now, this rhythm was steeped into Rika's body, and whether she was waking or sleeping, she couldn't rid herself of the sensation of running its course. Of the seventy members of the magazine team, ten were photographers, eight were admin, eleven were on the editorial desk, and the rest were journalists. Rika was the sole female journalist who was also a permanent-contract employee. Of the four other women who had joined the company at the same time as her, two had requested to be transferred to other departments, and two had left for health reasons. The women who had joined the company before her and shown her around had married and moved to other departments: books or sales. The job was impossible to manage alongside pregnancy and childcare, unless you had magical powers.

'If you keep landing scoops as you are doing, I wouldn't be surprised if Rika Machida became the first woman on the *Shūmei Weekly* editorial desk. That'd be so great.'

At the *Shūmei Weekly*, the task of writing up the journalists' reports into publishable articles was exclusively the work of the editorial desk. It was Rika's goal to one day have something printed that she'd written with her own hand.

'What are you saying, Kitamura? I know you're not remotely jealous.'

Kitamura's lack of professional ambition concerning anything other than shaving as many seconds as he could off the time he spent at work was so brazen that by this stage everybody practically respected him for it. He might not have come up with stories of his own, but this also ensured he had no emotional attachment towards what he was covering. As a result his work was accurate, and he got it done quicker than anybody else. Though today, for once, it seemed as though there was something he wanted to say.

'The scoops that you come up with are pretty wide in scope, from arts to sports, and there's no pattern to them. This might sound rude, but from what I've seen, however frequently female journalists meet with police and bureaucrats, they seem to find it hard to get those guys to open up, however attractive they're seen to be. The relationship between the weekly magazine journalists and their sources is a thoroughly homosocial one, and it's been that way basically since the Second World War. Female journalists put in the same amount of time and energy as their male counterparts, but it's the men who are trusted, and the women's stories get snapped up by them as a result ...'

Despite superficial similarities, the rice of the onigiri had none of the fragrance or the depth of flavour of Reiko's. Rika could feel its warmth on her tongue, yet as soon as the rice moved down her throat, a coldness spread out through her body. She washed the onigiri down with bottled green tea, driving out the grains caught behind her teeth with a pointed tongue.

In the corner of her vision, Shinoi was nodding at the presenter.

'If you're managing to line up so many scoops, you must have a pretty amazing source. Though I guess you're not about to reveal it to me.'

There was no way, Rika told herself, that someone like Kitamura could have figured it out. Even if he had, there was a limit to how interested he'd be. Not letting her smile slip, she met Kitamura's light-coloured eyes. In this industry, a casual utterance, a misjudged confidence, could cost you your life. Ensuring that your true feelings were well masked, inspecting each and every one of your actions and keeping yourself in check became a matter of habit.

'Um, excuse me, Ms Machida? Do you have plans to get rid of this box any time soon?'

It was Yū Uchimura, a university student who worked at the office part-time, the irritation in her voice palpable. Now it had been determined that Yū would be joining the company full-time next year, the restraint she'd previously shown had disappeared. Grateful for the interruption, Rika stood up and turned her back on Kitamura.

'Oh, sorry! I'll get it sent over to my place soon.'

Racing over to her desk, she pushed the cardboard box that was sticking out into the aisle back underneath her desk, and sat down at her chair. As it turned out, when three years' worth of the blog was printed out, it accounted for a whole boxful of paper. The entries were lengthy, and Manako Kajii had posted several a day, so the volume quickly mounted up. The blog had now been deleted, but one of her sources had saved a copy and that was how Rika had come to have it. She took five days' worth out of the box and flicked through it. Kajii's life, whose days were spent shopping and eating, seemed to float free from the constraints of ordinary people's lives, like that of an aristocrat. There were countless descriptions of the types of confectionery and wines considered the best that money could buy, endless lists of famous shops and restaurants in central Tokyo: Sembikiya, the New York Grill, Joël Robuchon, Nadaman, Maxim's de Paris, L'écrin … All of them were such traditional, established choices that even Rika had heard of them, which gave the blog's contents the feel of having been sponged from someone else, even when Kajii was ostensibly recording her own impressions. However many times Rika passed her eyes over the text, it wouldn't sink in.

Manako Kajii had been born in Fuchū, Tokyo in 1980. When it was decided that her father would help out his own father with his property business, the family had moved to Yasudamachi in Niigata. Kajii's mother taught flower arranging. Along with her sister, seven years her junior, Kajii had been brought up in relative affluence. She moved to Tokyo for university, but dropped out after three months. From that point on, she had been living in Fudō-mae in Shinagawa, taking no fixed employment and instead making her living as a professional mistress, protected by the peculiar network of rich, older men she'd established. She had been arrested in 2013, on suspicion of committing three murders that had taken place over the course of roughly six months. All of the victims were single men between forty and seventy, based in the capital, whom she had met through dating sites, and who were serious about marrying her. In response to Kajii's requests for money – the fees for her cooking school, medical costs for a family member who'd injured themselves, and so on – they'd handed over handsome sums of cash. Their various causes of death – an overdose of sleeping pills, drowning in the bathtub, falling in front of a train – could all be read as either suicide or sheer accident, but the deciding factor in Kajii's arrest had been the emergence of the information that in each case, she'd been with them right up until their deaths. She was also being tried for five charges of fraud. Despite a lack of concrete evidence for any of the charges against her, Kajii had been sentenced to life imprisonment, the jury apparently convinced by the prosecution's questionable psychologising. Kajii had appealed the decision that same day, and was currently in Tokyo Detention House, awaiting her retrial next spring. She was well known for refusing to meet anyone from the press, and was apparently particularly icy towards female journalists.

What the public found most alarming, even more than Kajii's lack of beauty, was the fact that she was not thin. Women appeared to find this aspect of the case profoundly disturbing, while in men it elicited an extraordinary display of hatred and vitriol. From early childhood, everyone had had it drummed into them that if a woman wasn't slim, she wasn't worth bothering with. The decision not to lose weight and remain plus-sized was one that demanded considerable resolve.

And yet, Kajii had given herself that permission. Ignoring other people's yardsticks, she had decided that she was enough as a woman. To be treated well, to be adored, to be showered with presents and affection, and to eschew that which she disliked, including work and group socialising – she went on demanding these things as though they were perfectly within her rights, and as a result, she had carved out for herself an environment she found comfortable, in which she could live apart from the world. It was this accomplishment, more than the close to 100 million yen she had managed to extract from various men, that seemed to Rika deserving of admiration. In principle, all women should give themselves permission to demand good treatment, but the world made doing so profoundly difficult. The women labelled 'the highly successful ones' whom Rika encountered through her work showed that ever so clearly. All of them seemed terrified of something. They reined themselves in to a degree that verged on asceticism, were abnormally modest, and seemed desperate to protect themselves. Rika herself, however much she was praised by others, however highly her work was esteemed, was unable to feel satisfaction with any aspect of her own self. On the nights when her confidence failed her, and she was struck by the urge to call Makoto and ask him to come over, she would keep herself in check, telling herself that she wouldn't get away with being so demanding. Even Reiko, who now seemed at peace, had been highly strung when she was younger, and struggled with social situations. She'd rarely had relationships. The fact that both Rika and Reiko had low self-esteem and found it difficult to rely on men perhaps had something to do with their relationships with their fathers. Manako Kajii, on the other hand, had adored her father – who had passed away several years ago – as if he were a lover, and was said to have been very close to him.

That said, Rika also understood the sense of loneliness and wretchedness shared by those who had been deceived by Kajii. She had no intention of aligning herself with such a woman, or driving nails into the coffin of those who were already dead. Her recent experience at Reiko's had reminded Rika of just how much comfort the thoughtfulness and home-made food of another person could bring to a tired body and dried-up heart. She could understand thinking that a person's appearance and personality didn't matter, that it didn't even matter if you were being deceived – that you just wanted a soft, warm-bodied member of the opposite sex to call your own. And yet, she thought, and yet … But when Rika tried to carry her train of thought any further, she brushed up against a rough, sore sensation like running her fingertips across sandpaper. It seemed that an anger she'd forgotten about for so long, kept sealed up all this time, was peeping through a crack in her skin. She didn't know who the bad feeling was directed towards. Was it contemporary society she was angry with, for still demanding that women be good around the house as a matter of course? She herself never cooked a meal for a man, and had never been asked to do so either, and yet …

Rika turned over the envelope lying on her desk where she imagined Yū had tossed it, light as a petal, and stifled a shriek. On the reverse of the envelope was printed the address of Tokyo Detention House. The letter was from Manako Kajii – it had to be. Until now, she'd not received a single letter from her, and yet Rika felt certain. Making sure that nobody was watching, she used a letter opener on the envelope. Inside was a single pale-pink sheet of paper.

You seem different from other journalists. I'd be happy to meet you.
Feel free to come and see me whenever suits you. Regards.

That was all the note said. Rika could see the stamp from the prison censor. Kajii's handwriting was mesmerisingly neat, with a rhythmical, fluid quality to it. 'She has beautiful writing', several people who knew her had testified – and, truly, she did. Rika's heart was thumping in her chest. She swallowed the impulse to make a noise. The room around her grew white and hazy. What had happened to bring this about? She recalled the letter she'd written to Kajii last week – one of several she'd already written. The only difference from her earlier missives was that, as Reiko had advised, she'd added a postscript at the bottom of the letter:

P.S. I'm really curious about the recipe for the beef stew that you made for Mr Yamamura. I'd be delighted if you'd share it with me.

On her phone, Rika checked the visiting hours for Tokyo Detention House: 8 a.m. to 4 p.m., with an hour break for lunch. If she left now, she'd get there by ten. She had no guarantee that Kajii would meet her, yet she felt she couldn't bear to be still.

'I'll be back in time for the meeting!' she called out to Kitamura and Yū, sticking her arms into her trenchcoat as she rushed out of the office.

Tensing her skin against the biting wind, she hurried towards Kagurazaka Station. Was she better aiming for Ayase or Kosuge Station? After deliberating a moment, she decided to change onto the Chiyoda Line at Otemachi and get off at Ayase. Once past Kita-Senju Station, the train emerged above ground, and light flooded the carriage. Past the bridge over the Arakawa river, the enormous Detention House building came into view: four towers arranged concentrically around a central tower with a lift running up and down. Seen from above, it resembled a bat with spread wings. Rika got out at Ayase Station and hailed a taxi.

The Ayase river, once known as the dirtiest in all Japan, had been cleaned up considerably. Even with the windows open and the breeze rushing in, there was no nasty stench. The taxi crossed the river, drove in a semicircle around the Detention House, and headed towards the visitors' entrance. This part of Tokyo had a melancholy feel to it, but it wasn't bleak. There were houses and apartment blocks dotted around with washing strung up outside, and in a park next to the Detention House, mothers and children were laughing and playing together. Opposite the gate, a grassy riverbank stretched on and on, and beyond the Arakawa river you could see Tokyo Skytree glinting. Rika got out of the taxi, passed through the prison gates staffed by security personnel, and hastened up the slope that led inside. Because many of the prisoners awaiting trial had considerable social influence, the buildings were fitted with cutting-edge technological equipment. Rika filled in the visitor form on the ground floor, and waited for the number on the piece of paper in her hand to be called.

Thirty minutes later, her number appeared on a screen, and was announced over a loudspeaker. Entrusting all her possessions save a pen and notepad to a member of staff, she passed through the metal detectors, then walked down a long corridor towards the brightly illuminated hall with lifts that connected the various parts of the building. When the lift doors opened, Rika found her way to the room with the number she'd been given. Opening the door, she found a small room partitioned by an acrylic screen. On the opposite side of the screen stood a single chair. As she sat down gingerly on the metal chair on her side of the screen, it occurred to Rika that at this very moment, she was being watched by Manako Kajii from outside the room. She felt her whole body tense up at the thought. It was now that Kajii would decide whether or not to meet her visitor. The nerves that came from being sized up by a prisoner were something that

Rika could never get used to, however many times she experienced them.

'Sorry to keep you waiting.' Kajii entered the room accompanied by a male prison officer.

With her plump hands clasped in front of her waist, she bowed in Rika's direction. Her high-pitched voice had a sugary sweetness to it. There was something intensely graceful about her entrance, as though the curtains had been raised and the princess had emerged to present herself, which felt at odds with the bleakness of the setting.

'It's great to meet you. I'm Rika Machida, a journalist on the *Shūmei Weekly*. I came straight away when I got your letter. Thank you for taking the time to see me.'

The woman settled herself down on the chair on the other side of the acrylic screen. The prison officer waited behind her.

'Nice to meet you. I'm Manako Kajii.'

She's not that ugly, or that fat, either ...

Taking extreme care not to be rude, Rika observed the woman opposite her. She may have spent most of her time alone in her cell, but perhaps owing to the three calorie-controlled meals a day that she was served at set times and the regular exercise she was encouraged to take, she looked considerably slimmer than at the time of her arrest. Ample she may have been, but she was small in stature, meaning the impression she gave was not an imposing one. She had a feminine quality to her, and it was only her dark eyebrows on the verge of joining in the middle and her big round eyes no less extreme in their darkness that gave her face a stubborn cast. She wore a long skirt of a soft fabric, and a salmon-pink jumper that stretched taut across her breasts. The hair cascading down onto her jumper shone glossily, the tips lightly curled. It must have been forbidden in the prison to wear make-up, but her flawless ivory skin seemed to glow from the inside, and her plump, baby-doll mouth was pale pink in colour. Quite possibly she looked fresher than Rika, whose hair was pulled back into a bun and whose only beauty regime consisted of applying BB cream to her tired skin. Yet Kajii looked older than her thirty-five years. There was something over-whelmingly old-fashioned about her – although that same quality could be described as a kind of class, or poise. The fact of her imprisonment seemed to lend her a sense of nobility. Rika imagined that her feeling right now was not unlike that of the prince when he finally got to meet Rapunzel, sequestered away at the top of the tower. The sense of being on the back foot that came from pleading with Kajii and finally being permitted to meet her, mingled with a sense of gratitude that she alone had been selected from the other journalists, and Rika found herself wanting to think well of the woman before her. She tried to tell herself that she had to remain unbiased.

In the end, though, it was Kajii who spoke first. Her eyes like ripe black grapes opened wide and she said, 'I've no intention whatsoever of speaking of my case. That position is in line with the counsel I've received from my lawyer and everyone supporting me. But you want to talk about food, am I right? So I thought that meeting you might prove a nice distraction. I don't have anyone around me I can talk to about such things. I'm absolutely starved for conversation about delicious food. So long as it's just as my conversational partner, I don't mind if you continue to come here.'

While she was thrown off by Kajii's affected way of speaking, Rika also found herself troubled by the contents of her speech. She shouldn't have pretended to be like Reiko, she thought, when she had so little knowledge about food, and she knew that it would take Kajii a long time to open up to her. She could hardly strike up a conversation about the convenience-store onigiri she'd eaten for breakfast.

'To start, why don't you tell me what you have in your refrigerator at home?'

Rika was relieved to be asked a question. The length of prison visits depended on how busy it was on a given day, and while they were sometimes cut off at ten minutes, they could last for as long as thirty. In any case, conversation seen as time-wasting was not permitted. At the same time, she felt that this was not a good start for their first ever conversation.

'Let's see … There's fruit and vegetable juice, some sports drinks, and some margarine. I'm not the type to put time and effort into cooking, like you are. I'm not good with my hands, and I hate anything domestic. My entire day is taken up by my work. I was so surprised to read your blog and see how much love and care you pour into everyday tasks.'

Rika could see how brazen she was being in her flattery, but she couldn't stop herself. Being around this woman, she felt herself to be a kind of court jester, who had to offer up something diverting to her. Kajii's thick unibrow shot upwards.

'Did you just say margarine?'

'Yes, it's lower in calories than butter. And isn't it better for you, because it has less cholesterol? And besides, you know there's a butter shortage going on at the moment …'

'Your problem is you've decided that butter is bad without even understanding what it tastes like. Margarine is far worse for your body than any butter. It's all fake, full of trans-saturated fats. Listen, the thing you must know about dairy products is …'

With her voice faintly trembling, Kajii launched into a diatribe on the poisonous effects of margarine. Her eyes grew darker, and a frown surfaced on her face. Oh yes, Rika thought, this was just what her blog was like. While she spoke endlessly about good breeding and behaving in a ladylike fashion, Kajii was quick to look down on people, watching out for her chance to scorn others over some trivial issue. Her words, just as smooth as cream, were laced with ferocity.

All of a sudden, she fell into a sullen silence. I've got to say something, Rika thought, but the moment she started to move her dry tongue, Kajii resumed her monologue.

'I learned from my late father that women should show generosity towards everyone. But there are two things that I simply cannot tolerate: feminists and margarine.'

Rika smiled uncomfortably, and murmured, 'Then I should apologise.'

'You must make yourself rice with butter and soy sauce.'

For a moment, Rika failed to process Kajii's words, and she let out a quiet, 'Hm?'

'Add butter and soy sauce to freshly cooked rice. Even someone who doesn't cook can manage that much, I'm sure. It's the best meal to truly understand the glory of butter.' Her manner of delivery was so grave that it made it impossible to even think of ridiculing her.

'I want you to use salted Échiré butter. There's an Échiré shop in Marunouchi Station. Go there and look at it, properly, before you buy it. The current shortage is a perfect opportunity to sample first-class butter from overseas. When I'm eating good butter I feel somehow as though I were falling.'

'Falling?'

'Yes. Not floating gently upwards, but falling. The same feeling as when the lift plunges towards the ground floor. The body plummets, starting from the very tip of the tongue.'

Rika attempted to recall the feeling of gravity that she'd experienced in the lift she'd just ridden. So sucked in was she by Kajii's way of speaking that she'd forgotten to take any notes. Now, she was startled to notice Kajii's eyes and lips growing moist. Her entranced gaze was directed somewhere else – some place that wasn't this room.

'The butter should still be cold. Remove it from the fridge just before. Superior-quality butter should be eaten when it's still cold and hard, to truly luxuriate in its texture and aroma. It will begin to melt almost immediately with the heat of the rice, but I want you to eat it before it melts fully. Cool butter and warm rice. First of all, savour the difference in their temperatures. Then, the two will melt alongside one another, mingle together, and form a golden fountain, right there inside your mouth. Even without seeing it, you just *know* that it's golden – that's the way it tastes. You'll sense the individual grains of rice coated in butter, and an aromatic fragrance as if the rice were being fried will ascend to your nose. A rich, milky sweetness will spread itself across your tongue …'

Rika felt her mouth growing moist. She knew that if she swallowed now, she'd let out a loud gulp, which she very much wished to avoid. Kajii sat up straight and clasped her plump fingers in front of her chest.

'If I speak to you again, it will most likely be after you've decided that you will never again let margarine pass your lips. I wouldn't like to waste my time on anyone except those who know the real thing when they see it. Oh, and one last matter: it's not "beef stew", it's "boeuf bourguignon". It's a French recipe. I corrected them several times in court. I'm astounded by how ignorant you all are when it comes to food. I'm tired now. Would you mind if we broke off here?'

Rika hurriedly jotted down the unfamiliar recipe name. It was usually the prison officer who signalled the end of the visit, but this time Kajii herself voted to end the session. Embarrassingly, Rika had been carried along entirely at Kajii's pace, from start to finish. Kajii was in the starring role, and everyone else was the supporting cast – was that how it was? Rika stared in bewilderment at the fleshy back and glossy hair of the retreating figure now making its way out of the room.

Back in the lift, Rika recalled Kajii's description of the taste of butter – *it tastes like you're falling.* In truth, Rika didn't really understand what that meant. She walked down the same long corridor as when she'd arrived and put the prison grounds behind her, heading to Kosuge, the station closest to the Detention House. Just as after she'd been swimming, her body felt heavy and her head wasn't working properly. She felt like she wanted to fall to the ground and sleep, but she summoned what remaining energy she had. Walking along, she noticed a spot where someone had laid flowers beneath the guardrail at the side of the road. Some unfortunate soul must have had their life cut short immediately after their release from the Detention House, she thought. Or else, it was a member of the public who had happened to meet their end in an accident here. The sight of those two round eyes like black grapes and the sound of that sickly sweet voice were trapped inside Rika's chest. She boarded the train, still feeling giddy and unreal.

Before returning to the office, Rika stopped at an electronics store and bought the smallest rice cooker she could find, along with a kilo of rice. Once the editorial meeting was over, she had to go out to Kasumigaseki to research a story, which gave her the opportunity to stop at Marunouchi Station. In the Échiré butter shop, which looked like a fancy boutique, she bought a pat of butter that cost almost 1,000 yen for just 100 grams. Never before had Rika spent that kind of money on ingredients. Both the label on the butter and the blue carrier bag she was handed had a pretty, romantic design, not the sort of thing you'd expect from a food item. She regretted that she hadn't thought to take Reiko a gift like this when she'd visited the previous week. The cashier gave Rika a sachet of refrigerant to make sure the butter didn't melt, and when she got back to work, she put it in the office fridge. She felt as though she were accumulating equipment for going into battle.

That evening, Rika took the various items home to her Iidabashi apartment, fifteen minutes' walk from the office. It had been a long time since she'd returned home this early. From tomorrow until the end of the weekend, she'd be so busy that she'd barely have the chance to catch her breath, so she needed to see to this task immediately.

Rika knew that it had been an oversight on her part not to prepare topics of conversation that Kajii would be interested in. That said, Kajii hadn't explicitly stated that she wouldn't meet her again. In other words, there was a chance that she would open up to Rika, depending on Rika's approach. Standing in front of her kitchen sink, which looked as new as it had done when she moved in ten years earlier, Rika washed one gō of rice, using her wrists to apply pressure.

She programmed the rice cooker, fresh out of its box, to cook the rice, and let her eyes rove around the place. It was rare for her to spend any time in her apartment, which she had chosen for its proximity to the office, and which cost her 85,000 yen a month in rent. She wasn't especially taken with it, but neither could she see any reason to move. The curtains and bed covers were the pale blue-grey ones that Reiko had helped her choose, back in her first year at the company.

When the rice cooker began to emit a sweet smell, Rika felt a sense of industriousness rising up in her. For the first time in what seemed to her an age she dusted the flat. It was as she was vacuuming that the rice cooker beeped. Lifting the lid, Rika saw the rice glistening beyond the plume of steam. Quite unexpectedly, she found herself entranced by the sight of its translucent gleam. She didn't own any rice bowls, so she used the plastic paddle that came with the cooker to spoon the rice messily into a café au lait bowl. Next she retrieved the butter, which she'd kept in the fridge as Kajii had stipulated, peeled off the wrapping paper, and gazed at its smooth buttercup-hued surface. What lay ahead was unknown territory. She had sampled the buttered rice that was sometimes served with burger patties, but she'd never encountered rice with soy sauce and butter – let alone piping-hot rice with top-class butter.

She perched a sliver of butter on top of the rice. From one of the sachets of soy sauce that came with convenience store bento boxes and which tended to accumulate in her apartment, she squeezed a single drop into the bowl.

Just as instructed, she moved the butter and some rice to her mouth before the butter had a chance to melt.

The first thing Rika felt was a strange breeze emanating from the back of her throat. The cold butter first met the roof of her mouth with a chilly sensation, contrasting with the steaming rice in both texture and temperature. The cool butter clashed against her teeth, and she felt its soft texture right down into their roots. Soon enough, just as Kajii had said, the melted butter began to surge through the individual grains of rice. It was a taste that could only be described as golden. A shining golden wave, with an astounding depth of flavour and a faint yet full and rounded aroma, wrapped itself around the rice and washed Rika's body far away.

It was, indeed, a lot like falling. Rika stared down intently at the bowl of rice with butter and soy sauce and let out a long sigh, feeling her breath rich and milky.

The meal that Reiko had cooked her was so delicious that Rika could still now recall every part of the sensation of eating it. Its fragrance, its restrained yet impactful flavours, had seemed to gently embrace her exhausted body. The seasonal ingredients had filled her with a sense of vitality that had carried over to the following day. This was a different kind of deliciousness to that – a more blatant, forceful deliciousness, that took hold of her from the tip of her tongue, pinned her down, and carried her off to some unknown place.

The next thing Rika knew, all the rice had vanished inside her stomach. And Rika wasn't done eating. In fact, it seemed that with every bite of butter and rice, her taste buds were developing new capacities, pleading with her for more.

So this was the butter that Manako Kajii loved so much – the symbol of all the succulent food she'd eaten with the money she'd extracted from her men. It was the same cruel, bright yellow as the butter that the tigers had melted into in *The Story of Little Babaji*.

Rika got to her feet. Reiko had told her she should eat more, and she was skinny enough as it was – possibly too skinny, in fact. Nobody could blame her for treating herself occasionally. Besides, this was part of her research. If this would endear Kajii to her, then she had little choice in the matter.

Placing the still-warm metal cooking pot in the sink, Rika turned on the tap and ran a stream of water across it. The surging water cooled the bowl. She would cook another gō of rice – no, make it two. Was that too much? If there was some leftover she could always freeze it. Glancing at the clock, Rika saw it was already long past midnight.

CHAPTER TWO

The spaghetti was done.

Hearing the alarm she'd set on her phone, Rika took her eyes from the report draft filling her computer screen. Wading through the warm, wheaty-smelling vapour to grasp the handles of the pan, she poured out its contents into the colander inside the sink. The stainless steel of the sink buckled, making a sound like a drum being struck, reverberating at her waist. A great plume of steam rose up, whitening her entire field of vision, before dispersing throughout her late-night kitchen with its single-plate hob. The steam wafted up to her cheeks and nose, wetting her skin. So intensely was the spaghetti glistening that it looked as if it were alive. She transferred it into a bowl, then opened up the fridge and took out the packet of Calpis butter, the pollock roe in its polystyrene tray sealed with clingfilm, along with a pack of shiso leaves, an unusually dark green for the season.

The previous week, Rika had thrown out her packet of margarine, so despised by Manako Kajii, with the burnable rubbish.

Since their previous meeting, Rika had once attempted to visit Kajii at the Detention House, and sent two letters.

I tried out the recipe you told me right away, I was astonished to discover that something so delicious could be so easy to rustle up, I'll never again eat anything that's just a heap of trans fats, I'd like to hear more of your thoughts on fine cuisine, and to develop my own knowledge as well, so I can be an interesting conversational partner to you.

Rika had chosen her words with great care, attempting to see things from Kajii's perspective as much as possible, but her efforts had been in vain. Still, she wasn't about to give up. She had to find a way of piquing Kajii's interest in her again, whatever it took.

She knew the Kagurazaka supermarket stocked a wide range of imported goods – its customers were principally affluent housewives and people from overseas – and she'd scooped up the last packet of Calpis butter on the shelf. There was something soothing about its subdued brown and white packaging, with its banner reading 'Superior Quality'. December was already more than half gone, and Christmas was fast approaching, and yet standard butter was still nowhere to be found in Tokyo. These expensive brands were the only kinds to be easily had.

A sliver of butter perched atop a mound of steaming rice garnished with a single drop of soy sauce was a taste that had quickly become an addiction for Rika. She'd used lashings of the same butter on her morning toast, too, and as a result the hundred grams of Échiré that she'd bought in the Marunouchi store had vanished in just a few days. In the midst of the end-of-year rush at work, where she was having to shave off hours of sleep, she had no time to buy more. When her hunger became too much to bear, she decided to sate it with whatever was close at hand – such had been her rationale for buying the Calpis. As it happened, though, this alternative brand brought together a creamy richness reminiscent of condensed milk, with a clean, fresh aftertaste. It was a different species of deliciousness to Échiré, whose umami-rich flavour lingered on and on eternally, and Rika took to it immediately.

Rereading Manako Kajii's blog, Rika discovered that Kajii repeatedly sang the praises of Calpis butter, and felt a kind of pride that her taste buds had not misled her. Previously Kajii's prose had seemed to her ever so turgid, but now, since her butter awakening, the odd phrases here and there would fall into her like droplets.

Rika had asked for the cardboard box full of blog printouts, which Yū had been so impatient with her to tidy away, to be sent to her apartment. There was no space for it there either, so she had put away her table and resorted to perching a tray or placemat on top of the box so that it doubled as a dining table, resenting all the while how student-like it made her living situation.

The recipes for the French dishes and cakes featured on Kajii's blog were far beyond Rika, reading to her like arcane magic spells hailing from another world, but this tarako pasta, which required that its components be simply mixed together, seemed like something she could manage, and what was more, she had succeeded in locating the necessary ingredients at the late-night supermarket. These days, Rika hardly ever went into diners or bento take-out shops on her way home. She felt like the kind of meals she made – putting butter on hot rice or toast, and eating that together with salads, instant miso or other cup soups she'd bought – hardly deserved to be called 'cooking', but at least she no longer felt an aversion towards using her kitchen. In the past, she hadn't even been able to summon the energy to make instant ramen. She'd harboured the sense that using water or heat in any way would drain her stamina – a stance that now seemed to her very grudging.

The dusky-pink pollock roe she removed from its polystyrene packaging gleamed wetly and, for an instant, the image of Kajii's puckered lips passed through her mind. Leaving its outer skin on, she broke up the roe with a fork and mixed it unfussily into the spaghetti. She sliced off a knob of the Calpis with a knife and perched it on top, then watched as the pale-yellow solid gently began to change colour, spreading out to the sides and turning golden, mingling with the fish eggs. The full, milky aroma of the butter married with the salty marine tang of the roe as the scent of the dish went rising up to her face, and she breathed it deeply into her lungs. She garnished the pasta with a scattering of shiso leaves she'd torn up with her fingers, then moved the bowl of pasta over to her cardboard box. There was a rosy-cheeked frankness about the pink of the roe, and in combination with the oozing butter, it looked positively carefree. Rika took up her fork and wound up the spaghetti, before lifting it to her mouth.

Cloaked in a coating of minuscule fish eggs and butter, the spaghetti strands sprang around on Rika's tongue as if in excitement. The dish was adequately salted, but there was a relaxed, mellow quality to its taste. What a wonderful combination pollock roe and butter made! Though she said it herself, the spaghetti had been cooked to perfection. You didn't find restaurants that served meals with this much butter, Rika thought. The more expensive the butter, the better the quality; the more that you used, the richer the taste. Rika felt the deep and generous flavour of the dish pushing into the distance her sense of irritation with herself and how gutlessly she'd behaved that day.

In its upcoming issue, the *Shūmei Weekly*'s cover story was to be about a young, popular politician who was currently making great strides in his career, and the editorial desk had been pestering her for dirt on him. Rika had been covering him closely in the lead-up to the election, but from what she could make out, he was a truly good egg. And yet, she'd managed to pick through his plain-dealing behaviour and root out some slight idiosyncrasies and changes in expression, which were then exaggerated so as to paint him as the very picture of arrogance.

As if to banish all thoughts of the issue, Rika chewed enthusiastically on the flavoursome noodles. The bright, fresh taste of the shiso stimulated her appetite, and she found herself letting out an 'mmmm' of satisfaction. The fact that she'd created this taste herself added to the preciousness of the moment.

This was all it took, she thought, to experience a sense of satisfaction of a kind she'd not had before. To make something yourself that you wanted to eat and eat it the way you wanted – was that the very essence of gratification? Until not long ago, she'd had no idea what it was that she wanted to eat, but since she'd begun using her kitchen, she was becoming able to picture, albeit vaguely, the objects of her desires.

With its prose littered with brand names and borrowed phrases, Kajii's blog exuded a refined, composed impression, but the more

Rika read of it, the more she was noticing: the articles Kajii wrote about butter had a hot-bloodedness to them that differed from the rest. As she went on slurping her pasta, Rika picked up the page that she'd put in a clear plastic file.

Fish roe and butter makes for a truly exquisite pairing! By adding butter to pollock roe, with its clusters of firm little orbs just like miniature egg yolks, you take away any unpleasant fishiness from the roe, instead producing a sauce with an inexplicable fullness of taste that forms a perfect coating for the carbohydrates, setting off their plumpness and texture like a dream. Perhaps best of all is the pretty pink hue of the roe, like a gorgeous spring evening (you may know by now that pink is my favourite colour!). The butter and rosy-coloured roe combination coats each and every spaghetti strand, bringing out that delicious semolina scent and generating a flavour that feels like a wave of kindness rising up uncontrollably from inside your chest. I like to top my version with a plentiful sprinkling of chopped shiso. The blend of pink and fresh green puts me in mind of a countryside field in April. Some prefer to garnish the dish with black nori, but I've never been fond of that trend, which kills off the delightful pink shade. Your gentleman friend won't be too pleased if you get nori stuck in your teeth, either!

The blog post featured a camera phone photograph of two plates of pasta, which even the most generous reader would be hard pressed to call a good shot. It looked as if an octogenarian, pressed by the need to message one of her grandchildren, had taken it with great trepidation, and it evoked neither the scent nor the flavour of the dish. The intricately patterned plates appeared to be made by Royal Copenhagen, but they clashed with the shade of the tablecloth. Rika knew she was in no position to criticise others when it came to the presentation of meals, but there was no denying that Kajii's seemed sloppy. She looked to have spent good money on both her ingredients and her tableware, her choice of which reflected her conservative-leaning taste, but it seemed safe to say that she lacked a refined aesthetic sense, and was untidy by nature. Rika found herself comparing the tabletop pictured with Reiko's, where the meals were rustled up from seasonal ingredients you could get hold of anywhere, and whose unbranded tableware arranged seemingly at random still managed to look refined. Rika noted the time stamp on the photo, which read *20 04 2012*.

In May the following year, her first victim, seventy-three-year-old Tadanobu Motomatsu, had died from a sleeping-pill overdose, at his home in front of Shōin Shrine in Setagaya, Tokyo. He was a wealthy bachelor and, like Kajii's late father, had had numerous properties to his name. His struggle with insomnia had gone on for several years, but he had never been prescribed sleeping pills by a doctor. He'd overdosed on barbiturates which he seemed to have acquired privately. The young care worker who came in to help him had testified that he'd appeared dazed for a few days before his death. The overdose might have been an unfortunate mistake caused by the onset of dementia symptoms, and it was also possible that he had taken his own life. It had, however, been established that Motomatsu had had large sums of money squeezed from him by Kajii, that he was having doubts about her pinned on her reluctance to get married, and that he had been adopting a more confrontational approach, putting pressure on her and acting the detective as a way of establishing how serious her intentions were. Kajii had been seeing multiple men at that point in time, which made it hard to be certain, but it seemed probable that the pasta in the photograph had been made for him.

Tucking into a delicious meal cooked for you by a girlfriend young enough to be your granddaughter, before falling into an eternal sleep ... Was that really a death tragic enough to merit the fuss the world was kicking up about it? Even Rika's attempts to put herself in the victims' place couldn't diminish the deliciousness of the spaghetti in front of her. The way the fork kept on moving relentlessly up to her mouth struck her as a sign of her unfeelingness, and she slurped up the pasta strands with exaggerated noises. As it cooled, the butter formed a hard film which adhered the roe to the pasta, bringing out an added layer of umami. Just as Rika was regretting not having boiled more pasta, her phone vibrated from its place on top of the box. She had a new message: *Sorry it's so last minute, but can I stay over tonight? I lost track of time at the Nishihashi launch and missed the last train, and I need to be in early tomorrow.*

It was from Makoto – the first text from him in what felt like a while. His messaging her last minute in search of a bed was not a new occurrence, and she typed her reply without hesitation: *Yeah, sure. If you want anything to drink, pick it up at the convenience store. I've got a clean toothbrush here you can use. I'll get your futon and pyjamas out.*

On a whim, Rika turned on the hob to heat a panful of water. She brought out the second futon kept folded up at the back of her closet, along with the change of clothes that Makoto kept at her place. She finished making up the futon just as the water came to the boil. Adding salt to the pan, she let the strands of spaghetti fan out around its perimeter like the petals of a flower. She wiped down the mirror in the bathroom, set out the new toothbrush, and tidied up the room until the alarm announced that the pasta was done. Then she stirred in the pollock roe and butter as she had before, and was just sprinkling on the garnish of shiso leaves when the intercom rang.

Makoto appeared at the door in a suit, then unfastened his tie as he stepped inside. When his eyes fell on the plate sitting on top of the cardboard box, he let out a startled cry. 'What's this? Have you cooked?'

'Yeah, I had tarako pasta for dinner, so I made you some. If you want it. It's nothing fancy – you just boil the spaghetti and stir in the rest.'

Makoto seemed to have drunk quite a bit, because the tip of his nose and cheeks were bright red. Since getting to the point in his career where he was in charge of editing some of the top authors, his jowls had begun to sag – most likely because of all the lavish socialising it entailed. When he'd first joined the company – the same year as Rika, both of them fresh from university – his dreamy looks had earned him the nickname 'The Prince of Shūmeisha', and he'd been wildly popular among the young female authors, but age had rounded his corners, and he'd become more approachable. He was humorous, with a never-ending supply of conversational topics under his belt, and never drove the person he was speaking to into a corner, which meant that Rika could talk to him for hours on end without feeling ill at ease. Makoto had been brought up in a single-mother household like Rika, and was if anything better around the house than she was. He had no interest in the sorts of power games that were so prevalent in the publishing industry, and was neither showy nor intimidating in his behaviour. As a result, he won over the hearts of his colleagues and the people he worked with. Though he and Rika saw one another very occasionally, as if they only remembered from time to time that they were a couple, and in fact hadn't had sex for over a month now, just holding hands with Makoto or having her hair stroked by him brought a warmth to Rika's heart. In a clear attempt to make himself look younger than his years, Makoto had dyed his own hair a lighter shade of brown than its natural colour and wore it permed, but it matched his round, light-coloured eyes well.

'It's been so long since I was at your place. This smell!'

'Does it smell funny? It must be because I haven't properly cleaned in a while! Sorry.'

'No, no, that's not what I mean. It's a you smell. It's comforting.'

With that, Makoto turned his back to her and changed into the clothes she'd laid out for him. Looking at the soft skin of his bare shoulders, flushed with the alcohol, she was taken by the urge to reach out and touch it. In the early days of their friendship, she'd seen Makoto as an ally to whom she could talk about anything, but the first time she'd held him, she'd felt the heat of his body loosening a deep part of her which had been stiff with tension. He'd told her, that first time, that he liked the way she smelled. They'd been friends for so long that it had made becoming lovers feel a little ticklish, and they both avoided overt displays of sentimentality, but she did wish they had more of the kind of time they'd had when they first started dating, when they could sit and simply wallow in one another's smell and body temperature. Back then, going into work unslept had not been the trial it was now, and they'd spent whole nights lying awake embracing. In any case, this was the longest relationship she'd had with a man.

Makoto hung his suit on a clothes hanger and sprayed it with anti-crease spray, before finally sitting down at the table, legs crossed. He looked like a student, she thought. She found herself casting glances at his mouth as he began to slurp the pasta. Thinking about it, she realised this was the first time she'd ever cooked for him.

'Is it okay?'

'Yeah, of course, it's good. Not that I'd have expected any less.'

Something about the way he was moving the pasta to his mouth seemed awkward to her. He chewed in silence. Knowing that he was partial to noodles after drinking, she'd been expecting more of a reaction, and she felt disappointed. Having polished off the spaghetti in no time at all, Makoto put his hands together in a gesture of thanks, then turned to look at her.

'Thank you. That was really good. But it took me by surprise. Isn't this the first time you've cooked for me?'

'Is it?' she said, carrying his empty plate to the sink and rinsing it off. She was on the verge of telling him that it was all part of her professional research, then thought better of it. Makoto might have been her boyfriend but he was also in the same industry. You never knew how things got leaked. Swearing him to secrecy would make it seem as if she didn't trust him. She didn't want to have her exclusive coverage of Kajii thwarted by anyone.

Poking his head out of the bathroom as he brushed his teeth assiduously, Makoto went on, his words just about comprehensible.

'You know that you don't need to make an effort when I come over, right? I don't need you to act all domestic or anything. I just wanted to see you. If I'm hungry I'll pick up food for myself. You must be so tired with all the end-of-year work.'

'Domestic? Me?'

Repeating the word she found impossible to connect with herself, Rika stared ahead in bewilderment, before murmuring, 'Oh I get it,' and sitting down on the bed. Her actions had been misconstrued, she saw now. Feeling as if whatever she said would only deepen the misunderstanding, she felt incapable of speaking at all. There was a loud gargling sound, then a damp-faced Makoto came into the room smelling of peppermint.

'I know you're my girlfriend, but I don't need you to take care of me in any practical sense, you know? I hate the idea that that burden falls on you when you're working just as hard as me. I saw what my mother had to go through.'

He kissed her on the cheek, and lay down on the futon she'd made up for him, rolling heavily onto his side. 'Night,' he mumbled, and turned out the light, so Rika lay down on her own futon along-side his. He reached out his hand towards hers and held it, but his grip grew slack almost immediately.

Why was it, she wondered as she pulled up the blanket, that a silly little interaction could bug her this much? Makoto hadn't said anything out of line. He cared about her and understood her better than anybody. Had their future as a couple grown uncertain because he'd rejected the idea of her cooking for him? No, that wasn't it. She couldn't clearly see herself marrying Makoto anyway, and she was sickened to the core by the idea that housework must be a woman's job. The word 'domestic' made her picture her mother, cowed and fearful around her late father, breaking down in tears after he picked endless holes in the meals she'd cooked.

Why, though, had Makoto had to take it that way? All she'd done was cook him a plate of pasta, on a whim. Lying in the darkness, replaying each of her actions in a bid to locate the problematic component, Rika felt herself growing ever more awake.

Next to her Makoto was snoring in a way that sounded too agonising, too earth-splitting for someone of his age.

*   *   *

The northerly wind coming off the Ayase river slipped effortlessly through the fabric of her coat, seeming to take hold of her by her very bones and rattle her around. Her frozen fingertip once again sprouted a small hangnail. This was Rika's third visit to the Tokyo Detention House this month. As she emerged from the visitor's exit, pulling the lapels of her coat tightly about her, her eyes fell on a sign across the road reading 'Masuda-ya'. There was a nostalgic look about its small, weathered wooden facade, which put Rika in mind of the regulation stationery shop outside the entrance to her primary school. This must be where you could buy items to give to people in the Detention House, she figured. The shop next door seemed to fulfil the same function, but its shutters were down. Glancing at her watch, Rika saw it was just before four. She had ample time before her next meeting. Before she knew it, she was making her way across the road. Again there were fresh flowers laid beside the guardrail, blowing in the wind.

Today, once again, Kajii had refused to see her.

Maybe, Rika mused, Kajii's recent crankiness wasn't down to her. Next week was Christmas, after all. Rika was beginning to understand that for someone with tastes as extravagant as Kajii's, being barred from going out during this season, being limited to the foods on a menu determined by others, was a profoundly unfortunate turn of events.

The final update to Kajii's blog was dated from the day before her arrest, 28 November of the year before last:

Not long now until Christmas! I adore this time of the year, when the outside world is at its most captivating. This year I'm throwing caution to the wind and cooking a succulent turkey stuffed with chestnuts and rice, complete with a sumptuous honey-rich gravy, just as we learned in cooking class. They'll be taking orders for Christmas cakes in no time, too. I'm currently debating which to plump for …
No, scrap that, I've decided!

Such was the buoyant note on which the blog concluded. This would be the third winter Kajii had spent in the Detention House, Rika calculated. Her patience must be reaching its limits.

The interior of Masuda-ya was lined with shelves made of the same aged wood as the shop's exterior, crowded with stationery, towels and underwear, bags of sweets, weekly magazines, and all kinds of other items. The brands of confectionery on sale were extremely old-fashioned; Rika remembered seeing them in the supermarket as a girl but was astonished to discover they were still being produced. Walking around convenience stores, where the newest goods were deliberately placed in the customer's line of sight, Rika would frequently feel twinges of temptation, but here she felt a surprising absence of any urge to buy anything.

Still, the only food items that the Detention House permitted to be brought inside were those bought either from here or the shop next door, which was currently shut. The customer would inform the cashier of the name of the prisoner they wished to send the items to, and the shop would deliver the purchased goods to the inmate in question. The grey-haired woman behind the counter, whom Rika assumed must be the owner, was glaring at her. Rika didn't want the woman to think that she was just idly browsing. She knew she had to decide on something. Calm down, she entreated herself. Kajii would know that only food from the designated shops could be sent in. Besides, didn't having such a limited range of options make things easier?

The family pack of assorted cakes in the glass case was the kind she had shared with her classmates during middle school parties. The green Sanyo cans arranged in a row on the shelf caught her eye. It was a long time since she'd seen canned fruit. Back in middle school, whenever she caught a cold, her mother would place a can of peaches in the fridge for her before setting out to work. She didn't know whether Kajii had access to a refrigerator, but those canned peaches that slipped so smoothly down the throat seemed like something that she might enjoy. Then there were chestnut manjū, canton fruit jelly, cigar-shaped sweets made of wheat gluten, Castella cakes stuffed with sweet bean paste ... Among the rows of Japanese sweets in austerely designed bags made by brands she'd never heard of, the boxes of Morinaga cookies struck her as the most appealing. There were three types: Marie, Moonlight and Choice. Which to go for? She'd probably sampled all three at some point, but couldn't recall how they tasted. She probably should have checked their ingredients or descriptions, but they were kept in the glass case and she was reluctant to ask the stern-faced woman to get them out and show them to her. After some deliberating, Rika made her selection.

'I'd like to have a can of peaches and a box of Choice sent to the Detention House.'

Of the three, the Choice box was the only one whose illustration featured butter. The shop woman clicked the beads on her abacus, then held out a piece of paper and a ballpoint pen to Rika. In the 'Prisoner's Name' box, Rika wrote in Manako Kajii's name, and then filled in the other required information. The refrigerated case caught her eye, and on impulse she asked the woman, 'You don't stock butter, do you?'

'We used to, but there's a supply shortage at the moment,' the woman replied brusquely. Rika paid up and left the shop. Even if there had been butter, it would doubtless have been either the bog-standard Snow Brand or else a cheap unbranded kind. Nevertheless, Rika felt that was the thing that would have most pleased Kajii to receive. She hoped that by the next time she came, it would be back in stock.

Rika hailed a cab to Ayase Station, where she caught the Chiyoda Line to Hibiya. Stepping off the train, she headed straight for the bathrooms. Standing in front of the mirror, she took out her make-up removal sheets and vigorously wiped her face clean. She balled up the wet wipe now streaked with black and beige, and threw it in the bin under the sink.

A young woman emerged from one of the cubicles and came to stand alongside Rika at the sinks. She applied a coat of pink lipstick, and then flashed a smile at herself in the mirror. Rika watched the girl leave with a feeling of goodwill in her chest.

With deliberate roughness of touch, Rika rubbed a thick coat of Nivea cream into her bare skin. She removed her contact lenses and replaced them with glasses, and pulled back her hair tightly with an elastic band. She needed to get rid of all traces of softness and sweetness about her before joining the man she was about to meet. The sight of the person in the mirror before her, tall and wiry and of indeterminate gender, gave her a sense of deep satisfaction. The bluish-white skin, suggesting exhaustion, worked well too. Yesterday a succession of things had not gone to plan at work, and she had only managed to sleep for three hours.

Painfully aware of her lack of exercise, Rika decided, when she emerged above ground, to walk the short distance to Shimbashi along the railway tracks. It was still early for people to be heading home from work, and yet Yūrakuchō at dusk was spilling over with people in suits. From here and there she heard the sound of dry coughing, and noticed several people whose eyes stood out because their faces were half-covered by masks. I need to get my flu vaccine, Rika thought to herself. The cold, dry wind slapped against her exposed, moist skin. Above her head, Yamanote and Keihin–Tōhoku Line trains went slipping by one after another.

Rika knew that in her industry there were women who used their sex to their advantage. She'd heard rumours of female journalists who entered into physical relationships with their sources. Yet personal relationships between men and women was not a domain in which others would intervene. It was up to the individual how they comported themselves, and in this world, where the quality of the story was everything, it would have been seen as crass to find fault with and lambast such methods. The women in question weren't open about what they were doing, and nobody could prove that it was going on.

To build a unique relationship that defied categorisation, and to then allow that relationship to morph until it just about justified itself – of course Rika hadn't spoken with any of the people whom the rumours were about, but she felt sure that inside, this was how they articulated what they were doing, resolute in their determination to feel no compunction about their actions.

In other words, even the high-earning and independent women in the media industry engaged in an alternative form of prostitution to get their hands on the hot tip-offs. And while Rika herself didn't employ her femininity to win over bureaucrats and police officers, she couldn't, hand on her heart, swear that she'd never behaved flirtatiously. She'd recently discovered that a female journalist from a rival newspaper, who'd landed several major political scoops, and whom Rika secretly admired, had in fact been sleeping with a Diet member for a long time and that all her information came from him, and her disappointment was still fresh. Not knowing who to blame, she looked up at the sunset sky, boxed in by buildings.

This was why a woman like Manako Kajii – a woman who didn't hide the fact that she used her sexuality as a weapon – was met with such fierce scorn, and even a kind of terror. In a statement in court, Kajii had asserted that her body had a special value, that she granted her lovers a fantastic experience, and that as such, it stood to reason she'd be rewarded financially. With no way of verifying the truth of her claims about the experience she and her body afforded, those listening to her found their rational faculties shutting down. The only response possible was to nod and say, 'Really, is that so?'

Trying to remember the woman who'd stood beside her at the sinks in the public toilet, Rika noticed that her features had already faded in her memory. That made sense, for it wasn't the girl's face that had drawn her attention, so much as the sense of taking good care of herself that she gave off. Since getting married, Reiko had begun exuding a similar kind of aura. For what was about to take place, Rika told herself now, she had no need for that soft-edged, fragrant presence.

She and her source met once a month in an izakaya with private rooms under the railway girders of Shimbashi Station. The izakaya was a ramshackle, sepia-toned place where every object looked like it had been simmered in mirin. They met on the third Thursday of the month at 5 p.m., before it got busy. They would be finished in an hour and a half, and subsequently return to work. Yes, they had a drink or two, but it hardly qualified as drinking together.

From the kitchen at the back, Rika could hear the sizzle of old oil boiling, and smell it too. The owner of the place, who must have been in his seventies, gave her a drawn-out cry of welcome: 'Irasshai!' He indicated to the room furthest from the kitchen, shielded by a screen, its two seats sunk into the floor.

'The giving up smoking didn't last long, I see!'

Rika let out a dry cackle as she sat herself down heavily opposite the suited man smoking a Highlight cigarette and threw her bag on top of the tatami. With the moist hand towel on the table, she wiped her brow and cheeks. The rules for their rendezvous were set: they didn't pour one another's drinks or serve one another food, didn't attempt to show respect for the other as one was obliged to do in other forms of professional entertaining, and spoke at length and as one-sidedly as they wanted about whatever they wanted to. When he was appearing on television as a commentator, Yoshinori Shinoi had a lot to say, but when you encountered him in real life he was taciturn. Sometimes Rika would spend their whole time together complaining, at which times he would display neither great interest nor irritation in response, but simply nod and make the appropriate noises, drinking at his own pace. On screen, he had a glint in his eye and appeared sturdily built, but the person sitting in front of her now was a slender, unassuming middle-aged man, his hair liberally streaked with grey. The way he jiggled his long arms and legs and hunched his tall back gave him an air of an adolescent boy. She noticed his shirt was slightly creased, but it didn't look dirty.

'I never said I'd given up. Just that I'd succeeded in cutting down,' he said quietly. Stubbing out the cigarette he'd begun in the ashtray, he raised his steamed-up glass to his mouth.

'I'm guessing that with all the TV work you've had even less time for sleep than usual. Wow, quite the classic old-man selection you've got there!'

Spread out on the table in front of Shinoi, alongside his shōchū with hot water, was an array of traditional izakaya dishes: braised burdock root, edamame, Atka mackerel, and tofu simmered in dashi. When she'd first started meeting Shinoi, his order had always been beer and deep-fried chicken, and the change made her realise that he'd started taking care of his health. Rika ordered a flask of hot sake, along with buttered sweetcorn and grilled spicy pollock roe. She tucked into the appetiser that the server brought her along with her sake flask and cup, using her chopsticks to lift up the slimy contents of the small dish with evident distaste.

'As usual, I've no idea what this is … Some kind of seafood? Or is it konnyaku?'

However many times she visited this place, she never got to the bottom of what exactly was in the sweet-and-sour gunk that they'd serve just a mouthful of as the obligatory appetiser. If the food here wasn't offensively bad, it wasn't particularly good either. The draw of the place, for her and for Shinoi, lay mostly in its lack of customers.

'I had something sent to one of the inmates at Tokyo Detention House for the first time today: cookies and canned peaches. A female inmate. I just figured that she must feel deprived at this time of year, not being able to eat cake and fried chicken like everyone else in Japan.'

Rika hadn't yet told Shinoi about Manako Kajii, but she felt close to confiding in him now. He was the only person she could talk to about work matters without concealing anything.

'I don't know, I hear the food in Kosuge is pretty good. You have three meals a day cooked for you by prisoners with chefs' licences. I've even heard talk of people who commit crimes just to get a place there …'

'Are you serious? Don't people call prison food "rank rice"?'

'I think that's probably an outmoded perception, from back in the days when people thought anything other than white rice was an insult to the taste buds. The rice they serve in the Detention House is mixed with various types of grains. I guess people took umbrage with that. Nowadays all of that stuff – barley and millet and what have you – has undergone a reappraisal, and is seen as very healthy. My guess is that they eat far better than you or I do.'

'You're right, that sounds a lot healthier and more nutritious than my diet. I never cook, and I get all my meals from the convenience store.'

For some reason, Rika felt loath to mention to Shinoi that she'd been using her kitchen of late.

'I'll see if I can get my hands on the latest "Special Occasions" menu for the Detention House.'

Shinoi jotted something down in his battered brown leather notepad. Whenever I see this guy he looks tired, Rika thought, observing him surreptitiously from across her sake cup. His skin had a greyish hue, and the whites of his eyes were clouded. Maybe she was not so different from him, but Shinoi's tiredness seemed to have sunk even deeper into his body, a kind of resignation that couldn't be erased. She'd caught wind of a rumour that he'd been divorced for years, but he barely ever spoke about his private life, and she didn't know whether or not it was true. Now she said, her tone deliberately blunt, 'After my parents divorced, my dad started leading an unhealthy lifestyle. Eventually he became an alcoholic, more or less, and one day he keeled over and died, all alone in his flat. You should be careful, you know. He was about your age, I think. How old are you now?'

'Forty-eight. And please don't come at me with that kind of ominous stuff. My diet might be a bit rough around the edges, but I have health checks pretty regularly. I've started jogging in the mornings around the Imperial Palace, and I buy a carton of vegetable juice whenever I catch sight of one in the station.'

Perhaps he was offended by her words, because for once Shinoi took a hand in steering the conversation.

There was no denying that he looked exhausted, but there was nothing about him that suggested that things had got out of hand. He didn't bring his frustrations or his bad physical condition into the conversation, either. She imagined that he had the strength and the wisdom it took to recuperate. It was for that reason that he was easy to be around. That was a feature he shared with Makoto, in fact. When it came to members of the opposite sex, Rika got along well with these types who didn't require women to play hostess or manager. She was fairly sure that Shinoi felt similarly about their connection. It was because they got along that he made the time to see her. He took care of Rika just like he would a male peer or colleague younger than him.

'I guess for someone of your age, you're on the careful side. It's weird, isn't it? Why is it that with nobody to watch over them, men can't stop themselves from falling into disrepair? And that disrepair is then looked upon kindly and excused by the world, seen not as a failure of personal responsibility but something poignant and tragic.'

Recently the disorderly behaviour of a former sportsman in his fifties, who had given up his career after being suspected of involvement with criminal gangs, had been making the news. After his wife of many years had left him and taken their children with her, he had gone off the rails, and had been seen out late at night on several occasions, drunkenly losing his cool. People suspected he was dabbling with drugs as well. To one journalist who'd interacted with him directly, he'd apparently said, 'Eating alone is so lonely, and the food tastes terrible, so I end up going out. I don't know how to cook rice by myself. Shit, I don't even know where the salt's kept! What did I do wrong, to have ended up with such a miserable life? I want my family back.' After this lamentation, he'd sent a public message to his sons, whom the family court had ruled he could no longer see, entitled 'From Dad.' The men's weekly magazines unanimously covered the story as a hero's tragic fall from grace, writing sympathetic articles portraying the occurrence as something that could happen to anyone.

Rika couldn't feel the slightest bit sorry for him – and not because he was a man who had for years been dogged by shady rumours, whose behaviour tended towards emotional blackmail, and who had caused his wife and children much suffering by having an affair. No, what bothered her was that he didn't even think to make the effort to improve his eating habits by himself. He was still of an age where he had no trouble getting around, and although on paper he might have been unemployed, he was still gifted with more money and time than the regular person, not to mention plentiful contacts and information sources. These days you could even find healthy choices at convenience stores and diners and late-night restaurants. Even someone incapable of cooking could still, by applying themselves just a little, live a passably healthy lifestyle. Perhaps his reckless, self-destructive bent was a curse directed at the fans who'd deserted him, at the media who'd built him up then abandoned him, and above all at his wife and sons, who'd walked out on him and started afresh. It was as if he were saying: *May this image of how low I've sunk brand itself into your minds, because it's all your fault.* The patterns of behaviour were so familiar. Choosing to kick up a stink until help was proffered him, instead of explicitly asking for it. Stubbornly refusing to change his way of living even a fraction. Insisting that family was the most important thing to him, while broadcasting to the world that his wife had left him to die.

Couldn't he simply go about rebuilding his life, and if he failed and died in the process, then so much the better? But wasn't the attitude of this man the same, to a greater or lesser extent, as the men that Kajii had killed? The things those men had said while they were alive, and the testimony of their family and friends, came filtering back to Rika now, one after another:

—*I'm scared of getting old alone. Before, my lifestyle was getting progressively less healthy. I wanted a woman to make me meals and take care of me, I didn't care who it was. I do feel suspicious of her. It's occurred to me that I might be being conned. My family's told me time and time again to break up with her, but I don't care. Even if it means cutting ties with my family, I'm choosing to be with her.*

—That woman found the cracks in the hearts of those poor victims who were living miserable, lonely lives, and went worming her way in. Men are inept creatures. They can't build a life for themselves without the support and kindness of a woman.

—There are things that every woman can learn from Manako Kajii. There's not a man in the world who can't be won over by a kind female presence who knows how to cook. The way to a man's heart is through his stomach, after all.

Whichever aspect of it you considered, Rika thought, the Kajii case was tinged by misogyny and the excessive self-pity felt by lonely men. Was thinking that way tantamount to victim-blaming, though? Usually, she loathed the all-too common take that people were responsible for their own destinies.

Perhaps I'm lacking in compassion because I'm still physically fit and capable of working, Rika thought to herself, trying to adopt an even stance on the matter. After the divorce, Rika's mother had raised her single-handedly, and Rika was aware that she was perhaps overly aligned with her mother's perspective. But it was possible that she herself would spend her old age alone, neglecting to take good care of herself – she might even have the wool pulled over her eyes by a younger man and have everything stolen from her.

But if it *were* me, she thought, I wouldn't go down the road to self-destruction solely because I was lonely. I'm pretty certain that I'd guard my savings with my life, too, and be wary of any propositions that came my way that sounded too good to be true. Among the people she was least likely to place her trust in were significantly younger unemployed men whom she'd met on the internet and asked for money from their first meeting. Even if she were on the verge of being conned, she was confident that Reiko, who by then would be just as old as she was, would notice, and step in to warn her. Even if Reiko were to die before her and she had nobody to talk to, then surely, so long as she had internet access, she'd find an online community of old people in the neighbourhood and join their circle. Or was she supposed to chalk up the fact that she was able to think all this through in a matter-of-fact way, not to mention her adaptability and her communication skills, to her being a woman? After all, two of Kajii's three victims had been of an age that still barely merited terming elderly, and had plenty of money.

But no, she was better off not thinking about this any more. A sense of foreboding loomed over her like a heavy cloud. In a bid to prevent the cloud from casting a shadow over their meeting, Rika took a gulp of sake. Her eyes on the sizzling hotplate with the buttered corn that had been brought to the table, she said, 'I wanted to ask you! Do you know the book *The Story of Little Babaji*? I was reading it the other day at the house of a married friend of mine.'

'I do. The one where the tigers turn into butter?'

'That's the one. Do you feel sorry for the tigers? Do you think Babaji's family are cruel?'

'It's just natural selection, isn't it? That's the way things work. Nobody's in the wrong. The tigers need to eat to stay alive.'

Shinoi strung his thoughts together as he de-shelled his edamame. The skin on his hands was dark and his middle fingers were very long.

'Babaji responded to the situation the only way he could, and the tigers went and killed themselves, no? And when the father brought the butter home to eat, he didn't know what it was – didn't know it came from a bunch of dead tigers. That's how order is preserved in the natural world, across various ecosystems – by the ones who've just so happened to make it through by getting their own way. I know it can seem cruel. We've come to use the word "evolution" as though it were a resolutely positive thing, but all it means is that the species best-adapted for a particular environment survive, and the others die out. Like how people often say that our print media here in Japan will gradually be driven out by the digital forms, like you see happening in America. That can hardly be called progress, can it?'

Shinoi fell silent, and his words turned round and round in Rika's head. When he continued, it was in the same tone as before.

'Do you know the members' club La Vie in Ginza? The owner was seen coming out of a maternity clinic in Kioichō that all the celebrities go to.'

Choosing her words carefully, Rika decided to venture inside the small jungle that had cropped up in front of her.

'Oh, I've heard rumours about her! Is she still single? She's the famously beautiful one, right?'

'She used to be a model, and she's apparently still quite something.'

'In that case I imagine her customers are a glamorous bunch.'

She caught sight of a gentle flicker at the back of Shinoi's irises.

'There's the former pop-star Tomomi Otani, and Toyohashi, the baseball player. And then ...'

As Shinoi pronounced the name of the politician upon whom so many hopes were pinned at the next elections, the corner of his mouth curled unmistakably. Rika felt the floor sway a little beneath her.

'Thank you.'

To this day, Shinoi had never given her a clear-cut tip-off. Instead, in a tone that suggested he was relating the kind of gossip known to everyone, he would drop into conversation nuggets that lay peripheral to the heart of the story in question. This was why she couldn't tell anybody about their relationship. They'd met two years previously at the magazine department's end-of-year party, when he'd still been writing articles for them, and had ended up sitting next to one another by chance. She'd been struck by his reserved persona, which seemed to indicate a distaste for rowdiness – very different to how he came across in the media. The next time they'd run into one another was outside the house of a Diet member. It had been raining. Spurred by her desire for information about the politician in question, she'd invited him for a drink, and he'd brought her to this place as somewhere close by where they could shelter from the rain. It was from that point in time that Rika's run of scoops had begun.

'I didn't say a thing.'

For the first time that day, Shinoi smiled a little. His eyes crinkled up to nothing, and a cluster of small lines formed around his mouth. It was an intimate smile that made the room feel smaller – it reminded Rika that they were alone together.

There were certain things that newspapers and national news channels couldn't report on: the backgrounds of crime victims, the personal lives of people in the limelight and politicians' affairs. People like Shinoi felt that they didn't want to let the information they'd happened to get hold of go to waste, even if they themselves couldn't use it. Passing it along to a new journalist at a weekly magazine was perhaps a perfectly natural thing to do, not dissimilar to serving the leftovers of yesterday's dinner to a pet. But why *me*? Rika was often left asking herself. The question unsettled her. She didn't have anything to offer Shinoi in return. Several times, she imagined herself through his eyes. There was nothing about her that would rouse his interest in her as a woman. He had never tried to steer things down that route, and she'd never even had a premonition that such a thing might happen.

'Can I have one?'

She scrounged a cigarette from him. His lighter was running out, so Rika called to the middle-aged waitress with a disinterested manner and asked her to bring the lighter from the kitchen. Putting the dry cigarette to her lips, she held up the gas lighter that looked a lot like a pistol and lit it. At the sight of this, which she fancied looked like something from a hard-boiled detective movie, Shinoi gave a wry smile. Rika didn't usually smoke, and had to make an effort to make sure she didn't cough with the first drag. She found Shinoi's look of incredulous amusement deeply comforting.

I just picked up something that he tossed away in front of me, that's all it is. No different to Babaji's dad bringing home the butter he'd found in the jungle.

While it was still warm the buttered corn tasted aromatic and flavoursome, but as it cooled, an acridity began to emerge. They must have been using margarine, she thought.

Dear Ms Machida,
It's been a while since we've been in touch. Thank you for the canned
peaches and biscuits that you kindly sent me. Choice are my favourite
Morinaga biscuits. I'm aware that Moonlight are the more popular
selection, but both they and Marie are made with margarine.
Christmas is fast approaching. The year before last, I was planning
on ordering a Christmas cake from West. Regrettably, I never got to
eat it. Well-made buttercream is truly delicious, but unfortunately
it's so hard to come by of late. Would you be so good as to eat the cake
on my behalf? If you were to eat 'the real thing', and tell me your
impressions immediately afterwards, we might have ourselves some
fun.
    Manako Kajii

Rika found the letter waiting on her desk after coming back from
her meeting with Shinoi. It was now the following day.

After reading the letter twice through, Rika had picked up her
phone and pressed the phone number listed on the West home page.
After a few rings, a softly spoken woman whose manner reminded
Rika of a school prefect picked up.

'I'm terribly sorry, but our reservation period for Christmas cakes
runs only from the first to the twentieth of December. This year we
received an unprecedented number of reservations … I'm terribly
sorry.' Her words came out smoothly enough that Rika could tell
she'd repeated this message many times, but still avoided sounding
robotic. Rika put down the phone. Wondering to herself whether the
unprecedented popularity had something to do with the butter
shortage, she booted up the computer on her desk. A search for the
term 'West Christmas cake' yielded numerous articles describing its
taste, from personal blogs to the sites of well-known food writers.
The writers were united in their lavish praise for its classic, refined
flavour. Yet Rika knew that borrowing another's words wouldn't do.
She couldn't fall into the trap of thinking that she understood simply
because she'd read about it. Unless she could articulate in her own

words something she'd experienced with her own tongue, there was no point. Manako Kajii would see through her lies immediately.

I'm being tested, she thought to herself.

Rika wracked her brains for any contacts that might be of help: bureaucrats, police officers, celebrities, sports journalists … but no, none of them had anything to do with cakes. She was starting to think half in earnest about standing outside the shop and paying someone who'd come to collect theirs to hand it over to her. Just then her eyes fell on the various weekly magazines in the rack by the desk. The *Shūmei Weekly* ranked third in the industry. She recalled what Shinoi had been saying about natural selection. Everyone thought of this as an age where magazines didn't sell, but you could be sure that everyone in the industry passed their eyes over them without fail every week. You could even go as far as to say that the people reading the magazines the most avidly, the ones dropping the most money on them, were fellow media employees.

'Aha!' she found herself saying aloud. She picked up her phone. Reiko answered almost immediately.

'This is unlike you, to call at this time! Aren't you at work? What's up?'

From the sound of running water in the background, she guessed that Reiko was preparing dinner.

'Do you know if Ryōsuke's company buys the cakes made by rival companies, for research?'

'Of course! Apparently on Christmas, Valentine's Day and White Day they buy all the products made by the other companies, spread them out in a line in a meeting room, and photograph and taste them. Sometimes if there's cake left over from one of the famous brands, he'll sneak some out and bring it so I get to taste it too.'

Rika briefly outlined her situation and Reiko understood right away.

'A West Christmas cake … Okay, got it. It's a pretty classic choice, so I can't imagine they won't have one. I'll ask. Leave it with me.'

There was a bounce to Reiko's tone now, and Rika could sense her friend's enthusiasm for this new mission she'd been entrusted with. Reiko excelled at whatever she turned a hand to and enjoyed helping others out. Being tasked only with housework every day offered little outlet for those qualities, though, and it seemed as if she'd been waiting for just this kind of opportunity.

'Thank you so much, I mean it. I know I said this in my text, but it was entirely thanks to your advice that Kajii opened up to me in the first place. I owe everything to you.'

Barely any time had elapsed between putting down the phone to Reiko and receiving a message from Ryōsuke.

Now it was Christmas Eve, and Rika had come to the Tokyo headquarters of Ryōsuke's confectionery company, not far from Gaiemmae Station. When she reached the top of the subway stairs, she saw fine snow falling on Route 246. The office building contained a company-run cafe on the ground floor, and Rika spotted Ryōsuke through the glass, chatting with a woman she assumed was the owner. The inside of the cafe was adorned with red and green decorations and a Christmas tree with twinkling lights, and she could see a stylish couple tucking into identical slices of cake. The Ryōsuke who lifted a hand to her in greeting struck her as somewhat off colour, brimming with less youthful vitality than usual. Even the trademark pink tint to his cheeks was gone. She broached the topic hesitantly, thanking him for responding to such an audacious request, and he smiled feebly.

'Every Christmas, everyone working at headquarters gets sent out to the factories to work on the cake-decorating lines. We do that all night, and then come morning, trot off to the city-centre department stores to do research, without any sleep at all. I know a lot of people think that working in a confectionery company sounds like a dream job, but the truth is that the people working in firms like ours are all well-built, sporty types. You have to be, otherwise you wouldn't last a minute.'

'At least when you finally get home you'll be eating Christmas dinner with Reiko.'

'That's true,' Ryōsuke said, smiling and looking a little bashful, before leading Rika to the employee lift at the back of the lobby. The small enclosed space smelled of chilled fresh cream.

'To repay the favour, I'd like to do a feature on your company at some point. Our readers love all that kind of stuff: insider secrets about product development and the backstories to the marketing campaigns and stuff.'

'What I'd love to say right now is, "There's no need to do anything in return, you're my wife's best friend!" But the truth is, that'd be much appreciated. We can't even scrape together an advertising budget at the moment, and it'd be great to be featured in a magazine with a readership as wide as yours. When times get tight, confectionery is one of the first luxuries people scrimp on. These days, when you can buy decent cakes in any convenience store, it's tough for middle-grade manufacturers like ours.'

It struck Rika acutely now how true luxury when it came to food demanded determination and energy, even more than it did money. You had to keep abreast of which products were in season, search out a bevy of go-to shops, and be forever researching new products and trends. You had to be perpetually asking your body, calmly, what it was craving at that particular time. In Kajii, that energy was so strong you could have termed it an obsession, the flame that kept her alive. However much time and money Rika were to have, she would never be that way.

The lift reached the third floor. Ryōsuke opened the door to the meeting room, and Rika was greeted by a fresh, fruity scent. The long table positioned centrally in the empty room was lined from one end to the other with Christmas cakes created by all of Japan's most famous confectionery companies. It made for quite a sight.

'They've already been photographed, so it's fine to tuck in. The product innovation bunch are coming for a tasting session later, so I'd rather you didn't polish off the whole thing, but one slice shouldn't be a problem.'

With a smile Ryōsuke pointed her to cake number four. The buttercream creation was different to the cakes around it, their surfaces crowded with strawberries, ivy and edible sugar decorations. Aside from the wreaths and candles rendered in cream on its white top, the only decorations here were three flame-shaped biscuits and a sprinkling of ground pistachios and walnuts. Its surface was as smooth as a snowscape, but Rika could tell that innumerable glistening particles of high-quality animal fat lay cloistered away inside. Like the stars, which are still twinkling up in the daytime sky though we can't see them, Rika thought.

'I have to say there's something quite compelling about doing away with all the strawberries and Santas and message plates and so on, and aiming to win the battle on the strength of their buttercream and sponge alone. West always go to town on their ingredients, fully aware it'll leave them in the red.'

'Wow. I've only ever heard of them before for their Leaf Pie biscuits.'

Saying this, Rika pictured the leaf-shaped pastry biscuits in their white box that someone had left in the corner of the break room at work. The vast proportion of the employees at her company were men, and yet those biscuits had vanished in no time at all. Rika had been slow in making a move, and missed her chance.

'They say that the West cafe in Meguro that shut two years ago never made a profit, despite being always full. That's pretty amazing to think about. You have to respect them.'

Meguro lay within walking distance of Fudō-mae, where Kajii had lived. The cafe had to have been one of her favourite places. If that was the case, Rika thought, it was likely that she'd been aiming to pick up her West Christmas cake from there.

With practised gestures, Ryōsuke cut into the cake, transferred a slice onto a plate and held it out to Rika, along with a plastic fork. Thanking him, Rika broke into the slice. She could sense its density beneath the fork's prongs. Its graceful white and light-yellow cross-section brought a smile to her face.

'This is actually the first time I've ever tried buttercream.'

No doubt because it had been refrigerated until very recently, the cream retained a certain firmness. As it melted under the heat of her tongue, the sweet butter expanded lusciously, rousing all the cells across her body capable of apprehending its rich goodness. The dense sponge saturated with the rich, weighty aroma of milk made her think that she would never again be satisfied by fluffy shortcake with its sweet and sour tang. True taste came with a high price tag, and a high calorie count to match. You had to traverse mountains to come by it. Rika shut her eyes and let the memory imprint itself onto her tongue. Somewhere in the distance, Rika could hear Ryōsuke's voice teasing her about how serious she looked.

When she stepped out of the office, the snow was still falling. Buying an umbrella seemed too much effort, and her coat grew dusted in snow as she walked at a clip towards Omotesandō Station and took the Chiyoda Line to Ayase Station. She caught a cab to Tokyo Detention House and filled in the usual visitors' application form. She passed through the metal detectors, walked down the long corridor and then took the lift to the specified floor. Standing in front of the numbered door, Rika found her chest ablaze with conviction that today she would get to see Kajii. After a little while, Kajii appeared with a look of great poise, accompanied by a male prison officer. It was three weeks since Rika had last seen her.

Her first thought was that Kajii looked prettier than the last time. Her skin seemed even paler and smoother than before. Stained a paleish pink shade, her cheeks and eyelids appeared somewhat swollen, as though she'd been crying, but that look wasn't without allure. She wore a white sweater above a long checked skirt – an outmoded sort of outfit, which left the impression that its wearer was ill-adapted to the times she was living in. But it was also a sophisticated look, and suited Kajii's face. What's more, it was ideally suited for Christmas Eve. Kajii was, in her own way, attempting to enjoy her life in the Detention House. Rika recalled Shinoi's mention of natural selection. She had the sense that come war, come famine, this woman would find a way of surviving.

'It's good to see you. I, um ... I just ate some of the West Christmas cake you mentioned, so I came to thank you for telling me about it, and share my thoughts.'

Kajii didn't smile. Her sleepy-looking eyes seemed a little out of focus. Partly thanks to the bobbly white sweater that she was wearing, there was something humorously snowman-like about her appearance. Rika didn't feel afraid of her today. The taste of the cake still lingered on her tongue. Fighting back her impulse to rush ahead, she parted her lips, still oily with the grease of the butter.

'A simple wreath design, with candles in the middle. The intricate cream piping looked like a sculpture. Aside from the sprinkling of ground nuts and the biscuits in the shape of candle flames, a total absence of decoration. I'm no expert when it comes to confectionery, but I understand that unsalted butter is used as standard in baking. By contrast, the West buttercream uses salted butter. That salinity really brings out the overall sweetness of the cake, adding depth to its richness. The sponge has a satisfying density to it, declaring itself roughly on the tongue, scented like eggs and flour. The Christmas cakes I've eaten up until now have all been shortcakes, and it's always seemed to me that the delicate, fluffy whipped cream and the sweet sourness of the strawberries obliterate the aroma and the texture of the sponge. You talked previously about the sensation of falling that you get from eating butter. The West Christmas cake is ...'

One day, Rika thought to herself, I'm going to be writing my own articles. I'm not the sort of person to reach for trite phrases. Desperately she groped for the right words to command Kajii's attention. She wasn't prepared to lose out to Kajii's speech about rice with butter and soy sauce. Suddenly, the image of the powder snow she'd encountered outside Gaiemmae came back to her – those crystal flakes whirling and dancing down from the grey sky.

'A fall that never ends, that leaves you spinning and spiralling as if waltzing as you plummet ceaselessly down.'

Those perfectly black eyes looked at her straight on, taking her in. Even through the acrylic screen, Rika could tell that Kajii's lips had grown moist. Her neck heaved up and down. She's hungry, Rika realised instinctively. Rika's description of the cake, her explanation of the sensation of eating it, had roused desire in Kajii. Rika couldn't remember the last time that she'd induced desire in anybody.

A memory surfaced. Back when she'd been at an all-girls' school, a classmate had begged Rika, tearfully, to let her kiss her. 'Please, just once,' she'd entreated. Rika had politely refused, fighting back her surprise. When Rika had re-encountered the girl many years later at a class reunion, she had transformed into a cheerful, good-natured woman, married with two children, and had said nonchalantly to Rika, 'I was so desperate back then to fall in love, but there were no boys around, and since you were the most boyishly handsome person in sight, I had no choice but to become obsessed with you. I went a bit funny in the head.' It was clear she was attempting to write the whole thing off as an amusing anecdote from the past, but Rika could remember the episode with an almost cruel level of detail. There was no doubting it – in that moment, the girl had desired Rika. Her eyes and her lips had grown moist, just like Kajii's were now, and she stared at Rika fixedly with a gaze hot enough to burn right through her. She'd known back then that lots of girls wanted her. Even though she'd understood that she was desired as a substitute for a man, Rika had felt as though she was being validated in her entirety, in a way that made her special.

Come to think of it, it was from around that point on that she had taken care that her body didn't become rounded and soft. Ensured, too, that she was the best in both her studies and in sport, that she was boyishly rugged and aloof in her behaviour, all the while taking care that these efforts went undetected by people around her. In order to fulfil the wishes of the girls around her for a prince, she needed to excel at everything with cool, calm composure. Sometimes, with a classmate of her choosing, she would open the first couple of buttons of her school shirt, allowing a glimpse of the sturdy nape of her neck and collarbone. She would casually drape her arm around them, brushing shoulders in a way that seemed totally unaffected. Through their uniforms, she could feel their pulses racing.

Instilling desire in someone was a lot of fun, regardless of whether that person was male or female.

But Rika had always believed that using your own wiles to excite someone was a malicious thing to do, in some ways – a base act, a dirty deed. Who had made her think that way? she wondered now. Knowing she'd instilled desire unwittingly in someone whom she wanted nothing to do with would send shivers down her spine, and she'd be swallowed up by a wave of self-hatred. But if the person in question was someone she'd deliberately targeted, then surely her success didn't devalue her in any way. A true emotion, one that she'd been holding back all this time, moved through her body. Would she be able to put a stop to this? she wondered with concern.

'Merry Christmas, Rika,' Kajii said in a voice thick and sweet as savarin syrup. The sound reverberated, until it was absorbed by the cold, hard walls of the visiting room.

CHAPTER THREE

On New Year's Day in Tokyo Detention House, the prisoners are served ozōni soup and red and white manjū, as well as a tiered bentō box containing a selection of osechi. The contents vary slightly according to the budget, but this year it's likely to be: deep-fried chicken, nishime, pork kakuni, grilled fish, simmered prawns, kazunoko, yōkan, datemaki, pink-and-white kamaboko, kuri-kinton, kuromame, and fruit. It's the only day of the year when they're served pure white rice, rather than rice mixed with barley. I hope this coming year treats you well!

The first message that Rika received in the new year was this one from Shinoi. She poked her head out from the gap between the down duvet and the futon, which was thin enough that she could feel the hardness of the floor beneath, and reached for her phone, which lay beside her pillow. She smiled as she read the text, clearly written by someone unused to composing messages that weren't strictly business-related. The sunlight filtering through the blinds declared the start of an as-yet unblemished new year. She was pleased that Shinoi had remembered her request. She brought up the keyboard to reply, then decided to do it in the evening. For today, at least, she wanted to avoid any kind of rushed communication. Tomorrow she would be going back into work.

It was now 10 a.m. By the time she'd got here last night, the annual Kōhaku New Year's Song Contest had already finished, and it was a few minutes before the TV began to show the ceremonial ringing of the bell. Seeing her daughter somewhat unsteady from drinking, her mother had smiled and rolled her eyes, and presented her with a small bowl of New Year's Eve toshikoshi soba, topped with a piece of yuzu rind. Rika had soaked in the hot bath until she was filmed by a faint sweat, and then slept for over nine hours beside her mother and her occasional teeth grinding. Even that was sufficient to make her feel like her body, ground down by the spate of end-of-year parties, had been restored to life.

Would Kajii be satisfied by the taste of the osechi she'd be served in the Detention House, presumably now for the third time? Staring up at the unfamiliar ceiling, Rika tried to picture the scene, aided by the contents of the message she'd just received. According to her past blog entries, when the year began to draw to a close, Kajii and her younger sister would set about preparing the various dishes that made up the osechi served in multi-tiered bento boxes. Added to this repertoire would be the traditional dishes particular to the Niigata region, such as noppe – a simmered vegetable stew made with taro and shiitake – and hizunumasu – pickled cartilage from the salmon's head. To make the ozōni mochi soup that was a must on New Year's Day, she would use her grandmother's recipe with salmon and cod roe, plenty of strong dashi and lots of vegetables. Just the thought of those small plump white hands carefully simmering and grilling all the ingredients roused a sense of hunger in Rika.

She got up and folded her futon, then looked around at the apartment in which her mother lived alone. She hadn't been to visit since the previous New Year. A Jeanne Moreau film poster, a photo book showing stylish elderly women walking around New York, a vase with some haphazardly arranged orchids, a few jazz records – she saw now a similarity between her mother's apartment and Reiko's house. Hadn't she read somewhere that people unconsciously selected close friends of a similar personality type to their mothers? As it happened, Reiko and Rika's mother got along very well. Compared to Rika herself, who was so sloppy when it came to her domestic environment, both women had a distinctive sense of style and created an environment where they could be surrounded by things that they liked, aspects of themselves that they put to use in their working lives too.

Rika's mother still worked three days a week in the Jiyūgaoka branch of her shop, a boutique aimed at women in their fifties and sixties that sold a wide range of items from clothes to imported knickknacks and interior goods.

There was no sign of her mother in the apartment. On the round IKEA table lay a note reading: 'Happy New Year! I've gone to visit Grandad. Come along when you're up. Remember to lock the door.'

Her mother's rent was 78,000 yen per month. The fact that her mother, who would turn sixty-two this year, was living in a place ever so slightly cheaper and smaller than her own would sometimes cause a prickling in Rika's chest. However much Rika tried to convince her, though, her mother wouldn't accept any money from her. She was adamant in her stance that a woman never knows what's going to happen in life. 'If you've got the money to give me,' she would say, 'I'd far rather you put it in your own savings.' When Rika's grandfather died, she said, she would think about using his inheritance to see about getting somewhere more permanent, but until then she was fine living in this place. Even now, when business was on track, her mother would never spend unnecessarily. Nobody would ever guess to look at them, but all the items of furniture and objects in this flat were bought from mass-retailers, antiques got on the cheap, or gifts she'd been given.

Her parents' divorce, which had occurred when Rika was just starting at a private middle school, had gone through on the condition that the only money they'd receive from her father were monthly maintenance payments, and so Rika had never once been on holiday with her mother. Perhaps because her school was relatively laid-back and unpretentious, and the fees weren't extortionate, she has no memory of them ever struggling to get by. The one-bedroom apartment in Hatanodai that the two of them had shared until Rika left university was smaller than her mother's current flat, and the rent had been 62,000 yen a month. When Rika had eventually discovered how little her mother had been earning at that time, she'd been shocked.

Rika got changed and slowly drank a glass of water. Her grandfather and uncle's family lived in the red-brick apartment block which she could see from the window.

It was now twelve years since Rika's grandparents had sold their house and come to live in this spot, ten minutes' walk from Okusawa Station. Rika's grandfather, who was about to turn ninety-three, was still physically mobile, but since he'd begun showing the early signs of dementia, he'd started finding aspects of daily life more challenging. These days he relied on Rika's mother and Rika's uncle's family for support, alongside his care workers. Rika's mother and her aunt – her mother's younger brother's wife – had long been on excellent terms, and referred to one another affectionately as Misaki-chan and Etchan. Although her mother was staying over at her grandfather's place more of late, she seemed to have no intention of giving up her own apartment, saying she wanted to keep hold of a space that was all her own.

Rika heard the sound of the key in the door. Poking her head out of the kitchen, she saw her mother come in, taking off her coat. She had a patterned scarf wrapped around her head, and wore a black turtleneck together with chunky jewellery of a bold design. Her mother was always dressed so chicly that she often looked out of place.

'What's happened? I was about to head over.'

'It's okay, you don't have to go. Grandpa lost his temper, and it's impossible with everyone there trying to soothe him. He's put his duvet over his head and won't come out.'

Her mother laid a package down on the table. 'Some mochi for you.' She moved in front of the extractor fan and lit a cigarette. Through the thin veil of smoke, her profile looked exhausted.

'It seems he took offence to the osechi that Etchan bought in the department store. He kept going on about how grandma used to make it herself, standards were slipping, and so on. Then he said that it was no wonder I ended up divorced.'

'If it was Etchan who bought them, why does he take it out on you and not her?'

Without answering, mother pointed to the package on the table.

'Do you want to grill them? Apparently they're fresh ones that he ordered from the local confectioners.'

Rika's grandfather was judicious in his treatment of Rika's aunt, but had never showed any mercy towards his own daughter. The tendency had grown even more pronounced after her divorce. There was no denying that, until a few years before her death, Rika's grandmother had made the time-consuming osechi from scratch, from kuromame – simmered black beans – to the datemaki – omelette rolls. Unlike Rika's mother, her grandmother had been a talented cook, but back then Rika hadn't really appreciated the fact, and had simply eaten her osechi out of habit.

Suddenly, a scene came flooding back to her. It was the New Year's Eve of her final year at primary school, and her father had stormed out of the house. He'd taken a dislike to the kamo seiro – chilled soba noodles with chicken dipping sauce – that her mother had made. Her father, an English literature professor, had grown up spoiled, and was still fussy when it came to food. He was forever finding something to complain about in Rika's mother's slapdash cooking. When Rika had told people about the episode in the past, they'd attempted to dress it up as a pleasant memory, saying 'Wow, your dad was a real foodie!' or similar. In reality, though, her memory of that New Year's Eve – which should by rights have been spent with the whole family sitting in front of the television, laughing together, but which had suddenly turned so that the air grew tense and her mother began to cry – was such that even bringing fragments of it to mind now caused her stomach to tense up. Rika had disliked kamo seiro ever since.

Rika's mother had formerly been a pupil of her father's. Back when the student protests had been in full swing, her father had been an idol to his students: the young professor kicking back against the system. The two of them had ignored the vehement disapproval of her parents, and their marriage was practically an elopement.

And there was she, thinking that both she and her mother had long ago escaped the kind of icy tension that used to descend upon the dinner table loaded with dishes of her home-cooked food.

'Etchan was saying that a kid she works with sprinkles sugar and soy sauce on her toasted mochi, and finishes it off with a slice of butter. Don't you think that's disgusting? Apparently it's how the younger generation like to eat them these days.'

'Butter, eh …'

Rika felt the inside of her cheeks puckering, and saliva welling up slowly in her mouth. She knew by now that the taste of butter in combination with any kind of carbohydrate was one of inexplicable fullness. There was no way that the trick wouldn't work with mochi too. Rika washed her hands then arranged the smooth, pre-cut mochi dusted with rice flour inside the toaster.

'Grandpa's just grumpy because his care worker doesn't come at New Year. The one he's got at the moment is a pretty young girl who listens and nods to whatever he says, and he's grown ever so fond of her. He was getting all excited telling me about how the two of them were going to go on a date.'

Rika opened the fridge to find it sparkling clean and, like her own, on the bare side. On the shelf was a jar of Koiwai butter. When she opened the lid, a fresh, sweet scent rose up to greet her. She found the image of her grandfather, whom she had once loved so much, coming together in her head with Manako Kajii's victims, in a way that made her feel quite melancholy.

Watching the corners of the mochi slowly filling out against the toaster's crimson-lit insides, mother and daughter fell quiet.

Rika recalled again the conversation she'd had with Shinoi. The variety of species on earth is in continual flux because most species are incapable of truly adapting to their environment and are consequently wiped out. It's not that the species that manage to survive the process of natural selection form the minority – it's that those who are wiped out form the majority. Extinction is a crucial phenomenon. Seen through the long lens of human history, the fact that Rika and her grandfather were alive simultaneously was an unnatural state of affairs. The mochi gradually began to take on colour and swell out. When their skin seared with brown grill marks started to split open, revealing glimpses of their sparkling white insides, Rika took them out of the toaster. She perched a generous wedge of butter on top of each, and prepared the sugared soy sauce in a small dish. Watching as the molten butter flowed gently over both the burnished surface and the soft white interior, her stomach rumbled. Though she knew it was bad manners to eat standing up, she stuffed one of the mochi in her mouth right there at the counter.

The heady aroma that rose up through her nose, the crispiness of the skin as it broke open beneath her teeth, the silkiness of the gooey insides that spread themselves flat across every bit of flesh in her mouth and refused to let go ... The hot butter fused the sugar and soy sauce together, clinging to the sweet, soft, shapeless mass in her mouth, swimming around its outside as though to ascertain its contours. The grease of the butter melded with the grit of the sugar and the pungent soy sauce. By the time she'd finished chewing, the roots of her teeth were trembling pleasurably.

Rika said with a sigh, 'I can see how you could get addicted to this combination. I'll grill some more, shall I? Four? Six?'

'Didn't you say you've got a sensitive stomach after all the end-of-year parties?' her mother said, her eyes widening as she watched Rika loading up the still-warm toaster with more mochi.

'Mum, once we've eaten these, shall we have an outing?' Rika said. 'We could do our New Year's shrine visit at the Megura Fudō temple, and then go for coffee somewhere.'

Rika knew from experience that, at times like these, the best strategy was to lead her mother away somewhere in order to take her mind off things. She couldn't keep track of the number of times that she'd witnessed the tragic sight of her mother, hurt by something her grandfather or father had said, trying to recover her equilibrium without letting anyone notice that she'd been affected. Her mother still seemed somewhat dazed, but she assented to the plan, donning again the coat that she'd taken off and stumbling outside. The two of them piled into the backseat of a taxi they'd hailed on the street and, after telling the driver their destination, Rika said very casually to her mother, 'Isn't it hard, having Grandpa taking things out on you like that? I know he's going senile and everything, but still.'

'Of course it is! It's exasperating. Thank goodness I don't live with him, and he's got Etchan and the care worker as well, so it doesn't get me down too much, but I don't know what would happen if it were just the two of us. I'm sure that would sound pathetic to all those people caring for their parents full time.'

Rika was still listening to her mother, making the appropriate responses and helping her to purge her frustration, when the taxi pulled up in front of an expensive apartment building, complete with a concierge, located along a cherry-tree-lined street very close to Meguro Fudō-mae. When her mother shot her a look of confusion, Rika whispered playfully in her ear, 'This is the building where Manako Kajii was living. I've been wanting to come and look at it when I had a moment. Apparently the rent's 300,000 yen a month.'

'I was wondering what had got into you! So this outing of ours is all work-related, then?' her mother asked indignantly, but it was clear that she was already on the way to casting off her earlier sadness. 'You mean that food fanatic who defrauded all those men from dating sites, right? Wow, quite a spot she chose for herself. Paid for with the money she extorted from them I suppose! Impressive!'

Just like Reiko, Rika's mother had a healthy curiosity, and was fascinated by whatever was making a splash in the news. Her tone now was high-spirited, and together they stared at the well-tended flowerbeds outside the building, the New Year's decorations, and the art object made out of driftwood adorning its glass-fronted entrance, which made it appear more like an art museum than a residential building. Even when a resident came out and gave them a withering stare, Rika's prevailing feeling was still one of relief that her mother's mood had shifted.

She looked up again at the twelve-storey apartment block, this time with the eyes of a journalist. It was certainly opulent in its construction, but it was the kind of building she often came across when covering celebrities and sports stars – there was nothing about it that promised to reveal a new aspect to Kajii's personality. For what Rika understood Kajii's tastes to be, it seemed lacking in individuality and overly contemporary, with very little about it that struck her as distinctive.

Mother and daughter walked around the outside of the building, in the direction of the Meguro Fudō temple. In the temple heaving with people, they lined up to make their New Year's prayer and drank the warm amazake being served. By the time they came to draw their fortunes for the year ahead, written on slips of paper, any sense of tension had disappeared. On their way to Meguro Station they passed by a fruit parlour, and recalling the taste of the Christmas cake, Rika said, 'This place used to be owned by that confectionery company, West. It was one of Kajii's favourite spots.'

There was a 'Closed for the Holidays' sign up in the shop window.

'Was it now?' Rika's mother said, her eyes sparkling.

She didn't want to go to Starbucks, she said, because she couldn't smoke there, so instead they entered a Doutor by Meguro JR Station. No sooner had she lifted her mug of coffee to her lips than she began her confession.

'You know, I feel like I can really understand why Manako Kajii was so popular with men. The truth is … You promise you won't mention this to anyone?'

She giggled like a schoolgirl and leaned across the table to whisper in Rika's ear. What Rika heard nearly made her choke on her mouthful of milk tea.

'What! You worked as a decoy at a matchmaking party? I need to hear more about this.'

'Oh no, I get scared when you get that journalist's face on … You're not writing an article on this, you hear? I told you in confidence.'

Her mother slid a Mevius cigarette out of the packet and lit it. The request, she told Rika, had come via a friend of hers who worked in a matchmaking company, who she'd initially met as a customer of the shop, and had begun occasionally going out for drinks with. The woman pleaded with her, saying that having someone so attractive there really helped the mood, and so Rika's mother had agreed to go out of curiosity. The party, which was limited to people over sixty, had taken place in an event venue in a Roppongi hotel. It had been, to borrow her mother's description, 'utter hell'.

'I never thought that at this age, I'd be treated like a hostess! When the truth is I wouldn't want to listen to a babyboomer grandpa boasting about all his past triumphs even if I were getting paid for it. Women like me aren't interested in a dazzling list of accolades – we want to meet men who can hold a decent conversation. It wasn't just me who was sickened by it, either. I found two other like-minded souls. As soon as our eyes met, we could tell that we were all feeling the same. When it was over the three of us went to Amando for tea – I've not been there in ages. When it comes to Roppongi, us women are far more in the know than the men!'

'That's so you, Mum. Still, I bet that looking the way you do, the men still had the hots for you.'

'That's the thing – not at all! That sort of man isn't looking for a partner with whom they can communicate equally, to share their life with. Nope, what they want is a capable hostess, who'll listen to them wittering on. Those women do exist, but most of them are employed by the party hosts. Professionals, in other words. I shouldn't go blurting this around, but apparently these matchmaking parties for seniors are rife with actual prostitutes – they're their main hunting ground. I heard that from the women I went to tea with. I suppose there were a few at the one I was at too. In fact, now I say that, there was a woman who I thought was behaving a bit peculiarly, snuggling up to the men and so forth.'

'Professionals ...'

Wasn't the great tragedy of Kajii's victims that they had mistaken a service, for which they should have paid a professional, with a woman's natural kindness and consideration?

'I say professional, but you'd never in a million years be able to tell by looking at them. To do that job you have to look like a *regular* middle-aged woman. You can't surprise the men, or make them feel anything new. And then the men come flocking. And that's okay, no? If they're meeting each other's needs, and having a good time,' her mother finished dryly, breathing out smoke. Her latest relationship, Rika deduced from this, had now ended. Between her mother's brows lay traces of disappointment that had been formed over decades, and were now impossible to erase.

Her mother was a highly serious and fastidious person, but was destined to be seen by others as reckless, and to suffer as a result. Both Rika's grandfather and father had done nothing but criticise her, but she would laugh it off and end up catering to their selfish whims. Their strategy worked because they knew full well that she was the kind to worry about the feelings of those around her, keep her own feelings inside, and never explode. Housework, work, childcare, and now caring duties – her mother had always performed a complex juggling act, but had never complained about it, even to Rika.

After the divorce, her mother's income had been taken up more or less entirely by the rent for their Hatanodai apartment and their living costs, and for a while her grandfather had covered her school fees. When Rika formulated the idea that she might be the reason that her mother still felt indebted to her grandfather, she felt a rush of guilt.

'Have you been to visit your dad's grave recently?'

'I've been thinking that I should find the time to, but haven't quite managed it.'

'You should go to see him from time to time. He's your blood relative, after all. I'm nothing but a stranger and even I went twice last year.'

Caught off guard by this announcement, which was delivered with the utmost smoothness, Rika stared at her mother. It wasn't as though the subject of her father was taboo between them, but neither was it one they tended to bring up.

When her mother had asked for a divorce, her father had been bewildered. His initial reaction was one of childish confusion, and then he'd flown into an uncontrollable rage. Rika was confident that up until that point, he hadn't even imagined that the situation had been stressful for her mother, or that she might want to leave him. She remembered now the sight of her mother's neck and shoulders filling her field of vision from where she was sitting in the child's seat on the back of the bicycle. As she pedalled up the hill, her top was stretched taut across her sweaty skin, and the nubs of her spine stood right out. While still a full-time homemaker, her mother had used to cycle from library to library, taking out the new novels that her father had reserved. It was not out of the ordinary for her to cycle to five libraries in a day. Rika had enjoyed those trips on her mother's bike to the libraries that she so loved, but if her mother failed to pick up even one of his reservations, her father's mood would turn sour and he'd fall silent, so there had always been a desperate quality to her mother's expression. Thinking back on it, it was from that point on that the financial difficulties had begun. Towards the end of Rika's time in primary school, her mother had taken a part-time job in spite of her father's resistance, and refused thenceforth to do the library run. After her parents had split, Rika's father had carried on living by himself in the Mitaka apartment where Rika had been born.

Apparently misinterpreting Rika's silence as consternation, her mother now said, 'What's wrong with that? I happened to be on my way back from checking out an import brand in Minato Mirai, so I called in to the graveyard in Yokohama. I don't have a single good memory of your father. Do you know, right before your middle school entrance exams, he started saying that he was going to quit his job at the university and dedicate himself to the novel he'd always dreamed of writing. He was really messed up. Did he have any *idea* how much we suffered?'

Even in complaining about Rika's late father, there was a lightness to her mother's tone, and her words didn't bring Rika down. Did she really feel as carefree about it as she made out, though? When a sentimental old song came on in the cafe she snorted with laughter, but then glanced down at her watch, making Rika suspect she was thinking about getting back to her grandfather.

It was the evening of the 4th, after the three days of official New Year's holiday were over, that Momoe Ōyasu, owner of the Ginza members' club La Vie, agreed to an interview with Rika, who was stationed outside her Hiroo apartment. Naturally, she had told Ōyasu that the magazine was planning to run a photo of her visiting the Kioichō Maternity Clinic, as well as a picture of her with the up-and-coming politician who was a regular visitor to the club.

'You're certainly determined, spending your New Year's holidays like this,' Ōyasu had said in apparent exasperation with Rika, who had been standing outside her apartment since the 2nd, before reluctantly agreeing to talk to her there on the street. Her diminutive figure, like that of a young girl, was swaddled in an expensive-looking coat, and Rika was unable to ascertain whether or not she was showing. Like Rika's mother, she'd tied back her long hair with a scarf, her bare white forehead gleaming in the dark of the street. A beautiful woman of indeterminate age, there was something about her pointed chin and the fierce glimmer in her large eyes that exerted pressure on the person she was speaking to, depriving them of the opportunity to look at her with any ill will.

'It's true that he's a regular customer, but I don't see him outside of work. That photograph was taken when we both happened to be walking in the direction of the club, and bumped into one another on the street. I don't deny that I'm expecting, no. I don't intend to make the father's name public, but when I become a mother I'm planning to hand over the club entirely to the girls working there. I intend to step back from the world of entertainment, and go into beauty treatment.'

The dignity with which she made this announcement struck Rika. And yet, although the article that the editorial desk wrote up from Rika's report preserved some of this statement, they omitted the part where she denied the courtship, and moulded the story into the kind of sex scandal about a major politician deemed fit to grace the front page of the first *Shūmei Weekly* of the year.

The relaxed time she'd enjoyed on New Year's Day soon disappeared without a trace under an onslaught of one hectic day after another, and she didn't even have time for the nanakusagayu – rice porridge containing seven spring herbs – that it was traditional to eat on the morning of the 7th. At least I'll be getting out of the office for lunch today, Rika thought as she struck the enter key with a force that immediately made her embarrassed.

'Rika, have you put on weight?'

Hearing the mocking tone of the question – not by any means the first today – Rika turned around in exasperation. Now even Kitamura, who as a rule showed zero interest in other people, was talking to her about her weight, with evident surprise on his face.

'How did you manage to gain so much weight when you barely took any time off?'

The fact that what he was saying was spot on made her even less inclined to reply. In all likelihood she had been accruing fat since before the turn of the year. Then there were all the mochi her mother had given her, which she'd been tucking into as a nightly snack.

She had, of course, been faintly aware of the changes to her body. There was a heaviness around her jawline, and her breasts had got bigger, so that the underwiring of her bra felt tight. She could see the fat gleaming pale and white on her lower abdomen. Having a sense of what was happening, she'd got on the scales kept in the medical office at work, only to find that she weighed more than she had ever done. Unable to believe it at first, she'd stepped on and off the scales repeatedly.

The text that she'd received late last night from Makoto also irked her.

Have you put on a few pounds?

He'd followed this up with a sticker of an anime character slapping their hands to their cheeks and screaming. Rika had felt a flicker of anger. If he'd caught sight of her at work, he could at least have said hello! Alone in her apartment, she felt her cheeks flush with embarrassment.

It's probably because you've been eating that stodgy pasta late at night. Still, what's done is done. Just watch yourself now and you'll be fine.

What did he mean, 'you'll be fine'? This was the first time since they'd started dating that Makoto, who could barely summon the enthusiasm to send a Happy New Year text message, was showing such strength of conviction.

Hey, you can hardly talk! Your belly's huge these days, thanks to all that drinking. You've started snoring and everything.

Men putting on weight is different from women putting on weight, though. I'm only saying this for your sake, Rika.

She knew from his tone that he was angry. She didn't reply. This morning another message had arrived from him, hammering the point home.

I'm being deliberately harsh when I say this, but for the record, I definitely don't think it's a good idea for you to put on weight. I haven't got fixed ideas about the way women should look or anything, but if people around you think you're not making an effort, you'll lose their respect.

Putting a forcible end to the task she'd begun, Rika slung on her coat and dashed out to Kagurazaka. The short jog to reach her destination on time made her break out in a light sweat all over her body – she wondered if this might help her shift some weight.

Reiko was already sitting on the cafe terrace that looked out across the moat in front of Iidabashi Station, drinking a cup of herbal tea. With an appointment at the maternity clinic she'd started attending in Suidōbashi, she'd got in touch to ask Rika to lunch, if she could find the time. Her hair, worn loose over her soft chestnut-coloured jumper, had the lustre of a woman with time to devote to her appearance, and just the sight of it calmed Rika's heart. The two wished one another a Happy New Year, spread out the menus in front of them, and quickly placed their orders.

'Sorry to make you come out all the way to my part of town,' Rika said.

'Don't apologise! I've got time on my hands – I'm happy to come to you.'

Reiko was sneaking glances at the man in a suit slurping pasta at the next table. Rika cocked her head inquisitively.

'He tried to light up a cigarette and got told off by a female customer,' Reiko whispered. 'She was so harsh I felt sorry for him. The sharing dishes look exactly like ashtrays, so it's hardly his fault if he got confused … Even as a non-smoker, I feel like this new anti-smoking drive is a bit extreme.'

Rika saw that the man was slumped over the table, lifting his fork to his mouth in a slightly forlorn manner.

'The doctor I went to see today has a reputation as *the* infertility expert. The surgery doesn't take reservations, so you have to wait at least three or four hours. When I gave my name at reception they told me to come back in two hours' time.'

'Wow, they're that popular? When's your next appointment? If you tell me, I can keep that day free. I'd love it if we could start having lunch regularly.'

'I think it'll depend on what happens today. It's all down to when you ovulate, so sometimes you're told to come back the following day. It was a right pain when I was still working. Having to take several afternoons a month off causes all sorts of problems for your colleagues, obviously. In that sense, it's good to have more time on my hands than I know what to do with.'

It was the first time Rika had heard Reiko admit to having too much time. Taken by surprise, she was unsure how to respond.

'Sorry, I shouldn't talk like that. It's bad form when I'm the one who chose to stop working. Forget I said it. What's been going on with you?'

Even if they only had a short time in each other's company, Rika would have liked to ask Reiko more. With the conversation now directed at her, though, she made a confession of her own.

'Actually, I've been taking Manako Kajii's advice and eating like crazy, and in the process I've put on five kilos. I currently weigh fifty-four kilos.'

Fighting back her embarrassment, she confided to her friend what everyone in the office was gossiping about. Reiko tilted her head and scrutinised Rika.

'Now you mention it I can see you've filled out a little. But how tall are you again – five feet five? At that height, fifty-four kilos isn't even plump. The beauty standards in the mass media are crazily exacting. If it's bothering you, though, why don't you try exercising to make up for the extra food you're eating? I'd recommend weight training rather than aerobic exercise. You're so sporty, you'll easily be able to shed a couple of kilos and enjoy yourself in the process. Then you'll not just be slim, but really toned.'

Where Makoto's suggestion had caused a visceral reaction in her, Reiko's advice made its way inside her frictionlessly. Reiko was right – the situation wasn't yet beyond repair. She just had to take a look at her lifestyle and make gradual adjustments. From this vantage point, it suddenly seemed strange to think that she'd lost her confidence and been so thrown by a few offhand comments.

'Still, Manako Kajii must be quite something, to change the habits of someone like you – you'd give a cave-dwelling hermit a run for their money. For better or worse, she must have heaps of charisma. It makes me want to meet her.'

'I'm trying to imagine you two together and all I can see is a pit viper and a mongoose at each other's throats. I can't think for a second that you'd get on.'

'Why not? Are you saying I'm savage enough to rival a convicted serial killer?' At this Reiko puffed out her cheeks sulkily, and Rika giggled. You wouldn't know it to look at her, but Reiko was especially adept at getting her own way, often in defiance of the people around her. Her love of food, also, matched Kajii's in its ardency. Rika couldn't imagine that Kajii, who needed to be in pole position at all times, would ever open her heart to Reiko. Perhaps, she thought now, it was precisely her own lack of sexiness, of in fact any kind of intensity, that allowed Kajii to relax and let go of her compulsion to compete with those around her.

'Anyway, we live in an age where knowing what's a good amount for you gets a bad rap. Same with the smoker from before.'

'A good amount?'

Reiko reached out and drew the sugar pot closer to her, sprinkling half a teaspoonful into her cup. 'You know how in recipes it'll say "sugar to taste" or "a good amount of salt" and so on? A friend of mine who edits cookery books for a living said that they've started having complaints about recipes that leave things to the individual's discretion. She thinks it's because people are increasingly worried about making mistakes, and losing faith in their own judgement – they don't know what "a good amount" looks like for them. When in fact, cooking is all about trial and error.'

'This is hard to hear. I think I'm probably that type too.'

Reiko set her cup down on the table and smiled, then looked towards the Chūō Line tracks that ran along the other side of the moat. Every time Rika saw her, Reiko seemed to have shrunk a fraction, as if she were a grain of rice whose outside layers were being gradually polished away. It was less that she looked unhealthy, and more as though, little by little, she was reverting to her younger self. There was no difference between the person sitting before her now and the eighteen-year-old Rika had first met. She didn't know if that was a good thing or not.

'Nobody has to be fully satisfied by just one thing, and nor do they have to aim to be like everyone else. It's plenty if people can enjoy things a good amount, and be satisfied with their life overall.

Enjoying a cigarette after a meal is okay, and putting on a little weight isn't anything to merit fussing about. I guess some would see that as a slacker's take, though.'

With this final line, Reiko cocked her head. Rika wanted to reach out and squeeze her pale hand. Neither she nor Reiko had really changed. Rather than making her happy, the fact seemed tinged with pathos.

'But that means knowing what's a good amount for you personally.'

'Right. Which is why you may need to eat all sorts of different foods, and find the tastes and the body size that work for you. Hey, why don't we make a habit of having lunch together, and try out new restaurants together? There's loads of good places in this neighbourhood. I think it's so great that you've had your eyes opened to the wonders of good food! I suppose I have Kajimana to thank for that.'

'I like that idea. I'll try expanding the boundaries of my taste buds, a little at a time.'

The pasta and salad they'd ordered arrived. The surface of the moat spread out in front of them was calm, absorbing the high blue January sky.

'Mochi with butter? That sounds scrumptious. Despite the intensity of its flavour, butter can accommodate any ingredient, and I imagine it would make a seamless combination with warm, softly stretching mochi.'

As she spoke, Kajii's eyes moistened and her lips took on a faint sheen. It was the first time Rika had seen her since the new year. The osechi had apparently been to her satisfaction, and no sooner had Rika enquired about them that Kajii started in on her detailed assessment: the nishime vegetable stew had not been a triumph, but the kuri-kinton weren't bad, and so on. In this manner, Rika was able to broach the subject of New Year's meals in the house where Kajii had grown up.

'What makes mochi delicious is the way that, beneath that endless surface of soft, plump skin, the mochi rice still retains a vestige of its former shape, and grazes roughly along the tongue. I remember how, back at home, we would roast kiritanpo skewers and eat them with butter and soy sauce. With kiritanpo, the granular texture of the rice is deliberately preserved during the pounding, and it's then moulded onto cedar sticks. The way the textures on the tongue alternate between chewy and abrasive is thrilling. When you add the ooze of butter to that it's just – ahhhh!'

Observing the sensual way that Kajii squirmed and sighed, the prison officer standing behind her shifted his eyes uncomfortably. Rika found herself saying, 'Thanks to all those mochi I ate, though, my colleagues are teasing me for having put on weight. I'm thinking about how best to lose it.'

A shadow descended across the plump pale face on the other side of the acrylic screen. The crease in her chin deepened, and was joined by others.

'There is nothing in this world so pathetic, so moronic, so meaningless as dieting.'

Damn, I've blown it, Rika thought. She could have kicked herself. The door which had begun to open in front of her was now slammed shut.

'My mother was a truly ignorant woman who was utterly fixated on dieting, and demanded the same of her daughters. A woman with a cold, impoverished soul and not a trace of femininity about her, who ignored her own husband to pursue her trifling hobbies, her social activities and her work. An utterly miserable creature. Not an iota of charm about her. My father can't ever have been loved in a way that truly satisfied him.'

Hearing Kajii alluding to her parents' sex lives with perfect equanimity left Rika a touch startled. She felt certain that this was an important pronouncement Kajii was making. If her memory served her correctly, Kajii had become tight-lipped in court whenever the subject had turned to her mother.

'For what purpose, exactly, do you want to lose weight? Are you worried about not being attractive to men? Because in that case, you have nothing to fear. Men are naturally attracted to shapely, full-figured women. When I say men, I'm of course referring to *real* men, who are emotionally mature, affluent, and capable of generosity. Men who favour women with bodies like skinny children are the ones with no confidence in themselves. They're without exception servile, sexually and emotionally immature, with no capacity for financial generosity, either.'

Kajii simply didn't permit the people who wouldn't accept her into her field of vision. That was how she was able to remain so full of confidence. The scent of camphor that clung to her was one unique to women who had only dated older, affluent men. The reason that Rika couldn't feel any envy towards her, however much her blog flaunted her luxurious way of living, was that it all seemed to belong to a bygone age – wealth as a codified form of belief in the dominance of the rich and powerful.

'No, I'm not particularly bothered about how men see me. This is a very mainstream view that I'm expressing, so please don't take offence, but here in Japan, it's thought that it's beautiful to be thin. It's better for your health, and clothes look more flattering on you that way.'

'You should read Madame de Pompadour.'

'Wasn't she the lover of Marie Antoinette's grandfather?'

'You people working in the media all graduate from good universities, and yet you don't know a thing, do you?'

Even this mocking tone of Kajii's didn't grate on Rika. It came as a surprise to her, but she was starting to enjoy Kajii speaking to her in this condescending way.

'She was a noblewoman who became Louis XV's chief mistress. She mused constantly about how to soothe the spirits of the king, so ground down by the war as they were. She educated herself in all kinds of disciplines, and came up with wonderful ideas on practically a daily basis. She invited men of letters to the palace, thereby originating salon culture. She produced plays, treading the boards herself, and convincing the Royal Family about the joys of acting. She became a connoisseur of wine and created the trend for selecting wines based on their region of origin. Many of her innovations form indispensable elements of French cuisine as we know it today.'

Rika found herself rapt by Kajii's speech. In a different way from Reiko, Kajii opened up a new world to her, expanding her perspective. She thought to herself that she would try gathering material about Madame de Pompadour. At the same time, she felt the story had a common thread with her mother's tale of the matchmaking party. At the end of the day, men were not looking for a real-life woman, but a professional entertainer.

'What lay behind Madame de Pompadour's actions wasn't any personal ambition or desire to show off. Her enduring innovations came from an earnest desire to devote herself to someone else, from a natural, feminine kindness.'

While Rika hated to admit it, she knew that what people would be talking about a hundred years from now would not be the articles she had busted a gut to write, but Manako Kajii and her case. This was no time to withdraw, though. She had to find a way of writing up this interaction between her and Kajii, which had been going on now for a month. She thought about how to broach the subject with Kajii. She'd have to wait for the right moment, then ask Kajii if she'd consent to being featured in an interview, so long as its content had nothing to do with her case. Her retrial would begin in spring.

'Are you listening to me?'

Rika was pulled back to the cramped visiting room by Kajii's imperious voice.

'In the same way that real men understand the beauty of a full-bodied woman, real French cuisine uses oodles of butter. Present-day Japan, enamoured by phrases like "low on sweetness", "low in calories", "light", and "simple-tasting" wouldn't know the real thing if it hit them in the face. Preferring simple-tasting food once you know how good butter can be, I can just about forgive. But these people can't even tell the difference between butter and margarine! For women like me, who are only interested in the real thing, it's unbearable. You too, though – it's imperative that you taste classic, orthodox French cuisine at least once. I suggest Joël Robuchon in Ebisu.'

'Is that the one in Ebisu Garden Place that looks like the Disneyland castle?' Rika asked unthinkingly, surprised by the appearance of this familiar name. Perhaps feeling that she'd been looked down on, Kajii pulled a huffish face.

'That's right. With these sorts of things, the orthodox choice is the safest route. I used to be taken there often on dates. I believe I went there two or three times with Mr Yamamura.'

Rika felt sweat forming between her fingers. It was the first time the name of one of her victims emerged from Kajii's mouth. This was why she'd spent the last month gorging on butter, like someone possessed, she thought to herself.

Tokio Yamamura, who had fallen under a train in November 2013, was the final victim in Kajii's case, a single man of forty-two who worked in one of the country's most prominent think tanks. He'd met Kajii in July of that year on a matchmaking site, and the two had immediately started dating with a view to getting married. Not only was he younger than Kajii's other victims, but as a keen trainspotter he was also something of a well-known figure online. His knowledge of the Odakyu and Hankyu lines, which he trotted out on his blog, was viewed as unrivalled in its thoroughness. He lived with his mother in central Tokyo, but when he started dating Kajii, he moved into his own apartment with a good view of the tracks near a station on the Odakyu Line. Photographs of him showed a man with a slender, boyish build. His clean-shaven face and polo shirt with its neatly ironed collar gave the impression of a meticulous character.

'Was Mr Yamamura knowledgeable about French cuisine?'

'Not in the slightest. He didn't know the first thing about wine, and he'd never even eaten game before. He would often lapse into silence, a troubled expression on his face, which was highly embarrassing. He wasn't the kind to savour conversation or cuisine, but I could sense his earnestness and loyalty to me.'

Rika could see that if she didn't intervene, Kajii's boasting would continue indefinitely. She decided to go on the offensive, armed with a key piece of intel.

'If I remember rightly, this is the person who mistook your boeuf bourguignon for beef stew, am I right? I looked it up, and discovered that in French, boeuf bourguignon means 'beef done in a Burgundy style'. In other words, stewed in red wine. I have to say, I don't feel like it's such a terrible error for someone who knows little about cooking to call it "beef stew" …'

No sooner were the words 'boeuf bourguignon' out of her mouth than Rika saw Kajii's expression change dramatically. It was as Reiko said: her spirits soared at the very mention of food. It was unexpectedly easy to manipulate her feelings.

'But in Japan, the words "beef stew" refer to a different dish altogether! Boeuf bourguignon is the very first dish we learned to make at Le Salon de Miyuko. I made it for Mr Yamamura as a sign of my gratitude to him for allowing me to frequent the school.'

Once again, Reiko's intuition had proved correct. Perhaps everything led back to that cooking school in Nishi-Azabu, and to that group of women.

'Then, to cap it all, he said he wanted to eat it not with bread, but with rice!' Kajii shook her glossy wavy hair as if in disgust.

'But it seems he appreciated the food you made for him, no? He texted his mother before he died to tell her about the meal, saying how delicious it was.'

'It was less that he understood the taste of the dishes I prepared, and more that he simply wanted to take his meals by my side. He used to often say, "I'd sooner die than end up living a solitary life eating takeaway bento boxes by myself."'

This again, Rika thought. For Kajii's victims there seemed to be only two types of meal: the warm, comforting kind eaten at a dinner table clustered with dishes lovingly prepared by a woman's patient hands, and the sad, lonely takeaway meals for one. Why so extreme in their thinking? Even if they were alone, even if they were eating food from the convenience store, it only took a little bit of imagination and application to transform the moment into a pleasurable one. Also, while these men seemed obsessed by food and meals, their understanding of taste was totally undeveloped. They didn't know what a 'good amount' was for themselves, either. Rika decided to air these doubts with Kajii.

'How did you manage to make such delicious meals for men whom you had no intention of being with long-term? Wasn't it a bore?'

'You really don't understand anything, do you?'

Rika was sure that she heard Kajii click her tongue.

'It gives me pleasure to give men pleasure. It's not 'work', at least as you conceive of it. Caring for, supporting and warming the hearts of men is women's god-given role, and, without fail, performing it makes women beautiful. They become goddesses. Don't you see? You find so many hard, spiky women these days because they lack love towards men, and are unsatisfied as a result. You have to understand that women can never hope to rival men's power. That's nothing to be ashamed of. When you acknowledge the differences between the sexes, when you accept men for how they are and work to support and please them, a future of freedom and abundance awaits you. Everyone is suffering because they're trying to rail against the natural order of things.'

As she spoke, Kajii's face was contorted by a violent anger and frustration at odds with the content of what she was saying. Her mouth and nose took up unusual positions, giving her a wholly different face to the one that Rika had become accustomed to. Her eyes grew bloodshot, and her irises startlingly dark.

'Women's obsession with work and independence and so on is the source of their dissatisfaction. When women surpass men, their chance for romance slips away from them. Men and women alike need to understand that they can't find happiness without each other.

If you scrimp on butter, your food will taste inferior, and if you scrimp on femininity and a wish to serve your partner then your relationships will grow impoverished – why can't you fathom that? My case is attracting this much attention precisely because there are so many totally misguided women out there. They can't bear to see me acting so uninhibitedly!'

Growing more and more heated, Kajii began enunciating the end of her sentences with great force. Rika was surprised to hear her refer to how others were perceiving her. She had thought Kajii barely registered such things.

'That's why you're worthless, all of you!' she howled, her face a deep tomato red.

'That's the end of the meeting!' barked the prison officer as he came rushing over, restraining Kajii. She had entirely forsaken her usual affected composure. Her nostrils flared and her shoulders heaved up and down as she breathed. Noticing Rika staring at her astonished, Kajii seemed to come back to herself.

'I'm tired,' she murmured.

For a while, Rika found herself unable to get to her feet. When she finally stood and passed down the long corridor and out of the Detention House, the sight of the buildings with no sign of any life inside struck her as even more bleak than usual.

The flowers placed by the guardrail had been replaced again with fresh ones. Pheasant's eyes – Rika wasn't at all good with flowers but she had a sense that was what they were called. They were the New Year's flower.

In order to have sufficient time and money at your disposal and to generally enjoy yourself while serving as an entertainer for men, and to do this so well that you never once presented them with a glimpse of what went on behind the scenes, you needed to treat the role as your career, as Kajii had done. You had to give up working, give up being a mother. Even Momoe Ōyasu, the ultimate professional, had decided to throw it all away and brave the world alone the moment she became a mother.

On the one hand you had the men seeking a professional, and on the other, women looking for a partner to share their life with. Sensing the sheer depth of the rift existing between the two positions, Rika felt dizzy. But men weren't all like that, she tried telling herself. Think of Makoto – but then she remembered their recent message exchange and felt as if she had accidentally crunched a mouthful of sand.

What was it that Makoto wanted if not a woman slender as a board who never said anything troublesome, didn't tie him down, and wasn't in any way too much for him? Would he not, in fact, drop her with surprising abruptness if she failed to meet even one of those requirements? Rika didn't want to believe it, she wanted to think that Makoto wasn't the kind of man to force a particular role on a woman. She'd fallen for him because he was someone with whom she could share her feelings.

When the two of them had first met, they'd spent hours talking about their childhoods and their favourite books. Every time they found things they had in common, the sparkle in his eyes would grow brighter.

There she went, reminiscing on the early stages of their relationship again. She found it impossible to picture their future in a way that seemed appealing. But this loss of confidence in their relationship was surely the result of their spending so little time together, so that her sense of him as a person was starting to fade. This year, she said to herself, she'd make an effort to see as much of him as possible.

Effort, effort, effort – this word that seemed to attach itself to her every waking hour, as pervasive as a curse. How could she try any harder than she already was? She barely ever saw her family, or her boyfriend, or her best friend. She took one day off for the New Year break. Even after Reiko's advice, she was finding it hard to create the time to exercise. This lunchtime, being mindful of her calorie consumption, she'd shovelled down a seaweed salad that she hadn't even wanted to eat. Cold seaweed on a midwinter day had chilled her to the core.

Was the future that Rika dreamed of for herself exactly the kind of thing Kajii had been warning against? Would becoming the first woman to make the editorial desk make men fear her? Could she become strong enough to genuinely no longer care what men thought of her? She didn't understand how you were supposed to decide how much was enough. She had no idea what a 'good amount' for her would be.

Rika took out her smartphone and put in a call to the Joël Robuchon. Asked how many people her reservation was for, she hesitated, then requested a table for one, for dinner next week. She would have loved to go with Reiko but it seemed cruel to ask her out to a costly dinner when she wasn't working. Asking her mother was fraught, too, when she was busy caring for Rika's grandfather on weeknights. She suspected Makoto wouldn't want to go, either. The atmosphere in those kinds of places set him on edge, and she thought he might well complain about the rich, buttery taste of the food.

If she was going to fork out that kind of money, then she would ideally sit opposite someone with whom she could fully share the experience. If that was impossible, then she didn't mind going alone. She knew this way of thinking couldn't be further from Kajii's conviction that when eating out it was essential to have a male companion. Rika felt that a boyfriend was someone you should meet only at those times your needs perfectly corresponded. She was pretty sure that Makoto felt the same.

So, really, we're in the same boat, Rika thought as she raised an arm to hail a taxi. The cold wind coming off the river stung the inside of her nose and slapped at her cheeks, instructing her: *Make an effort! But be sure not to surpass everybody else while you're at it!*

Out of the corner of her eye, she thought she saw the pheasant's eyes wavering about in a gust of wind.

CHAPTER FOUR

Finally reaching the end of the covered walkway that snaked along for what felt like an eternity, Rika was met by a blast of wintry night wind that seemed to strip off not just her clothes but the flesh of her body as well, mercilessly lashing the bare bones beneath. Once across the street, she was afforded a view of Ebisu Garden Place in its entirety. In the distance stood the palatial facade of the Joël Robuchon, lit up grandly from outside. The wide open space yawning between Rika and the building made her hesitant, and she was struck by the urge to turn around, go home and eat the butter-and-soy-sauce rice topped with a fried egg that had become her new favourite dinner. By the time she reached the entrance on the right-hand side of the building, she was weary with cold and nerves.

She had deliberated long and hard, but eventually opted to wear the chocolate-brown tweed suit that was her go-to for formal occasions. Solo female diners must be few and far between at Joël Robuchon. What would the people working here think of her?

'Irasshaimase!'

In front of the reception desk, a tall woman in a black suit with a chignon slipped off Rika's coat. Her fluid movements made the heavy, well-worn garment feel feather-light. Rika followed her up the staircase with its ornate banisters to the first floor.

The glass doors opened. Rika blinked at the scene that unfolded in front of her, as dazzling to her eyes as if she'd dived into a glass of champagne. The whole space sparkled with honey-coloured light.

The faint sounds of glasses clinking and forks against plates became themselves flashes of light, bounding around the room.

Shown to a table in one corner, Rika took her seat. Behind her, a pane of glass protected the dazzling display of Swarovski crystal that studded the walls. The waitress ran through the day's menu, but her speech was so strewn with words Rika had never heard before that none of it seemed to sink in. She looked down at the menu and ordered a glass of what looked like the cheapest champagne. This wasn't officially part of her professional research so she couldn't put it on expenses and she'd be paying over 30,000 yen for the dinner already.

She glanced up at the chandelier laden with so many crystals that it seemed likely to fall from the ceiling at any second. Was this the real world? Was the world in which Rika usually lived the fake one? The experience was making her unsure. She took in her surroundings. As she'd anticipated, the restaurant was full of couples. With just a cursory look, she could make out three pairs of elderly men with young women. She could tell that they weren't fathers and daughters, either. The women's hair and skin were singularly lustrous, and they were dressed in a way that suggested that doing so was their profession, while the men looked affluent.

A serving of clear jelly was brought out as the amuse bouche. It came in a heavy, elegant porcelain dish which she felt sure would have made her swoon if she'd known the first thing about ceramics. The neatly lined up forks and knives were immaculately polished, and caught the light from the chandelier. Rika put a spoonful of the jelly to her mouth and was hit by the sour tang of lemon rind. The mouthful glided across her tongue and plummeted down her throat. There was no sweetness to it whatsoever. While the jelly slid slowly across the lining of her stomach, she felt a hunger stealthily rising up in her, from deep in her belly. This, she thought – this is a magic potion to enliven the senses. As if to prove this, she now distinctly overheard a scrap of the conversation from the next table.

'I've reserved a hotel room for us for afterwards.'

Was the room at the West Inn, just a few dozen metres away, she wondered? Met by this announcement from the grey-haired man, the young woman sitting opposite him continued to chew her fish, nodding very slightly but not meeting his eyes. Rika found herself thinking of her own teenage years. Back then, talk of 'subsidised dating' was all over the media. It was the era of the high-school girl as a sexual commodity. Walking around Shibuya in uniform, the eyes of men of her father's generation had pored over her, sizing her up, before they held up a certain number of fingers to indicate the price they'd be willing to pay. It wasn't just once or twice that this had happened to Rika, but on numerous occasions. Those memories were ruptures within the peaceful stretch of her adolescence surrounded by other girls, and just thinking back to them gave her a rush of fear.

Kajii was two years older than Rika and must have experienced – to a greater or lesser extent – the same kind of cultural climate. Rika didn't know how high school girls from Niigata had spent their time after school, what they might have been exposed to, but according to Kajii's testimony in court, her first romantic partner had been a married salesman in his forties who travelled back and forth between Niigata and Tokyo for his work. She'd been seventeen at the time. It was this man who had enticed Kajii away from her hometown. Yes, thinking about it, Rika realised that was something that Kajii had which she didn't – a hometown. Rika had been born in Tokyo, had lost the home she'd grown up in after her parents' divorce, and had never lived in any other city. She had neither a place to leave nor a place to go back to.

She looked up to see a knob of canary-yellow butter being carried towards her in a glass-lidded container.

'All this butter just for me, when there's a national shortage …'

Hearing Rika mumbling these words, the maitre d' smiled and lifted the lid of the dish.

'This butter has been flown in especially from overseas. Please help yourself to as much as you'd like.'

Confronted with an overwhelming selection of different kinds of bread on the trolley, Rika chose the simplest option she could see – a piece of baguette. Once again, she thought that she should have come with Reiko. Reiko would have told her which to choose. Rika spread a thick layer of butter on the bread. The butter, of a firmness that would break apart slowly on the tongue, went sinking into the crumb of the baguette. That alone was enough to make Rika glad she'd come.

The next course to be served was a chilled dish of avocado and snow crab stacked delicately like layer cake, topped with a generous helping of caviar. The acidity of the pomegranate seeds that exploded juicily in her mouth accentuated the creamy richness of the avocado and the sweetness of the crab flesh. Their unabashed scarlet hue brought the colour palette of the whole plate to life. Chased by the champagne, the taste of the crab and the caviar expanded like light suffusing her mouth.

If Kajii's account of her own past was to be trusted, she had first emerged on the scene as a muse-like figure, protected and supported by a network of prosperous old men. While it seemed too loose in its set-up to merit the term 'prostitution ring', there was no doubt that the association, which Kajii had described as 'an intellectual salon frequented by those with an appreciation for *the real thing*', was at least a little shady. What had Kajii been like at that age, as a young girl fresh out of Niigata?

Rika waited until a waiter came to clear her empty plate, then ordered a glass of red wine. Her selection procedure was based entirely on the reasonableness of the price. The wine brought over had a smoky taste reminiscent of bacon, which spread out plump and round at the back of her throat. The base of her tongue grew hot and tingly.

Of the numerous sensational things Kajii had come out with in court, the one that had caused the biggest ripple was her statement that, looking back on her twenties, she felt she'd 'lived a life like

Holly Golightly in *Breakfast at Tiffany's*. 'Were you making your living as a prostitute?' the lawyer for the prosecution had snapped back, to which Kajii had responded with great composure, 'I lived as Holly did. I belonged to nobody, either spiritually or physically. I was "travelling".' The sports papers and magazines had written this up in articles with titles like 'Fatso Serial-Killer Thinks She's Hepburn', deriding her lack of self-awareness. And yet, if you took Kajii's identification with Hepburn's character at face value, things started to fall into place.

Before joining Le Salon de Miyuko, Kajii had been a student at the Daikanyama branch of Le Cordon Bleu cooking school – the Paris cooking school attended by the female lead in the film *Sabrina*, also played by Hepburn. There, Sabrina is taught not only cooking skills but a sense of style, an entire way of life. When the chef tells her to lose her ponytail, she swaps her long hair for a pixie cut, transforming into a beautiful, sophisticated young woman. Her stubbornly flat soufflés begin to swell as they should. Maybe Kajii had thought of her dalliances with older men as being in the spirit of Audrey Hepburn coupling with Humphrey Bogart and Fred Astaire. According to her blog, Kajii's father, a man of refined tastes, had taken her along to the cinema showing old classics in Niigata. Had the films she said she'd seen there – *My Fair Lady*, *Funny Face*, *Roman Holiday* – come to shape her unique set of priorities?

Rika thought now of Holly Golightly. Between Truman Capote's original novel and the film adaptation, there was a big difference both in Holly's personality and the ending to her story. With Hepburn portraying her, Golightly had come to be known as a metropolitan pixie with a lucid, ethereal quality, but the original Holly was a failed actress turned high-class hooker. Dating was her profession and she went flitting from man to man, seeking only her own comfort. As an adolescent, Rika too had admired and envied Holly and her New York life. Had Manako Kajii simply attempted to stage a recreation of *Breakfast at Tiffany's* set in contemporary Japan, with herself in the starring role?

The grilled foie gras brought out next was accompanied by dried persimmons sautéed in butter. The saltiness of the butter drew out the persimmons' clinging, pervasive flavour. So tenaciously umami-rich was their taste, it was almost impossible to believe this was fruit that had once grown on a tree. It seemed more like a sweet flaky meat – no less so than the foie gras, in fact, which was so exquisitely tender that it broke apart on the tongue, oozing thick blood-scented liquid. Though she hadn't planned it so, the dish made a perfect match with the smoky notes of the red wine. Rika sighed. Piece after piece, the foie gras melted away softly in her mouth. She felt a sense of melancholy at reaching the end.

'The truffles are excellent, no? This is the season for them,' the elder gentleman sitting beside her said solicitously to his companion. As before, the young woman was chewing away in silence. There was virtually no conversation between them, and yet the look on the man's face was one of intent satisfaction. This wasn't the kind of relationship where the people in it drew pleasure from communicating, Rika thought. This was an old man dabbling in the costly pastime of cultivating a young girl so that her tastes matched his. Seeing it happening in real life, it appeared utterly unilateral, something only someone horribly self-satisfied would think of doing. The man's tone was not dissimilar to that of Rika's increasingly senile grandfather as he vented at her mother. Rika was starting to believe that women who were expected to accompany men in their pursuit of self-satisfaction had the right to make demands of their own.

The image of a face now surfaced in Rika's mind. It belonged to the second of Kajii's victims, who had died after Tadanobu Motomatsu and before Tokio Yamamura: Hisanori Niimi. Back in mid-August 2013, Niimi had been found drowned in the bathtub of his Hatagaya apartment, where he lived alone. Had he and Kajii had dates like the couple sitting alongside her? Rika wondered. While Kajii had only been explicit about coming to Joël Robuchon with Tokio Yamamura, in all likelihood she had also come with Niimi.

Kajii had met Niimi online at a much earlier stage than she had the others, and they had begun seeing one another when Kajii was still in her twenties. Neither wanted to get married, and it seemed to have been a comfortable relationship. Why, then, had she needed to kill this former patron of hers? The question niggled at Rika. That phrase she'd heard Kajii use several times, 'a mature man, with the capacity for both emotional and financial generosity' surely referred to Niimi.

The waiter brought over a plate of flounder in a white lemony sauce. The delicate yet fresh flavour palette, reminiscent of early summer, sent a welcome breeze rippling through Rika's feverish excitement.

There were further differences between Niimi and the other two victims. Niimi was a divorcee, and had a child with his former wife. He was of medium height and build, with a handsome, masculine face, tanned from his frequent golfing expeditions, and put some effort into maintaining his looks. He had handed over the reins of the small import company he had run for years to his son, but he remained a social creature, and would sometimes take Kajii out and show her off. He had boasted to his colleagues and the staff at the bar he often frequented that he was going out with an innocent princess young enough to be his daughter. He had gourmet tastes, and enjoyed touring a wealth of different restaurants with Kajii.

A plate of caramelised pork served with truffles and a silky corn mash was set down on the table. The candy that was secreted inside the mash popped on Rika's tongue, and she felt her eyes opening wide. 'Ah!' she exclaimed, her face growing hot. As with the magical jelly she'd been given as the amuse bouche, the dish suggested that food here was not just food, but an expertly designed form of entertainment. The ride started out gently, slowing down and speeding up before finally reaching the climax, where all the hints dropped along the way fell into place. Kajii had pulled a face when Rika had said it, but this place really was like Disneyland, Rika thought now. Her palate was still not refined enough to appreciate the truffles, though;

eating them felt like crunching on fragrant dry leaves strewn on the floor of an autumnal forest.

With dessert – an Impressionist painting composed of fig confit and mascarpone – behind her she felt like her stomach was about to burst, and when the trolley full of tiny cakes that looked like a stall from a summer festival pulled up to her table, she almost moaned.

Once she'd reached the bottom of her strong coffee, she would have to leave this place. Thinking about her journey home and how cold it was outside, her reluctance to leave grew became overwhelming. Taken by the urge to slump down onto the black tablecloth, Rika closed her eyes. She'd been so nervous before arriving, yet she now felt she wanted to do it all again, right from the amuse bouche on. Could she say with any confidence that she'd tasted it all? When would be the next time she came? In a few years' time, or would this visit be her last? The sadness swelled in her at the very idea.

Through her eyelids, the lights of the chandelier swayed provocatively.

'Your digestive system's just upset after all that heavy food. It's nothing to worry about. I made you some soup that's great for indigestion. Fingers crossed you'll like it.'

Saying this, Reiko took out a thermos flask from her tote bag and poured a cupful of the cloudy white liquid into its lid. Rika made out the tingle of ginger on her taste buds, and her throat immediately grew hot. The soup of scallions, daikon and goji berries slipped down smoothly into her stomach. With almost no salt and only the sweetness of its ingredients, its taste was subtle, yet full and rounded nonetheless, and impossible to imagine tiring of. Her stomach made a noise like a small creature mewling, and the two women locked eyes and laughed.

They had arranged to meet for lunch somewhere near Rika's office on the day of Reiko's next appointment at the Suidōbashi maternity clinic, but with the previous night's Robuchon feast still lying undigested in her stomach, Rika couldn't face the idea of eating anything else. Her whole body was heavy, as though swollen with salt and fat, she felt devoid of inspiration, as if her brain had been caramelised in honey. She was so sluggish that she didn't feel like doing a thing. She'd told Reiko as much in a message that morning, and hours later Reiko had showed up at the office reception desk with a wicker basket containing a flask of her special soup. Now, in the crowded staff canteen, Reiko carefully studied the samples in the glass case, before selecting the most popular teishoku lunch.

'This is amazing! Trust the Shūmeisha canteen to have such great food … I'd be happy paying for this sweet-and-sour black pork in an upmarket hotel! I can't believe you can eat this for four hundred yen. They say that the publishing industry is struggling, but the big places must still be doing all right.'

Reiko was smiling as she spoke, her lips glistening with sweet and sour sauce. In her white mohair sweater, she looked a bit like a rabbit. Looking intently at her friend, as she would someone she didn't know well, a peculiar feeling came over Rika. It was funny to be sitting across from Reiko in the staff canteen like this. Until a year and a half ago, Reiko had been an accomplished PR person, forever dashing from one place to another, yet now here she was, coming into Rika's workplace like she were on a field trip, savouring the whole experience. She wondered at how far her friend's sense of herself had shifted in the interim.

'How amazing that you went to dinner at Robuchon, though! He's a real Japanophile, and an expert on Japanese ingredients. Persimmon and foie gras sounds like such a rich and delicious combination!'

'Honestly, the tableware and the interior design alone put me in a daze. It was so much extravagance crammed together in one place I could barely take it all in. It's possible I didn't even properly taste the food? Maybe I'm just getting old. The biggest surprise was that the meat course contained this kind of popping candy – like the stuff I ate at primary school.'

'Right, when it comes to ingredients, anything goes with Robuchon. But popping candy! Wow. I never got to eat that at school. My mum's parenting might have been slapdash, but she was very strict about buying sweets and things.'

Reiko's expression looked aggrieved. When it came to gastro-nomic experiences, her covetousness rivalled that of Kajii.

'It made me think how much sheer physical strength Kajii must have, you know? To be able to eat a feast like that, go back to the West Inn to have sex, and go restaurant-hopping again the very next day, before writing it all up on her blog ...'

Sensing that something wasn't quite right, Rika looked up. The expression on her friend's face – a kind of discomfort – was not one she'd ever seen before. Thinking she must have put her foot in it somehow, Rika traced back over what she'd just said, and then it dawned on her. She'd almost never spoken with Reiko about anything sexual. Reiko was fastidiously prim. She didn't let men get away with telling even remotely dirty jokes around her. Even the pair's reports to one another about their first times had been vague.

'We should go together one time. I've only ever been to the more casual branch in Roppongi, where you sit at the counter.' Taking charge of the conversation, Reiko lifted the corners of her mouth into a bright smile. Rika brought the topic back round to Kajii regardless.

'I think she might have gone to Robuchon quite a lot with her second victim, Niimi. It's amazing that her suitors could keep up with that kind of diet and lifestyle when they were hardly spring chickens. That really struck me while I was there. Although saying that, there were plenty of those couples in the restaurant.'

'Is Niimi the oldish one who was a bit of a player – already a foodie before he met her? All this info of mine comes straight out of the weekly magazines, I should say ...'

'He may well have been, but there was also an element of him wanting to impress Kajii, to put on a show for her. I, for one, couldn't keep up with her lifestyle. It seems Niimi had high blood pressure, which makes me wonder if the whole bathtub thing might just have been an accident. Surely anyone, eating so lavishly ...'

As she spoke, Rika registered that Reiko's eyes weren't smiling in the slightest. The fat from the undigested foie gras instantly cooled inside her body, so she could feel its shape distinctly.

'Aren't you coming dangerously close to siding with her? Are you telling me all three men died of natural causes, their demise brought on because they couldn't keep up with her lifestyle? You think she's innocent, is that what you're saying?'

Rika felt the clamour of the canteen slip away like a wave receding. Reiko's words formed sharp angles, cutting into her flesh, seeking out her vital organs.

Hearing Reiko put it into such plain language, Rika thought it didn't sound so ridiculous. If she was honest, it was a possibility she had found herself considering. Tadanobu Motomatsu and his overdose of sleeping pills, Hisanori Niimi found drowned in the bath and Tokio Yamamura run over by a train – there was no material evidence that Kajii had killed any of them. The only thing to incriminate her was the fact that she'd been with them until soon before their deaths. Reiko was frowning at her reproachfully. With trepidation, Rika spoke.

'You're a Kajimana fan too though, no? Do you remember when I came to your house last year, and we talked about *The Story of Little Babaji*? I remember you saying that it was the tigers' fault – that they brought about their own death by turning into butter. I just mean …'

'You're trying to say that Kajii's men are like the tigers?' Reiko cut in sharply. She seemed oblivious to the sauce of her sweet-and-sour pork gradually congealing on her plate. 'You want to imply that Manako Kajii simply brought home the butter that she stumbled across and used it to enjoy a good meal, and that there's nothing wrong with that? She has no awareness of lying, therefore she isn't a liar? She has no awareness of having killed, therefore she's not a killer? Is that what you think? Her appetite and her sex drive run to such extraordinary degrees that they took a toll on the lives of the people, and eventually threw their lives off course? If that's how you really see it, then I think you're already under her spell.'

Rika tried to smile, but it didn't feel as though she was doing it right. Reiko was attacking her. Over the course of their fourteen-year friendship, they'd argued several times, but she'd never before experienced the stony expression that Reiko's face wore now, or this sensation of having no idea what to say in response.

'I think you want to be like her in some way.'

'Want to *be* like her? What do you mean? Why would I want to be like a convicted serial killer?'

Why is my voice trembling like this? Rika wondered as she spoke.

Reiko couldn't know anything. It was a terrible misunderstanding. But the large, pale-brown eyes hovering before her permitted no escape route.

'If eating exactly what she wants and having men following in her footsteps results in their deaths, then that's a perfect crime of truly delicious proportions.' Pursing her lips tightly, she gazed fixedly at Rika. Finally, she said, 'You seem tired recently, Rika. You don't seem to have any motivation to exercise, either.'

There was an unfamiliar cruelty to the gaze with which Reiko now surveyed her body. Was even Reiko hinting for her to lose weight now? As it happened, Rika had gained another kilo. Her expression must have been pretty dejected, because Reiko let up.

'But look, never mind that. I'm sorry, let's change the subject. Did you know that Joël Robuchon is a freemason? Apparently he talks about it in his autobiography.'

From then until the moment she had to leave to make her appointment, Reiko kept up a stream of conversation so cheerful as to seem contrived. Rika walked her to the door of the building to say goodbye, and Reiko went pattering off in the direction of Kagurazaka, her wicker basket dangling from one arm. When Rika returned to the editing room, Yū approached her with a clipboard in hand.

'That girl you were with before – was she a prospective employee? Visiting from one of the universities or something?'

On the verge of bursting out laughing, Rika took the clipboard.

'No, no, she's a friend. The same age as me. We were in the same year at university, and now she's married. Until last year she worked for a big film company. She's much older than you are!'

'Seriously?! Sorry, in that case. She doesn't look it at all, though. Carrying that straw basket, I thought she had to be a student.' Yū widened her eyes dramatically.

'I'm sure she'd be delighted to hear that. She's always looked young for her age, though.'

'I mean, she definitely looks young, but it's not just that …' Yū seemed to be struggling to articulate her thoughts. Her irises swam, and Rika felt sure that she was seeing a Reiko who wasn't actually in front of her. And the real Reiko – what was she doing right now? Was she at this very moment spreading her reedy legs for the famous fertility doctor, whose praises she sang so highly? Rika quickly pushed the image from her mind, feeling a surge of self-hatred.

'I think it's her aura. It's like she's not resigned herself in any way. She's so intense. She was looking at you with such sparkle in her eyes, it seemed less how you'd look at a friend and more the way you look at someone older, whom you look up to and aspire to be.'

'Oh, no way! Reiko's got her life far better sorted than I have, and she's got a lovely husband.' Saying this, Rika switched on her computer. Lots of people in her department came into the office past noon, so the office was at its busiest after lunch. But Yū seemed like she wanted to continue talking.

'Everyone starts to become resigned to things sooner or later, don't they? As adults.'

'Hey, what's with all this glumness? You've passed our internal exam, you're on easy street now. Oh, I get it! You've got the post-finding-employment blues. I remember that, actually.'

'Do you really? It's like I can see my future as this straight line stretching out front of me. I know it's a luxury complaint to have. Anyway, I'm going to see my favourite idol group play live tonight, which should perk me up. I'll be full of beans again by tomorrow, I promise.'

'An idol group? One of the boybands?'

'They're called Scream. They're all middle-school girls. Have you heard of them? They've not had much media coverage yet, but before long they'll be on the Kōhaku New Year's Song Contest and become nationwide stars, and then all the magazines for middle-aged men like ours will be covering them. They're so talented!'

Yū's way of speaking was usually clipped, and it was rare to find this degree of excitement in her tone. When Rika looked up at her in surprise, Yū flushed, waving her hand in front of her face as if to bat away any misunderstandings.

'Don't get me wrong, I'm not an otaku or anything like that. They have quite a few fans here in the company. Mr Fujimura from the books department loves them. Apparently one of his authors is into them and dragged him along to a concert, but then he grew to like them himself.'

'Really! Mr Fujimura too, eh? That's unexpected.' Rika could sense she was pulling an odd expression. The subject had never once come up between her and Makoto. As soon as Yū had turned her back Rika pulled out her smartphone and sent him a text. She heard him reply instantly. All at once, her feeling of indigestion had eased.

Makoto had suggested meeting at a Japanese bistro currently in vogue on the main Kagurazaka shopping street. As soon as Rika descended to the basement where the restaurant was located, she understood that the cuisine here was not what Kajii would have called 'orthodox'. Both the jazz playing in the background and the voices of the staff were too loud. She was escorted to a private room that was softly lit with indirect lighting, yet something about the space left her unable to relax.

Makoto, sitting opposite her, now spread his napkin and said, as if reassured, 'I get it, finally. It's all because you're reporting on Manako Kajii. It stands to reason that you'd be eating a lot, if that's the case. Getting an exclusive interview with her would be a real coup.'

Rika had arranged to meet Makoto in a restaurant not solely to talk about the idol group issue. She also wanted to tell him that she'd been meeting with Kajii. She was trying to persuade herself that it was okay to trust Makoto, and in order to do so, she wanted to share something important with him.

'That comes as a real relief. I'm sorry for saying all that stuff. If that's the reason you're putting on weight, then it doesn't bother me at all. I was out of line, and I apologise. It was insensitive of me.'

Why was it, Rika wondered to herself, that this apology didn't take away her doubts?

Judging from Makoto's interactions with the serving staff, he had come here before. The restaurant's concept was healthy meals that used plenty of organic vegetables. In this, too, she sensed a powerful pressure to lose weight, which made her insides contract. Yet she was finding she didn't have the energy to get down about each and every thing – yes, that was it, she just didn't have the energy. She was tired of living her life thinking constantly about how she appeared to others, checking her answers against everyone else's. The organic noble rot wine slipped down her throat like water.

'The food here is low on calories, so you can eat as much as you like,' Makoto said smiling kindly, but Rika soon found herself irritated by the taste of the dishes that showed up one after another on their table. Tofu caprese, root-vegetable ratatouille – the meals were neither Japanese nor Western, neither rich nor simple. She was bored by this kind of cuisine, with its taste that didn't seem to be making any kind of statement. As she failed to make headway with her portion of brown rice paella with basket clams, Makoto looked curiously at her.

'We don't come on dates like this often, so why not forget about your diet for tonight and just enjoy yourself?'

Why didn't he realise how contradictory his demands were? The worst of it was that he thought of himself as one of the good ones – an enlightened man who understood women. Until not long ago, Rika had thought the same of him. She would usually have felt grateful for his consideration in this situation.

'You say that, but if I eat, I'll definitely put on weight. Rice is still a carbohydrate, even if it's brown.'

'Are you still worrying about what I said? I've told you, that was my mistake. I don't think you have to be thin or anything. All I was saying is that it's not good to let yourself go. You've been forcing yourself to eat for professional reasons, no? That's not your fault. If you're gaining weight as a result of the effort you're making for your work, then it's unavoidable. Just look at how I've ended up, thanks to all the socialising I have to do for work.'

Rika felt like she was being roped into an alliance against her will, and she wanted no part of it. She felt no inclination to carry on the conversation.

'Oh yeah, I wanted to ask ... Is it true that you're into that idol group Scream?'

Before leaving the office, Rika had looked them up online. Five middle-school girls who had just made their debut, managed by a small talent agency. The group's selling point seemed to be that its members looked like any other girls their age, but on stage they transformed into dazzling performers. Makoto nodded, as though it were no big deal.

'Oh, did Yū let the cat out of the bag? Yeah, I do like them. If you're interested, why don't you come along to their next concert, with the bunch from work? You'll enjoy it, I think. They've got quite a few female fans.'

'But all teenagers, no? I think I'll pass. I'm not sure I can get into music made by girls young enough to be my children.'

'Oh, they're totally different from all your run-of-the-mill idol groups. There's a strong emphasis on talent, and the girls really give it their all. Every time I see them they've improved. They always show so much gratitude to their fans, and they're very modest. Watching them gives you the feeling that you want to try your hardest, too.'

Makoto took out his smartphone and showed her a photo of him in a Scream T-shirt. Seeing him looking the very picture of an otaku made her smile. Indeed, there was nothing about his objective, reasoned way of speaking to cause discomfort. Still, the more she heard Makoto praise the Scream members' determination and modesty, the greater the feeling grew inside Rika that she couldn't get on board. You had to have a reason for liking something – that was what she heard him saying. He liked these girls because they made an effort, and anyone who didn't wasn't worthy of his praise. It struck her that she'd have found it much easier to accept if he'd come out and said he liked them because they were cute.

'Don't you have any idols?'

At this unexpected question, Rika abandoned her struggle to remove the basket clam glued tightly to its shell and looked up at him. In the glow of the soft lighting, Makoto's friendly round eyes made him look ever so kind. There are lots of women out there who'd want to date him, she thought to herself, as though the fact were quite unconnected to her.

'I guess you don't really go for that kind of stuff, do you?' Makoto continued. 'It doesn't have to be a celebrity. I was just wondering if you've ever had someone you aspired to be like, who made you feel brave or inspired or whatever. When you were in your teens, for example.'

Someone you aspired to be like – with this phrase, her conversation with Reiko came flooding back to her, and she felt the firm, salty tofu masquerading as mozzarella break apart underneath her tongue. An unpleasant, fishy taste spread through her mouth.

'Life is hard without someone to admire or yearn for, don't you think?'

They paid the bill and were climbing the flight of steps leading up to the street when Makoto said to her from behind, 'Hey, can I stay over tonight?'

It was the first time he'd asked in a while, and Rika felt her heart start to race anxiously. She wasn't yet fully recovered from her bout of indigestion, and despite the healthy dinner, her body still felt sluggish and heavy. Even lifting her feet to climb the stairs was a trial.

'Not tonight I think, sorry. I've got a very early start tomorrow.'

Turning around, she saw Makoto nod, before reaching out his hand to gently intertwine his fingers with hers. He was so understanding that her previous moment of panic seemed like wasted energy.

'He's stingy. With both his wallet and his spirit,' Manako Kajii pronounced matter-of-factly. She was in such a good mood today that it was hard to believe this was the same woman who'd gone at Rika with such ferocity on her previous visit. Kajii had responded favourably to her request for another meeting because Rika had been to Robuchon as instructed, and written up her impressions in a letter. When she now confided to Kajii about her bistro date and how the food hadn't been to her taste, Kajii found fault not only with the cuisine, but with Rika's suitor as well.

'Have you ever dated a man of influence, with generosity of spirit?'

'No. I can count on one hand the number of men I've ever dated, and all of them have been my age.'

At some stage, Rika's reservations about revealing elements of her private life to Kajii had vanished. In her letter, she had confided to Kajii that her parents had divorced when she was in middle school, that her mother had started up a small boutique with a friend, that her father had died, that she'd gone to an all-girls' school, that she'd met her best friend at a mixed university, and that she was dating someone her age at the company. Yet Kajii grew bored by the topic of Makoto almost immediately.

'Well, in any case, let us talk about Robuchon. That champagne-gold interior with the black tablecloths to draw out its luminescence is simply glorious, isn't it? I adore it there!'

'Did you go there with Mr Niimi?'

'Hmm, did I, I wonder? I can't remember. I went there with so many people, I don't recall all the individual occasions.'

'In all honesty, I think it was too glamorous for me. It made my eyes spin.'

Rika was starting to learn that it was her most unaffected reactions that lodged the deepest with Kajii. True to form, Kajii's expression now softened. If only she looked like this all the time, Rika thought. She felt closer to understanding the lengths her male suitors had gone to keep her in a good mood.

'There's something rather boyish about you, Rika. Like a middle-school boy.'

It was the second time ever that Manako had said Rika's name. Hearing it from her lips gave her a ticklish, embarrassed feeling. Kajii giggled, mockingly.

'Do you not think you need to learn to love yourself more? That way you'll come to realise that it's a waste to diminish yourself by going on dates with people you aren't matched with. Your estimation of yourself is too low.'

'I wonder whether I can do that, though. If I give this guy up, I don't have any confidence I'll find someone else. He's a good person, generally speaking. I feel that all women would like to learn to love themselves the way you do, to act with confidence, but it's actually the hardest thing of all.'

'Rubbish! It's easy. Ignore all that nonsense about making an effort and so forth. All you need to do is to eat as much of whatever it is you most desire at any given moment. Listen carefully to your heart and your body. Never eat anything you don't want to. When you take the decision to live that way, both your mind and your body will commence their transformation.'

The seaweed salad she shovelled down her throat at her desk, the gritty dried fruit she snacked on while on the move, the Japanese bistro Makoto had taken her to – of late, Rika was so scared of putting on any more weight that she was subsisting entirely on things she didn't want to eat. But no, that was misrepresenting the situation. In her thirty-three years, had she ever spontaneously eaten anything that she wanted to? The meals she'd eaten since becoming acquainted with Kajii had been delicious, but even those she'd ingested purely because she'd been instructed to by someone else.

Kajii had rolled up the sleeves of her jumper to reveal her fleshy arms, which she began stroking and caressing with her fingers. Conscious of Rika's admiring gaze on her skin, she spoke in a nasal, cooing voice, 'My arms, my breasts, and my bottom are packed to bursting with all my favourite food. My body is made up entirely from steaks from the New York Grill, sukiyaki from Imahan, and the Gargantuan Chaliapin Steak Pie from the Imperial Hotel. When I grow fatigued by the food they serve here in prison, and I feel like I'm going out of my mind imagining all the delectable things I could be eating, I gently touch and squeeze myself. My upper arms are particularly cool and soft. When I stick out my tongue and lick them, I can taste their sweetness.'

Kajii winked mischievously at Rika, who couldn't take her eyes off her. Stroking her upper arm, groping its flesh through the fabric of her jumper, she rolled her eyes back in her head suggestively. A picture floated into Rika's mind of Kajii stark naked, her huge breasts pressed together and her chin thrust forwards to fit her nipples into her mouth. This woman wanted to eat herself whole.

Maybe she masturbated this way when the prison officers weren't looking, Rika thought now. The object of Kajii's desire wasn't past lovers or celebrities she had crushes on, but her own body. Was that why, even stripped of her freedom and faced with the possibility of having to live out the rest of her life here, she seemed so satisfied, exuding such potent femininity? She was like a self-pollinating plant in full bloom. For all she scorned other women for eschewing men, wasn't it Kajii, above anyone, who least needed a male partner?

'Since I was young, I've always been delectable to insects. When the weather's balmy, they come flocking to me. Mr Motomatsu used to say that even my breath must be sweet.' Saying this, she exhaled an affected puff of air. The acrylic screen between them grew foggy.

'Your office is situated in Kagurazaka, isn't it? That's an excellent location. Do you like teppanyaki? The aged sirloin steak from Miyazaki is wonderful, naturally, but it's the garlic butter rice that they bring out at the end that is truly exquisite. Give it a try. Then let me know what you think. At the moment, your culinary tales are the only thing I have to look forward to.'

Saying this, she shot Rika an unstudied smile, and for a second, Rika felt unbearably sad for her. She wanted to smash the acrylic screen and lead Kajii away from here. She wanted to watch Manako Kajii devouring a plate of food, to feel the thrill of it right to the marrow of her bones.

Why had she put on lipstick?

Instead of taking off her make-up when she left the office, instead of removing any trace of softness, Rika had gone into the bathroom and reapplied her lipstick. She almost came to a standstill midway up the hill. At first, she'd thought about inviting Reiko to the restaurant and offering to pay, but she felt that right now even so much as mentioning Manako Kajii's name was liable to put Reiko in a bad mood, so she decided to leave it. She and Shinoi had formed a habit of meeting in the same cheap izakaya, but it couldn't hurt to go somewhere nice for once, and besides, there was something she wanted to talk to him about. So she'd told him there was a restaurant she wanted to visit, and they'd decided on today to meet.

As she headed along the route that would take her there, the narrow, labyrinthine backstreets of Kagurazaka twisted and turned off at a multiplicity of angles, tempting her in different directions. She passed a white couple with a touristy air about them. In front of a small torii gate she was noticing for the first time, bunches of flowers had been left in offering. The smell of dashi emanated from a restaurant. Looking up at the night sky, it was hard to believe that all of this lay behind the scenery she encountered day in, day out. She'd passed along here multiple times for work drinks, yet tonight, strangely enough, everything seemed vivid in a way it never had before.

'Sorry for keeping you. It was hard to get away from the office today.'

When she arrived at the restaurant five minutes late, Rika found Shinoi sitting at one side of a full counter, facing the long teppan – hotplate – and drinking a beer. Exposed to the sizzle and the smell of frying meat, her tongue moistened. The fact that she was craving meat when the memory of her recent bout of indigestion was still so vivid was a sign that she was getting more gluttonous. Feeling the slick of her lipstick heavy on her lips, she glanced towards the door of the bathroom, designated by a noren curtain.

'I've put on some weight.' Rika had decided to announce it herself, before he could point it out.

'Have you?' Shinoi cocked his head and looked at her with his distinctive round eyes. Their whites were cloudy, and beneath them lay the usual heavy dark bags. It had been a long time since she'd been inspected by a member of the opposite sex in such a blatant way, even if she'd been the one to prompt it, and she felt her midriff grow hot and the blood course thickly through her. Shinoi averted his gaze to the gleaming hotplate and said, somewhat bluntly, 'Sorry, I'm not good at noticing things like that. I'm kind of clueless when it comes to changes in women's appearance. But I think you're fine as you are, no?'

The appetisers were brought over. As the watershield served in its little glass bowl went slipping down her throat, she felt a fresh spring well up in her stomach.

Polishing off her first beer, Rika thought back to the events of the previous night. She'd been out to a members' bar in Akasaka with a budget examiner from the Ministry of Finance. After making her sing two duets with him on the karaoke machine, he'd reached out a swollen hand, wedding band glinting on its finger, towards her thigh.

Similar things had happened to her in the past, she was sure, but it was the first time that the other person in the equation had displayed their desire so brazenly. Maybe there *was* something different about her after all. If she were being totally honest, she didn't utterly dislike her new physique. When she was in the bath and her eyes fell on her naked thighs and her stomach, glistening and gleaming as if lit from the inside, speckled with beads of water, she found herself staring at her own body if she were eyeing up a slab of Échiré butter. Maybe, if she weren't receiving so much criticism from the people around her, she would be fine with the way she looked.

The budget examiner's fawning attitude as he tried to cosy up to her flipped the moment that Rika brushed his hand away.

'Think you can still put on airs now that you're fat like a pig?' he spat out, affecting drunkenness with his tone. The contradiction at the heart of his actions seemed ridiculous and pathetic, to the point that she'd had to stifle a smile. He was like the men who'd given money to Manako Kajii, she thought. She had only just about managed to stop him from touching her, but she was curiously free of fear or shame. She had no doubt that if something similar had happened previously, she'd have been plunged into violent self-loathing for days, for having given him the opportunity to act as he did.

Rika had held his icy, mocking gaze, and this morning she'd received a fearful-sounding text from him: *I drank too much last night so I don't remember what I said, but if I was rude then I apologise.*

It was the first time that Rika had ever experienced someone grovelling like that, when she herself had no sense of having lost anything. Maybe this way she'd be able to get some information out of him about the upcoming budget.

Now, she decided to stop fretting about her lipstick. It would rub off while she was eating the meat anyway.

Just as the two of them finished their plump white asparagus spears in white sauce, they were served a selection of grilled vegetables. To think that onions could become so sweet and rich simply by grilling them! Rika had never been a fan of shishito peppers, but the ones on the plate in front of her were fragrant, with a gentle taste. Before she knew it, she'd devoured many more vegetables than she had the other night in that Japanese bistro, just a few dozen metres from here.

She was fairly sure that the red meat being cooked on a section of the hotplate not far from where they were sitting was for them. Eventually, clear jus began oozing from its surface. Even the smell of the melting fat was appealing and mild – not aggressive or meaty. She watched transfixed as the red turned to pale pink, as the white fat grew translucent.

The meat was cut up and served to them in pieces. Rika imagined it would be steaming hot, but when she brought one of the chunks to her lips, she found it to be just the right temperature. The comfort it brought was that of a warm, affectionate tongue entering her mouth. When she bit into the aromatic seared surface of the meat, the juices from the moist, rare sections came seeping out, making the lining of her cheeks tremble. A blood-coloured filament flickered across her vision.

'Apparently the garlic-butter rice here is truly out of this world. They use plenty of butter, as well as the leftover meat juices.'

Rika was looking at the rice cooking on the hotplate as she spoke. Cloaked in their mantle of amber butter, the grains shimmied and danced before her eyes. There was a sizzle as the chef poured on some soy sauce, and then the short, spirited tango was over.

Bowls of the glistening bronze rice appeared before them. Swathed in meat jus and butter, each and every grain shone potently. The rich, heady aroma of the soy sauce stoked Rika's appetite. The garlic singed to a deep brown unleashed a perilous bitterness and astringency across her palate. Slippery with fat, the rice slid across the plane of her tongue and down her throat. The meat she'd eaten before had been fantastically flavoursome, but this rice that had absorbed its juices was truly formidable in its taste. With each movement of her jaw, she felt a new lease of power surging up her body. The sense of fullness brought on a comfortable lethargy, and Rika felt she could happily drop off right at that moment.

'Ahhh, this is so good,' she mumbled several times. Glancing towards her companion, she saw that Shinoi's chopsticks had stopped moving, and he was looking at her.

'Do you not like it?'

'No, no, it's not that. I was just thinking how contented you looked.'

He sighed, and Rika smelled the butter and garlic on his breath. Seeing his skin and lips, usually so cracked and dry, now gleaming with fat brought Rika a sense of pride. Shinoi held out his bowl towards her.

'If you like it that much, you can have the rest of mine.'

As embarrassed as she felt about the situation, Rika's hunger won out, and she ended up polishing off the rest of Shinoi's bowl. Then, whether because her tongue had grown loose with all the fat she'd ingested or because she'd already confessed the same thing to Makoto, she looked around and said quite smoothly, her voice lowered, 'You know, I'm thinking I'd like to do an interview with Manako Kajii for the magazine. I've been visiting Tokyo Detention House since last year, and I've spoken with her at least four times now. I've managed to get close while avoiding the subject of her case, but moving beyond that point feels hard. How would you approach it, in my situation?'

'If you've got this far you must be pretty determined, so I'll tell you what I think.' Shinoi rested his chopsticks on the counter. The sound of frying meat grew louder. 'Offer your heart to her on a plate.'

As she turned to look at him, his profile looked neither particularly austere nor especially serious. It was the same Shinoi as ever, with his sunken cheeks and puffy lower eyelids, but she could tell that his mind was somewhere else. Who was the person he had once handed his heart to on a plate?

'You need to instil in her a sense of unbreakable trust in you. It's not about sucking up or telling lies. You show the other party your most vulnerable part, give them a piece of your life.'

Dessert was caramelised apple with ice cream. As usual, they split the bill. Stepping out of the restaurant, they walked side by side along the narrow street. They were enveloped in a rich darkness, and the commotion of the main street seemed a long way off.

'That was a really good find. I'm surprised – I didn't know you were into the restaurant scene.'

'I haven't been at all, until recently. But a friend of mine who really knows her food told me about it.'

A friend – that was how Rika had just referred to Manako Kajii. All her adult life, Reiko had been the only person she'd used that word about. Reiko had occupied that throne so squarely that nobody else had even approached it. Rika was fairly sure that Manako Kajii had never once had a female friend she felt she could trust.

'I feel like I've eaten a proper meal for the first time in ages. Thanks. If you find another place like that, take me along. Next time it's on me,' Shinoi said. When Rika turned to him in astonishment, he laughed sheepishly.

'What?' he said, then quickly looked away.

'Okay, I will,' she said. As she stepped forward, walking alongside him, she felt the hardness of his body against hers. Her breast was touching his upper arm. Her body had swelled out so rapidly that she was still not used to its new dimensions, and hadn't readjusted her movements yet to keep the right distance between herself and others. When she'd had her bra size measured at an underwear shop in the station between work appointments, she found she'd shot up from a B to a D cup. Her body was the type where excess weight went immediately to her breasts. When the older female shop assistant had grabbed her breasts roughly and pushed them inside the cup, she'd felt her nipples throb from the inside. The three new bras that she'd bought, grabbing hastily from the shelves while darting glances at her watch, didn't match the pants she owned, in either colour or material. They weren't the kind of underwear she could show to anyone. Rika caught herself and thought about it.

Who, exactly, would she be showing her underwear to, anyway? The man next to her was a member of the editorial team at a major news firm, and a reliable source of hers. That was all.

She hadn't brushed up against him on purpose, and she felt that if she pulled back hurriedly she'd be confirming it as a regrettable fact, so instead she continued walking as she was, her breast softly crushed against his firm bicep.

'Where do you live?' she asked him.

'Suidōbashi.'

'This might be a silly question, but what's your favourite food?'

'Hmm, maybe Castella cake. I recently discovered how good the packaged slices they sell in 7 Eleven are.'

'That's a cute answer,' she replied, and she saw him smiling, his white teeth glinting in the darkness. Pleasantly full as she was, Rika felt like crying. She might dine with someone, but at the end of the meal they would go their separate ways. She couldn't stay with that person forever. Even with her stomach full of warmth and the taste of delicious food lingering on her tongue, she remained alone. It didn't matter who she had for company. She was beginning to understand that the more delicious the time she spent with others, the more alone she felt.

That morning, as she filled in the admission form on the ground floor of the Tokyo Detention House, Rika had been hit by the sense that something wasn't right, as though she'd been drenched by an invisible downpour.

'Did someone come to see you yesterday?' she asked the moment she was shown into the visiting room. Manako Kajii flashed her a smile in response. It wouldn't be unheard of for a member of her family to have visited, and Kajii had plenty of supporters. Yet Rika couldn't shake the feeling that the visitor had been someone of a similar position to her. The thought made her unbearably anxious. Was Kajii leading other journalists on at the same time? There was no room for hesitation. Today, Rika decided, she would broach the matter of the interview.

'You know I can only have one visit per day. Why are you so uptight? It's very odd.'

Rika was overcome by a desire to subjugate the woman sitting before her, separated only by the acrylic screen. The urge to touch her, to dig her fingers into that huge bosom, took her with startling force. Kajii's body was so unlike that of the women she knew. Her mother exercised regularly and was complimented by people on her figure, her youthfulness. Reiko's firm body was like that of a young girl's, its lack of any excess seemed designed to resist the gaze of the opposite sex. Her classmates back in school who had brushed up against her had been the same. Endlessly full and seemingly capable of absorbing anything that it touched, this body in front of her now operated according to a different aesthetic. Rika longed to feel it, to explore with her own hands that uncharted territory into which all those men had poured so much of their money.

'I have a request. I want you to let me interview you. I want to make it a special feature in the *Shūmei Weekly* – a major serialised article. If we do it, I think it'll help you with your next trial. I'm not yet in a position where I'm allowed to write my own copy, so the editorial desk would use the draft I gave them to write up the article, but I'd be responsible for making sure that there's nothing in there that could be detrimental to you.'

Kajii drew in her chin as if dismayed, and looked fixedly at Rika.

'I believe I was clear the first time you visited. I have no intention of speaking about the case. Have you still not given up on that idea? The only thing I have a mind to talk with you about is food.'

'Of course. I'm not looking for any information about the case or the victims. All I want to do is ensure the public has the right impression of you. I think we should try to bring public opinion over to your side. To that end, I'd like you to tell me honestly about the kind of life you've lived, about your feelings and your experiences, without hiding anything.'

'And just what good would that do me? I've had quite enough exposure to the public's greedy curiosity already.'

'I think that hearing about your approach to life could offer something like salvation to so many women out there who are struggling. You say that women should acknowledge their inferiority to men, and let them take the lead, but the very fact that someone like you is here, breathing, is continuing to inflict damage on a lot of men. You're a paradoxical figure. The people whose noses you really put out of joint in court were all men in a position of social authority. There are many men who, even if you didn't actually lay a finger on them, had their lives thrown off course simply by having met you. You don't deny that, I presume? Japanese women are required to be self-denying, hard-working and ascetic, and in the same breath, to be feminine, soft and caring towards men. Everyone finds that an impossible balance to strike, and they struggle desperately as a result. Even when they do manage to strike it, there's no redemption to be had. They're never fully free. That's what women are feeling.'

'I don't care about other women. I've no desire to try to save them. You know how much I despise most women.'

The cold, hard surface of Kajii's tone allowed no room for Rika to burrow her way in. She held on desperately, as if clinging with her nails onto a shiny rock face.

'Maybe it's not about other women. Maybe it's me who's looking for salvation. Can you think of it as something you're doing for me?'

'But why?'

Kajii looked up at Rika, unconvinced. This, it seemed, was still not good enough for her. As Shinoi had said, Rika had to give herself up completely – to become a tiger and go whirling round and round until she melted into golden butter that Kajii could slather over her lips.

'I think it's maybe because you're … No, forget that. I want to do it because …'

From the day Rika had met Manako Kajii, she'd thought about her constantly. Kajii took up a greater place in her mind than Makoto, than Reiko, than her mother. Her words and behaviour so riddled with contradiction, her stubborn fidelity to her own desire, her unshakeable confidence which came from averting her gaze from that which she did not want to see – all of it affected Rika deeply. She couldn't look away from her. All that reasoning Makoto needed to defend his support of the idol group wasn't necessary for Rika. Even if idolising Kajii seemed to go against the greater part of her life as she knew it, she couldn't give up.

'I want to do it because … I really like you.'

However you analysed Kajii's expression, you would find no trace of her being moved by these words. Rika felt the hurt take form within her instantaneously, a sharp object boring into her abdomen. It was the first time she'd told anybody of her feelings for them, the first time she'd summoned up her bravery like this, and her confession had been taken as utterly pedestrian.

'Can we be friends?'

'I don't want friends.' As she shook her head of glossy hair, a smile floated across Kajii's face. 'I don't need friends. I'm only interested in having worshippers.'

CHAPTER FIVE

Observing her dimly lit hands grow suddenly light, Rika spun around.

Someone had opened the blinds in the office. The end-of-January sunlight streamed in at an angle, bleaching the rough brown recycled paper in front of her to a bright white. Her fingertips grew warmer beneath its rays. Noticing how dry and powdery her nails were, streaked here and there with vertical lines, she recalled that she was out of hand cream.

The heavy feeling in her stomach had dragged on, and at the doctor's surgery in the station, which she'd dived into between work appointments, she'd been diagnosed with light inflammation of the oesophagus. The doctor had prescribed several types of powder and pills that made her oesophagus feel cold, and left her acutely aware of the shape of her stomach. On the doctor's advice, she was restricting herself to plain food. In the morning she had warm milk and a banana, and her lunch was chunky vegetable soup from the bento shop. She got home as early as possible in the evening and was making rice porridge with vegetables, using the small portions of rice she'd frozen in advance. Now that the new year was properly under-way, she'd stopped overeating. The medicine she was taking three times daily was restoring her to her senses. Her weight gain seemed to be finally subsiding.

The experience of putting on weight so suddenly meant that Rika was starting to understand what a 'good amount' was for her. She realised that she'd been negligent in the way she'd been eating. At that rate, she now thought, she would have fallen ill sooner or later. It was okay to seek out good food, as far as time and money permitted. If anything, she preferred her upper arms and belly as they were now, with a bit of meat on them. For a height of five foot five, her current weight was not unhealthy. She had previously been too thin. She didn't mind forgoing the compliments on her figure that she'd received before, though she meant to ensure she didn't exceed 55 kilos, to avoid having to buy a whole new wardrobe.

Still, the consternation that her weight gain had elicited in the people around her seemed to her extreme. The changes to her body hadn't caused them any trouble, and yet people's reactions were critical, even fearful. Rika couldn't be sure that she herself wouldn't react in the same way to someone else filling out a little. Being on the receiving end had made her determined not to do the same to someone else in future.

Sitting at her desk, Rika used a glue stick to stick a pile of cuttings into a scrapbook. She'd got into the habit when she had a few minutes to spare at work, of going through the *Shūmei Weekly* back issues kept in the editorial office, or the newspapers and magazines in the materials office, taking photocopies of any articles she found concerning the Kajii case and cutting them out. She now flicked briskly through the pages of the special feature that had run in the second week of December 2013, when the world had been paying full attention to the case. The feature included articles about the reputation Kajii and her family had in her hometown, insider information on Le Salon de Miyuko and shots of its students, speculations about her annual revenue, revelations about the private lives and personalities of her victims, and quotes from their families. This latter category, though, didn't comprise many members. For a start, Motomatsu, who had been advanced in years, seemed to have had little contact with his relatives since splitting with his common-law wife. Niimi's wife was dead, and his son – in his late forties and running the company his father had left him – was largely silent, making no secret of his ill will towards Kajii and his exhaustion that came from being pursued by the press. He did state that his father, once a man of common sense, had been deceived by that 'deranged woman' and lost himself, that Kajii's promises of marriage had been 'a trick', and she had 'killed him, while making his death look like a heart attack'.

But a quote given by the sister of Kajii's third victim, Yamamura, stood out from the rest: 'My brother wasn't her fiancé. Maybe I shouldn't say this as a member of his family, but I think he was just one of her numerous worshippers. As I said in court, he always spoke badly of her in front of me – saying she was ugly, or fat, or strange and naive. As a woman, it was horrible to hear him say those things. But I could tell that that was all just talk, and actually he was crazy about her.'

Worshipper – that was the word that Rika had been unable to get out of her head since her meeting with Kajii last week. Feeling a sudden itchiness around her neck, she tugged at the collar of her turtleneck. Kajii had batted away Rika's offer of friendship, making clear her lack of interest. The issue of the interview remained unresolved.

'I don't think that woman has had a single real relationship in her life,' Yamamura's sister said. 'My brother got sucked in by her impressive way of talking. He was just an audience member at the play she was putting on. That said, I've never met her outside of the courtroom.'

Her way of speaking might have been detached, but it didn't seem cold. She said she'd been against the idea of her brother dating Kajii from the beginning, but had been worn down by the strength of his fixation. Not wanting to get into arguments with him, she'd avoided bringing up the subject when they met.

What was the time that Kajii had spent with these men really like? Rika now wondered. If you believed her testimony, it sounded as though she'd wielded a well-judged combination of kindness and wilfulness to make them devoted to her. Yet as besotted as Kajii's victims had been, they'd kept making derogatory remarks about her to others. Rika found it hard to comprehend falling head over heels with a person while also looking down on them.

Rika found herself gazing at the blinds from which the light was streaming through. Maybe her father had been exactly the same as those men. He'd found fault in her mother's execution of household tasks, told her constantly that she didn't understand how the world worked, and mocked how cosseted she was. Yet when she had made to leave, he'd been profoundly perturbed. Images of her father's self-destructive lifestyle after the divorce, which she usually tried not to remember, now came flooding back to her, making her stomach clench up even further. She definitely had some of him in her. She couldn't help but feel that she resembled him more by the year. When he'd been younger, his well-defined nose, placid gaze, and almost unhealthily slender frame had captured the hearts of many of his female students. Yet there was no trace of that person to be found in the figure he'd cut before his death, bloated from all the alcohol, his stomach jutting out as though it might burst open at any moment. An unearthly protuberance that seemed somehow wilful, as if he were housing a living creature inside.

Rika had been focused purely on how she could offer Kajii her fidelity, but maybe that approach was misguided. If she simply remained in her thrall, then she was no different from the victims, and Kajii would only take advantage. Rika had no intention of ending up as one of her worshippers. She wanted to build a real human relationship with her. The question was how to go about it.

'This Manako Kajii feature from three years ago. Was it your team who did it?'

Rubbing her glue-sticky fingers together, Rika addressed Kitamura who was sitting two desks away across the aisle. She held up the issue in question, pointing to the article.

'Yep. I did the interviews with the victim's relatives.'

Kitamura came over to her desk and looked at Rika's scrapbook over her shoulder.

'With Yamamura's sister? She must have agreed to the interview pretty readily, then? I know you're not one to push.'

'True, although she wasn't at all cooperative at first. Yamamura's mother fell ill after the press descended, and was taken to a hospital in the city, and the sister took time off work to care for her. She agreed to answer my questions in the hospital waiting room, on the proviso that I didn't come back – I was disturbing the other patients. Her mother died soon after. The whole thing left a bad taste in my mouth, which is why I still remember it.'

Kitamura's expressionless tone as he narrated this made Rika shudder.

'When I spoke to her she was obviously exhausted, but she seemed like she was quite well sorted as a person. I think she might have been head of department at an architecture firm? I don't know if she's still there now.'

'Do you have her contact details? I'd like to meet her.'

Rika couldn't help sensing that this woman had formed an accurate understanding of Kajii, simply through her brother's actions. Of all the people embroiled in the story, it seemed Yamamura's sister had a perspective that most closely resembled her own.

'You're not planning to start covering this case, are you? After all this time?'

'I sure am. The retrial kicks off in May and the world will catch Kajimana fever again.'

'Don't do it. It might be different if you were with a women's magazine, but with a publication like ours, that kind of coverage was barely warranted last year, let alone now. You'll just be wasting your time.'

'Why do you say that? That feature we did recently on "professional second wives" did really well.'

The article had reported on the various techniques employed by women who married elderly affluent men with the intention of inheriting their fortunes, and had caused a stir. The humdrum approaches the wives had used to hasten their husbands' death, such as over-seasoning their meals and getting them accustomed to greasy food, had made her think of Kajii's case. For someone that gifted at cooking, doing away with one's spouse would be a piece of cake.

'That's different, though. It's fun for people to gossip about because it's something that only happens to rich men, and therefore doesn't concern them. The Kajii case is different. Yes, people took an interest in it at the beginning, but our readers find it unpleasant and unsettling. Everyone's scared that it could happen to them – being lured towards catastrophe by a woman. We should leave the victims alone, not flagellate them any further.'

Kitamura was getting riled up, his excitement the polar opposite to the indifferent way he spoke about Yamamura's sister.

'But don't you think that finding out more about Kajii's methods could teach men how to protect themselves? We might be able to lure in some new female readers, too. Wait, are you reacting like this because you've had a similar kind of experience?'

She was only teasing, but Kitamura turned away with a distasteful expression, saying, 'You're acting weird recently.'

After a little while he came back to her, holding out a tube of hand cream.

'Thanks,' she mumbled, taken aback. Kajii might have been a liar, Rika thought, but she found it hard to imagine her ever feeling strongly enough about another person to kill them.

As soon as the door to the visiting room opened, and she saw Kajii's lips twisted into an expression of sulky displeasure, Rika smiled to herself. Her plan had worked. Leaving a good gap between her visits had been wise. During the ten-day hiatus, she had not been entirely inactive, either: she'd sent Kajii several volumes of the latest Joël Robuchon recipe books. She now surmised that its pictures of butter-rich recipes had not only diverted Kajii, but stoked a fierce longing in her.

'It's been a while. Have you missed me?' Rika asked.

Kajii widened her eyes as if in surprise, then immediately sucked in her chin, deepening the creases in her flesh. If she always acted subserviently then she was going to be seen as a pushover, Rika had realised.

When she'd settled herself on the chair on the opposite side of the acrylic screen, Rika said, 'I was wondering how you'd feel about telling me a bit about your life, from your girlhood until now? Or perhaps I can start by telling you how I conceive of your case. The men who you met on the internet imagined you to be unworldly and naive, and treated you like a maid. As they were inducted into your values and lifestyle, though, their lives started to fall out of sync. They got ill and lost sight of themselves, and died in unfortunate, but preventable, ways. In court, it was said that you signed up to a members-only site for serial killers which you were accessing several times daily, were researching ways to murder someone in a way that would look like suicide, and had bought various books about poisonous substances – but all of that is circumstantial evidence. Even if you had plotted to kill those men, I can't see why doing so would benefit you. You understood that, if they did die, you'd be the first to be suspected.

'Your first victim, Mr Motomatsu, was so worried about you cheating on him that it exacerbated his insomnia. In his confused state, it would hardly be difficult for him to accidentally overdose on the sleeping pills he'd got hold of without a doctor's prescription.

'Next we have Mr Niimi. His blood pressure was high to begin with, and yet he put on a show of taking you out on dates and eating fancy meals with you, sending his cholesterol levels rocketing. According to his doctor, he'd already suffered multiple heart attacks. It's highly likely his death in the bath was purely accidental.

'As for Mr Yamamura, his death could quite feasibly have been suicide. His fall onto the tracks wasn't caught on CCTV because he jumped from a blind spot on the platform, but no footage of any suspicious individuals has been found. His work at the think tank must have been very exacting. He was doing overtime to fund his relationship with you, and his exhaustion levels were peaking. Going by the testimony of his family, his love affair with you was his first ever romantic liaison. He was physically and mentally satisfied after eating your beef stew – sorry, your boeuf bourguignon, and yet if he'd been made to think that the engagement might not go ahead or sensed the presence of other men in your life … Maybe he hadn't explicitly intended to commit suicide, but just grown unsteady on his feet on his way to work.

'If you can be accused of anything, then it's extorting money from men, pledging to marry them while simultaneously leaving them feeling insecure of your affection, and ignoring the signs of their worsening health. Since I swapped margarine for butter, at your suggestion, and began eating at the restaurants you recommended, I've gained six kilos, and had stomach problems that drove me to the doctor's office last week. But I've also been unable to return to my former way of eating, and my outlook has changed significantly. Would it be too much to say that you've killed off my past self?'

Even confronted by the word 'killed', Kajii's mouth remained twisted in a lopsided sneer. She seemed aware that speaking would only be to her detriment. Rika waited patiently. Eventually, with a palpable sense of regret at being the first to break, Kajii slowly opened her mouth.

'If I've told you once I've told you a hundred times. I shan't give you anything. Besides, you're not my only supporter.'

'I'm aware of that. You do realise, though, that if we could change public opinion, you might be able to overturn the verdict in your retrial?'

Rika saw Kajii's eyes flicker.

'Besides, you can make this connection work for you in other ways. I've given up on the idea of forming a relationship with you. What I'm saying is: why don't you use me?'

Rika placed particular emphasis on the word 'use'.

'I'll eat things, feel things, see things in your place. I'll engage with the world as a part of you. As long as I keep coming, you can remain free, at least in spirit.'

Rika pictured Kajii swanning around Tokyo. The city, the very act of consumption, suited her. She didn't belong in a small, dark cell. A pause, and Rika felt the air between them waver.

'There is something I'm desperate to eat right now.'

Kajii flicked her eyes up seductively.

Rika almost blurted out 'Finally' but she clamped her lips together and pulled out a pad, ready to take notes.

'There's a particular ramen restaurant on Yasukuni-dōri in Shinjuku. I would like you to eat their butter ramen and provide me with an accurate description of its taste. In your own words, as always.'

Rika had heard of the place – it was one of the few ramen restaurants from the northern Tōhoku region of Japan that had opened up branches across the country. The mission appeared suspiciously simple.

'Eaten in normal circumstances, their ramen isn't particularly outstanding. In order to make it delicious, a specific condition must be fulfilled.' Kajii paused, taking Rika in with her black-grape eyes.

'You have to consume it immediately after having sex. At three or four in the morning. The colder the weather the better. This is the perfect season.'

Kajii's request was so ridiculous that Rika found herself smiling. There was something ephemeral about Kajii's look today – an ice-blue knitted jumper – that formed a perfect mismatch with the words that had come out of her mouth.

'I'm recalling one February, three years ago, when I stayed with Mr Niimi in the Shinjuku Park Hyatt. The steaks we were served in the New York Grill were exceptional. That hotel has a sensational view of the city at night.'

Rika called to mind the images Kajii had uploaded onto her blog from that day: a great hunk of meat, and a night sky so crowded with stars that it was hard to believe the photo had been taken in Shinjuku. How extraordinary, Rika thought to herself, to manage a bowl of ramen just hours after consuming something of that volume.

'I woke up in the early hours, my stomach rumbling. I longed to eat something warm, with its own distinctive flavour, but there was nothing on the room service menu that spoke to me. I pulled on my coat, leaving Mr Niimi asleep in the bed, and jumped into a cab outside the hotel. It was exactly this time of the year, when the weather is at its coldest. We drove for a while without a destination in mind, and just as the taxi meter was about to creep above the starting fare, my eyes fell on that place on Yasukuni-dōri.'

'But why ramen?'

'After sex, you're left emptied out. I'm seized by the urge to fill up that starved self with something hot, rich and juicy. I told you, didn't I? Eating what you want when you want it makes your senses come alive.'

Rika couldn't relate to the sensation Kajii described. Was that in part because sex felt like a distant reality to her? She couldn't actually remember the last time she'd had it. For the first time, her gaze met that of the prison officer, who stood there erasing his presence as if he were a shadow. She could see he was making an effort not to let his feelings seep into his facial expression, but the whites of his eyes gleamed with vulgar curiosity. This man is currently picturing me naked, she thought, and felt herself growing hot all over.

'I purchased my ticket at the vending machine and then sat down at the counter. The other customers – all men, drivers and postmen and so on – stared at me. I ordered salty ramen topped with butter. For the noodles, I selected the firmest kind, the harigane.'

'I thought you only frequented classier establishments.'

Rika hadn't intended this as a compliment, but she could see that it pleased Kajii.

'I don't believe good taste has anything to do with price. When you date all kinds of men, you start to understand a variety of different tastes. If you can tell me with accuracy how the salt butter ramen tastes, I'll think about granting you an exclusive interview.'

Pronouncing this with self-satisfaction, Kajii puckered her pink lips and lifted her shoulders.

'I don't believe that the taste of something can change so dramatically depending on what you've done before eating it.'

'Ha! You blather on and on about women's rights, but in actual fact you're too proud to ask a man for sex.'

At Kajii's mocking tone, Rika sensed the back of her neck flush. The room felt stifling. She wanted to be out of there as quickly as possible. She wanted to breathe fresh air. If she stayed any longer she'd be sucked into Kajii's madness, lose her powers of judgement.

'When you place your order, you mustn't forget to say "plenty of butter".'

When Rika eventually nodded, it wasn't out of submission to Kajii. Rather, she decided she'd really quite like to taste ramen with oodles of butter straight after sex.

'You're left feeling "emptied out"? Isn't that a very male way of looking at it?' Reiko's eyebrows lowered, taking on the outline of a dove in flight. Seemingly embarrassed by her own words, her cheeks reddened. Lately, lunching opposite one another in Rika's staff canteen had become a habit. Their exciting plans to explore different Kagurazaka restaurants had come to nothing, because Reiko's visits to the maternity clinic were all dependent on her ovulation, and difficult to predict.

'I get sleepy right after, so I've never experienced that. In any case, surely that's not the sort of thing that you go around telling people.'

The area around Reiko's eyes grew dark and her tone combative, so Rika apologised immediately for bringing up the topic. Reiko shrugged and pursed her lips.

'Reiko! Reikooooooo!' Rika called in a silly voice, but got no reply. Rika thought for a while, then spoke.

'Okay, I bet this will make you talk. You know how when I came to your house at Christmas, Ryōsuke was saying that you stunned one of his colleagues with a whole lecture on how to make the shūmai dumplings he'd complimented you on? Will you tell me how to make those shūmai?'

'You've no interest in cooking, though!'

'Do you remember that my letter to Manako Kajii only worked because I took your advice? I know you worry that I've grown too close to her, but I want you to remember that this is all thanks to you. It was you who told me that when dealing with a real foodie, the first thing to do is ask them for a recipe.'

'Are you implying that I'm to blame for this entire situation?' Reiko said poutily, her mood apparently worsening. The topic of Kajii was on its way to becoming a taboo between them. Rika felt that, at least between her and Reiko, she didn't want there to be subjects that heralded disaster.

'No! I'm grateful to you. What I'm trying to say is that following this story is, of course, important for my own professional life, but it's also – as grandiose as this sounds – a way for me to repay the good that my friendship with you has done me.'

Reiko looked up at her uncomprehendingly. Her jaw looked more sharply pointed than the last time Rika had seen her. The wrists sticking out of her jumper looked as though they might snap in two at any moment.

'We'd both been feeling stifled by life before we met, hadn't we? We became friends because we felt the same.'

Reiko fell into silence. Rika had no doubt they were both picturing the same thing: Reiko as she'd used to be. Back in university, she'd been so outraged with the male teacher for the misogynistic things he said that she'd got into an argument with him in the middle of a seminar. She'd been reproved by a classmate for rejecting a man who wouldn't leave her alone on a cafe terrace, which had only made her angrier. At her first job out of university, she'd been shocked when a married colleague higher up in the company whom she'd respected had come on to her. She'd complained bitterly when a client rejected an idea of hers on the grounds that people didn't watch films with female protagonists unless they had a romantic plotline.

'I'm still the same today,' Rika said. 'All of this stuff stops me in my tracks, even now. I can't help but feel that the sexism we face on a daily basis is underpinning this whole case. That's what I want to pursue. If possible, I want to write about it in my own words.'

'The me from the past was so ...' With this, Reiko dropped her gaze into her plastic cup. The fluorescent ceiling lights were reflected in the surface of the weak green tea from the dispenser.

'I'm different to you, Rika. I used to get angry about those same things, but I ran away.'

Rika had suspected that Reiko had been feeling this way, but hearing her voice so thin and wavering now made her panic. She felt her solar plexus constrict. Whenever she saw Reiko sad, she was taken by the sense that she had to do something to help, right this instant. *It's everything about this world that's wrong*, she wanted to shout at the top of her voice, *you're the one who's in the right.*

'You've not run away. You're no different from how you always were. You quit your job so as to figure out a way to do what's right for you.'

Reiko looked at Rika. Her light brown eyes sparkled and her long eyelashes formed bouncing canopies over them, so voluminous they looked like they should be making a noise.

'Ryōsuke won't come with me to the clinic. He doesn't want to do the ... the sample stuff. We've made two appointments, and he's missed both. And of course, me going alone won't lead anywhere.'

'I'm surprised to hear that. I didn't have him down for that kind of person.' Rika couldn't think of what else to say. She'd always thought they were united in their desire for a child.

'I thought that he was different too, but it turns out that he's worried about saving face, just like all the other men. He keeps saying that things haven't come to that yet, that we should see how it goes, leave it up to nature a bit longer. He's convinced that if they discover some problem on his side, it'll take something fundamental away from him. Of late I've been feeling like I'm trying to make a baby on my own.'

Rika found herself wondering if there wasn't some kind of justification for Ryōsuke's actions – if he wasn't just exhausted from work, if Reiko wasn't misunderstanding in some way – and felt a flash of disappointment in herself. She didn't want to start disliking him, but she also knew that it was society itself, and the provisions it made for men like Ryōsuke, which was responsible for causing Reiko so much pain.

'Isn't there a fairy tale like that?' Rika said. 'A woman who's desperate for a child sets off on a long adventure all alone. By a lake in a forest, she finds the arms and legs and various other parts of a child, which she assembles to create a real child. She and the child live happily ever after. The father never makes an appearance, and everyone's content.'

Rika could picture it – Reiko in a big hood, roaming the forest gathering up tiny arms and legs, carefully assembling them into a whole. The saddest part was how perfectly the scene seemed to suit her.

'Pork loin,' Reiko said now, tonelessly. Not having the faintest idea what she was talking about, Rika awaited her next words.

'My shūmai recipe uses tenderised loin meat, as well as the usual pork mince. You knead the meat with plenty of finely chopped onions, load the mixture into the dumpling wrappers and steam them once, then freeze them. The freezing breaks down the cells of the onion, so that when you steam them again, the filling is smooth, juicy and slightly sweet.'

'Will you make them for me next time?' Rika said pleadingly.

'Honestly!' Reiko replied, but her mouth relaxed in a way that made Rika feel relieved.

'You're right, it's like you said. For someone who likes good food, asking for a recipe works like a magic spell …'

Reiko rolled her eyes, then asked, 'Does it never occur to you that you should try out cooking school?'

Seeing Reiko back to her usual forceful self, Rika felt the tension in her stomach loosen.

'Me? I can barely peel an apple.'

'That's exactly why I'm suggesting it. There's a limit to how far you can keep up with conversations with Manako Kajii if all you're doing is going around eating fancy meals. You're smart, and are getting used to good food, so you should be quick on the uptake. Pay for classes with a professional and you'll improve in no time. If you go, I want to go too.'

If she was going to attend cooking school, Rika thought, there was only one place in this whole world she was interested in signing up to.

Since waking that morning she'd had the nagging thought that she needed to go out and buy some new underwear, the kind that some-one else was likely to find sexy. She hadn't managed to find the time, though, and now it was evening. She wanted to face the mission ahead as a perfect version of herself, with no cracks showing.

Staying at the Park Hyatt had proved impossible – quite aside from budgetary considerations, it turned out to be fully booked in advance of Valentine's Day anyway. Now Rika stood on the twenty-fourth floor of the Century Southern Tower Hotel, looking down at Shinjuku Gyoen Park, a patch of complete darkness amid the sea of neon lights.

She was still waiting for a reply from Makoto, but she sent him another message to let him know the room number. If he couldn't make it, she told herself, she'd have a long sleep, then go into work the following morning. She was so nervous about his reply that she couldn't look at her phone. She'd turned down his most recent offer to spend the night together, but now that she'd been set a mission by Kajii, she was the one issuing the invite – was her behaviour too selfish?

And more to the point, why was it that she felt this guilty and embarrassed about asking her boyfriend to have sex with her? Rika sank down onto the double bed, without peeling back the covers. She caught sight of a coffee percolator, the same type that they had in the kitchen at work. What would she do if he said no? What if he thought she was sexually dissatisfied? The thoughts went round and round in her head. She felt as though there was a hidden camera in the room, and on the other side a crowd of people roaring with laughter. She covered her face with a pillow.

It was past 1 a.m. when she heard a knock on the door. Brought back from her peaceful doze to the smell of green-tea-scented air freshener, she sat up and got off the bed.

'Sorry I'm so late.'

'That's okay. It's me who should be apologising for the last-minute invitation.'

Rika could see from Makoto's body language that he was hanging back. He looked at her wordlessly from where he stood by the door, then finally trudged into the room. As always, he turned his back to her, took off his suit, and hung it on the hanger.

'Man, I'm tired,' he said, settling down heavily on the bed.

Rika sat next to him and reached out a hand towards him.

'Sorry to ask, when you're so busy.'

His hair was so soft that it offered no resistance to her touch at all, and she liked the feel of it wrapping itself around her fingers. His round eyes, the same colour as his hair, were bloodshot, and he blinked restlessly.

'Even if Nishihashi wins, I might not be working with him by the time he claims the award.'

The established author whose book Makoto was editing had been nominated for a prestigious award, and the winner would be announced in the spring.

'Will you be switching jobs at the end of the fiscal year? They move people around so much in books. Did you hear something to that effect?'

'Look, honestly, there's not even any point talking about it. When the order comes you just have to obey them. It happens to everyone, not just me.'

Though he sounded resigned to his fate, Makoto's eyelid was twitching.

'You don't have to be pragmatic for my sake. I don't mind you moaning. It'd be sad if you got taken away from him now. You've been involved with that book since the very start.'

'It's fine, it's fine. It's a waste to talk shop when it's just the two of us.'

Makoto's intonation was forceful, and Rika fell silent. Once again, she felt she'd brushed up against the obstinate part of him. Did he believe that strength lay in not complaining, not showing weakness? In the past, he'd spoken more about the less admirable sides of himself, without hiding them. That was why Rika had felt like she could share anything with him. At some point, they'd started carrying the tension they felt at work into their relationship. Was that really just a result of the lack of time they spent together?

Rika's father had been the same.

She'd liked the father who'd read her picture books, who'd secretly made her instant yakisoba, which her mother forbade her to eat, in a frying pan, who ostensibly had such highbrow tastes but at New Year would always watch a Tora-san film and cry. When his inflexible character had got him in trouble, and he'd veered off the path that led to prestige and glory at his university, he'd begun to change. He stopped looking Rika in the eye when he spoke to her. As their family fell into financial difficulties, he grew increasingly taciturn, going out drinking and returning home in the early hours. The alcohol meant he was more aggressive with her mother. Yet neither Rika nor her mother expected him to be a perfect breadwinner: Rika wouldn't have minded not going to a private girls' school, and her mother was more than willing to work. All that they'd wanted was a father who'd engage with his family.

'I'm begging you, talk to me. That's all I'm asking you.'

Hearing her mother's tear-choked voice from behind the sliding door, Rika would snuggle down deeper in her futon. Still she heard nothing from her father. As though he believed that if he said so much as a word, his entire body might split open.

Weren't Kajii's men bound by this same need to be manly? Forced to keep up with her extraordinary stamina, luxurious tastes and desire for high-calorie meals, their whole bodies had screamed out in protest, and still they'd been incapable of saying that they were tired, that they needed a rest. Wasn't that less about their fear of losing her and more because they didn't want to lose *to* her? The media coverage had portrayed the victims as shy men with poor communication skills, but they hadn't been totally isolated. Yamamura's sister and his mother, Niimi's former colleagues and his eldest son's wife, and Motomatsu's care worker and the wives in the neighbourhood – all those people had been worried about them. According to the articles, all the concerned parties had been women. If the victims had listened to just one of them …

'My back hurts. I think my eyes are tired as well.'

Saying that, Makoto threw himself down onto the bed and, groaning, rolled over onto his front. Rika noticed, for the first time in a long time, the surprising pertness of his bottom, and patted it.

'I'll give you a massage.'

'No, that's okay. You must be tired too.'

Before, Rika had always thought his hesitancy came out of consideration, but was his reluctance to accept from her not just the meal she'd casually rustled up but even a massage in fact a species of rejection? With all those small rejections in the past, she had become incapable of showing him vulnerability.

Now she straddled his body intrepidly, her thighs pressed against his lower back, and moved her hands up inside his vest. He yelped – her hands were too cold. Rika rubbed them together before once again returning to massage his lower back. His skin was smooth and moist, and stuck to her hands. Touching him like this brought memories from the last time they were physically intimate, over three months ago now, seeping back to her. She felt Kajii's instructions begin to grow fuzzy. Maybe she didn't really need to have sex. If she told Kajii honestly that she'd been unable to carry out her mission, it might gratify Kajii's self-esteem.

At first, Makoto had moved his body from side to side ticklishly, but his movements soon stilled. As Rika's hands began to warm up, she could tell that Makoto's lower back was terribly stiff, and his body was chilled all over.

As she went on massaging, the blood began to circulate through his skin and she could feel a lively pulse beneath her fingers. With his warmth underneath her, her groin began to grow hot and moist.

Suddenly Makoto sat up, catching Rika off balance so she toppled to the side. She was still giggling when he grabbed her arm. At the feel of his unexpected grip, everything else seemed to fade into the background. Makoto threw off his vest. His naked chest swelled out awkwardly like that of a pubescent girl. There was hair growing around his nipples. When she touched the skin there, her fingers slid across with surprising smoothness. His body had grown very hot.

Rika raised her bottom so she could ease off her pants and tights at the same time. She heard his bag opening, papers rustling as he pushed them aside, and then the snap of the condom. At the touch of his fingers on her pelvis, her nipples pointed stiffly up at the ceiling.

She had been in her head too much, trying too hard to put things into words. She could tell that sensations that had gone unfelt for so long were now mobilising en masse within her. The heat of Makoto's body felt good. Her legs were prised tenderly open. She felt all her joints tingling softly. A sweet smell, which didn't seem like her own, filled the room. She wasn't fully wet yet, and at first her insides stung a little, but she began acclimatising with a hungry speed. Feeling a drop of tepid water on her forehead, she looked up to see a pair of intent, bloodshot eyes above her. The sweat continued to drip from Makoto's face, splashing down on her body. The feeling of being with him spread right out to the tips of her toes. Rika understood in the deepest part of her that this, or else something that was an extension of this, was what had been lacking. She didn't know what was going to happen with her and Makoto from now on, whether or not this relationship was what she really needed. She guessed he felt the same. Yet right now, half of Rika felt satisfied. The rain of Makoto's sweat fell on her like a blessing. The pristine ceiling above seemed to get higher and higher.

Finally Makoto rolled off her, panting. She felt the heat slipping away. She waited for her breathing to return to normal, for her vision to grow light, and then she lifted her head and surveyed the room from within this brand-new feeling. Their sweat had left semi-transparent patches on the sheets. She didn't feel like taking a shower at all. She could hear Makoto's breathing gradually getting quieter.

'You can't talk,' she said, reaching out an arm and slapping his rounded stomach. Just then she didn't feel embarrassed about the weight she'd put on. Rika kept on fooling around, and finally, as if relenting, Makoto smiled.

'Your body's so sexy like that.' The words he whispered in her ear felt so ticklish to hear that Rika flapped her feet. His dry lips snagged on her skin. She heard a noise like the coo of a small bird coming from inside her throat. Clinging to his neck, she rested her forehead on his curved shoulder. All the childishness she'd been desperately trying to keep inside was now coming out, and the feeling was unbelievably comforting.

Why, when her desire was the most natural thing, was she not brave enough to look it in the eye?

'I'm sorry for abandoning you. I know I don't take you anywhere … I'm really sorry,' Makoto mumbled, as if sleep-talking. He looked up at the ceiling and then closed his eyes. Rika gazed at his nostrils, glistening with drops of sweat. He seemed to be humming something. Maybe it was a song by that idol group. His belly rose and fell.

One thing all of the Scream songs she'd listened to on YouTube had in common was their fixation on effort and perseverance. *Grit your teeth, don't rely on others, the answer is right in front of you* – in the mouths of those cute young girls, these phrases seemed not gallant but stifling. The idols Rika knew from the nineties had all sung about love and sweets and lip balm, and seemed to be having a whale of a time.

'I don't need us to go anywhere. We're both so busy that I'd rather spend the time we do have together relaxing. I'm happy to just loll around like this.'

Rika realised that the more she said, the more it sounded like she was having a go at him for not being attentive enough, and so she stopped. It was the tarako pasta all over again: the more she emphasised that she'd not put any effort into it, the further he'd shrunk back.

'I've got to get up early tomorrow – or today, even. There's stuff I didn't manage to do yesterday, and we go to print the day after tomorrow. You should take it easy and sleep in.' Once again Makoto's words were mumbled as if he were sleep-talking. Rika could tell he was slipping into sleep.

'When we do things like this, do you feel like you're slacking off?' she asked.

Rika wanted them to lie together cuddling, to fall asleep savouring each other's body heat. She linked her fingers with his, and slid her leg between his thighs.

'Don't you think that's a disease of the contemporary age? It feels like these days our value is determined by how much effort we make from day to day. That matters even more than our results. After a while, the concept of effort starts to become mixed up with things feeling difficult, and then you reach the point where the person seen as the most admirable is the one suffering the most. I think that's the reason people are so vicious towards Manako Kajii. She refuses to live that life, refuses to suffer.'

Hearing snoring, Rika broke off her monologue. Makoto's Adam's apple was moving, his stomach heaving up and down. Inside, she berated herself for broaching the subject of work again. She was hardly in a position to reproach him.

Her inclination to sleep snugly next to Makoto was intensely strong. She had faith that if she could just keep on living her life somewhere as comfortable as this, satisfied with the small world she inhabited, then nothing bad would happen to her. If they spent more time together, Makoto might gradually open up. But she had to keep her promise, however minor a promise it was.

The bedside clock read 2:45.

Rika roused herself and got up from the bed. She put on her underwear, her trousers and a jumper, her shoes, and finally a coat. After deliberating for a moment, she decided to leave her phone behind. Her soft, moistened skin resisted the fabric of her clothes, and her mind was unable to acclimatise to the reality of being dressed, so that as she took her wallet and room key in hand, she still felt herself to be naked. Stricken by a pang of guilt towards Makoto, who was sleeping with his mouth open, she pressed her hands together at the door in a gesture of apology, then walked down the long, deserted corridor and took the lift to the ground floor. She walked past the reception desk, behind which a solitary male employee was sitting. No sooner had the automatic doors opened than she felt the night breeze strike her, as though someone had thrown a sheet of ice with full force in her direction. The uncompromising cold and dark promptly blew away the magic of before.

A starless night sky, close to blue in colour.

Nobody looked at her. She was a tall, mediocre-looking woman. It was relief that she felt, more than sadness. Maybe Makoto did like her after all – the thought made her faintly happy. If you were accepted by just one person, then you didn't need to be someone whose beauty was acknowledged by everyone. The flood of neon signs, oblivious to any demands to harmonise with their surroundings, coursed past her as she moved, and she could smell the odour of garbage blended with the cool air.

That intimate playfulness exchanged by two people in bed – it occurred to Rika now that Manako Kajii's entire identity could be summarised by the way she took such a thing totally seriously, assigned it value, and attempted to integrate it into her daily life.

Her blood had stopped circulating properly, and every inch of her body felt chilled. The back of her nose twinged with the cold, and her toes had grown numb. All these unpleasant sensations came together to form a deluge, and her own self, which had until just now seemed to her like such a smooth, simple thing, became a difficult, unwieldy being.

Seeing the red and gold sign for the chain ramen restaurant, Rika dived inside the shop as if chased, not even stopping to take in its exterior. A rotund middle-aged man sat dozing in front of a half-eaten bowl of noodles. A young man with prominent cheekbones wearing a sweatshirt with the shop's logo on it looked at her with disinterest from behind the counter. Rika pressed the right button on the ticket machine and then sat down close to the door without taking off her coat. Surrounded by the smell of the stock and the warmth of the room, she felt her body relax. Holding out her ticket, she called out, 'Salt butter ramen, please, with harigane noodles. Plenty of butter.'

With the vapour from the soup and the steam rising up from the pan where the noodles were boiling, her taut skin began to loosen. After a while, the sound of noodles being drained echoed round the restaurant. She could barely see into the kitchen for all the steam. Rika had always liked ramen. When she'd first joined the company, she'd been out to eat ramen with Makoto, and with other colleagues too, and when it came to the restaurants in the Kagurazaka area, it was the ramen places she knew the most about. Her favourite kind was simple soy sauce flavour, with nothing fancy added to it. Now, a bowl was placed unceremoniously on the counter in front of her. Its solid weight and heat unthawed her numbed fingertips. She took a pair of disposable chopsticks from the dispenser and snapped them apart. Their woody scent blended with the smell of the soup.

The only garnish for the noodles was sesame and spring onions. The two perfect squares of butter on top were already beginning to lose their shape in the clear broth, their outlines blurring messily. Beneath them floated the crinkled noodles with their potent yellow hue. Dissolved in the soup, the butter formed golden circles on its surface. Rika deliberately passed the noodles through those circles on their way to her mouth. The taste of lye water was a little strong, but they weren't badly cooked, and retained their bite. She sipped the soup. Against the faint chicken base of the stock she could detect the flavour of bonito. The broth was hot but it slipped down easily, lubricating her painfully dry throat. Alone, the cheap butter had an overly milky tang, but in combination with the noodles and the soup, its flavour grew golden and staked its territory, with a kind of violence. A certain depth of flavour began to assert itself, and as the droplets plummeted to the centre of her body, its arc of influence expanded. The back of her nose grew hot, and she reached for the tissue box on the counter. Feeling the moisture flowing, she blew her nose loudly. A film of butter was forming across her insides. The hot broth and the hot noodles were more assertive, more forceful than Makoto's warmth and smell. As she raised them to her mouth alternately, Rika's body regained more and more of its heat and softness. She was already warmer than she had been back in the hotel room.

She noticed the man behind the counter with the cheekbones staring at her. Undeterred, Rika remained focused on her ramen.

An uninterrupted flow of cars made its way up and down Yasukuni-dōri. Rika felt as if Shinjuku, a part of town she knew well, had been transformed into a foreign country.

She slurped her noodles noisily.

Ramen that she'd waltzed out to eat after having sex – the experience wasn't, as she'd been imagining, an extension of the sensuality of the physical contact. No, the taste was one of freedom – the kind of freedom that could only be savoured alone.

Kajii could pursue her desires so wholeheartedly precisely because she wasn't tied to anybody. For the first time, Rika understood what Tokyo meant to a woman like her, who'd abandoned her hometown, and who had no fixed employment or friends. As someone born and brought up in the city, Rika was unable – for better or worse – to escape the sense of customs, family and history attached to it. For Kajii, though, Tokyo would always be a place to see and be seen, a great stage that was perfectly suited to special occasions, a foreign land where she could toss away her shame and tear around just as she wished. Maybe the idea of 'travelling' wasn't just something that she'd borrowed from Holly Golightly. She'd been masquerading as a woman in search of a marriage partner, but the truth was that she had no intention of belonging to anyone.

It came to Rika now that it was the year after Kajii's father had died, back in her hometown, that the men around her had begun meeting their demise. Was there some connection between the two? By continuing to eat as she had been doing, perhaps Rika had finally grasped Kajii's perspective. Or was it more accurate to say her taste?

Cradling the bowl in her two hands, she drank down the last of the buttery broth. When she held it up, the bowl shrouded the entirety of her vision. A starry sky formed of grease glinted at her out of the darkness. Sensing eyes on her, she raised her face from the bottom of the bowl and looked towards Yasukuni-dōri. She couldn't shake the sense that Kajii was standing there in the night, watching her.

CHAPTER SIX

'Rika!'

Hearing her name called, Rika lifted her eyes to see an almost-white bob catching the sunlight illuminating the dark corner of the soba restaurant.

'I haven't seen you in ages! Do you mind if I sit with you?'

It was hard to work out where the woman's hair ended and her silky alabaster skin began. She was only in her forties, but rather than ageing her, the white gave her an ageless, fairy-like charm.

'Of course, have a seat!'

Rika rested the bowl of wakame soba she'd been sipping on the table with a clunk. Yoriko Mizushima, formerly a well-regarded journalist at the *Shūmei Weekly*, sat down on the cushion lying on top of the low, angular chair. Rika had barely seen Mizushima since she'd transferred to the sales department three years earlier.

She caught a glimpse now of Mizushima's gleaming loafers. As far as business attire went, there was no faulting her crisp look made up of blazer, stylish button-down shirt and chino trousers, but it said 'woman in her forties' less than it did 'dapper young boy'. All of the materials looked like they could be washed at home, and she wore only the lightest coat of make-up. This woman understands what a good amount means for her, Rika thought to herself. At the corners of her eyes, set far apart in her face, she was accumulating wrinkles. Even the downy hair growing out of the large mole on the side of her nose seemed harmless, and somehow cute.

'How odd to bump into you. I wouldn't have thought you had lunch in places like this! Although I guess it's not really lunchtime, is it? I was busy going around bookshops and forgot to eat!'

Mizushima and Rika were the only customers in the establishment. The smell of dashi filling the restaurant and Mizushima's matter-of-fact way of speaking, which took Rika straight back to when they worked together, made her heart feel lighter. Mizushima had once occupied a unique position at the magazine, both among colleagues and when out on assignments. Even when interviewing policemen and bureaucrats, she hadn't pretended to be someone she wasn't.

'The food in the canteen is great, but I get claustrophobic if I spend too long in that building,' Rika replied. 'It's important to get out sometimes, and not only for work engagements. Do you come here often?'

The soba restaurant, in a back alley just two minutes' walk from the office, was not especially well frequented, no doubt due to its obscure location and its understated exterior that made it hard to distinguish from a regular house. The elderly couple who ran the place relied mostly on takeaway orders for their business, taking turns to run in and out, and the service was rough and ready. Yet their freshly made soba was fragrant, and drinking the water it had been cooked in, which was served after the meal, would leave your legs feeling toasty and warm throughout the afternoon, in a way Rika felt sure was good for her. Now that Reiko was no longer inviting her to lunch, she had no need to stick to the staff canteen.

Reiko, it seemed, was taking a break from the fertility clinic. Rika hadn't heard as much from her directly, but her texts, which had previously been arriving weekly, had dried up entirely. It was obvious that Ryōsuke's reluctance was having an effect on her. Given the delicate nature of the topic, Rika felt she had no choice but to wait until Reiko confided in her to speak of it. Rika didn't know whether that meant she was being considerate or not.

'Today was bring-your-own-bento day at the nursery, but I didn't have the time to make one for my husband and me.'

'Do you make bento boxes for your child?'

'Only on the odd occasion – she's normally given lunch at the nursery. Besides, my daughter's four now, so even that's only until she gets into primary school. I never bust a gut making the fancy ones with anime characters and so on. I just do rice, umeboshi, rolled omelette, some meat or something left over from dinner the previous night, then stuff in something green, and that's the lot.'

'That's still so impressive!'

Rika still couldn't summon the interest for getting married and having kids. She knew it was expected of her, but sometimes she felt that the day when she'd truly want to do it would never come. Mizushima ordered a rice bowl topped with eggs, meat and onions, then turned back to Rika.

'Not at all. I've got much more time these days than when I was working for the magazine. I can go home on time most days. And the biggest thing is the sense of safety that comes from having no unexpected demands made of you. What about you? Do you have anything exciting on the go?'

In most firms, the sales team was perceived as the face of the company, but at the Shūmeisha offices there was a tendency to see it as behind-the-scenes work. Employees might move into the department after giving birth or if they had long-term health issues. When Rika had heard that Mizushima was going to move to sales because she couldn't juggle childcare with her magazine work, she'd felt a pall descend over her own vision of the future. The sweet-salty smell of Mizushima's soba wafted over from behind, where it was being prepared. Rika lowered her voice to answer.

'I've just come from the house of the victim in the Shinonome case. Though she didn't agree to an interview.'

The mother of a middle-school boy who'd lost his life in a brutal attack at the hands of a friend was being publicly excoriated. A single mother working two jobs, she'd not been at home with her son as much as she'd have liked, and had missed the warning signs. The son had first met the boy, who would befriend and then kill him, while walking to a convenience store to buy dinner. Of all the takes people had on the case, the one that stood out was that this was a tragedy brought on by the failings of contemporary culture that prioritised ready meals over home-made food. Even the *Shūmei Weekly*, though it hadn't overtly criticised the mother, had featured some opinions on the subject of food that were directed at working mothers in general. Rika, responsible for covering the story, had vehemently opposed the article right up to its publication, but her opinion hadn't been heeded. The issue was just out, which had only exacerbated her feelings of reluctance about going to see the mother today. She still couldn't get the sound of that weak, wavering voice on the other side of the intercom out of her head as it spoke: 'I'm terribly sorry to have inconvenienced everyone like this. It was all my fault.'

Mizushima lowered her thick eyebrows and her mole twitched.

'Oh, *that* case … I can't help but think of my own situation, of course. It's ridiculous to blame it on the mother – it's just sheer bad luck that it happened to that household. I'm sure there'll be plenty of times in the future when I'm too busy to make dinner and tell my kids to go and get something for themselves.'

If only Mizushima were on the editorial desk, Rika thought to herself. It was so hard to make her opinion heard – she felt like an insignificant bit player, gathering up the components the desk needed to write the pieces their way, looking on at a current whose momentum exceeded her own.

'You're being so patient, Rika. Everyone of my generation is so impressed. If you become the first woman to make the desk, I won't even be envious! I'll simply feel pure delight.'

Mizushima was almost certainly the first woman at the *Shūmei Weekly* to have taken not just maternity leave but childcare leave as well.

'I really tried to make motherhood and a career work. I used everything at my disposal, spent so much of the money I'd saved up when I was single. I employed a babysitter until a space in nursery became free, because I was so determined not to be a burden on the people around me. But it turned out that I wasn't superhuman. That's not a bad thing, I know now, but back then I believed that I had to be.'

She lowered her eyelashes and a shadow fell across the bags under her eyes.

'Nowadays I think that maybe it would have been all right to be a bit of a burden to the people around me. Young people like you are paying the price for people like me gritting my teeth, bearing it all myself and not showing any weakness. I didn't ask for help, and that stopped other people around me from asking for it.'

Mizushima's lunch was brought over, and she energetically broke her chopsticks in two. Fluffy egg enveloped pieces of pork and kamaboko on a bed of rice stained with soy sauce. As she chewed, she looked at Rika.

'You seem different somehow. You used to have the air of a monk in training.'

'It must be because I've put on weight recently, from eating so much. I've swelled right out.'

'Oh, you look far better like this. You used to be so skinny it made me concerned to look at you. You seemed to throw yourself headlong into your work, and didn't take care of yourself at all. When I see people who don't look after themselves, I end up feeling guilty myself.'

There was the sound of the glass door opening. The old woman returned from her delivery and headed silently towards the kitchen. As if he'd been waiting for her cue, the man pointed the remote control at the TV and turned up the volume. The lines from the dubbed Western drama flowed clearly and brightly through the restaurant.

No sooner were they sitting face to face across the acrylic screen than Kajii smiled and said, 'Well, was the salty butter ramen to your liking?'

Rika willed herself not to blush, but she could feel her ears growing hot. She went through her memories of that dawn excursion four days previously, attempting to ignore the prison officer's gaze.

'Is it the cold that makes a bowl of ramen from a regular chain restaurant taste that good?'

'Why are you asking me, when you know the answer better than anyone?'

There was nothing wheedling about her way of speaking today, and what she said landed with Rika with alarming ease. She didn't need Kajii to point out to her that having sex with Makoto just once had made her feelings toward him a lot clearer.

'Men are simply very warm creatures, aren't they? Where I grew up, February was freezing, so you feel ever so grateful for that warmth. I was at high school when I cottoned on to the fact.'

'Your first boyfriend was a salesman who came and went between Tokyo and Niigata, yes? Where did you meet him?'

Rika opened up her memo pad and held her pen poised. Usually Kajii would assume a wary look as soon as Rika began to write, so she'd been trying to keep her note-taking to a minimum, but today Kajii's eyes were roving around as though she were dreaming, and she seemed quite unbothered by what Rika was up to. Seizing her chance, Rika began scribbling.

'He approached me as I was perusing the works of Carl Sagan in my local bookshop. I was very into reading as a young girl. He told me that he liked Sagan too, and he would love it if a girl like me would show him around the town. He tried to persuade me to be his lover immediately, but I brushed him off. I took him bento boxes and sweets that I'd made, and he was so overjoyed that I kept it up. Each time I saw him, he would do his very best to seduce me. On Valentine's Day, I baked him a cake. For the first time, I lied to my parents, and the two of us stayed over at a hotel near Niigata Station. There was a snowstorm that night. That was how things began between us. Then someone at my school who saw us coming out of a love hotel together spread the rumour that he was paying me for my time, as was very much the trend back then, and we were forced to separate. It was only then that I found out he was married. But that's neither here nor there to me. I treasure my memories with him.'

To Rika's surprise, Kajii brushed away a tear from her eye with the back of her little finger. Rika fought away her feeling of discomfort. She had to remember the intensity of the time spent in the hotel room with Makoto, and the chilly reality when she stepped out onto the street. She mustn't forget that feeling of the magic fading away – or else she would end up being sucked into Kajii's view of the world.

'It seems as though you've patched up things with your boyfriend, so why don't you make him something for Valentine's Day?'

'I've never once given him anything for Valentine's, let alone something I've baked myself. He doesn't go for all that stuff. He finds it too heavy.'

'In that case, avoid sickly sweet chocolate, and do something like a quatre quarts. It's a simple recipe, perfect for beginners.'

'Quatre …?'

'It's French for "four quarters". It's a pound cake that uses equal amounts of egg, flour, butter and granulated sugar. 150 grams of each. It's easy to remember, no? No, don't write it down, *memorise* it. It's outstanding with lemon as well. Organic, Japan-grown lemons – grate in the zest. You can add vanilla essence too, if you have some, and glaze the finished product with rum.'

'Cake-making sounds so hard, though. I'm not sure I'm up to it.'

Rika was sure she'd sampled more home-made confectionery than most. Back at her girls' school, she'd received a constant stream of home-made pound cakes and cookies from her admirers. Frequently the cakes were undercooked, or coated the tongue and refused to come off, or were hard and dry as rock. Eating them, she'd felt that she could sense her admirers' saccharine scent, their body temperature. The stuff you could buy at the convenience store tasted far better. When Rika had first got to know Reiko and sampled her home-made apple pie, she had been blown away by how good it was, how sophisticated the flavour. Oblivious to Rika's musings, Kajii went on speaking.

'Oven-baking is a perfect pursuit for busy people like you. It'll give you an understanding of what it means to put your time to good use. If possible, you should try to serve him the cake when it's fresh out of the oven. Pound cake is at its most flavoursome the day after it's been baked, when it's had a chance to take on its full richness, but I personally love a thick slice of it when it's still warm. You say that he has an aversion to home baking, but I'm certain that's because he's never sampled a freshly baked cake.'

Rika knew that after Makoto's father had died, his mother had worked in sales for a cosmetics company to earn money for the family, and hadn't been at home very much. Like Rika herself, Makoto wouldn't have grown up eating the food his mother had cooked.

'Did you always make cakes on Valentine's Day for the men you were seeing?'

Knowing that Kajii had dated several men at one time, the thought of the effort involved made Rika feel almost faint. The new mission she'd been assigned seemed to her nothing but a hassle. She had no faith she'd be able to make a cake rise, and she couldn't conceive of Makoto being pleased by the gift.

'Absolutely. In the days before Valentine's Day, my apartment would be transformed into a patisserie.'

In her conversational element, Kajii seemed to be genuinely enjoying herself. Feeling as if something sweet had become stuck in her throat, Rika gave a dry cough. She remembered her reason for coming.

'Is it okay to assume that you're agreeing to an exclusive interview?'

'Yes,' Kajii said, nodding, and Rika promptly dropped her pen. She lifted herself from the seat to fetch it, and as she looked down at it rolling across the floor, she felt her vision go double.

'But I haven't said that I'll do it with you,' Kajii said coldly, as Rika sat back down. Rika took a sharp inhale. Cocking her head with an expression of distaste, Kajii was looking baldly at her.

'Sitting here looking at you, I feel my heart drying up like a desert. It's so *exhausting* to watch people who live in such a sacrificial way. It makes me feel as though I'm being accused of something. What are you pulling that face for?'

'So you are actually noticing me, after all?'

'What are you talking about, you idiot!' Kajii spat out dismissively, and Rika could see her fleshy jowls trembling furiously.

That look again, Rika thought – of late, even when she was cruel to Rika, there was a certain curiosity, a desire for affection mixed up in Kajii's expression. Did she really hate women as she said? Was it not that she was trying her best to convince herself of the fact? If so, then why, when she was otherwise so true to her desires, would she try so persistently to push away this wish to be close to another woman? Rika only realised that she was staring intently at Kajii when, for the first time, Kajii turned away from Rika in embarrassment.

'In any case, you should master cake-baking, even if you only learn how to make one kind. It will help you understand the art of wall-building. You don't have any walls in your life, you see. Your work and your private life, your true feelings and your social self – everything is mixed up. It's frankly tiring to watch. Once that roughness about you has disappeared, I'll be happy to tell you everything. For the quatre quarts recipe, consult my blog. The trick is to aerate the butter well, and mix in the flour with quick strokes.'

Kajii nodded as if in satisfaction at something beyond the room in which she sat. She looked like a master chef, tasting her stew and finding its flavour thoroughly intoxicating.

From the next room came the sound of a woman, not too young by the sound of things, singing an off-key pop song. Rika thought she'd heard the melody before. When it came to the bridge she realised it was Scream's latest hit.

In the dim interior of a karaoke box five minutes' walk from Iidabashi Station, Rika and Shinoi sat at right angles around a low table. This was their chosen spot when they needed to meet in proximity to the office, the booths meaning they could remain unseen. The two mics lay on the table, still clothed in their cellophane covers, and the muted TV screen played commercials for the most recent big-hit bands.

'The victim's mother had just moved to Shinonome from Fukui Prefecture, and wouldn't have known about any of the rumours circulating about the boy's family. I guess there was nobody to warn her. She was probably just glad that her son had made a friend and was spending time at his house. A colleague of hers at the hospital said it bothered her that whenever she called nobody picked up, but she had no time to visit and check that everything was okay.'

The assailant's father had once got into a disagreement with a parent of one of his classmates, and as a result his friends stopped coming round to his house. In his loneliness, the boy had been looking for someone to hang out with who didn't know the rumours. All this Shinoi told her freely, guided by her questioning, as he drank his shōchū and iced oolong tea. Rika put her memo pad away in her bag and bowed her head in gratitude.

'Thanks so much. I'll try speaking to people around the assailant's house again.'

'And how are things going with Kajii?'

'I finally got her to agree to doing an exclusive interview, but apparently she's reluctant to do it with me, another woman. She said she'll do it on the condition that I bake a cake,' Rika said with a smile, and raised her pu'er tea, now thoroughly cold, to her lips. Shinoi tapped his cigarette that rested on the edge of the ashtray.

'A cake? Why?'

Rika brought him up to date on the situation, leaving out the part about Makoto, then pulled from her bag a printed blog entry in a clear file, dated October 2013. There was the recipe for quatre quarts, together with a section of Kajii's writing about her love of confectionery, so long as it was 'the real thing' and used lots of butter, and her loathing of the individually wrapped slices of pound cake that were given as gifts or bought in convenience stores.

'I'm in a bit of a bind with it, though. For a start, I don't have an oven at home. Then, you need all kinds of equipment to make cakes, right? I asked my friend who loves cooking if I can borrow her kitchen, but her husband's got the flu and I don't think it's going to be possible. And there's only four days left until Valentine's Day!'

Rika didn't know if what Reiko had written in her text was true, or if she was simply avoiding her. But even if she'd succeeded in baking a cake at Reiko's house, she'd be way down the Den-en-Toshi Line, which made serving it to Makoto fresh from the oven out of the question. She could hire one of the kitchen studios used for photo shoots, but most of them were daytime only, and besides, right before Valentine's Day, they'd be fully booked up.

There was a pause, and then Shinoi said, without changing expression, 'You can come over to my place now, if you want. It's got a built-in oven that's actually quite high-spec. I've got cake-making equipment there, too. There's a supermarket on the ground floor of the building, which I think will still be open. Anything I don't have, you can buy there.'

She glanced at him to check for the signs of any hidden intention in his eye, but a second later she swallowed back her doubts and her words. Looking at her watch, she saw it was already past half ten. She would go to his apartment – it was only one stop away and close to the station – go to the supermarket and bake a cake. Makoto was just about to send a book to print, and would almost certainly still be at work. She couldn't miss this opportunity.

Seeing Rika nod, Shinoi got up and opened the door to the booth. He paid the bill, then went down the stairs by the reception. Rika followed. When she stepped outside, he was already hailing a taxi. She got into the passenger seat, conscious of the people around her. Shinoi gave his address, and the car set off in the direction of Yotsuya. Rika started.

'I thought your apartment was near Suidōbashi?'

'That's just the cheap one-room apartment that I'm renting. My real home is where we're headed now. I don't go there much. It's very close – in Arakichō.'

By 'real home', did he mean the place he'd lived before his divorce? Rika wondered. Did that mean his ex-wife would be there? She felt concerned by the thought that his ex might come waltzing in on the two of them, but this feeling was surpassed by her sense of curiosity and her worries about baking a good quatre quarts.

'I'm fairly sure there's a bowl, a whisk and a spatula there.'

Their eyes met in the rear-view mirror; she was the first to look away. When they turned off the main road, they came to a quiet residential area that felt a million miles from the parade of endless neon outside Iidabashi Station. The taxi descended the hill of Arakichō, which was shaped like a bowl, stopping when it reached the base. The apartment block, clearly designed for families, looked out over a tiny park, furnished with just a sandpit and a swing.

From the ground-floor supermarket open until 1 a.m. spilled a bright white light that gave the swing in the park a long shadow. The supermarket chain was known for its selection of organic vegetables, imported sweets and coffee. In the dairy section, where Rika headed first, was a notice reading *Due to supply shortages, sales of butter are currently limited to one item per customer*, but luckily there were two remaining packets of Yotsuba unsalted butter. She added a roll of aluminium foil, Japanese organic lemons, bags of flour and granulated sugar, and a carton of eggs into her basket, and headed to the cash registers. The cashier loaded her shopping into paper bags. As she and Shinoi walked out through the automatic doors together, Rika was taken by the sensation that she'd slipped into a parallel world. In that world, she'd started living here, close to the office, with an older man from the same industry whose first marriage had collapsed, and some day in the future they would get married and have children – the thought didn't cause her excitement, but it did seem somehow grounded. They climbed a short flight of stairs and passed by the caretaker's office, now empty. Shinoi took out a bunch of keys held together with a key ring featuring the cartoon mascot for his news agency, and used one of them to open the door. While the lift with its old metal doors headed for the fourth floor, only the rustling of her paper shopping bags saved them from total silence.

As he inserted his key in the door to his apartment, Rika found herself holding her breath. Moving into the room first, Shinoi switched on the lights. A silver carpet, its pile thoroughly flattened, led from the lobby down the hall and into the living room that spread out beyond. The dry, chilly air made her sneeze. She took off her shoes and lined them up, before following Shinoi inside, still wearing her coat. She was cold, but she also wanted to avoid exposing the contours of her body.

Judging by the number of doors, it was a three-bedroom apartment. The only items of furniture in the living room were four chairs and a table, a plasma TV and a cabinet for kitchenware, mostly empty. Shinoi turned on the heating. The dark kitchen with its island seemed mostly bereft of objects. There was none of the stuffy smell characteristic of other people's houses. Instead the air had a clean, whiteish quality, not dissimilar to a brand-new office. On the other side of the kitchen counter, Shinoi set out paper towels, sponges and washing-up liquid.

'The bowls and whisk are in the rack under the sink, but they haven't been used in a long time, so it might be best to give them a wash first. The cleaner comes once a month, so the kitchen itself shouldn't be dirty. I did a deep clean of the oven and the sink, so I think they should be okay. Since my wife and daughter left, I only come back three or four times a month, but I pay all the bills – the water and the gas will work. The divorce finally went through the other day, so the time has probably come for me to sell it, or else to get rid of the other place, but I can't seem to decide. I'll just sit here and work, so do whatever you need to.'

Shinoi made for the kitchen table. He took his laptop from his bag and began tapping away at its keys, apparently unfazed by her presence. Hesitantly, Rika moved into the kitchen with Kajii's recipe and the ingredients in hand, and turned on the lights. The bulbs made a buzzing noise, and the surroundings slowly lit up. From over the counter, she glanced at Shinoi's profile. Had his wife stood in this same place and looked at him? The room wasn't that large, and yet he seemed terribly far away. The kitchen was a lonely place, she thought.

She waited until the tap water ran hot, then washed her hands and dried them with a paper towel. The beige four-plate was spotless – not a single smudge or burn mark – making it impossible to get a sense of the family that had once lived here. When Rika opened up the oven, out wafted the smell of baked caramel. She wiped the insides with a paper towel, but all that came off was a little grease. Knowing this was hardly the time to hesitate, she spoke out straight away.

'The recipe says to preheat the oven to 170 degrees. I've never done this before, so would you mind having a look for me?'

Shinoi came over and fiddled with the controls. A blue flame rose up, flickering, inside the pitch-black cavity of the oven. When Rika opened the cupboards beneath the sink as instructed, she found a whisk, knives and a plastic spatula. She couldn't see any pans or chopping boards, though. There were several cake tins, and Rika reached for the oblong pound cake one. She found the burn marks at the edges, dating back to who-knew-when, very reassuring. She pulled out the large, medium and small bowls and a sieve. To be safe, she washed them all with a washing-up sponge, then dried them off with a paper towel. Laying a sheet of paper towel on top of the scales, she measured out 500 grams of flour.

As she was sieving the flour into the bowl, Shinoi said, still looking at his laptop screen: 'You might want to put some baking powder in, just to be sure. That recipe looked pretty authentic. This is your first time making a cake, right?'

Rika stopped moving. The flour falling softly through the metal mesh formed a tiny tornado the width of her fingertip. The remaining clumps rolled forlornly around in the sieve.

'I know from the recipes I've seen online that it's normal to put baking powder in a quatre quarts, but I want to make it according to Manako Kajii's instructions.'

'So earnest! You know she's not watching you right now, don't you?'

No, Rika thought, she's here. Can't you sense her presence? She's looking at us and grinning. When she was attending to the ingredients, Rika could always feel Kajii's gaze. But if she said any of this to Shinoi, he'd think she'd gone mad. She measured out the granulated sugar, then beat three eggs, the equivalent of 500 grams.

'It's you who told me to offer my heart on a plate, remember? I want to be sincere with her.'

'Despite the fact that she's robbed several innocent men of their lives?'

Rika pretended not to hear. She took the butter from its box and opened up its foil wrapper. It was hard and cold. She didn't want to create more washing-up than necessary and she still hadn't located a chopping board, so she sliced it on top of the paper and placed it on the scale. There was a tiny fragment left over on the knife, which she raised to her mouth. The lack of salt meant it coasted across her tongue like a placid midwinter wave, leaving her with an impression of silkiness and concentrated fat.

She transferred the butter, cut up into pieces, to the bowl. Gripping the whisk in one hand, she plunged it into the centre of the butter chunks, but the butter simply broke apart. It seemed to be still too cold, and refused to loosen. Even once it began to grow softer, it would cling to the edges of the tulip-shaped wire, making its way inside, so that there was barely any butter left inside the bowl. Rika felt her forearms growing heavy, as if waterlogged. After darting a succession of glances at Rika wielding the whisk, Shinoi sighed. He stood up as if he'd been waiting to do so all along, and came over to stand behind her. Rika felt her body tense up at their proximity.

'That whisking technique is no good. It said to aerate it, right?'

'I don't really know what that means, though. Aerating butter? Are you quite knowledgeable about baking?'

The oven had started to warm up. The kitchen, so chilly before, was now filled with soft air. Once again, she could smell that toffee-like smell. She wondered what had last been cooked in it. Crème caramel, perhaps?

'It was always my job to do the bits that required physical strength.' Saying that, he took the whisk from Rika. Their fingers brushed. She was surprised to notice that in comparison with his, her own skin – which she thought of as very rough – seemed soft and smooth.

'So your wife and daughter were into making cakes? But why did they …'

… *leave their cake-making stuff behind in your kitchen then?* Rika was on the verge of asking, but stopped herself. There was plenty of baking equipment here, but not much else in the way of general cooking implements. She shouldn't intrude any further. Maybe the two of them had actually died, and Shinoi had been lying to cover up his grief.

Ignoring her half-finished question, Shinoi grasped the bowl with his large hand and gripped the handle of the whisk at a different angle to how Rika had been holding it. Now all the buttercup-yellow fragments filling up the whisk's tulip were propelled outside. Not allowing the whisk to strike the side of the bowl, Shinoi summoned a gentle breeze as he carried on blending the ingredients. Rika took the opportunity to remove her coat, which she no longer needed. Draping it across the back of a chair in the living room, which was beginning to warm up, she turned around to face Shinoi behind the counter. Looking at him from here he seemed far away. She felt the depth of the rift that opened up between the person cooking and the person not. When she re-entered the kitchen, he began issuing her with instructions.

'Add in the sugar in three equal parts.'

She tilted the paper towel, letting a single stream of light rain down on the butter, which was gradually taking on the texture of

cream, losing its yellow tint and becoming mostly white. Feeling that
the slightest word might hurt Shinoi in untold ways, Rika said nothing. Directly in her line of sight, his shoulders moved busily.

'They don't make cakes any more. Either of them.'

A light film of sweat now shone on Shinoi's forehead. When all
the sugar had been added into the bowl, Rika let her hands hang
down by her sides and looked at him.

'When my daughter entered middle school, she began dieting.
Apparently she was being bullied for being big. From my perspective,
it was just a bit of puppy fat, hardly anything to worry about. I
thought it was just kids being kids, and didn't take it very seriously. I
didn't listen properly to what my wife and my daughter said. I was
busy with work, and I guess I was insensitive. Gradually we stopped
being able to talk to each other properly. I didn't really notice
anything was wrong until my daughter developed an eating disorder
and had to take time off school. By the time they left, cake-making
was a topic we all avoided.'

It was hard to know from Shinoi's age when the last time was
they might have been here together as a family. Rika felt that any
words of consolation she might have offered at this point would feel
trite.

How old was his daughter now? Where was she and what was
she doing? Was she happy with how she looked? Had she developed
the strength to brush off the demands of the people around her,
whose blade-like nature Rika herself had experienced only recently?

'It should be okay now, so give it a go.'

Shinoi passed the bowl and the whisk back to Rika but remained
standing beside her, perhaps still concerned about her messing it up.
Now, as she moved the whisk, she let out a little noise. It was so
much lighter. It wasn't simply soft, coming away willingly from the
whisk – the butter was fluffy and white, light as a cloud. This was a
totally new guise for butter to take.

'There's something I've always wanted to ask you. Why do you
pass on your tip-offs to me? Of course I'm grateful for them. I truly

appreciate it. I have a lot of respect for you as a person. But I do sometimes feel anxious about the whole situation, because I'm not in a position to be able to give you anything back. I know this might sound rude, but sometimes I wonder if I'm exploiting my own femininity. If something might be expected of me, at some point, to pay you back. I know that's a terrible thing to say.' Rika did her best not to look at him. Shinoi poured glugs of brightly coloured beaten egg into the bright white buttercream Rika was whipping.

'It'll separate if you stop, so carry on.' It took her a few seconds to figure out that he was talking about the mixture.

'No, that's not what my intentions are. I've not … there's been none of that sort of thing in my life for almost five years now. If I've misled you in some way then I apologise.'

Rika assiduously mixed in the thin dribbles of egg that Shinoi poured into the mixture, trying as best as she could to retain the air that he'd integrated. The yellow and the white came together to form a beautiful hue.

'This is probably a crass way of putting it, but I think I wanted to do something for someone, and experience their gratitude. I guess I was missing that, in my life. I'm just your typical old dude wanting to pat themselves on the back. Of all the weekly magazine journalists I know, you seemed to me the most honest and trustworthy. At the same time, you also struck me as someone who was bad at lying and would therefore find it difficult to form a relationship with sources.'

Confronted by this evidence of her own excessive self-consciousness, Rika felt her stomach boil over, but the feeling soon died down, and the cold tension she'd been carrying melted away too. She knew that from now on, she would find it easier to be around Shinoi. The eggs, butter and sugar combined gently to create a soft mountain. Rika was about to add in the flour with the rubber spatula, but Shinoi stopped her.

'This part is tricky, so you'd better watch me do it first.'

Rika found it funny to see this side of him, but she decided to trust him. When he took the spatula, their fingers brushed together again, but this time she didn't think anything of it.

'It seems like you're good at cooking, and yet you don't. It's a waste.'

Shinoi cut through the mixture with the spatula and went about mixing the dough choppily. The flour and the yellow buttercream took it in turns to hide behind one other, giving the insides of the bowl a chaotic appearance. She suddenly felt concerned about the grey tinge of his skin.

'If it's just for myself, I really can't be bothered to cook good, healthy food. There's not much point in making sure I live to a grand old age, anyway.'

Saying this, he held out the bowl towards her. Inside, the shiny mixture rose up in a nicely rounded little mound. To save the bother of looking for a grater, Rika had used the back of a knife to remove the zest of the lemon, which she now added into the dough. She poured the mixture into the cake tin, and dropped the heavy tin on the counter to get rid of any excess air. Finally, she cut a slit in the top with a knife, put the tin on a baking sheet, and opened the oven to slide it in. A blast of hot air struck her cheeks, and she marvelled at the flames burning in the darkness. She set the timer for fifty minutes, shut the door of the oven and let out a small sigh. Then she went towards the washing-up.

'I think not taking care of yourself properly is a form of violence.'

Shinoi had returned to the table and was gazing at his computer screen as if he were uninvolved in the discussion, but Rika went on.

'Treating yourself badly is a way of directing your anger at someone. I myself ...'

But she couldn't say it. Right now, she couldn't say it. She kept her eyes fixed on the foam oozing out of the washing-up sponge. Could it be true that, quite unconsciously, she'd been hurting people? That by living her life the way she had, she'd been hurting her mother, Mizushima, Reiko and Makoto, just like her father had once done to her? By treating himself badly, he had accused the people around him.

When it came to cleanliness, this apartment in which she now stood and her father's Mitaka place were worlds apart, but in atmosphere they closely resembled one another. Both were former family homes that had become ruins. She didn't hate Shinoi's apartment, but she wouldn't have wanted to be here for long. It wouldn't take much time, she sensed, for her fifteen-year-old self to come flooding back to her.

Now Shinoi spoke in an emotionless tone, different from before, 'You're saying that even a man with not a single person in his life who cares about him has an obligation to take care of himself properly? That's a pretty exacting view.'

Rika dried off the bowls and other cooking implements and returned them to their original positions, then wiped down the counter and left the kitchen. Putting on her coat, she sat down opposite Shinoi. A sweet smell drifted over to her from the oven.

'I would argue that even thinking that way is a form of wordless violence. Refusing to look after yourself because there's nobody around to care about you is a form of violence towards somebody. To my eyes, you're not living a reckless sort of life, but if you truly don't care what becomes of you, then that's really sad. Won't that wind up hurting your daughter eventually, even if she doesn't know about it now? I believe that Kajii's victims could have been happy without a woman, if she hadn't been around. Even if there was nobody to care for them, they could have cared for themselves. Or they could have looked for help. That's not that difficult a thing to do. I think that maybe, as a journalist, that's the thing I most want to say.'

Shinoi dropped his eyes to his computer, saying nothing. Rika wasn't sure if her words were reaching him, and even if they were, she wasn't confident about what she was saying. After a while she rested her head on the table and shut her eyes.

As she was shaken gently awake, she realised the oven timer was going off. The room was filled with the heady smell of the cake.

'Have a look.'

Peering into the open oven, Rika let out a yelp. The copper-coloured dough had risen up over the top of the tin to create a mountain range whose central rift offered a peek of its golden insides. With a towel-wrapped hand, Shinoi pulled out the baking sheet. The sweetly flavoured heat fanned at Rika's fringe.

'It's amazing that it's risen so well with just four ingredients. It's all thanks to your whipping.'

So this was the kind of wall that Kajii had been talking about, Rika thought. They didn't have to be made of hard bricks and cold concrete. They could be made of sweet, soft dough – and still offer protection.

She removed the cake as quickly as she could from the tin, for fear of burning herself. Placing the freshly baked quatre quarts on a piece of aluminium foil, she quickly cut it into ten even slices. Seeing the bright yellow of its inside and the steam rising up from within, her cheeks flushed in pleasure. She wrapped two slices in aluminium foil and held them out to Shinoi.

'I know it's not much, but this is for you. I've got to go and take the rest to somebody while it's still warm. It's all part of the agreement with Kajii.'

'Your boyfriend?'

Rika nodded. Shinoi waved his hand as if to say go. Something about the gesture gave Rika to understand that this man was still a father. She wrapped up the rest of the cake loosely so as to keep in the warm air. The bundle felt soft, like a baby. She washed up the still-warm baking tin, knife and baking tray, and dried them off with paper towels. She opened the oven and checked that it was properly turned off.

'Are you leaving now too?'

Rika didn't want to leave Shinoi alone in this room, suffused with its sweet smell.

'I need to do a couple of things before I go, and I want to air the place a bit too. You go ahead, before the cake gets cold.'

Rika left the apartment, turning back several times to glance behind her. The sight of Shinoi's profile getting narrower through the crack in the door made her chest feel tight.

Outside the apartment block, she broke into a run. The cold didn't make her flinch as it had before. On reaching the main road, she hailed a cab, and got to the office having only just exceeded the starting fare. She hadn't come to the seventh floor, where the books department was, since her initial training. It was well past 1 a.m., yet there were still a few people dotted around the office. Spotting Makoto poring over some proofs with a serious expression, she caught his eye, and nodded towards the kitchen, indicating for him to come. He had a cold, aged look that unsettled her.

'What is it?'

His expression as he came in hunched to the chaotic office kitchen was one of confusion. Remembering the night of the pasta, her resolve flickered, but she knew she had to get him to eat the cake as soon as possible. She didn't care if he thought the gesture too much, too domestic – he had to eat it before it cooled. She created a space on the trolley piled with shop-bought biscuits and cakes, set the quatre quarts down, and spoke quickly to cover her embarrassment.

'I baked a cake. At my friend's house, who lives just over there. It's just come out of the oven, and I wanted you to taste it while it's warm. Valentine's Day's just round the corner after all. I'm begging you, please don't overthink this. I just wanted one time to do something like this, that's all.'

She washed her hands and unwrapped the foil. A burst of sweet steam rose into the room. Hesitantly, Makoto reached for a piece and lifted it to his mouth.

'Mm, it's warm,' he said, and then began chewing, his expression somehow troubled. His hair looked more bouffant than last time she'd seen him, and he had stubble on his chin.

'I always thought that I'd be imposing on you if I did something like this, but I think that, on reflection, that's exactly what's been lacking. I've started to realise that nothing ever happens if you don't impose on people.'

After a little while, Makoto reached out for another slice. It was all thanks to Shinoi, Rika thought, that it had turned out a success.

'I've never had cake fresh out of the oven before.' Makoto's breath was sweet and hot. His voice sounded better lubricated than before.

'Or actually, that's not true. Maybe once, at a friend's house in primary school. His mother baked madeleines. They were still warm, and they tasted different to anything I'd eaten before, I was amazed. When my mum came home from work I said I wanted to eat them again, and she looked really sad. I told myself then that I'd never again ask her to make me food. This has the same smell as those madeleines did. Fresh, and sweet, and sour.'

'It's the lemon zest. It's not "the taste of authentic home cooking" or anything – it's just lemon zest. Your mum didn't have the time, and that's okay. Doing this takes time. It's not about affection, I've realised – it's just about time. You don't realise that until you do it.'

Rika knew that she'd succeeded in her mission because she'd acted quickly and decisively. If she'd hesitated about taking up Shinoi's offer, she couldn't have done it. If she could hone her powers of decision-making about the rest of her life choices, was it possible that she'd find the time to cook, and read, and bake quatre quarts for fun at the end of the working day? Maybe that was the kind of wall that Kajii was talking about.

'Do you want to meet my mum sometime? I feel like you and her would get along.'

Rika nodded. She'd been avoiding this for so long. If it ever got out that both the ramen evening and this cake-baking experiment were carried out at Kajii's instruction, would Makoto be hurt? she wondered.

'Why did you leave, the other night?'

In the time it took her to comprehend his words, Rika polished off two slices of the still-warm cake.

That other night, getting back freezing cold from the ramen restaurant, she had been so relieved by her full belly and the warmth of the bed and Makoto's smell that she'd immediately fallen into a deep sleep. When she woke up in the morning, there was no sign of Makoto next to her, as he'd warned her there wouldn't be – only a note on the bedside table. She'd been convinced he hadn't noticed her escaping.

'I had a real craving for ramen. I couldn't resist.'

'That stomach of yours really leads you around, eh?' he said in disbelief, but there was a new note of sweetness and kindness to his voice. 'Don't just disappear like that without saying anything again. It made me worried.'

Now he reached for her wrist, pulled her close to him and kissed her. It came to her then that on that night, their lips hadn't touched. Now, their chapped lips made a funny rustling noise as they brushed together. Both their tongues tasted of lemon zest and butter.

Tokyo had seen its first snowfall of the year, and the toes of Rika's leather shoes got wet on the way to the Detention House. For the moment the snow was mixed with sleet and seemed unlikely to settle, but she resolved to dig out her wellies that evening. Listening to Kajii, her attention kept being drawn to her soggy toes inside her shoes. Kajii was wearing a baggy ribbed sweater over a shirt, covering up the outline of her body that was usually on display. The tip of her nose was faintly red.

'His mother is like mine, then. Neglecting the household in the name of self-expression, and depriving her children of sufficient affection as a result. That murder case in Shinonome amounts to the same thing. It only happened because the mother insisted on having her own way.'

'The desire to express themselves isn't the only reason that people go out to work, though. That woman, for one, was under a lot of financial pressure.'

'That doesn't mean you should sacrifice your children! Both your mother and his could have gone out to matchmaking parties and found someone to remarry. Why did they try to make it work all by themselves? I can't think of any reason for doing that other than being enamoured with themselves. That someone should reach adulthood without tasting a freshly baked cake is a misfortune of irredeemable proportions!'

'How come you knew the taste, then, when your mother didn't bake for you?'

'My father was interested in cooking, and was a big influence on us, so from primary school on my sister and I used to bake cakes ourselves. My paternal grandmother – she's dead now, but she used to make us fresh doughnuts and ohagi. She was a beautiful, domestic woman, with a great talent for supporting men. My aim is to become like her.'

'Do you still want to have children?'

At this unexpected question, Kajii's eyes began to glisten.

'I do. The ultimate happiness for women is to find their soulmate, raise his children, and make delicious food. And to do so is to make a contribution to society.'

This wasn't far off the sort of things Reiko came out with, Rika thought. Kajii was trying to sever her ties with the past and change the present, as a way of obtaining the childhood she had never had – and doing so all alone. Even in her current situation, Kajii still hadn't given up on the idea of children. Her way of going about things might seem conservative, but in fact, it spoke more of a lack of expectations placed on the opposite sex.

'If I'm going to do an interview with you, I want to speak about my childhood. For that to happen, you need to know more about the place where I grew up. Don't you think?'

Rika had, of course, thought about this before. She'd only taken paid leave from the company once since joining, to attend her grandmother's funeral, but now, with the possibility of an exclusive interview on the horizon, she might be able to take a few days off if she had a word with the editorial desk. She knew Yasudamachi in Agano was a peaceful village filled with dairy farms, forty minutes by car from Niigata Station and home to the factory for a well-known yoghurt brand.

'Yes, you must go and visit the house I grew up in.'

Rika hadn't predicted that Kajii herself would suggest the trip, though. If she went, she had been thinking, it would be of her own volition.

'My mother and sister live there by themselves. My mother is unwell and can't go out much, and she's pretty frosty towards journalists, but my sister is on my side. I've spoken of you to her, so she'll treat you kindly. I'll give you her contact details, and you can let her know when you expect to be there.'

Kajii's sister had got divorced and returned to her hometown after Kajii's arrest. It was unexpected, then, to hear that the two were on good terms after the sister had ostensibly had her life turned upside down by Kajii's actions.

'To be frank, I always thought you'd severed your ties with your hometown. I got that feeling when I went to eat the ramen.'

'Your way of thinking about and doing things is always so *painful* to behold. Severing ties, and so on. It's as if every day is a war. It's only a bowl of ramen! However many times I tell you this it doesn't seem to get through, so I'll make it very clear for you. My life up until coming here wasn't the teeth-grinding ordeal that you think it was. It was fun, easy, frivolous. I was on my own because I was too busy having love affairs and eating delicious food to need that cloying type of friendship where you go to the toilet together and dab away each other's tears and all that nonsense. With the support of my men, I could remain a princess.'

They were on the verge of being washed away by Kajii's relaxed tone, but with a struggle Rika brought back her memories of Yasukuni-dōri at dawn, as glimpsed from the ramen restaurant, and of the night she'd used up all that physical energy making the cake. Even now, the joints of her arms were faintly aching.

When they heard that someone was full-figured and liked cooking and eating, most men imagined someone quiet and domestic. Someone whose interior life would not surpass their own. But did that reasoning really hold up?

Eating was fundamentally an individual and egoistic compulsion, Rika was starting to realise. A gourmand was ultimately a seeker of the truth. You could wrap up their mission in all kinds of fancy language, but they were simply confronting their desires day in and day out. As you learned to cook, you became increasingly able to shut out the outside world and create a fortress within your own spirit. You hunted down your prey, using fire and blades to fashion them into the form you desired. Reading Kajii's blog posts, she'd been struck by her intense stoicism. It took a deathly earnestness to remain faithful to her desires at all times.

Mothers around the world didn't put in the work of coming up with and then cooking the day's menu because those foods were what they themselves wanted to eat, but because they were thinking of their family. From a certain moment on, Kajii had started making the food she wanted to eat when she wanted to eat it. She no longer heeded the physical condition or the palates of the men she was with. That was why her food had the wild deliciousness of something attained through black magic. She could enjoy the act of cooking because it didn't pain her in any way.

That was something that her victims failed to notice, Rika thought. Taking her cooking as an expression of her affection towards them, they'd happily eaten it. Wasn't the same true of Makoto? She'd made him a single bowl of pasta and he'd mistakenly assumed she was forcing her affection on him, hinting she wanted to get married, and rejected her as a result. But that was pasta Rika had made for her own sake. That was why it'd tasted so good.

Kajii's tone seemed unusually soft.

'I don't like my mother very much, but I'm close to my sister. She has always been a bit of a basket case who could never do anything unless I was around. Besides, there are so many delicious local delicacies where I'm from. I would love for you to try them. If you can, I'd like you to visit my father's grave. It must be totally buried in snow at the moment ...'

A warm loyalty coursed through her words like a pulse.

'If you do visit, I think you'll understand why I love butter the way that I do. Wrap up warm when you go – it's called the Snow Country for a reason. Niigata in February is bitingly cold. It's not like Tokyo, where everyone loses their minds at the first dusting of snow.'

The convicted serial killer, sending a journalist to her native Snow Country when the cold was at its most bitter, now flashed Rika a kind, maternal smile.

CHAPTER SEVEN

The slender ankles in front of her looked like they could easily have been snapped in two – like breaking a piece of meringue – if someone were so minded.

Rika was sitting on the lower level of the two-storey Max Toki 314. Outside the train window, the platform was exactly at eye-level. She couldn't take her eyes off those slim legs with no face attached to them, just ten centimetres in front of her, separated by a single pane of glass. The slender ankles shrouded in high-denier tights and the toes in their ballet pumps turned anxiously to the left and then the right, and Rika imagined their owner standing with a ticket in her hand, unsure of where to go. Perhaps the lack of information about the legs compounded her attraction. She tried on all kinds of possibilities for what kind of face, what kind of torso they might belong to. This desire to encircle her thumb and index fingers around their short circumference – did she feel that way because they represented something she herself didn't have? Finally, having apparently identified their destination, the ankles vanished from the pane of glass in front of Rika. She watched them go with a lingering disappointment.

Rika looked down at her own footwear, beyond the thick denim cladding her legs. Heeding Kajii's warnings, she had been checking the Niigata weather forecast regularly, and had come in men's waterproof boots that stretched up to her knees. Given the girth of her legs, she looked altogether like a strong, sturdy man.

Although she hadn't informed her colleagues at the *Shūmei Weekly* of her destination, she had obtained permission from the chief editor and the desk team to go away for three nights to conduct some preliminary research. When she'd told them that Manako Kajii had promised her an exclusive interview, they'd practically fallen from their seats, and said that she didn't have to scrimp on the budget. Kitamura had been concerned that the world was getting bored of Kajii, but their reaction suggested she was still deemed a topic worthy of the front page.

'Get you, Machida! This could actually win us some new female readers. I know she's said she won't touch on the facts of her case, but you've formed a relationship with her where she'll speak about her personal life and her love affairs, right? So all that weight you've put on in the last few months is because of this, eh? I get it now. You've got guts! I'm impressed.'

These words from the person whom she reported to directly at the desk had irritated her. But he would be the one to write up Rika's interview. Maybe she should feel grateful that he'd understood her intention in exploring Kajii's personality and way of seeing the world, as opposed to scandalous anecdotes or the overarching truth of the case.

Pulling the tab on the top of her can of whisky and water, Rika felt a sense of liberation she hadn't experienced for a long time. Tomorrow, she was due to visit the Yasudamachi house Kajii had grown up in, but until then she was free. Just the thought of spending two hours by herself on the train made her heart expand joyfully.

The bullet train bound for Niigata slowly began to move. Watching Tokyo with its indigo-stained buildings receding, Rika checked there was no one in the seat behind her and made to recline her seat – and that was when it happened.

'Sorry I'm so late!'

Looking down at the floor, Rika started. It was those tights, those ballet shoes from before. All at once, she realised that those ankles belonged to none other than Reiko. A surprisingly heavily laden Reiko – in addition to a wheelie suitcase, she had a Boston bag slung over her right shoulder. Rika would have thought that with her years working in PR taking all those business trips she would have been used to travelling light. With her make-up-free face swaddled in a tartan scarf, there was something childlike about her appearance.

'Are you sure it's not a nuisance, me tagging along?'

'No, I'm really happy you're here. It's been ages! How long, since I last saw you?' Rika's thoughts couldn't keep pace with the situation, and her voice grew squeaky.

Reiko uncoiled her scarf, and removed her arms from her coat sleeves. Rika noticed the scent of fabric softener wafting over to her, a smell that she was not used to on the people around her. Who in their right mind would find this woman's presence a nuisance? Who could have sent her away?

'Apparently it's really cold up there. Snowing and everything. Will you be okay dressed so lightly?' As she spoke, she took care with her intonation so as not to make Reiko feel like her presence was a burden.

'It's okay. I might not show it, but I'm a Kanazawa girl at heart! I've brought boots for walking in. I'm sure I'm way more resilient to the cold than you are. I've got plenty of warm clothes in here too.'

Wheeling her suitcase close, she lifted it into the overhead rack together with her Boston bag, then sat down beside Rika. The carriage was almost empty. Rika looked down at hers and Reiko's feet – hers in boots, Reiko's in pumps. They looked exactly like those of a man and a woman. Through Reiko's blue sweater Rika could see the ridges of her bones. Perhaps Rika only felt this way because her own had expanded, but Reiko's body seemed to her worryingly delicate, her skin as white and transparent as paper.

The previous night, when she'd sent Reiko a message saying that she was going to Niigata for the Kajii story, and that she'd bring her back a present, she saw the word 'Read' flash up next to it immediately, and then, for the first time in what felt like ages, a reply came from her friend. *I want to come! What time is your train? Let me have your seat number and the name of your hotel. I'll change the reservations.*

The reply had left Rika flustered. Her research trip was, of course, supposed to be secret. She'd sent Reiko the details, feeling doubtful all the while. A part of her felt that her friend accompanying her would present problems, but she heard nothing more from her, which made it hard to write and tell her not to come. She'd wanted to believe that Reiko's response had been a joke. The Reiko now sitting in front of her seemed, in a way, like a person from a dream. It wasn't just the ethereal aspect to her appearance, either – she felt that even if she reached out a hand, she wouldn't be able to touch her friend.

'Is Ryōsuke okay with it?'

'Yep. I told him I was coming with you and he seemed fine about it – he just told me to have a good time. I made some business cards on my computer yesterday, just in case.'

Looking at the simple card that Reiko handed her, Rika widened her eyes in shock.

'What's this? "Freelance photographer"?'

'Yeah, I thought it'd be a good idea if I masqueraded as a photographer so I can come with you to Kajii's house.'

'You're kidding, right?'

Rika tried to laugh it off, but Reiko spoke with total composure.

'I've got a professional-looking camera that I used in my old job. If they insist it must be you alone, then I'll do some solo sightseeing in Niigata. Can I accompany you for whatever bits I'm able?'

'I'm not sure … I've not told either my boss or Kajii's sister that you're coming.'

'Listen, Rika. I'm going to be straight with you – you can't carry on like this. If you do, then for all you've been granted an exclusive interview, you're just going to reinforce the image of Kajimana being dished out by the media already. It might cause a stir at first, but it won't be the groundbreaking article you want it to be.'

Reiko's tone was stern. Outside the window, the city where Rika had been brought up slunk further and further away. The fluorescent lights overhead looked strong and harsh in their whiteness.

'You're in her thrall, Rika. You don't try to see anything she hasn't shown you. You've got to seek out the truth in a place that she's not focusing on, ask her the sorts of questions that cut to the chase. You need to find a way to draw out the self that she intended not to show anyone.'

Rika tilted her head, affecting a nonplussed expression, but inside the panic was rising, together with a feeling of aggravation. The aggravation was directed not at Reiko and her frankness, but rather at herself, as Reiko had described her.

'Have you decided where to eat tonight? It'll be nine by the time we get there. If you've not sorted anywhere, how about we try this place I found? It's inside Niigata Station, and it serves local delicacies and rice dishes, with a wide range of sake. Niigata will be freezing at night, so it's better not to have to walk too far. I'll make a reservation now, for about the time that we get in.'

Rika nodded equivocally. Reiko decided, and Rika went along with her decision – it had always been this way, since their student days. But it was also true that following behind Reiko meant getting to see things that she would never get to see – never even imagine – if she were alone.

'I wonder if that place is on Kajii's list?'

'What list? Show me!'

Rika got out the list on which she'd noted down Kajii's recommendations for restaurants and foods to try, and Reiko practically snatched it from her hands.

Kajii's memories of Niigata were cut off at the age of eighteen, when she moved to Tokyo. Going by the research Rika had done online, some of the places Kajii had suggested had since closed down. She had nonetheless made detailed plans to eat whatever local delicacies she could from the list: the praline cake eaten at festivities and gatherings; the raisin and buttercream swirl pastries; the Le Lectier yōkan; butter from Sado island; the Kenshin junmai ginjō sake that had been Kajii's father's favourite; the buttery waffles at the chain of restaurants owned by Kajii's local yoghurt factory; the place in the old town serving a rice bowl topped with a large cutlet; the set meal served on a tray in the restaurant that specialised in rice cooked in a traditional stove … As Reiko and Rika discussed various entries in the guidebook Rika had brought with her, they drew closer to the Snow Country. Their conversation from before, still unresolved, was now far behind them.

Looking out at the darkening landscape outside the window, Rika could just about make out the snow-covered mountains and fields stretching off into the distance, a hushed blue-white peacefulness that sparkled on and on. Watching the passing scenery, seemingly uninhabited by a single living creature, she felt her heart sinking, little by little, into a place of deep coldness.

Stepping onto the deserted platform, the first thing she smelled was the gentle scent of moist sand and sweet water. The next moment, she felt a grinding sensation in the bones at the back of her nose, and her thoughts grew fuzzy. This cold was of a different species to that in Tokyo. The humidity of the air lent it a softness, and there was something even comforting and soporific about it. It seemed to Rika that if her skin split open and she began bleeding, she might simply not notice. From her eyes up to her scalp, the parts of her that the air was touching quickly lost all sensation.

'Thank goodness the restaurant's directly linked to the station! Thanks for making the reservation.'

Her diction was slurry. Escaping the platform, they jumped onto the escalator leading up to the ticket gates. The souvenir shops were already closed, and a statue of three naked young girls stood before them, somewhat lonely looking. Looking at the plaque, Rika saw it was *The Three Graces*; she knew there was another version in Agano. She saw promotional banners advertising sasadango – bamboo-leaf-wrapped sweets – and sake, Niigata's iconic products. The pair passed through the ticket gates, going up and down various flights of stairs until they arrived at the restaurant, which lay at the bottom of a long escalator.

Informing a young employee in a samue cotton jacket of their reservation, they were shown a room containing two tables separated by a screen. The restaurant's interior was dimly lit, save for the bright spotlights on the pampas grass arrangement and the shelves lined with sake bottles. Rika ordered sake and rice, and Reiko an onigiri with salmon roe, as well as several kinds of vegetable and meat dishes unique to Niigata. Rika clinked her sake cup full of lukewarm Shimeharitsuru to Reiko's cup of hōjicha. After the pleasurable flutter on her tongue, a calm fire kindled at the back of her chilled throat. They were brought over a mix of different kinds of rosy-seabass sashimi. The surface of its skin had been lightly scorched. On her first bite, Rika widened her eyes at the deep sweetness of the meaty flesh.

Next to appear was her bowl of rice, its shining white grains forming a mound over the rim of the bowl. Rika picked up her chopsticks and tucked in. On the other side of the table, Reiko was biting into her onigiri wrapped in dense black nori. Both of their expressions took on an ecstatic cast. Each individual grain of rice was so intensely sweet. She could sense not only the flavour of the grains on her tongue, but their shape as well. When she chewed them, the inside of her mouth loosened, and when she made to greedily absorb them and taste them, she could feel the insides of her body whirring round as if all its cogs were moving. A soft heat rose up from her solar plexus. Cutting the taste with the pumpkin pickles, pale pink millet roe, and the umeboshi brought out with the rice, she worked her way through in small mouthfuls.

Reiko murmured, 'Humans just need rice, don't they? Basically.'

'There are people who say that so long as they're drinking alcohol, they don't need carbohydrates. I envy them, but I'm not like that at all. Excuse me, could I have a refill?' Rika called out to the server who was stacking up the dirty plates at a nearby table.

'You've really got into your food, haven't you?' Reiko was looking at her as she spoke.

'I've put on more weight, you know. I'm now ... wait for it ... fifty-six kilos! It's so cold that I don't feel like doing any exercise. And

I end up eating a lot.' Rika's tone was jokey, but Reiko stared back at her blankly, holding her rice ball from which she'd still taken only a single bite. The reaction didn't make her feel ashamed. Together with her fresh bowl of rice, the server brought over a seasonal dish called noppe – vegetables and kamaboko were simmered in a light dashi, and the whole thing decorated with a sprinkling of salmon roe. As she felt the part of her that had tensed up with the cold begin to thaw in the face of that unbridled nourishing flavour, Rika sighed.

'You know you spoke to me before about "good amounts"?'

'Did I? Oh, you mean in cooking?'

'The more I come to know about all the different flavours out there, the softer I seem to become on myself. I don't really mind any more if people call me lazy or fat. I feel like I'm just going to keep going until I'm satisfied. I still feel a long way off fully understanding what the right amount is for me.'

Reiko was looking at her with a dazed expression. Just as Rika was starting to suspect that her friend was totally despairing of her, Reiko began to speak.

'I feel envious, actually. You've gained confidence in yourself. You seem really good. Maybe that's what "a good amount" is truly about. Also, I know this is going to make me sound like an interfering old woman, but they say that the ideal weight for someone of five feet five is actually sixty kilos.'

Rika spluttered. 'What? There's some incredible yardstick out there that says it wouldn't be weird for me to weigh sixty kilos? I want to go by that! Why isn't it better known about?'

'Ha, that's true, why isn't it? Have a look on the home page of the Japan Medical Association. You're right, it is ridiculous. It feels like the Japanese desire to be thin is less about beauty and more ...'

Reiko looked down at the onigiri she was chewing on. The orbs of the cod roe were peeking out from inside like scarlet crystals. Did she see those eggs as tiny little Reikos?

'It's like we're all being controlled, so that when you come across a person who's shaken off that control you feel irritated. I'm sorry for telling you before that you should diet. Seeing you becoming softer and rounder and more relaxed made me anxious. It's embarrassing to admit, but I felt like you were moving away from being the prince you used to be, whom I'd loved.'

Seeing Reiko casting her eyes down and her earlobes reddening, Rika felt taken aback.

'It's okay! Really, don't worry about it. It's amazing to me that you always stay so thin, when you love eating so much. Is that just your metabolism?'

'No way! During puberty, with all the stress of everything with my parents, I put on loads of weight. It was while I was studying nutrition that I got into the habit of calculating daily calorie intakes.'

This was the first time Rika had heard any of this. She couldn't imagine Reiko the slightest bit overweight.

'Wow, trust you to be so in control! I'm genuinely glad that you are so beautiful. But – and I know I'm hardly one to say this, but I've been a bit concerned about you recently. You seem to be getting thinner and thinner. It's like you're reverting to being a young girl.'

As soon as these words were out of her mouth, Rika worried that she should have been more careful in her phrasing, but Reiko cocked her head in an adorable look of puzzlement.

'Hmm, I feel like I'm eating the same amount as usual, though? Maybe it's got harder for me to put on weight as I've got older. I guess now that I'm trying to get pregnant, I've been trying to eat healthily. I've cut out alcohol and luxurious foods. Nothing's wrong, though.'

The shiokara squid went so well with the rice, drawing out its flavour and sweetness, and Rika found that in no time her second bowl of rice, too, had vanished. She set down her chopsticks.

'What you said to me on the train before – it's something that I've been thinking about. You were spot on. It's as if, when you get involved with her, you end up becoming a part of her or something. I know it's pathetic, but I end up only being able to see the bits she wants me to see.'

She immediately felt lighter for admitting it. She was too embarrassed to order a third helping of rice, but she felt that she could, in fact, have managed one.

'I think women like that want to lead people like you around.' Reiko drew the omelette closer to her. Her lips traced a shape that looked both ironic and sad, and Rika didn't know what to take from it. With her eyes roving around, Reiko strung her words together slowly. 'But seeing only the things you want to see means *not* seeing the things you don't want to, right? Don't you think in actual fact, she's a weak, unconfident person? I'm sure there's parts of you that are stronger than her.'

Rika looked hard at her friend. 'I feel like you understand her a lot better than I do, despite never having met her.'

Reiko made to speak, but stopped herself and reached for the sake list. Rika checked the messages on her phone to find one from Makoto: *Wrap up warm, and be careful you don't catch cold! Give me a call later.*

The message roused no particular emotion, and she decided to put off replying until later.

The two of them finished off their meal with Le Lectier pears dripping with delicious juice, whose flesh dissolved the moment they were inside the mouth. Then they paid up and left the restaurant, venturing out into the city of Niigata, where there'd been a big snowfall a few days previously. By the bus station, blackish snow was heaped up beside the road. Rika could sense how high the sky was, despite the darkness. Even with all the heat from the food they'd just eaten, their bodies were instantly drained of warmth. They trudged along the wet asphalt until they arrived at their hotel. The snow reflected the light spilling from restaurants and bars, shooting it up towards the night sky in beams like searchlights.

Reiko checked them in at the front desk, and they got in the small lift, still trembling with cold. Inside their room, Reiko went straight into the bathroom, hosed down the bathtub with the shower, and began to fill it. Reiko had offered her the first bath, but Rika decided to go after her friend.

When she did get in, the hot water clung to her body with velvety softness. It had only taken them a few minutes to arrive from the station, but in that time she'd grown chilled to the core, and the sensation was now so pleasurable she could have cried out in ecstasy. From the other side of the curtain, she heard Reiko brushing her teeth.

'The bath water's so soft and slippery. I guess that's what everyone means when they talk about how good the water is in this part of the country. Which is why the rice and the sake are so tasty, too, I suppose,' Rika said.

'When you get out, don't drain the water, okay?' Reiko's voice coming through the curtain was muffled. 'Leave it in, and open the door.'

When Rika came out of the bathroom with a towel wrapped around her head to keep in the moisture, Reiko, who was sitting reading on the bed in her flannel pyjamas, looked up.

'I ordered a humidifier.'

Now that Rika looked, she could see white smoke billowing up from a humidifier placed beneath the bed. The room was warm and plentifully moist. She took comfort in the fact that she and Reiko smelled of the same shampoo. Turning on the desk light, she took out her laptop from her bag. The narrow mirror in front of her reflected the white, childlike face of the person sitting on the bed.

'I'm going to do a bit of work before bed. Feel free to go to sleep before me. Will it be too bright for you if I keep this light on?'

'It's a nuisance, isn't it, me tagging along?'

Rika had turned off the lights in the room and was tapping at the keys when she heard Reiko's voice again.

'Me and Ryōsuke, we don't – we haven't done it for ages.'

Rika felt a pang of relief that she could have this conversation without needing to look at her friend. 'Since you fought about the treatment?' she ventured cautiously, keeping her eyes from the mirror.

'No ... since way before then.'

She realised that the revelation did not surprise her. For a while she had been vaguely aware – no, if she was honest, it had been a robust awareness. Had it started that time she'd been to their house? No, it predated that. Maybe Rika's awareness of this aspect of her friend went back to before she'd even met Ryōsuke. Reiko went on, as though something in her were spilling over.

'Since I quit my job, the year before last. Up until that point we'd both been making an effort, but I think when I packed everything else in and decided to focus my energies on having a child, he felt a sense of pressure. Which is why it's all useless – going to the clinic, and taking the Chinese herbal medicine, and everything. I thought that if I gave it my best shot then he'd eventually feel like doing the same. But the more obsessed I became with it the more he ... I don't know. I think I felt like if we pretended that we were having sex then we really would start to have it. If I could have people believe my lies then they'd become true. I'm hardly one to fault Kajii's compulsive lying. For Ryōsuke, it all seemed to become this burden. The tension just grew between us. Suddenly it struck me how ridiculous it all was, and I stopped going to the Suidōbashi clinic. Stopped everything.'

'Ah, really,' Rika said with a sigh. It was all that she could say. The powerful sense of pity now rising up in her chest would only hurt her friend if she expressed it.

'It seems that ever since I gave up my work, my desire to have children has been oppressive to Ryō. We talked about it a lot. I know it sounds like we had communication problems, but that's not true. Do you think he's just a bad husband? That it's a form of abuse? Is it me, am I a bad wife? This stuff aside, everything between us is going very well. Truly. Although I've no way of proving that to a third party.'

Reiko let out a little laugh. Her breathing sounded as if she might be crying, and her voice gradually grew quieter.

'I don't really like talking about this, but I've never been a big fan of all that … stuff. Initiating it myself, or having the other person initiate it – either way. Ryōsuke is the only man I've met who I can talk to without clamming up. When you think that, however hard I try, I can't even put my own husband in the mood, Kajii's really something. Having that many people besotted with her …'

Even Reiko, who had railed so hard against society's double standards when it came to men and women – it had even got to her, in the end. The ceiling in the hotel room suddenly felt low. The same kind of pressure the victims of this case had endured was now pushing down on her best friend – on Reiko, who had always been so good at managing herself, at driving things forward.

'It's just like you said. I shouldn't have given up a job that I liked so readily. I was in such a fluster that I didn't take your words on board. I was really stupid.'

Reiko was crying. Rika could tell, even without looking.

'I'm running out of time. I'm only getting older, and I can't change anything about my situation. Manako Kajii's not given up hope of getting married and having kids, despite being in prison for life. I see that and wonder how it's possible to feel such optimism, when I'm this panicked. I'm sorry for tagging along. I just didn't want to be in that house waiting for him any longer. I had no intention of getting in the way of your work. I'll stay behind tomorrow.'

'You should – you need to …' *Take it a bit easy, relax, don't blame yourself* – all the phrases Rika could think of didn't have any meaning. Why had she grown so scared of drawing close to her best friend? It was just that she was desperate not to lose her. Rika stood up, went over to Reiko's bed and hugged her. Burying her face in her hair, she smelled a rich, sweet smell that made Reiko's words from before seem like a dream.

'Thanks for ordering the humidifier, and thinking to leave the bath water in. If I was here by myself my throat would most likely have got all dry and hoarse. The person who gets to live with you doesn't know how lucky they are.'

How very delicate she was. She couldn't say it to Reiko, but hugging her now, her body felt so fragile that the idea of it giving life to another being seemed almost unthinkable. She could feel Reiko's breathing through the duvet. For a while they stayed hugging, until Reiko said, 'You're so heavy!' and Rika said, 'And you're so mean!' and the two of them laughed.

The next morning when Rika woke, there was no sign of Reiko. On the table was a handwritten note: *Gone for breakfast! R*

Rika arranged her hair and put on some make-up, then sat on the toilet lid as she brushed her teeth. Scrolling through her inbox and the internet news, she saw an email from Kitamura, with the subject line 'Can I talk to you about something?' It was rare for him to be in touch, but she decided to leave it for the moment. She made a quick call, then left the room.

In the ground-floor restaurant she found Reiko, polished as ever, sipping her coffee among a sea of single men who were no doubt travelling for work. Rika watched with a feeling of pride as they flicked glances at Reiko's lowered eyelashes and glossy hair. The 1,200-yen buffet breakfast appeared at first to be a standard spread, but on closer inspection, Rika found an ample assortment of things to eat with the rice in the cooker, sparkling in the morning sunlight. Sitting opposite Reiko and taking her first mouthful, sensing its sweetness and fragrance, Rika's shoulders trembled in pleasure. The rolled omelette was made with plenty of sugar, and was nicely browned on the outside.

As Rika was standing up to fetch seconds, she said to Reiko, 'I want you to come with me today. I checked with the Kajii house if it was okay to bring a photographer and they said yes.'

'No, forget about that. I wasn't thinking straight when I suggested it.'

'Come! I'll notice things if I'm there with you that I wouldn't otherwise – all the things about Kajii that I haven't been able to register so far. I'm asking you now as a journalist. This is my assignment, and if I say you can come then you can.'

Reiko nodded. Her eyes looked faintly red.

'I'll go and get my camera,' she said and stood up to leave. After her second bowl of rice, Rika took out her phone and called a taxi.

When the two friends emerged from the hotel entrance several minutes later, a well-built taxi driver in his fifties was standing by his car. Slivers of blue sky poked out temptingly from between gaps in the clouds.

'You're visitors here, yes?' the driver said when they told him their destination, looking at them in the rear-view mirror with an enquiring gaze. 'You know there's nothing to see in Agano at this time of the year?'

Beyond the windscreen, the black asphalt twinkled wetly from between the banks of snow.

'It's amazing that the roads are so well-cleared after such a big snowfall,' Rika said, promptly changing the subject.

The driver replied, 'You know that there's snow-melting pipes in the roads? They sprinkle water from beneath.'

Even when she pressed her cheek to the glass she couldn't get a great view, but there did appear to be tiny holes lining the middle of the road, from which water spurted out. Rika hadn't slept well the previous night, and her eyes grew heavy as she stared out of the window.

She woke up to hear Reiko whispering, 'Hey, that's Kajii's middle school, right?'

The scenery had transformed to snow-blanketed fields and mountains. Rika's mouth felt parched, and her shoulders hurt. The school Reiko had been speaking of was now far behind them. A way off in the distance, Rika could see a huge fairground wheel and the coiled silhouette of a rollercoaster.

'What's that theme park over there?'

The driver's response came immediately. 'That's Suntopia World. I believe it's closed between December and mid-March, though.'

The taxi pulled up outside a triangular clump of houses surrounded on all three sides by paddy fields. No sooner had they paid the fare of almost 10,000 yen and stepped out than Rika let out a squeal.

'I'd describe it less as cold, and more just *painful*. I feel like my blood vessels are going to freeze up and burst.'

It would have made sense to her if her ears and nose had dropped off and fallen to her feet, leaving red stains on the dirt track below.

'You Tokyoites, you're all wimps,' Reiko said, but her cheeks were a vivid red, and her teeth were chattering.

This was a different cold again to what they'd experienced getting off the train at Niigata Station. And there was no comparison between this and the evening that she'd been to eat ramen in Shinjuku. She understood now how Kajii had so easily torn herself from the warm bed where her lover lay and waltzed out into the night. The Tokyo cold must have been nothing to her.

The house with 'Kajii' on the nameplate looked about 160 square metres in size. There was an old Prius parked outside. Rika took a deep breath and looked up, determined not to miss a detail. It was a two-storey house designed for families – the kind you saw many of, even in Reiko's part of Tokyo – and repainted a pale yellow. As Rika was staring up at the cracked layer of snow on the triangular roof above the door and thinking how it might come falling down at any moment, she heard a thump behind her – a clump of snow had fallen from the telephone wire. In the tinted-glass windows sat several aged soft toys, arranged so that they faced the street. A huge beige bear smiled out, its button-eyes wide open.

Reiko whispered in her ear, 'It's just a normal house! Somehow I was imagining some kind of mansion.'

The two of them took off their coats and down jackets and held them in their hands. With a gloved finger, Rika pushed the intercom button. After a while, the door was opened and a reserved-looking woman poked her head out. Rika introduced herself. Then it was Reiko's turn.

'I'm Reiko Sayama, the photographer. It's a pleasure to meet you.' With this, Reiko bowed, an almost irritatingly polite expression on her face.

'Nice to meet you both. You've had such a long journey!'

Anna Shōji – maiden name Anna Kajii – looked nothing like her older sister. She had colourless lips and swollen eyes. Not many would have called her a beauty, but she was small and slim. The positioning of her mouth and nose wasn't unlike Kajii's, but her eyes had a lot of life in them, and it was clear, as she looked at you, that she was properly taking you in. Rika was fairly sure she'd read she was twenty-eight, but with her beige sweater, her long, checked skirt and her black hair worn in a simple ponytail, she could have passed for a student. The only clear commonality with her sister was her pale, soft-looking skin.

Asked inside, Rika and Reiko took off their shoes in the lobby and handed Anna their coats. Her gestures didn't convey the wariness towards journalists that was common among the family members of suspected criminals. The way she held back the door and beckoned them in suggested a sense of trust.

Inside the living room, Rika felt a burst of nostalgia. The smell of the kerosene stove, she realised, reminded her of her school chapel in mid-winter. The room was spacious, and its underfloor heating made it warm, but it was very dusty. She took in its contents: a piano, long-haired shag carpet, a table and chairs, a dresser, a soft couch with lace covers, a glass table, a plasma TV. It wasn't messy, but the carelessly stacked magazines, the jumble of soft toys, and the many plants of different heights lined up along the wall made for a creepy ambience. It would seem that, just like the elder daughter of the family, neither the mother nor the younger daughter had a talent for cleaning and organising. Next to her Reiko, who was sensitive to such things, gave a small cough.

'My sister often mentions you in her letters, so it doesn't feel like the first time I'm meeting you. The press barrage has died down now, and it's a long time since anybody's come to visit us like this.'

Anna gestured for Rika and Reiko to sit on the chairs at the table. Faded cushions had been tied to their backs. The table was covered in a vinyl cloth with a tiny flower pattern. Anna pulled a large hot-water dispenser towards her and filled the teapot with boiling water.

'She's always been misunderstood as a person. In a town like ours, she couldn't help but stand out. I was about the only woman who was capable of conversing with her.'

Her tone was serious, yet there was a hint of pride in her words.

'But the real Manako isn't the one that the media have painted her to be. She liked taking care of others from such a young age, and as the eldest child, she's always found it hard to say no to people. I think it's true that the victims were in love with her, but my guess is that she was unable to turn them down, so they got the wrong end of the stick. I think it's possible that some woman jealous of my sister killed those men and made it look like it was her.'

Anna's small nostrils quivered as she spoke. As the chill from before receded, Rika came to realise that the room they were in was, in fact, overheated. Although now was hardly the time for it, she felt her head starting to droop sleepily.

'Is your mother, erm …?'

'She's asleep upstairs. I told her you were coming, but after everything she's been through with the media, I don't think she wanted to see you. She's had problems with her back these past few years, and finds it difficult to walk. She's doing okay, now that I'm living here.'

Kajii's mother, the same generation as Rika's own, was a loquacious type, known for being cooperative with journalists. She had seemed almost proud of the fact that her daughter was a suspected criminal, and would readily offer her opinion on the state of public education or the justice system. According to one of the journalists covering the story at the time, she was not at all like Kajii. It seemed that of the two girls, it was Anna who had inherited the mother's characteristics.

The tea set appeared not to have been used for some time. The cups were marked with stains that had been there since goodness knows when. To accompany the green tea, they were given rice crackers wrapped in cellophane.

The piano didn't look like it had been played in a long time, either. There was a lace cover thrown over it, and its top was cluttered with souvenirs – dolls, cheap-looking stuffed toys and ceramics. The rug beneath was visibly dusty, and everywhere you looked there were stray hairs. Yet you could also sense that a rigid order governed the space. If you moved anything, you'd be shouted at – that was the sense that the room exuded.

All of the indoor plants were dark green with visible veining, their leaves and stalks tracing long arcs. While the impression they gave was that they'd simply been left to grow, the fact that they'd retained their vivid colouration through the winter was proof that they were well tended to. And perhaps there was also an organising principle behind the stacking of the magazines and the arrangement of the toys. Rika cast her eyes to the door with its frosted glass inset. Was it possible that Kajii's mother was in the room behind it?

She studied the blown-up photos arranged on top of the piano. Judging by their resolution, they were from quite some time ago. Two children – a young girl in baggy matching skiwear and a toddler – were standing against a background of white snow building a snow hut. The large, chubby older girl had a dignified air about her, and was looking fixedly at the camera.

'Is this you and your sister?'

'That's right. My sister was in her third year of primary school then, and I was two. She always took the lead, ever since we were little.'

'I don't mean to be rude, but she looks very grown up for a kid in her third year of primary school.'

'Yes, she got her first period at around this age.'

'At nine years old? That's really very early …'

Rika attempted to remember how old she herself had been, but she couldn't retrieve the information. She could remember how her chest and her hips had remained flat as boards, and how, even into middle school, her period had stubbornly refused to come, but she hadn't been in any particular hurry. In fact, while all around her girls were undergoing puberty and having to reckon with the difficulties that being a woman brought, it had been pleasurable to retain a body like a young boy, and act so freely. Still, she somehow felt sure that being the first to develop lay at the core of Kajii's unerring self-confidence.

After clearing with Anna that it was okay to take photos, clarifying that they wouldn't be published but just used as materials, Reiko took her heavy black camera out of its bag, and turned her lens on this framed memory.

'It was around then that my mother and my sister stopped getting on so well. My mother was at a loss with how to deal with her daughter maturing so early. She's quite active and masculine in her demeanour, and liked it when we looked like little boys. She was flustered by how girlish my sister was from a young age. My sister got fed up with this aspect of my mother, but it wasn't a problem for her, because my father was around. She and my father were extremely close – so close that I couldn't even feel jealous.'

As far as Rika could see, there were no pictures of either of the parents in the room. Rika had the sense that after their father had died, the pictures of them as a couple had been removed.

'Oh, and I had a message from my sister. She told me to take you to the house of a nearby dairy farmer.'

'A dairy farmer?'

'His name's Akiyama. He's a childhood friend of ours, of sorts – he was in the same class as my sister in high school. As kids we often used to go round to his place, and once we saw a cow giving birth. It was one part of our father's education. Shall we set out there now? It's about five minutes' walk away. We'll get him to show us round the cowshed, and then on the way home we can visit my father's grave. My sister asked that we do that too.'

Perhaps because she was relaying her sister's instructions, Anna spoke clearly and compellingly, her delivery bright. Right away, she

changed into wellies and opened the door. With firm steps, she went
trudging through the snow. Rika and Reiko followed after her, trying
to tread in the tracks she'd left.

Outside, every bit of Rika's energy was consumed by withstand-
ing the weather. Over and over, her mind returned to how much she
wanted to be somewhere warm. Once again, all thought had shut
down.

At last, they reached the cowshed that was positioned alongside a
family house. As they approached, they heard loud, drawn-out
mooing, and were met by a ripe animal smell mingled with that of
soured cream cheese. The hay stacked in bales exuded a warm, spicy
and sweet scent. Instructed by Anna, they put vinyl covers over their
boots and stepped inside. The cows of different colours and sizes
behind the fence all began mooing apprehensively. Rika's body
immediately stiffened. Whether from the warm breath of the cows or
the air conditioning, the shed was surprisingly warm.

'Hi, it's Anna! I've brought some visitors from Tokyo. Rika
Machida and Reiko Sayama,' Anna called out towards the
back of the shed. Hearing a loud male voice respond, Rika turned
around.

'A pleasure to meet you, I'm Akiyama. I've heard about you!'

If he was the same age as Kajii, that would make him thirty-five.
Yet the sturdily built man before her with a pale complexion and rosy
cheeks seemed of a different species to Rika's colleagues of the same
age.

'The spot you're standing in right now is believed to be the birth-
place of Niigata's dairy farming industry. We've opened up our
cowshed so that visitors can get a sense of what dairy farming is
really like.'

He turned and went striding along the fence through which the
cows were poking their noses. Rika and Reiko followed behind.

'The number of dairy farms like ours has been dropping off
dramatically in recent years, because there's a shortage of young
people who want to take over when the elder generations retire. It's

all because the Japanese are consuming less milk. You could say the same of rice farmers too.'

Catching the gaze of one of the cows through the railings, Rika started. Its bulging eyes were pointed in different directions.

Noticing her reaction, Akiyama said, 'Cows can do this thing where they look not in front of them but behind. They sleep with their eyes open, too.'

She watched the cow's big wet snout twitching like a creature in its own right.

'In order to keep producing milk, cows need to calve once a year. So we keep them permanently pregnant, through artificial insemination. Feel free to touch them, if you like.'

Rika snuck a look at Reiko's profile, but her gaze was directed with fascination on the cows.

'They're so warm!' Reiko said, running her palm along one cow's mottled caramel back. From under its smooth-haired hide surface the outline of its backbone looked powerful enough to go ripping through its flesh at any moment.

'Have a go at feeding them,' Akiyama said, handing them each a handful of hay. As soon as Rika held her hand up tentatively beneath its nose, the cow bit at the strands poking through her fingers, making to pull them roughly away. Rika felt her courage recede as the fear of being bitten surfaced in her. Next to her, Reiko was calmly feeding the cows, passing over the hay little by little.

'We choose the sperm donors from a catalogue. The key is to choose the best-looking bulls, which you can tell have a good bloodline.'

Just like with humans, Rika thought. Kajii's view of romance, whereby men should be chosen based on their financial and social status alone, had been criticised in court, but if your objective wasn't a communion of minds but simple reproduction, then perhaps it was a sensible way of going about things.

'We're planning to enter one of our cows into a beauty contest soon.'

'There are beauty contests for cows?' Rika asked.

'Now you mention it, though, out of these three, this one clearly seems the prettiest,' Reiko said, peering eagerly at the three cows standing in the pen. Rika could barely see any difference between them.

'There are eighty cows in this shed. In a group that size, you inevitably see the emergence of a hierarchy. What we do is put them all out to graze once, and get them to determine the pecking order between themselves. It means they make allowances and maintain order between themselves. Hierarchy isn't a bad thing. You need it, to prevent conflict.'

One of the cows let out a long moo. Its tenor sounded less anxious than before. The arrival of strangers must have set them on edge.

The tigers in *The Story of Little Babaji*, so set on proving they were at the top of the pecking order that they had turned into butter, had been males, for sure. She was certain it said as much in the book.

Women avoided that futile struggle if they possibly could. Wasn't that why they subtly informed one another of their respective positions and personalities? They created an invisible system of order so as to avoid hurting one another. Silently, rules came into being. *This is your territory and I'll take care not to encroach on it – in return, don't threaten my freedom.* By gently asserting themselves in this way, they protected their place.

'The interesting thing is that it's not always the strongest cows who are at the top. The hierarchy is not about size, or looks.'

'How is it decided, then?' Reiko asked.

'It's hard to say – in the same way that it's hard to say what it is that makes women admire other women. Some cows have just got that special something.'

Why was Rika so subservient when it came to Kajii? Why had Kajii got under Reiko's skin, even though Reiko seemed to resist the fact? Why was it that Anna looked up to her sister so much? The cow that Reiko had deemed the prettiest before now pushed some hay in the direction of a black cow in the same enclosure, offering up food that could have been its own.

'We ensure this place stays clean, and we feed and water the cows well. That's what determines the taste of the milk. Milk starts out as part of the blood, after all.'

'I didn't know that. How does that red blood end up so …'

Could it really be that the meticulous white of butter and milk and cream was once the red liquid pumping through the body of these giant creatures? She felt as though she was starting to understand something. Everything Akiyama said seemed to stir things up inside her.

'Would you like to try milking them?'

Akiyama slid a bucket beneath one of the cows, then held down the cow's back legs. Rika bent over and stretched out a tentative hand towards the udder. At her touch, it dented and flopped softly towards her. At first she gripped the teat softly, but nothing came out, so she squeezed again with force. A straight white line emerged from the tip of the teat, shooting into the bucket.

Milk was originally blood. In that case, was the butter in the Babaji story actually a metaphor for all the carnage that took place under the cover of the jungle? What seemed pure, white and creamy had its origins in vivid, bloody red – was that not the essence of this whole case? A scene rose vividly to Rika's mind: the menstrual blood that had gushed between the legs of nine-year old Manako Kajii staining crimson the pure white of Agano.

Maybe the victims hadn't been murdered. Maybe they had all killed one another – but not in a confrontation. Hadn't they brought about their own destruction out of the jealousy they had come to feel towards one another? She imagined them now, chasing one another in circles around Kajii, until they had met their respective ends …

Rika felt as though she could see a red stain diffusing through the white milk that had collected in the bucket. Something about this vision was making her tremble. The image of that spreading patch of red made it hard for her to breathe.

Then, she saw it – the ivory carpet, stained with blood.

In its very centre lay her father. It had been Rika, back when she was in middle school, who had found his body in the Mitaka apartment three days after he died. The blood had been dark, almost brown, as if it had taken on the colour of his insides before spilling out of his body. It was a scene that she'd kept locked up in the very innermost chamber of her memory – a scene she'd told herself she mustn't remember. What had happened wasn't her fault, and it wasn't her mother's fault either.

Rika swallowed and breathed in a lungful of air smelling of manure and cows' saliva. Something was not right. Why was her thinking so disarrayed? There was no connection between her father's death and the Kajii case. Feeling a gush of liquid between her legs, she began to tremble all over again. It was too early for her period, of that she was sure. She'd have to check in the bathroom later, see what had happened. Would she be able to use the bathroom here?

Just then it came back to her: it had been straight after her father had died that she'd got her first period.

'What's wrong, Rika? Are you feeling all right? You're very pale.'

The sound of Reiko's concerned voice tugged Rika back to reality. The cows were drinking, their noses pressed to the base of the trough. Akiyama suggested that they put the cowshed behind them.

'In winter, because it's this cold, the cows eat a lot, and so their milk is sweet and rich. In the summer it's runnier and lighter in taste. You should try some fresh milk. I'll warm some up for you. We shut our shop over the winter, so you'll have to come to my kitchen.'

Akiyama's home adjoined the cowshed. It had a dirt floor, which meant they could enter without taking off their shoes. In the corner of the room were bikes and a rice-polishing machine. Though not tidy, the atmosphere was different to that of the Kajii household – it was well ventilated, and there was no stuffy feeling. On the hob in the kitchen at one corner of the living space, a steaming pan was letting out a bubbling noise. A woman of Akiyama's age, who Rika assumed was his wife, handed Rika and Reiko two warm paper cups.

'My sister used to love the soft-serve they made here,' Anna said, looking through the window at the shop with its snow-laden corrugated-iron roof. 'She said it tasted like rich, creamy cheese. It's still a bit cold for ice cream now, though.'

Rika could picture the scene – a young girl with the air of a woman about her, licking a soft-serve ice cream as she leaned on the fence, gazing at the cows. Inside Rika, a premonition began to emerge, recalling the words Reiko had said to her last night: *As I went on telling lies, I started to feel as though they were becoming the truth …*

'Oh, this is delicious! It's like it's got nectar inside,' Reiko exclaimed on her first sip. She was right – the milk tasted like sunlight spreading out across the tongue. Rika let out a sigh of satisfaction. She knew that it was just her imagination, but somehow Reiko already looked slightly softer and rounder, which made her happy.

While Reiko was busy taking photographs, Rika whispered to Akiyama, 'I heard that you were childhood friends with Manako Kajii.'

Handing him her business card, she noticed his breathing grow shallower.

'I'm a journalist at a weekly magazine. I think the innovations you're making with the farm are wonderful. I'm sure there's scope to feature it in our magazine … I'd like, if possible, to hear your memories of Manako Kajii, it doesn't matter how inconsequential. Will you call me on this number? I'll be in Niigata until 5 p.m. tomorrow.'

Hesitantly, Akiyama reached out for the card, which he secreted in the pocket of his overalls. All of a sudden the steam from the milk was no more.

CHAPTER EIGHT

With practised gestures, Anna cleared away the snow from the tombstone.

The clumps of compacted snow went sliding down the stone, breaking apart on the ground. The sparkling wet surface of the stone came into view, the deep grooves of its etched characters glinting in the afternoon sun.

This small graveyard, a fifteen-minute walk from Akiyama's cowshed, also offered a clear glimpse of Suntopia World. The Agano landscape was composed of snow-covered rice paddies, with no buildings tall enough to block the view of the theme park. Most of the graves were heaped with snow, so that you could tell at a glance which households had been to visit their dead today. The cold air was clear and pure, yet something about its extreme transparency made it hard to breathe.

'It'll be frozen solid in no time, I'm sure, but this was my dad's favourite, and my sister told me to leave it for him.' Saying this, Anna took a big bottle of Kenshin sake from her canvas tote bag and set it down in front of the stone with a chink. She then laid the chrysanthemums she'd brought on the grave. The incense refused to light, and Rika could see the movement of Anna's finger flicking the lighter take on signs of irritation. Even when the line of smoke began finally to rise up, it was immediately absorbed by the snow, its heady fragrance intercepted by the clear cold air.

'It was at exactly this time of the year that he passed, back in February 2012. It was an accident. He was hunting with some neighbours, and he fell on a snowy path on Hōshu Mountain and hit his head. The only time my sister has been back since leaving for Tokyo was to attend his funeral. I mean, I saw plenty of her when I went to Tokyo, as did my father. We saw one another much more frequently than most siblings do.'

Reiko and Rika copied Anna in putting their gloved hands together in prayer, and closing their numbed eyelids. Rika could feel that the tips of her eyelashes were frozen.

After a respectful silence, the two of them opened their eyes and lowered their hands, but Anna showed no sign of moving, so Rika asked tentatively, 'Did your parents meet and get married in Tokyo?'

At this, Anna finally opened her eyes.

'That's right. My mother took an office job at a small manufac-turer in Shinagawa where my father was working. My mother would often boast fondly that all the women in the company loved my father, because he was knowledgeable and good at languages and behaved like a real gentleman, so everyone envied my mother when he chose her. From as far back as I can remember, my mother wasn't at home much, and her relationship with my father was somewhat rocky, but by all accounts when they first got together my mother adored my father. She treasured those early memories, it seems.'

Anna returned her tote bag to her shoulder. Once out of the graveyard, they walked along beside the road. It felt considerably warmer than when they'd set out from the Kajiis' house. Big patches of blue sky showed between the clouds, and the surface of the road had grown wet. The snow beneath their boots had changed from the texture of ice-pops to that of shaved ice. Rika felt the moisture oozing into her insoles.

As they retraced their steps, she asked, 'Why did your parents come back to Agano?'

'My father got embroiled in some trouble with a client, and grew increasingly fed up with working for a company. At around the same time, my grandfather's health began to get worse, and they decided

to move back when my sister was three.' Rika exchanged a quick
glance with Reiko.

'Your father must have been a wonderful person. Your sister
always looks so happy when she speaks of him.'

At this, Anna pouted proudly. Having little colour to them, her
lips didn't stand out, but a closer look revealed them to be surprisingly full, not unlike her sister's. Overall, the impression she left was
a childlike one, but those lips gave off the sense of passion with no
place to go.

'He was a very stylish, attractive man. He was an avid reader and
film lover, and very knowledgeable about computing, even back in
the early nineties. Alongside his estate agency work, he set up his
own company designing websites for people. He built the homepages
for the village hall here, and Akiyama's farm, I believe. The internet
enabled him to order everything that he wanted from overseas. The
people around here must have sensed that he was in a different league
to them. I dearly loved him, but he was so clever that the things he
said often went over my head. My sister and he were very well
matched in that sense. They were less like father and daughter and
more like … Let's say I could understand why my mother might have
felt jealous.'

Anna gazed down the road into the distance as she spoke.

'My father would often tell her, "You're not like ordinary children." But I never felt envious of her. We were so far apart in age,
after all. I liked to see my sister and my father getting along so well.'

There was something about Anna's unstintingly positive account
of her sister that made Rika suspicious. Did she really not feel any
resentment towards someone who'd wrought so much disruption
upon her life? Did Anna have pastimes, or friends with whom she
could share things? Rika found herself wondering. She wanted to
believe that Anna had at least a sliver of a world for herself which
had nothing to do with her sister.

'This car park here used to be my grandparents' house. My family
is the landlord here.'

Saying this, she looked at the stretch of asphalt over the field. The five or six cars parked there were heaped with snow, and there was a large faded sign positioned by the road. From the letters she could make out reading '... metres ahead' Rika surmised that it was for Suntopia World.

'My grandfather passed away when I was in my fourth year of primary school, and my grandmother a year later. My sister was close with my grandmother, and I think her death came as a shock. I imagine that was another reason for her not returning.'

They arrived back at the Kajii house. The dustiness and the smell of the kerosene heater that came spilling out as soon as Anna opened the door already seemed like something from a long time in the past. Rika felt her body warming and relaxing. She was starting to get used to the place, she supposed.

'Would you mind if I used your bathroom?'

It went against the code of etiquette while visiting somewhere professionally, but Rika didn't feel she had much choice.

'Of course. It's just in there.'

Rika entered into the small room beyond the door in the living room that Anna indicated. There was a strong smell of air freshener. Rika pulled her trousers, tights and underwear down in the same movement, and checked for blood. Her thighs were frozen cold. There was no sign of any stain in her underwear, and she felt a rush of relief.

Returning to the living room, she found Reiko and Anna on the sofa leafing through a photo album – they looked like they could be good friends, she thought.

When Rika sat herself down alongside Reiko, she saw a plume of dust rise up, sparkling in the beam of light filtering through the gap in the curtain. From this position, Rika noticed that there was a fireplace behind the TV, filled with stacks of magazines.

'This is my father,' Anna said. Rika looked at the page which she was pointing at. As far as she could tell from the photograph behind its cellophane coating, he wasn't remotely handsome. The man in the image, somewhere in his forties and standing in front of a barbecue in what must have been the garden of this house, was far shorter than she'd imagined. His narrow eyes and heavy eyelids contributed to a somewhat blank expression. His hair was set in place with so much product that it looked as though he were wearing a black cap. A different photo showed him relaxing in front of the fireplace, and in another, he appeared holding a rifle. There were pictures of him with Manako and Anna as young girls wearing expensive-looking kids' clothing, but not a single one featured their mother, Masako. Rika squinted at the image of middle-school-aged Manako standing close beside her father, but her eyes contained only an indistinct darkness, and her mouth was a stubborn straight line. There was nothing there to point to any kind of incestuous relationship.

'This is me in my fourth year of primary school, with my sister. For a while, the principal asked that students be accompanied by an adult on their way to and from school. My mother was busy, so my sister offered.'

Here was Manako at around seventeen in a caramel-coloured double-breasted coat, leading Anna with her school rucksack by the hand down the snow-covered road. Her stature lent her a sense of dignity, so that she fitted in to an almost alarming extent with the mothers around her. Rika found herself smiling.

'Why did you need someone to take you to school and bring you home? You were in the fourth year by this point, no?' Reiko asked unexpectedly, her tone sharp. Anna's gaze stayed focused on the album.

'My mother had started to teach a flower-arranging class in a new cultural centre in Furumachi. She got her teaching qualification when she was living in Tokyo. She got her driving licence, too, so she could drive in. She was a social person, but she didn't fit in well with the housewives around here, so she was delighted to find a job.'

Were all the plants crammed into this room left over from that era? Rika wondered. And the dried flower bouquets and wreaths strewn around – were they, also, Masako's handiwork?

That was why my sister accompanied me … Oh, Mum! You're awake. You should be resting.'

Anna pouted as she spoke, her intonation immediately growing more childish. Rika and Reiko hurriedly stood to their feet and looked in the direction of Anna's gaze. A backlit figure stood in the gloom of the kitchen.

'The pain's not too bad today, so I'm fine to be up. The sekihan should be ready soon. I've been soaking the cowpeas for it since yesterday.'

The woman before them looked to be around sixty.

'I'm Masako, Anna and Manako's mother. Thank you for coming all this way.'

Her low voice had a teacher's clear, firm tone. While Rika and Reiko introduced themselves, Masako began moving around busily, taking out bowls, arranging the chopsticks on the table.

They'd been told that she couldn't move around much on account of her bad back, and she certainly had a pronounced stoop, but both her facial expressions and her movements seemed controlled. She must have changed clothes knowing that they had visitors, Rika thought, taking in her black woollen jumper with sequins worn over leggings. Her hair was dyed a dark brown and cut short, and her diminutive face with its sunken cheeks was almost eclipsed by a pair of spectacles with light purple frames. Her skin was dusted with white powder, and there was something about her youthfulness that made it impossible to take your eyes off her. Rika remembered that herself and Manako Kajii were only two years apart in age, yet owing to her calmness of demeanour and distinctive way of speaking, Rika had been imagining her mother as a woman in her seventies.

'I don't personally like sekihan that much. Please don't feel any obligation to eat it.' Anna's delivery suggested her own reluctance to be put out in any way rather than any consideration of her guests' feelings. Even when they heard the sound of running water from the kitchen, she didn't stop flicking through the album, or show any signs of going to help. Rika had been thinking of her as the strong-willed second daughter who'd sacrificed a marriage to take care of her ailing mother and protest her sister's innocence. But she wondered if in fact living with a parent in her hometown was simply easier than looking after her husband and their household in Tokyo, where there also happened to be a strong media presence. Was it possible that she relied quite heavily on her mother, both financially and in terms of housework? They heard the rice cooker playing a melody that announced the rice was finished.

'Really? But you can tolerate it once in a while, can't you? We've got visitors after all,' Masako said placatingly, looking at Rika and Reiko encouragingly.

'Oh no ... but we wouldn't want to ...' Reiko began, and was cut off by a firm voice.

'No, you must have some. You're hungry, no?'

Steaming plates of sekihan – red rice – and cream stew were arranged on the plastic tablecloth. The dusty interior had taken away their appetites, but Reiko and Rika both sat down at the table, voicing exaggerated compliments.

The bowls and plates were all of assorted shapes and colours, and when Rika thought that these same vessels might, decades ago, have come in contact with Manako's saliva, she felt her throat constricting. She told herself that if she could just ingest some of this food, which Kajii herself had doubtless eaten at some point, then she would be drawing a step closer to her. Manako had said her mother was bad at cooking, but the way the rice was cooked and seasoned impressed Rika. From among the grains of mochi rice stained a faint red poked large, puffy cowpeas. When she lifted the rice to her mouth, it resisted her bite with a pleasing stickiness. The flaky insides of the cowpeas spilled out from their skins, breaking up the rich taste of the rice. The stew, on the other hand, tasted only of the cubed roux, and the carrots and potatoes didn't even seem properly cooked.

'Does this sekihan have a dash of soy sauce in it? It's delicious, it's got real body to it. The cowpeas are perfectly cooked as well. It makes me want another portion.'

Rika could see Reiko's eyes glinting as she spoke. The fact that Reiko was thinking the same as her gave her confidence in her tastebuds' verdict, and she shovelled the rice into her mouth.

'Well spotted! You're absolutely right. When I first ate at my husband's home, around the time I moved to Niigata, I thought how delicious my mother-in-law's sekihan was. That was about the only thing she taught me, the recipe for this.'

Masako's pale cheeks were flushed. Rika didn't have her pinned as a domestic type, but her tickled look after having her cooking complimented made Rika think of a new bride.

'I've never been much of a cook. When we moved here, there were fewer options for eating out, and with my husband being a real foodie, he would make all kinds of demands on me. I grew quite fed up with it, and ended up relying on microwaved and pre-prepared food. The pre-prepared food in the supermarkets here is very good quality. The portions of the deep-fried meat they sell at the butcher's are huge! I'm talking like this!'

Giggling, Masako traced a square shape with her hands.

'At the weekend, my husband would experiment with smoking bacon on blocks of bricks in the garden, or caramelising kilos of onions at a time, or making curry from scratch. The sort of cooking that men do when it's a hobby for them, in other words. And it's fun, all that, because it's an experiment, a special activity that you do when you have the time, and that you don't mind spending money on. For me, though, it was nothing but a pain. In the week, the kids would go on at me to cook the types of dishes their father made.'

Masako frowned, the expression on her face a vivid illustration of the 'pain' that she'd found it to be. There was not a trace of that experimental spirit in this cramped living room. Remembering the fireplace behind the TV, Rika thought of something.

'Did you dispose of your husband's things after he passed away?'

'Yes, we redecorated soon after he died. I threw away all his trophies and paintings that used to be in here.'

Now it was pointed out to her, Rika realised the room didn't even have an altar, as was conventional for a house in which one of the family members had died.

'Seeing his things every day would make us too sad.' Masako lowered her eyebrows into a suitably sombre expression, but Rika could tell she was lying.

'My sister was very angry about it,' Anna said. 'After the funeral, she came back to find all my father's things gone, and the place looking entirely different. She said it was no longer the house that she knew.'

Masako said something conciliatory in response.

It was the winter of her third year of middle school. Right after she and the caretaker had found her father's body in his flat, Rika had called her mother from a public phone box while waiting for the police and forensics team to arrive.

'He's dead? He's definitely dead? Or you still don't know?'

Rika could tell that her mother was being mindful of her feelings, yet she could still hear the trace of exhilaration in her voice. Rather than probing the possibility that he was still alive, her mother wanted to know whether it was established, beyond doubt, that there was no such chance.

'I'll come right away. You don't need to do anything.'

Since finding his body, Rika hadn't set foot in the apartment at all.

Once the post-mortem was complete and the cause of death ascertained, her mother raced into action. Her father's family stubbornly refused to lift a finger, and so her mother organised the funeral more or less single-handedly. Even when, at the wake before the funeral, his parents and relatives had grown hysterical and effectively accused her mother of killing him, she hadn't so much as flinched. Her mother arranged for a professional cleaning firm to visit the apartment. They cleaned the carpet stained with her father's blood and the rooms now stained with tobacco smoke and dust, and threw away all of their family mementoes, save for a few photo albums. When the transformation was complete, the place was sold off. His bank account, together with the small sum of money left in it, were legally handed over to Rika. Rika's mother put the money in it towards Rika's education. She moved with speed and efficiency. She must have played out this scenario in her head several times before it happened, Rika figured. Needless to say, she had no objections to anything her mother did. She was grateful that there was no need for her ever to return to that apartment.

And yet, she couldn't help but feel that her mother had been waiting for her father to die. The indolent lifestyle he led as a form of accusation had continued to cause her suffering.

Rika, who went once a month to visit him in Mitaka, had kept on lying to her mother, telling her that her father was doing well and enjoying living alone, but her version of events was always undermined by other people's accounts. Various interfering women – those living in his block, and the mothers of the kids whom Rika had been to primary school with – would give her updates on what a sad, irresponsible sort of life he was living. Her mother wasn't close with any of these women, and since the divorce they had no connection with her at all. One of them had come to her boutique and, feigning concern, had managed to elicit her mother's new phone number, which made the rounds in no time.

The women would make comments to Rika's mother like: 'His eyes look hollow and I'm worried about him', or, 'the very idea that someone once so stylish has come to disregard his appearance completely', or, 'it seems as though he lives off convenience store food'. 'He's just past fifty but he looks way older,' they'd say, or, 'it's been long enough now, why don't you just go back to him?'

The way the women spoke, it was as if her father was an oversized baby that her mother was neglecting. Even as they affected kindness, their voices were full of envy and anger towards her mother for fleeing her father in pursuit of her own freedom, and for being now in the process of getting her life back on track. Several times Rika had observed her mother put down the receiver and sink to the floor, her hands covering her face.

'I didn't cook her sekihan when she got her first period, like you're supposed to,' Masako said quietly now. 'She was still in her early years of primary school. It seemed so early that I was worried something was wrong with her, and I didn't celebrate it. Is that why she's turned out this way? I wonder. But that can't be the reason, surely.' Masako spoke as if trying to convince herself, and then pursed her pale purplish lips. They were very thin and perfectly straight, nothing like her daughters'.

'My mother never cooked sekihan for me either,' Rika said.

Reiko shook her head dramatically. 'Me either! My parents were barely at home while I was growing up. I get the impression yours is a wonderful home, and everyone under its roof lives so well.'

'Oh! Do you really think so?'

With these words Masako's expression immediately relaxed. Rika understood: here was a woman starved of validation. She had been waiting for it for a long, long time, and her wishes had been continually betrayed.

'My sister used to say that nobody seemed to care that she was the first to get her period. The teacher didn't even congratulate her, although the kids who came first in races and who were top of the class would always be praised.' Anna smiled as she recounted this memory. '"It's so unfair that you don't get praised for what goes on between your legs," she used to say. "You have to publicise it yourself."'

Stunned, Rika rested her chopsticks on the table. The rice in her mouth suddenly tasted faintly sour. There was no indication that Masako was shocked by this pronouncement. With graceful movements, she was serving Reiko a second bowlful of rice.

'That's typical of Manako, only ever thinking about being praised. She was forever neglecting the important things, all the effort and the preparation that go into making a thing happen. All she really liked was eating, and she got so big! I was always telling her to exercise, to cut down on sweets, but she wouldn't listen. If she'd tried a tiny bit harder at school she could have gone to a decent university, but she quit. Such a waste.'

Holding out the bowl to Reiko, Masako smiled a little sheepishly.

'Having you two here like this feels a little like being a mother to lots of daughters!'

It seemed as though their visit had satisfied something within Masako, and she had particularly taken to Reiko. The gaze she turned on her was brimming with affection.

'Manako never brought female friends round, you see. Anna didn't either, really. That was sad for me.'

The look on Anna's face as she ate her stew gave no sense of any awareness she was being spoken of. It appeared that she really did dislike sekihan, and made no move to tuck into her portion. Masako continued speaking, her words pouring out like water released from a dam.

'I'm not suited to staying at home, that's the thing. I was so bored by village life. When I started working at the cultural centre and made friends with the other teachers, I felt like I'd been brought back to life. I started going to tennis and ballet on my way back from work. It was great. I used to be really sporty as a girl – not that you could tell, to look at me now. My husband didn't like me doing all that, though. He put on a good show of being liberal, but he was nothing more than a spoiled boy brought up in provincial Niigata who wanted a stay-at-home wife. His view of women was terribly conservative. You find a lot of left-wing men his age like that.'

'My father was the same. My parents divorced and we lived separately from him, but I know exactly what you mean. My mum and dad met in the student protests, so in theory his politics were progressive.'

At this interjection from Rika, Masako's eyes twinkled.

'Did your mother raise you all by herself then? How impressive. And you turned out to be a journalist on a weekly magazine! You grew up with your mother as your role model. I failed to make either of my girls independent. I wanted to raise them as women with proper jobs, who could fend for themselves.'

Midway through her impassioned outburst, Masako suddenly lifted her head. In the light reflecting from the blanket of snow outside, Rika could clearly see the lines on her face and the loose skin on her neck.

'My daughter didn't kill anybody. I'm sure of that. She was ostentatious and terribly lazy, but I didn't raise her in a way that would allow her to stray from the path that badly. The meaning behind her name is "living close to the truth". My husband spoiled her rotten, and was only interested in the fun parts of childcare, so I also took on the role of the father in his place, and instilled a sense of rules and manners in her. If she hates me for it as a result, it doesn't bother me.'

Masako's eyes were tinged red and her lips trembled. Rika wondered if the mismatched impression she created was to do with the conflict between her confidence in her child-rearing and her lack of trust in her daughter. If she was going to say something, she knew, it had to be now.

'Would you be happy to show us Manako's room?'

'Of course,' Masako said. She got to her feet, ignoring the look that her daughter was casting in her direction.

Anna got up reluctantly after her, and Reiko and Rika followed, climbing the steep staircase in a line. Now that Rika's body was so thoroughly warmed, she felt the coolness of the bare floorboards and the air filtering in through the cracks around the door.

At the top of the stairs were three doors. When Masako reached out an arm towards one, Rika asked, 'If you don't mind my asking, which was your bedroom?'

Anna answered. 'That's my parents' bedroom, there.' She indicated the door opposite. 'My mother now sleeps there alone.'

How had the fast-maturing Manako viewed her parents' bedroom across the hall? Rika tried to recall her own childhood. She'd not once detected any kind of sensual air between her parents, but there had perhaps been times when she'd been frightened by the sexual impulse that she sensed lying behind her father's attacks on her mother.

Finally, they reached Manako's bedroom. An eternity seemed to elapse before the door was opened.

Confronted by a smell like a mixture of glue sticks and mould, Rika blinked. Before her was a smallish room with a grey carpet, furnished with a school desk, a bed, and a bookshelf stretching up to the ceiling. Immediately inside the door was a fitted closet. The bedcovers and curtains were the same navy and green checked pattern. What appeared to be a sheaf of school printouts spilled chaotically from a binder. The electric pencil sharpener was the same model that Rika herself had used, and its chamber was full of pencil shavings. There were no dolls in sight, nothing lacy or frilly.

'Manako loved reading. She was a real bookworm. At her father's insistence, she read from a very young age. She got a commendation from the local library!'

Now Rika looked, she could see several certificates for book reports framed on the walls.

The bookcase was crammed with French classics and contemporary Japanese literature. Hadn't Kajii said that it was Sagan who had brought her together with the first man she dated? Masako was gazing at the books on the shelf with a satisfied expression. When Rika looked at Reiko, she saw she had her camera out again.

'Is it okay to take some photos? Of course they'll only be for internal use. If Rika's going to interview Manako, it'll be really helpful for her to have this room in mind.'

Masako thought for a while, then nodded.

'This interview will change the way the public sees her, I'm sure of it,' Reiko said. 'If we can get people to understand what she's really like ...'

Rika saw that Masako's eyes had teared up at these words. Suddenly the wind hammered at the window, and all of them looked up.

'Oh, the snow's got heavier. Why don't the two of you stay the night, and leave in the morning?'

Surely there could have been no more precious experience as a journalist than staying the night in Manako Kajii's house? Rika was all ready to accept, but Reiko got in first, politely refusing the offer.

As soon as she'd sat herself down at the heated table sunk in the floor, Reiko rolled up the sleeve of her jumper and held out her wrist towards Rika, showing her the inside of her arm.

'Look.'

Reiko's milk-white skin was speckled with swollen red marks. Rika cried out and winced. They were in a restaurant that Kajii had recommended, a place fifteen minutes' walk from Niigata Station, serving rice cooked over an open flame. By the counter that they could see from their seats, skewered fish were hung up in a line at the back of an open fireplace, to which an employee was adding straw. The entire scene resembled something from a fairy tale.

'I'm so itchy! Are you okay?'

'I'm fine. What is it, are you allergic to something?'

'It's fleas! The carpets and the stuffed toys in that place were crawling with them. I just loathe cluttered, unhygienic places like that. They make me feel itchy all over.'

Reiko scratched her bites so forcefully that Rika was sure they would start bleeding. It pained her to see her friend's actions, so uncharacteristically rough.

'Really? Can you still get fleas when it's this cold? Maybe they got you in the cowshed?'

'The cowshed was clean. It was well-ventilated, so the air could circulate.'

'What did you think, then? Of the house.'

The two of them had been avoiding the topic since they got into the taxi outside the Kajiis' door.

Reiko now raised her eyes from her bites and said, candidly, 'It freaked me out! Have you ever seen anywhere that creepy before?'

Her reply startled Rika. She hadn't known Reiko could be so two-faced.

'They're totally bonkers. But I learned a lot. That's the kind of place that serial killers grow up in, I guess. The mother had clearly lost her marbles – going on and on so proudly about her stance on education, when her daughter's a convicted serial killer! And the sister was the same, brushing off anything that wasn't convenient for her. It makes sense that a family like that would give rise to someone like Kajii. There's not a smidgen of doubt in my mind that she's a murderer. Which then makes me think: did she do the father as well? What they said about her only having been home for the funeral was definitely a lie.'

'What would be her motive?' Rika asked, feeling somewhat over-powered by Reiko's fervour.

'My guess would be that he caught wind of the fact that all these old men in Tokyo were giving her money, and gave her a dressing down for the first time. She flew into a rage and pushed him over on the snow. Or else it was a financial issue. One of her men asked her to return his money. When her father refused to give her any, she flew off the handle. Yeah, that must be it.'

'You had a second helping of the sekihan!' As she spoke, Rika could hear she sounded like a petulant child.

'That's what you do to make sure you're liked, though. You're a journalist, surely you know better than anyone that flattery gets you everywhere? It wasn't totally inedible, either. But when I peeked into the kitchen, it looked filthy, and the sink was all greasy and gross. And what's with serving sekihan to journalists when your daughter's been convicted of murder? Plus, using ready-made roux for cream stew when you live in a place with the best dairy products in the country is unforgivable, if you ask me.'

There was something about the tinge of snobbery permeating Reiko's words that made Rika think of Kajii. What was going through Kajii's head right now, as she sat in the Tokyo Detention House on a February evening? Was she thinking about Rika and her trip to Agano? Rika felt sorry for her, sitting alone in her cold cell. The server brought over rice and miso soup, salted salmon, pickles and shiokara, and omelette. In awe once again at the unbridled sweetness of the rice, Rika wished that she could have given some of this repast, the taste of her hometown, to Kajii.

'I don't know … I agree they were somehow out of kilter, set apart from the rest of the world, but I wouldn't have said there was anything particularly *abnormal* about them. It made me think that no matter how good a mother's intentions are in raising her kids, things can go awry, and you end up with a daughter like Kajii.'

'Rika, I think you're losing it. What were you *seeing*? Why didn't you feel it? Did you truly not sense something about that house? I've never been anywhere so creepy in my life.'

Rika felt her earlobes reddening. Was there really something not quite right about her? Or was it Reiko who was the odd one, interfering this much in her friend's work? She felt that her confidence in her powers of judgement had disappeared.

'Where are the bulls kept, I wonder?'

These were Reiko's words after they'd paid and settled into the back seat of a cab. For a moment, Rika had no idea what she was on about. Their time in Akiyama's cowshed already seemed like the distant past.

'They must have their semen taken from them artificially. And if they're producing semen for dairy cows, then they're not being used for meat. How do they live out the rest of their time, in between sperm donations? Is that all there is to them? It's kind of sad to think about.' Hearing Reiko say this, Rika knew instinctively that she was thinking about Ryōsuke.

She'd barely thought about Makoto since coming to Niigata, she realised, but she'd stopped feeling any guilt about such things. The snow outside the window shone, as if competing with the city's neon lights.

* * *

Upon waking, Rika checked her phone. The sky beyond the curtain looked significantly darker than it had the previous morning.

She heard the noise of a hairdryer coming from the bathroom. In a bid to outdo it, she cleared her throat and shouted, 'Akiyama texted! He says he's free from two. If I leave now, I should make it. I'm meeting him in a cafe in the yoghurt factory in Agano. He's only mentioned me, though, so do you mind if I go on this one alone?'

Rika suspected her friend would put up a fight, but the glossy-haired Reiko who now poked her head round the bathroom door nodded docilely. Rika felt a burst of relief at the contrast to yesterday.

'Got it. I'll spend the day doing some Niigata sightseeing, then. I'll pick up the souvenirs on the Kajimana list, too. Where should we convene this evening?'

They ate a leisurely breakfast and then Reiko saw her off at the entrance to the hotel, where Rika got in a taxi to Agano as she'd done the previous day. According to the weather forecast, tonight would bring a snowstorm.

The factory was only small, but the brand of yoghurt they manu-factured was one you often found in Tokyo supermarkets. The place appeared to be a tourist spot, and when she mentioned its name to the taxi driver, he nodded immediately.

Having arrived early, Rika decided to walk around the factory grounds. A long pipe extended from a giant tank, connecting up to a truck emblazoned with the company logo. Was there milk running through it, she wondered? She felt the contents of the pipe were somehow linked with the snowy landscape around. Reiko's words from last night came back to her, and she thought about the fate of the sperm-producing bulls.

She located the small pre-fab cafe in front of the factory. The outdoor terrace with its stone statues and flowerbeds stood covered in a blanket of snow. Stepping up to the entrance, Rika found her nostrils filling with the scent of butter. The staff behind the counter dressed in naval-style uniforms greeted her.

Akiyama was sitting in the bright white interior of the cafe. He got to his feet when he saw her. Dressed in a down gilet and jeans, he looked so much younger than he had done the previous day in his overalls that it was as if she were meeting a different person.

'Thank you so much for agreeing to meet me, I know you're very busy. And thanks again for showing us around yesterday.' Rika took a seat opposite him. A girl in uniform came over to take her order. She requested a yoghurt waffle with whipped cream and a café au lait, apologising to Akiyama for eating on the job. The waffles here had been on Kajii's list, and she felt she needed to try them.

'It's perfect timing, as it turns out. I managed to get hold of a stand-in who occasionally covers for me. It's good to give my wife and parents a break sometimes, too. You're going home tomorrow after all.' As he spoke, he poured sugar and a generous helping of milk into his paper cup full of coffee.

'A dairy farm stand-in? I didn't know such a thing existed. If you let me have the receipt, I can reimburse you.'

'Could you? That would be great. Traditionally, us dairy farmers have no days off, you see. Recently, though, by getting outside help, I've been able to make time for studying and training. That would be unthinkable for people of my parents' generation, but if we don't go on updating the industry and finding new approaches, we'll never manage to make it an appealing job for the younger generations, and we'll be left with nobody to take over.'

Rika's coffee and waffles were brought to the table. The whipped butter had already started melting across the waffles' latticed brown surface, creating a golden trickling waterfall that pooled in their hollows. Rika bit into the dough, savouring how juicy and moist it had become with all the butter it had absorbed, with a pleasant salt-iness. She must have been making a satisfied face, because Akiyama now snickered and looked embarrassed.

'That reminds me … Manako loved the waffles here. She used to come here often and eat several at a time. Her mother would tell her off.'

'What were your feelings about her?'

'I didn't feel much either way, to be honest. Our families were friendly, so we used to play together a lot when we were younger. She'd sometimes come to watch our cows giving birth. Her father would give us sweets and gifts from Tokyo, which I loved. Her mother was still healthy at that time but she always seemed a bit prickly, and I wasn't so fond of her. By middle school, though, we'd stopped saying hi when we ran into each other.'

Rika wondered what Kajii had made of this manly boy of her own age.

'She's said repeatedly, both in court and to me directly, that she was always mature for her age, and as a result she stood out and was the subject of a lot of attention. Her sister said something similar. Is that true?'

'It might be true that she stood out, but I think that was mostly because she was a little bit odd … She was very quiet, and you could never really tell what she was thinking.'

A couple with two children sat down at the next table. Akiyama raised a hand in greeting and the man bowed his head. Had this man also been to school with Kajii? Rika wondered.

'As for whether she was mature, she always seemed a bit babyish to me. She was a slow child, who ate vast amounts like a cow, and never seemed quite all there.' At this, Rika rested her plastic fork, which had been hovering above her second waffle, on her plate.

'She might have been big, but she wasn't bullied or anything. Our class at school were a good bunch.'

This is the kind of person, Rika thought, who is forever a member of the majority, and lives a perfectly smooth life. She felt a pang of pity for Kajii, for having to live as a girl with an irregular-sized body in this landscape, where crops were hard to grow, and everyone could see everything for miles around. The little girl at the next table had managed to get the creamy waffle she was eating all over her face.

'It's not like in the weekly magazines, where they make out that a particular someone is the talk of the town. It's the same in Tokyo and everywhere else, right? I know this is a small town, and there's little in the way of entertainment, and it might look to you as if there's nothing here, but everyone's busy thinking about their futures, their families. So long as you have the internet, you could be living anywhere.'

His voice had taken on a pragmatic tone.

'I don't know anyone in our class who fancied her. We were neighbours for all that time, but I never heard of anyone having a crush on her. Doesn't that seem unusual to you?' He tilted his head, without malice.

This is it, Rika thought, opening her eyes wide. This is what Kajii had stolidly averted her eyes from: this unrestrained, unflinching evaluation made by men of her own age with a very ordinary perspective.

'Hearing the reports of the case, though, I didn't find it particularly bizarre. All of the men were people she met online – they were either elderly or didn't have much experience with women. It makes sense that there'd be a demand for someone like Manako among people like that. After you gave me your business card, I thought for a while about whether I should meet you or not.'

The girl at the next table was being scolded by her mother. Akiyama smiled and took a sip of his coffee. Rika suddenly found herself nauseated by the smell of sweet waffles and butter pervading the restaurant.

'Like I said, I used to be quite close with the Kajii family, so I feel a little guilty, talking to you like this. We've had requests for coverage from journalists in the past, but my parents have turned them all down. But I felt I wanted to speak to you. I guess at heart, I like a bit of entertainment. Maybe I've been lacking in stimulus. And something occurred to me.'

Akiyama put down his coffee and leaned in slightly.

'Could it be that a certain impression of someone is fabricated after the fact? One winter, when I was seventeen, I heard rumours about Manako and a weird older man. At the time, everyone had their heads full of getting into university and what they were going to do after school ended, so we forgot about them almost immediately.'

'You're talking about her going around with an older man from Tokyo, right? Rumours circulated that it was compensated dating, and it was on the back of those that she left the area.'

'That's the story that's been told by the weekly magazines, for sure. And I guess that's right in a way. There's nothing inaccurate about that story. Nobody's telling lies. But it doesn't really capture the way things felt at the time. The reality was a bit different. Our high school was about two kilometres from here. These days it's a school specifically designed to prepare kids for university, but at the time it had a lot of dropouts and so on, and there was plenty of dating going on among the kids. If anything, Manako seemed kind of babyish in comparison to the others.'

Nobody praises you for what's going on between your legs unless you yourself say something about it …

'It wasn't really that people saw her in a different light after that. Maybe they'd grin and give her the look, but it was done in a protective way. Her being seen walking about with an old man was really neither here nor there. The media at the time was flooded with stories of older men paying to date and sleep with schoolgirls, anyway.'

While Rika hadn't experienced being an adolescent in a mixed school, she could imagine it well enough. Most likely, the lack of interest that the boys of her own generation showed in her had been the toughest thing for Kajii to bear.

However hard she looked at him, she couldn't see any strong emotions in Akiyama as he sat before her. She couldn't sense any of the curiosity, irritation and envy toward Kajii that the people around Rika all displayed. In this town, where it was impossible to hide anything, Kajii had just been an unremarkable sort of a girl who ate a lot. That was the sum total of his knowledge about her.

Since he'd taken the trouble to make the time to see her, Rika asked him a few questions about the latest developments in dairy farming, and Akiyama answered each of her enquiries clearly and cogently.

By the time that she thanked him and took her leave, the sky was fully clouded over. She considered a tour of the factory, but it seemed wiser to get back to Niigata. When she took her phone out to call a cab, she noticed a missed call from Reiko. As the ringtone sounded, she gazed at Suntopia World in the distance. When would she next see this place? she wondered. Then she heard Reiko's voice.

'Rika, I'm in Agano. I followed you when you left the hotel. I lied to you. I think we should go to Kajii's house again. I'm heading there now. Come as soon as you can.'

'What? You can't just do that, Reiko!'

But Reiko had already hung up. As Rika took in the situation, the anger came spurting up inside her. She couldn't keep up with Reiko's furious pace any longer. The Kajii house wasn't far, so she decided to walk there. While feeling bad for even thinking it, she found herself wondering if the reason Ryōsuke had begun keeping his distance from Reiko had nothing to do with finding her sexually attractive, but because he was sick of her rushing headlong into decisions without taking others' feelings into account. She had her vision of how things should be, and anybody who didn't agree was excluded from consideration. Just like when Rika had warned her friend in all seriousness about the dangers of giving up work, and Reiko had refused to listen.

It wasn't even evening but the sky above her was as dark as night. When she rang the intercom at the Kajiis' house, Anna's voice announced that the door was open.

Inside the living room, Reiko was already sitting with Anna on the sofa. Reiko glanced at her, and then, before Rika could utter a word, turned her body towards Anna and said, so that Rika could hear, 'There's something I've always found strange, and that's how nobody knows anything about the man your sister was going out with in the winter of her seventeenth year. Did he really exist?'

'There was definitely an older man who my sister was close to, yes.' Anna seemed visibly perturbed by this question. Her voice was hushed.

'Leave it, Reiko. I mean, Ms Sayama,' Rika interrupted, but Reiko ignored her. Feeling she had no choice, Rika sat down next to her.

'I think the media have talked to most of the people in your sister's class at school, and I didn't expect any new information to emerge from any of them, so I decided to try another route. I went to visit the primary school I saw in your photo album. There was a teacher there who could remember back to when you two were at school. He introduced me to a girl who was in your year, and is now working as the librarian there.'

Rika looked at Reiko, her eyes wide with disbelief. Reiko was no longer even making eye contact with her.

'They both remembered the incident well. The reason she started taking you into primary school in your fourth year wasn't because of the snow – for the kids around here, a bit of snow is nothing. No, it was because of reports that there was a prowler in the area. What concerned the local parents wasn't the safety of the children, though, but that of the prowler. The children had developed a game among themselves. They used to go after the man in a group and torment him. The rougher boys would throw stones at him – one time they even hit his legs with a baseball bat. The parents started coming along to keep a watch over the boys' violent behaviour. The time it was happening perfectly coincides with the time when your sister started seeing her older man. Apparently he took an especial liking to you, is that right? The teacher found it strange even now how your parents hadn't seemed particularly worried about it when they'd been told.'

Anna's eyes seemed to be taking in nothing. Reiko leant forward, so as to encroach upon her field of vision, then gave a shrug in Rika's direction. While overpowered by Reiko's force, Rika felt her confidence in herself wavering. The whole situation was too much to be borne.

'Both Rika and I went to girls' schools, albeit different ones. In Rika's school, she was the prince, a kind of substitute for a male presence. There's always one, in every girls' school. Get a bunch of girls together, with no opportunity for romance, and everybody ends up wanting something to feast on, even if it's not the real deal. Everyone wants somebody of their own to fall in love with, even if that love is fake.'

A young girl maturing faster than everybody around her.

A girl who had formed the powerful sense that she was different from others. Yet her rich inner world was of woefully little interest to those around her. Leaving aside her father and her sister, nobody paid her any attention. Her brain and her body were developing, but nobody attempted to come near her. Yes, thought Rika, she must have been impatient. Back at her girls' school, even as she'd joyfully played the role of the school prince, Rika had also felt a sense of urgency. Sometimes the worry she had – that this period of her life when she was at her most beautiful would be all used up by the girls around before she was *discovered* as a woman – would grow so intense that she wanted to curl up into a ball.

'Your sister wasn't the focus of everyone's attention, as you keep claiming. I'm right, aren't I? Your sister as you saw her and your sister as she was perceived by the town are two separate entities. You must have been aware of that rift.'

'But my sister—'

'There was just one time when she attracted attention, and that was when, in the winter of her seventeenth year, she was seen around town with an older man. The exact same period that the prowler was lurking around your primary school. What happened then, between you and your sister?'

Reiko's gaze was transparent and unerring as the bright white snowscape of Agano.

'How old do you think I was when I got my first period?' Anna said, after a pause. 'Fifteen. Six years later than my sister.'

About the same age as me, Rika thought.

'When I finally got mine, my mother cooked me sekihan out of relief. My sister's first period was unusual, but mine came at a normal age. Compared to the kids in my year I was immature, and physically petite as well. I wasn't bullied, but I think they saw me as a bit stupid. But my sister was always kind to me. More than either of my parents, it was my sister who looked out for me. When they found out that the man had been speaking to me, my parents weren't particularly concerned, even when the teachers warned them about it. They were always fond of me, but to them, I was a cute little thing, like a pet. I was never really seen as a person in my own right in this house. Maybe the idea that I'd be seen in a sexual light didn't ring true …'

As she spoke, Anna's gaze was fixed on the photograph framed on the wall of her and her sister as young girls.

'It started off as a kind of a game. I can't remember how old he was, the man. He wasn't exposing himself or anything, but as I was leaving school he'd stare at me, and ask me where I was from. He wore a face mask, so nobody could make out his features properly. The fact that he'd singled me out like that earned me the class's attention, which I was more pleased about than scared by. Like the teacher told you, we began developing these games with him – let's get the weird man! and all that. At the time, there was a craze for these manga and anime series featuring a gang of young detectives. Kids getting together to solve a problem in a way that won them the admiration of the grown-ups. I happened one day to bump into him on my way home from school, and I followed him. I was thinking I'd impress them all the next day with my reports of how brave I'd been. He went inside a barn on Akiyama's farm, in which they kept hay for the cows to graze on. When I peered in through a crack, the door suddenly swung open. I fell inside onto the hay. The man reached out a hand towards me. The next thing I knew, I was lying looking up at the ceiling, and his hand was inside my knickers. I was so astonished, I got to my feet and bolted outside. I found a hoe leaning against the shed, and without thinking about what I was doing, hit him on the head with it.'

The words fell falteringly from Anna's mouth.

'Blood flew across the snow. I remember being startled by that. It was the same bright red you saw in films and TV programmes. The man was crouching down, cradling his head in his hands. I thought maybe I'd killed him, and if the truth ever got out, I'd be in huge trouble with my parents. As soon as I got home, I broke down in tears and confessed to my sister. My sister told me to leave it to her. Leave it with me, she said, and don't tell a soul about it. She went out that evening by herself to find him, and didn't come home all night. My mother was furious, my dad was out of his mind with worry, and I couldn't sleep a wink. The next morning she came back. She refused to say where she'd been, even when my mother slapped her. Later on, she told me that he hadn't died. She'd found him collapsed by the barn and taken him to hospital. She said that he was mentally ill, but he wasn't a bad man.'

In fact, Anna should have been angry. She should have cried, and been repulsed by what had happened to her. She should have got the adults around her involved.

'My sister said that he was just starved of female tenderness. If he had only been given some female affection, he wouldn't have ended up that way. She told me that she'd become friends with him.'

The first person outside of her immediate family to look favourably at Kajii was a sex offender. She had reworked the story to give it a more palatable taste, transforming it into the one of a mysterious older man and a precocious young girl in a secret relationship. It was through making contact with the worldview of a sex offender that her life had changed.

In that worldview, the woman was to blame for everything. Sexual assault took place because women led men on, then gave them nothing. Men who were introverted, timid, and couldn't express their feelings well couldn't find partners. The reason behind Japan's declining population was all those women who judged men solely on their appearance and the size of their pockets.

It was all women's fault. But she was different. She was a goddess, shining bright.

'She told me that men are weak, sensitive and tender creatures, so you had to forgive them a bit of rudeness and interference. That he probably approached me because I led him on in some way. He'd only behaved the way he had because he was lonely. It's a situation that's come about because women are frosty towards men, and treat them like idiots. It's the fault of women like our mother. She told me I had to do everything I could to make sure I didn't turn out like that too.'

Rika heard Reiko stifle a gasp, but Anna carried on.

'I remember that when my father passed away my sister said the same thing – that it was my mother's fault. That if she'd taken better care of him, it wouldn't have happened. She shouldn't have let him go out on a snowy day in boots with such little grip.'

According to Kajii, men were like children with no capacity to make decisions of their own – even her most beloved father. But could Rika really claim to be that different?

She wanted to say that she hated her father, that it was only natural that he'd died in the way he had given the choices he'd made. And yet, there was part of her that felt sorry for him. When she thought of her father dying all alone in that apartment full of memories of their family, the sadness was unbearable. It was because she and her mother had left him that her father had died – there was no doubting that. She and her mother had killed him. If they'd stuck with him, managed to keep him in check just as the good wife and good daughter that society required them to be were supposed to do, managed the juggling act needed to maintain his good mood, then they might have been able to live together as a family. Even though Rika knew in her heart of hearts that any kind of connection that demanded that much effort to sustain was fraudulent, even though she was aware of how hurt her mother would be if she ever knew Rika thought this way, there was no doubting that some part of her did believe all this. If she'd been better at suppressing her ego and her feelings of hatred towards her father, if she and her mother hadn't gone after their own freedom, if they'd hadn't ignored her father's cries for help … What Rika regretted above anything was …

But no, this wasn't right. She was being sucked into Kajii's way of thinking. She bit down hard on her lip, desperately trying to bring herself round. Her own past wasn't relevant right now. If she didn't manage to draw a line between the two, she really would become just as Reiko suggested she was becoming.

Anna continued in a feeble voice. 'Talking to my sister, I started to feel like it was all my fault. If I hadn't set out to get him, then none of it would have happened. From that point on, I never spoke about it with anybody. Not even to the teachers at school.'

Anna gave a helpless smile.

'It was at that time my sister started cooking. She'd make bento boxes and bake cakes to give to him. She told me that it made her happy to see how, each time he ate her food, he'd get a little better. She didn't tell me what he did, or where he lived. All she said was that he lived alone, and that he was starved of home-cooked food.'

The two were co-conspirators, and comrades. Out on those cold, exposed fields, they had each other.

'I don't think he was interested in grown women. At seventeen, my sister already had the body of an adult, so I doubt that there was anything of that nature between them. My sister was a terribly serious person with a strong sense of personal responsibility. She attempted to give him a new life, and continued to cover up my crime. It's possible that he's on her side, even now. Maybe he was jealous of the other men, and killed them off. Maybe my hitting him in the head sent him crazy. If that's the case, then it's all my fault.'

With this, Anna burst into tears.

'Stop your crying.'

Masako had appeared and stood directly behind her daughter. Looking up at her from where she sat on the sofa, Rika thought she looked exactly like Manako – those huge, blank eyes like black grapes. She was petite, but there was a certain girth to her chest, an overpowering sense of weight. Rika felt as though the plants in the room were reaching out to wrap their tendrils around her. She met the button gaze of one of the soft toys.

'Not in front of guests! It won't do. You shouldn't be dredging up the past like that. What's the point in remembering those things now?'

She knew it wasn't the time for it, but Rika's attention was captured by the snowstorm outside the window. Would they be able to get back to Niigata that evening? Maybe this time they really would have to sleep in this house.

Feeling an itch on the inside of her arm, she turned over her wrist to see several of the same swollen red marks that Reiko had shown her the previous night.

CHAPTER NINE

It was early evening but the sky above the platform was already a deep indigo. The cold, clear air seemed to absorb all the noise in the vicinity – the sounds of the train, the tannoy announcements, even the chatter of the other passengers seeing each other off. It was a peaceful colour, peaceful enough to make you forget the snowstorm of the previous night. Rika's body had grown accustomed to the cold now – it was hard for her to imagine that this time tomorrow, she would be back in her office, soporifically warm and so dry that her skin would grow chapped.

'I hope it doesn't melt before you get to Tokyo. The train will probably be well heated.' Reiko gestured to the Sado butter at the top of the paper bag full of edible souvenirs. In accordance with Kajii's list, they'd hurriedly picked up the yellow box with the cow on it in the dairy section of the supermarket at Niigata Station.

'Will you really be okay by yourself?' Rika asked Reiko, who had announced that she would stay one more night and explore Niigata before taking advantage of the newly opened Hokuriku Line to visit her hometown in Kanazawa Prefecture. If Rika's memory served her right, it was at least five years since Reiko had last been back. The previous time was to attend the funeral of a beloved teacher from primary school, and while there, she'd barely seen her parents. The alarming intensity she'd displayed in pursuing Kajii's family had vanished like melted snow.

Both of them had spent most of the morning in bed. The previous evening, resisting Masako's entreaties to stay, they had got in a taxi that had crept across the snow up to the house. The visibility had been terrible and they'd stopped several times, but eventually reached Niigata. By the time they arrived at the hotel they were both exhausted, but the adrenaline coursing through Rika's body had made it hard to get to sleep.

Past midday, the two of them had visited the head of PR at the Niigata Prefectural Police Department. Their hope was to investigate the sex offenders who had been arrested in the area from December 1997 onwards, but the officer hadn't been able to help with cases that far back. Rika would try to get hold of the list once she was back in Tokyo. Naturally, there was no telling whether Kajii's guy would be on it or not. It was perfectly possible that he had remained on the run, had never been tried in court, and continued to prey on young girls to this day. Perhaps he had gone along with Kajii to Tokyo for her university entrance exams, and lived with her from that point on. For someone with as much financial clout as Kajii, it wouldn't be so complicated to provide for a man and keep him hidden.

With an almost beatific expression on her face, Reiko said, 'I'm not anticipating that my relationship with my parents will change. If I can just meet with Mrs Tajima, the housekeeper, then I'll be happy. She's the only person I truly think of as family. I don't know if she still works at my parents' house, but she sends a New Year's card every year and her address hasn't changed, so she must still live close by, with her husband. I really hope Melanie, our collie, is doing well.'

What a strange person Reiko was, Rika thought. She considered her best friend of ten years. There was the woman with the air of a thirteen-year-old girl, and there was the woman who had shoved Rika aside to obstinately interrogate Kajii's family. It didn't seem that just one of those was the true Reiko, but rather that both personas were aspects of her whole. The Rika of this moment could appreciate that fully. The person she'd been in the past hadn't been able to accept the slightest contradiction. She hadn't tolerated the incursion of even a tiny bit of seasoning to enrich the overall taste.

'I'm sorry, Rika,' Reiko now said, her voice so quiet it was almost drowned out by the roar of the wind. 'I've been a real pain. I got ahead of myself. Hearing you talk about Kajii made me anxious. I felt like you were being consumed by her, just like her victims. Although really, that's a fancy way of saying I was just jealous.'

After spurting this all out at once, Reiko bowed her head sheepishly. With her thumb and forefinger, Rika pinched what little flesh there was on Reiko's cheek to take hold of. Reiko squirmed ticklishly, and Rika saw the sparse flesh turn pink and tremble. The white vapour of their breath blended in the air. There was the faint scent of the piping hot onigiri that they'd eaten in the restaurant just before. Reiko had ordered salmon, and Rika the salted salmon roe. It was incredible to Rika how easily her appetite had returned, even after everything she'd gone through the day before.

'I like that unstable, typhoon-like part of you, Reiko. Even if it takes me by surprise sometimes and, if I'm honest, infuriates me too. Besides, of the two of us, it's me who should be apologising. I got so invested in Kajii that I wasn't seeing certain things. I'm so glad I had you here with me. My eyes have been opened, honestly. You're way better suited to journalism than I am. I realised that yesterday, and felt ashamed.'

Reiko's big eyes were open wide, looking up at her. Her lips trembled. The wind went rushing past them.

'Reiko, you should be working. It doesn't matter what kind of job. It's such a waste to leave all that talent of yours untapped. I feel pretty sure that once you're no longer spending all your time at home worrying, your relationship with Ryōsuke will gradually improve. You just have to choose a workplace that makes it possible to combine your work with having a family. I've got your back. And let's book a holiday, a proper holiday, the two of us. I'll take time off. Your relationship with Ryōsuke is important, but that's not all that you are. If it gets too hard, you can always come to me.'

'My prince is being princely,' Reiko said. Her tone was light-hearted but her eyes were tinged red. Looking up at the LED display on the platform, Rika saw that her train was about to leave. The two friends were interlocking gloved fingers, like a young couple reluctant to part from one another.

As Rika stepped up onto the train, Reiko said, 'I think there's something I got wrong, before. It's not that you've become consumed by Kajii ... It's all to do with your dad, isn't it? The reason why you're hooked by this case.'

Her look was one of total seriousness. Rika had never had a proper conversation with Reiko about her father's death. The gap between the train and the platform separating them seemed dark and fathomless.

'Misaki told me about it once when you were out. Back when we were at university. She was really concerned that it had scarred you.'

An announcement rang out down the platform, advising of the train's imminent departure. Passengers slipped past Rika. Realising that she was in the way, she hurriedly flattened herself against the wall by the train door.

'I think it would have turned out the same way, whatever anybody had done, however hard they'd tried. It wasn't your fault. But I'm guessing you feel like you ... caused it somehow, right?'

Rika found herself unable to nod. Reiko looked embarrassed. Rika could tell that her friend was selecting her words carefully so as not to hurt her, even though the time they had to speak was fast running out. Her hair was stuck to her face with static. Rika succeeded in raising her frowning eyebrows and lifting up the corners of her mouth into a smile.

'Thank you, for being concerned about me. But I'm fine. Look after yourself, okay? Enjoy Niigata, and your trip back home.' She gave a little wave, her hand hovering at her chest, like a schoolgirl. In truth – in truth, she hadn't spoken to anybody about her father's death. Not even to her mother. Reiko dropped the subject, let her shoulders relax and smiled.

'You too! Look after yourself. And make sure the butter doesn't melt before you get home.'

No sooner had Reiko finished speaking than the automatic doors hissed shut in front of them. They both mouthed 'Bye!' Before she knew what she was doing, Rika had pressed her hand, her forehead, the tip of her nose against the ice-cold glass of the window. Reiko's figure on the platform grew smaller and smaller, until she disappeared behind a veil of snow. And yet, Rika continued to stand there, straining her eyes, attempting to brand the after-image of her friend onto her retinas. She couldn't fathom why, but she had the feeling she might never see her again.

Turning the door handle to her apartment, she was met with a blast of cold air. A crisp smell, like mechanical pencil lead and washing-up liquid, rushed at her, only to disperse in the air of the corridor behind her. It was her own smell, which had for the last few days been wrapped up in Tokyo's cold air and vacuum sealed.

The next moment, Rika was stifling a scream.

In the darkness of the space beyond the narrow entranceway lay her father. She darted into the room without removing her shoes, switched on the light, and let out an enormous sigh.

What had looked like a person face down on the floor was in fact her own trenchcoat, which she'd taken off and left lying there. She remembered now, as if it were an event of the distant past, how days ago, as she was stepping out of the apartment, it had occurred to her that the trenchcoat wouldn't be warm enough for the cold of Niigata, and she'd swapped it for a down jacket.

Inhaling deeply, she returned to the entranceway and took off her boots. She dragged in her bag of souvenirs and overnight bag, and set the air conditioner to heat the room. Without washing her hands, without even taking off her down jacket, she lay spread-eagled face up on her bed. Passing her eyes across the room, she thought to herself again how devoid of character it was. The footfall, the din of the cars and the trains was incomparably louder than it had been in Niigata. Why, then, did it feel so quiet and lonely? Was it because Reiko had been by her side these last few days? Rika lay dozily on her bed until the room got warmer, then sat up to take off her jacket. She didn't have the energy to clean the floor, which she'd dirtied with her outdoor shoes. Visions of the floor of the cowshed and the snowy paths she'd trodden floated up and then disappeared.

Rika's internal kaleidoscope of images and memories settled on Reiko's parting words, and she leapt up off the bed. Reaching inside the bag of souvenirs, she peeled back the lid of the butter box and wailed. The silver-wrapped oblong dented at her touch, its creamy contents ready to ooze out at any second. It needed to be refrigerated immediately, but she'd read that re-chilling melted butter led to a significant deterioration in taste. She'd gone to all that trouble to buy Sado butter; she wanted to eat it at its best. What recipes involved large amounts of softened butter? Mulling the question, Rika opened the fridge door. If she were a baker like Kajii, she could use up a whole stick of butter easily, but not only did she not have an oven, she didn't have any flour or eggs either. Nor any rice, bread or noodles, come to think of it. In fact, all she had were two large, sprouting potatoes, cowering in the vegetable drawer. How had they got there? She hadn't bought them herself. Then it came to her: one of her colleagues had been handing them out at the office, wrapped in paper. Had they been growing at his parents' house, or had he bought them while on a work trip? She couldn't recall.

Rika shifted the potatoes into a colander and moved them over to the sink, trembling involuntarily at how cold the tap water was. She gouged out the malevolent-looking sprouts with a knife, then put the potatoes in a pan, filled it with water, and lit the stove. After a little time, white steam with a delicate, starchy aroma filled the bone-dry apartment. The feeling of desolation from before began to wane, and Rika stood looking down at the two potatoes, sitting lumpen amid the rising steam.

Still standing, she checked her phone, and started replying to her work correspondence. With every message she sent, she felt herself being dragged back into the world of normality. She had texts and emails from both Makoto and Kitamura, but she put off replying to them for the moment. Periodically she would stick a cooking chopstick into the potatoes to check on their progress. After a few tries, the chopstick passed smoothly through the potato flesh without any resistance. She transferred the boiled potatoes onto a plate and brought them over to the table, together with the soy sauce and the butter. The skins had split open, and their soft white insides sparkled generously.

She took a knifeful of the butter clinging to the silver paper, so soft it offered virtually no resistance, and dropped it into the holes in the potatoes' skins. It was absorbed mercilessly fast by the granules inside, which soon took on a yellow hue. Rika sprinkled on a few drops of soy sauce, then pressed her hands together. 'Itadakimasu,' she said, and tucked in to the potatoes with a fork. The hot potatoes engorged with butter crumbled apart in her mouth and the steam rose up to the back of her throat. Inside her mouth, the mixture transformed into a smooth-textured cream, heavy and rich, which spread out hotly across her tongue.

The Sado butter was relatively light in its taste, but had the same warmth and body as the other dairy products she'd sampled in Niigata. The soy sauce drew out the sweetness and texture of the potatoes, and the hand with which Rika held her fork moved incessantly.

The next thing she knew, the two potatoes had disappeared, along with almost all of the butter. She lay down, a delicious sated feeling in her stomach. She had managed to soothe herself, and of that she felt proud.

Maybe there was little separating Kajii's victims and Rika. Maybe, if you had to pin it down, the difference resided in whether or not you were able to boil up some vegetables when the mood took you and season them to your taste.

'Dad,' Rika mumbled, and felt her windpipe constrict. Perhaps a fragment of potato had got stuck. The word – dad – was one she'd not said for almost twenty years. He had been only fifty-two.

He hadn't been such a bad person. All this time, she had taken care only to remember the bad things about him, because otherwise the sorrow was too much to bear. Her childhood birthdays, Christmas – she'd definitely felt his love for her then, as something real.

If the ambulance men were to be trusted, he'd died a painless death. It had been a 'curtain suddenly falling' sort of a death, they'd said. What had he felt in his last moments? What had he seen, lying in his home that was crowded with memories of his family? Rika's vision momentarily distorted.

When she lifted her head, the thin potato skin left on her plate was quivering in the hot draught of the air conditioner. Rika burped a potato-scented burp. She would grow old and most likely not have kids, until one day she died alone, either in this apartment or in a place not unlike it, leaving nothing behind her. This much she realised now, with clarity. She was her father's daughter. That was inescapable. What mattered, then, was not to let those aspects of her get out of hand. She had to do all she could, under her own steam, to make the small details of her life as rich and fulfilling as they could be. That way, she thought, things would feel less desolate, even if the outcome was the same.

A resolution came to her, in a flash. Before she died, she wanted to pour everything she had into cooking a proper meal for someone – the kind of feast she'd seen in picture books as a child, with a whole turkey and an iced cake. Merely thinking about it made her chest light up. It wasn't in her nature to cook proper home-made food for someone else. But the truth was, she was sick of cooking just for herself.

And there was one thing she knew for certain: Makoto wouldn't be the person she cooked it for.

She swept the layer of brown film that had formed across the surface of the milky tea to the side of the cup, creating deep pleats. The cafe was decked out in wood, and crowded with a young female clientele. Having realised that they didn't need alcohol to feel comfortable around one another, Rika and Shinoi had decided it was better to meet in places like this one.

'Soy sauce and home-made miso … Quite unexpected gifts for a bachelor,' Shinoi laughed as he took the presents she'd bought him out of the bag.

'I considered getting you sake, since it's a rice-producing region, but then I thought that you probably drink enough with people from work. So I figured I'd get you something that you'd have to use at home. With this, you'll be able to boil and fry vegetables, right?'

'I've been played … This is your way of ensuring I'm no longer incapable of cooking at home.'

Despite the proliferation of young women in the cafe, Shinoi didn't seem like a fish out of water. There was no intimidating quality to his face, in a way that Rika sensed was tied up with him being the father to a daughter.

'It's okay, I bought the same things for myself too. You and I can make an effort together. Look at this app I found. It's got all these straightforward recipes using simple ingredients, which only take five or ten minutes to prepare. The first step could be to boil some rice, and combine it with miso soup and an easy side dish.'

Rika held out her smartphone. Since she'd decided that she didn't mind being seen as interfering, the tension between them had vanished, and their interactions had taken on a nice rhythm that resembled what she had with Reiko.

'Learning about Agano's culinary culture helped me understand Kajii's scathing attitude towards the Japanese pressure to be thin, and her willingness to be fixated by food. I'm going to take this as an opportunity to start cooking properly. I'm thinking I might attend Le Salon de Miyuko.'

'Isn't it closed, still?' Shinoi spoke in a lowered tone, shifting his gaze from the presents he'd received to look at Rika.

'I got one of my contacts to look into it. Apparently she's giving classes in her home, away from the eyes of the paparazzi, and only to former students. I'm going to see if I can get in.'

'They'll be on high alert. It'll be no mean feat to muscle your way in. That said, I do think that Le Salon de Miyuko must have been the turning point for Kajii.'

'I think so too. Why on earth would she have voluntarily taken part in exactly the sort of gathering of women that she was so wary of? If she wanted to learn authentic cooking methods, there are other, more reasonably priced schools with more brand power out there. She could have gone to a mixed cooking school. They must be perfect places for men and women to meet.'

Shinoi took a sip of his milky tea, still hot, and looked openly at Rika.

'You found something in Niigata, didn't you? You seem totally different from before you went.'

When she dug into her apple pie, the caramel-coloured insides came spilling out.

'I need a list of the sex offenders arrested in Agano from December 1997 onwards. You don't have contacts for any journalists who were in Niigata around that time and might have some affiliation with the police there, do you?'

'I'll look into it,' he said, nodding. Rika had given up feeling guilty about asking for information and offering nothing in return. She now believed that if Shinoi wanted something, he would ask her for it. If that happened, she would use whatever means available to her to get it for him. Even if it was impossible right now, she would build a relationship between them that was, in the long term, of a give-and-take nature.

Back in the lift of her office building, she pulled out her phone to see a message from Makoto.

Are you free to meet tonight? I'd like to hear about Niigata.

On reading the message she realised that she'd forgotten to buy him a present. She hurried to the staff kitchen where that morning she'd left two Le Lectier-flavoured yōkan on the trolley, along with a note saying 'Presents from Niigata! Help yourself.' It was just past 3 p.m. Her hope was that there might be one left, but as she got inside Yū was helping herself to the final slice.

'Ah, all gone, is it?'

Without any guilt, Yū placed the last bite of the bean jelly in her mouth and said, 'Of course it disappeared in no time! It's so juicy and delicious. It's like biting into a whole pear. I'm definitely going to buy some just for myself. Do you think they'd sell it in the Niigata shop on Omotesandō?'

'I didn't even know that existed! And they sell Niigata souvenirs there? Where is it?'

Rika memorised the address Yū passed on, thinking she'd have to find a way of dropping in. She felt sheepish about telling Makoto that she'd forgotten to buy him anything. Yū was wearing her Scream hoodie. Noticing Rika's gaze, Yū looked down at herself, and said, 'I couldn't make it home last night, and this was the only change of clothes I had with me.'

'Does Fujimura wear that kind of stuff too?'

'Yeah, I think he spends quite a lot on merch. I know he buys several copies of all the CDs: one for keeping, one for listening to and then the rest for giving out to other people to spread the word. My guess would be that he only wears stuff like this when nobody's looking, though. I think it must be quite tough for the wives and girlfriends of those types of fans, you know?'

Rika had begun the conversation in the spirit of idle chitchat, but it had managed nonetheless to strike right at the heart of things. Yū seemed oblivious, toying with the yōkan box as if wishing she could magic more into existence.

Making an effort to keep her tone light, Rika said, 'But he seems like a good person, no? He works a lot, and seems to understand women.'

Yū moved her gaze up to the shelves over her head, and nodded slowly.

'Yes, he'd be the kind of boyfriend you could feel proud of in front of other people. But he's a bit ...'

Yū peeled off a paper-thin sliver of yōkan that was stuck to the knife, and put it in her mouth. Her tongue was a shade of pale pink that reminded Rika of a small animal.

'Don't you get the sense that he's the type who wouldn't really let you in? I get the sense he'd never volunteer the information that he liked an idol group, for example.'

Rika forced a smile.

'But maybe that's nothing to worry about,' Yū went on. 'It sounds like he's giving up on Scream, anyway.'

'Really?'

'Yeah, his favourite member, Megumi, has put on loads of weight. It was all over the news – didn't you see it? She's the front girl of the band. She's fourteen and smack bang in the middle of puberty, so it's totally normal for her to swell out a bit, but Mr Fujimura was saying he felt disillusioned with her. That it showed she wasn't really trying hard enough. It's a shame, I really liked having a fellow Scream fan at work.'

Rika smiled and left the kitchen. Leaning against the wall of the corridor, she replied to Makoto: *Sorry, I can't tonight. I'll message you soon.*

Her fingers did all the work for her. All of a sudden, it struck her that she and Makoto had switched places in terms of their affection for each other. Had that night in the hotel been the turning point?

Back at her desk, a Post-it note in handwriting she recognised announced there was a visitor for her on the ground floor. It was rare for people to show up to see her without an appointment.

Her body was stiff with tension as she made her way downstairs, but the sight that jumped into her vision when she stepped out of the lift brought a sense of relief. Standing in his duffle coat in the lobby while severe-looking editors came and went around him, Ryōsuke appeared defenceless, like a large, good-natured, warm-blooded dog. Perhaps because of the cold, his nose and cheeks looked redder than ever.

'Sorry for showing up out of the blue like this, I know you must be swept off your feet. I heard Reiko went along on your work trip. I hope she didn't cause you too much trouble.'

'No, I'm sorry for depriving you of her for all that time! I haven't seen you since the Christmas cake incident – thanks again so much for that.'

Perhaps his company was thinking of opening up a shop in the area, or else he happened to be passing close by for work, Rika thought as she guided him towards one of the clusters of sofas by reception.

Ryōsuke bowed his head several times apologetically. 'I'm here because I don't know where Reiko is. I can't get through to her on the phone.'

Rika was startled. She, too, had messaged Reiko several times but her messages weren't showing as read. Assuming that Reiko was either absorbed in her sightseeing or else was somewhere with a patchy signal, she hadn't been especially bothered by it. She sat down in front of Ryōsuke.

'I wonder why. The last time I saw her was yesterday, at Niigata Station. She was planning to stay on one more night there, then travel to her parents' in Kanazawa. I thought you knew.'

'That's what she told me too. But when I called her parents, they said Reiko had no plans to stay there that they knew of. I'd imagine she'd at least tell them if she was thinking about going back. Although saying that, these are the parents who didn't even come to our wedding ...'

Ryōsuke's square forehead was filmed with sweat. He frowned and said, as if struggling to get the words out, 'She's been really worrying about not getting pregnant. We haven't been speaking all that much recently. Even when I try and start a conversation with her, she seems a bit out of it. A lot of the time, she doesn't do any housework, but just sits staring at the computer all day. I know it's all my fault though. I'm not a fit husband for her.'

'I heard from her that you disagreed about fertility treatments,' Rika said hesitantly, and Ryōsuke's cheeks flushed an even deeper shade of crimson. He rested his hands awkwardly on his knees.

'When Reiko first told me she was interested in me, it took me totally by surprise. What could someone like that, who attracts so much attention wherever she goes, possibly see in someone like me? I've never been particularly popular with women, and I don't have all that much to talk about. My salary was far less than hers, too.'

Rika said nothing, remembering her own doubts when Reiko had got engaged.

'Even after we got married, even once we were living together and having a great time together, I couldn't fully push that sense away. You know how determined she is about having a family. When I heard that she was going to quit the job she loved to concentrate on getting pregnant, it came as a surprise. I tried to stop her, but she wouldn't listen to me.'

Rika recalled Reiko's hand stroking the cow.

'Something shifted in her feelings towards me. Maybe she started thinking it didn't have to be me. When I began to suspect it didn't matter to her who she was with as long as they'd give her children, I just couldn't … you know. I deliberately scheduled meetings for the day I was due to go to the clinic and be checked out. I know that's awful. But I was scared that if it turned out to be my fault she couldn't conceive, she'd leave me. I'm sorry to be telling you all this personal stuff out of the blue, I'm sure you don't want to hear it.'

Ryōsuke was hunched as if braced against the pain. His voice was faltering, sometimes growing high, close to a wail. Rika felt certain this was the first time he'd spoken about this to anybody. His tone, usually so jokey, took on a formal edge. As Rika leaned in, her phone rang. She took it out of her pocket, meaning to turn it off, and saw Kitamura's name flashing up on the screen. Apologising to Ryōsuke, she picked up, covering her mouth with her hand and whispered quickly.

'I'm with a client right now. Is it urgent? Can we talk after?'

'It won't take long. I'm in the staff canteen. Come straight away, please.' With this, he hung up. Rika intended to ignore his request, but Ryōsuke was already getting to his feet.

'I'm really sorry to barge in like this, right in the middle of your working day. I'm going home. If something happens, please call me. You're the only person I can turn to at this point.'

As Rika watched his figure growing smaller beyond the glass-fronted entrance, she felt the unpleasant premonition she'd brushed up against in Niigata swell out and take on a sense of reality. She ran down the stairs to the staff canteen in the basement, trying her best to get a handle on the situation.

Had Reiko run away from home deliberately, to try to make Ryōsuke realise the severity of the situation? It might make sense, yet that brand of childishness wasn't Reiko's style. The strangest part of all was that Reiko was now uncontactable. And yet it was hard to believe that Reiko, as cautious as she was, would have got embroiled in any kind of trouble. Also, barely any time had passed. Maybe come the evening, she would be in touch to say that she'd arrived at her parents' home in Kanazawa.

Kitamura popped his head round from a table in the corner of the mostly deserted canteen, separated off by a partition.

'Who was that guy you were with? It was me who took the call from reception.'

The inquisitiveness of his tone bothered Rika, and she sank down on the chair with deliberate force. She was also annoyed that, owing to Kitamura, Ryōsuke had gone home. Even Kitamura's immaculately ironed shirt and the lustre of his skin, so rare among the editing department, now appeared irritating in her eyes.

'Does it matter? What is this about? Is it the sister of Manako's victim? Have you found her contact details? If so, then give them to me.'

Rika felt her tone become peremptory, although that wasn't her intention. Kitamura glared back at her with a combative glint in his eye that she'd never seen before.

'I saw you, last week, getting in a taxi with Mr Shinoi from the news agency outside Iidabashi.'

His eyes now glimmered with evident pride.

'I followed you. You headed to Arakichō, went down the hill and got out at a block of flats with a supermarket on the ground floor.'

'This is unbelievable. You know that's a violation of privacy?'

Rika settled herself back in her chair. Right now her sense of surprise was overridden by a feeling of hatred. It was spooky that someone as unconcerned with other people's affairs as Kitamura was would involve himself to this degree.

'You went shopping in the supermarket, and then entered the building together.'

'That's right. We're friends, who sometimes drink together. What's wrong with that? There were other people there with us. We all cooked and ate together.'

The lies flowed out smoothly. She felt no sense of guilt. Explaining what had really happened in that room would mean exposing both Shinoi and his family. It seemed to be a source of irritation to Kitamura that she was so unemotional. He pushed back his neatly styled hair.

'I heard the news. You've got an exclusive interview with Manako Kajii, right?'

'How do you know that?'

'The whole magazine knows. People all across the company are talking about it.'

That explained the stares she'd been getting since returning to work. She felt a wave of fatigue cresting inside her.

'Apparently a journalist at a rival newspaper asked her for an interview. She refused, and mentioned your name. The journalist then tried to find out if it was true. He questioned someone at the desk about it when they were out drinking, who admitted it. It all got out very quickly while you were away.'

There was no particular reason to hide it. It was to be announced publicly next month anyway, and the fact that Kajii had mentioned her name roused Rika's courage.

'Has that come about through Mr Shinoi?'

The connection between the two things seemed to her for a moment so absurd that Rika burst out laughing.

'I always thought of you as someone who didn't use sleazy tactics to get ahead, but it looks like I was wrong. I thought you and I were of the same kind.'

Feeling disgusted with the prim, righteous look on his face, Rika shook her head.

'I don't care what you think. It's true that Shinoi gives me advice occasionally, but he's totally unconnected with the Kajii thing. I wrote to her several times before she gave me permission to go and see her. In other words, it came about through totally fair means. Similarly, the relationship I have with Shinoi is one I've built up over time. If you want to spread it around, then go ahead.'

There was a pause and then all the tension dropped from Kitamura's expression. A little of his usual nonchalant self returned.

'I used to respect you. You and Mizushima were the only journalists in our department who I truly rated. You're both rational, but you've got heart as well. While everyone around was blindly clinging to tradition, it seemed like you two alone were trying to do something new.' He was mumbling now, not looking at Rika. Rika had never heard him mention Mizushima before.

'In order to build relationships with their sources, journalists are out drinking all the time, spending vast sums of cash. They go on about how badly the print media are faring, but they have no issue spending money like water on entertaining. The whole industry accepts that that's just the way it is. While the rest of the world has woken up to the dangers of wastefulness and nepotism, this industry seems to operate on the rules of a bygone age.'

Rika made to say something, and then thought better of it. It seemed to her strange that this man, who she was convinced thought only about going home earlier than his colleagues, would share her sense of discomfort on such matters.

'The working hours of the magazine section are timed to fit in with night-time entertaining of clients. If we could find decent things to write about without going for dinner and drinks, then there's no reason why people couldn't come in before nine and leave at six. But nobody does that. If those rules were put in place, maybe

Mizushima wouldn't have moved to the sales department. It's because those meaningless conventions are prioritised over all else that both quality and sales are dropping off, don't you think?'

Kitamura and Mizushima had overlapped only for a short period, during which time Mizushima had been critical of Kitamura's attitude to work. And yet, Rika now sensed that Kitamura had shown his real self to Mizushima and her alone.

'If you could build a relationship that was based on real trust, you wouldn't need to spend that much time together or drink that much. Can you say with confidence that Shinoi's not interested in you?'

Ignoring the prickle in her chest at this question, Rika said, 'I'm quite confident our relationship is entirely about the information he provides me with.'

'You've really changed, you know? I think you should drop the Kajii case. I think you might be getting in over your head.'

Rika stood up without looking at him. Even once she was out of the staff canteen, she couldn't shake off the itchy feeling of his gaze on her.

'Everything in Niigata is delicious, don't you agree? Well, how was it? What was your favourite thing you tried?' Kajii asked in a sing-song tone of voice. Seeing her this relaxed and carefree, the events of Niigata started to seem like a dream. Maybe Rika had just been on a pleasant holiday with Reiko – a Reiko who was now back at home, making dinner as she waited for Ryōsuke to get in from work …

The reality was, though, that Rika had been unable to reach Reiko the previous evening. Ryōsuke had been in touch with Reiko's parents again, and they'd confirmed that she still hadn't arrived.

It was nearing the end of February, but the Tokyo Detention House was as cold as ever. On the other side of the acrylic screen, Kajii's cheeks were flushed a rosy pink, as if she were in some tropical land.

'And I heard you met Taiichi Akiyama! Honestly, that name really takes me back. He used to be such a rogue when he was younger. He played it cool but I could tell that he was secretly in love with me. So adorable.'

As soon as the topic turned to the opposite sex, Kajii's delivery grew animated, her eyes narrowed, and her lips moistened.

'Are you sure you aren't getting your wires crossed?'

'What do you mean? What's with that stern face?'

'I'll tell you what Akiyama told me. He said that back when he knew you, you were a fairly unremarkable girl.'

Kajii opened her mouth wide and laughed.

'Has Anna been saying peculiar things to you, by any chance? She's not all there these days, you know. I mean, it stands to reason, having to spend all that time with my mother. You'd be best off ignoring them. In his heart of hearts, Taiichi wanted to come with me to Tokyo. Instead he was forced to stay at home, and to marry some dullard from his year at school.'

Rika regarded Kajii coolly. Why had she ever been taken in by this woman? Her own actions from just a short time ago seemed now both idiotic and pitiable to Rika. That version of herself had no confidence in anything she did. She hadn't even known what she wanted to eat.

'The only man to give you a second thought was the child molester who went after your younger sister when she was still in primary school.'

'What are you saying? I've no idea what you're talking about.'

Suddenly, it all seemed pointless to Rika. However hard she attempted to comprehend Kajii's way of thinking, would it not all end up as a wasted effort?

'I'm talking about the first man you dated. He was after your sister, wasn't he? All that stuff about him being a business man from Tokyo is just made up, isn't it?'

Rika knew, even without having to look at Kajii. The thick wall she had erected couldn't be broken down from this direction. Rika decided to change tack.

'Listen, I'm thinking about attending the cooking school you went to. I'm planning to go with my friend Reiko. It was thanks to her coming along with me to Niigata that I was able to find out all the information that I did.'

'How will that work? I thought you had no interest in cooking?'

'Why did you start going to Le Salon de Miyuko? My sense is that it represented a last ray of hope for you.'

'What are you talking about?'

'To find people who understood you. To find kindred spirits.'

'I told you. I don't need friends.'

'You did tell me. But while the men you dated were attracted to your body and your caring and maternal qualities, those were all attributes that benefited them in some way. They wouldn't share your worries and your pain, would they? They always wanted something from you.'

'That doesn't bother me. I never had any worries or any pain to begin with, so that wasn't a concern of mine.'

Rika cut her off.

'In any case, I'm going with Reiko. Attending with her means I'll see things that I wouldn't be able to alone.'

'Reiko, Reiko – what's with this Reiko? Are you two in love or something?' Kajii spat out the words as if they were pieces of gum. Her normally blank eyes assumed a merciless look that somehow suited her. 'Reiko's not the woman that you think she is. You still can't see anything.'

Rika countered cautiously, 'Do you ... know Reiko?'

Kajii cocked her chin and looked down her nose at Rika, as if observing someone in a cage.

'She's come to see me. Twice.'

Rika saw the snow-capped mountains of Agano, the whitened big wheel of Suntopia World, flash before her eyes. Her cheeks felt cold, her insides frozen. She could sense her temples twitching. Maybe this was how it worked, she thought. How Kajii had killed off her victims without actually needing to lay a finger on them.

'When?'

'Hmm, let me recall. Once just after New Year, and again at the beginning of this month. She wrote to me after you'd begun visiting. She said that you were losing your grip, and it was my fault. Would I please agree to meet with her, just once. She was so persistent that I consented, and then she showed up. She told me with a deadly serious face that, thanks to me, her friend was going off the rails. Do you want to know what she said when I asked her in what way?'

Kajii paused, then spread her arms and leaned forward menacingly.

'"She's put on so much weight!"' Kajii exclaimed theatrically, her eyes wide. 'I was wondering what on earth it was you'd gone and done, and that was it! You'd put on weight. She said she was hopelessly worried about you. You'd left the world of reason behind. That sickened me to hear. Is the woman daft, or what? Being that upset about what happens to somebody else's body! How can someone be so conscious of what shape another person takes, of the extent to which they've liberated their desires? It's not normal to feel such anxiety about that. If you're paying more attention to the form other people are assuming than what's taking place inside yourself, it means something is seriously wrong with you.'

Kajii spoke with clarity, and her words sounded more sincere than anything she'd uttered before. She was right, Rika thought. She had perfectly voiced the sense of discomfort Rika had felt for the last few months at people's reactions to her.

'She's clearly mentally unstable. I'm not surprised her husband wants nothing to do with her. She's got a stingy little body like an anaemic twig and she talks in such a grating, high-pitched voice. I could tell, as soon as I met her – here's a woman who has never been properly caressed. Just like my mother. Women like that are headstrong, and ever so good at making high-handed pronouncements, but they don't win the love of men. They don't know true pleasure, and that's why they're never satisfied. They can't relax until they've found a target to attack. Everything she was spouting about her friendship with you and so on is just an outlet for her unfulfilled sexual desire. The way she talked about you as if you were her lover gave me the shivers.

'So I told her: people who don't have sex regularly, for whatever reason, are all maladapted to society. What right do you have to call yourself a person if you're not having sex? It's no use thinking that time will heal things. If you're not loved by your husband at this very moment, things will never resolve themselves. It's useless, you're beyond help.'

A wave of pain now ran through Rika. Maybe what drew her to Kajii was the anger that had accumulated within her over the years. Kajii couldn't resist the urge to tear apart even Reiko, with whom she had no relationship at all. She felt sure that Kajii's very essence was a rage like an inextinguishable flame that burned everything it touched.

'You and Reiko both seek a paternal quality in your men. You're expecting men to live up to this figure of the warm father that you never had. My father and I loved and trusted one another deeply, so I don't require men to be my father. I don't thrust my twisted desires on them, as people who have never really known a father's love do. That is why I can be loved by anybody. You look down on men who are secretly pining for a mother figure, seeking kindness and care from women, but I don't see how you're any different.'

Before, Rika thought, she would have been felled by this criticism, left reeling for days. She was faintly aware that she viewed Shinoi as a kind of father figure. She also knew that by encouraging him to live a healthier lifestyle, she was hoping to atone for what had happened with her own father. Yet she knew that neither she nor Reiko were people who sought to control others without giving anything of themselves. She sat up straight, not falling into the pit Kajii had dug for her.

'Did you say that to Reiko?'

'I did. She turned white, then red, and then began to cry great globules. I burst out laughing. She started telling me, utterly straight-faced, how she was going to win you back from me. It was painful to watch.'

The woman sitting in front of her was only suspected of killing three people. Rika had met plenty of people more dangerous than her in the past.

'I don't dislike Reiko at all. She has some strange aspects to her personality, and she can be quite conceited. Sometimes she drives me mad. But even if what you say is on the nose, she's still fun to be around.'

'Fun?' Kajii turned the word around on her tongue like a boiled sweet, as if she were encountering it for the first time. She repeated it again: 'Fun.'

'Yes. Talking with friends is fun. Perhaps you never had any because people found your company tedious and monotonous.'

'That's a fine thing for you to say, when you've been spellbound by my conversation!'

'At first I was spellbound, you're absolutely right. But then I realised. All of your knowledge is within anybody's reach if they read the right books and pay the right money. The reason you appear so special is because people these days don't spend all that time and money. Because they all count calories and have abandoned the arts of home-cooking and fine-dining, which they didn't receive a proper education in. That's all.'

'That's not true. It's because being with me is painful for them. It's the same for all you women. You can't be comfortable with a member of your own sex unless you feel that she's inferior to you in some way.'

'It must be easier for you to think that way.'

Kitamura and Kajii were both attacking her in a similar way, she thought now. Kitamura had never had a source, and Kajii had never had a friend. As a result, their words were rooted in the realm of fantasy. There was no need to quake in fear at their vitriol, or to feel pained by it. Rika could sense that Kajii was beginning to recoil in the face of Rika's refusal to be fazed by her onslaught.

'Do you have any idea where Reiko is right now?'

Regaining her sense of advantage, Kajii broke into a smile and refused to answer. She rubbed her lips together so that they resembled two creatures caressing.

'I admit that I was drawn to you. The way you affirm yourself so completely, are so resolute, so without doubt. But don't you think that the way Reiko – and I, for that matter – put ourselves through these troublesome head-on encounters with people makes us stronger than you?'

'Strong? You two?'

Kajii drew in her chin and studied Rika.

'To me, you seem like the far weaker person,' Rika went on. 'You exclude everything you don't want to see from your sight, deny the existence of anybody that won't engage with you. Until going to Niigata, there was some part of me that was scared of you. But now I think that was a disservice to your humanity. You're not a monster, like the world says you are. You're just a person.'

Saying this, she deliberately cast her eyes downwards. When Kajii spoke, her voice was trembling.

'There's a limit to how much rudeness I can tolerate. If you don't like me, then you can scrap the idea of the exclusive interview.'

'Maybe we'll have to.' Rika looked up to see Kajii lost for words. Her mouth hung open. Only her white fingertips were moving restlessly.

'If I go padding around blindly after you, I'll only end up repeating your narrative. Who's going to read that, if I publish it? The world is beginning to get tired of your story.'

'This is exactly why I hate female journalists. They're emotional, hysterical, ridiculously needy, and incapable of acting professionally. I'm done with it! Consider the interview off! This is why I hate women!'

Rika herself found it bizarre how unruffled she felt, even with Kajii screaming in front of her like this, her nostrils flaring and her face bright red.

'I'm on a permanent contract at the magazine, so even if the interview comes to nothing, I'll keep my job. At the end of the day, I lose nothing. I'd go as far as to say that it's you who'll be losing something. You'll be losing the first person who's understood you. Things will just go back to how they were for you. Back to how they were in Agano, when everybody ignored you.'

The grapeskins ruptured. Rika could see it happening. Just a little further, Rika thought. Her armpits grew sweaty. She had to appeal to her senses, gradually draw Kajii into her rhythm. It wouldn't do to rush.

'Visiting Agano, I started for the first time to feel genuinely sorry for you. Maybe if you'd had someone like Reiko in your life – it wouldn't have mattered if they were a man or a woman, just someone you could talk to about what was on your mind – then things wouldn't have worked out this way. Maybe then you wouldn't have needed to be so impossibly self-contained, to do everything on your own. If I'd taken a wrong turn somewhere, I could have easily ended up like you.'

For the first time since she'd met her, Rika returned Kajii's gaze directly, challengingly, with the conviction of a journalist who demands her question be answered immediately.

'Will you please tell me where my friend Reiko Sayama is right now, and what she's doing?'

CHAPTER TEN

22 FEBRUARY

Ryō is really into his sake recently. He must have developed a taste for it when out drinking with his colleagues.

After saying goodbye to Rika on the platform, I went to get my stuff – which I'd secreted in a locker when she wasn't looking – and hung out in the souvenir shop inside the ticket gates, although I had no intention of buying anything. I had to catch the bullet train, and head to my hometown of Kanazawa. I hadn't the slightest intention of exploring Niigata any further, or of going to meet my parents. I had just one aim. Once that was completed, I had to return to Tokyo, head for the house in Kawasaki, and do my best to keep my cool. I went down the escalator to the correct platform, wheeling my suitcase. The train was pulling into the station, dusted in snow.

Before boarding, I took my phone out of my coat pocket and switched it off. These days it was only Rika and Ryō who ever contacted me, but I didn't want them to throw me off course or interfere with my plans. If I was only out of reach for a few days, I could make the excuse that I'd lost or broken my phone. I took out the other phone I'd prepared in advance, and turned it on. The handset was the same icy temperature as the air, and the dark, unwelcoming screen reflected my contours hazily.

Settling down into the seat I'd reserved, before even leaning back in my seat or taking off my coat, I looked at the message from the

only contact I had saved in my phone, and immediately sent a
one-handed reply:

Dear Jelly Wizard,
Today I managed to leave without my husband catching me. I'll be
at your place tonight. You're the last person in the world I have to
rely on. I'm looking forward to meeting you.
	Custard

Then I took out a notebook, and noted down my finds from my
visit to the police station in Niigata with Rika. On my to-do list, I
crossed out 'Go to Kanazawa', then memorised the list of things still
remaining.

My findings from my research of the last few months are beginning to come together with what emerged yesterday at the Kajii
residence. If my line of thinking is correct, Kajii has a collaborator.
Maybe, like Rika said, she didn't actually lay hands on anybody, but
in that case there must be a fourth man, who killed the others
according to her instructions. That person has made an appearance
already, both in her testimony and in the investigation. I have to go
about this carefully, take one thing at a time, not become impatient.

Before too long, the train pulled into the city in which I was born.
Stepping out onto the platform, I was enveloped by its gentle, cold
air, very different to that I'd experienced in Niigata. A smell like
burnt grass grazed my nose. I felt irritated by the wave of nostalgia
that rose up in me.

I climbed into a cab and gave the address of my parents' home in
Korinbo: a Western-style building with a red triangular roof built in
the Shōwa Era, standing in a classy residential district around the
back of the shopping area. The kind of house that tourists would stop
outside in flocks to take photos of. When the evening sun lit up the
stained-glass window on the first-floor landing, the Virgin Mary's
face would appear in profile. Back at school, the other kids in my

class had been jealous of where I lived, saying it looked like the houses you saw on TV.

The flyers in the pocket on the back of the driver's seat were for my father's hotel, well-known in these parts. If he needed to be putting flyers in taxis, I thought, business really had to have taken a turn for the worse. My eyes met that of my father's in the promotional photo. He had clearly been having Botox, because his face looked even more artificial than I remembered it. The bright white of his hair made his skin, thoroughly tanned from the time he spent on his yacht, appear even darker. He was tall, with handsome features, and in his younger days had been scouted as a model. His eyes were very similar to my own, a fact I hated.

'It's the biggest hotel in the area. If you haven't got a room booked for the evening, you could give it a try?'

It seemed the thick-necked taxi driver in his sixties was monitoring me in the rear-view mirror. When I made a non-committal noise, he said in a slightly malicious tone, 'You won't need a reservation. It's empty as anything of late.'

When I was a child, our hotel was viewed as the best Kanazawa had to offer for its food and service. Yet when my father took over the business from my grandfather, the quality gradually began to decline. Outside the window, the sky was a far more cheerful shade of indigo than that in Niigata.

The taxi pulled up outside the entrance to the residential district. As I was paying, I saw the taxi driver's eyes flit down to my wallet. It was stuffed to bursting with 250,000 yen in cash. I'd left my bank and insurance cards and anything else by which my location could be traced in a drawer at home. In the event that anything happened to me, I had no identifying documents on me.

'I'll be back down in ten minutes. Could you wait here?' I said to the driver, and stepped out of the cab into the street where I'd been born and brought up.

The house I hadn't returned to in five years appeared to me overly large, not unlike a haunted mansion. It towered before me, black and quietly menacing. My parents seemed to be out, as usual. We had been the first people in the area to install a surveillance camera at our entrance. I went round to the back and put my key in the door. If it no longer fitted, I planned on phoning Mrs Tajima and enlisting her help. The key turned, and I let out a sigh of relief, pushing the low wooden door open. In the middle of the back garden, through which a path ran to the kitchen door, stood a dog kennel. Inside was Melanie, seemingly smaller than when I'd last seen her. I had thought she might bark, but instead she turned a longing gaze on me, wrinkling her nose. I crouched down and held my breath, using her collar to pull her close. My eyes grew hot and my throat dry. Just knowing that Melanie was still alive and well justified having come all this way.

'Do you remember me, Melly?'

She and Ryō were alike after all, I thought, my first impression hadn't been wrong. Burying my face in Melanie's warm back, I felt a deep sense of relief. Blood still pulsed through her small body. The fur on her throat smelled of sweet bread.

'What is it that you like about Ryōsuke?'

I remember Rika had asked me that question, hesitantly, when I told her we were getting married. One of my former colleagues said quite plainly that she didn't think the two of us were a match, but I hadn't understood what she meant. My attraction to Ryō, the man who resembled my beloved Melanie, had been immediate. Ryō was far better loved by people than I was, and was the kind of person who could get along well anywhere he went without pretending – that much was obvious at a glance. I've always been drawn to people like that.

Melanie's fur was stiffer than it used to be, and I had a harder time running my fingers through it. Her eyes were crusty with sleep. But I had my worries about her – was she being walked enough? My parents would have tended to her out of the fear of what people would think if they didn't. And failing that, there was always Mrs Tajima to take care of her.

Melanie was a black and white Border collie. The characteristic traits of the breed – obedience, loyalty and trust – ran deep in her. She was just a puppy when she first came to our house, the Christmas of my third year of high school, bought by my parents as an attempt to keep me close to home. She had, in theory, been a gift to celebrate my getting a scholarship to my first-choice university, but it was obvious that I couldn't take a puppy that still needed so much attention with me to Tokyo, or, indeed, look after her while I was still accustoming myself to living alone. Sobbing, I said goodbye to my parents' house, leaving Melanie behind. I had been hoping to leave with a greater sense of liberation, so their scheme angered me.

Now I was about to drag the same poor creature away from the place she was used to. From my wheelie suitcase I pulled out a carrier for medium-sized dogs and assembled it. I took off the lid, and arranged several items inside so that they'd take up as little space as possible – her brush, her lead, her bone-shaped toy, a portable toilet, a little bit of food, and a training pad – all things that I'd bought yesterday in the pet shop of a nearby mall, after Rika had left the hotel room. When we'd set out from Tokyo, Rika had been surprised at how much stuff I'd brought with me, but my luggage had been virtually empty. Tempting Melanie with a biscuit, I coaxed her inside the carrier.

I took out a folded polyester tote bag, put the last of my clothes and toiletries inside, and then slung my empty suitcase and Boston bag into the corner of the garden. My calculations had been correct, and Melanie fitted snugly inside the carrier. As soon as I closed the door, she began to bark furiously, so I took out my notepad and scribbled a note in ballpoint pen. I thought about addressing it to Mrs Tajima, but then it struck me that she didn't often pass through this part of the house. In any case, however much I hated my parents, I had to let them know that Melanie was safe:

I've taken Melanie. She was mine to begin with, so I guess that's allowed, right? Reiko.

I tore off the page and tossed it inside the kennel. With my tote bag and pet carrier in hand, I left the garden. As soon as I turned my back on the house, I could feel my breathing growing less laboured. Suddenly my own behaviour seemed to me a bit like a child throwing a tantrum, and I stomped the asphalt underfoot as hard as I could. Inside the carrier, Melanie went on barking.

To Ryō and Rika, I've always painted a picture of my home situation whereby I was the overlooked daughter whose parents wouldn't give her the attention she wanted, but the reality is a little different. In fact, it was me who cut the ties. To this day, my folks still try to get in touch and offer to send me money, but I bat off their advances. I have confidence that they won't report me for kidnapping Melanie.

Fifteen is seventy-six in dog years. Starting tomorrow, I thought, I'll begin taking Melanie out for walks. I'll give her massages, and sort out her fur. The list of all the things I needed to do grew longer by the minute, making me so dizzy that for a moment I had the impulse to abandon my plan entirely.

Returning to the taxi with the pet carrier in my right hand and the tote bag in my left, I instructed the driver to head back to the station. Melanie was still barking, and he shot several glances over his shoulder with obvious irritation, but by the time we reached Kanazawa Station and boarded the bullet train bound for Tokyo, she had grown tired and fallen asleep. There was a sad look about her sleeping face, and I felt a pang for all the times I could have come back to see her and chosen not to. But now she was an indispensable part of my plan. I had no confidence I could pull this off alone, so I had to take her with me. I was selfish, and I exhausted the people around me. I felt fairly sure that everyone who got involved with me would come to regret it someday.

I'm more like Kajii than I care to admit.

As it happens, I've lied to Rika about a number of things. I told her that my parents' relationship had broken down although they continued to live in the same house, but the truth was that they always got on well together, and were adoring parents with a romantic view of building a household. Mrs Tajima did all the cooking and the housework, but that was just how things were, and as a youngster not knowing the taste of my mother's cooking didn't bother me in the slightest. The three of us often ate out at classy restaurants or my dad's hotel, and at New Year and birthdays we enjoyed the feasts that Mrs Tajima prepared for us – all heartwarming memories. Our family lived affluently, no sacrifices were demanded of us, and as a result, we were all, for the most part, smiling and cheerful.

Everything I wanted was given to me. I went to a local girls' school with a good reputation, and had a busy schedule of extra-curricular lessons. I can concede that the teaching and the knowledge I inherited from my parents form the cornerstone of who I am. When I think about it now, my parents' love for me seems a bit like that for a beloved pet, but I was always their pride and joy, and they rejoiced in what a bright and earnest child I was. From time to time I modelled in the adverts for the hotel, and its most luxurious suite is named after me. Having got married as students, my parents always seemed younger than the parents of the other children in my class, and I was proud of them too. They seemed to me so beautiful, like a couple of young lovers.

One day, in the spring of my first year at junior high school, while walking home from a piano lesson, I spotted my father strolling around Kenroku Park with a young woman who worked in the hotel. It didn't occur to me that they were having an affair, and I followed them as a kind of game, but I soon lost sight of them. The incident stuck with me, and I kept on wondering what it had been about. I told my mother what I'd seen but she didn't look remotely fazed, saying, 'Your dad is good at giving advice to young women, so lots of the staff members rely on him. He's always been that way, ever since university, when he'd do the same with younger members of the tennis club. It doesn't bother me at all.' Behind these words, I sensed something peculiar.

There were plenty of girls at school who followed me around and wanted to be friends, but I didn't have anyone I was close to, who I could share things with. Thanks to the environment I'd grown up in, where my parents were my best friends, I'd not learned to seek a place where I belonged outside the home. Aside from my relatives, the only person I could talk to was Mrs Tajima. One day, I decided to ask her about my parents as she was preparing dinner, and for the first time ever she evaded my question, a nervous smile on her face. I didn't give up, though. I persevered with following my father and observing my mother, and carried on talking to Mrs Tajima. As time went on, I started to see what I hadn't been able to until then.

The turning point came when I hit thirteen. That both my parents had numerous lovers turned out to be common knowledge not just in our immediate neighbourhood, but among all the hotel staff and across the whole area. Their unique interpretation of marriage, I learned, had been passed down through the family, dating back to before my grandfather's generation. Their lovers included the nice men and women who had often visited the hotel and played with me, and who I thought of as uncles and aunts.

In the summer of my second year at middle school, I presented my parents with the proof I'd gathered, and accused them of infidelity. Initially, they both stubbornly denied it, but setting eyes on the photos I presented them with, they fell silent. Finally, with fear in their eyes, they met the gaze of their daughter, who had grown so icy in her attitude towards them of late that she seemed like a different person entirely. From then on, I would go on to experience that same look in lots of places, from lots of different people. Yesterday Rika, my best friend in the world, turned it on me. Which means, I suppose, it's only a matter of time before our friendship will come to an end.

'Your mother is the only person I love, and she feels the same about me,' my father said.

His tone suggested he was simplifying something difficult for my benefit. No, it's *you* who doesn't understand, I thought to myself. That's not love. It's that you've become co-conspirators with one another, because your needs match. I could feel myself glaring at them. My mother kept her eyes fixed on the scenery outside the window, never dropping the act of the poor victim. She can't have been that dissimilar in age to me now. In my memory, her appearance is irritatingly similar to mine: a smooth-skinned, delicate woman, reminiscent of a porcelain doll. There was nothing she wanted to express, no desires piercing her body. She was a tedious woman who caused no friction with anybody – who couldn't have caused any friction, even if she wanted to.

'Taking other lovers is what allows our relationship to stay fresh, and what enables us to get along so well,' my father told me. 'Our way of going about things might be a little different from other people, but I'm sure someone as perceptive as you can understand that adults have needs. We want you to know that there are lots of different kinds of marriages.'

I decided to put to use all of the knowledge I'd accumulated up until that point, all the debating skills I'd developed at school. Calmly and logically, I explained why their approach to marriage was mistaken, why it showed they had misunderstood love and responsibility. At first, my parents seemed flummoxed, then afraid of this daughter of theirs who had changed so much. In time, their expressions began to register their irritation. That was how I came to realise: for all their knowledge of literature and the arts, my dear parents weren't in the habit of thinking deeply about anything. They were, in fact, profoundly superficial people who were happy if they could spend their days enjoying themselves, surrounded by things they liked and which were pleasing on the eye. Eventually, my father got fed up with my talking.

'It can't be helped. I just can't have sex with someone who's so close that they feel like family.'

I don't think I'll ever forget the look on his face as he said this. The twist of his lips, the dark flash in his eyes spoke of an insatiable thirst for pleasure. Alongside his indulgence, I could also detect a determination, too – the determination not to change his way of life, at any cost. This was a man who was content to bend the rules, if doing so would feel good.

'I just can't have sex with someone who's so close that they feel like family' – since becoming an adult, I've heard these words in various different contexts. This line of thought, which has become so common all of a sudden, casts a contemptuous gaze on all married couples, indiscriminately. I suppose I must have been giving him a frosty glare, because my father hurriedly tried to smooth things over.

'I'm sure you'll understand one day, when you're older.'

But I am older now, and my feelings on the subject remain unchanged. Back then, the thought that went through my head was this: if I never come to understand the kind of pleasure that makes you lose respect for your partner, for the rules, I will consider myself fortunate.

It was at that moment that I made the decision.

I would reject my parents' way of life with everything I had. I would leave home, and live entirely independently of them. I would go to Tokyo, and build a new life from scratch – find new friends, a boyfriend, a job. I would never have sex with anybody other than my husband. I resolved that for me, sex would be exclusively tied to having children. I decided to remain a virgin until I married. It was around that time that I got my first period.

As it turned out, my will wasn't sufficiently strong to uphold that promise to myself, but I did make sure not to sleep with any men with whom I wasn't seriously considering a future. My image of what an ideal home looked like was borrowed from the house of Mrs Tajima, which I had visited so often since I was small. I would choose a man like Mr Tajima, a cuddly man working as a middle-school teacher, and his wife's double. It was my dream to become part of a happy couple blessed with many children.

When I got to Tokyo Station, I changed to the Keihin–Tōhoku Line. Melanie was still sleeping quietly. Eventually, I made it to Kawasaki. My long journey was finally nearing its end.

Inside the chilly stall of the station toilet, I wrapped a bandage around my wrist, stuck a plaster to my left cheek, and put on an eye patch. I left the stall, and looked in the mirror to check that I had transformed into the kind of unfortunate, powerless woman I wanted to be seen as. By now, my make-up had worn off totally, and I was so tired that I had a natural pallor. I had to hand it to myself: the look was perfect. I got into a taxi outside the station and gave the driver an address one block before my destination. There was no way of telling where he'd be watching from, and I wanted to make him think I'd walked from the station.

He lived in a small residential strip at the edge of Kawasaki's industrial belt.

Right beside the house was a river with a grassy bank – the perfect spot to take Melanie for a walk tomorrow, I thought.

The three-storey building was tall and narrow, shaped like a slice of cake. The place had originally been an office building adjoining a factory, which had gone bust two years before and been knocked down. If his explanation in court had been correct, then the kitchen and living room were on the ground floor, the first floor comprised the bathroom, toilet, and his bedroom, and the second floor was storage space. What he'd said about the thin walls and harsh winters seemed plausible. I could imagine that looking after his ageing mother here had been no easy task.

I knocked on the flimsy plywood door, pressing at the same time on the button to the intercom, which was blackened by soot. Steeling myself, I made a pledge that whatever happened I wouldn't run away. After a little while the door opened, and I was hit by a rush of the sweet, stale smell that other people's houses have, but at ten times the usual concentration. A flabby, round face with greyish skin stared out at me. Through his fingerprint-smeared glasses, our eyes met. A faint smell of semen and artificial flavourings stung my eyes, and I felt the nausea rising up from the pit of my stomach. But I was not going to turn back. I lifted my head, held my breath and looked around the triangular space spreading out from the entranceway. A small kitchen at the back, and in front of it a living room with tatami flooring. A low kotatsu – foot-warmer table – sat in its centre, its perimeter littered with magazines and instant-ramen containers.

The blanket for the kotatsu was yellowing. I was stirred by the impulse to yank it off and toss it out of the window.

'Nice to meet you, I'm Custard. I mean, I'm Sonomi Ikeda.'

I was borrowing the name of a hapless-looking classmate of mine from high school. Taking care to ensure my voice was as feeble as I could make it, my nose grew itchy and I sneezed loudly. The itch quickly became uncontrollable and spread to my throat, so that I choked violently. The same complacent lack of hygiene as I'd experienced at the Kajiis' house confronted me from all directions. I held my breath again, and stepped inside the flat. The door shut behind me. I heard him lock it. There's no turning back now, I said to myself.

'I'm Shirō Yokota.'

I took a good look at the small-framed, pudgy middle-aged man in front of me. His voice was far more high-pitched than I'd expected. His small stature was reassuring. I could definitely take him on, if necessary. I took another big step into the room, steeling myself again not to turn around.

'It sounds awful, what you've been through. I'm happy to help if I can. Make yourself at home here. You don't need to feel shy about it. Your husband sounds like a bad man.'

As he spoke, spittle built up at the corners of Yokota's chapped purple lips. The edge of his mouth was speckled with small white pimples. I knew his age to be fifty-two, but his facial expressions and gestures were more like that of a student. He was clearly intoxicated by the show he was putting on of being a valiant knight in shining armour, apparently undeterred by his beer belly and greying hair. I observed him carefully. How did he see me? I couldn't detect any sign of lust, but I could tell that beneath his filthy sweater his heart was racing at the appearance of a new living body in his personal space.

I pulled an apologetic face, exchanging the occasional glance with him. As far as I could see, the layout of the place was just as he had said.

In November three years previously, Kajii had been arrested at Yokota's house. She'd been staying with him for two days. If you went by their version of events, they'd met in 2012. They'd started chatting on a dating site, hit it off with stories about their shared place of origin, and begun exchanging emails. Immediately before her arrest, realising that her Meguro apartment was being staked out by the police, Kajii had crept out with just the clothes on her back and turned up at this house, whose address Yokota had given her, telling her she was welcome at any time. It was the first time they were meeting in person. Kajii described Yokota as a 'kind-hearted man, like an older brother'. He hadn't touched her. They had slept in separate rooms, with Kajii staying up on the second floor. He had been so overwhelmed with gratitude at the meals Kajii made for him and her considerate nature that he had essentially proposed to her, saying that all he wanted was for her to live alongside him, that that was enough for him. He'd testified that when she was arrested, he'd been astonished. In the courtroom, he had spoken at length about how lonesome his life had been after his mother had died, and how much he missed her. He had talked about Kajii's kindness and how much he had appreciated her warmth. The public had sympathised with him as a devoted, unselfish man, with little experience of women.

Using the courtroom records and the internet, it had been straightforward enough for me to track down his address and real name. Since giving up my fertility treatment, I had bags of time on my hands.

This last month, he and I had been corresponding through a dating site. My interest in him had been sparked by something Kajii had said when I'd met her in person relating to the number of men involved in her case. On the site, I went by the nickname 'Custard', and he by the name 'Jelly Wizard', which he claimed was a character from his favourite anime series. I posed as a housewife from Saitama in an abusive marriage. By not mentioning Kajii at all, and making out that I liked the same anime, I'd managed to squeeze a bunch of information out of him.

Yokota was born in a hospital a couple of kilometres away from Kajii's house in Agano, and his father had died when he was a young child. Initially he'd taken a job in the computing department of a local rice-cracker company, but the work had started to take its toll mentally, and he had repeatedly been signed off with stress. When his mother fell ill, the two of them had moved to Tokyo, where they had relatives around to help. She had died four years earlier. He had never been married. I knew that Kajii targeted idlers with no money worries. Sure enough, it appeared that Yokota owned the house he lived in.

The possibility had come to me in a flash in Niigata: was the mystery man who had gone after Kajii's primary-school-aged sister, and who'd become the first person to understand Kajii in fact Yokota? I'd been told that he was in his forties at the time, but that was from a child's perspective – in reality he may well have been younger. The court records stated that the two had bonded over the fact that they both came from Agano. Had they not, in fact, known one another for longer than they attested? If so, the absence of a physical relationship between them would add up. Yokota's testimony had improved the public's impression of Kajii, if only slightly. Wouldn't it make sense that he was her co-conspirator, with whom she had been secretly corresponding for over a decade?

Three days – that is how long I'd told my husband I'd be staying in Kanazawa for. Long enough, I was hoping, to obtain proof that Yokota was a paedophile, and that he was still in touch with Kajii. If I could show that proof to Rika, I'd be able to win her back, and prove Kajii's guilt.

I realised that Yokota was staring at the pet carrier dangling from my right hand. Smiling inwardly, I rested the carrier on the floor, opened the flap, and showed him Melanie's dry nose.

'I brought my dog Melanie with me. You don't mind, do you?'

'Erm, I'm not so keen on dogs. You didn't mention that in your …' Yokota trailed off. I was of course aware that he hated dogs. I had tracked down his blog, in which he wrote about his favourite anime series. From his conversations in the comments column with the blog's handful of readers, I had managed to put together a complete picture of him as a person.

'I'm sorry. It's just that she really can't do without me. I don't know what my husband would do to her if I left her with him. She's getting old, and needs care.'

I had to get my way on this. I summoned the negotiating skills I'd acquired while I was working at the PR company, working to eliminate my partner's choices and leave no opportunity for counter-arguments.

'My parents live in Yamagata, but we don't have a good relationship, and I haven't seen them in years and years. My best friend, who I've known for a while, is here in Tokyo. She's travelling abroad on business at the moment, but she'll be back next week, and my plan is to go and live with her. Could Melanie and I stay here until then? Just three nights.'

There was no way I could tolerate the stuffy air of this room any longer than that. I stepped into the living room, forcing Yokota to move out of the way and trampling across magazines and ramen cups as I moved, and went around opening all the windows. The air that filtered in smelled faintly of petrol, but it was clean and freely circulating, and I inhaled deeply. Far off in the night sky, the lights of what looked like an incinerator flashed red. Behind me, Yokota mumbled, 'You're a bit different to how I imagined.'

I hurriedly affected a weak smile as I turned around to face him. I was lucky that I was petite and looked young, I thought. He had rejected a physical relationship with a full-bodied woman like Kajii, but maybe someone with a childlike physique like mine would activate his sex drive. That would be my chance to confirm his sexual predilections. The thought filled me with fear, but also expectation. Would I be able to fight him off if I needed to? As far as I could read the situation, though, he seemed hesitant around me.

'It's okay, though. Do as you like,' he mumbled, acquiescently. I wanted to clap my hands together in gratitude.

'Where do you keep the vacuum cleaner?'

Yokota scratched his head. His sweatshirt was peppered with dandruff. After a pause, he pointed to a yellowing sliding door.

'You don't need to worry about vacuuming. You must be tired, you should sleep. The spare room's on the second floor. There's a bed there, which used to be my mother's. I'll show you where it is.'

'I'm okay for now.'

I didn't want to be in the same room with him and a bed.

'You really don't need to clean, though. I don't have any cleaning products or anything like that.'

I smiled and shook my head. Amateurs tend to think that cleaning needs the right equipment, when in fact, making use of whatever is around to clean a room produces a space that feels even cleaner. Besides, I had cotton wool buds, bicarbonate of soda and plastic gloves in my tote bag.

'I feel so bad about staying here for free. Cleaning is about the only thing I'm good for, so let me at least repay you in that way.'

With that, I headed into the kitchen. There I found a portable one-ring hob, a stainless-steel sink and a hot water dispenser, all filthy with grease and mould. Under the sink I located a bottle of vinegar long past its expiry date that I guessed Kajii must have bought, together with a jar for storing rice. In the sink was a well-used sponge. That was sufficient. Yokota was still standing looking at me.

'Are you sure you don't need to sleep? You must be tired. You've cut your hand and everything.'

Recalling at last the role I was supposed to be playing, I affected a pained expression as I sheepishly hid my wrist, then put on the plastic gloves.

'I'm going to do the tiniest bit of cleaning, and then I'll sleep. Please feel free to go up before me.' I smiled broadly to shut him up. I had to deal with at least this kitchen and the room I'd be sleeping in. Luckily the house was smaller than my own, so the task would be quick enough if I put my mind to it.

When Yokota finally made his exit, I took off my tights and tore them into four strips. I tied up my hair and put on a mask, changed into a tracksuit that I'd brought with the intention of throwing it away afterwards, and took off my eye patch. Eventually I planned to rip up those clothes also, and use them for cleaning. Using a piece of cardboard I found lying around and the pet training pads I'd brought, I created a toilet for Melanie. I found a comparatively clean-looking bowl, into which I poured bicarbonate of soda and water, stirring the mixture with a disposable chopstick I picked off the floor. I felt as though if I stopped at any point I'd be swallowed up by anxiety, so I kept on moving single-mindedly. I cleaned the sink, used the sponge to wipe the place down, threw everything on the floor into the bin, then vacuumed. Melanie emerged nervously from the carrier, sticking her nose into one of the ramen cups. I frantically whisked it away from her, pouring some water into a bowl that I offered her. I gazed down at the pale pink tip of her lapping tongue.

I set my phone to play some music at a low volume, to keep up my morale. After I'd worked non-stop for just under an hour, the ground floor was unrecognisable. The flooring was now totally visible, and the strange smell had vanished. Taking Melanie, I climbed the creaky flight of stairs to the floor on which Yokota was sleeping. The tiled bathroom and the toilet were horrendously dirty. I gave up on the idea of washing this evening. I found a container of toilet cleaner with a little bit remaining, laid some toilet paper over the seat and then poured the fluid on. From through the green wall with its grainy texture, I could hear the high-pitched voices and frenetic music of an anime programme.

Every time Melanie sidled up to me, I would bend down and stroke her neck, from time to time offering her a dog biscuit or some of the food I'd brought with me.

'I'm really sorry, baby. You're tired after that long journey, aren't you? I'm going to make somewhere for you to rest now.'

When I finally dragged my heavy body up to the second floor, it was past four in the morning. I stepped inside the room with Melanie, then closed and locked the door behind me. The room was an unusual hexagram shape, only about twelve square metres in size. Its only contents were some stacks of magazines tied up with plastic string, an electric heater, seven empty cardboard boxes, a dusty plastic Christmas tree, and a low bed of the kind used for nursing that must have belonged to Yokota's mother. There was also a mouldy-looking futon folded into four. This was the room in which Kajii must have slept. The very thought made me feel like no amount of scrubbing would be sufficient to clean it to my satisfaction, but my physical strength was reaching its limit, and I kept my dusting to a minimum. I turned on the heater, and decided to cover the futon in newspaper and sleep on it. Whatever happened to me, I told myself, Melanie would protect me. If Yokota were to force open the door, while I couldn't rely on her to bite him sufficiently hard to keep him off, I knew that she'd least bark and alert me to the danger. I made a bed for her out of a pile of towels, but she seemed anxious in her new environment, padding round and round in circles and beginning to whimper. I had to do my best to keep her quiet. I called her over and massaged her, lying down on the futon as I waited for her to calm down. I pictured Kajii's large body occupying the space that mine did now.

'Goodnight, Melanie.'

I missed Rika. A cold sensation spreading through my body alerted me to her newly unfamiliar absence.

The truth was, I wanted to go on travelling with Rika forever.

23 FEBRUARY

I woke up to the sensation of something soft and warm touching my cheek. It took me a moment to realise it was Melanie's nose. She was whimpering, so I scooped her up and brought her into the bed with me. She was getting old, I thought again. It saddened me how her nose was no longer wet. Sleeping on a futon covered in newspaper had left my body chilled through, and thanks to my late-night cleaning spell, I'd only had two hours' sleep. Stroking Melanie's ruff, I found myself growing sleepy. But no, I thought to myself, I had to get up.

As I was making my way down the stairs, I heard Yokota's loud snoring.

'Let's go for a walk before breakfast, okay, Melanie?'

I put on the eye patch and applied plasters to my bare face, pulled on my coat, and stepped outside with Melanie. After my trip up north, the cool air of the morning felt soft. I heard the hammering of metal, and saw trails of smoke rising up here and there, feeling with my whole body the town shifting into motion, as if wound up with a key. Melanie stayed by my side, her lead hanging limply between us like a ribbon – not taut as it had always been when I took her out for walks in the past. I figured that this recent change to her environment might well have been a stressor.

I came to a flight of stone steps leading up to the bank of the river having barely encountered a soul.

The air by the river smelled of cool, wet soil, and I breathed it in deeply, letting the back of my throat swell out. Thanks to the haze in the air, the river appeared to go on forever, and the Keihin–Tōhoku Line cut horizontally through the sky. The wide-open scenery felt good. I passed a group of girls out jogging – the volleyball team at a local middle school by the looks of it, doing their early morning practice. I had heard that Yokota helped out with the admin at a local cram school, which was run by an acquaintance of a relative. The cram school was aimed at kids taking their middle- and high-school entrance exams, so girls of exactly this age would doubtless be passing in and out all the time. That detail of his life only strengthened my conviction in my hypothesis.

I'm really sorry this is happening. It's like … I care about you too much or something. Out of nowhere, I heard Ryō's voice in my head. As I let my feet follow where Melanie led, I remembered his face, the feel of his hand.

I feel weird about doing that stuff with someone when they feel like family to me. You're like a younger sister or even a daughter to me, Reiko – a breakable thing, whom I love so much. I can get a bit rough with that stuff, and I never want to do anything like that with you.

That was the first time I discovered Ryō's preference for rough sex. When I asked him how long I'd have to wait until we could do it again, he'd looked pained and said, 'We will have kids someday. Please trust me. I need you to be patient for the moment.'

I'm the opposite of Ryō. It's with the man that I've chosen to be my family, and only with him, that I want to do it. As the boundaries between mine and Ryō's two bodies grew so close I could scarcely tell them apart, my sex drive, which had been so weak before getting married, grew stronger and stronger. I felt desperate to have sex with the familiar presence who was sleeping soundly next to me, utterly relaxed, our bodies' smells so intermingled as to be practically the same. Ryō's words echoed my father's so closely as to be uncanny.

I stood staring into the river until Melanie tugged gently at the lead, bringing me back to myself.

On the way home, we passed a twenty-four-hour supermarket. I popped in and bought bathroom cleaner and kitchen sponges, as well as some eggs, butter and other dairy products, seasonal vegetables and fruits, meat and seasonings. It wasn't at all expensive. This would be a good area to bring up children, I thought. In a hundred-yen shop, I bought a thin, papery apron. I had no intention of being here for long, so I wanted to keep my expenditure to a minimum.

When I got back to the house, I felt a wave of satisfaction to see the sparkling-clean kitchen lit up by the morning sun. I remembered a recipe for pancakes made with yoghurt and cream cheese I'd once found in a book called *Anti-Ageing for Dogs*. I poured the mixture into a heated frying pan, cooking a whole stack of thin golden-coloured pancakes one after another. Hearing the sound of footsteps coming down the stairs, I looked around. It seemed Yokota had finally stirred.

'Can't you keep that dog quiet? It made such a racket last night I didn't get a wink of sleep,' Yokota said, his tone so irritable he seemed like a different person to the one I'd met the previous evening. Now dressed in a black sweater and jeans, he looked like an ordinary middle-aged man, one you might expect to come with a wife and children. If I'd messed up somewhere along the line, I might well have found myself married to a man like this. 'At this rate, I wouldn't be surprised if the neighbours complained. Then it's you who'll be in trouble.'

I found myself tensing reflexively. There I'd been, thinking that Yokota didn't have it in him to make demands of or threats to a woman. He seemed totally uninterested by the transformation that had happened to his house, sitting with his legs under the low heated table, and staring down rudely at the breakfast arranged there.

'You're serving me the same food as the dog?'

He appeared to have worked out that Melanie was eating the same meal from her dish on the kitchen floor. I smiled broadly, resisting his overt disgust. I was far more concerned about Melanie's health than pleasing Yokota.

'They're just as tasty for humans!' I said, taking an exaggerated bite out of one of the miniature pancakes. Yokota's expression remained stern. I couldn't suppress the irritation inside me. He'd presented himself as someone so helpless, fretting about his diet of ready-meals, yet here was someone serving him proper home-cooked food, and all he did was find fault. This is why people like you stay single, I thought to myself. The longer I kept a smile plastered across my face, the harsher the words inside my head grew.

'Forget it. I'm not hungry, anyway.' He threw down his fork. My hatred assumed clear contours inside me.

Pouring a cup of coffee, I said, 'Is work busy at the moment?'
'Yep.'
'How many children are there at the cram school?'
'Depends on the day.'

This was like an interview, I thought. Over email he'd said often how much he wanted someone to talk to, but you'd never have guessed it to look at him. Now Yokota got up from the table without touching his pancakes, put on a down jacket with protruding feathers hanging from the wall, and headed for the door.

'Don't go into my room. Under any circumstances.'

'Have a good day!' I called out, but no reply came. Would the scorn I felt come leaking out, I wondered, regardless of how well I painted over it with a smile? I'd thought that wrapping a man like him around my little finger would be easy. I waited for the sound of the door closing, then darted upstairs to the first floor. As I suspected, his bedroom was unlocked.

Did he trust me, or was he just careless? Or another possibility: was he trying to test me? It appeared as though his experience of caring for his mother hadn't smartened him up at all. Or maybe all of his tales of caring for her were in fact a lie. It seemed entirely possible that he had left all of that to relatives and care workers.

The smell of sweat in his room was so strong it stung my eyes. I took in the yellowing futon left out on the floor, a rack crammed full of anime DVDs that looked ready to come tumbling down at any time, and endless figurines and posters with illustrated pictures of young girls. All of it just as I'd imagined. I set to work immediately.

And yet, however hard I looked, I couldn't find the incriminating material I was after – actual pornography.

I decided to take a look at the anime he appeared to have been watching most recently. With a rubber-gloved finger, I pressed the sickeningly sticky play button on the DVD player. Shoving his futon and the manga out of the way, I cleared a space for myself to sit. I had confidence that I'd be able to stand whatever scenes would appear, but in the end my sense of exasperation outdid any feeling of distaste. So much was demanded of the fourteen-year-old heroine: she had to be cute, innocent, strong, obedient, hard-working and sexy. If this was all you watched, it stood to reason a real woman was going to seem difficult to handle and more trouble than she was worth.

I ejected the DVD and booted up the PC on the desk. I'd thought in advance about options for what his password would be, but I still rolled my eyes at how simple a code it was to crack: the birthday of *Jelly Wizard*'s heroine. I pored meticulously through his email and chat history. I found some conversations with Kajii, but they dated from before her arrest, and their content was more or less the same as what had been read out in court. Everything I found seemed to suggest that they'd met after 2012, and their relationship had developed in a short time online.

Which meant that, placed in exactly the same circumstances as I was currently, Kajii had managed to win Yokota's love and trust. Starting to feel dizzy, I moved away from the desk, crouching down on the floor and wrapping my arms around my knees. I wasn't yet ready to abandon my hypothesis. Was it possible that, unperceptive as that would make him, Yokota had got close to Kajii without ever realising that she was the elder sister of the young girl he'd targeted back then? It was plausible that he'd come to be manipulated by her without realising it.

Just like how I'd been guided to this place by what she'd told me, from the other side of that perspex screen.

At our very first meeting, Kajii had somehow seen through me, and perceived the things that I'd been covering up all these years: the distance between me and my husband, the fact I'd hidden my true feelings from Rika, how I never felt truly relaxed around other people, that my malice towards my parents was the main driving force in my life.

I had liked my job. I'd given it my all, and I'd built up strong, trusting relationships with several people. And yet, in the same proportion that I'd done things right, I'd got things wrong. Whenever I put all of my energy into promoting some product or other, people would timidly caution me that maybe I was 'going too far'. Through a number of conflicts, I came to be a person whom others spoke ill about.

What a poor soul you are! Here am I, all locked up, yet you're far, far more lonely than I am. Rika's desperate to be my friend. She's adorable, isn't she? She's become so fixated by me that I've grown quite fond of her. It looks like you're about to lose her …

Since the day I met Kajii, my mind hasn't stopped racing. Whatever happens, I can't bear to lose Rika. In a way, it's as if I've had a crush on her ever since we met in our first year of university.

Feeling a warmth beside me, I looked down to see Melanie. I reached out a hand, touching her long, soft fur, slightly coarsened by age. I felt the stagnant sensation in my fingers disappear. Ever since touching that cow in Akiyama's farm, I had been dying to stroke my Melanie. How much I'd like to become the kind of creature whose very presence soothes, I thought – the kind of creature who can unconditionally affirm someone's existence just by turning their black eyes on them.

The rest of the day, I cleaned for over eight hours, transforming the bathroom, toilet and the second-floor storage room so it would have met the approval of the most exacting of clean-freaks. Come evening, I set about preparing dinner. I figured that someone like Yokota would feel wary of any dish that was new to him. After thinking it through carefully, I used the ingredients I'd bought that morning to make potato croquettes and vegetable stew.

Yokota came home just after seven. Casting one look at the meal set out on the low table, he said, 'I don't like konnyaku. And I don't eat carrots, either.'

He was lying. 'But you ate the oden and the borscht that Kajii made you!' I wanted to scream. 'You told her how delicious it was, and asked for another serving. You poured the soup over your rice, making her frown disapprovingly!'

As Yokota stabbed at the freshly made croquettes with his chopsticks, he murmured, 'This reminds me of her.'

Here we go, I thought, finally. I pushed down my exhilaration as best I could, and served his rice with as nonchalant a face as I could muster.

'You mean the woman you lived with for a little while? I think you've mentioned her to me before. You met on the same site we met on, right?' As I made my careful enquiries, I scooped up the soup with a ladle, avoiding the konnyaku and the carrots. In his emails to me, Yokota had boasted of how a woman had once lived in this house with him – neglecting, of course, to mention that Kajii had only been here a couple of days before she was arrested.

'Yeah. She'd make loads of different dishes that she'd set out on the table. It reminded me of when my mum was still well. It was a lot of fun, eating with her.'

'She must have been a wonderful woman.'

'Nah, she was ugly as anything. Fat, too. Fat as a pig.' Saying this, he snickered, and I felt a shiver running down my spine.

In contrast to his schoolboy way of speaking, his eyes flashed defiantly as if he were taking on the world.

It struck me then that I'd encountered many people like this before: boys who approached the girls with an obsessive attachment, mingled with both desire and sadism. Luckily, I wasn't the type who people like that went for, but their cruel teasing and bullying of other girls that I witnessed in the classroom had stunned me. If you told the teacher or confronted them about it, you'd be ostracised not only by the boys doing the teasing but also by their female victims as well. My mother always said that was just how boys were, that they were shy, and so teased the girls they liked, but it still made me hate them. That hatred had informed my decision to go to a girls' school.

When the topic at hand was Kajii, Yokota seemed like a totally different person. His gestures became animated, and he spoke so fast that it was easy to lose track of what he was saying.

'When you looked properly, though, there was something kind of pleasing about her roundness. She was fat, for sure, but just about within the tolerable range, I guess. Her skin was good, or okay, at least. When you were sat opposite her, she started to seem kind of attractive. She had a nice voice. Women are five times hotter when they've got nice voices.'

My voice is comparatively low, for a woman. As I was thinking this, Yokota was going on about how Kajii's voice resembled the voice of an anime character played by a particular voice actress, seemingly oblivious to the dinner set out in front of him. I got the sense that he didn't really care whether I was there or not. I watched as the crispy spikes on the croquette batter gradually wilted and grew soft.

'She was really devoted to me, as well.'

Even after his romance had ended the way it did, Yokota seemed to have learned nothing. If I'd had the same experience, I wouldn't have gone back to internet dating, and I certainly wouldn't have let a strange woman in my house again.

'Do you still love her?'

In response to this direct question, Yokota pulled an exasperated expression, the exact same face that boys my age had made at me when I was a kid. Maybe within this tiny body of mine was secreted the special power to make any desire in members of the opposite sex shrivel up.

'Were you romantically involved with her?'

Yokota sucked in his cheeks and pouted.

'No way! I couldn't do it with someone that fat if they begged me.'

Even when the woman in question was Kajii, I found it hard to hear a man denigrating a woman's appearance like this. I decided to change tack.

'You and her were from the same part of the country, right? Is it possible you'd met one another before, back when you lived there?'

I looked at him, determined not to miss the look that passed across his face.

'If we did I don't remember it.'

Was it suspicious that he ended the conversation like this?

He didn't comment on the taste of the food, either, which further fuelled my irritation. He couldn't have faulted it if he wanted to. The crispy croquettes were a magnificent golden brown. I'd put in curry powder for maximum flavour, and melted cheese hidden in the batter.

'Do you like the food?'

Yokota looked momentarily nonplussed by the question, then mumbled something incomprehensible as he chewed. He hadn't said a single word of appreciation this whole time. It seemed that, even if I did the same things as Kajii had done, there was something different about me. I had the urge to yell out, 'What's missing? What am I doing wrong?' It was clear that the two of us despised one another.

'Would you prefer toast for breakfast? Or rice?'

Even the way that he snapped back 'Toast', as if it were totally obvious, I found almost unbearably objectionable.

A desire that I didn't usually confront suddenly flashed before my eyes as if lit up in fluorescent lights: *If only Rika were a man.*

24 FEBRUARY

Breakfast this morning was home-baked bagels with bacon and eggs and home-made jam.

'I made these bagels myself. You know you can make them in a frying pan?'

Stop it, I said to myself, and yet I seemed incapable of preventing myself from seeking his approval. When I showed off like this to Ryō, he would look impressed and stroke my hair, but this guy simply nodded, not showing the slightest bit of interest in what I was saying.

'Roughly what time will you be home?'

'Did you go into my room yesterday?'

Knowing that if I gave a firm answer in either direction I was doomed, I smiled as ambiguously as I could. Yokota turned to me with the look of someone who felt they held the monopoly on common sense. Around me, he acted as though he were perfectly well adapted to society.

'Are you lying to me? You don't look to me like someone who's the victim of domestic violence. You don't seem scared of men, either.'

The bandage on my wrist was long gone, and today for the first time I'd left the eye patch off, thinking it was probably no longer necessary. I'd underestimated him. It stood to reason that he might feel wary of me, and that it would top even his hatred. I found it bizarre. He clearly wasn't satisfied by me waiting on him hand and foot. And yet, Kajii had been accepted by him – and accepted with a readiness that had stunned the world.

'Well, whatever. You're leaving today or tomorrow anyway, aren't you?'

It shocked me to realise that I'd totally forgotten about that element of my plan. I felt far from at home here, but I hadn't yet accomplished my aim in coming.

'What's your real goal?' Yokota's gaze was acutely direct. I found it stranger and stranger that someone with a sense of suspicion this healthy had managed to live with Kajii.

'Will you be back about eight?' I responded, avoiding his question. 'I'll make something nice and warming for dinner. Try and be back as early as you can!' I smiled, attempting with all my might to affect a maternal aura, but Yokota stared back at me as if beholding something horrifying. After the door had closed, I stood for a while at a loss. Melanie placed her nose on top of the table, gazing with interest at the remains of the breakfast spread. I gave her one of the dog biscuits I'd made, then went over to the sink and turned on the tap to wash up. The spray hit my face and I snapped back to myself with a start.

What was I doing, trying to win him over like this? I could hardly believe my own behaviour. What was I trying to achieve? How could I possibly attain a pass mark in this task I'd set myself? I was already well beyond an age where I could blame this on my parents.

My plan was to make a cream stew with potatoes, onions and broccoli. No carrots, of course. As I always tried to do, I'd curated a menu that took into consideration the physical state of the person I was cooking for and the ingredients I had at hand. The trick to making lump-free béchamel sauce was not to scrimp on butter, and to add in the cold milk in one go. I wanted, at least once, to make a meal that Yokota would compliment. I felt like I couldn't leave this place until I'd at least got a pass mark from him.

But hang on … This is …

My hand gripping the ladle paused, and I looked up, through the wire mesh, at the sparkling clean extraction fan with not a single speck of dust on it. For a moment I felt a flash of satisfaction at what I'd achieved in such a short space of time.

I hurriedly tried to push away the thought that was taking shape in my mind. If I accepted it, I knew I wouldn't be able to go back to my life as it was before. It would mean accepting defeat to her. The fan twisted before my eyes. And yet, I couldn't stop myself from voicing it.

This is no different to living with Ryō.

The two were totally different people. Yet was I not exactly the same whoever I lived with? What I did was identical. I immersed myself in the housework, scrubbing and polishing away, making meals tailored to the needs of the person I was living with. I would ask, again and again, whether they liked it. There was no sexual tension, no flirtatious interaction. And then an uncontrollable rage would begin to form inside me. Could I really say that I loved Ryō? I enjoyed being around him, of course. Enveloped by his large body, I felt a sense of safety. I valued him, and I felt total confidence that he felt the same about me.

Yet I couldn't rid myself of the sense that if I stopped moving, the merry-go-round called our family would simply cease to rotate. If I stopped moving, then I wouldn't be loved. And if I was the one moving, then I had no proof that I was loved. What did it mean to be loved, in any case? Was it to be needed? Why, then, when I was helping people in this way, did I feel this hollow and miserable?

I had begun to forget that I was here to help Rika, to prove Kajii's guilt. Owing to my own efforts, my sense of belonging was shrinking away. My breathing grew more laborious. Why was this house so cramped, so oddly shaped?

The doorbell rang. A dull sound. Maybe it needed fixing. Had Yokota come back for something he'd forgotten?

I sighed, wiped my hands on the front of my apron and headed to the door. Melanie looked up at me anxiously, padding obediently behind me.

It was just the same, whoever it was, wherever I was.

Whoever might be standing outside the door, it wouldn't alter the fact that I was all alone in this world.

CHAPTER ELEVEN

Was it because she herself had put on 8 kilos since her first visit? It had been three months since she had started visiting Kajii at the Tokyo Detention House and now, considering the woman before her, Rika found it bizarre that her looks had been so roundly criticised. She wasn't young and she certainly wasn't stunningly beautiful, but her appearance was very ordinary. The soft, pale-blue jumper she wore today matched her long, heavy, white skirt. The sense of self-acceptance that welled up from inside her lent her gestures and expressions a springy bounce. But that was all. She was an entirely average woman in her mid-thirties.

Rika saw a trace of fatigue cross Kajii's face as she considered her demand. Now, as if giving in, Kajii broke her silence and spat out, 'How would I know! I'm no magician. How would I be able to tell where your friend is right now?' She shook her hair from side to side in apparent exasperation. The circle of light ringing the crown of her head dissolved. Rika knew she couldn't turn back now. Besides, Kajii's words only strengthened her conviction: there was no doubt she knew where Reiko was.

'Won't you give me the tiniest hint? Can you think of what you said to Reiko that might have made a strong impression on her?'

Kajii's gaze roamed the air as if tracing an invisible butterfly. Rika could tell that she was enjoying savouring the stress she was inducing. She hummed, lifted her chubby index finger to her chin and pouted.

'Perhaps I'm not totally without ideas. But there's a condition attached to my telling you!' she squealed. Her eyes once again assumed an ominous glint. Not again, Rika thought, trembling inwardly. 'How did you kill your father?'

Rika had no memory of having told Kajii about that day, but these kinds of conversational developments no longer surprised her.

'Answer the question, and I shall do my best to remember what I might have said to Reiko.'

Rika had known since her all-consuming experience in the cowshed in Agano that she could not go for much longer without facing the subject head on. Now, she carefully regulated her breathing, working through each bump of fear one by one.

'The reason you're so attached to me is that you feel a sense of responsibility for the death of your father while you were in the third year of middle school. That's what Reiko told me. It was her opinion that that was probably all bound up in your head with cooking.'

'I broke a promise to him.' Rika finally managed to squeeze out. She had a sense that in doing so, she might have elicited a little sympathy – that even Kajii wouldn't have it in her to probe any further. But Kajii now leaned so far forward that her face looked ready to brush against the acrylic screen.

'What kind of promise?'

Rika made up her mind. The truth would come out anyway, so she might as well be the one to tell it.

'I promised to make my father the macaroni gratin I'd learned how to cook in home economics class, and I didn't.'

'You? A gratin? I thought you didn't know even know how to chop an onion.' Seemingly oblivious to the sensitivity of the subject at hand, Kajii rolled her eyes playfully. Her long, soft eyelashes had been curled to form perfect semicircles.

'The truth is, I used to really enjoy cooking when I was in middle school. I'd become determined to take over the housework from my mother, who was kept so busy with her work. As a result, I was top in our cooking classes. The teacher would praise whatever group I was in. I was her firm favourite.'

The moment was engraved in Rika's memory – when she'd taken the gratin out of the oven and held it up proudly in an oven-gloved hand, a round of applause went up across the classroom. She could recall perfectly the golden-brown breadcrumbs, the melted yellow cheese, and the thin skin that had formed across the white sauce.

'What was the recipe? I am fond of a good gratin. It's the season for them now, isn't it? This is rousing my hunger.'

'You fry chopped onion dusted with flour in butter, and stir in the milk a little at a time. When that's all absorbed, you add in the macaroni and broccoli boiled in salted water, and prawns simmered in white wine. Then you pour it all into the gratin tin, sprinkle it with cheese, breadcrumbs and parsley, and bake it in the oven for twenty minutes, if I recall correctly.'

To Rika's surprise, the recipe flowed fluidly from her lips. She could even picture the font in which the recipe had been printed, the rounded lines of the illustrations depicting the various stages. In fact, since the age of fifteen, whenever she'd attempted to make a proper meal, all of it would come back to her vividly – the scrap of loose leaf paper on which she had jotted down various tips for doing it extra well, the branches of the school magnolia tree visible from the window, the path to the home economics classroom which she had walked with her friends, chanting lines from the recipe as if they were lyrics to a song. That was why she had avoided even venturing close to a kitchen ever since.

'Surprisingly orthodox! I imagined it would be a less painstaking version.'

'I told my dad about it when I spoke to him on the phone, and he said how much he wanted to try it. I would stay with him one weekend a month, so he asked me to make it for him next time I went round, and I agreed.'

Back then, what Rika had feared the most was silence. When she was with her father, she would talk incessantly, continually coming up with new topics of conversation, intent on allowing no space for him to ask questions about her mother. She felt that if she didn't play the role of the optimistic, high-energy kid who was unfazed by her parents' divorce, if she wasn't perpetually providing entertainment, then she would be eaten up by the loving glances her father sometimes threw her way, by the reckless things that he said. The prince she was at school and the version of her that existed before her father were altogether different creatures. Around her father, Rika was an easy-going, scatter-brained jokester, a chatty young girl who was easily swept along by the latest trends. Even if the alcohol and the bad diet had made him balloon beyond recognition in the two years since she and her mother had left the house, even if he was permanently red-faced and dressed in the same yellowing zip-up hoodie, so long as he was rolling his eyes at something silly she'd said, she could pretend to herself that he wasn't so changed after all, and find a comfort in that.

'Okay, next Friday then. I'm looking forward to it. At seven? It's fine if you're early.'

That day, Rika's volleyball practice had dragged on. It was that time of year when the sun had begun setting earlier. As Rika looked up at the deep blue of the sky and pulled the lapels of her regulation pea coat tightly around her neck, the thought of getting on the Chūō Line, shopping for ingredients in the supermarket by the station, and then heading to her father's apartment seemed impossibly arduous. She hadn't told her mother this, but since the two of them had left, there was no sign that the Mitaka apartment had been cleaned even once, and the sinks and the bath were now so mouldy it made her hair stand on end. She wouldn't wash when she stayed, and always requested to eat out if possible.

These days, her father barely went into university any longer, instead staying home and writing papers the whole time, and the wallpaper had been stained brown by all the cigarettes he smoked. If she was going to cook, she'd have to first clean the kitchen, at the very least. She felt envy bubbling up in her towards her classmates, innocently joking around, of a kind she'd never felt before. Rika was the only girl in her class whose parents were divorced.

When she called her father from the pay phone and told him that she couldn't go over that evening after all because they'd been informed there was a test on Monday, which she had to revise for, it was the first time she'd ever lied to him. 'Oh, okay,' her father had said, calmly, and made to put the phone down, but she'd heard him give a loud sigh. In that moment of silence, Rika's stomach had squeezed into a tight ball.

Then he said, in a cold voice, 'You think I'm an idiot, don't you? You and your mother both. Some daughter you are.'

When she made to reply, to laugh and deny it, saying, of course I don't think you're an idiot, what are you saying, she realised that this was the same sort of accusation he'd hurled at her mother night after night. She lost the power to speak. Standing in the phone box, she wanted to hold her head and scream. She'd been so committed to making sure he never felt that way about her, and now, with one bad judgement call on her part, all her efforts had gone to waste. She put down the phone without saying a thing.

'My father was all on his own,' Rika said now to Kajii. 'I was the only person who went to his apartment. He was too proud to ask for help from anybody. He had a few drinking buddies by the sounds of things, but nobody he could talk to about his worries. He was starved for the kind of meal you eat with other people. I found the look he'd given me when I was leaving, that lingering gaze, too much to bear. That day, I lied to my mum too, and told her that I'd been round to see my dad but decided not to stay the night, because the test was approaching. She didn't suspect a thing. When I tried to call him on Monday, there was no answer. At first, I thought nothing of it. But come Wednesday morning, when he still didn't pick up, I had a bad feeling about it. I told my teacher I wanted to leave school early, and went rushing over to Mitaka.'

She could remember the looks that her friends shot her then. Of course they were worried about Rika, dashing off pale-faced, but they were also excited by the dramatic nature of the tragedy which their prince-like classmate was going through, and which they themselves almost certainly never would.

'He died of a stroke. By the time I found him, he'd been dead three days. I only glimpsed him lying face down on the floor from where I was standing in the door, but his body was already beginning to decay ... Afterwards, I read up all about it. If I'd met him that Friday, made him dinner, stayed overnight and the next day, I might have noticed the early signs of a stroke.'

After a while, Kajii finally said quietly, 'It wasn't your fault. You were just a child, and besides, it doesn't sound as though his death was avoidable, whatever you might have done.'

Her eyes, which had narrowed to fine threads suddenly popped wide open. 'Is that what you thought I'd say? Hmm?'

Her nostrils flared and the flesh of her cheeks jutted out. Her lips glistened. With the smile of someone full of their very favourite food, Kajii pointed at her.

'I've finally understood why you're so attached to me. As you yourself know full well, you're a murderer. Virtually the same as me. The reason you can't take your eyes off me is because you seek validation. If I'm proven innocent, you'll be able to forgive yourself. It'll be two birds with one stone.'

Rika felt the tension she'd been holding inside her body relax. She felt a far greater sense of redemption at this pronouncement than by the words Reiko had uttered at Niigata Station: 'It's not your fault.' This woman who didn't tolerate other women had made an exception for her.

Kajii was right, Rika thought. I killed him. For the first time she accepted the fact calmly: Rika Machida was a murderer.

It wasn't an oversight. She had deliberately forsaken her father, and killed him as a result. Thanks to her doing, both she and her mother had been liberated. She loved him, she felt sorry for how incapable he was, not a day went by that she didn't think of him, and she couldn't forgive herself, but killing him had enabled her to move forward.

'If I did kill anybody,' Kajii said, 'then my method was the same as yours. I simply stopped making myself available. I withdrew the lavish care I had been providing for them up until that point. Somewhere in your heart you're glad that you killed your father. You were relieved to find out he'd died, were you not?'

She was right. The ambulance workers who'd spread a blue plastic sheet from the entranceway of the apartment had dealt with her father's body out of her sight. One of them then returned to where Rika was standing with the caretaker and said, 'I'm sorry to inform you—'. What had come out of Rika's mouth was a line even she knew to be unfeeling:

'He's dead, isn't he?'

She wanted him to be dead beyond doubt. If he'd somehow managed to survive in a compromised state, it would have been even more restrictive for Rika and her mother.

'I was the same. When they died off, one by one, I felt a weight lifting from my shoulders. That's one less person to take care of, I thought.'

Rika did have regrets. If she could have that time again, she would go to her father's place and make the gratin. But she also imagined what it would have been like if her father had carried on living as he was. The father whose very existence felt like a weight around her neck – she still didn't know for sure if she loved him or hated him.

'You really didn't kill them, then? You never actually laid hands on them?'

Kajii shook her head. In that moment, Rika believed her entirely. This is the truth, she thought. This is what I've been coming here all this time for – this moment.

'Did you have the intention to kill them, though? That will be what the trial hinges on.'

'You could say I did, or you could say I didn't. Isn't that always how it is? Spend enough time with someone and there'll inevitably be moments when you find them a nuisance and wish they'd disappear.'

Rika recalled the enormity of the irritation she'd felt towards Reiko and her stubbornness in Niigata. Had Reiko sensed that somehow? she now wondered. She felt a shiver down her spine.

'My motive was the same as yours. One day, out of the blue, they just became too much. The faces of people who thought nothing of making endless demands, of being constantly given things. The way they sat at the table simply waiting to be served, not lifting a finger. Their certainty that they would be taken care of, without even having to try. I began, in an instant, to hate them. I couldn't be bothered to buy seasonal ingredients, prepare them, cook, choose the plates, serve up the food, then clear away the dishes and wash up for people like that. When I stopped being in touch, when I stopped doing the housework and the cooking, they panicked. Some of them became hyper-suspicious and their behaviour took on a stalkerish air. Some of them, after returning to life alone, began neglecting themselves, and suffered physically as a result. Like babies, all of them, whose mother had ceased looking after them. It's odd, isn't it? Once I had found their incompetence, their reliance on me adorable. I believed, up until that point, that I liked pleasing them. Yet I suddenly saw that it was always just me, working away frenziedly, all alone.'

Rika didn't fail to notice the slight change in Kajii's expression, the note of sorrow that went sliding across her peach-hued face.

'Don't get the wrong idea. I like serving men and giving them pleasure. Women who don't don't deserve the name. But being with just one man, a changeable woman like me gets bored.'

'And yet you haven't given up looking for a marriage partner?'

'It's just that I haven't met the right person yet.'

'I feel like what you're saying isn't—'

'Cooking is enjoyable, but the moment it becomes a duty, it grows boring. The same is true of sex, and fashion, and beauty. When you're forced to do something, it becomes a chore, and the pleasure disappears.'

Rika's body felt heavy. She knew this was important, and yet she couldn't bring herself to ask a question.

'The kind of wife that the men on those sites are looking for is, at base, a woman with no sense of life about her. Their ideal partner would be a kind of ghost.'

It wasn't at all hot in the room, and yet Rika's armpits were slick with lukewarm sweat. Even the gap between her sleeves and her wrists felt clammy.

'The quickest way for a modern Japanese woman to gain the love of a man is to become corpse-like. The kind of men who want those women are dead themselves. Indeed, it's because they're dead that they're so terrified of anyone with a sense of life about them. If those men hadn't met me, if I hadn't rejected them, they'd quite probably have died anyway. They were never really here to begin with.'

Maybe it isn't only the victims, Rika thought. Maybe I, also, have been dead for a long time. And not just me, either, but Makoto, and Reiko, and Ryōsuke, and Shinoi, and my mother. The only truly living person is this woman right in front of me. Which is why, as furious as everyone is with her, they can't take their eyes off her. They have to keep on watching her from across the dividing line between life and death, as she burns through the rest of her life, living out her desires.

'But why, when you're so full of that life force, were you attractive to those half-dead people then?'

'I wonder. Ghosts are souls who can't cross over to the afterlife, aren't they? They float around in this one, attaching themselves to the living.'

'What you're saying is so bizarre, and yet I feel like I understand it.'

Rika's mouth seemed to be moving of its own accord. Her thoughts were coming out unadulterated.

'I don't really know what it's about, but there are times when I feel as though I'm not participating at all in the scene in front of me.'

'Talking to you is so much fun,' Kajii said, smiling innocently. It was a smile like a warm breeze carrying a flurry of petals into the room, a smile that instantly made the space more vibrant. 'Talking with women can be fun, after all. I suppose we've opened our hearts to one another. I feel like I've finally understood what you've been saying all this time.'

Don't go along with this any further, Rika warned herself. She could tell that the prison officer was eyeing the clock. Perhaps there were fewer visitors than usual today, because he'd let them talk for over twenty minutes, but their limit was surely approaching.

'To return to your promise. Will you tell me where Reiko is?'

Kajii shot Rika a bored look. She opened her mouth and spoke slowly, as if the very act of doing so were extraordinarily bothersome.

'This was what I said to her. How many tigers did it take to turn into butter?'

The Story of Little Babaji. Reiko was the only person that Rika had talked to about that story – but she supposed that Kajii had managed to figure it out from something Reiko had coincidentally let slip. When it came to information that would help her manipulate others, Kajii's nose was nothing if not acute.

'When I said that, her expression totally changed ...' Kajii's expression, too, was changing as she spoke. Her face crumpled like a baby's on the verge of crying and her skin took on a deep red tinge. 'You go on about this woman all the time. Are you *that* concerned about her? And on the day that I'm prepared to open up to you, too! I've told you things that would get me in trouble with my lawyer if he found out about them, and you don't even seem pleased.' Kajii made no attempt to hide her anger with Rika. 'I'm tired. Leave now.'

Rika had planned to end the meeting herself for once, but in the end Kajii got there first.

It was three months since Rika had last got off at this particular station on the Den-en-Toshi Line. On leaving the Detention House, her plan had been to go to a restaurant near Ayase Station, but before she knew what she was doing, she was standing in front of the ticket gates, calling Ryōsuke.

'I've still not heard from Reiko,' he told her. His voice had a floating, ungraspable quality to it. 'I'm think I'm going to go to the police.
I can't get any work done, so I've left work early.'

'Can I come over? There's something I'd like to talk to you about.'

Outside the station, in Reiko's neighbourhood, Rika headed
straight for the same supermarket that she had visited before.
Hunting for butter here at the end of last year now seemed to her
like a distant memory.

Rika was fairly sure that Reiko would have cheese, flour and
breadcrumbs at home, so she didn't bother to look for them. Into her
shopping basket she tossed macaroni, frozen prawns, and onions. In
the dairy section, she deliberated before picking up a 500ml carton of
milk and then began looking for the butter.

*Due to product shortages, sales of butter are currently limited to one
item per customer.*

It was the same notice as before, but there was far more stock
lining the shelves than there had been last December. She picked up
a pack of salted Snow Brand butter and headed to the cash registers.

With the sunset sky as a backdrop, the lines of tightly packed
houses snaked their way up the hill. Housewives doing their shopping for the evening meal came and went. Once upon a time, Rika
would have felt overpowered by their unerring sense of purpose, but
now she blended in among them with no discomfort.

She pushed the button to the Sayama house intercom. The planters housing a mix of violas and daisies looked as well-kept and
brightly coloured as ever. She reminded herself that it had only been
five days since Reiko left the house.

'Hi. Thanks for letting me come.'

Something felt markedly different about the house from her last
visit. It wasn't that it was messy. Perhaps it had something to do with
Ryōsuke's large form filling the hall, but it felt narrower. Rika hadn't
thought he smoked, but she could smell cigarette smoke in the air.

His feet were bare, he wore a sweatshirt and tracksuit bottoms, and she surmised from the pallor of his face that he hadn't been sleeping properly.

'Is it okay to use your kitchen? I want to make macaroni gratin. Will you taste it for me?'

'What's this about? Gratin? Right now I ... I'd feel bad about you going to all that trouble.'

Rika insisted. She wasn't trying to express her gratitude – she had simply come to use his oven. She thought too that knowing someone else would be tasting it would make her up her game.

'I'm sure it won't be as good as Reiko's, but still. If you tell me where the knives and chopping boards live, I'll figure out the rest.'

Ryōsuke followed her into the living room and gazed at her with a worried expression.

The moment Rika stepped into the kitchen, she felt all the sensations that she'd kept locked away since that day she'd planned to go to her father's come rushing out in one go. Ryōsuke, it seemed, rarely ventured inside the kitchen, and he couldn't tell her where anything was. Luckily, it was tidy, and both the sugar and salt were kept in labelled transparent containers, so that Rika got the feel for things soon enough. She had expected to find dirty plates piled up in the sink, but its metal bowl was sparkling clean, and all the taps were spotless. Thanks to her experience at Shinoi's place, she understood better how to use an oven. The fitted oven beneath the hob was new, and its door less heavy than Shinoi's, making it easier to open and close.

Beside the microwave stood a row of cookery books. She pulled out one called *Home Cooking*, which featured a range of Japanese and Western dishes, with dated-looking brightly coloured photographs. She checked the index to find the page number of the recipe for macaroni gratin. Given how yellowed the pages were, it seemed to have been used a fair amount, but there was not a single oil or food stain on it, proof of how carefully Reiko treated her possessions.

'For lump-free béchamel sauce, use plenty of butter and pour in the milk in one go,' Reiko had noted in pencil. Seeing her smooth, fluid writing felt to Rika like coming across a much-appreciated road sign. And she hadn't known that white sauce was also known as béchamel. The instructions didn't say to dust the chopped onion with flour before frying it, as she'd learned in home economics. In fact, there was no frying the flour at all – instead, you simply stirred it into melted butter. She set the oven to heat to the stipulated temperature.

Just as she'd expected, she found cheese, breadcrumbs and dried parsley inside the spotless fridge. She washed the onions, the cold of the water chilling her to the bone. With reddened fingers, she began peeling their skin. When the smooth white appeared beneath, she placed the onions on the chopping board and inserted the knife. As she'd learned in home economics, she cut it in half vertically, then chopped it perpendicular to the direction of its rings. Her eyes stung, and she blinked repeatedly. She boiled the macaroni according to the instructions on the packet, and stirred in plenty of butter. Once she'd shelled and de-veined the prawns, she poured in some white wine and heated them gently. Watching the prawns curl up and turn a rosy pink, she felt the sticky feeling that had been clinging to her since leaving the Detention House falling away.

Looking for somewhere to throw away the prawn shells and onion skins, her eyes alighted on a square plastic container by the wall. She opened the lid to find separate compartments for burnable and non-burnable waste. The non-burnable section was crammed with empty bento boxes from the convenience store. Now she understood why the kitchen looked untouched. She glanced at Ryōsuke sitting at the table, staring down vacantly at a stack of work papers.

She dropped a knob of butter into a frying pan, waited for it to turn a golden colour, and then added in the flour she'd measured out with a tablespoon. In a matter of seconds, the flour began to absorb the butter, growing sticky. Greedily, it sucked up more and more butter. Mixing the contents of the pan with a whisk, she poured in the milk in one go, watching it transform into a runny cream-like béchamel, then blended in the prawns and the onion.

Opening the overhead cupboard, she found a pair of gratin dishes right away – a bright sunny shade of yellow, which seemed to speak of a happily married couple. She poured in the béchamel sauce with the macaroni added, then sprinkled on the cheese, breadcrumbs and parsley. When she'd transferred the baking tray with the gratin dishes into the preheated oven, Rika took off the oven glove and left the kitchen. Her sense that the gratin was going to turn out well put a bounce in her step.

'Can I have a look at your bookshelves?'

She waited for Ryōsuke to nod, then made for the bookshelves that occupied an entire wall of the living room. Without hesitating, she pulled out the book she was seeking.

This was where it had all started. If Reiko hadn't told her about this book, Rika wouldn't have got close to Kajii. For the three months since encountering this book, Rika had been making her way through the dense jungle, with Reiko by her side, whispering hints to guide her. Yet when she looked around her now, she could only make out herself and Kajii in the hot, humid forest. Reiko was nowhere to be seen.

The pool of golden butter spreading out from the roots of the trees.

Just then, a slip of paper escaped the book's pages and fluttered to her feet. It looked like a cutting from a weekly magazine. Instinctively sensing that she mustn't let Ryōsuke see it, she hurriedly picked it up and slid it into her pocket.

'Would you mind showing me Reiko's computer? I think it might provide some clues.'

He nodded and took out her laptop from the drawers at the side of the room.

'I tried to, but I didn't know her password.' Ryōsuke shook his head from side to side as he spoke. Rika tried entering Reiko's birthday, phone number, and the birthdate of her favourite actress, but none of them worked. A rich smell of butter, milk and cheese all melting together came drifting into the room.

'I don't think she's caught up in any kind of trouble,' said Rika. 'My sense is that she's got involved with something of her own volition. Would you mind holding off until tomorrow afternoon to file a police report? It would really help.'

'Do you have any idea of where she might be?'

Even without looking at Ryōsuke, who was standing behind her, casting his large shadow over her, she could tell his expression was one of exhaustion.

'Someone from our year at university says she's got a lead.'

Rika knew that if she turned around now, she'd be outed as lying. At that very moment, the oven timer bleeped. Thanking her lucky stars, Rika slipped past Ryōsuke, turning her back on him. She opened the oven door, her senses drawn to the blue flame and blazing hot air filling the dark space. For a moment, she recalled her moment of glory in the home economics classroom. The cheese was making a seething sound. She smiled to see the burnished brown of its surface.

At least its appearance was passable, she thought in relief, and reached out an oven-gloved hand.

She transferred the gratin dishes onto white plates, brought them over to the table along with forks and cups of water, and sat down opposite Ryōsuke.

Then Rika picked up her fork and pierced the crispy top layer of breadcrumbs. The béchamel sauce cascaded out from underneath like molten lava, and the macaroni and prawns came into view. Feeling a rush of confidence, Rika lifted her first forkful to her mouth. Just as she was exalting in how both the taste and the amount of salt seemed spot on, she felt something rough graze her tongue. A soil-like texture, which ruined the mellow fragrance of the butter and cheese, the smoothness of the sauce, and the squidgy texture of the prawns and macaroni. She tried to ignore it, but it scraped away at the inside of her mouth. After moving her tongue for a while, she dropped her shoulders and put down her fork.

'The sauce is lumpy, isn't it? It's horrible. I'm sorry.'

'That's not true! Thank you for doing this.'

It wasn't that in the intervening eighteen years Rika's cooking skills had got worse. More likely, on that day, the result would have been the same. She felt her stomach lurch. Rika had been a favourite not just among the other students, but even among the teachers, perhaps because of her home situation. In that small world, whatever she'd done had been praised to the skies.

Ryōsuke went on eating, his face registering no particular emotion. Rika finally understood. Even if she'd made her totally ordinary macaroni gratin for her father that day, he would still have died. His demise had been inevitable. Even if he'd managed, with Rika's help, to avoid the stroke, he wasn't the sort of person to amend his ways after a hospital visit or two. He would have collapsed again, afterwards.

The idea that a single home-cooked dish could save a person was a delusion. But how much suffering, how much bondage did that delusion cause for women? To think that a badly made meal like this could have saved somebody's life was arrogant and self-obsessed in the extreme. However hard she tried, Rika couldn't have erased her father's loneliness. Playing the good daughter on that day wouldn't have altered the situation a jot.

'I've discovered one thing,' Ryōsuke said now, flatly. 'I always thought Reiko was popular. But over the last few days I've got in touch with people whose contact details I've found noted down in her things. It didn't seem as though any of them really liked her that much. Talking to them, there was no trace of the Reiko I know.'

Rika was about to reply when she saw her phone vibrating in her bag. It was Makoto. He'd called several times today. Still, Rika decided to leave it until later.

'She was always finding her own way to do things, wasn't she? It was the same with her relationship with me, and with you. With the flavours she used in the kitchen as well. It was as if in everything she did, she was conducting experiments, figuring things out for herself.

Please don't think that Reiko chose you only because she thought you'd be a good person to have children with.'

When their meal was finished, Rika said her goodbyes and hurried towards the station. She had to get back to the office.

There were four tigers in the story.

Three of Kajii's lovers were dead. Who, then, was the fourth? Was it not the man who may well have had a narrow escape? That's who Kajii had been leading Reiko towards. If that was so, then that was where she needed to go too.

At 10 p.m., Rika met Shinoi outside a Belgian beer bar next to the office, and they entered together. There'd been no time to find somewhere low profile. Right away, she saw someone staring at them from the corner of the counter, but she decided to ignore them.

'I think this must be the guy. The first person who she felt really understood her.'

With these words, Shinoi set down on the table a file that he'd received earlier that afternoon from a journalist previously based in Niigata. Opening it, Rika found a collection of newspaper cuttings.

'He lived alone in a flat in Agano, from 1995 on. His parents were wealthy and had a home near Niigata Station, people of influence who were often featured in the papers. He lived with them as a recluse until he was in his forties, and then they gave him his own apartment, as a way of forcing him out. They sent him money, but rarely went to see him. There were several reports of him behaving strangely – screaming in the middle of the night, being rude to his neighbours, speaking to small children. The only reason he wasn't arrested, despite hanging around Manako's sister and people causing a fuss, was his parents.'

Rika stared down at the young man profiled alongside his parents in the now-faded article from the local paper. At the time the photo was taken he must have been in his twenties. His face itself was handsome. His eyebrows were thick, the gap between them narrow and his eyes were the deepest black, like Kajii's own. His lips were forming a strange expression, so that it was hard to tell if he was smiling or about to cry out in fear.

'He died last year. Suicide. He hanged himself in his Agano apartment. He was fifty-six.'

'So including her father, he's the fifth person she was close to who died. Do you think there's the possibility they were secretly in touch all those years? I'm thinking about what Anna said, that maybe it was in fact him who killed the victims ...'

'I don't know about that. But he did die straight after the verdict of her first trial. As far as I can tell from what you've said, Reiko is a smart cookie. My guess would be that she's trying to solve this case herself. I imagine she's trying to contact Shirō Yokota, to check if there's any connection between him and this guy. To help you out.'

Rika took a swallow of her over-chilled beer and winced, then shovelled some nuts into her mouth.

Shinoi carried on speaking. 'You know that after Kajii's arrest, they found enough pesticide in Yokota's house to kill a person? Kajii stated that she'd bought it for the herbs she was growing, but it's possible that she intended to kill Yokota, if he got in her way.'

'That's strange, though. Even if Kajii has killed people, she's always made it look as if they were accidents or deaths from natural causes. Why would she take down the fourth victim in such an obvious way?'

'Maybe once she knew the police were onto her she got desperate?'

'I found this cutting in Reiko's house.'

Seeing the slip of paper Rika held out to him, Shinoi's eyes turned pale. The clipping was taken from a trashy article in a woman's magazine, not the kind of thing Reiko normally read:

Never fear, even if you're overweight or unattractive! Manako Kajii's tried and tested techniques for winning a man's heart

Mr A said that he had his heart captured by Manako Kajii after living with her for just two days! One of her most alluring

attributes was her home cooking, he told us enthusiastically. The
staples of her weekly menu were dishes such as stews, hamburgers,
macaroni gratin – very orthodox choices. It turns out that fancy
options are the go-to for arrogant women trying to assert their egos.
If you find the man of your dreams, best to appeal to him with tastes
that remind him of his ma's cooking, and don't give him any nasty
surprises! Mr A still has several of the condiments that Manako
Kajii left in his kitchen. He says he's keeping them there for when
she comes back …

'Yokota really garnered people's sympathy, didn't he? He seemed
so pure and naive, and kind of tragic.'

What would Shinoi say, Rika wondered, if she vocalised the question on her mind? Namely, were the tigers – which was to say, Kajii's
so-called victims – dead to begin with, as she had said? Was that why,
when the police told Yokota that he may have had a narrow escape, it
hadn't registered with him at all? Are we really alive, you and I, she
wanted to ask Shinoi now – Shinoi who still couldn't part ways with
the house his family had lived in, and she herself, still so preoccupied
with her dead father.

'I come across this kind of advice for how to get ahead in life all
over the place, with regards to all kinds of things, and it always
sounds to me as if the advice hinges on closing off your intuition
about the person in front of you, not perceiving anything about them
with your own senses but just going by the rules you've been given.
Do you know what I mean?'

Shinoi looked at her. 'Do you think that maybe Kajii's crime was
not being able to see people as people, living their own lives?'

His eyes were now so wide they looked like they might drop out.
The lower lids just about managing to keep them in place were mauve
with lack of sleep.

'You know I said my daughter was bullied after she started
putting on weight?'

Rika nodded.

'It wasn't really that she'd put on weight – she'd just started puberty before the others. Her classmates were afraid of the changes she was going through. And I was too, in fact. I was scared that developing a woman's body meant she'd come to me with questions I'd be hard-pressed to answer.'

Rika attempted to picture Shinoi's daughter now, a young girl with features like his.

'I didn't realise what was going on at the time, although maybe deep down I sensed it. But I deliberately didn't cut back the hours I was working. With everything I was doing for her as her father, I thought, it wasn't my fault if I didn't notice. I was ticking all the boxes. Not the boxes of my daughter's needs, but the boxes as they were defined by society. I don't ever want to make that mistake again. I've been doing everything that I can to help you, but …'

He trailed off and took a sip of his beer, as yet untouched, then scrunched up his face.

'Are you thinking it's best I don't involve myself any further in this case?' Rika asked, and Shinoi looked at her, his gaze more piercing than she'd seen it before.

'As a journalist, I think you should keep going, but as a friend, I wonder. For Reiko's sake as well, I think you'd be better to step back and leave the rest to the police.'

'Speaking of which, I asked Reiko's husband if he would wait until tomorrow to file an official report. I don't want to make more of a big deal of this than necessary. I want to bring Reiko back as if none of this had ever happened.'

Rika turned around and shot a bald stare at Kitamura, for it was he who was watching them from the corner. He attempted to shield his face with the latest edition of a literary journal, but she'd recognised him the moment she stepped inside. Now she walked up to him and plucked the magazine from his hand.

'You were in charge of covering the Kajii case three years ago. Do you know where Shirō Yokota's house in Kawasaki is? The man she was living with when she was arrested.'

'I do, but what's this about, out of the blue?'

Kitamura's usual composure had vanished. Even in the dim light of the bar she could tell that he had flushed right up to his ears.

'I think there's a chance someone I know is with him. Will you take me there?'

Kitamura's eyes flicked to the space behind Rika. Turning back to where he was looking, she saw her mobile phone flashing insistently from her bag.

'Hold on a second,' she said. She grabbed the phone and stepped outside to answer the call.

'Why won't you pick up? What's going on? Have I done something?'

'Sorry, I'm just really busy right now.' She'd left her coat in the bar, and even as she spoke she could hear how cold she sounded. To meet Makoto, who was almost certainly still at work, would take only two minutes of her time. His voice, just about maintaining a veneer of cheerfulness, was trembling.

'Do you want to break up?'

In the years they'd been together, this was the first time that these words had been uttered between them. Rika hadn't conceived of the possibility at all, but now she accommodated it without any particular feeling of disturbance.

'Let's talk about it properly when I see you.'

'What the hell have I done, Rika? Tell me! What's this about?'

So now he's talking to me like this, Rika thought. He's talking to me like a man. With the power her mobile afforded her, she cut off the wailing. His reaction was perfectly natural, she thought. Why didn't she feel worse about behaving so cruelly? It wasn't because her head was full of Reiko. In the last few days, Rika had come to realise with clarity: she just didn't love him.

She'd been able to stay with him for as long as she had in part because they'd barely seen one another, but also because neither of them had really understood what it was for two people to love one another. She had been convinced that it was a good thing for men and women not to stir up one another's emotions, not to encroach on one another. It wasn't just their bodies they hadn't been using, but their hearts and their time as well. They had both, in a sense, been all but dead. Suddenly Rika realised Kitamura was standing beside her, and Shinoi was stepping out of the bar behind him.

'I'll be in touch,' Shinoi said, nodding at her and Kitamura, then slipped past them down the road towards the station. It had started to drizzle, still so faintly that even when you put your hand out, it took a while to feel the droplets.

Would Makoto go on to die alone, like Rika's father had done?

Looking up at the office building in the dark, she directed her eyes to the light coming from his department. She'd never seen it with the lights off. Though she knew it was conceited to do so, she pictured his death, down to the smallest detail. If that happened, she really would be a killer.

Alongside her, Kitamura was looking perplexed. She made to write a message on her phone, then thought better of it and put it away in her bag. If something were to happen to Makoto now, Rika still wouldn't regret the choice she was making. There was a limit to the time they had. Once she'd found Reiko, she'd speak with him properly, she decided. For the moment, she resolved to put him out of her mind.

In the darkness at the bottom of her bag, her phone continued to flash. All night long, it lit up the scraps of paper, paperclips and pen caps lying there, as if confronting Rika with her own heartlessness.

The breeze was mixed with the smell of gasoline, but she found it a fragrant, pleasant smell. Was it because her face was so painfully cold? In the morning, Kawasaki's industrial belt was home to several different kinds of smoke, each with its particular smell, and she felt as though she could differentiate them just by sight. Rika had taken the Keihin-Tōkoku Line to the nearest station, and for the last hour she and Kitamura had been keeping watch outside the three-storey building which lay on a corner of a strip of houses, and which was, they believed, owned by Yokota.

It was a fiendishly cold morning, of the kind that made it hard to believe that March was just around the corner.

'Do you have any proof that this Reiko person is in there? And what kind of decisive evidence proving Kajii's guilt is she hoping to obtain by moving in with him?'

'I know I'm a fine one to talk, but Reiko's the kind of person who's prone to acting in extreme ways. She's always been like that.'

'It's amazing that you've managed to maintain this friendship since university, when you're as busy as you are. I'm envious.'

'I never thought I'd hear you admit to envying anyone or anything.'

'I don't have a single friendship like that – one which has nothing to do with what both parties are getting out of it. That was why I couldn't believe that your connection with Shinoi would be without that kind of motive.'

Rika was about to reply, when Kitamura jutted his left shoulder forward.

A short, plumpish man in a down jacket had come out of the building. Was this Yokota? From his profile, he didn't look particularly happy or satisfied. The image of him lying naked with Reiko flickered before Rika's eyes and then vanished. She waited for him to disappear, then ran towards the door and rang the bell. If nobody replied, she thought to herself, she would try turning the doorknob. What would happen if it was open?

If Reiko was lying there spread out on the floor, like her father had been that day, would she ever recover? If she'd lost two people she cared about through her own bad choices, would she be able to keep on living?

The image rose vividly to her eyes: Reiko's graceful body lying in a room littered with old ramen containers and magazines. She could tell that Kitamura, standing next to her, had noticed her legs were trembling. The door opened slowly from the inside.

'Reiko!'

Inside was her friend, standing forlornly in the doorway. There was no lobby in the place – the porch opened immediately on a triangular living space. Reiko stood at the tip of that equilateral triangle.

'Rika,' she said, her tongue moving unsteadily, as if she were saying the word for the first time. The dog at her heels growled at Rika nervously.

The kitchen and the living room with its low heated table somehow put her in mind of Reiko's Tokyo house, although both the area and the positioning of the furniture were different. She must have spent time cleaning the place up, Rika thought.

The cheap apron Reiko was wearing didn't suit her in the slightest. An expression Rika had never seen before was papered across the tidy contours of her face. She was pale with nerves, the tightness of her lips and the creases around her eyes all suggested she was as tense as a piano spring.

It dawned on Rika that the proper name for what Reiko was doing wasn't 'running away', or 'infidelity', or even 'research'. Reiko had been using this little building to play house. In fact, what she had been doing for the last few years was a grand attempt at playing house. This place, Rika understood, was just like a doll's house. When she looked towards the small windows in the kitchen, she felt she could see those black eyes peering through at her. This room, the furniture in it, Rika, and Reiko and Kitamura – all of them were little playthings that Kajii had arranged as she wished.

She had to say something. Maybe, just as it had been with her father, everything rested on the one thing Rika would say next. Compared to the pressure on her that day when she was fifteen this was nothing. Her dry lips moved as if of their own accord.

'Is that white – I mean, béchamel sauce?'

She could hear the sound of something simmering in the kitchen. The smell of smooth béchamel sauce with plenty of butter had wafted over and rose up between them. Rika was certain that the sauce would be glossy and scorching hot, with good body to it. That it would have a velvety feel in the mouth, and slip gently down to the stomach. She wanted to eat Reiko's food. She loved the food Reiko cooked. It was well executed and delicate, and yet there was a liveliness, or rather an ardency, about it. Yes, thought Rika, the good thing about Reiko was how extreme she was, honest to a fault, incapable of concealing her passion. She had a stronger sense of individuality about her than even Kajii.

Reiko ignored calculations based on profit and loss, winning and losing, and plunged headlong into the unknown. She got hurt more, lost more, than anybody else. It wasn't Kajii whose side Rika needed to be on – it was Reiko's. This pure-souled woman, whose next move nobody could read, needed Rika more than anybody. Rather than sink down to Kajii's depths, Rika wanted to ascend to Reiko's heights. Now, suddenly, it struck her: it wasn't Kajii who was really alive – it was Reiko. She'd been so close to her all this time that she hadn't even noticed.

Rika hadn't brushed her teeth since the previous day. She could still feel the unpleasant texture of the lumpy macaroni gratin on her tongue. Beside her, Kitamura was growing irritated and signalling to her in some way, but she didn't have the space to pay him any attention.

'It's cold today, so I thought I'd make him a stew. I was frying the flour in butter, and I just poured in the milk,' Reiko said, her eyes focused on the middle distance.

Rika could see it: a sweet stew, with a rich milky taste and large chunks of floating vegetables. A cream stew with depth and a certain austerity, which didn't even bear comparing with the one Kajii's mother had made from the solid roux. She heard her stomach rumble. Even at a time like this, her stomach rumbled, faint yet indubitable proof that she herself was alive. Rika was simply waiting, silently, for the moment when Reiko would tell her to tuck in.

CHAPTER TWELVE

The second she made to take off the grey lid of the bathtub, Rika recalled the bath and the sink in her father's apartment, and the inside of her mind was stained the colour of mould. Holding her breath, she forced her hands to peel back the lid. Shinoi said he hadn't taken a bath here for years, but the tub that appeared was immaculately white. It was hard to believe that it had once taken on the dirt and sweat from the bodies of a family of three.

Nevertheless, Rika carefully washed down the tub using the showerhead and the palm of her hand – she couldn't find a sponge – before filling it with hot water. The apartment was dry, so she left the door to the bathroom with its frosted-glass panes open. Moisture, dust, yellowing wallpaper, and the short, straight hairs in the corner of the room, which could have been Shinoi's or her own – did the fact that she no longer felt aversion to Shinoi's smell and skin this close to her mean that their relationship was verging on a familial one?

Rika dried her wet soles, went into the living room and washed her hands thoroughly. She boiled some water, made tea, which she poured into a thermos flask, then wrapped three of the chilled onigiri she'd made in silver foil.

The gentle melody of the chimes signalling the start of fourth period drifted in from the nearby primary school. This neighbourhood was steeped in the rhythms of people's lives, which she found soothing.

These days, the moment she crossed off something from her to-do list, something else would pop up to take its place. Her mind didn't have a second's rest. Is this what it was like being a housewife?

She called out to Reiko, still in bed in the room that had once belonged to Shinoi's daughter.

'I've left the water at room temperature. The yoghurt's in the fridge. I made some onigiri and some tea, too. Oh, and I opened one of the cans of dog food I bought and left it on the floor, just for the meantime. There's a supermarket on the ground floor here, so I'll leave out some money and a key. I'll keep an eye on my phone, so if anything comes up, however small, then call me, okay? I'm off to work. There might be people coming in and out, but you don't have to do a thing. I'll be home as soon as I can.'

Reiko hadn't uttered a word since the previous day, when Kitamura and Rika had brought her here. Now Rika heard something bumping the bottom of the bedroom door. When she twisted the handle and opened the door a sliver, Melanie poked her damp nose through the crack. Her moist black eyes stared up at Rika. Rika had never shared a space with a pet before, and she found this small black and white body with its bulging eyes more terrifying than adorable. She hadn't yet adjusted to being around a creature that moved so far beneath eye level, or to its smell. She found herself worrying about what she should do if the dog injured itself or got away, and she was relieved to have it out of her sight. She caught a glimpse of Reiko's back, as she lay there in the bed. It seemed that in the few days they had been apart, Reiko had shrunk yet again. Melanie slipped past Rika's feet and padded towards the can of dog food on the kitchen floor.

Rika closed the door. Turning her back on the wet noise of Melanie munching the food, she took one of the rice balls on the plate and brought it to her lips. The film of sushi nori clinging to the still-warm rice burst open beneath her teeth, and the taste of the bonito-flavoured umeboshi filled her mouth.

'So she's safe? She's not hurt in any way?' Ryōsuke had said, when Rika had called him last night in front of Reiko and told him everything, his voice so dry-sounding that it made the core of her being shrivel up and twinge in pain.

'I'm going to take care of her for a while. I'll keep you updated about everything.'

There was nothing seriously wrong, it was just that married life had left her exhausted and she needed a bit of a break, Rika had said repeatedly. She didn't have it in her to refuse Ryōsuke's plea to just hear her voice, so she'd passed the phone to Reiko, then stood outside on the balcony for a few minutes. Whether the two had actually talked during that time, she didn't know.

Rika's initial plan had been to let Reiko stay in her own apartment, but the building didn't allow pets. She knew that she couldn't separate Reiko from her beloved Melanie in her current state. When Rika had dragged Reiko from Yokota's house, she had clutched Melanie to her chest like a little girl, oblivious to almost everything else going on around her. It was as they got in the taxi that Rika first thought of Shinoi's Arakichō apartment, which lay virtually empty. She checked and found out that pets were permitted.

Shinoi had agreed to Rika's desperate request to use the apartment until Reiko was better. Not only that, but he also offered to stop by and check up on her himself from time to time. Since the two of them had arrived, Reiko had been sleeping like the dead. Rika, on the other hand, with the help of Kitamura, had been running around, going to the pet shop to buy a dog toilet and dog food, getting spare keys cut, collecting her stuff and her work things from her Iidabashi apartment and preparing for this new living arrangement, having no idea how long it was likely to continue.

What had Reiko heard, what had she witnessed in those three days she'd been in Yokota's house? She worried that Yokota might have reported the incident to the police, but Kitamura had managed to track down his blog, and had reported that he'd updated it this morning with a new piece on a favourite anime series, which seemed a sign that Reiko's absence hadn't greatly disturbed him.

Rika had no intention of comparing Reiko with Kajii. She understood how meaningless an exercise that would be. Yet it was hard for her to accept that, over the same period of time and under similar circumstances, Kajii had been chosen by Yokota while Reiko hadn't. It gave her the feeling that it was not only her, but her best friend also who was having her feelings trampled over by Kajii.

Exiting Yokota's apartment, they'd locked the door and posted his key into the post box with a note, leaving the half-cooked stew sitting on the hob. Rika then took the smartphone that Reiko had bought to communicate with Yokota.

Now, leaving the apartment and chewing her second onigiri, Rika walked along the sloping streets that led to the office. The temperature had to be far higher than in Niigata, but the dry, hard Tokyo wind bit into her skin. On a tree in someone's garden she spotted plum blossoms, but she couldn't smell any of the scents of spring. How she wished she could spend all her time taking care of Reiko! As she walked, Rika was aware that she'd left most of herself behind in that apartment. At this rate, she was very likely to mess things up in some way at work, which scared her. Was this the feeling that Mizushima had had every day, heading into work with a young child?

There was nothing for it. She would have to rely on people who had more time and energy than her.

Arriving at the office after one o'clock, she called Kitamura and Yū to the sofa outside the smoking area and, lowering her voice, said, 'I'm sorry about this, guys, but there's something I could really use your help with. I've texted you the address of an apartment in Arakichō. It's owned by Mr Shinoi, from the news agency, but my friend who's left home is currently staying there, along with her dog. She's mentally fragile at the moment. I'm going to try to get home as early as I can, but I was wondering if you two might take it in turns to pop in and check on her, when you have the time? It's about five minutes away by taxi. I'll pay. You can sit there and work, or do whatever. I just need you to be there. These are the keys.'

Apparently unruffled by the urgency in her voice, Kitamura nodded in agreement and took the key before returning to his desk. Rika felt grateful to him for not commenting on the situation. Yū, on the other hand, was frowning, clearly confused by this development. Her zip-up hoodie emblazoned with the idol group's logo looked faded and creased. Quite possibly, she hadn't had enough time of late to go home and rest.

'When you say Mr Shinoi, do you mean Yoshinori Shinoi, that famous editor? And who is your friend?'

Rika had intended to skim over the sensitive elements of the story, but she found herself explaining to Yū everything that had happened with Reiko. By the end of the account, Yū seemed buzzing with excitement.

'That's amazing! That's so incredible that she'd do that! It's like something from a movie. That's the young-looking pretty woman who was at reception a while back, right? We should definitely give her a job at the company, in that case!'

'At the moment she's pretty weak, and isn't her usual self.'

'You know, people of my generation aren't that into the whole Kajimana thing. It feels very bubble era, somehow. To me, Reiko seems far more lively and interesting than Kajii. Of course I'll help. I'd love to meet her. I can do my research anywhere, anyway. I'll go over right away,' Yū said. Her burst of enthusiasm made Rika a little nervous.

'Thanks, I'm so grateful. Just don't go in too strong, okay? She's a delicate soul.'

Informed that she had a call from the chief editor on the internal line, Rika got up.

When she entered the editor's glass-fronted corner office, he placed an opened envelope on the desk between them. It bore a logo she knew well by now: Tokyo Detention House.

'It's from Kajii. Is it true that you were curt with her?'

Rika had imagined that, sooner or later, it would come to this. It was Kajii who had been the first to notice that Rika's interest in her was waning.

'It's amazing. She seems besotted with you. She starts by getting angry that you've not shown much interest in her lately, then practically begs for you to go and see her.'

Rika exhaled. For Kajii, this was doubtless the first time that a person who was supposedly crazy about her had turned their back on her.

'I think she's fed up because I'm distancing myself from her.'

There was no point trying to hide it any more. After being so frank with Yū and Kitamura earlier, Rika no longer felt any hesitation in trampling on the rules she'd been following up until now.

'I wouldn't mind if it were just me, but she's endangering the people around me too. I'm going to step back from this case. Would you look for someone to take over from me? I know it's irresponsible of me to do this, and if I end up having to move departments as a result, I'll understand.'

Rika gave her boss a brief run-down of what had happened to Reiko over the previous few days. As she expected, his eyes began to bulge – the glint they took on was more cynical than the one that had appeared in Yū's.

'I know this might be a poor choice of words, but this is a genuinely fascinating turn of events. Your friend sounds like a real character, no less than Kajii herself. Will you think about writing up this story? Just as it is. I know this is unprecedented, but I don't mind making it your journalistic debut.'

'Sorry, but I'm washing my hands of it. I've realised that I can do the work I want without Kajii.' Her voice was hard and quiet. Overriding any feeling of anger inside her was a sense of the danger she faced, and the impulse to protect herself. She could tell that the editor was going to go on the offensive.

'I've got some good news, though, about Le Salon de Miyuko. We got the go-ahead for you to attend. One of our freelancers who writes food articles for the women's magazine used her connections and got in touch with them. The owner and his wife seem to trust her. We registered you under a false name, said you're working in overseas sales. You can take someone else along with you. That Reiko woman, perhaps. It might be a nice change of scene for her.'

'What are you saying? Did you hear what I told you about the sort of state she's in?'

'Are you a journalist, or aren't you? I don't know why you're pulling back now, when you're so close to where you've been trying to get to. You're not far off a place at the desk. You've worked so hard to get Kajii. You're so nearly there. Turn back now and you'll regret it for the rest of your life.'

His unkempt grey eyebrows moved about a lot, but the eyelids beneath them were heavy and creased like an elephant's foot. The whites of his eyes were clouded. He was in his fifties, but his body looked swollen to the very tips of his fingers with fatigue and suspicion. After getting married he had gone back to smoking heavily, and his clothes and body were so deeply infused with the scent of tobacco that Rika could smell it from where she was sitting.

And yet she also knew that what he was saying was true. She remembered how he had desperately tried to stop Mizushima when she'd requested to move departments. The shade of envelope Kajii had chosen was reminiscent of the cherry blossom whose season was rapidly approaching. It seemed out of place in this office soaked through with exhaustion.

She sensed the cafe door opening. Something told her that it was Makoto who had entered, but she didn't lift her head from her phone screen. The sleeve of his coat was reflected in the window that looked out over Kagurazaka, on which darkness had fallen a couple of hours before. Seeing the paper bag with the Shūmeisha logo that he was carrying, she guessed that he was on his way back from delivering proofs to a writer.

'Megumi's really cute, isn't she?' Rika said, finally peeling her eyes from her phone, on which a YouTube video of a Scream song was playing. Makoto's reaction was reflected shakily on the surface of her coffee. He turned around to halt a server, and pointed to something on the menu.

'I was watching videos of her online. Her whole face lights up when she smiles, and she's such a good singer. From what I can see, she's going through puberty, so her body has filled out, and her figure looks a bit unbalanced, but it'll sort itself out in a couple of years. What's more worrying to me is how her weight seems to be fluctuating since being criticised by her fans, and she's smiling less than she used to. Why have you suddenly stopped supporting her?'

Eventually, she heard the noise of Makoto's lips parting. When he spoke, he did so in a clear, gentle tone that she could tell he was adopting to mask his irritation.

'Why are you asking me that? Have I said anything to you about it? Has someone been saying things about me? Look, that's not what we're here to talk about. It's like you're doing research for an article or something! I've come here to talk about us. Surely you're not going to tell me that's the reason you've been so cold?'

'I want you to tell me why you stopped feeling able to be her fan.'

Makoto seemed to understand that if he evaded the subject any longer, they'd keep going round in circles. He spoke at speed, a pained look on his face.

'I don't like people who can't control themselves. I thought she was more disciplined than that. What? Why are you looking at me like that? It's just a pop star we're talking about, no? Do I need a reason to stop liking her?'

'It's not that, though. It's not that you've stopped liking her because she's stopped trying. You're not that sensitive to beauty or aesthetics or any of that stuff. It's that you're just not brave enough to keep on supporting someone whom everyone else has turned on.'

Makoto's eyes were directed at the people on the next table.

'The reason that you never told me about them in the first place was because you felt embarrassed to be a grown man getting all excited over a bunch of young girls, right? But I wish you'd talked to me about it. When two people are going out, they need to talk about all those little things that are important to them, so they can get to know each other properly. That's what I wanted.'

'I'm sorry, Rika. I just didn't have the time. That's what almost everything comes down to: the lack of time.'

She guessed that Makoto thought there was no point arguing about it any more. He frowned in an exaggerated rendition of a sorry face.

'I was really happy that time when you asked me to – to the hotel. I felt so warm after that. I wanted us to have more times like that. That was how it started out, you and me. Didn't you feel the same? Given our lifestyle, I thought we could ...'

Rika nodded, as if to cut him off. A sliver of the heat and the pain of that period flooded back to her. The days when they'd first started going out, when they'd stayed awake having sex all night. She'd enjoyed doing that with him, but looking back at those times from the place where she now stood, they seemed to her like a single ray of sunlight, without any depth. She felt sure that if they stayed together, it would always be her who would have to initiate things, for as long as they lived.

'Yes, but I think I'm a different person now to who I was then. I keep on changing. And there's something I need to apologise to you for.'

She was going to tell him that she'd only initiated sex with him that time because Kajii had ordered her to, but at the last moment thought better of it. If she did tell him, it would only be to rid herself of the burden of guilt. Instead she said, 'It wasn't because I was covering the Kajii case that I put on weight, you know. Until recently, I associated cooking and eating with guilt. I didn't like doing it because it made me think about my dead father, waiting all alone for me to come over. But I like tasting things, and absorbing things into my body. Right now, I've no plans to lose weight. I'm going to stay this way until I've understood better what feels right for me.'

'If I said something about your figure that's bothered you, then I apologise. It was wrong of me. I was being insensitive. I'll really try harder.'

Both Makoto's tone and his posture suggested such exhaustion that she was taken by the impulse to reach out a hand and help him. She could see that he felt at a loss for what to do. Suddenly she felt as though she were in the wrong in some way. Why wouldn't she give in? Everything she was agitated by was so minor. Her own behaviour seemed bizarre to her.

She knew that there would come a time when she would regret her current decision. Would it not be better to restore her body to its previous state and carry on seeing Makoto occasionally? Why was it that she could no longer do that? Maybe the same question could be asked of Reiko. If she just shut her eyes, accepted the situation and returned to Ryōsuke, everything would be fine. Why is it, Rika thought, that we're both incapable of that? It wasn't that she disliked Makoto, or that Reiko disliked Ryōsuke. Yet, having said all that, she and her friend were terrified of being alone.

Just then, Rika's eyes met Makoto's. She saw the same question floating there. She could tell that however composed and accepting he was trying to act, he was irritated. He wanted to make unilateral demands of her. He had no wish to budge an inch, either.

Maybe, Rika thought, we are confronting one another as fully formed individuals for the first time. If Rika were to lie now, and the two of them were to move past this, she would only end up betraying and hurting him in the long run.

'These past few days I haven't been able to concentrate on my work, and I haven't been sleeping well. If I'm doing something wrong then tell me, and I'll fix it. I have so much fun with you, and I think we're pretty compatible. I know we haven't seen each other that much, but I'll make time from now on. I want to hang out with you more. We're both busy, so let's not squander the time we do have together by fighting.'

His tone was sincere. He was about to send a book to press.

Staring at the cars outside the window, Rika reminded herself not to get carried away by the moment.

'It's not about that, though. It's not just about now. I'm talking about the future.'

'You mean getting married? I'll do my best to think about that, as much as I can.'

'No, that's not what I mean. If I get an exclusive interview with Kajii and become the first female member of staff on the editorial desk, I'm going to get a lot of flak. Will you still want to date me then? Could you take it if people start saying to you, "How can you stand to go out with a woman like that?" The same sorts of things people say to Kajii's victims, even though they're already dead.'

For a little while now, Rika had been harbouring a premonition: in the not-too-distant future, she would be attacked by a vast horde of people. The thought made her cower in terror, but she sensed that it was inescapable.

'You just have to do everything you can to make sure you're not criticised. The truth is, I'm not as laid-back as I seem, at all. I'm the type who has to work twice as hard as everyone else to keep up. That's how I've always lived, and it's tough for me when people deride that way of being.'

As he spoke, Makoto's tone grew heavier, even slightly sleepy. She wondered whether he'd be angry if she pointed that out. A wave of sadness went crashing through her. He wasn't saying this because he was fed up, she realised. He really did believe that if you tried your hardest then everything would turn out for the best. He believed that every tragedy was a matter of individual responsibility, and that it was wrong to rely on the help of others.

'I don't think I'm a lazy person, necessarily, but I'm not confident that I can maintain the effort needed to keep you and the rest of the world happy twenty-four-seven. I'm not young any more, and I don't want to give myself up to other people for their consumption. I want to decide how I work and interact with other people based on what I think really matters.'

Rika took care to speak as kindly as possible. Seeing that it was becoming too much for Makoto to bear, she let out a big sigh. She would put an end to this herself, she decided.

'Even after the Kajii assignment is over, I'll probably stay as I am. Maybe I'll put on even more weight as I get older and my metabolism slows. And it's not just my appearance, either. I'll be even busier, and I might not have the time to sit and talk with you like this.'

She was trying to gently let go of his hand. And yet there was a part of her – a part she felt ashamed of – that was also, faintly, pleading with him. *You don't have to drive yourself into a corner*, she wanted him to say. *Let's stop seeing one another in this way that ends up grinding us both down. If we can just be alongside one another, sharing each other's heat like we did that night in the Shinjuku hotel, that's enough for me. However the world thinks of you, it won't change what I feel about you …*

She saw his mouth contort. Without intending to, Rika let out a sound. His lips, which mostly refused to settle on a fixed shape, had just smiled. It was the end. Two seconds before he actually said it, she knew what was coming.

'Well, then, I guess that's that.' The weak smile on his face bore a trace of relief.

Rika tried to remember the first day they'd met, or at least the first day she'd become aware of having feelings for him, willing herself to feel the prick of tears in her eyes. Yet all that had happened in the last few months with Reiko and Kajii was too bright, and she could barely summon a single memory.

Reiko, dressed in the sweatshirt and tracksuit bottoms that Rika had lent her, was sitting on the sofa with Kitamura, their bodies some distance apart as they faced the 50-inch plasma TV screen. Rika greeted them as she took off her coat. Physically she was exhausted, yet emotionally she felt strangely unruffled. She laid her shopping bags down on the table.

Opposite her, Yū was sitting with her laptop. Barely making eye contact with Rika, she said, 'Welcome back. I've had to resubmit my graduation thesis, so I've been glued to my computer. But Reiko isn't really responding when I talk to her, anyway. These two have just been playing this game the whole time.'

Rika had forgotten that until the end of next month, Yū was still a student. 'Right,' she murmured. There was neither any anger nor longing for Makoto left inside her. Instead, she felt a chill that had seeped down into the deepest part of her.

After deciding to break up, she and he had talked about work and various trivial things for nearly an hour, before parting ways. She felt that now, if she were to message him, it would be easy for the two of them to meet. He had said that they'd 'gone back to being friends', but to Rika's mind, their relationship had always been simply the extension of a friendship. Maybe it had just become clear that they had no future together. A bright light had shone down and cast into full view their future, which had hitherto been concealed to just the right degree.

The screen was taken up by the image of an old, rusty theme park. A white man and woman in combat gear were running around carrying guns.

'This is the game I'm hooked on at the moment,' Kitamura said, only half glancing at Rika. Reiko, on the other hand, made no attempt to prize her eyes from the screen. Melanie was sitting on her lap.

'My people skills aren't the best, so I thought I'd try this out. Mrs Sayama got really into it, as you can see. She's very quick on the uptake, so she's a good person to play with.'

The rusty Ferris wheel and the motionless merry-go-round on screen made her think of Suntopia World.

Without looking at her, Kitamura went on, 'I found out where Yamamura's sister is currently working. It turns out she's joined a small estate agency. How do you want to go forward?'

Rika didn't answer immediately. After she'd made him go to all that effort, she could hardly tell him that she'd lost the passion she'd felt for the case, that it had been replaced by a sense of burden and fear. What with this, and the Le Salon de Miyuko news … She put on a cheerful voice to mask her true feelings.

'Is anyone hungry?'

Everyone's eyes turned to look at her, like a group of primary school kids.

'I'll make something. It's cold, so I was thinking of making a nice warming pot-au-feu. What do you think?'

Saying this, Rika lifted the supermarket bag containing potatoes, onions, carrots, and beef.

Yū nodded disinterestedly, her eyes already back on her laptop. Reiko and Kitamura had returned to exploring the theme park, pointing their guns whenever a zombie appeared. With her work life and private life jumbled together in this way, Rika felt unsure of how to act.

Just then she heard the sound of a key in the door, and Shinoi entered wearing a winter coat. As she was wondering how to introduce him, he said, 'I was here before, so we've all introduced ourselves already. Kitamura, Reiko and Uchimura.'

With this, Shinoi placed a red and white package on the table. A familiar smell of oil and seasoning followed him from the entrance to the table.

'I brought you guys some fried chicken. Coleslaw and biscuits as well.'

Kitamura and Yū immediately got up and clustered around the table, reaching for the grease-stained box. The lid was lifted to reveal tightly packed pieces of golden-brown fried chicken. Even Reiko took a piece and bit in. Perhaps in response to the smell, Melanie began barking loudly, circling round and round the chicken-eaters.

Rika didn't feel in the mood for fried food, and looked on as her colleagues and friends hungrily devoured the chicken, as if their expressionless faces from before had been a dream.

'So you and Shinoi are an item, then?' Kitamura said out of the blue as he sucked on a bone, making Rika almost drop the biscuit that she'd finally reached a hand out for.

'Listen, Kitamura. I sometimes go mountain climbing, as a hobby,' Shinoi said, oblivious to Kitamura's confusion. 'Of late, you find lots of climbers with no clue about mountain-climbing etiquette. A friend of mine said that they recently found a ton of disposable nappies that had been tossed away. I wonder what on earth that can have been about? Come to think of it, I think there's an old people's home at the foot of the mountains. Run by that company … You know, the one that's also started opening up bars …'

Kitamura's expression grew stern. He glared at Shinoi, not concealing his wariness.

'Why are you telling me this? You know I'm not going to give you anything in return. Are you trying to make me your accomplice?'

'What are you talking about? I'm just shooting the shit, in the same way I do with Rika. If you take that information away and do something with it, then that's got nothing to do with me. It's the same as me letting you stay in this house. I'm lonely, so I ask you to lend me an ear sometimes. Just like Rika does.'

Kitamura fell silent, and Shinoi kept on 'shooting the shit' until Kitamura took out his jotter pad.

'It feels a bit like summer camp, doesn't it?' Rika said to nobody in particular, and her eyes met Yū's. Reiko had started playing the game again without Kitamura.

Glancing at her, Yū said, 'I think Reiko finds it embarrassing with everyone staring at her. I reckon it's best if we all just get on with what we're supposed to be doing, and don't pay her too much attention. My place is a long way away, so is it okay to stay over? There're futons, aren't there?'

'I was wondering if I might stay too. It's close to the office, after all.' Kitamura broke off his conversation with Shinoi to say this to the group, and Rika started.

'You're a man, different rules apply!' Yū snapped back.

'That's discrimination!' Kitamura pouted, his lips slick with chicken grease. Rika looked over at Reiko, who nodded to indicate it didn't bother her.

'Okay, well, I'm going to go back to Suidōbashi,' said Shinoi. 'The guest futons are kept over there. Kitamura, you can sleep in the living room, and Uchimura, you can sleep in what used to be mine and my wife's bedroom.' With this, he began preparing to leave. Rika felt a pang of guilt – it was his apartment, after all.

And yet, she realised, however hard she tried, these people wouldn't behave in the way she wanted them to. Given which, it was best if she did what she wanted as well. She felt reluctant to go home now. She stood up, deciding she would lay a futon on the floor of Reiko's room and sleep there.

'I've had dreams that you stopped coming to see me,' Kajii said in a sickly tear-stained voice the moment Rika stepped into the visiting room. She had sworn to herself she'd never come again, but here she was. Had the chief editor got his way, or was it that she still wanted to get to understand Kajii better? Not really knowing the truth, Rika sat down roughly on the metal chair.

'I was going out of my mind, I couldn't concentrate on a thing. I couldn't even sleep.' It was true that Kajii looked exhausted. Her hair was flat and lifeless. Her skin was dry and her eyes sunken. The beige sweater she wore looked cheap and was pilling.

'I thought you didn't want any female friends,' Rika said, in a voice that seemed melodramatic in its iciness even to her. And yet, it appeared that Kajii was delighted to be talking to her nonetheless. Her eyes drooped tragically at the corners.

'That's only because I didn't know what a friend was back then. You're my first! The first person in my life that I can speak to like this.'

'Are you aware what you did to me?'

'I apologise for teasing your friend. But it all worked out okay in the end, didn't it? She spent a few days with Yokota, but couldn't rise to the occasion. She spent the entire duration cleaning and cooking, and returned exhausted. Yes?'

Rika didn't want to hear any more. She couldn't abide the look of superiority that came over Kajii's round, sagging face when she spoke about Reiko.

'I'm guessing that was all part of your plan, too?'

To mask the sound of her own tutting, which she'd let out unthinkingly, Rika slammed her heel on the floor then ground it in.

'Manipulating people is your only real skill, isn't it? You seem to think that getting other people to act as you wish them to is part and parcel of human interaction, but it's not. People are unpredictable, and they don't do as you want them to, and they keep on changing. You're someone who can't take pleasure in anything that transcends your understanding. You can't feel safe if something's unpredictable. You're a lonely, cowardly and dull person.'

Kajii looked down, sadness written across her face, and shook her hair.

The gesture riled Rika up even more.

'Do you know what kind of state Reiko is in now, thanks to you? If something happens to her, I'll never forgive you.'

Rika hoped that Kajii would explode, and the whole thing would be over. Yet she showed no intention of veering from her usual modus operandi.

'Have you eaten anything particularly delicious recently?'

'I'm done. I'm sick of this. I'm going home.' Rika stood up from her chair to show she meant what she said. Kajii immediately lowered her voice.

'Don't go. I'll never forgive you for leaving me on my own. This time I really shall take everything from you. Although saying that, you and Reiko are both such weaklings, you can't even be properly ruined.'

Rika turned pale. Kajii immediately grew apologetic.

'I'm sorry. Ignore that. It's wrong to say such things about one's friends. I like you, which is why I got a little jealous. You can write whatever you wish about me in the article. If you're the one writing it, I'll accept whatever you include.' Kajii joined her hands together pleadingly. There was a goofiness to the whole performance. Rika warned herself not to let her guard drop.

'The reason I went to the cooking school, to Le Salon de Miyuko, was just as you said. To make friends. I hate other women. Groups of women, especially. But I thought there might be at least one person there who I could converse with on an equal footing.'

'Wasn't a boyfriend enough?'

'I was consorting with various men. Whichever of them I was with, though, I never felt truly satisfied. I wanted to talk with someone about delicious food, about my everyday worries and pleasures. I wanted to enjoy the art of conversation! But they all grew distempered when the talk turned to things they didn't know about. If I made them something whose taste was new to them, they became anxious and silent. When I made them boeuf bourguignon, all they saw was beef stew. Speaking with them, I never had the sensation of a new world unfolding before me, and felt lonely as a result. With you, it's the opposite. When you encounter a new taste, you grow excited, and you savour it. When I'm with you, I feel my field of vision expanding. I feel like I begin to see things I haven't seen before. It reminds me of when I started going to Le Salon de Miyuko.'

Rika reluctantly accepted that she understood exactly what Kajii meant. After seeing Kajii, she would feel as though a fresh breeze was blowing through her body. Still, she found it disconcerting how Kajii was repudiating what she'd said until now, and aligning herself with Rika's way of seeing the world all of a sudden.

'I felt as though there I would find women on my level. It was, after all, a salon, of the kind originated by Madame de Pompadour.'

'Did you find anyone like that?'

'There was one person I felt optimistic about, but …' Kajii broke off. Rika couldn't stop herself from grinning. Kajii hadn't been able to integrate herself into the group. Rika had heard from numerous sources that those stylish, affluent ladies, well versed in communicating with other women, found Kajii's behaviour and her appearance ridiculous, and hadn't admitted her into their circle.

'The time you started going to Le Salon de Miyuko coincides

with the point in time when people around you started dying. There was some link, wasn't there?'

As she asked the question, Rika had the sense that something was off. She felt like Kajii was holding the reins, after all. Kajii bowed her head and kept it bowed, and the visit came to an end.

Rika noticed that her whole body was filmed in sweat. Even after she left the Detention House and began walking, the moisture enveloping her showed no sign of drying. A cold, sleet-blended rain had soaked the pavement. Only the knowledge that she was heading to an apartment where someone was waiting for her kept her feet moving forward.

Rika couldn't understand why people favoured the taiyaki and takoyaki and fried chicken that Shinoi bought over the Japanese food that lately she was putting so much time and energy into cooking, even getting home early from work to prepare. Today, Shinoi had brought katsu sandwiches that he'd picked up in a shop in the station between appointments. Most of them had disappeared the instant the box was opened, and now there were only two left. Only Reiko, who seemed a little vacant, hadn't tucked in.

'It's strange, isn't it, this set up? It feels really relaxed somehow.' It took Rika a while to realise that the person speaking to her was Reiko. Her friend was standing right beside her at the sink, drying one of the wet plates Rika had washed. Even while busily moving her hands, Rika could tell that Reiko was making an effort to return to her ordinary self. Desperate not to mar the atmosphere, Rika inhaled deeply, turned on the tap and affected as casual a tone as she could.

'Maybe it's because there's lots of rooms, and it feels like a family habitat in a way? So people are free to use it how they want. And everyone here is a night owl. It's special because everyone's doing exactly as they please.'

'I don't think so. I think it's because you're here.'

Rika now surveyed the apartment from behind the kitchen counter. Yū, finally liberated from her graduation assignment, was engrossed in a game with Kitamura, while Shinoi was at the table cutting out articles from a newspaper. Melanie lay at his feet.

'When you're around, everyone feels freed from their normal roles. They forget their gender and their position in society. It's as if the magnetic field shifts. I think you've always had that aspect to you, but it's grown stronger recently.'

'Really? I can't see that all, myself. Do you think it's because I'm more approachable now I've put on so much weight – like some kind of cuddly mascot? Oh, and the editor told me that two places have opened up at Le Salon de Miyuko. If I start going, I'm only going to gain more! I'm not even interested in the Kajii case any more.'

Even listening to Rika prattling away, Reiko didn't crack a smile.

'I think it's because you don't mind if your acquaintances get to know one another when you're not there. You're not bothered by the idea of them forming new connections or talking about you, right? That's a rare quality. People are usually desperate to hold on to what they've got, desperate not to lose anything.'

'Maybe you're right. Also, I haven't told you this yet, but Makoto and I broke up.'

'Oh, did you?' Reiko said, and nodded. Rika squeezed on the washing-up sponge in her hand, so the foam inside burst out.

'I don't imagine I'll find anyone else now. I'm guessing I'll be single for the rest of my life. If that's how it has to be, then so be it, I guess. It was my decision, after all. I never thought that I wanted to get married, but maybe I'm more conservative than I realised.'

'Why do you think that it's impossible to fall in love unless someone appears before you and tries to win you over?'

Reiko's large pale eyes were focused on Rika.

'Why do we think that nothing will ever happen unless a man singles us out? Why do we have to wait to be chosen, doing nothing, as if we were dead or something?'

The water came spilling over the side of the washing-up bowl, and Rika turned off the tap. The clear water sloshing around brightened up the kitchen.

'... Not voicing your hopes or what you really feel, enticing the other person to behave as you want, watching them to see how they act so you don't mess things up – that way of going about things seems no different to Kajii and her victims. I really understood that, spending time at Yokota's house. I thought that a man who was unused to women, the kind of man who would fall for Kajii, would be easy to win over, just by cooking and cleaning for him, but all I did was scare him off.

'I think maybe the same was true with Ryōsuke, too. I was so concerned with trying to get Ryōsuke to act in the way I wanted him to that I was actually running in the opposite direction from him, without ever really telling him what I wanted. I'd abandoned the idea of having an equal conversation. I was always waiting for him to initiate everything. I wanted to be the princess who was forever wanted by others. I felt so embarrassed when Kajii pointed that out about me. When I was rejected by Yokota, a man I didn't even like, my pride was in tatters. I was an idiot. I'm not a cute little girl any more, I should know that. I really think you should stop waiting on others' approval, too. I'm pretty sure that you'll fall in love with someone else, in due course. Then you need to tell that person, honestly, how you feel.'

'Do you think it could ever work out, though? With me as I am?'

Rika's voice was trembling, and she felt herself blush. Reiko was the picture of seriousness.

'What does it mean though, for things to work out between a man and a woman? What state is that indicating? Sometimes you can go as far as getting married and it still doesn't work out, like in my case. And being desired by men doesn't always make you happy, as we know from Kajii. You need to trust yourself, Rika. If you find someone you truly like then that person is enormously lucky, and if you told them how you felt they'd be pleased, regardless of whether it develops into a romantic relationship. The kind of person you'd fall for wouldn't treat you cruelly or use you. I can guarantee that.'

Out of the blue, Rika was hit by the desire to have an apartment of her own, the same size as this one. Or no, the size didn't really matter – the thing was to have lots of individual rooms, so that people could have their privacy.

'Thank you, Reiko. I really mean it. And look, if you're feeling a bit better, send Ryōsuke a text or an email, will you? He's really worried about you. Forget that he's your husband, and think about him as a male friend.'

There was a little pause, and then, without changing her expression, Reiko nodded and raised her right shoulder in assent, then wiped her hands with a towel. With Melanie padding after her, she headed off into Shinoi's daughter's bedroom.

Looking at the three people left sitting in the living room, Rika felt the haze that had been clouding her vision start to take on clearer contours.

All this time, she had thought that she alone could protect Reiko. She'd wanted to make Shinoi feel less lonely, and she'd been plagued by guilt about her mother, who was so tied up with taking care of her grandfather. But actually, thinking that she could solve their problems was sheer arrogance – just as she'd been unable to do anything to save her father in the final stretch of his life. Her loved ones' issues were their own domains, as individuals, and not places that she could go stomping into. Quite possibly, the only thing she could do was to create a place of refuge where the people close to her could come when they needed to.

Saying they'd go back to their respective homes that evening, Kitamura and Yū left while the trains were still running. Rika had a shower, changed out of her work clothes and returned to the living room to find Shinoi sitting opposite Reiko. For one moment, their faces overlapped inside her, and she started.

Shinoi glanced up at Rika, who was drying her hair. These last few days, he seemed to have grown visibly younger. His skin looked softer and shinier, possibly as a result of all the fried food he'd been eating.

Across from him, Reiko was slurping a bowl of noodles.

'It's my culinary speciality: Sapporo Ichiban salt ramen with butter on top. It looked like she didn't have much of an appetite earlier. For once, she asked.'

Rika sensed a glimmer of pride in his long, thin profile. Reiko had a sensitive palate, and was hyper-aware of additives and nutritional values, and yet here she was eating this? Rika felt a small sense of betrayal.

'There are times in life when this sort of instant food tastes better. With homemade food, absorbing the feelings of whoever it is that has made it can feel draining. Everyone needs some distance some-times – from tasty things as well as anything else,' said Shinoi. Rika guessed that he had eaten instant ramen alone in this room more times than he could count. He must have noticed Rika's critical expression, for he went on.

'Reiko's old enough to take responsibility for her diet herself. It's not good to fuss over her too much. She's spoilt enough as it is. A spoilt little princess – or no, maybe she's more like a prince.'

Reiko looked up from her bowl and glared at Shinoi. The fact that the two of them had grown this close so quickly seemed perfectly natural to Rika. She also knew there'd not been a single man in Reiko's past who'd teased her like this.

The only noise in the room was that of Reiko slurping her noodles. Rika could smell the spices in the powdered soup.

Shinoi's way of speaking was somehow warmer and fuller when he was speaking to Reiko. Maybe there were similarities between her and his ex-wife, she thought. Certainly the kitchen here and in Reiko's house had points of similarity. The air that wafted out when you opened the oven, the creak that the table made when pulling it out were identical. Maybe Rika was like his daughter, and Reiko like his wife. If that were true, it would make sense why they felt so comfortable as a threesome.

Reiko slowly set her bowl down on the table.

'I want to go to Kajii's cooking school, the one you were talking about. If you're not going to go, then I'll go alone. I'm not doing it for you. I just want to see what it's like.'

Reiko wiped her shining lips with the back of her hand, then stood up and opened the window. Envisioning the ice-cold night-time air flooding in, Rika tensed her body. The pale ochre curtains flapped in the breeze, for a moment obscuring Reiko's delicate shoulders. Rika whispered to Shinoi, who was next to her.

'Would you mind making me a bowl, too? With plenty of butter.'

He grinned, and strode over to the kitchen, empty bowl in hand. The night breeze that blew in was unexpectedly mild, caressing the exposed sections of Rika's skin. As it grazed her cheeks, she smelled the scent of spring. It came as a shock to her that the warmer season was finally arriving, kicking away the cold, dry wind. And there she'd been, until a few minutes ago, thinking that nothing would change, that she couldn't change a thing.

Even without her lifting a finger, the world would keep on changing. The fact stunned her. Even without her trying, the people around her would form connections, intertwine in complex ways, and keep on growing, like the roots, leaves and stems of a plant. She felt as though she could see their rich green spreading out behind her eyelids.

Maybe spring was a good season to take up a new hobby. Manako Kajii's retrial would start in two months' time.

CHAPTER THIRTEEN

I was born in Fuchū, in Tokyo, but from as far back as I can remember, I was brought up in a village called Agano, recognised as the origin of the dairy farming industry for the entire prefecture of Niigata.

It's about forty minutes' drive from Agano to the station in Niigata city, where you can get hold of more or less anything you might need. My father was an adventurous type, and thanks to his influence, my family took pleasure in eating out and taking trips. My mother was a sociable person, absorbed in her job teaching in the cultural centre and the various lessons she attended, so I often used to go with her into Niigata and wander around. Accordingly, I never had much of a sense of myself as living in the countryside.

Yet come winter, the plains would be blanketed in snow as far as the eye could see, and I would be cooped up in that tiny village. It seemed to me then as though the world was quiet, and everything around me was dead. The one place which stood out to me, and seemed to exude a sense of life, was the cowshed next to my house. Even when all around was silvery white, the shed remained pleasantly warm from the cows' body temperature and their hot breath. In winter, the cows stock up on nutrients, so their milk is sweet, with a creamy richness. Milk is originally part of cows' blood.

For me, dairy products are both my life and my blood. It's these memories that I have to thank for my love of sweet things and buttery food, particularly butter-rich French cuisine. Looking at the cowshed, with its rows of female cows, I was overcome by their sheer

*power as they stood, unbothered by the stench and the flies, with their
big teeth and protruding eyes. The strips of flypaper black with flies
made me shudder. At the same time, I found myself wondering about
the absent bulls. I felt unnerved by how, so long as they had some
way of getting hold of the semen to make them pregnant, these cows
could do without the opposite sex entirely.*

*The thing about Tokyo that initially took me aback when I came
here to study was how bland the dairy products and the rice tasted. I
was surprised, too, by how the women around me tended not to eat
much of either. If they did, it would be in tiny quantities. Their
ascetic, abstinent attitude applied to all aspects of their lifestyle.
Looking at them living in that finicky, pious way made me so angry
I wanted to slam them against the wall.*

*One lunchtime, not long after first arriving at university, I was
on my own in the university cafeteria. I hadn't succeeded in
making any friends. Sitting there, I overheard a group of four girls
talking. All of them originated from outside Tokyo, and were
living alone or in the girls' dorms. None had boyfriends. They were
confessing things to one another with great earnestness – one of
them hadn't fitted in well back home, one didn't like the big city,
one wanted to save money, one wanted to lose weight. At the
beginning they hadn't sounded at all lively, but I suppose that as
they went on chatting, it brightened their spirits. Gradually they
began smiling, and eventually concocted a plan for the four of them
to go on holiday together. By the time they stood up from the table,
they looked like regular university students, having a whale of a
time. I felt wounded by the speed of their transformation and the
depth of their self-interest, and angered by how they seemed
satisfied when not a single one of their original problems had been
solved. I didn't understand it at all. I am alone, I thought. I don't
need solace. I decided at that moment to live my life without
becoming involved with other people. Not long after that I quit
university, and began to make my living by going on dates with
affluent gentlemen.*

I'll confess to something here. I know I'm perceived as man-crazy, but the truth is, I'm not the kind of base, lascivious woman who thinks only of men's bodies. It's more that I loathe women.

My loathing doesn't stem from jealousy, and nor is it my revenge for not being accepted. I will admit that many of the men I met on dating sites were spoiled and needy, but such tendencies are far easier to bear than women's inscrutable behaviour, overpowering ferocity and endlessly mercurial natures.

There's a statue in Agano of three hardworking maidens, known as 'The Three Graces'. There's a similar statue in Niigata Station, too. Ever since I was very young, I have despised those statues. I will admit that, on occasion, I stuck old chewing gum and left my melted ice-cream on the Agano Graces. It's inconceivable that a number of women – beautiful ones at that – could get along with one another while working together. With three of them, it's certain that one would always be left out. I also couldn't forgive the fact that all of them were so slim. Having been subjected from such a young age to my mother's pathologically persistent attempts to make me diet, I despised reduced-calorie food and exercise above anything.

I know that people ridicule my figure. People have commented in the past that if I'm so set on pleasing men, it makes no sense that my appearance would fail to meet their requirements. I say that people who come out with such things don't understand the mechanism by which men fall for women. They've probably only ever had a very malnourished sex life. I can only feel sympathy for them.

To forgive, envelop, affirm, reassure and never surpass men – that's all it takes. Why do the women of this world not understand this? You think that doesn't sound like something which a human is capable of? I would like to say very loudly and forcefully: all women should become goddesses. If my imprisonment here – for crimes I didn't commit – would only enable that message to spread across the world, then I could make my peace with it a little better.

I'm not saying that women should suppress their desires. If they're hoping to maintain superlative powers of tolerance, women can't be holding on to stress, worries or conflict. They are goddesses, after all! Which is why I eat exactly what I want to. I don't repress desires of any kind, and that isn't confined to luxuries either.

'Nice to meet you! My name's Kazuko Minami. I'm a friend of Ms Shigemori, the food writer.'

This wasn't the first time Rika had used a false name for work, but her pronunciation of this one came out sounding awkward. Unlike on previous occasions, the person she was speaking to wasn't a politician or a celebrity, but rather Miyuko Sasazuka, known to everyone as 'Madame'.

Together with her husband, Madame oversaw the running of the renowned Balzac restaurant. Her personality and hospitality won over even those VIPs visiting from overseas, and it was no rarity to see her featured in classy women's magazines. Her sharp gaze gave the impression of someone who wouldn't let anything slip past her, but there was a quality to her that made her impossible to dislike, like a small dog looking out serenely from the soft blanket in which it had been carefully wrapped.

'I'm Mariko Iino, Kazuko's friend from university. I'm a house-wife,' Reiko introduced herself smoothly. Rika had been concerned about how Reiko would cope with her first excursion into the outside world since her ordeal, and had been sneaking furtive looks in her direction since they'd met at Roppongi Station, but her friend's movements seemed carefree and assured. She wore a navy jumper she had borrowed from Yū, and had swept back her hair, which had by now grown quite long, leaving her forehead exposed. A slick of lipstick graced her otherwise un-made-up face. These small details already made her look more like she had when working at her old job, which Rika was happy to see. Reiko was still staying at Shinoi's house, but recently she'd been corresponding with Ryōsuke unprompted, and had started taking Melanie for morning walks. Shinoi didn't seem to object to her presence, and with Yū and Kitamura there all the time now as well, Rika was starting to relinquish the sense that the situation was one she needed to sort out. She herself was staying in the apartment about half the week.

It was already midway through March. The air was still chilly, but the cherry blossoms were forecast to bloom a little earlier than usual, and she had a crop of work-related hanami parties in the diary for the end of the month.

She and Reiko had arrived at Roppongi Station, deep below the ground, and taken several long escalators that carried them above ground in stages until they finally found themselves outside Roppongi Hills. The apartment was a five-minute walk down a gentle slope towards Azabu Jūban, in a cream-coloured fortress of a building that was practically indistinguishable from the many embassies in this area.

They were let into the building then walked a carpeted corridor to a glass-fronted lift. On reaching Madame's apartment, they changed into large comfortable slippers in the marble-floored entranceway. Guided by their host, they walked down a corridor, rounding two corners before they came to a huge open-plan room. Everything was arranged around the centrally positioned square kitchen, with two ovens and six hobs. The sink and the work stations were made of a material Rika hadn't encountered before with no light or gloss to it, which gave the space an unintimidating feel. It was hard to imagine that all the kitchens in the building were like this – the Sasazukas must have had it designed to their specifications.

'Everyone, this is Ms Minami and Ms Iino, who will be joining us from today. They're friends of Ms Shigemori.'

The six students sitting around the long table draped with a starched white cloth now looked up. All were women in their thirties or forties, whose stylish attire, lustrous hair and glossy skin spoke of their affluent lifestyle. Several of them Rika recognised, and she averted her eyes. She was all too aware that, were it not for their contact with Kajii, their lives would've continued without scrutiny. Outside the window, Tokyo Tower twinkled in the night sky, astonishingly close.

From the ceiling hung a small vintage chandelier. Lined up on the caramel-coloured bookcase were numerous trophies and pictures of the Sasazukas alongside the French ambassador, along with various snow domes, Mexican dolls, ceramic thimble-sized trinkets and other souvenirs she imagined they'd received as gifts. Hung on the wall was a baroque painting of a noblewoman playing cards which looked familiar. Jazz piano was playing at a low volume in the background, vigorous and striking.

Madame went around the students handing out stapled sheets of paper on which the day's recipes were written.

'Shall we make a start? Today we'll be cooking soupe de poisson, which we'll make by straining a mixture of fish and seafood. That'll be followed by carrot, onion and cumin pie, lamb with orange, and a strawberry mousse.'

'Ahh, cumin! My favourite! I should have a healthy appetite today,' said a woman with short hair of a vibrant brown, clapping her hands together and instantly lightening the mood of the room.

'You really love cumin, don't you, Aki!' The other women laughed.

Rika tentatively raised a hand. 'Are we going to make all of that? Here and now?'

'We certainly are. But there's eight of us, so we'll be fine! Shall we get down to business?'

The students stood up as one. The cloth was removed from the table they'd been sitting at, heralding its transformation into a work station. All the ingredients were brought over.

Rika widened her eyes to see the lamb joint with its row of bones sticking out from its crimson flesh. Then her attention was caught by the dull gleam and vibrant hues of the mussels, crab, sea perch and marbled rockfish. Madame went on arranging ingredients on the table – a basket heaped with colourful vegetables, containers of butter and cream. The students discovered tasks for themselves without being directed, and Rika soon found herself at a loss. Seeing this, a woman wearing a spotted apron over her cashmere cardigan handed Rika a chopping board and knife. As instructed, Rika set about chopping up the carrots, celery and onions into a brunoise. There was no denying that her movements were slow in comparison to those of the women around her. Not just that, but she felt that the task required her entire focus, in stark contrast to everyone else, who managed to talk and laugh as they worked. At Madame's instruction, Rika transferred her irregularly diced vegetables into a pan, and began to heat them. She was handed a wooden spatula, and stood at the hob, her heart still pounding in her chest. The other students gathered around her.

'We'll start with the soupe de poisson. First of all, we suet the vegetables that have been cut into a brunoise. "Suet" means to sweat, and with this, we're literally making the vegetables sweat, heating them slowly on a low flame until they're veiled with a light moisture. Don't overdo it, you need to watch the heat.'

Rika could sense people's gazes focused on her hands. Finally, the moisture began to seep from the vegetables, and steam dampened Rika's cheeks.

'Try lowering the heat, Ms Minami.'

It was a pointer, not a telling-off, and yet this alone was enough to make Rika's stomach clench. Perhaps sensing her nerves, Madame smoothly took over with the spatula, and Rika stepped back. The food processor whizzed, a torrent of flour and butter moving up and down. This mixture would become the pie crust.

'We don't want to let the fragments of butter melt, so we pour in the cold water little by little.'

When the lid of the food processor was removed, the flour danced up into the air, grazing Rika's nose.

Next, the roughly chopped seafood was added into the suet pan. The air in the kitchen grew lively with the smell of saffron. The refreshing acidity of the tomatoes that were tossed in next cleansed her chest. Cumin seeds were sprinkled on the carrots and onions being braised in the pan, and the moment they met its moisture, a smell that seemed to combine fragrant smoke, fried meat and nuts rose up, tickling the back of Rika's nose with a comfortable heat and bringing a smokiness to her throat.

'Madame, the pâte brisée is finished,' someone said, and Madame turned around.

'Now use the pastry cutter to cut it into circles. If you don't have a round cutter at home, you can always use a glass.'

Rika could tell that Reiko was being restored to life. She fitted in so well that nobody would ever guess it was her first time, deftly chopping vegetables and sprinkling salt over the lamb from a height. Madame was complimenting her in language that Rika didn't even understand. The oranges for the sauce were squeezed, the sweet-sour smell of their juice drifting through the kitchen. Breadcrumbs, coriander and orange peel formed a whirlwind inside the food processor, creating an aromatic mixture that was to be smeared onto the lamb before roasting.

Standing next to Madame, Rika found herself mumbling, 'Coriander and orange with lamb … I can't even imagine how that will taste.'

'But tastes you *can* imagine are dull, no?' Madame responded brightly. As she spoke, a fine orange ribbon of carrot peeled with the spine of her knife spiralled onto the chopping board. She wound it up as if creating a corsage.

'Wow, that really looks like an orange flower! You'd never think it was made of carrot!'

The strawberries pureed in the mixer were placed in a bowl submerged in ice water, then mixed with the cream. Their fresh red combined with the soft white to create a bright pink shade, the very sight of which set flowers blossoming in Rika's chest. Seeing her standing by, doing very little except for watching all that was going on around her, Reiko handed her a grinder-like device with a handle.

'You can be in charge of straining the soup, Kazuko.'

Rika pulled a puzzled face, and Reiko pointed to the device's handle. In the strainer at the top of the bowl lay the cooked fish and crab.

'It's the hardest thing to mess up. See?'

It seemed as though all you had to do was turn the moulinette handle, and out would come the soup. Rika could feel the bones, tails and eyes of the fish being pulverised beneath the force of her arms. Her arms soon grew tired, and she put her whole body weight into it. She grasped the moulinette, thinking that if she could just keep up with this task, she would get away without embarrassing herself. A tall woman called Chizu coiling the carrot ribbons behind her whispered in her ear.

'You're the same as me. You're not here to get better at cooking, are you?'

Rika had been drawn to this woman from the start – amidst a sea of soft knitted fabric and dresses, she was the only student wearing trousers beneath her apron. Unable to meet the woman's gaze, Rika stared down at a marbled rockfish eye in the moulinette. From the moment she stepped inside this room, she'd had the sense that she recognised the woman from somewhere. There was something familiar about her freckled skin and thick, shapely lips.

'You've come to look at all the pretty women, right?' Chizu said with a grin. As Rika fell into stunned silence, she went on, 'I know your game! I come here because it reminds me of club activities back at school.'

A woman in her forties, full-figured but very beautiful, joined in their conversation. Rika guessed that she had been the target of the comments online that said, 'There's other people there just as fat as Kajii!' As she spoke, she continued whisking the contents of a bowl.

'I don't think that's true, Chizu! I think you'd go anywhere in the world so long as there was plenty of cheese, be it France or Switzerland …'

'Today's cheese is your favourite: Mimolette! Just make sure you save some for us, okay?' Now Madame broke into the conversation, and everybody laughed.

A worryingly meagre amount of soup had emerged from the moulinette. In time, the hot, buttery scent of the baking pies began to fill the room. From the other oven flooded the aroma of lamb and oranges. The sweet-sour scent of the fruit commingled with the wild tang of the meat, stimulating the appetite.

By the time all the courses were done, it was already past ten. Rika, who'd been envisaging the lesson to be a far more casual affair, felt overcome and exhausted by the amount of work involved, as well as everyone's reserves of energy and their wealth of knowledge.

The flowers placed on the table were mimosas, to chime with the red and orange tones of the meal. The tablecloth was a pale blue – 'Choose complementary colours to make the food really shine,' Madame said as she spread it out – lending the table a lakeside picnic ambience. Rika's levels of hunger were starting to grow unbearable, and the moment she sat down, unable to wait for the food about to be served, she reached for a slice of baguette, which she spread with a thick layer of butter. So extreme was her hunger that she couldn't absorb the lengthy tasting notes for the wine.

Barely paying attention to the colour combinations of the plates, she lifted to her mouth a spoonful of the tomato-coloured soup in front of her. From all around came the sound of sighing. She'd been disappointed by the small quantity of liquid she'd managed to extract, even after putting so much effort in, but the finished product was like liquid umami. It seemed to comprise the sweet, bitter and mellow tastes from every part of each of the fish – from the very centres of their eyeballs.

Tucking into the bite-sized pie decorated with the orange carrot flower, her eyes widened at how delicious the braised new onions and carrots were, the cumin perfectly drawing out their sweetness. The main dish of lamb, cut from the bone as soon as it was placed on the table, was so glorious to behold that it made her heart race. Protected by its wall of sweet breadcrumbs, orange peel and fresh coriander, the meat had the robust smell of a grassy plain. The strawberry mousse served as dessert, brought out after the hard rich orange cheese that reminded her of dried mullet roe, was fluffy and soft, sweet yet tart. For the first time this year, Rika felt that the season when all the flowers would come into bloom was at arm's reach.

Rika was fascinated by the lecture that Madame gave about table-setting, and differences between Japanese and Western approaches to lighting. The other students showed no hesitation in asking questions.

When the meal had drawn to a close, Madame looked over at Rika and said, 'Ms Minami, is there anything in particular you'd like to learn to cook? Any requests are welcome!'

Lulled into a sense of safety by the relaxed atmosphere, Rika couldn't resist. She replied, 'Hmm, well, I imagine it might be quite basic for everyone here, but I'd love to learn how to make boeuf bourguignon.'

A hush fell around the table. A petite, pretty woman that people called Hitomi stood up, her head down, and left the room. Rika had read about her online – she was the wife of a department head at a major manufacturing firm, and of all the group was the one whose identity had been most widely divulged by the media. Chizu followed hurriedly behind her. Madame looked after them with a concerned look, but then, perhaps out of consideration for Rika, narrowed her eyes into a smile.

'I'm sorry. We've done that recipe so many times by now, I think we'll leave it for the moment.'

After a while Hitomi returned and, though still a touch pale, began conversing with the others as though nothing had happened. It was palpably clear that everyone was taking care not to make a big deal out of it. Rika felt unbearably guilty, but didn't know what to say. When Hitomi's colour had returned and she was talking normally, Madame got to her feet.

'Well, ladies, I'll see you in two weeks' time. We'll be learning about apéritifs and digestifs. I know that drinking sweet liquor with a meal isn't something that's really done in Japan, but it can stimulate the appetite, and be very delicious.'

The lesson was over. A bevy of different-coloured scents wafted through Rika's body. As if intoxicated, she found it hard to summon the energy to get to her feet, until Reiko prompted her. They folded up their aprons and left the apartment. The warmth inside her body made the outside air feel especially cool. The moment she sank into the subway seat, Rika felt a heavy, dull ache in her arms and back. She and Reiko looked at one another, simultaneously registering their tiredness. It struck her that this was the first time she and Reiko had cooked together. The sensation was a mismatched one: the satisfaction of a full stomach, together with a profound exhaustion. She'd definitely been nervous, but her heart had been singing for most of it. A sense of achievement filled her body right down to her fingertips.

'I think Kajii actually killed them. That's my bet.'

Of late, the two of them had been avoiding the subject of Kajii. To hear Reiko speaking of her unprompted like this came as a relief, even as it astonished her.

'There's so much physical force involved in that kind of cooking. It's serious business. If you were to hit someone with one of those terrine weights, they'd probably die. Or if you crushed someone's fingers in the moulinette.'

Rika burst out laughing. The sensation of crushing the sea perch and marbled rockfish to a pulp came rushing back to her.

'You're right. When I hear about cooking schools, my image is of something dainty and domestic, but it's actually a strength contest.'

'The students are all way nicer than I was expecting, though,' Reiko said. 'They're not affected, and don't give off the super-rich vibe. I feel bad for them for being exposed like that, just on the back of having been in the same room as Kajii. That person who ran out in the middle – I guess she must have been thinking of Kajii.'

'I felt terrible when that happened. Even knowing it's for the article, it doesn't make the guilt any less. Why do you think the school attracted that much media attention, though? There was a while when it seemed like it was getting more coverage than Kajimana herself.'

'It must be wrapped up in people's prejudice and sense of inferiority toward the kinds of women who attend cooking schools, don't you think? They're seen as being part of this privileged elite, and everyone's envious.'

'Yeah. If I'm honest, I had the same preconception,' Rika admitted. 'But I feel like I understand better, now I've started cooking a little myself. Cleaning and cooking are much more rock and roll than I thought. What you need above all is strength … A fighting spirit that can withstand the tedium of everyday life without getting blunted by it.'

At this, Reiko's eyes sprung open wide. 'Yes! It's rock and roll! A means of resisting authority!'

Rika could tell that the suited man leaning his whole body weight on the leather strap was listening in to their conversation.

'When the world is this unfair and unfriendly, people want to do the things that give them satisfaction, that fortify and protect them. It doesn't necessarily require money – just time and innovation. Making the very thing you want to eat for yourself can be a pain sometimes, but it's fun, too.'

Seeing Reiko so full of beans was immensely heartening. Ryōsuke might find her power overwhelming, but it was exactly that power which was protecting his way of life.

Rika's lips stayed slick with grease from the lamb until she got back to the office.

'Where on earth did you meet someone like that?' Rika asked, interrupting Kajii's monologue.

She was beginning to write up her interview with Kajii in the form of a first-person diary, which was to be the main feature in the New Year's issue of the *Shūmei Weekly*, but she was having a hard time with it.

By now, with a fair amount of jumping back and forth, Kajii had told her story up to the point at which she'd quit her women's university. She claimed that she'd begun earning a living by dating affluent older gentlemen, and that she'd done so on the back of a suggestion made by a man whom she'd stumbled across one day in town. This part of her story was particularly vague, so Rika followed up in a harsh tone of voice. Kajii shrugged.

'I was having tea in the lounge at Hotel Ōkura when he approached me and said, "I've been searching for you all this time." A white-haired gentleman in a finely tailored linen suit.'

'Please just tell me the truth. I know when you're lying.'

Perhaps because Rika screwed up her face with a look of such displeasure, Kajii reluctantly amended her account. Maybe she'd misremembered being scouted – maybe she'd in fact begun looking into it by herself on the internet, and an elderly gentleman she'd met that way had introduced her to many others. But she didn't forget to add, in a tone so forceful that it indicated, on this point at least, she was not budging an inch, that, 'It was *not* prostitution. Few of them were physically capable of having sex, anyway. They'd treat me to dinner in extravagant restaurants, I'd converse with them, go along with them to the opera, or kabuki, or sumo wrestling, and then we'd retire to a famous hotel, where we'd either cuddle and sleep next to each other, or I'd give them a massage or let them rest their head in my lap. That was all.'

Rika only half believed this statement, but however you looked at the matter, there was no doubting that Kajii had been selling her youth. The truth about Kajii's prostitution had already been revealed in other magazines, and Rika knew that even if she did pursue the matter further, it wouldn't make for print-worthy news.

'Thanks to them, I was able to lead a lifestyle that other girls of my age couldn't even dream of. I felt that fulfilling men's desires was an ideal profession. All of them told me how enjoyable it was to be with me, how I allowed them to lose track of time. Of course, just like Madame de Pompadour, it kept me busy. I would read *The Nikkei* so that I could converse satisfactorily with company presidents, and I studied the classics and the traditional arts. I made an effort with my skin and my hair.'

'Did your family realise that you'd stopped studying and were making a living from, uh, dating men?'

'My father was aware. He had a word with me about it once, when he was visiting Tokyo. I informed him that I'd quit university, but I was attending a cooking school in Daikanyama and getting an education in real life, and that convinced him. Dating older people, I said, was my way of studying society, and I didn't let them touch me. My father was always saying that women shouldn't cheapen themselves, that they should be mysterious untouchable beings, like the Virgin Mary. All that time, he was sending me money. He'd often come to Tokyo, and take me to an assortment of restaurants, as part of my education. When Anna moved to Tokyo, she came to live with me. She was still very young at the time, really, and didn't seem to understand what I was doing for a living. But when it was the three of us – my father, my sister and I, without my mother – it was such great fun. Living in Tokyo seemed in my eyes like *the real thing.*'

When Kajii spoke about her early twenties, she grew genuinely animated. It was hard to resist the conclusion that she'd had a far more fulfilled sort of existence than Rika and Reiko when they'd first ventured out of university into the world. At that time, Rika had been so taken up with trying to acclimatise to her work that her personal life had been practically non-existent.

'It seems like that way of life suited you. Why did you decide you wanted to get married, and begin looking for a husband? It sounds as though you needn't have done that.'

Kajii calmly lifted her cheeks and cocked her head. 'I wanted to have a daughter.'

'Madame de Pompadour never became a mother, did she? I remember reading she was physically weak, and had numerous miscarriages …' Unable to form her thoughts into a coherent shape, Rika changed her question. 'Why a daughter, though, when you dislike women so much? Doesn't that contradict what you're always saying?'

'Oh no, I love my sister Anna. It's different when it's family. I have a profoundly maternal streak.'

'Were your fellow students at Le Salon de Miyuko another exception?' Rika stopped when she saw Kajii's startled look.

The longer she spent with Kajii and heard what she had to say, the more strongly Rika felt it. It was the same as the way that using complementary colours and aromas brought out the flavour of one's ingredients. The more extreme Kajii's pronouncements, the more they were drenched in loneliness.

The vinegar in the beurre blanc sauce brought the creamy smooth-ness of the sea urchin into even starker relief. As the warm sea urchin was crushed on the surface of her tongue, it was transformed into sea-flavoured cream that blended seamlessly with the similarly rich taste of the flan pastry, redolent with egg yolk.

By the second lesson, Rika's embarrassment about making mistakes and being slower than the other students had disappeared. She now felt assured in the fact that, with Madame's instructions and the abilities of the other students, the meal would get made whatever happened. A far more important question, she had come to under-stand, was how to enjoy this time to the fullest.

'Are you free after this? We could go and get a coffee, if you like?' It was after the meal and Madame's lecture were over, when Rika was folding up her apron and wrapping the cords around it, that Chizu approached her. Rika nodded.

'How about you, Ms Iino?'

Now Chizu glanced over Rika's shoulder at Reiko, but most likely out of consideration for Rika, Reiko smiled and said no, walking briskly out of the classroom with her ponytail swaying from side to side.

On the way out of Madame's apartment, Chizu put on a well-worn but still trusty-looking trenchcoat that was almost identical to Rika's, a fact which made the two of them exchange glances and smile. They went into the Starbucks in a corner of the Tsutaya in Roppongi and sat facing one another at a table near the entrance.

The air outside was chilly, and Rika was startled to see several customers drinking Frappuccinos on the outside terrace, all of them white. Both Rika and Chizu had just had a coffee with the crepes they'd eaten for dessert, so they ordered cups of tea and chai respectively.

'You must have got a real surprise when Hitomi took a funny turn all of a sudden,' Chizu said, with no preamble. Rika sat up straight. This was exactly what she'd been angling for; in the lesson they'd just had she'd made a point of speaking to Chizu and expressing concern about Hitomi.

'I don't think there's any point hiding it, so I may as well just tell you ... You know Manako Kajii, who was convicted for killing those men she met on dating sites? Were you aware of some connection? I guess it figures you'd know, if you're a friend of Ms Shigemori. She's in the media world, after all.'

When Chizu came to the crucial part of her tale, Rika widened her eyes in shock just as she'd practised doing. She moved her eyes around as if to imply that, come to think of it, she had read something like that in the past, and nodded.

'If you search for the name of the school online, you'll probably find photos of us all. People say that we're a group of nauseatingly rich women who exacerbated Kajii's insecurities and drove her to become a killer, a group of bored housewives who think of our husbands as cash machines and nothing else. It's all way off the mark, but Hitomi's a very sensitive person, and it seems she took those comments to heart and went through a rough patch. I think she was traumatised, in a way, by having cooked in a room together with Kajii, so that subject has become a taboo in our lessons. Would you mind passing the message on to Ms Iino as well? Sorry, I've probably said too much.'

'No, not at all. I imagine it's a hard thing to talk about with other people, but I'm very happy to listen. This might sound impolite, but I'm fascinated by it.'

'I can see that. I bet if I weren't involved, I'd be captivated by it, and looking stuff up about it, and all the rest. With the sort of work

I do, I'm fairly used to being criticised and insulted, so I've developed a thick skin as a result. I can take an objective view of things, if needed. Talking with you like this, I keep thinking of more I want to say. I really feel like I've met you somewhere before.'

Rika smiled ambiguously, although she was coming to feel the same. She'd probably met Chizu as the secretary or aide of one of the people she was covering for work, she thought, but it seemed uncouth to probe further.

'Boeuf bourguignon, the dish you said you wanted to learn how to make, was a dish that Kajii loved, and was obsessed with learning. She mentioned it in court. I feel like she might have made it for one of her victims? Anyway, it was after that the media onslaught began. It was so petty and awful. Women's magazines getting in touch and saying, "Teach us how to make meals so mouth-watering that they'd allow someone as ugly as Kajii to win the hearts of multiple men! Help us save the women of this world who want to get married and can't find a guy!" It's just a regular cooking school, you know? I got so sick of the press making out that it was some kind of training school for brides-to-be, or an academy teaching women how to attract guys. It was such a horrible thing to happen, and it messed everything up for us. But I guess it did bring us all closer as a result.'

Aha, Reiko thought, maybe that was where the lively ambience that reminded her of her girls' school came from.

'Starting up the lessons again has helped all of us to heal. Now we've got new students joining, it feels like we're finally returning to business as usual. I think you and Ms Iino's arrival has helped with that. Maybe in time we'll be able to do lessons in the restaurant again. Madame's apartment is great, but the power of the hobs in the restaurant kitchen is on a totally different level.'

'I don't know if I'm allowed to ask this, but what was she like?'

'Impossible to forget. A truly odd character. She came for about half a year – so I guess about fifteen times in total? She was some-thing of a troublemaker from the start, even leaving aside everything that came later. She came to us through a company president who was a regular at the restaurant – they may well have been together. In her first lesson, after we'd finished cooking and she took a bite of the food, she burst into tears. I was shocked! It was so delicious, had such a *generous* taste, that she couldn't help but cry, she said. Everyone could see they were fake tears. She was like an overly self-conscious teenager.'

Chizu stared at her half-drunk tea and then looked towards the bookshop outside the coffee shop.

'She'd ask us so many questions – where we came from, what schools we'd been to, where we'd bought our clothes and our bags. Whether or not we were married. What did our husbands do? If someone had a boyfriend, were they planning to marry him? Don't you think that's weird behaviour? When we weren't even close.'

Rika had begun to notice that, although Kajii would say how much she despised the clamminess of female interaction, her inner world was the stickiest, clammiest and heaviest of all. In one-on-one conversations she could remain aloof in the belief that she had the upper hand, but Rika could easily imagine how once she joined a group of women, she'd hover around fretfully, trying to find her place. She felt a sensation she'd never experienced before rising up from her waist, flummoxing her. Was this sympathy? Pity? Was she finding Kajii sweet? But no, that wasn't right. This was nothing but an unpleasant sense of superiority, Rika attempted to tell herself.

'It was exhausting, and it caught me off guard. I started attending lessons precisely because I was sick of all that in the outside world, and then it found its way in.'

'When you say "all that"?'

'How can I explain it? The yardsticks by which women are measured, I guess? The reason the cooking school received as much attention as it did is the preconception that women are creatures who are forever comparing themselves with one another. But that only happens because men try and use their yardsticks to establish some kind of order among women. I feel like Kajii was more man than she was woman. That's a bad way of putting it, isn't it? When I say "man",

I mean one of the dominant ones in society. I guess that figures, though, doesn't it? Anybody would turn out that way if they were mixing exclusively with old men who buy young women for money. I was getting to be like that at one point myself, too.'

Seeing the look Rika was giving her, Chizu waved her hand in front of her face and burst out laughing.

'Ha, sorry, I don't mean romantically! I just mean that my work is full of old men and old-men-in-training. There are no women my age, and all the women older than me who looked out for me quit because they couldn't balance their work life with their duties as wives and mothers. Before I knew it, I was the only one left. Several times, I've found myself becoming desensitised, and taking on that kind of old-man attitude myself. I'd start to see groups of women as naive, and they would get on my nerves, or I'd suddenly start feeling irritated with my older sister, whom I usually get on with, because I felt like, as a housewife, she couldn't understand how hard the working world was. Then I visited Madame's restaurant with some people from work. I'd never been all that interested in food, but it struck me that time how enjoyable dining could be. Of course the food was delicious, but the ambience was just as lovely. It was so relaxing. Talking to Madame, I found out that she ran a cookery school, and I immediately applied. Back then I couldn't even peel a potato.'

'I know just what you're talking about. When I tried the food that Ms Shigemori had made at the cooking school, I was so impressed. The next thing I knew, I was asking her how I could apply.'

Rika had the disconcerting sensation that what she was saying was in fact the truth. It barely seemed to her as though she were lying. It was as if Kajii's ways had rubbed off on her. In fact, she'd only ever seen Ms Shigemori's photo in a magazine, but she felt that she could not only imagine her voice and her presence, but could even clearly picture the inside of her house. She could picture her laptop left open, how she enjoyed cooking but didn't have the time to devote hours to it, and yet would still end up buying unusual spices and oils when she found them, which now lined the shelves of her kitchen. How the spices she'd bought would often be past their sell-by date. In the attempt to use them up in time she'd make over-seasoned pasta, which made her wince as she ate, washing it down with wine. She tried not to think what this woman – this extension of her – would feel about betraying her friends from the cooking class on behalf of someone from the same industry.

'I thought so. I had a feeling you and I were two of a kind. We're not good at cooking, but we enjoy good food. We're similar, too, in the way we gravitate to those tasks that require a lot of brute force but are difficult to mess up.'

Hearing this, a genuine smile spread across Rika's face and she felt some core part of her untense. Even the bitter taste of guilt became a welcome ingredient in the dish of her current feelings, somehow accentuating its texture.

'The way Kajii viewed marriage as the be-all and end-all, the fact she seemed a bit of an unknown quantity, the way she didn't quite get things ... All that stopped us from opening up to her, I think.'

'I really get that.'

'It was like she brought in all these external standards, then got right up close to us and started forcing them upon us. I got fed up with it. Up until then we'd all enjoyed cooking together without having to know what everyone was doing in their lives outside the school. That's true again now. It's a bit like building a boat and setting it afloat altogether. You collaborate to make the things you want to eat, and then eat them. That's it. Those classes are a safe space. I'm so busy with my work that I barely get to see my family, but I desperately protect the time to go to those lessons, and somehow manage to get off work early that day. As a result, I don't mind cooking for myself as much as I used to, and I've started being more conscious about eating vegetables and meat. I'm getting by somehow.'

Rika gave a deep nod.

'You need a place like that, don't you? Everyone does. Life is hard when you don't have a place where you can feel safe, and it's easy to find yourself stuck.'

'We didn't know anything about one another – ages, jobs, work-places, whether we're married or have kids, even surnames. We only knew one another's first names. There was none of the kind of competition that the articles insinuated there was.'

Rika nodded again. She'd only attended two of the lessons so far, but could tell that the students came not only to learn cooking, but because they loved the atmosphere.

'What we do know about one another is our favourite and least favourite foods, whether or not we can make a sauce with a nappe consistency, if we've been on a cheese holiday to France, which department store's food section we like the best, which meal scenes from films we take inspiration from when laying the table – that kind of stuff. That's the crucial info, as far as we're concerned.'

Was it not in those details that a person's soul resided? It seemed to Rika that she'd lived her life underestimating the importance of such things.

'But Kajii wasn't like that?'

'Madame's way of teaching is to make sure that her students master the basics, so you first learn to do everything in an orthodox way. Then, once you've grasped that, you can go your own way more: make new additions and adjustments to suit your palate. The same principle is true at Balzac. That's how true originality is born, she says. I like that sense of freedom. It feels good to me. But Kajii was fixed on doing things in the classic, orthodox way. Breaking the rules even the tiniest bit, giving a new twist to something, made her ever so nervous.'

'I think I read that she was really into luxury brands. I guess that's all related.'

'Exactly. She didn't like working with ingredients she'd not seen before, or new combinations. It really bothered her, and she'd talk about it all the time. Asking again and again, "Do men like this taste, though?" and "Wouldn't men object if you did this?" with a perfectly straight face.'

Rika did her best to appear unaffected by these revelations. The backs of her knees were cramping, and not just from standing in the kitchen for so long that evening. She had always supposed that Kajii's attitude to food had been with her since childhood. Now she saw she'd been wrong. Until Kajii had started attending lessons, she'd seen cooking as a service that one performed for someone else.

'So one day I just came out and told her: "We're not here to make food to please our boyfriends and our husbands." Madame followed up, kindly, telling her that it wasn't that that way of thinking is mistaken, and there are other cooking schools that teach you how to do exactly that, but if this approach didn't work for her, she'd be best to find somewhere that suited her better.'

'What did she say?'

'She looked shocked. Mumbled something like, "Can you really cook just for yourself, though?" When we asked if she ever had, she said no. She said she would spend time making food when she was with her sister or her boyfriends, but when she was alone, she would simply make things like rice with butter and soy sauce, or rice with a fried egg on top, or tarako pasta. She looked kind of dejected as she said it. I told her that, from where I was standing, as a total lazybones, those all sounded like haute cuisine, and everyone laughed. That was the first time I saw her smile.'

Could it be that the person at Le Salon de Miyuko who Kajii had identified as a potential friend was Chizu? Rika wondered now.

'That smile floored me, I have to say. She was always putting on airs in this irritating theatrical way, but in that moment all that fell away, and she seemed like a little girl. I remember thinking that, although she's kind of weird, she's not so unlike me and the others, after all. Maybe she's just lonely and ground down. She was a talented cook, and her movements were very precise. She was always cleanly presented, and handled the ingredients with real care, which was a joy to see. She was quick to pick up new information, and serious, and very keen to learn. She was the only one who would consistently practise cooking the recipes we'd made in class at home, to make sure she mastered them. Lots of people didn't like her, but everyone would admit that much. However much she stuck out, she was never asked to leave.'

Chizu spoke of Kajii as if talking about a girl she'd been at school with. Even if she didn't seem friendly towards her, there was no whiff of malice in her words.

'She looked as though she were really enjoying herself in the lessons. Sometimes she seemed to get so revved up that she'd come over a bit strange, clinging to me in a way that became annoying. I guess she was probably very lonely, starved of friends of her own age and conversation on an equal footing. People found her difficult, but I – this is a secret, okay? Sometimes I found her sweet, in her own way. It must have been so dull for her, hanging out with old men all the time to earn a living. They didn't go to work, her men. It must have been exhausting. Like nursing someone, twenty-four seven.'

'Nursing someone ...'

'And then one day, in the autumn, Madame suggested that as a special treat the following lesson we'd make whatever meals people wanted. It didn't matter what cuisine it was – Chinese, Italian, Japanese, Vietnamese, anything went. Someone made a request that Kajii vehemently objected to, saying that it wasn't suitable for Le Salon de Miyuko, it wasn't in the spirit of French cuisine and so on. We were all so excited by the plan, though, we didn't take much notice. Maybe that wasn't particularly mature of us. Anyway, we took a vote, and the majority went for the idea. And Kajii suddenly kicked off, shouting and saying all this crazy stuff. We were stunned.'

Chizu paused, looked around her and lowered her voice.

'I don't think the police know about this. Madame didn't want us to be the subject of any more curiosity. Anyway, she marched over to the kitchen, and tipped over a pot of fond de veau that was sitting on the hob, covering the floor in steaming brown liquid. She threw the heatproof glass containers on the floor, making a huge racket and sending pieces of glass flying. Everyone screeched, and Madame went to call the police. But Kajii saw her reaching for the phone on the wall, and fled out of the back entrance. Nobody went after her. We just set about slowly but steadily clearing up the mess she'd made. We had no idea what was going on, and we were tired, and frightened. She didn't come back after that. Not all that long after, we heard about the case on the news.'

Chizu turned over her hands and inspected her fingernails. In today's lesson, she'd been tasked with peeling the skins of red peppers that had been chargrilled to a rich black, and she hadn't managed to get all the dirt out.

'I've said too much, probably. It must be shocking to hear. I really do get the sense we're quite similar, you and I.'

'Yes, you're right. I really related to what you said about your working environment, and the way people there think.'

'I'm also the kind who throws myself headlong into my work. It's only since I've started coming to these lessons that I've begun to understand the power of combining different ingredients, and of leaving a dish to develop for a while if the taste isn't working yet.' Saying this, Chizu gave a bashful smile. Rika was the same. By experimenting during the lessons, she wanted to learn how to create meals that tasted uniquely hers. She hoped that Reiko wished the same for her.

The classic and the new, the bitter and the sweet, the costly and the easy-to-come-by seasonal ingredients, the soft and the hard, the powerful and the delicate – she wanted to include anything that appealed to her, trusting in her instincts as she combined things. That was the true pleasure of cooking and, it seemed to Rika, a route to enriching her life. Quite possibly, it was in this that true style, flexibility and wisdom lay. Kajii was a talented cook, faithful to the basics, but the art of innovative combination was beyond her. She could only do extremes, only black or white. Did she ever tire of herself, despair of herself for being that way?

Kajii had been arrested two months after quitting Le Salon de Miyuko. Her men had been dying off, one by one, since she'd begun attending. *I began cooking for myself*, she'd said. In other words, she'd begun focusing the phenomenal energy that all this time she'd been pouring on them on herself, and the men who'd been so hungry for her attention had stopped taking care of themselves, and strayed towards death – if that were the case, Rika could understand it.

'What was the dish that Kajii objected to? Do you remember?'

'Oh, did I not say? It was roast turkey, though the lesson was still a little while off Thanksgiving. They eat turkey in France, of course, but I guess in Japan the associations with the US and the UK are stronger. There are lots of embassies in this area, and supermarkets catering to foreign people. I think someone discovered one that sold frozen turkeys and said they wanted to try cooking one, and everyone else got on board. We wanted to create one of those roast turkeys like you see in pictures of Thanksgiving dinners.'

Chizu looked out at the street beyond the window. The cherry blossom was approaching full bloom, and the air tonight seemed almost white.

The roast turkey as it existed in Rika's imagination was sizzling hot, gleaming all over with a golden sheen thanks to its coatings of butter, singed here and there to an aromatic dark brown. This unfamiliar dish somehow corresponded perfectly with the features of Rika's vision of an ideal life: a radical improvement in her cooking skills, an affluent, full life, a warm household where people came together ... But no, what it really symbolised, she thought, was something you make on your own, and give with generosity to your loved ones – not so unlike a safe space.

Surely, it had signified something similar to Chizu, too. But maybe for Kajii the turkey had meant something different. Maybe for her, it had held the diametrically opposite meaning.

Rika was becoming able to gesture towards the contours of what it was that she wanted, even if they were still vague. Attending the cooking lessons was making her more sensitive to smells, textures and temperatures.

She was starting to get the hang of it. She just had to keep going a little bit further.

When she looked up at Tokyo Tower on her way home, she found it glinting as if smeared with animal fat. The fat flowed from it, becoming luminescent trails that lit up the spring night.

CHAPTER FOURTEEN

The nights were still chilly, and Rika wore her trenchcoat out in the evening, but the days were warm enough that she'd be sweating even in a light jumper.

Rika now weighed 59 kilos – 10 kilos heavier than when she'd first started covering the Kajii case.

Now that there was no chance of her appearing slim however hard she tried, she had resolved to wear whatever she wanted. Today she wore a jumper of an acid-green shade like apple sherbet, which she'd bought in a sale but always thought too girly for her, complete with a brooch that her mother had given her. She was still perpetually short of sleep, but her hair and skin looked more lustrous. Was that the result of a better diet?

Now, looking out the window, her estate agent said, 'It's the perfect spot for a hanami picnic. You've got shops selling nice ready-made food in the arcade nearby, so you wouldn't even need to prepare.'

A constant stream of pale petals from the cherry trees in full bloom outside the window floated down onto the puddles on the ground, blanketing them. In the end, the cherry trees had bloomed later than expected, so the hanami parties with work people that had been arranged for the end of March hadn't been the liveliest of affairs.

For a time, the two women said nothing, gazing down together at the park below. Encircled by the cherry trees sat several groups of mothers and children on small picnic sheets spread with grilled chicken and bento boxes.

* * *

The property Rika was viewing was a three-bedroomed apartment with a large open-plan kitchen, built some thirty years earlier. It was a fair walk from the nearest station, but it was of a price that meant Rika would feasibly be able to eventually pay off her mortgage, even if she took early retirement. If Rika's ideas about getting her own place were starting to assume a tinge of reality, it had a lot to do with her estate agent, Hatoko Yamamura, sister of Tokio Yamamura.

The information Kitamura had provided about Kajii's victim's sister had led Rika to an estate agency in Nishi-Shinjuku. In the third-floor office of a tall, narrow building, with a water dispenser that gurgled loudly placed in the entrance, she'd asked for Hatoko Yamamura. As she was explaining to the young male employee that she was a single woman looking for a property with as many rooms as possible, and that she'd heard Hatoko was great to work with, the woman herself had poked her head round a door at the back of the office. With hot water from the dispenser, she'd made them weak matcha tea. From that point on, they'd been meeting once every four or so days, when Rika found space in her working schedule. Today was their third appointment.

Rika had given her real name and profession, but Hatoko showed no sign of suspicion. Perhaps she could tell that Rika was truly interested in the properties, and wasn't pretending.

Attempting not to lose track of her real objective in all of this, Rika would sneak looks at the side of Hatoko's face, trying to imagine what it must be like to have a member of your family stolen away permanently by a woman like Kajii.

'It's amazing that you manage to cook properly, when you're so busy with work.'

At Hatoko's comment, which seemed to come from genuine admiration rather than a wish to flatter, Rika snapped back to herself. Without fully knowing what she was doing, she'd gone back into the kitchen and was opening and closing the oven door. Hatoko looked at her from where she stood in the living room. The sunlight pouring in through the window illuminated the downy hairs around her mouth.

'Oh no, I've just started learning. But I do think it'd be great to have a proper oven like this. If possible, I'd love a hob with at least three rings.'

Just through interacting with Hatoko, Rika could feel her wishes assuming a more visible form. At first, Hatoko had come over as a little frosty, but Rika was starting to understand that her way of working consisted in listening carefully to what the other person said and not butting in too much, so as to best ascertain their needs.

'Are you going to cookery classes? I find them so …' Hatoko began, and then shook her head, saying, 'Ignore me.'

When Rika encouraged her, she said hesitantly, 'I suppose they're attended by very domestically minded women, with lots of time and money on their hands.'

She didn't sound subservient, but there was a hint of resignation to her words. Was she thinking of Kajii as she spoke? Rika found herself attempting to smooth things over.

'I'm not remotely domestic myself, I just like eating. I'm happiest when I'm cooking for myself.'

Hatoko began talking at speed, as if to justify herself.

'I don't cook. I'm bad at it. Since my mother died, I don't even set foot in the kitchen. My mother wasn't that fond of cooking either, so when I see someone using an oven, I think, wow! I feel a sense of inferiority, I suppose.'

Despite the personal nature of what she was saying, Hatoko's expression didn't change as she spoke. The roughness of her skin made her black hair appear glossy, almost wet, in contrast. Her eyes were set closely together, as were her nose and her mouth. Her thick, unkempt eyebrows cast dark shadows over her eyelids.

She didn't look very like her baby-faced brother, Kajii's victim, who seemed to be pouting in every photo taken of him. Rika had heard that the mother had been overprotective of her son, but what had her relationship been like with her daughter – his older sister?

Rika got the sense that Hatoko may have been very capable from a young age, the kind who thought nothing of taking care of herself. Rika attempted to change the subject.

'I'd like to have as many rooms as possible. It doesn't matter if they're small. When my grandfather dies, my mother might want to come and live with me. I'd like to make the place into a kind of refuge that people around me can use.'

'A refuge?'

'Yes, a lot of my friends, both male and female, get quite lonely. Sorry, I know that's quite a particular ask. But that's the main reason I want to buy a place of my own.'

Rika was surprised to hear herself referring to Shinoi as a friend, and yet it felt right. Of late, they hadn't been talking about news items, and all his tip-offs had been going to Kitamura.

'One day I might need to rely on them, so I want to help them out while I still can. When I was in middle school, I found my father's body in the apartment where he was living by himself, and I can't shake off the feeling that I'm going to die alone as well.'

'He died alone?' Hatoko murmured, then fell silent. Rika knew that she had abandoned her former career as a result of what happened to her brother.

Rika wondered whether she'd be able to carry on working at Shūmeisha in the long-term. Thanks to the Kajii feature, her path to the editorial desk had come into sharper focus. But when she thought about whether she'd have the physical and mental strength to continue doing that job into her forties and fifties, she wondered whether she'd be able to keep up mortgage repayments for a place of her own. She'd decided that when she came to the end of the Kajii feature, she would need to take stock of what was possible for her at thirty-three.

'I started thinking about those things, too, when I was your age.'

Hatoko tilted her oval face. There was something hard and stiff about her aura, and she didn't smile readily. But the more Rika saw her, the more she caught glimpses of a different side to her – the sassy movement of her eyes when explaining the plumbing system, or the way she would go after the landlord with an unfazed expression when something in a property wasn't quite working as it should. Now, she was gazing at a young boy and slightly older-looking girl playing in the park below.

'I live on my own, and I don't anticipate that ever changing. I'm really glad that I bought a place of my own around forty. It meant I was able to start using the time I'd spent worrying about it doing other things I enjoy.'

Hatoko's tone was light, but it was the first time that she'd spoken in this much depth about her own life. The best thing to do, Rika thought, would be to conceal the fact that this had all been part of her research, and slip away quietly from Hatoko's life.

'I've understood what it is you're looking for,' she said now. 'Rather than a sealed-off space, you want a place where people can come and go, and where you can customise things. An inviting space that can be a point of intersection for lots of different people. A space to rest and rejuvenate.'

A gust of wind blew in from the window. Several cherry petals clung to the mosquito netting, trembling for a few moments before falling lightly to the ground.

'So it's okay to think about it in that way?' Rika said.

Hatoko made to close the window as she replied.

'As long as somewhere has got a roof, and a place to let the air in, then it's good as a home. I think a place's inhabitants should be free to decide how it's going to be used. When people are bound by rules, they find it difficult to choose a property that suits them. I'll have a think about what might work best for you. Even among properties of the same sort of area, the layout and the direction in which it faces can make a big difference to the feel of a place.'

Rika was doing the cooking lessons and the house-hunting for entirely professional reasons, yet both had somehow come to soak through into her life. It was just like how, as you went on folding the dough for pie crust, the lumps of butter would all of a sudden cease to be visible.

'It's the first sell-out issue in ages!'

When Rika arrived at work, the desk editors' ears and noses were flushed with excitement.

The issue of the *Shūmei Weekly* with the Manako Kajii interview as its lead article was making waves. They had received more letters and emails from readers than ever before. It had been talked about online before its publication, and even women in their twenties who would not usually go near the *Shūmei Weekly* were buying it.

The first part of the six-part feature focused on Manako Kajii's life in Niigata.

Kajii had been very reluctant to admit to any connection with the man who'd molested her sister, but when Rika happened to mention that he'd taken his life, her attitude had grown more compliant. 'He protected me. He fed me, enveloped me, and helped me, like a mother should. We were similar, and we only had one another. You could say that we had a physical relationship, and you could also say we didn't.' Her manner of speech was as overblown as ever, but in essence amounted to a roundabout confession. When confronted with how, in her testimony in court, she'd morphed this man into a salesman from Tokyo, Kajii pinned her large, grape-like eyes on Rika and said in a clipped tone, 'He was always vague in what he told me, always mixing reality and fantasy. To a young girl like me, he seemed like a sophisticated adult.'

Now, Rika passed her eyes over some of the emails sent in by readers that a temp had printed out for her.

'Why does the world get *this* worked up about Manako Kajii?'

Rika turned around to see Kitamura standing next to her, shaking his head. He had sleep in his eyes and his hair looked still rumpled, a far cry from his usual appearance. Thanks to one of Shinoi's tip-offs, he had a scoop in this same issue. The illegal dumping of waste by a care home run by a certain izakaya chain was the second biggest article, after the exclusive Kajii interview.

'I think everyone's starved of calorific substances. They're super responsive to anything with a whiff of crunch or excess about it.'

Kitamura looked unimpressed by this answer. Rika felt that he wouldn't understand even if she were to explain, so she ignored him and returned her eyes to the emails.

She passed her eyes across the criticism that she had known would also come. However conceited it might sound, she sensed that the article's success wasn't solely down to the fascination with Kajii as a subject. It was because she'd put in the time, and stuck with it until she was satisfied. Even if that didn't mean much to other people, she planned to keep on working like that in the future, honing her own unique style. Would that be possible at the *Shumei Weekly*?

The temp came to tell her that the editor wanted to see her. When she entered the glass-fronted cubicle, the first words he said were not any words of praise or gratitude, but: 'Can you increase the number of parts?'

'No, I don't want to water it down. It'll be a six-parter, as agreed.'

The editor raised his eyebrows, startled.

It was the first time that Rika had ever pushed back on an order from above.

'That's amazing, Kazuko! You mean you practise everything we learn here at home?' a red-faced Chizu asked as she mixed the hollandaise sauce. She appeared to be struggling to get it to the state of 'thick and gloopy, with minuscule bubbles', as per Madame's instructions. The yellow liquid had been splashing around in the bowl for some time now, sending spray flying.

'I don't manage to get everything right, by a long stretch! But I just move on to the next thing without worrying too much,' Rika replied as she cut off the hard bits at the base of the white asparagus spears. The chicken roasting in the oven was giving off a delicious aroma.

Rika wanted to do everything the way Kajii had done it. In these two weeks, at home she had made all four of the dishes they'd learned to cook in their second lesson. Once every three or so days, she would go over to Shinoi's apartment relatively early in the evening, and try her hand at one of the recipes. She attempted to reproduce them faithfully the way she'd been taught, without changing too much. The recipes given out in class all served six people, but she found that if she made them at Shinoi's, where there was always somebody staying over, it would all get polished off. Admittedly, the lamb with orange that she'd made first of all had been underdone, the volume of soupe du poisson she'd produced had been very small, and the crêpes Suzette had fallen to pieces. Yet even when she messed things up, she didn't stop, didn't permit herself to be disheartened, but simply moved on to the next thing. The previous evening, when she'd carried the sea urchin with beurre blanc sauce over to the dining table, the others had cheered in a way they'd not done before. Was it because this was her favourite of all the dishes they'd made in class so far that it had turned out so well? She'd also splashed out and bought herself a new apron.

Now, overhearing her and Chizu's conversation, the other students began to chip in.

'That's so good of you to do that! I almost never make the stuff I learn here at home.'

'Yes, I'm definitely absorbing techniques and knowledge, and I've made some dishes several times, but never all of them.'

'I mean, even if I did rustle up French cuisine for my husband and kids, I'm not sure what they'd make of it ...'

At this comment from Aki, everyone tittered in embarrassment.

'Someday! One day, when the time comes, I'll do it! I just haven't given it my all yet,' Chizu exclaimed in a high voice. Her hand holding the whisk finally stopped moving and she slumped against the table as if exhausted. Everyone burst out laughing. Madame smiled knowingly, and dropped the white asparagus spears into the boiling water.

'You should all take a leaf from Kazuko's book. Practising something immediately after you've learned it is the best way to master it.
Asparagus is all about fragrance, so be careful not to overboil them.'

Rika now whispered into the ear next to her, which was pink with
excitement, 'You know the turkey you told me about last time – what
recipe were you going to follow? I couldn't find any in my French
cooking book.'

Chizu shook her head from side to side, perhaps trying to
dislodge some of the hair that was stuck with sweat to her neck, and
replied hesitantly, 'I guess Madame would remember.'

Rika snuck a glance at Madame, who was lending a hand whisking the meringue. She waited until the lecture had finished, and the
students were getting ready to go home, then asked her in as gentle a
way as she knew how. The instant Rika pronounced the word 'turkey',
she saw Madame's shoulders tense up, but her reply was as composed
as ever.

'I've got a friend from university who's been living in the States
for a while, with her husband's work. She had a real struggle at first,
adapting the meals over there so they'd agree with her family's taste
buds, and making Japanese food from things she could get her hands
on when Asian ingredients were less readily accessible. I was thinking
of making it according to a recipe she gave me. I've only made it once
myself. I had it in a notebook, which I took out and showed to everyone. I think that was when …'

Madame frowned slightly. Before she had time to suspect
anything, Rika said quickly, 'Would you mind if I copied that recipe?'

'Yes, that's fine. It's so long you won't be able to copy it out now,
so I'll lend you my recipe book, if you like. You can give it back
whenever.'

Leaving Rika no time to demur, Madame went over to the bookcase on the wall. The notepad that Madame held out to her was
covered in brown oil stains. Magazine clippings of recipes for
simmered vegetables and Chinese dishes had been stuck into its
pages, with handwritten notes in the margins. Seeing how unthink-

ingly Madame had shared this part of herself, a sense of guilt dug into Rika's tenderest part.

Rika remembered Reiko's advice on approaching Kajii: to ask a woman who loves to cook for a recipe is to strike them in their weakest, most unprotected spot. In other words, all this time, Rika had been playing the dirtiest game imaginable.

Thinking to herself that some day, eventually, she would get her comeuppance, Rika slid the notebook into her bag.

Rika had initially been imagining cooking the turkey as an extension of her research, but she soon gave up on the idea. According to Madame's notes, a 5-kilogram turkey took three whole days just to defrost. Once it was defrosted, you had to prepare it, leave it overnight, and then roast it for three hours, keeping watch over it all the while. The following day you boiled the bones to make stock, and could make sandwiches and gratins with the remaining meat. A five-day long task wasn't something that she could easily perform alongside her professional duties.

The bird's hollowed-out insides were stuffed with its other parts, such as its gizzard, heart, liver, neck and even, sometimes, its head. Imagine being killed, Rika thought, having your insides scooped out, and then being stuffed with your own internal organs, your own head. The thought robbed her of her appetite, yet the description of the stuffing made of giblets, chestnuts, pine nuts and mochi rice made her salivate. The description of how you would boil the turkey's neck to make gravy, something she so often read about in novels from overseas, gave her a rush of excitement.

For once, Shinoi's apartment was deserted. Rika shut her laptop and headed to the kitchen. She took out eggs, butter and white asparagus. She wanted to practise making the recipe from the lesson the day before, before she forgot how to do it. It was already past two in the morning, and she wanted to make sure she was in bed within the next hour. She'd sleep for four hours, then she had to go and see a government minister in Kasumigaseki.

She melted the butter in the pan. She warmed the egg yolks by immersing them in a bowl of hot water and mixing them with vinegar, then pouring in the shining golden butter little by little. She moved the whisk ceaselessly, making the contents of the bowl whirl round and round. Having observed Chizu's troubles up close, and learned how to avoid them, she succeeded in producing the fine egg-coloured foam relatively quickly. Her whole hand, from the wrist down, was dancing a waltz.

The tigers in the book, whose desires had kept them spinning round and round until they transformed into butter, had ended up in the stomachs of Little Babaji's family. Even after their deaths, Kajii's victims continued to be exposed to and consumed by the curious gaze of the general public.

Rika had stopped believing that any blame lay with the victims themselves. Being sucked into the vortex of Kajii's ominous power, like she herself had been, was something that could happen to anybody. Thinking this, she went on single-mindedly whisking the butter.

Through her adventures with the quatre-quarts on Valentine's Day, she'd learned that waiting on the far side of all of this seemingly endless whisking was not stasis or evaporation, but emulsification. If she couldn't tear her eyes away from Kajii, if she couldn't stop herself from spinning round and round, then maybe all that was left to do was to grip on to Kajii with all her might, so as to ensure she wasn't shaken off.

'Done!' Rika said to herself and lifted up the whisk. The sauce of warm, bright yellow that came dripping off the whisk was smooth as cashmere.

Rika heard the door open, and then Shinoi's voice, apparently having seen the number of shoes, saying, 'Is nobody around today?' Soon after, she heard the sound of him gargling loudly in the bathroom.

'Yū's at a welcome party for the new recruits, and Kitamura's chasing up your latest tip-off, so I'm on duty tonight. Though it seems as if Reiko's out. I don't know where she's gone, but I guess she might be having dinner with Ryōsuke.'

'Aha,' Shinoi said, finally appearing in the room and draping his suit jacket over a hanger. Of late, he smelled less strongly of cigarette smoke.

'Try this, if you'd like. It's white asparagus in a hollandaise sauce.'

Rika carried over to the table a plate laid out as beautifully as an artwork, together with a low-carb beer. Sitting down, Shinoi thanked her, and took a long gulp of the beer. He let out a contented sigh, and gently skewered a spear of asparagus with his fork. He lifted it straight to his mouth and chewed vigorously, his throat moving up and down.

'This is great. It tastes of spring.' Clearly embarrassed by what he'd just said, Shinoi laughed, avoiding Rika's eyes.

'This might sound rude, but I think your cooking has really improved. Until now, the things you've made tasted like you'd cooked them well according to the recipe, but this one somehow has a Rika sort of flavour.'

'What kind of a flavour is that?'

'Strong and assertive, but delicate at the same time. The kind of taste you don't get bored of.'

'I actually amended the recipe this time. I felt like I wanted a tiny bit of natural sweetness, so I added a drop of honey.'

'Honey, eh?' Shinoi said nodding and reached out with his fork for another spear.

'Under Kajii's influence, I was eating lots of very heavy, orthodox dishes, but recently I've started to understand my own tastes better. I like relatively classical flavouring but with an extra something to pep it up – a bit of spice, or something to give a hint of acidity or bitterness. I also really like simple recipes, with not too many flavours.'

'Sounds like you're finding your own style. Speaking of which, the article is great. You present her viewpoint and way of thinking just as they are, while also managing to touch upon the background that gave rise to all of this. It's genuinely fascinating, and has got its own flavour to it that stays with the reader. I guess that's your style, too.'

Feeling embarrassed, she glanced at him to check his expression.

'Reiko's way better at cooking than I am.'

'Is she?' he said, covering his asparagus spear with lashings of sauce.

'Reiko's face softens a little when she's talking with you.'

'I enjoy her company too. She looks so serious, but she's a real oddball, and fun to be around. We never run out of things to say to each other. I feel like I learn new perspectives on things from her, which is odd when she herself seems to operate with such tunnel vision.'

The two of them laughed, and Rika suddenly understood what it was that had drawn her to Shinoi. She felt she could trust him because they liked the same things.

'Right. She's got such a narrow focus, and yet you feel your world opening up through being with her.'

All of a sudden, Rika felt herself tearing up. All this time, she had been waiting for the moment when she could share everything she liked about her friend with someone else. She'd often worried whether anyone apart from her would notice the good points about her friend, which weren't immediately obvious – if anyone else would cherish them like she did. You could say that Ryōsuke's way of loving the shiny, cheerful, good parts of Reiko and failing to notice any of her darkness was just his own way of loving her, but you could also argue that it was exactly that which had driven Reiko into a corner. Rika had always wanted to joke around with someone else about her best friend's reckless tendencies, her self-righteousness, her painful seriousness.

'I still don't feel I've got my head around marriage, but I'm sure it must be easier when you've got an escape. I don't mean infidelity, obviously. I mean a place that you can go to drink a cup of coffee when you feel stuck. Then your husband could come and collect you.

I feel like that alone would be enough. Just because you're family doesn't mean you have to share absolutely everything.'

'That's heartening to hear. I've been thinking recently that I'm going to try and see my daughter.' Shinoi's voice wavered slightly as he spoke. 'One of the conditions of our divorce is that I'm allowed to see her. But I asked to meet her once and she said no, and it hurt me so much that I haven't tried again. I just hear about her through my ex-wife. I don't have any intention of trying to be a model father to her, like I did back then. I just want to aim to be a person she can have a cup of coffee with, when she feels like it. Eating here with all you lot, I feel like I've understood a bit better what spending time with other people is about.'

As Rika nodded, it struck her that in the not-so-distant future, their little group would disband. Everyone was already beginning to return to their former routines. Shinoi needed to sell this apartment. They needed to move on. That seemed sad, but something new awaited all of them.

She stood up and headed into the kitchen, then turned on the hob. Watching the large bubbles forming and then vanishing on the surface of the water in the pan, she felt Kajii's reason for objecting so strongly to the turkey taking clear shape in her mind. Caught up in the torrents of boiling water, the asparagus spears were being thrown violently up and down.

'If you want seconds, they'll just take a moment.'

She must have looked as though she were away with the fairies. Shinoi stared at her, saying nothing. The second round of asparagus, which she overcooked, was as fluffy and elusive as a spring breeze.

'People must have so much time on their hands! Are they really that obsessed with me?' Kajii said. She affected irritation, but her eyes were sparkling with glee. This person simply adores attention, Rika thought. When she told Kajii that the edition featuring her interview had sold out, Kajii became as high-spirited as a child, and brandished her own copy of the magazine, apparently acquired at the Detention

House shop. But instead of turning immediately to the interview, as Rika expected her to, Kajii opened it onto a double-page colour spread featuring a young actress. Screwing up her face, she said bitterly, 'So cheap of her to do something like this. She must be losing favour.'

The twenty-year-old actress was wearing a white sleeveless dress, her bright eyes open wide in an expression that said how impressed she was by all she saw and heard.

She's forever looking at women, Rika thought. The image of a plump young girl licking ice cream as she stared fixedly at the female cows rose before Rika's eyes.

'I came today to talk to you about something else. I heard that, at Le Salon de Miyuko, you stormed out after taking objection to the students' plan to cook a turkey. I've finally understood why it is that the idea was so abhorrent to you.'

Kajii looked at her. There was an uncertainty in her.

'It seems like you were the only one of the students who'd always practise the meals you'd been taught at Le Salon de Miyuko until you had them perfect.'

Rika hadn't told Kajii in so many words that she was attending Le Salon de Miyuko, or that she'd had contact with Hatoko. She figured, though, that Kajii being Kajii, she would have already realised.

'A 5-kilogram turkey feeds about ten adults, yes?'

That afternoon, Rika had had a lunch meeting at Balzac, and caught a glimpse of the kitchen where Le Salon de Miyuko lessons had once been taught. As she looked over, a stout grey-haired man who she took to be the owner-chef was tasting the sauce in a small pan that a young chef held out. The big commercial kitchen contained several huge sparkling clean ovens and drains in the floor. The idea that one person could cause such destruction in that impenetrable fortress was extraordinary.

'You can buy mini turkeys that would probably be suitable for two people, but then the defrosting and roasting times would be different.

It would become a different meal, with a different recipe. You're someone who wanted to do things exactly as Madame had taught you. Even for someone with as healthy an appetite as yours, polishing off a turkey that feeds ten people would be out of the question.'

Kajii showed no sign of upset at this, and Rika felt her confidence start to waver. Still she went on.

'The reason you objected was because you understood immediately that even if you learned how to roast a turkey, you'd never have the opportunity to cook it. The other students at the lessons didn't make the recipes they'd learned because they had in their heads the idea of a "someday" when they'd get the chance to. If "someday" all their friends got together, they'd make that particular meal. But you – you didn't have that notion of a "someday". That's been the case ever since you were a child. However optimistic you make yourself out to be, you can only believe in the things you see before you with your own eyes, the things you can get hold of this very instant.'

Rika stopped speaking and looked at Kajii. She realised that, in her eagerness for the words to hit home, she was adopting the tone Madame took when explaining things to the students.

'Whatever you did, however hard you tried, you couldn't have had ten friends over to your house. You had plenty of worshippers, but you could hardly have the men you'd met on the dating sites together in the same place. Your maximum guest count would have been a man you were dating and your sister, which is to say, two people. Or maybe even that would have been impossible – perhaps it would have been too risky to let someone you'd told all those lies meet a member of your family. Even if you were more serious about your cooking than any of the other students, you weren't blessed with a place where you could do it in the way you wanted to. Quite possibly, the same applied to every aspect of your life.'

Rika shot a look at Kajii. She looked as though she were smiling.

'Maybe, if you'd had enough ease and space in your life to believe in a "someday", then everything would have been different. Believing in a "someday" isn't a sign of weakness or stupidity, and it isn't an escape either. When you realised that you didn't have anywhere you could cook and serve a turkey, you felt like you couldn't breathe, like you had nowhere left to go. You felt hatred towards all those students who weren't even thinking about their futures, and wanted to leave the Balzac kitchen that very moment. When you realised that what you'd done meant you could no longer return to the one space where you felt safe, you grew sick and tired of everything. Am I right?'

Kajii smiled a wholesome smile without any hidden significance. Rika could understand very well what Chizu had said. This Manako was undoubtedly really sweet.

'Chizu told me that you've got a really sweet side to you, and that you're a very talented cook. Is she the woman you were talking about, that you thought you might have become friends with?'

Kajii eventually answered in a drawn-out, honeyed voice.

'What are you talking about? I don't know who that is. I've not even heard the name before.'

Even as she cocked her head, playing dumb, her voice was trembling slightly and her eyes were moist. Rika watched as she pursed her soft-looking lips. Their peach blush transformed to a blueish purple, and the skin on her face darkened.

'I've decided that I'm going to roast a turkey someday. Just for my own enjoyment.'

Rika decided to bring an end to her attack, and try something new.

'I don't feel particularly sorry for you, you know. Not having any friends isn't especially unusual. I thought about whether, if I was to roast a turkey, I could invite ten people over to eat it. I don't have a large circle of friends, and there isn't an oven big enough in the place I'm living at the moment. Ten people couldn't even fit inside my apartment, and I don't have enough chairs or tableware. So I couldn't do it. In fact, I feel like the people who can are in the minority. But if I can rent out a big room, and get that number of people together, then maybe I'll give it a try. If you're free by then, if you're out of prison ...'

Rika hesitated for a moment. An image of the apartment in front of the park that Hatoko had shown her rose up before her.

'Then I hope you'll come and have some of the turkey I'll cook. I'd love it if you came.'

Unable to control herself any longer, Kajii burst into tears.

They weren't fake, either. She sniffed, and her hands rose to her eyes, trying to keep back the tears that were spilling out. Through Kajii's fingers, Rika glimpsed her red bloodshot eyes, her swollen eyelids. The painful sounding sobs kept on coming.

If the acrylic screen hadn't been there, Rika would have handed her a handkerchief from her bag. Even playing out the hypothetical scenario, she felt embarrassed at the thought of her utilitarian hankie, which felt so mismatched with Kajii's style. She decided on her next day off that she'd pop into a department store and buy some hand-kerchiefs in a sophisticated floral pattern, of a kind that Kajii would like better.

CHAPTER FIFTEEN

The three-digit number she'd been assigned was an alternating combination of a number believed to be lucky, and one said to indicate death.

She'd persuaded Kitamura and three part-time university students from the company to join the queue with her from early morning, but in the end, it was Rika herself who'd landed the winning ticket. On so many occasions in the past she had lined up like this, but this was the first time she'd got one of the admittance tickets everyone was craving. It was a weekday, yet more than three hundred people had joined the queue for sixty-five courtroom seats. Scoring an entry ticket made Rika think that she and Kajii did have some kind of connection, after all.

Around them stood the not-so young women who were the spitting image of Manako Kajii, dubbed the 'Kajimana Girls' by the mass media. They wore dresses of sky blue and baby pink teamed with cardigans, their half-up half-down hair held in place with bow-shaped barrettes. Rika felt like she had stumbled into a science-fiction novel where the world was ruled by Kajii clones.

The trees lining the pavement gave out the smell of young fresh greenery, and their leaves dappled the sunlight cast upon the ground. May had only just begun but the air was dry, and it already felt like summer was on the way. After thanking Kitamura and the others and seeing them off as they vanished inside the subway, Rika slipped inside the entrance to the Tokyo High Court. The other men and women lucky enough to get their hands on tickets packed

into the lift like sardines in a tin. When they got to the correct
floor, Rika was spat out along with them, and waited in a long line
to have her bag searched. With a jotter and a pen in hand, she
joined a different line, this time to enter the courtroom. Reporters
wearing armbands slid past her several times, ducking as if to erase
their presence.

The wood-effect door opened, and the line began slowly disappearing inside. Anyone who wished to was allowed to remain outside
while the press photographers were taking pictures of the courtroom.
Rika stood in the corridor now mostly emptied of people, gazing
down at the trees blowing about in the wind outside.

It had been a year since the first trial, and the fervour had cooled
somewhat, yet there had still been almost five times the average
number of people waiting for tickets. Thanks to Rika's article, whose
final instalment had been printed the previous day, public interest in
the case was resurfacing. There was already talk at Shūmeisha about
publishing the article as a book. The sixth and final part of the article
touched upon what Kajii had felt at Le Salon de Miyuko, how she
had behaved, how hurt she had been, and how she felt now, after her
arrest and detention.

To write it, Rika had had to forget everything she herself had
seen and heard at the cooking school, and reconstruct the events
through Kajii's eyes. At first, Kajii had portrayed the lessons as far
more showy than they actually were, and the students as ever so
prim, but after Rika confessed that she'd used a fake name to attend
the lessons several times and mentioned Chizu's name, Kajii had
become less insistent. After various digressions, she even admitted
how comfortable she'd felt there. Generally, when she spoke about
women Kajii would without fail turn to insulting them, but her tone
became slightly kinder when speaking of Madame and the other
students.

'I asked them lots of questions. That was my way of doing my very
best to show my interest and get close to them.'

But she couldn't altogether stop herself from criticising them.

'I was the only one who practised what we were going to learn in advance, and revised what we had done already. It seemed as though they weren't really serious about learning to cook, and they didn't care much about their husbands and lovers either. Cold-hearted women.' When Rika feigned agreement, Kajii's tongue grew even looser. By bringing up elements of Chizu's account, Rika managed to elicit a version of the turkey incident from Kajii's perspective: how she'd been enraged by the way they'd decided on what to cook without her consent after she'd shown them such goodwill, and had run out of the classroom. It was Rika's hope that this portrayal would help disperse at least some of the prejudice surrounding the school.

When she got to the visitors' gallery, Rika looked around. Staring straight ahead in their allocated seats, the defence lawyers and prosecution all wore perfectly blank expressions, seemingly calculated to cool the excitement of the crowd. She looked for Hatoko but couldn't see her. Of late, Rika had put her apartment-hunting on pause. Her feelings of guilt towards Hatoko, for pouring so much effort into the search, were winning out after all. Most of those in the gallery were women. She spotted the faces of a few writers, journalists and others she recognised. For a second it occurred to her that all of them, herself included, had come together to inflict an injustice on Kajii. A bitter taste spread out from the back of her throat and through her body.

Eventually the judges entered, and the voice of the chief justice rang out, announcing that the court was open. Then a tangible ripple ran through the room. Kajii had appeared in handcuffs from the door on the left, accompanied by a prison guard. Rika felt a wave of relief. Kajii had told her that she intended to attend the court, but there was no obligation for the defendant to make an appearance at the retrial, and she had wondered if she might, in fact, not show.

Directed by the chief justice to state her name, she replied in a voice so quiet as to be almost inaudible, 'Manako Kajii.'

After confirming her date of birth in a feeble voice, she sat down alongside the defence lawyers.

Outside the small Detention House visiting room, in this high-ceilinged courtroom devoid of decorative excess, Kajii looked like a giant blancmange. There was a tenacious fragility to her – she was not repelling the piercing gazes directed her way, and seemed sunken into herself, just about succeeding in retaining her shape. Her lips, rosy pink against her smooth, opaque, white skin, were drawn together in a tight bow, creating a dimple on her chin, and her eyes, whose lids looked heavy as if she'd recently been crying, were focused on a point in the middle distance, as though she were seeking help. Her defiant attitude in the first trial, the lack of manners she so often showed, now seemed like a fiction.

Above all, her appearance seemed remarkably slapdash in comparison to the times Rika had met her in the visiting room. Over a pair of leggings, she wore a charcoal-grey dress of a sweatshirt fabric which masked all the contours of her body – the kind of outfit you'd expect someone to wear exclusively around the house. Even from this distance, Rika could tell that she was wearing a sturdy push-up bra, making her think that perhaps the rumour that she wore underwear sent into the prison by her male supporters – of which there were supposedly quite a few – was true. Yet leaving that aside, with strands of stray hair stuck to her forehead, the impression she gave was an unkempt one.

Rika turned her glance on the male lawyer with the well-defined jaw sitting next to her, his long hair tied back. He wore round glasses and his face was dusted with stubble. His way of narrowing his eyes made him seem overly self-conscious, but he was famous for being supremely talented. She had interviewed him twice in connection with other cases.

For the most part, Kajii kept her eyes pinned on the ground, but from time to time she would open them wide, batting her eyelashes and hunching her shoulders forlornly. Only her eyebrows looked as potent as ever.

The lawyer began to read out the reasons for the appeal in a low, mumbling voice.

From time to time, Kajii would turn to him and nod her head, as if in support. Rika stared fixedly at her, feeling much as if she'd just woken from a dream.

How was it that these past six months she had been so mesmerised by this woman? Surrounded and protected by people as she was, she now seemed in Rika's eyes a thoroughly weak-willed character, incapable of deciding anything for herself. Maybe she was, in fact, utterly lacking in things she wanted to do or to say. Perhaps it was her lies, which had nothing to do with her real wishes and which she'd simply used as a way of getting through whatever circumstance was currently at hand, that had carried her to the place where she was now. Quite possibly, when it came to her online dating and prostitution, she had made no decisions herself, but simply reached for whatever was esteemed by the world. The fact that everything she'd sought was so pricey seemed to support that hypothesis.

All of a sudden, Kajii looked towards the public gallery. The movement of eyes suggested she was looking for someone. Rika tried to catch her gaze, but like a firefly, it eluded her time and time again.

The new evidence presented by the defence was very minor. Four days before he died, Hatoko's brother Tokio had been in a cafe in Hachimanyama he used for meetings. In a guestbook which the regulars passed around, he had written something hinting at his desire to take his own life – perhaps in response to sensing Kajii's change of heart about their relationship. This had come to light because the cafe had recently closed, and the owner had stumbled upon the note while reading over the messages from the past ten years. The handwriting analysis had returned the conclusion that it almost certainly belonged to Tokio.

Even including the back and forth between the defence and the prosecution, the first hearing was over after thirty minutes. There was no opportunity for Kajii to speak, and the chief justice called for a re-examination of the notebook. The date for the next hearing was not yet determined.

Along with all the other people there, Rika watched Kajii as she disappeared from the courtroom accompanied by a prison guard: rounded back, swollen cheek glimpsed from the side, dishevelled black hair. Their eyes hadn't met once the whole time.

She could have invited her mother, whom she hadn't seen since New Year, to join her, but Rika felt she wanted to come alone. It had been eight years since she'd last visited the Yokohama graveyard where her father had been laid to rest. The graveyard was located in a neighbourhood where her father had lived for several years during his adolescence. For a while now, she'd been thinking to herself that she'd come as soon as the retrial had begun.

Somewhere far off, Rika heard the sound of a ship's horn. She could see the expanse of calm yet lonesome-looking summer sea in the distance. After checking that nobody was around, Rika began speaking to the gravestone, on which her father's posthumous Buddhist name was inscribed.

'I've started going to cooking lessons. I've learned how to make hollandaise sauce. It's soft-tasting with an acidic kick, a bit like mayonnaise.'

She remembered his smell, the last time she'd seen him. She hadn't found that scent – a mixture of old tobacco, the sebum of middle-aged men and sake – unpleasant. It wasn't a good smell, but it wasn't a bad one either. It was his smell, her father's smell. She remembered, too, the feel of his beard when he rubbed his face against hers.

'I wish I could make it for you. Not at your apartment, though. It's too dirty. I wouldn't want to be in charge of cleaning that place. I'd rather invite you over to mine.'

Perhaps she'd been getting it wrong all this time.

Maybe what had been eating away at her father wasn't loneliness, but rather a sense of shame. That was why he hadn't been able to ask for help. The reason he'd had such a strong reaction when Rika had told him why she couldn't go over to his wasn't anger or despair. He felt ashamed that he'd been treated with cruelty by his daughter, who was the only one he could rely on.

Rika recalled what Reiko had said when she came back to the apartment one morning the previous week and told Rika that she'd seen Ryōsuke.

'We had dinner in Naka-Meguro, and took a walk,' she said. 'He seemed relieved to see that I was doing okay. He actually cried, even with all those people around on the weekend. I cried a bit too, I don't really know why. It'd been so long since we ate out, just the two of us. On the way home, he invited me to a hotel and I said yes. It's weird, isn't it? I've only ever been to a hotel with him before we married, and even then only a handful of times, so many years ago. Lying in that bed with him in a totally unknown space, our house, and the question of kids, and us being married and all that felt very far away. I just knew that I was lying next to a man, and that his name was Ryōsuke. It feels dumb to be so affected by the space you're in.'

As if suddenly snapping back to herself, Reiko screwed up her face.

'It made me think, you know. I really do disagree with my father's way of life. I still hate that idea of not wanting to have sex with someone who feels like family to you. But maybe, my parents believed that was the best way for them to stay married. Thinking about it that way makes me feel kind of sorry for them.'

What had made Reiko want to escape wasn't Ryōsuke himself, but that house by the Den-en-Toshi Line, her hopes for how things would be, and the family set-up that they had built. Similarly, what Rika was afraid of wasn't her father himself, but that apartment as it existed within her memory. In the yellowing wallpaper and the dirt stains she had seen sadness. In actual fact, it was just that her father was a lazybones and had slacked off the cleaning. Yet she'd used those elements to stoke her terrifying visions. Blaming herself brought a comfortable kind of pain. As long as she believed that she was in the wrong, she didn't have to worry about forgetting her father, and thereby becoming an even more heartless daughter.

The reason she hadn't made the macaroni gratin for her father wasn't because she disliked him and was avoiding him. It was because she didn't have the confidence that she could clean his kitchen and make a smooth béchamel sauce. Maybe if she'd lifted up his body as it lay there face down on the floor, she might have seen that the expression on his face was one of unexpected tranquillity. Quite possibly her father didn't resent Rika and her mother. Even if he did, Rika would accept that resentment.

'Even if I end up dying alone, I don't think I'll resent people for it. I won't sit around waiting for other people. I'll use my own money to buy ingredients, make the food I want to eat, eat it how I like, and then die.'

Rika turned from the stone and walked towards the graveyard entrance. She was headed to the cafe looking out over the sea where her parents had been on their first date. Her mother would usually look pained when speaking of her father, but when she talked about that day, a smile would come over her face. Once again, Rika heard the sound of a ship's horn.

Rika was now used to being called into the glass-fronted editor's office. It was rare for the editor to be in the office early in the morning, though. Lately, Rika had started coming in early and leaving by the evening. Even if it put her schedule at odds with the rest of her colleagues, the number of hours she worked remained the same, and so long as she made sure to attend all the meetings, nobody minded. She no longer stayed on late into the night, as she used to. In a bid not to lose the young female readership they had acquired with the Kajii feature, the *Shūmei Weekly* was now doing a feature on the grievous lack of available childcare and its effects on parents. Freed from the burden of futile preparatory research and fruitless dinner dates, she felt less frenetic.

'I just had someone call me up to check some facts about a story that's going to print as a lead feature in three days' time. I'm guessing it'll cause a stir, so I want you to be prepared. For once the person who tipped me off seemed sympathetic.'

With this, the chief editor held out a faxed copy of an article from a rival magazine. Seeing the headline, a blue flash blocked out Rika's vision.

Exclusive Kajii Interview!
Her marriage in prison and her relationship with her father!
She told us all, right before her retrial.
'The stuff in the Shūmei Weekly *was all lies!'*
Discover the sordid truth behind the famous Shūmeisha journalist's twisted affection.

Rika felt her legs growing soft, as if her entire body had turned to playdough. She pulled up a metal chair and sat down. Licking her dry lips, she flicked through the pages, surveying the topics covered by the article. A part of her had suspected something of this kind might happen one day.

It appeared that Kajii had started a relationship with the article's author – a freelance editor in his fifties – and they were now engaged to be married.

'I recognise the guy's name. Ever since we published our article, he's been shopping it around to all the other publishing houses. I'm guessing he sold it to the one who offered him the most money. He's an oddball, a self-important type who used to work at a major newspaper. He's been banned from a lot of places for causing trouble.'

There was so much new information for Rika to absorb. The letters in front of her quivered like winged insects.

I believe that female journalist from the Shūmei Weekly *harboured warped feelings for me. She imitated various aspects of my life: the way I lived, what I ate. I think she was trying to live my life as it was before my arrest. She clearly deviated from the journalistic ethical code. To my utmost surprise, she even confided in me about her sex life at times. Maybe she was trying to impress me with her fidelity to me, but I could only see it as sexual harassment.*

'Is this true?'

Rika looked down at the toes of her loafers. She'd not taken good care of them, and the patent leather was peeling off.

'It's true,' she said weakly. She knew, without lifting her head, that however she tried to excuse her behaviour, the editor would just groan. Though they didn't want to, her eyes kept on scanning the words on the page.

Her feelings for me were a burden. I don't dislike her, though – even after reading the article she wrote, which was a bundle of lies. So subjective! My lawyer has suggested I press charges, but I've been blessed with this opportunity to speak the truth, and that's taken away my will to do anything more. She simply had a crush on me, that's all. In order to get her point across, in order to ratify the clumsy, selfish, man-hating women that the world is so full of, she's written about the person she wants me to be: a lonely woman full of insecurities who was unable to fit in with other women. That's fine by me. This article by my husband will be the first time that a writer or author represents me as the woman I really am. I've experienced the same kind of misrepresentation many times, from my childhood on. People are attracted to me, foist their illusions onto me, and when I don't go along with it, when I don't live up to their expectations, they turn on me, and start behaving in strange, inexplicable ways. I think this will allow the world, finally, to understand that I haven't taken anybody's life. I have no end of regret that those men died, and I have so many memories of our good times together, but unfortunately their lives were lost through their own doing. It has nothing to do with me.

Her attack on Rika was only the beginning. Kajii went on to speak about her father:

This is the first time I've told anybody this. On that fateful snowy morning, I was actually back visiting my hometown. I didn't return to my parents' house, but met my father in a local hotel. I told him that everything I'd been saying to him about my life in Tokyo was a lie, and I was having my lifestyle financed by men. I said, too, that I had no intention of changing my ways. Well, things grew heated, and I said some things I now painfully regret. It didn't help that I had for a long time been harbouring a powerful sense of vexation with my father for keeping up his fraudulent marriage with my mother, whom he didn't love. My father became enraged, and slapped me. He wasn't disappointed so much as he was jealous, the kind of jealousy you find between men and women. What my father felt for me was of a different kind to the affection one feels for one's family members, you see. We were more like lovers – emotionally speaking, that is. I think my mother was painfully jealous of that. I believe that my father also took his own life and made it out to be an accident, as a man who'd sought his daughter's love and been betrayed.

Was it because she knew the ominous feeling that pervaded the Kajii house that Rika found it impossible to laugh off this statement as sheer delusion? Recalling that room crowded with dried flowers, and that all-over itchiness that had remained with her for days after, she felt a profoundly unsettled feeling working its way through her.

Maybe I won't live for all that long. But that awareness enables me to feel a powerful love for my husband. All that I've endured up until this point has not been in vain. When I met him, things began going as I wished. This is the first time he's been married, but he is kind enough to have taken in the child of a relative, whom he's bringing up as his own son. I feel the happiness of someone who's suddenly acquired a family. He is one of just a few people who can see me for who I am and understands me, without getting distracted by the clamour of what everybody else is saying.

Rika lifted her head, feeling in danger of choking. She gave a dry cough, and her thoughts finally began to assume some order. Thinking of the ordeal that was about to begin, she held her breath for a moment. When she let it out, it felt like an avalanche.

Rika took pride in the fact that she had thoroughly researched Kajii's mother and sister, but it was true that she hadn't pursued the matter of Kajii's father. This wasn't out of any lack of interest, but because she had been intentionally avoiding it, knowing that when the subject of fathers came up she would feel it striking against the darkest parts of her. Her article had touched on it only very lightly. She didn't know how accurate what Kajii said in this latest article was but, regardless, Rika's failure to probe this core issue amounted to negligence on her part.

'Her account differs quite significantly from the facts. All I did was to try and draw out Kajii's own words,' Rika finally managed to say, although it took all her strength. The article ended with the statement that Kajii and her husband would publish her biography together.

'I have a good sense of how you conduct yourself professionally, and I let you write the article in full knowledge of what a piece of work this woman is. But I suspect, for the time being, you'll be on the receiving end of a lot of scrutiny. We can't send you out to cover stories in the way you've been doing. I think it's best for you to take some time off. I need you to be prepared for your way of working to change. It's fine for you to go home for today.'

The editor's voice was gentler than Rika had ever heard it, and she bowed her head deeply in gratitude. She left the building, doing her utmost not to make eye contact with her colleagues. She knew that she had to go and meet Kajii, right away. Even now, a part of her wanted to believe that there was an alternative interpretation for what was going on.

She headed straight for the Detention House, taking a train and then a taxi, doing her best to keep her mind blank. The rails in front of her, the steps, the people she met, all lacked any sense of reality, as though they were images she was seeing on her phone screen.

Before Rika knew it, two hours had passed since she'd arrived at reception. She waited and waited, but her number wasn't called.

Rays of sun baked the black asphalt.

She stepped out into the road, realising too late that the light was red. A car went gliding past, brushing right by her toes, and her body was instantly drenched in sweat. She made to step back but her body wouldn't move.

She heard the car brake and her vision began to spin. A dull pain ran through the base of her stomach. She saw the bright blue sky spreading out above her, and the next moment her eyelid brushed against the hot concrete. Fine grit flew into her eyes. At the edge of her vision she could see the colour of blood, which she supposed to be her own, and she eventually realised that her right arm and leg were seized with pain the likes of which she'd not felt before. The shirt and trousers she was wearing had ripped, exposing her skin. She could tell by the vibration of the hot ground on her bare skin that the car had stopped for long enough for the driver to see what kind of state she was in, and then driven off. With her cheek scraping along the ground, she somehow managed to drag herself over to the pavement. The rough, uneven texture of the concrete, the flattened pieces of gum, and particles of dust and grit, none of which she ever noticed when she was walking, made her choke several times.

Smelling an acrid, herbaceous scent, she lifted her eyes to see some chrysanthemums arranged in an empty bottle and placed under the guardrail, just like they had been that first day she'd come here. Maybe the person commemorated by these flowers had lost their life because of Kajii, or someone like Kajii.

Lying curled up on the pavement, Rika understood: this was how Kajii's victims had died. The thing they had treasured had been cruelly shattered. She had to face it this time: Kajii was a killer. It didn't matter whether or not she'd murdered her victims with her own hands. Clearly, there resided within her a violent loathing of other people. Rika hadn't been able to see it until she herself had been struck off. The situation had come about through her own lack of care, but without the damage Kajii had inflicted on her, she would never have sunk this low. There was no doubt that those three men had experienced the same flow of emotions, the same shock. The freelance editor now engaged to Kajii would probably, sooner or later, experience the same sorts of feelings. With trepidation, Rika ran the palm of her hand across her body. Her knees and elbows were badly grazed. Glimpsing the vivid red blood and the exposed pink flesh she shook and looked away. Her blood-wet fingertips were dusted with grit.

Rika thought back to when she'd hurt herself as a child – hadn't she stared tirelessly at her wounds, as if they were something un-related to her? She felt as though time was flowing slowly around her. She was lying on the pavement, but she felt tremendously calm, as if she were lounging around on the floor of her own room. The blue sky fell down towards her. If she shut her eyes now, she could go to sleep. Just as she was thinking that, she caught sight of the hem of a pair of jeans and a pair of trainers, connected by two slim legs.

'Are you okay?'

Hearing the woman's voice, Rika looked up. The young woman with a child looking down in concern at Rika from far above was, without doubt, a person standing in safety on the shore. She wore a striped jersey top, and her cheeks were a healthy-looking shade of pink. Even in circumstances like this, Rika found herself adopting the journalist's mindset, and wondering what it would be like to bring up a child right by the Detention House. Out of the corner of her eye, she saw the washing strung up outside the tall apartment blocks flapping in the breeze.

'Shall I call the police? An ambulance?'

The woman crouched down and looked at Rika with her bright brown eyes. Rika finally sat up, and looked back at the woman. She hunched over and folded her legs, thinking that she shouldn't reveal the sight of her blood to the little boy, who was currently hiding behind his mother.

'I'm okay, I'm sorry. I stepped out into the road without looking at the lights. It was my own fault. I've not broken anything. I'll go home and clean myself up.'

'All right, but you shouldn't move right now. I'll hail a taxi for you, okay? Do you live far away?'

'In the city centre. Thank you, sorry about this.'

'Don't worry about it at all. My son falls over all the time. He's constantly injuring himself. When he finds a friend he's particularly fond of, he's not satisfied until they've had a fight and have both got covered in mud and scrapes.'

Perhaps attempting to take Rika's mind off her injuries, the woman went on speaking light-heartedly as she took wet wipes and a towel out of her bag. Then she stood up and reached a supple arm towards the road and waved, then quickly drew it in with a disappointed face.

'You're gonna get a scab.'

Rika now noticed a pair of black eyes, pinned on her grazes. Showing no fear, the boy was bending down and staring at her injuries. His envious look took Rika aback.

'Hey, stop that! Gosh, I'm so sorry about him. He loves peeling scabs more than anything else in this world. He peels those of his friends as well.' The young woman's eyes were still trained on the road as she spoke.

Rika saw that the boy's palms and his knees that extended from his shorts were peppered with scars, presumably from peeling his scabs.

The boy whispered in her ear as if revealing a prize secret, 'Scabs taste really good.'

Rika looked in shock at those soft-looking cheeks. The young mother, waving her right arm, oblivious to what was going on between the two of them, finally managed to hail a cab. Rika thanked the woman, who helped her to her feet, and then got in. The doors closed. The smell of air freshener was too strong for the cab's small interior.

The taxi driver, a man in his late sixties, she'd have guessed, was looking at Rika. To ensure she didn't leave any blood on the seat, she took out a handkerchief, spread it out beneath her, and sat down again. The sight of the little boy standing beside his mother and waving slowly receded. Across the river, Tokyo Skytree shone even brighter in the distance. Rika closed her eyes.

Thirty minutes later, Rika asked the taxi to stop outside the biggest supermarket in the Kagurazaka area, which had a chemist inside. There she picked up bandages, antiseptic fluid, plasters and gauze. She had no appetite, but she needed to buy something nourishing to drink. She didn't feel like meeting Shinoi and the others, who would surely already know about Kajii's betrayal. She knew that once she got back to her own apartment, she wouldn't have the energy to go out again, or to cook. When she thought about the night she would spend alone, she felt scared, and searched around desperately for something that might take her mind off it. Just then, the white light spilling from the supermarket called to her.

She floated unsteadily over to the dairy section, and found her eyes immediately directed to the small packet with its crisp navy logo exerting enough power to eclipse all the other products around it.

To think that a regular supermarket such as this one would stock Échiré butter! Checking the price, she saw it was less than a thousand yen. Not just that, either, but there was a whole assortment of different kinds of butter filling the display: cultured, aged, salted, unsalted … Until just a few months ago, it had been so difficult to find. Things changed at such speed. For a while, Rika stood still, bathing in the white light of the dairy section.

It was the first time she'd noticed, in her ten years of living in that apartment, the peculiar shape of the ceiling. It looked like a building-block castle that had collapsed. Like the room above and those on either side were encroaching on her territory, little by little. The walls and the ceiling pressed in on her, and the space around her shrunk. She found herself hoping for the day when the walls would cave in altogether, obliterating everything inside this place, herself included. She closed her eyes. She wasn't remotely sleepy, but she couldn't get out of bed.

Today was the third day of the seven-day leave of absence the editor had given her. Her most recent class at Le Salon de Miyuko had been scheduled for four days earlier. After a lot of deliberation, Rika had decided to go along. Reiko had texted her several times, saying she was worried about her and wanted to go with her, but Rika had refused her offer, replying that she was sorry, but she'd prefer if she didn't.

When she pushed the intercom buzzer and hesitantly stated her false name, she heard Madame's soft voice say, 'That's not your real name, is it? Go home, please.'

'Will you at least let me return your notebook?' Rika had pleaded, cold sweat running down her back, but the door hadn't opened.

'It's yours now. You can keep it. Don't come back here again. Please tell Ms Iino as well.'

Her tone was business-like and devoid of emotion. From the silence in the background, Rika felt she could sense the anger of the other students.

It was a perfectly executed revenge. Since when had Kajii been hatching this plan? Had she had the idea from the moment that Rika made contact with her, or when she'd first pleaded to become her friend? Was it Kajii's meeting with Reiko that had triggered it all? Or was it a consequence of the time when Rika had pushed Kajii away?

The night before, Rika had hesitantly done an internet search of her own name and, just as she'd thought, had been met by a deluge of abuse. Photos from an interview she'd once done for the in-house women's magazine, without make-up and wearing clothes she didn't particularly like, had been published online, so people knew what she looked like.

There were more unpleasant comments about her appearance than she'd been expecting. In fact, she found far more comments directed at her figure and her face than opinions about the article itself. The fact that Rika had never thought of herself as particularly overweight or ugly made it all the more shocking for these accusations to be levelled against her. What stood out the most were the impassioned comments about how, as a woman in an industry where you had to engage with the public, failing to regulate her weight and put on make-up was lazy and showed a lack of effort. It struck Rika that this was the same gaze that had been turned on Kajii all this time, and she felt she understood why Kajii would choose to remain so stubbornly within her own subjective world. When it came to appearance, the world's standards were so harsh that, unless you built thick walls like she had done, unless you continued to affirm yourself with a great tenacity of spirit, it became difficult to lead your life with a sense of pride.

There were lots of comments, too, about how Rika had had feelings for Kajii, how she was projecting and glorifying the facts of her case, and how her love-hate relationship with Kajii stemmed from her own insecurities. Her eyes lingered on a suggestion that she could do well to learn from Kajii's resilience and wisdom.

What hit Rika the hardest was that these heartless criticisms made by invisible individuals were not all completely off the mark. Rika felt herself to have grown braver in recent months, but that was only a very slight change, occurring within a safe environment which she was lucky to have access to, under the protection of the people she was close to. Really, nothing at all had changed about her since she was at school. With every comment she read, a pain would go shooting through her head as if it were about to split open, and her oesophagus would burn as if someone had tossed a burning splint inside. Yet she carried on reading them for hours. Sometimes, a memory would come back to her – something from her childhood, an expression on her mother's face, her period of popularity in high school, the various encounters and successes she'd had since joining the company. Joining up the criticism in front of her with those memories, her life up until this point began to seem fictional.

Once she was past the initial shock, though, she began to take a certain kind of pleasure in the situation. The more she was denigrated, the more she felt that her body, her will, and her feelings had all melted away, and ceased to be visible to anybody else. She felt as though she herself had vanished, become just one part of the various episodes surrounding the Kajii case. Spending all that time on her laptop made her feel wired, yet bereft of energy.

She was incapable of contacting Reiko, or Shinoi, or her mother. Three days ago, she'd sent them all a message saying the same thing: she was so busy with work she was having to stay over at the office, and couldn't see them. She felt certain that if she met any of them, she'd no longer be able to rein in her emotions. She'd crumble and never be able to put herself back together again. She was receiving huge numbers of phone calls and emails from all kinds of people, but she had no will to reply. She knew that she should ask somebody for help, but she also knew that nobody could save her. She suspected that before long, she'd tender her resignation.

Going by how things had been progressing in the retrial, it looked unlikely that Kajii would escape a life sentence. The defence appeared to be pushing the angle that it was Kajii's sexuality that had wreaked confusion on the people around her, and led the victims to die of their own accord, but to Rika, this strategy seemed likely only to buy antagonism from the judges. Yet Kajii's way of life, her commitment to remaining true to her own desires even while she wrecked the lives of those around her, was far more fulfilling than Rika's was currently.

Even if she'd not voiced her feelings to anyone, Rika had in the past been critical of the victims for simply waiting for someone to step in to help them, for being too proud to ask for help.

You should reach out to other people, you should rely on others, Rika had preached to the people around her. *Helping and depending on one another is nothing to be ashamed of.* But now it was her own turn to be in trouble, she found herself incapable of doing what she'd been advocating. Just the thought of being seen in this state by someone like Reiko or Shinoi, who knew everything she'd done and had been trying to do all this time, made her grow hot all over, so that her skin hurt. How strong Reiko and Shinoi must have been, she realised now, for taking the hand she'd extended to them. Maybe it was in fact them who had been supporting her this entire time.

The last time Rika had spent this long doing nothing was in her early childhood. She was realising she didn't have any pastimes outside of her work. Her empty stomach would feel hollow, but she had no urge to fill it. From time to time, she'd have a jelly drink. She turned over in bed again and again, trying to rid herself of the ache in her stomach.

As she was doing this her finger brushed up against something rough. She looked down to see her exposed knee peeking out from her sweat shorts. The graze was covered with a red scab of the sort that felt tempting to pick, just as the little boy outside the Detention House had said it would be. Rika sat herself up and inspected it.

Against the white background of her skin, the scab looked like a richly coloured meal of some kind. In fact, it looked quite a bit like bacon fried in butter. She could see why the boy had talked about how tasty they were. When he'd said so she'd been horrified, but before she'd entered kindergarten Rika herself had felt no hesitation in eating her scabs. She would also bite her nails, and if she came across a smooth pebble of a sweet-looking colour, she'd put it in her mouth to find out how it tasted. That had been at the camping grounds in Gotemba by Mount Fuji. She remembered her mother's face as she urged Rika to spit the pebble out.

As Rika went on caressing the scab, a chunk of it fell off. Holding the broken-off piece between her fingers, Rika looked at it, then moved it up to her mouth and licked it. That clump of blackish blood was perhaps a miniature version of what had formed in her father's head, when he'd died face down on the floor. All roads led back to her father – her face, this body of hers so ready to put on weight, her way of losing sight of herself …

She recalled that milk came from blood. The same must then be true of butter. She licked the blood on the scab again. It tasted of metal and sweat. Feeling a slimy sensation on her leg, she looked down to see a thin thread of blood trickling from the wound, though it didn't hurt in the slightest. Maybe the scab wasn't ready to come off yet. Watching the dark red droplets stain the sheets, she noticed the room was growing dim. What time was it?

Rika got out of bed. The blood in her body plummeted to her feet and she stood still with her right hand on the bed to steady herself, waiting for her vision to grow lighter again. She tentatively opened the curtain to see the sky was tinted the mid-blue of early evening. She opened the window and a warmer breeze than she'd expected came rushing in. Soothed by this, she headed to the kitchen. She didn't feel hungry, but she knew that she had to eat. She opened up the fridge but it was empty except for some seasonings and a packet of butter. She cut off a piece with a butter knife and put it on her tongue. Her body flinched at first at its sharp coldness, but the chunk soon melted like honey, forming an unctuous film across her dry mouth. It was a sign, Rika thought, that her body was still producing heat.

She wasn't like Kajii's victims. She could get up of her own accord, she could put things in her own mouth. She could taste them, too. She would ask for help.

Rika summoned up the last of her strength. She reached for her phone and found in her contacts list the name she was searching for. She had nothing left to lose. If he said no, that was fine, she said to herself, sending the text with a trembling finger: *I'm sorry to ask, but would you mind bringing me something to eat? Don't worry if you can't.*

Rika knew that to get herself out of this place, she had to traverse the bewilderingly long path towards the light. To do so, she had to line up the lowest hurdles she could find, and jump them. Starting by calling upon the people she felt able to call on.

She didn't know how long she had been lying down for when the doorbell rang.

Rika opened her eyes. Looking at her phone she saw it was past ten in the evening. The apartment was pitch-black. When she got up her stomach twisted, and she winced in pain. She could tell that her breath smelt terrible. She had had no energy for attending either to her appearance or the state of the apartment. She turned on the light and went to the door, dressed in her sweatshirt and joggers.

The man standing in the hall was a stranger. He had a towel draped around his thick neck. A slightly undersized emerald green T-shirt with a caricature and name of an idol clung to his body.

'I was at Megumi's leaving concert tonight, so I came straight over after it finished.'

I thought you'd given up on her, Rika made to say, but she stopped herself.

Makoto didn't seem particularly concerned by her appearance, taking off his trainers and stepping into the apartment. When he moved past her, a flat paper fan – with a photograph of Megumi's face – sticking out of his backpack grazed her nose.

As Rika was wondering what he'd brought for her, Makoto washed his hands in the sink and then took out milk, eggs and pancake mix from a plastic bag. He opened the packet of pancake mix into a small pan he found on the drying rack, stirred in the milk, then broke in the eggs.

There was no need to tell him where anything was.

'Thank you,' she mumbled, lying down on the bed and shutting her eyes. Just letting a living being inside her flat was the limit to what she could manage. She heard the sound of cooking chopsticks scraping against the side of the pan. The floury smell reached her. She didn't really want to eat, and she wasn't sure why he'd brought pancakes, but she was grateful for the simple fact that someone was cooking for her.

'I'm in such a miserable state, you're the only one I felt I could ask. I know I've got a nerve to be in touch, given the way we broke up. But I needed it to be someone not too close, or else I couldn't do it.'

She heard the fridge opening. He didn't seem to have heard her. 'Oh, good. You've got butter,' he said.

Soon after, Rika heard the sizzle of butter melting in a hot frying pan. It smelt to her like life itself. Maybe because it was animal fat, there was a rough, raw depth and fragrance to its smell, which you didn't get with vegetable oil or margarine. Rika addressed Makoto again.

'You read that article, right? I want to apologise to you. My guess is you're the one that it hurt the most. I told Kajii about the night that we stayed in the hotel. Not in any detail. Kajii went on so proudly about the taste of butter ramen eaten straight after having sex that I wanted to know what it was like. I felt that if I knew, I might better understand her, and so I—'

With his back still turned to her, Makoto broke in. 'I was definitely surprised when I first read it, and angry too. But I think I realised even in the moment that there was something going on. It was the first time you'd ever initiated things like that. I briefly wondered if the *Shūmei Weekly* was finally running the "Ten Ways to Keep Having Sex Until You Die" feature. That's just how you are – everything's related to your work. The same goes for me, I guess. Maybe in that way we were well-suited.'

'We really didn't talk, did we?' Rika felt a sense of relief flooding through her. As it did, a gust of cool air flowed through her throat, making the back of her nose hurt.

'I think if we were still together, I wouldn't be able to let it go, but we're not. I told you before about that time when I was a kid, and I felt so envious of the cakes my friend's mother made, right? My elder sister saw that and took pity on me, so she bought some pancake mix and cooked me pancakes. She said that the trick is to make them exactly as it says on the back of the box. You made me a cake for Valentine's Day ages ago, remember? So this is in return for that.'

'You say ages ago, but it's only been three months,' Rika said in a critical tone, surprised by how hurtful she found his comment.

'Wow, it really feels like years ago. Coming over to this apartment, as well.'

'At the end of *The Story of Little Babaji* they make pancakes out of the tigers that have transformed into butter, and eat them. I think they mix the tiger-butter into the batter. Or put it on top. Maybe they even melt it in the frying pan.'

But Rika's words got lost amid the sound of the pancake mix being poured into the pan. She heard the noise of the pancake being flipped and sticking again to the pan. After a while, Makoto came over with a plate in his hand. The perfectly round, golden brown pancake was steaming, the maple syrup shining, and the knob of butter on top beginning to melt. She brought her hands together, and said, 'Itadakimasu.'

With a fork, Rika broke off a small piece of the pancake, revealing its bright yellow insides. The way that the batter with its structure of fine air bubbles and countless little pillars supported the surface layer, burnished to a deep brown, was proof that it had been well mixed. The butter slid around sluggishly. Rika put a tiny sliver into her mouth. She instructed her teeth to bite, and with some effort, succeeded in moving her mouth, chewing the soft, warm pancake into which the salted butter and syrup had been absorbed. Her stomach let out a sound as if it were being wrung. She could taste what was in her mouth, could feel its texture and temperature – that in itself was proof she was past the worst stage. She felt a blockage in her chest, but she forced down another bite. Her throat felt hot and stuffed. She moved her fork again. When she'd eaten about a quarter of the pancake, she reached her limit. Fighting back the urge to throw up, she set down her fork.

'I realised,' she began, noticing how sweet her breath was, 'I was trying to sumo wrestle all by myself. I was going round and round in circles, and ended up compromising both my workplace and my sense of belonging, and hurting the people around me. Just like Kajii's victims. She'll keep on winning over people by trampling all over people. Maybe people like her will multiply, and people like me will be wiped out, and then everyone will be destroyed.'

She suspected that, as usual, Makoto would say something optimistic that effectively ended the conversation, but he said nothing.

When he did speak, it was after Rika had forced down another mouthful of the pancake.

'You know Megumi, the idol I support?' As he said this, Rika realised that it was her name written on his T-shirt. 'I figured she'd lose weight before her final concert, but in fact she was even chubbier. She looked really happy, though, like she was having fun. She put on a brilliant performance. It's just like you said – I stopped supporting her because she was being criticised. There were so many people laughing at her, and I became scared of supporting her because it felt like I myself was being laughed at, so I gave up on her. Even though there's no need to care about what other people think, with that kind of stuff. I was letting other people determine my tastes, without realising it.'

Makoto was talking at an alarming speed. Rika felt stunned, but she also felt relieved. It made her realise that Makoto had had these kinds of conversations with lots of people, even if he hadn't with her. This was the real Makoto, not the spotless, special-occasion version of himself he'd shown her while they'd been together. Come to think of it, before they'd started going out, Makoto had been the kind of person to speak ardently for hours on all kinds of things, from waste water pipes to classic films.

'I think that when I saw her putting on weight and becoming a different person I felt left behind, somehow. It made me feel neglected, as though she was ignoring the fans' hopes for her. But today she seemed to be having a great time. Do you find it gross, to hear me talking like this?'

'Maybe a bit gross. But it's interesting,' Rika said with a smile. She felt relieved that she could still do it – could still raise the corners of her mouth and let her voice go a bit higher. Even at a time like this, she was pleased to hear Makoto speaking at length about the things he liked.

'I'm really glad I went to the concert. I think it'll go down in history, and I'll be able to tell people I was there. And that's all thanks to you. I don't think I'd have gone if you hadn't said what you did.'

'You know, I don't know if I've been cheered up, or used as an outlet for your otaku ravings.' As she said this, it occurred to Rika that maybe her relationship with Kajii hadn't been too dissimilar to that between an idol and a fan.

'Okay, I'm gonna head off. Oh, this is their CD. Have a listen if you feel like it. The songs are really good.' Makoto handed her a CD still wrapped in polythene, and stood up. Seeing the mess he'd made of the kitchen, he winced apologetically, but Rika laughed and shook her head.

'No, no, you go to bed. I'm sorry for calling on you like this. Thank you. I'm genuinely grateful. The pancakes were really good. And I'll listen to this later,' Rika said, holding up the CD.

'Oh, yeah. You know the shorts I left here? Can I take them? I'm going to the Bōsō Peninsula for Megumi's final tour, and I thought I'd take them with me.'

'I haven't washed them,' Rika said, pulling them from their allocated spot in the closet and handing them to him. Why was it that she'd not thought of getting rid of them before? Makoto put on his shoes in the entranceway and waved. Rika waved back. The door closed, and the room was silent again. She could still smell his smell, but it didn't make her feel anything.

Maybe he had only come over because he'd wanted to share his post-gig elation with someone. He'd said what he wanted to say, then he'd had enough. Even so, Rika felt grateful, even just for that. It seemed peculiar to her that she'd ever slept with him, or had any kind of serious conversation with him.

If Makoto ever reached out to her in need, she thought, she'd help him out, whatever the situation. She got the feeling that he was going to be on his own for some time. She went back to her bedroom, and inserted the CD he'd given her into the disk drive of her computer.

She glanced down at the half-eaten pancake, which had grown cold and hard. She broke off a piece and moved it to her mouth. There was an artificial sweetness and bitterness to the taste that hadn't bothered her when they'd just been cooked. The butter which had hardened inside the dough now struck her tongue with a chilly sensation.

The sense of profound excitement she'd felt the very first time she tasted good butter, right here in this apartment, came back to her now as vividly as if it had happened a few seconds ago. Try as she might, she couldn't accept that the last six months had been for nothing. She tried counting up all the tastes and aromas that she would never have encountered if she'd hadn't met Kajii. However embarrassed she felt of what she'd been through, Rika suspected that the experience had been in some way necessary.

Glancing down, she noticed that the blood which had run when her scab had fallen off had now started to set. Touching a finger to it, she found it of a jelly-like consistency.

She remembered how the young mother had described her son as someone who felt compelled to start fights with the people he liked the most, who tried to peel off other people's scabs as well as his own.

To drink in a person in their entirety, to chew them up until there was nothing left of them – that was Kajii's mode of communication. It was maybe also her way of loving somebody – like peeling off a scab again and again to create a scar that would never go away. Had she not loved Rika, too, even if that love had been of a supremely warped kind?

Looking round the room, she noticed that the walls and ceiling didn't seem to press in on her as they had done before. The scabs on her elbow and knees were a sign that Rika was regenerating, or at least starting to.

The now-cooled butter left white tracks across the surface of the pancakes like the trails of a shooting star. Blood and butter both hardened in no time – which was why she would be okay. The song playing from her computer was a funky disco track, surprisingly lacking in saccharine sweetness, filling the lifeless room with a humidity and a burst of primary colours that put Rika in mind of the jungle. She tossed her dirty clothes into the washing machine, flung in a gel pod, and pressed the Night Mode button. The quiet sound of the machine whirring and the sound of the young girls' voices seemed to chase each other round and round, catching up with each other and blending together.

CHAPTER SIXTEEN

The rain wasn't falling hard, yet in the few minutes it had taken to walk here from Shinjuku Station, the water had soaked through the soles of her shoes. This endless drizzle had been going on for some days now, making it difficult to believe summer was really here. The atmospheric pressure today made her breath grow shallow, and she felt herself floating along amid the soft water.

Rika shared the lift with a young Middle Eastern woman who got out at the same floor, and the two of them stood together at the reception. The woman leaned over to take the ballpoint pen first, her clothing rustling as she did so.

By now, Rika could identify that the smell drifting over to where she stood and tickling the base of her nose was a mix of spices where cumin played a central role.

Madame had a fondness for cumin. Rika had been trying not to think about the cooking lessons and everything that had gone with them, but it came back to her now all at once, and she found her senses swimming.

Lately, Rika wasn't in the mood for making elaborate meals, and she didn't have the time for it anyway. As if performing a series of automatic movements that had been written into her body, she cooked rice and froze it in bowl-sized portions, peeled and cut up fruit to put in Ziploc bags, boiled and salted vegetables, soaked dried foods in water, steamed chicken breasts in sake in the microwave before pulling them apart into bits and putting them into Tupperware containers. All these tasks were impossible to mess up as long as you kept your hands moving, so she didn't need to engage her brain as she went about them. In this way she produced meals that she could eat straight from the container without even having to turn on the hob, for those nights when the memories of Kajii would return, making her body grow so heavy she felt incapable of moving an inch, and robbing her of her appetite. Preparing this food was like a quiet ritual that Rika performed, one necessary for her survival.

In the stand crammed full of umbrellas she spotted a blue-grey one with a flower pattern that she recognised, and slipped her see-through plastic one in beside it.

In the low-ceilinged room, tables and chairs were set out close together. Next to the wall stood a row of steaming pans and rice cookers, heaps of fruit and cheese, vegetables whose names she didn't know, platters of lamb, and small cakes and confectionery items arranged by colour. Stretching out in front of them was a line of people holding disposable foil plates. Young women of university age were circulating the tables, pouring out cups of cherry juice. On the wall was a projector with a slide announcing the purpose of the meeting and explaining key terms. Filled with people of all ages, sexes and nationalities, the space had a home-made feel that reminded Rika of children's parties.

When Rika was shown to her seat, her best friend – who she hadn't seen in about a month – looked up at her and pulled a silly face, no particular sign of concern on her face. It had been Reiko who had texted to invite her to an event about fasting, run by an organisation aimed at spreading awareness of Turkish culture in Japan. 'Try to come on an empty stomach', Reiko had said in her text. Rika had no idea what it was about, but she'd skipped out of work and, for the first time in a good while, made her way into the city for a non-work-related excursion.

'It's weird, isn't it, that I'd be this stressed out and still not lose any weight,' Rika said sitting down opposite her. Over the past month Rika had had many a sleepless night, and her appetite still hadn't fully returned, but she hadn't lost any weight.

And yet Rika had realised a while back that, even if she were to lose a few kilos, she still wouldn't pass. However beautiful she became, however well she did at work, even if she got married and had children, society didn't let women off that easily. The standards were getting higher, and assessments harsher. The only way to be free of it – however scary and anxiety-inducing it was, however much you kept on looking back to check whether or not people were laughing at you – was to learn to accept yourself.

'But thanks to all those nutrients I had stored away, I'm somehow still standing.'

'I'm glad. You look better than I was expecting.'

Reiko herself was looking slightly softer around the edges, and the colour had returned to her face. 'It's been so long since I've seen you,' Rika smiled.

She knew that if she could just get through this first meeting with her best friend, she would be past the worst. However she might have exposed herself to the world at her most pathetic, she still couldn't relinquish the desire to be a prince in front of Reiko. Her stomach clenched.

'I'm so sorry I couldn't do anything for you, when you were having such a bad time,' Reiko said, and stopped. In the space between them, the red juice trembled in the paper cups. The fragrance of a complex mix of spices enveloped them, and an elderly man began to pluck a stringed instrument.

'No, no, it's me who should be apologising. I was that intent on supporting you and then as soon as things started heating up for me, I left you on your own.'

Reiko had gone on meeting up with Ryōsuke outside the house and then, when Shinoi had decided to sell the apartment, had finally returned to her life as it had been before. This Rika had heard from Shinoi very recently. Reiko and Ryōsuke had filled in divorce papers, ready for her to file at any time. Now that she knew that she could be free of her marriage when and if she chose to be, she wanted to spend as much time with him as possible while she still felt the desire to – that was how she had decided to think about the situation.

'The iftar is the meal that people in Turkey have to break their fast. The point of this event is to allow Japanese people to experience what fasting during Ramadan is like. Did you manage to fast today?'

'Yes. Although I had some yoghurt for breakfast. I felt a bit hurt when you told me not to eat, because it was like you were telling me to diet. You know I've got all these people in the industry and online saying how huge and crazy I am.'

'It's not all criticism, though.'

Rika had meant her remark as a self-deprecating joke, but Reiko's face wore a serious look, and there was kindness in her eyes.

'Lots of people are saying what a talented journalist you are. There are loads who are on your side, who say that Kajii's either lying or has betrayed you. Whenever there's opposition there's also support, don't forget. You see, you shouldn't underestimate the research capabilities of a childless, internet-loving housewife with plenty of time on her hands.'

Reiko's calm tone of voice, the fact that she wasn't in any kind of panic, was a source of great reassurance to Rika. She knew that Reiko wasn't saying this to console her, either.

To conceal how close she felt to tears, Rika said, 'I've got way more time on my hands too. The only thing that's keeping me busy is running around apologising to people. They've not decided what department I'm going to be moving to yet, but for the moment I've been taken off any public-facing projects, and I'm just doing admin or research tasks in the office. Thanks for asking me along. It's nice to do something different like this. And to meet, just the two of us.'

The pair joined the line for the buffet, plates in hand.

The cheerful array of fruits and vegetables, all so much larger and more vividly coloured than those you could find in a regular supermarket, made Rika feel as if she were visiting a market in a far-flung land. She was drawn by the look of the kebabs and various kinds of bread, but it was the rice that called to her the most powerfully. The lamb pilaf, stuffed vine-leaves, and roast peppers filled with pilau particularly caught her attention. The smooth, boiled dumplings with their savoury yoghurt sauce fired up her appetite. At each bite of the bean salad, she could feel resolve rising up from the pit of her stomach. The teeth-tingling sweetness of the small hard pies lit up a honey-coloured light in a part of her brain she didn't usually use, so that it felt ready to melt.

Biting into the same kind of little pie, Reiko frowned, and said with a slightly troubled expression, 'Turkish sweets are so *sweet*, aren't they? I feel like my tongue has gone numb.'

'So sweet. But I think I like this approach. Having just one meal a day and having it as a feast must feel so satisfying. I misunderstood fasting. I imagined it to be this painful experience where you didn't eat or drink anything for days on end.'

'Right! Have a read of this.'

Reiko spread open a concertina pamphlet, and Rika read aloud: 'People who are permitted to abstain from fasting are: those travelling, the ill, pregnant women, children, women on their period, people who find their will bending, and people who break their fast by mistake.'

Rika burst out laughing. Reiko nodded, as if to say, 'Right?'

'So, basically, anything goes.'

'Yeah, apparently the thinking is that it's enough if the people who can do it, do. Whenever you can't, you can skip it. Apparently you can give zakat to compensate for the days that you didn't manage it. Ramadan is about creating an understanding of the feelings of the underprivileged, and the aim isn't hardship or reducing consumption. There are a lot of misunderstandings about Islam in contemporary society. This event has been created to promote understanding of religious teachings in Turkey.'

'Wow. It's enough if the people who can do it, do …'

'You could say that about everything, right? Which is why, Rika …'

Reiko leaned forward a little in her chair. Pointing to a line written in the pamphlet, she intoned, "'Allah desireth for you ease; He desireth not hardship for you.'"

"'Allah desireth for you ease, He desireth not hardship for you',' Rika repeated.

'Right. If God exists, He wouldn't take joy or satisfaction in the sight of suffering. Which means, you don't have to get through everything alone. You don't have to always be growing as a person either. The far more important thing is just to get through the day.'

Unprompted, Rika thought to herself, not for the first time, that she really liked the way Reiko looked. Reiko was made up of things that Rika herself didn't have. She was sweet and soft-looking, but she was enhanced by a dusting of pungent and bitter spices. She was like a strong-smelling, rich-flavoured petit four, which no recipe in the world could teach you how to make.

'This week I'm starting couples counselling with Ryōsuke, at the university hospital. We've given up trying to do everything by ourselves, and worrying about what other couples do and what we should be doing. Ryōsuke says he wants to try and create some escape routes for us, so that we don't feel driven into the ground by one another. I don't know if it'll work, but one thing I do know is that I'm not embarrassed any more about the fact that we've been having problems. I want to get help. It's going to cost money, so I might end up asking my parents. From now on, I'm going to stop thinking that asking for their support means admitting defeat, or taking advantage, or being sneaky, or any of that. My parents seem a bit bewildered by everything that's happened, but they say they want to hear what we've got to say, so I'm going to take Ryōsuke to meet them for the first time. Oh, and I've decided to take up a part-time job doing accounting for the Chinese pharmacist nearby. I figure it'll be a good way for me to learn about herbology. Don't worry, I'm not going to get carried away again. I've started to think that even if it turns out I can't have kids, I'll be okay with that.'

Rika nodded, saying nothing, but inside she was telling Reiko what a good idea she thought that all was.

'You've not messed up in any way, Rika, and I don't think you've done anything as shameful as I have. Anybody would end up like you if they got involved with a woman like Kajii. I reckon every woman ends up being hurt by her, and every man ends up dying. Just look at me.'

With a silly gesture, Reiko flung her arms wide apart.

'Thank you, for saying all that.'

In a casual tone, as if speaking about an old classmate, Reiko went on, 'What did we do wrong, do you think? Women like that really get under my skin, however much I try not to let them. Learning that Kajii wanted female friends comes as a kind of relief. Chizu said the same to me.'

'Wait, are you in touch with her?' Rika asked, surprised.

Reiko took a sip of her cherry juice and exhaled a burst of sweet-sour air.

'Yep. I've told her my real name, too, and about my connection with you, and where I'm from. I felt like I had to do that, if I wanted her to open up to me. I mimicked your way of working.'

'Your communication skills are really something else. You're way better suited to journalism than I am. She must be so angry with me.'

'Not really, not any more. I've been talking to her for a while, about all kinds of things. My relationship with you, and various embarrassing personal things. Besides, she was worried about you. About whether what happened would have affected you physically and mentally. You know she's the secretary to a Diet member, in Nagata-chō?'

'That's why she looks so familiar.' Rika thought back to the night they'd been to Starbucks – how she'd sat with Chizu, the two of them dressed so similarly, in the way that she'd do with a friend she'd known for years. It felt like it had happened several years ago.

'You did well to get in touch with her.'

'I felt I couldn't leave things as they were. I got the sense that she wanted me to listen to what she had to say, too. In the end, I think everyone who's fixated by Kajii, everyone who's been involved with her, needs someone to talk to.'

Was that because Kajii, more than anybody, needed someone of the same sex to listen to her?

'Would you like to meet her? Shall we ask her along with us next time? Or is it too soon?'

In that instant, something ribbon-like went sailing across Rika's vision and she averted her eyes. The fluttering string of letters formed a line of text from Kajii's blog:

Not long now until Christmas! I adore this time of the year, when the outside world is at its most captivating …

Of course! How could she have forgotten something so crucial, when she had read Kajii's witness report and blog so many times? On 28 November, the day before her arrest, Kajii had written a blog post detailing her plans to cook a turkey for Christmas, and her intention to follow the recipe to the letter. Rika had read it over and over, particularly around the time she'd first started visiting the Tokyo Detention House.

That same Kajii, who had objected so vehemently to cooking the turkey at Madame's, had written those words just two months later. What had happened in that time to bring about such a change of heart? Was she trying to impress someone? How had she got her hands on the recipe?

By the time of the post, she had left her house in Naka-Meguro and was busy making meals for Yokota in his house in Kawasaki. Rika recalled the small kitchen there, which she'd glimpsed when rescuing Reiko. She couldn't believe that there'd be an oven there big enough to fit a turkey inside.

'Reiko, there's something I'd like you to check with Chizu.'

* * *

'I'd like to buy this apartment. Please.'

The piece of paper Rika unfolded showed the layout of the three-bedroom apartment by the park with the big oven, which Hatoko had shown her three months before. The two sat facing one another at a table separated from the rest of the room by partitioning screens, in the small estate agency in the narrow, multi-storey building in Nishi-Shinjuku. It was after lunch, and the other agents were all out of the office with clients.

'I'd rather you didn't make your decision in such a half-hearted way. It's a big purchase. You only saw a fraction of the buildings I'd planned to show you. I couldn't get in touch with you.'

The coolness of Hatoko's delivery and the condescending note to her gaze informed Rika that she had sussed who she was. There was no way that Hatoko would overlook any news on Kajii, however minor. She must at least have been on top of all the information that found its way onto the internet.

'It's not a half-hearted decision that I'm making. I have two solid reasons, both entirely selfish. The first is that I want to get a mortgage before I have to give up working in a company. Luckily, I've barely spent any money since joining the company, and my mother won't accept any financial help from me, so I have plenty saved up for the deposit. I don't want to waste any more time. The second reason is that I want something that ties me indelibly to you, so that I can maybe interview you in the future. I'm a journalist at the *Shūmei Weekly* – although I guess you know that already.'

As Rika went on, it became clear that Hatoko's eyes were shielding her emotions, creating a barrier between the two of them.

'Not, of course, that I think that purchasing a property of 30 million yen from a capable estate agent like yourself will make you indebted to me in any way. I don't expect you to agree to the interview immediately, either. In fact, I don't mind if you ignore the idea entirely for the moment. But you know that this is a once-in-a-lifetime purchase for me, and I'm saying that I want to buy it from you. I want to block the path that leads away from being employed, and I need to do it as quickly as I can. Which is why I made my choice out of the properties you've shown me already.'

In an instant, Hatoko's expression grew severe. The angle of the sunlight streaming through the window made the down on her face seem as though it were standing on end.

'How nice it must be to be a journalist at a major media company,' she said, as if sickened. 'Even when you've been publicly lambasted, when you've messed up people's lives just because you can, you still have a safety net. How many professions do you think there are like that in the world? How many single women do you think there are in Japan who can take out a thirty-year mortgage when the urge strikes them? Don't think for a moment that you're isolated, or that you've got it hard. I don't feel the remotest bit sorry for you, even after everything that's happened.'

'I know that I'm lucky. I guess I'm of the same generation as your brother, with similar working hours and salary, and a similar personal life. Maybe the only difference between us is that I'm a woman and he's a man.'

Hatoko exhaled loudly. Rika was ready to be slapped, but instead Hatoko got to her feet, went over to the water-cooler and drank a glass of water. A big bubble rose up in the plastic tank and burst loudly.

When she returned, all of the strength had gone from her face. Her lips were wet. She sat down roughly on the chair, and said in a reckless tone, as if she no longer had any concern for Rika, 'Do you get a kick out of driving people into a corner like this? There are other surviving family members of her victims, aren't there? Why choose me?'

'Because you believe that your brother had some element of responsibility in his own death. At least, that's the sense I got, reading what you've said in the media so far and watching how you work. Your brother was drawn to an extremely domestic sort of woman. I wonder if that wasn't a source of hurt for you and your mother. I suspect that's why you're working in this field. Even after you gave up working for the architecture firm, you took up another job working with houses, from a different angle.'

When Hatoko lifted her head, Rika could smell the sweetness of water from her. As part of the retrial, her brother's personal life was once again being exposed. His life, consisting only of his work and the trains that were his pastime, was deemed terribly sad. Increasingly, what he'd written in that cafe notebook was being seen less as an expression of his feelings towards Kajii and more as a way of letting out the stress from his work life.

'What does that mean, anyway – to be domestic? For a taste to be "domestic", a woman to be "domestic",' Rika murmured. She didn't know whether or not Hatoko was listening. 'In today's world, when there are so many different forms the family can take, it doesn't really mean anything. Both men and women alike are being led round the houses and pressurised by a concept that doesn't even exist. I feel as though that's the very essence of this case.'

The water-cooler let out another big gurgle.

'My feeling of wanting this apartment isn't half-hearted. I want it because it has a really great fitted oven. Of all the places I've seen, it's the only one with such a big one. I want to roast a turkey, as soon as possible, before my determination dries up. That's the only thing that Manako Kajii couldn't make – that she didn't get to taste.'

'Can you roast a whole turkey at home?' Hatoko said, glancing at her suspiciously. Rika could tell she was trying not to make eye contact.

'Thanks to my time at Le Salon de Miyuko, I now have the recipe for boeuf bourguignon – the same meal Kajii cooked for your brother right before he died. I got it through a student who I know there, and I made it yesterday.'

'Why are you telling me this?'

Hatoko's voice was quiet, but it still sounded as though she were screaming. She glared at Rika's nose. Like this, Rika could at last see the similarity between her and her brother's faces. Perhaps they had looked quite alike when they were younger, she thought.

'I heard that he thought it was beef stew, and tried to pour it over his rice. Kajii scorned him for that in the courtroom, but when I made it, I discovered the recipe is basically the same as what we call "beef stew" in Japan. The Western dishes commonly served in Japan are an adaptation, devised in the Meiji era as a way of making European food suitable for the Japanese palate, so there was nothing mistaken about what your brother said.'

'So what?'

'Well, beef stew was your mother's special dish, wasn't it? You always poured it over your rice.'

Hatoko said nothing, just stared down at the plan of the kitchen spread out in front of her.

'It's not only bœuf bourguignon, either. In these last few months, I've been going through and making all the recipes Kajii made. I feel like I've come to an understanding of what it was that her victims were drawn to in her. What it was she was trying to satisfy in them, and what she herself felt.'

Hatoko leaned against the backrest of the chair and mumbled, 'Do you really need to do all that, as a journalist? It sounds excessive to me.'

'Seeing the way you work, I think you'd probably take a similar approach. Just from going to see two apartments with you, I know that you use your own time to walk around the neighbourhoods where the properties are, gaining access to the sort of information that you'd only know if you were a local.'

After a little while, Hatoko said with a sigh, 'My mother was more or less a single parent, and she was so busy working, she didn't have time for housework. To assuage her guilt about that, she spoiled my brother rotten, though she left me to my own devices. Whatever my brother wanted, she tried to give him. I told her that Kajii was bad news, but she stuck to her guns and said that if Tokio thought she'd make a good wife, then we should give her a chance. My mother also had insecurities about not being domestic enough. The beef stew she cooked wasn't the kind you make from scratch, frying flour in butter and all that – she used the roux you bought from the super-market. But she'd always put plenty of vegetables in, and I think she added in a bit of butter and miso.'

She folded her legs, unveiling her body's gentle curves.

'If you ask me, that's what cooking is about. That's real home cooking.'

With Rika's words, an awkward smile finally formed on Hatoko's face.

'Why on earth did I tell you all that? I thought I'd learned my lesson.'

'Will you let me interview you? Thanks to what happened, people now know my name and my face. Perhaps I didn't manage to see Manako Kajii for what she really was, but I can see the women who've had their honour dented by this case, because they're all like me. Would you give me a chance? I'll be very respectful of your privacy, and there'll be none of the kind of rude behaviour that you experienced before. I'll do everything I can to make sure it doesn't impact on your work.'

Rika thought she heard a child screeching, but in fact it was the brakes of a car travelling along the Kōshū Kaidō. Hatoko stood up and, using the hot water from the water dispenser, finally made Rika a cup of tea.

I'm having a small party on the evening of 1 August to celebrate buying a place of my own, and I'm planning to roast a turkey. I'd love it if all the important people in my life would come. Please bring whatever you'd like to drink, and a dish of some kind – home-made or shop bought, it doesn't matter. I don't have enough chairs or tables to go around, so please bring a cushion to sit on if you can. Rika.

The first person to respond to Rika's text and offer up her services was Yū. Usually it was Reiko who was first off the mark with these things, but she seemed so busy rebuilding her life with Ryōsuke that she didn't have the time to be helping out. Rika felt genuinely pleased about this development.

She asked Yū to accompany her to the international supermarket in Azabu after work.

Reiko, Ryōsuke, Yū, Shinoi, her mother, Kitamura, Mizushima, Mizushima's husband who worked for an editorial agency, and their young daughter – these were the nine people who Rika had thought of to invite. She had deliberated about whether to invite Makoto, knowing that would make it ten, but in the end decided to leave him off the list. Even if he and she were comfortable in each other's presence, she thought, the others would feel concerned.

At the top of the escalator leading up from the front entrance, they were met by baskets heaped with dragonfruit and lychees, and enveloped by the cool sweet air of the fresh foods section. It was past ten in the evening, and there were few other customers. Rika could smell oranges and meat. She had heard that the meat section here boasted the best selection in Japan, with creatures and cuts from various different cultures, and this appeared to be true – in the endless rows of glass cases, she spotted alligator meat and what looked like the fur-covered limbs of a large, unidentified beast.

In the frozen food aisle, they found a case extending for metres crammed full of turkeys. Like giant rugby balls, they were shrouded in netting under their plastic packaging. They ranged in size, from that of a small watermelon to that of a sleeping baby. All of them were frozen so solid that they could easily break your toe if carelessly dropped.

Rika saw no sign of the pre-marinated and seasoned type she'd been hoping to find. Left with no other choice, she investigated the unseasoned ones covered in frost, eventually selecting one weighing 5.8 kilos. She'd heard before that turkeys were inexpensive, but she still felt surprised, consulting the price label written in English, by how low the prices were.

The baking tray that came with the oven in her new place was shallow, and she had a feeling that the bird's juices would spill over its side, so she also picked up a large aluminium tray made especially for roasting turkeys, before pushing her shopping trolley in the direction of the tills.

'Do you not need to get some ice packs, to make sure it doesn't melt?'

'No, it'll be okay without. It takes three whole days to defrost, so I'm sure it'll be all right in just the time it takes to get back home.'

Unbidden, Yū was throwing paper plates, cups and plastic forks into the trolley. When Rika looked at her in puzzlement, she said, 'You've only just moved, haven't you? I'm guessing you don't have enough tableware for ten people?'

She hadn't been thinking about tableware at all, she now realised. Yū gave her an incredulous smile, then paid for all the disposable tableware herself, though Rika told her she didn't have to.

Stepping out of the cool supermarket into the warm, humid air outside felt good. Even when she shared the weight with Yū, the turkey was heavy enough to make her lower back ache. As they were walking along the street, Yū suddenly yelped and then winced. In front of them was a poster for a chain of major bookshops: *Manako Kajii's First Autobiography: On Sale 10th August*. Rika recognised the photo of Kajii – it was one often used for PR, but now touched up to make her look far younger and more attractive.

'I've heard that the proofs are already out. I really don't think it'll sell. This husband of hers is a money-grubbing, attention-hungry moron, who's running around trying to hawk it here, there and everywhere. Everyone says how boring it actually is. Not that I'd want to read it anyway,' Yū said at speed, suddenly furious. 'You know how subjective everything Kajii says is. If all that's in there is her own testimony, it'll turn out like a badly done Harlequin romance novel, I'm sure. The narcissism of claiming that it's written by "a talented third party" doesn't bother me all that much, but it's just so shoddy. Your article was far more real, not to mention interesting, and urgent.'

It had been decided that, once her training was complete, Yū would be working in the non-fiction section.

'What can you do, though. I mean, she …'

Rika swallowed the end of her sentence: *has nobody else to listen to her.*

Even wallowing in notoriety, even with a devoted man to support her, so long as she continued to bend the truth she would be perpetually alone. However much she shouted and screamed, it wouldn't change the fact that she was all by herself, and not a single person would accept the words she was spouting. Rika recognised that now. It made her neither disgusted nor sad – it was simply the truth. It was one way of living, and Kajii wasn't the only one to choose it.

Kajii stared silently out from the poster, her eyes turned directly on Rika. They looked as if they were challenging her: *What is the truth, though, really? What is a lie? There's such a small discrepancy between the two. Given that, what's so wrong about choosing whichever path seems more appealing to you? What's so wrong about coating barren, flavourless reality in oodles of melted butter and seasoning it with condiments and spices? That's my way of getting by in life, which has come about quite naturally. A kind of evolution, rooted in history. Do you really believe that everything deserves to be confronted in its true form? Does this world really deserve to be inhabited, as it is?*

'Maybe Kajimana's not really a food-lover at all,' Rika murmured. A plume of exhaust gas from a passing truck now separated her and Kajii.

Yū pulled a sceptical face. Rika picked up the handle of the bag, and set off walking again.

It wasn't as though Rika was only interested in eating exquisite cuisine that someone had toiled over making. The convenience-store bento boxes and cup ramen that she shovelled down in the office late at night, the cold rice and nattō she ate when she was alone at night, the meals she'd made and stored away in Tupperware containers, not to mention all the unknown combinations she'd not eaten yet whose tastes she couldn't imagine – she felt just as much affection for all these types of food. She imagined that the future would bring its fair share of bitter feelings, humiliation and fear, but now that she'd known all kinds of tastes, and had come through the worst, that prospect didn't seem so bad.

Rika looked away from Kajii towards late-night Roppongi, suffused with neon and exhaust gas. A drip of water fell from the turkey onto the pavement. Looking back at Yū to encourage her along, she headed for the steps leading down to the subway.

When she found a seat in the carriage, she rested the heavy, cold turkey on her lap on top of a handkerchief. In the time it took for the train to reach her station, she replayed in her head the voicemail message that Reiko had left on her phone while she was still at work: 'I checked with Chizu, and it's as you suspected. At first she denied it, but I could tell by how shaken up she sounded that she was lying. Just like you said, all the students at the school got an invite from Kajii in November 2013. It was around the time that the news of her arrest broke, so everyone tore them up. They didn't show them to the police either, because they didn't want people thinking that they were close to Kajii.'

Going back to her new apartment still made Rika feel as if she were on holiday. The lukewarm air as they stepped out of the subway station felt good against her frozen knees. It was more than a fifteen-minute walk to hers, so they took a taxi.

In the park outside her block, the cicadas were just as loud as during the daytime, and a group of five students were standing and chatting by the water fountain. She opened the door and headed to her apartment up the external staircase.

When Rika turned on the lights in the apartment, Yū looked around with great curiosity. Rika still didn't own any furniture other than a bed, or any curtains either. The brand-new wallpaper in the large, parquet-floored room shone almost blue in its whiteness, somewhat forbidding. She opened the window and pulled the mosquito nets shut, and a heavy breeze drifted in.

Right away, Rika put the turkey inside the aluminium baking tray, put it on the oven rack and pushed it into the oven. The oven gave a rusty creak when she opened and closed it, and the inside smelled faintly of baked apples. Without a flame, its inside was pitch-black and she couldn't see a thing, but having established that the turkey would fit inside, her anxiety waned.

Next, she opened up the new fridge. She had taken out the shelves beforehand, so the turkey fitted easily into that wide, ingredient-free space, bathed in white light. Yū's youthful forehead as she peered in behind Rika was reflected in the stainless-steel handle.

'Wait, you didn't buy a fridge especially to fit a turkey, did you?'

'Yep. The one I was using before was tiny, like the ones you get in hotels.'

'Surely if you left it out of the fridge it would defrost quicker, and you wouldn't need to wait three days?'

'That harms the outer layer of the meat, apparently.'

When Yū was ready to head home, Rika went to the door to see her off.

As she put on her shoes, Rika said to her back, 'By the way, I wanted to say … Don't work yourself into the ground so that you wind up quitting, okay? I don't think you will, but just in case. And I'm sorry for getting you to help out with all this extra-curricular stuff.'

Yū turned around and said, as she pushed open the door, 'I think you're amazing, Ms Machida. There's loads of people on your side in the company, even if they don't say it directly. I really don't want you to quit. Not over something like this.'

'Thank you,' Rika mumbled.

The following day, when she woke up and looked at her phone, she saw a message from Shinoi: *It turns out that they did find a rotten five-kilo turkey in her fridge after her arrest, just as you said. How did you know?*

Rika didn't feel surprise. This was the meal Kajii had wanted so badly to make that she'd had to kill three – no, five – men to do it. The meal that ended up rotting away unnoticed in her fridge.

All day at work, the turkey lay in the back of her mind. Whatever she did, her thoughts were focused upon her kitchen. She guessed that Kajii had been the same.

Even while she was staying at Yokota's house, Kajii had intended to return to that apartment. All that time, she'd been thinking about that turkey slowly defrosting. She hadn't ever really intended to live with Yokota. She would have a Christmas dinner at her house with her classmates from Le Salon de Miyuko. As a perfectionist with a strong desire to impress, she wouldn't be like Rika and roast it for the first time on the day itself – rather, she'd have done several test runs beforehand. If she was welcoming Chizu into her home, then she needed to make her cry out loud with pleasure.

As soon as Rika got home from the office that evening she went over to the fridge. A whole day had passed, but the turkey was still heavy as a rock, and its surface was still only half defrosted.

By the end of the second day, Rika could feel when she prodded the turkey with a tentative finger that, although its inside was still a lump of solid ice, its surface layer had regained its tender, fleshy texture.

She removed the net, peeled away the wrapping paper, and saw for the first time its pinkish-white meat. The mound of the turkey's breast traced a generous curve. Its plump legs, folded together so neatly, gave her a pang of sadness. A red pin stuck into the bird's flesh was designed to indicate when it was properly cooked. All in all, it seemed just as lifelike as a section of the human body twisted into a different shape, and the feeling she had that it might well start moving and talking to her at any moment made Rika feel as though her heart were ready to break.

She rubbed salt across the entirety of its body, the stubbly feeling of its skin making her hair stand on end. When she pictured herself reaching inside to pull out the head and the giblets, she felt desperate to put off the task for as long as possible. With a snap, she cut the hard, plastic thread with kitchen scissors. Peeling back the layer of skin, she saw the entrance to its dark cavity.

Rika felt a profound reluctance to stick her hand inside that unfathomable darkness, which reminded her of Kajii's eyes. She stepped back and attempted to subdue her fear. The cavity didn't seem like it was the entrance to a body that small. If she'd been told it was the passageway through to another world, she'd have believed it.

In less than twenty four hours, her friends would arrive. When she totted up all the things she had to do between then and now, she could feel her vision clouding over. Of course, this whole occasion was happening at her own initiative, but still she felt an enormous sense of pressure.

Stepping forward again and squeezing her eyes shut, Rika pushed her right hand into the cavity. With the back of her hand, she could make out a moist, open space, filled with cool air. With her palm, she could feel the bones behind the meat. A flash of anxiety that she might never see her fingers again ran through her. Her right hand might as well be floating through space, being ogled by various alien life forms. Finally, she found the long, sausage-like neck section, together with a little bag containing the liver, heart and so on. These she pulled out, then gazed down at her own hand as if seeing it for the first time.

She had to marinate the turkey. After reading numerous articles and recipes on the internet, she had decided to make a brine. She soaked celery, carrots, onion and cloves in heavily salted water, and since she couldn't find any wine, poured in the sake she'd been given as a moving-in present. This mixture she put in a plastic bag along with the turkey. When she peered inside, the fluorescent lights from the kitchen filtered through the polythene, illuminating the bag's contents. Watching the water swilling around, she felt as though she'd acquired a small, indoor pool. She fastened the handles in a tight double knot, tied rubber bands around the opening, and then placed it in the fridge.

There was no time to rest. Next, Rika boiled the turkey neck in a pan with a bouquet garni, then added in flour fried in butter to thicken it. But the gravy wasn't finished yet – tomorrow she'd have to add in the juices from the roasted turkey. When she'd done all she could, Rika collapsed onto her bed without showering, and fell asleep.

She slept soundly until past midday, and woke up feeling refreshed. The moment she sat up, a solemn feeling came over her. Finally, the big day had arrived. She folded up her futon and went to the kitchen, only to find that there was water seeping from the fridge. Opening the door, she discovered that, despite how assiduous she'd been in fastening the bag with the turkey in, brine had still managed to leak from it. She breathed deeply, trying not to panic, pulled a heap of kitchen paper from the roll and got down on all floors. Having wiped the floor and thoroughly washed her hands, she took the turkey out of the bag. Its meat was now sticky and soft, and when she held it up its shape changed, as if it were keen to slide right out of her hands and onto the floor. She blotted away the excess moisture, massaged it with salt and lemon juice, and placed it in the aluminium tray.

Now it was time to tackle the stuffing, which she was making with two kinds of rice: regular short-grain and sticky mochi rice.

Rika washed the heart, gizzard and liver that she'd pulled out of the turkey the previous evening and chopped them into small pieces. To this, she added beef mince, finely chopped onion, the two kinds of rice, pine nuts, bay leaves and herbs, and fried everything together. The recipe instructed to add water and boil the rice there in the pan, but Rika feared she wouldn't be able to get it right this way, and instead transferred the mixture into her rice cooker and set it on the speediest setting. This technique was adapted from a foolproof way of making paella that Reiko had taught her.

Soon enough, steam began to seep out of the vents in the rice cooker. Breathing in the smell of the umami-rich rice mixture, Rika felt the tension building. According to the food blogs and articles she'd read, stuffing a turkey brought with it the danger of food poisoning, because the stuffing came into contact with the raw meat. The important thing in that regard was to make sure that the meat was cooked through – yet if you focused exclusively on that, the whole thing may end up dry. She'd read that so long as you made sure

to stuff it just before cooking, not too tightly, and basted the turkey
with butter as you were cooking, you would probably be fine, but
Rika was very conscious of the fact that she was cooking for nine
people. Not only that, but it was mid-summer, and there was a small
child. If anything bad happened, it would be on her.

She set the oven to heat, and took a packet of butter out of the
fridge to bring it to room temperature.

When the rice cooker played its melody to signal that its contents
were ready, she spread out the golden-brown pilaf, its every grain
gleaming with the fat of the turkey's entrails, in a flat dish. Her lower
stomach cramped a little with the enormity of the responsibility. It
struck her now how easy it was for a woman tasked with feeding
others to kill them. She lowered the temperature of the air conditioning.

When the rice mixture had cooled sufficiently, she stuffed it
loosely inside the turkey's cavity, desperately telling herself not to let
it touch the inside walls, and holding one bowl's worth back to be
safe. She unwound some twine and trussed the bird's legs together.
With the help of four toothpicks, she used the turkey's skin to cover
over the entrance to the cavity.

Next, she smeared the now-softened butter across the turkey with
her hands. The way that the white butter went vanishing into the skin
with the heat of her fingers reminded her of that time she'd given
Makoto a massage. It was amazing how easily it melted in. She put
the slippery turkey speckled with protuberances like tiny grains into
the aluminium tray, placed the tray on the baking sheet and opened
the oven.

Lit up by blue flames, the oven made Rika think of the ring of fire
in the circus. If she could pass through, she thought, she would be
treated to feverish applause. Her cheeks felt hot. Finally, finally, Rika
put the turkey in the oven, closed the door, and let out a big sigh of
relief.

She had three hours. She washed her hands and sighed once
more. She had to ensure that great hunk of meat was cooked all the

way through, opening the oven from time to time to baste it with melted butter. If it wasn't cooked well enough, someone might get sick. Alternatively, it might turn out dry and flaky, and she would feel terrible about that too. To avert the latter eventuality, she had to be very careful and thorough with her basting.

She tasted the left-over stuffing. The mochi rice imbued with the sticky, rich taste of liver was heavenly to eat just as it was. She melted some butter in a pan, did some washing-up, and cleaned around the fridge with an alcohol spray.

Her phone timer went off, alerting her that an hour had passed. Putting on her oven gloves, Rika cautiously opened up the oven. The whole bird was now a light brown shade and its skin had grown tight. It was still far from being roasted, but the juice-laden mass sizzling in front of her had already ceased to be a lump of raw meat ridden with causes for concern.

Rika felt herself immediately calmer. She took out a cake-decorating brush and slowly painted melted butter over the turkey's surface. The butter was absorbed greedily by the hot meat, vanishing at an astounding speed. Not long after she'd put the turkey back in the oven, the intercom rang for the first time that day. She pressed the button to let her guest in, and washed her hands.

'Irasshaimase!' she said as she opened the door wide. It was Reiko and Ryōsuke, along with her mother and Kitamura, who they'd bumped into downstairs. A smile rose up on her face, totally naturally.

'Wow, this place is so big!'

'Congratulations on your new home!'

'Wait, you don't have a table!? I can't believe you'd think to invite this many people without one,' Kitamura said, apparently unfazed by the presence of Rika's mother. Her guests arranged the cushions that they'd brought on the floor, while Kitamura spread a rug from a Scandinavian brand designed for outdoor use. Immediately, the floor of the living room was transformed into a giant, comfortable sofa. Rika set out the low folding table she'd used at her previous

apartment in the middle, and it instantly became somewhere suitable
for a crowd of people to eat a meal.

'It's a nomads' dinner party,' her mother said with a laugh, sitting
down with her legs out to one side. Rika felt reassured to see her
making conversation with Kitamura and Ryōsuke, both of whom she
was meeting for the first time. Reiko arranged the mashed potato
and savoury home-made hot biscuits she'd brought on paper plates.
Then Mizushima and her husband arrived with their five-year-old
daughter, Miki.

'What's that yummy smell!' Miki cried out when she stepped in.
Outside the window a summer sunset was spreading out across the
sky. Inside, a smell of hot butter and cooked meat, with a far greater
depth to it than any chicken, was making its way throughout the
room. With cups of wine and juice in hand, the guests picked at the
cheese and snacks that people had brought. Yū arrived with a watermelon. The party began of its own accord, irrespective of Rika still
stationed beside the oven. Like a doctor's assistant, Reiko brought
over drinks and bite-sized sandwiches for her to eat.

The second time she opened the oven, Rika knew in her heart
that it was going to be a success. She bent over as she basted the
turkey once again, so that nobody could see inside.

Shinoi, the last of her guests to arrive, showed up fifteen
minutes before the turkey was done. Over the intercom he said,
'I've brought someone with me. Is that okay? I'm sorry it's so
last-minute. When I told her where I was going, she said she wanted
to come.'

'That's totally fine. The recipe's for ten, so it's perfect, in fact.'

When Rika opened the door, she saw a long-limbed, pale-skinned
young girl, dressed casually in jeans and a T-shirt.

'Hi, I'm Saya Kamiyama.'

Her short haircut revealed ears studded with small earrings of an
intricate design. Rika struggled to reconcile the stories of the young
girl she'd heard about from Shinoi together with the very ordinary-
looking student standing in front of her, and turned to Shinoi as if

for help. He looked both abashed and embarrassed, and seemed to be having difficulties getting words out.

Without looking at her father, Saya went on, 'My dad told me about your party. I've always wanted to try roast turkey. I'm studying nutrition at university – I'm in my third year – so I thought I might be able to help you out in some way.'

So, Rika thought, she was putting her past experience to good use. She knew she shouldn't stare, but she couldn't help herself from wondering about the state of the girl's health. She didn't seem overly skinny, but nor was she chubby – she looked, in fact, a regular sort of weight. Her wide, slightly downturned eyes had a sad cast about them, but she had an attractive face with black, wilful-looking eyebrows. She wasn't noticeably similar to Shinoi, so Rika supposed she must take after her mother.

The last time she'd spoken to Shinoi about his relationship with his daughter, it had sounded to her as though it was probably beyond repair – and yet here they were.

'I'm sorry for tagging along out of the blue, though. Thanks for agreeing to have me.'

'I'm Rika Machida. Your father has been very good to me. I guess if you're studying nutrition you must be a good cook? I'm still very much a beginner, so I'd love to learn more from you.'

While the two of them were talking, Shinoi and Ryōsuke introduced themselves, exchanging business cards and bowing.

'It's great to meet you. I understand that Reiko was staying at your place for a while. I'm really sorry for all the disturbance that must have caused.'

Rika was surprised to overhear this snippet of conversation, meaning as it did that Reiko must have told Ryōsuke where she'd been while she was away from home. She found it hard to imagine what their time together as a couple must have been like since her return.

'Not at all, it's I who should be thanking you. Reiko kept the apartment in good order. As a result, it looks like it's going to sell for a high price.'

Seeing Reiko and Ryōsuke standing there in front of Shinoi, Rika finally understood: Reiko had been liberated in some way. She'd started laughing and eating more, and led by her Ryōsuke had also regained his generosity. It was clear that Shinoi had played a big role in her transformation. He himself had started seeing his daughter. The idea that now floated into Rika's mind – was it just frivolous speculation? But even if it were true, who on earth would blame Reiko for it?

The timer on her phone went off, and Rika ran into the kitchen. She took a deep breath and, with both oven gloves on, flung open the oven door. The turkey that appeared before her was a burnished golden shade, sizzling in its juices. This was it – the physical embodiment of the image she'd been painting in her head for so long. It seemed like the symbol of ultimate victory. She would remember this time and time again in the future, she thought, whenever she felt discouraged. The red pin had risen up out of the turkey flesh. Her eyes stung from the heat of the oven.

Rika yelled from the bottom of her stomach, 'The turkey's done! Reiko, will you help me add the juices into the gravy?'

She picked up the foil tray whose contents were as heavy as a baby and carried it over into the centre of the room where everyone stood. A great cheer went up, which she knew instinctively to be one of genuine admiration. Everyone's eyes were sparkling. A few people held up their phones towards the turkey.

'Amazing! How are we going to carve it, though?'

'Yeah, I hadn't thought about that,' Rika said in response to Reiko's question. With her hands out of action, she shook her head, then set the turkey down on the table. Her lower arms were cramping with the weight of it.

'I found a video of Martha Stewart cutting a Thanksgiving turkey. This might do it,' Saya said, showing Yū her phone. The two were close in age, and they seemed to be getting on well. Saya didn't appear a particularly talkative type, but when the topic at hand was food, she grew more proactive in making conversation.

Watching the screen of her phone, Saya worked efficiently. She unwound the twine, now coated in jus. The bird's legs came off first, then the upper part of the breast. Her movements with the knife were clean and efficient. As the inside of the turkey began to show from beneath its crisp brown skin, steam rose up. Rika was surprised to find the flesh was more densely packed than she had thought. Her mother let out a sigh. Its cross-section looked like a joint of smooth pink ham. A pile of different kinds of cuts formed on the plate alongside the turkey, and its hazel-coloured bones were removed. Rika now understood how the turkey's bones were arranged in its body. The cavity that had seemed endless to her when she'd put her hand inside it appeared very small. The part filled with stuffing occupied less than a fifth of the bird's overall volume.

The rich sweetness of the butter and the delicious aroma of the meat had expanded to fill the entire room.

'Martha Stewart is the one who went to jail for insider trading, right? But made jam and generally quite enjoyed her life as a prisoner,' Kitamura said.

Mizushima immediately responded, 'Oh my God, she's the American Kajimana!'

People were having fun, not worrying about Rika. Even Saya was smiling a little. When she smiled her jaw grew round and her cheeks stuck out, so that her face appeared far younger, like that of a child. As the adults were peering with fascination at the video, making various comments, she went on carving the turkey. Rika remembered something that Madame had said once during a lesson: *Japanese people have a bad habit of trying too hard when entertaining. We try to do everything perfectly all by ourselves, and that's why the habit of inviting people round and enjoying it in a relaxed way hasn't caught on in this country.* She had a feeling that her life from now on was going to be a lot easier. She felt the tension that had accumulated from the move and the long hours cooking now draining from her body.

The plate with the carved meat and paper cups of wine and juice were passed around. Kitamura stood up.

'I think before we say cheers, we should have a little speech from the person who's put this all together.'

All eyes turned to Rika. A cup of wine in her hand, still mentally sorting through the things that had happened and the decisions she'd made these last few days, she opened her mouth.

'From next month, I'm going to be writing a feature for the company's women's magazine. It's going to be about what happened to me, featuring interviews with other women whose lives were thrown into disarray by Kajii. I've got permission to speak with one of the victim's relatives, with Kajii's mother and sister, with the person running the cooking school she attended, and with a few of its students too. After much pestering, the chief editor has finally agreed for me to do it, on the condition that it isn't published in the *Shūmei Weekly*. I'm not going to leave the company. For better or worse I'm famous now, and I think I'm going to make use of that fame as best as I can to get by. At the moment, my role at the weekly magazine is mostly limited to administrative tasks. I don't expect they'll let me return to public-facing stuff for a while, but I want to stay there, figuring out how best to go about it as I go along. I've got a mortgage now, so there's no turning back. I know it's not the most convenient place to get to, but I've got plenty of rooms, so I'd like you to use it, and stay over if you ever need to, like a dorm, as you did with Mr Shinoi's place. I don't have any furniture yet, but I do have three futons for guests. I guess what I really want to say is, I'm really grateful to you for all your support.'

The room fell quiet. It was Reiko who broke the silence.

'I'd love you to interview me as well,' she said, straight-faced. 'You wouldn't have to use my name or reveal my identity, right?'

'Of course not. Let me think about it.'

Everyone said cheers, and then fell upon the meat as if their patience could hold out no longer.

'This is the first time I've ever eaten turkey – it's so good! I can't believe it!' Kitamura said, a level of excitement in his voice that made him sound like a totally different person to normal. He wasn't the only one either – everyone had a compliment for the meal:

'It's different from both chicken and duck. It's flavourful and tender. Lots of umami.'

'The skin is crispy like Peking duck, but the flesh is so moist and creamy.'

'I've never eaten anything like this before! The stuffing in the middle is out of this world. Did you make it all from scratch? I'd love the recipe. Will you give it to me later?'

Rika was the last to pick up her fork and tuck in to the meat. The first thing she experienced was simple relief that the pink flesh was sufficiently cooked. It had a unique fragrance to it, which made her think of walking along a path with fallen leaves crunching underfoot, and its clear jus filled her mouth. The stuffing of mochi rice, mince and pine nuts, now swollen with all the turkey juices and butter it had soaked up, had a sticky texture and a concentrated richness of flavour totally different to before it had been stuffed, which made Rika feel that she wanted to carry on eating it forever.

'It's like we're having a feast,' Miki said smiling, her face streaked with gravy.

'All right, you don't need to advertise how half-hearted Mum's cooking is in comparison!' Mizushima said, wiping her daughter's face with a napkin, and everyone laughed.

'It's a feast because it only happens once in a blue moon,' Rika said.

The gravy that Reiko had put the finishing touches to was passed around the guests. Rich with the juices of the turkey, its taste seemed to contain the umami from all the parts of the bird. When soaked up with the hot biscuits Reiko had made, the combination of the crumbly pastry and the jus was unbelievably good. Both vanished in no time.

Rika said quietly to Reiko, who had come to sit next to her, 'It's a funny thing, sharing recipes. I got this one from Madame, who got it from a university friend who now lives in the States. It was a recipe that was the start of everything with Kajii as well. And the recipes she's taught me are almost all other people's.'

Reiko lowered her voice and asked, 'How did Kajii get her hands on this recipe, though?'

'My guess is that Madame gave it to her.'

'Even when she hadn't been back to the class after causing that huge spectacle?'

'In order to have officially quit, she'd have had to be in touch with Madame, no? I had to email her to un-enrol us. It was so awkward.'

Why had Madame given Rika her recipe book so readily? When Rika thought the matter through, she felt as though she could begin to understand Madame's feelings a bit better.

The more times you followed a recipe, the more it became a part of your own body. That was particularly true of a professional like Madame. Which is why the recipes in that notebook were no longer really for her. They were a public item – they existed to be shown to the women who came to learn to cook with her. Even if the school only admitted people through personal introductions, it stood to reason that when you opened up your doors, you would get outsiders like Kajii and Rika joining. Madame had no hesitation in passing on her recipes, not just to her beloved disciples who worshipped her, but to women she would not see again, and had no wish to either. Perhaps she felt some kind of satisfaction in the idea of the recipes she'd passed on spreading throughout the world. It wasn't a desire for fame or exposure, but a more personal kind of enjoyment and sense of openness. Kajii, too, must have understood that pleasure for her to have given all her recipes and culinary experiences to Rika.

Before too long, there was only a little of the turkey left. Looking at the variously shaped purple-tinged bones heaped up on the foil tray, Rika thought over the last four days, and a question came to her.

Where had the tigers' bones ended up?

The tigers in *Little Babaji* had spun round and round until they turned into butter, but there hadn't been any bones scattered beneath the tree. Had the bones melted into the butter as well? But no. If the bones hadn't been found, then it was impossible to say whether or not the tigers were really dead. Maybe they were living on in the jungle to this day?

The same went, too, for Kajii's victims – nobody really knew whether or not they'd had their hearts stolen by her. Rika had never once seen any proof that Kajii had been adored by anyone – the kind of visible proof that was in front of her now, in the way Shinoi looked at Saya, and Reiko served Ryōsuke his meat. There was nothing left beyond her own version of events.

People were stretching out now on the rug, allowing their distended stomachs to hang out.

With flushed cheeks, which led Rika to think she might be a bit tipsy for once, her mother said, 'There's nothing like this kind of post-meal satisfaction. But it's not so heavy it gives you indigestion, either. It was *so* good.'

'Apparently in the West, they use turkey to make meals the day after Thanksgiving as well. You can mash up the turkey with potato, put cheese on and fry it, or make turkey sandwiches. You see it in Hollywood films and overseas novels as well,' Reiko said. Rika now envisaged the smells and the looks of those meals. She wanted to try them one day, for sure, but they didn't feel quite right on this occasion. What she wanted to eat next was something completely different. She put a hand to her stomach, and tried to listen calmly to her own desires, to what her body wanted.

'Today's meal was really stodgy, so I feel like it'd be nice to do something light, with Japanese flavouring. Dashi and soy sauce, or something.'

'Cooking turkey in a Japanese style – is that possible?' Reiko said incredulously.

'If I feel like doing it, then of course it is.' The words came out of her mouth naturally. It was only once they were out that she realised how absurdly confident they sounded. Looking round at people's surprised faces, she felt a flush of embarrassment.

In a loud voice, she announced, 'If anybody wants to eat a meal made from the turkey leftovers tomorrow, you're welcome to stay over. It won't be anything orthodox. I'm going to do my own Japanese take.'

Her mother's eyes lit up as she said immediately, 'I'll stay!' Rika guessed that for her mother, who was so burdened by caring for her grandfather, staying away from home was a real treat.

Shinoi, who seemed tipsy, said in a far softer tone of voice than usual, 'I'd like to as well. Although I guess I should hold back, should I? If it's going to be all women.'

'Dad, do you have to be so insensitive? Please!' Saya cut in, and the atmosphere grew icy for a moment. Shinoi looked so crestfallen that Rika couldn't help but feel sorry for him. Then Saya went on, 'I'll stay. This place is close to my university, and I've got club activities tomorrow.'

'But …'

'There's three rooms, yes? I'll sleep in the room next to my dad. That'll solve the problem, right? Would you mind lending me something to sleep in?'

There was something so clipped and decisive about her way of speaking that everyone looked surprised.

'Are you sure that's okay? You're not doing anything you don't want to?' Shinoi looked bewildered, and his eyes had grown red, but Saya ignored him entirely, and began clearing up the paper plates. Maybe, Rika thought, if her father was alive and was here, she would do something similar. Maybe she would also have been able to find her way towards a third path, where neither she nor her father were acting purely out of obligation, and yet neither of them felt rejected.

'It's fine, I'm not. I'd like to eat turkey for breakfast.'

Her mother, Shinoi, and Saya – it was a combination that until very recently would have been unimaginable, yet now, the thought of those three sleeping together under this roof seemed to make sense. Was it because the apartment was spacious, or because they'd all shared the turkey? Everyone carried on talking, with little concern for what was going on around them. Only Shinoi stayed silent, gazing at his daughter's profile.

One by one, the guests started to leave, with Reiko and Ryōsuke the last to go. When Rika went back into the living room, after watching from the balcony as the pair vanished into the darkness, she and the three remaining guests set about clearing up. The cups and plates could be thrown away, so it didn't take long. All the food other than the turkey had been polished off. By the time they'd taken turns to wash, it was past one in the morning. Rika laid out the futons in the three rooms and handed people nightclothes, then they all said good night to one another. Shinoi wore tracksuit bottoms and a shirt that Makoto had once worn, his face flushed red from the bath.

Rika finally was able to lie down on the camp bed in the living room.

She knew that nights like these when she was surrounded by friends and didn't have to feel alone were a rare miracle. How many years would it be before there'd be another occasion like this? The knowledge of its rarity made it feel even more precious to her. She was reading her book when her mother came into the room wearing Rika's clothes, her skin gleaming.

'Do you need something?'

'No, no. Today was the most fun I've had in a while. The people in your life are all so strange and interesting.'

Saying this, her mother looked around the room with nothing in it and said hesitantly, 'I was quite worried about you, with everything that was going on at work. I'm relieved to see you're looking well.'

Rika moved the ribbon in her book to mark her page, then sat up. Sitting with her mother like this, it felt just like when they'd first started living alone, when her mother was in her forties. Rika had no confidence that she would be as cheerful as her mother had always been if she herself had a school-aged daughter.

'I've been so tied up in my own stuff that I haven't been helping you at all. I always feel bad about that. If it ever gets too much, you can always come here, you know? I chose this place so that you could live with me one day.'

'Thank you. I think I've still got a bit of fight left in me before that. If I feel I can't manage it any more, I'll tell you. I'd much rather you were doing what you wanted to and looking after yourself, than holding back and helping me. That's the best you can do for me, as a daughter. I'm going to take care of myself physically, and make sure I enjoy my life. That was what I got divorced for. It wasn't to make things harder for myself, but to make them more enjoyable.' Saying this, her mother left the room, looking a little embarrassed.

Rika turned out the lights.

Gazing into the darkness, Rika thought about the meal she was going to cook the following day. She remembered that she had noodles that she'd meant to eat after she'd moved in, as was tradi-tional – they were still sitting under the sink.

'Turkey seiro!' she murmured into the darkness. Since her father had lost his temper so badly on New Year's Eve, she'd disliked kamo seiro, that traditional New Year food, yet now she felt a burst of long-ing for the cold soba noodles dipped into warm aromatic sauce. The turkey had absorbed lots of butter, which went well with soy sauce. There was nothing so far-fetched about mixing turkey with Japanese flavours.

She would simmer the turkey bones and add in dashi, seasoning the broth with soy sauce and mirin. Then she'd boil the soba noodles, chill them in cold water and drain them. She'd put the last remaining pieces of turkey meat into the hot dipping sauce along with yuzu rind. Ideally she'd have used water celery, but she would make do with the cress she'd bought for the salad, and finish it off with some wasabi and chopped scallions.

Why had Kajii wanted to roast a turkey? Rika felt sure that it was to make amends with the women in the cooking class. Fortunately, she'd been arrested before she discovered that Chizu and the others had ripped up her invitations. Quite possibly, she was still thinking about the students, and about Rika too. What position do I occupy inside her consciousness, Rika wondered, as the woman she hurt so thoroughly – the woman she let in, and then succeeded in ruining?

But then, she asked herself, *was* I ruined? In the end, it was probably correct to say that Kajii hadn't even succeeded in doing that. 'You can't even be properly ruined!' Kajii had once bellowed at her, maliciously. The people who had wished not only for Kajii's ruin but Rika's as well must have been trembling in dissatisfaction and despair. And yet, however much scorn Kajii might pour on her way of life, which consisted in proceeding clumsily forward, stopping and starting, changing course as she went, Rika no longer had any intention of altering it. Now that she was able to produce with her own two hands what she felt to be lacking, she sensed that tomorrow and the day after would, if anything, be better than today.

She knew that she was brazen. Her journalistic career had been all but ripped apart at the seams, and yet she hadn't given up writing. She had clung on at the company, used her connections to cobble together a new project, taken out a mortgage, and now here she was thinking about what she was going to eat tomorrow. Maybe in the eyes of the world she was an impudent eccentric, just like Kajii. Seeing herself from the outside for a split second, Rika smiled.

Noodles with a turkey and soy dipping sauce was the first recipe that Rika had come up with by herself and for herself, based on her tastes, desires, and physical condition.

She wanted to invent many more original recipes in the future, and tell someone about the best ones. It didn't matter if that someone was a person she liked or disliked, or someone she'd never even met. If someone else could experience the journey she'd been on, and the joy she'd felt in coming up with the dish – just the thought of that prospect made Rika's chest fizz in excitement. She wanted for these nameless recipes she'd invented to go rippling out into the world, changing colour and shape as they went, just like the drop of a hidden ingredient which you added to the soup at the very end. Rika wanted to go on living with a sense of that chain reaction stored inside her.

She wanted to see Kajii again too. She wanted to meet her and tell her that this world deserved to be lived in. Or, no – that this world deserved to be tasted, greedily.

Rika's body sank comfortably into the bed with a brand-new sense of satisfaction. She'd done it. She'd taken great care with her cooking, and hadn't made anyone sick. Her labour over the past four days had been rewarded. She pulled her blanket up to her nose, sensing the presence of the father and daughter whose relationship was slowly being rebuilt a couple of walls away.

They'd eaten everything, and all that remained were bones.

Rika closed her eyes, and pictured the shapely hazel-coloured carcass in the fridge. As she was thinking through the steps she'd take in cooking it the following morning, she fell into a deep, delicious sleep.